SUMMARY

I'd rather fight than run.
I'd rather fight than submit.

Ruth was born weaker than most vampires. Because of that, she has to find a place on the fringes of the vampire world where she can call the shots in her own life. Doing bodyguard work at the mysterious Circus fits the bill, but it's there her even bigger secret is revealed. Unlike most vampires, she's not a Dominant.

She wants a Master she can fight, until he makes her submit. He must prove he's stronger on every level that matters, and win her trust, loyalty and love. Merc, part incubus, part angel, catches her attention, but his dangerous reputation makes him a bad risk. However, working alongside him to protect a fortune teller who has seen things that can endanger the vampire world, she gets a different view. Plus, out of all his mesmerizing qualities, there's one she finds irresistible.

He relishes a good fight.

VAMPIRE'S CHOICE

A Vampire Queen Series Novel

JOEY W. HILL

ACKNOWLEDGMENTS

Because so many characters and elements from previous books in the series had a part to play in this book, checking storyline continuity and character consistency was essential, and well beyond my time and capability to do. Enter the fabulous VQS expert beta team, readers who have read the series multiple times and enthusiastically volunteered for this arduous task.

Thank you Kathleen, Rosa, Christina, Jennifer, Kerry and Tammy. I owe you big time! Anything you miss is my fault. If I'd done the kind of series bible I should have been doing all along (take note, all aspiring authors!), I wouldn't have had to foist this monstrous challenge on you very kind readers.

Thank you also, ALL the devoted fans of the Vampire Queen series. It's been an amazing journey through these eighteen books, and the joy your insights and enthusiasm have brought to me are *immeasurable*.

One additional thanks (and smirk) to Mandy for the bathmat comment. I and my unoffended sweater HAD to use it.

CHAPTER ONE

*Y*ou *are weak. You should be afraid. You should run.*
Her subconscious alarm clock was prodding her from sleep, with its usual cheerful wakeup call.

Ruth opened her eyes. "Fuck off. And bugger off, too."

If she was using her father's preferred expletive, she didn't want to leave out her Irish mother's.

"Have a good day, motherfucker."

She added that herself, just to be nice.

Peering up at the night sky through the branches of the tree where she sat told her it was about one in the morning. Her father had been by not long ago. Since vampires had an ultrasensitive radar for one another, she could still detect his energy signature. The realization that she hadn't been roused by his approach gave that menacing whisper a bonus shot across the bow of her mind. She ignored it, though when she saw her father later, she knew the awareness would be in his eyes. The worry.

Tau lounged in the long grass below the tree. When she shifted against the sturdy branch that had served as her bed, the lion's ears swiveled and he tilted his head, golden eyes finding her.

"Yeah, about time I woke up, right?" Then she noticed the froth of white scraps around him. Her gaze shot to her lap. Before she nodded off, she'd been holding a book.

"Goddamn it, Tau."

1

She wasn't mad at him. Just herself. The novel had likely bounced right off of him. At least it had been a cheap paperback brought by the supply boat from the Florida mainland. The staff routinely grabbed a bag of them from a used bookstore's dollar bin. But this one had been pretty good. Maybe the store could find her another copy.

She dropped to the ground next to the lion. The marked human staff weren't allowed this proximity, because the sanctuary cats weren't pets. Those who could return to the wild were rehabilitated toward that goal, while the ones too injured or domesticated through captivity were still treated as wild animals. Mal—her father—offered them a life as close to the natural one as they'd had. Or should have had.

Which meant they were as dangerous to humans as they were supposed to be. Ruth, Mal and Adan, her twin brother, were the only ones allowed to be this close. As vampires, they were accepted as predators on par with the cats, but not in competition with them. Mal had given them extensive training on how to establish that balance and the proper level of vigilance.

Her lip curled. He'd been okay with Adan being around the cats a lot sooner than he'd been okay with Ruth doing so, but in fairness, acceptance from the cats that she wasn't prey had taken longer.

She squatted next to Tau. When he dipped his giant head toward her, she obliged, a glancing face bump, an acknowledgment that came with the brush of musky rough fur and a puff of meat breath. Ruth settled back on her heels, arms crossed over her knees, and tilted her head toward the wind much like he did, scenting what was there.

Fellow predator BFFs or not, her father still frowned on things like the face bump. Probably because Ruth had done it to a cheetah once when she was far less experienced in reading the animal's language. That had been a few decades ago, when she was in her early twenties. Only her father's anticipation of trouble and quick reflexes had kept her from getting her face ripped off.

It would have healed, good as new, with time and enough blood intake, but it would have hurt a lot. More importantly, it would have traumatized her mother. Otherwise, Mal might have let the cheetah do it, to hammer home the lesson. He was definitely a tough love kind of sire.

Tau's ears twitched to forward alert. He straightened out of his indolent recline, his sharp gaze searching the area around them. The two lionesses that shared this section of the preserve were nowhere to be seen, but if they were who he sensed, his body language would have been different. And Ruth wouldn't be reacting the same way, because she'd detected it, too.

She didn't rise to her feet, which would draw attention to herself as a target. She stayed motionless, and stretched her senses out farther.

No one could approach the island by air or water, or come through the portals, without triggering security alarms. In theory. Adan was a gifted sorcerer, and he'd told her father that magic was no different from technology. Someone was always trying to figure out a hack. Now that Adan was a Light Guardian, the elite of the magic user world and essentially a cosmic cop—she called him that just to annoy him—he himself could move through the portals without setting off the detectors.

He routinely did "upgrades" to their portal system when he had time to visit, to increase the alarms' sensitivity.

As routine maintenance, Mal also did plenty of tweaking to keep the sanctuary's fault line connections and protections running the way they should. Over the past decade, he'd been teaching Ruth how to do it.

"I don't have your brother's innate grasp of the magical workings of the universe," Mal had told her. *"But I've taken what little natural ability I do have, applied it to practical application, and worked hard to expand that. You can do the same."*

"So you're saying even if you took away his Harry Potter wand and Gandalf staff, Adan could do all this in his sleep, but we can use the tools and our brains to muddle along well enough?"

Mal had been amused, but hadn't disagreed with her assessment. For Adan, working with magic at any level was as easy as breathing. Him upgrading the island protections gave her father one less thing to handle.

Ruth's gaze latched onto a wind ripple through the long grass. It was a couple hundred feet away, but advancing in her direction, bringing a whisper of sound that suggested a language. A shadow came with it, spreading out into a more defined shape over the waving fronds. She had the impression of wings, and a human shoulder? Then

3

the silhouette contracted, like a bird who had turned and wheeled, lifting himself higher into the sky.

That shadow was too big to be any bird she knew. Unless Adan had screwed up the sanctuary's portals, tapped into time travel, and allowed a pterodactyl to get through. In which case, her father was going to shit kittens and she would have delightful fodder with which to tease her all-powerful brother.

After they figured out how to keep the creature from eating all the animals, including the humans and vampires.

Whatever it was passed above her. She'd taken her hair down while she was reading, and the breeze of that passage brushed the straight long strands against the round part of her shoulder, awakening nerve endings.

Predators attempted to flush prey by freaking them out enough they'd bolt. To resist it, the prey had to hold fast to the belief that, until he or she moved, the hunter had no visual fix on their target.

No surprise, that subconscious whisper was back.

Run. Run. *Run.*

A surge of adrenaline told her she might need to consider it. Sooner rather than later.

Her father had told her there *was* a time to run. *Run when your instincts tell you to, but do it with clarity. Think ahead. Be planning your next steps.*

Had he ever felt the need to have that talk with Adan? She'd never asked. She didn't look for answers that would only hurt and drag her down.

A rumble vibrated in Tau's chest. All the muscles beneath the smooth tawny fur became far more defined as they tensed. He bolted. Only her quick reflexes, which shifted her a few inches to the right, kept her in her squat. Otherwise the push-off from his powerful haunches would have struck and toppled her.

A male lion didn't run from an opponent, unless it wasn't something he could fight.

The shadow passed over her again.

If there'd been no island breach—and her senses didn't detect any —and this threat wasn't aimed at the cats they protected—she didn't feel that, either—this was something else.

Ruth tracked that shadow and its attending movement of grasses.

The prevailing wind was coming from the opposite direction. When the two met, the ripples melted into it and disappeared.

By the time she blinked twice, they resurfaced. Only now the grass bent in tight coils in several places simultaneously. Triangulating her position.

It was telling her it knew she was there. Playing with her, but not to be playful. This was a cat thinking it had stumbled on a mouse, a random opportunity.

It didn't know she was thinking the same.

Okay, yeah, maybe the day-to-day was becoming a little too routine. She loved it here, and intended to be her father's successor in caring for the sanctuary, but so far her only significant ventures outside the island on her own were limited to her use of her pilot's license to ferry goods and staff to and from the Florida mainland, outside of the supply boat's normal schedule.

Female born vampires reaching their seventies were the equivalent of a human in their twenties. Wanting to explore and experience... everything. And Ruth was in her eighties.

Maybe that was what kept her from sounding an alarm. The architect of the swirling wind projected some of the same pent-up restlessness.

Would it have been better if she *was* sensing a threat to her home, her family or the cats? Her protective instincts would have kicked in and she wouldn't be struggling with what was probably a really stupid reaction. She would have alerted her father through their blood born mind link and gone after the visitor with ferocity.

Instead, the taunt of the mini tornadoes only intrigued her more. Her hair lifted again, brushing her other shoulder.

Her father often ambushed her on the preserve, testing and training her. She'd not only picked up fight skills quickly from a young age, she'd loved learning them. She relished the warrior's dance.

The visitor was inviting her to take a turn on that floor with him.

Him. It was definitely a male energy. Her attention sharpened.

Heat along her back, a closer pass from the shadow, and she moved.

She spun, fangs bared, ducked and rolled. As she did, she felt the glancing strike of a grasping hand. She leaped away from the sense of something large and solid in her personal space, and ran right into a heated and dense net.

She tore at it, twisted and kicked. A male voice cursed. She rolled free, and when she opened her hands, what she'd torn loose fell free.

Feathers. Silky, long and strong, with points that scraped her palms.

Fae? No. She recognized the Fae, and, with few exceptions, most incited murderous rage from her.

He wasn't vampire, either.

Before she could surge to her feet, he landed on her, driving her to the ground, pressing her to her stomach.

She needed to call Mal. She wasn't an idiot. But before she could reach out over the mind link, her antagonist hit her with another weapon.

Pure lust.

It flooded her, accelerating the pumping of blood through every organ, swelling erogenous zones, tightening others, and bringing all nerve endings to full, erotic attention.

The desire's deliciously painful edge provoked a hunger so strong it would never be sated. Though it wouldn't stop her from trying.

Or so her opponent probably thought. Vampires were all about sex. A stake could be a millimeter from piercing her heart and she would still think about fucking. She laughed out loud, a rasping, sultry sound.

"You've chosen the wrong weapon. This is familiar territory." As need shuddered through her, she bit back a moan at the insane pleasure of it, but it didn't change her answer. "No. Not interested."

A long pause. He was stretched fully upon her, chest to her back, knees pressed to the ground between her forced open legs. Pelvis against her ass. He was big, heavy and strong. So strong. Stronger than the strongest vampire. He was also hot like a winter stove, and had a cock as stiff and ready to go as a pumpjack for oil drilling.

Thank you, Mike Rowe of Dirty Jobs, for the sexual simile. Her libidinous vampire mind had been way too caught up in the episode on the battered staff TV. Drilling, pumping, penetrating...

She shuddered. What *was* he?

"You don't say no to me. Not now. Not ever."

6

His voice was a summer day dense with electrical heat, the storm darkening the horizon. The timbre alone could cause an orgasm.

Her arousal ramped up impossibly higher, making her writhe and mewl. That cock and the solid force of the rest of him pushed her flatter against the earth. He could crush, overwhelm. He would definitely not be ignored.

She became a vessel for that desire, as if he'd forced open all entry points and poured it into her. And kept pouring, no matter her capacity to absorb it.

An aphrodisiacal waterboarding. Unique.

She'd never known the tips of her fingers, the crook of her elbow or the spaces between her toes could become aroused like nipples or cunt, her nape, or the small of her back.

Vampires might be masters at using sex for their own purposes, but compared to him, they were amateurs. Her soul—her freaking soul—screamed at her to give in and let go of control.

Holy fuck. Incubus.

She'd never met one, but thanks to anecdotes from her brother's travels, the word was there, ready to be called. Her heart skipped a beat. If she was right, she really was playing with fire. But sex demons didn't have wings. Did they?

Another moan broke from her lips, believable because it was real. She shifted her hips, a mindless invitation on the outside that masked the calculation on the inside. When his weight shifted, his grip loosening, she shoved against his less balanced side and broke free. She made it to her feet and kicked.

She thought she hit his face. Every time she looked his way, she saw only a shimmer in the air. Cloaking spell.

Moving back a few steps, she planted her feet. She was aggressive, worked up. Ready to get into it. She didn't know what the range of that sexual energy was, but she was still inside it. Ropes of it twined around her arms and legs, wanting to pull them out, open her up.

They circled her throat, making her want to lift her chin, offer it, arch her back, present her breasts for his tasting, the sucking heat of his mouth. If he moved down, that feast would be there for him, all prepared, her cunt slick and ready. To taste her, eat her, fuck her, bite her, suck her...

Oh God. The impact pushed upon her from all sides, like the ocean did the island.

"Did I hurt you?" she taunted, no matter that she had a throaty voice and quivering limbs.

A movement suggested a lifted arm, perhaps a hand to his nose or jaw, to determine if she'd broken either. She could almost see the outline of his head as he tilted it. He was tall. The air to either side of him moved, a disruption much farther than a wide shoulder span. The wings. She could still feel the prick of the feathers against her palms.

"Do you know how easy it would be to kill you?"

The menace held the promise to fuck *and* choke her into oblivion. He wanted her frightened.

Tough. She didn't do fear. She'd honed a trio of emotions to repel its invasion. Anger, determination and disdain. If they were being lazy, she had a backup bell ringer. She'd use disgust like a barbed whip, and flog the others into doing their job.

"You may be stronger, but I'm a hell of a lot braver. Nothing scares me. Especially you. As for your twisted mating call, not now, not ever. You need a lesson in what *no* means."

She took off. Her vampire speed was far beyond human capabilities, but she wasn't under any illusion that he was human.

A half chuckle, half sob caught in her throat. This was so ill-advised. But her body language matched the cats when they were playing catch-me-if-you-can. She wondered how smart he'd be at reading it.

She didn't have long to wait to find out.

A coil of male energy struck her left arm, trying to drive her right. She did a hard stop, reversed course, ducked left, and let strong fingers slide over her hip. Could he have caught her? Maybe. But she had him intrigued.

The game was predator and prey, and she knew which one she was. But it was an adult game, no coddling. She didn't want coddling. She wanted to be played with, like this.

A game with real stakes. No holding back. No one worrying about her, trying to protect her.

There's no one to run to. There were two ways to look at that. With terror and despair, or with anticipation for the unknown. For where that could lead.

She couldn't tell if he was using sorcery to do that air thing, pushing at her with energy, trying to corral or herd her. Maybe he was large and fast enough to be doing it with his own body.

Regardless, the next time he got ahead of her to make her change course, she tossed a look over her shoulder as she spun away. She said it again.

"No." Determined, with a *fuck-you* edge.

She dashed toward the trees, leading him into a winding chase among them. When he caught her, he pinned her against a trunk, bark biting into her back. Her arms dropped to her sides. That male energy pressed near, and she shuddered as his hands closed over her wrists, moving them behind her. Gradually, inexorably, like that tide of desire that hadn't abated, and was only getting more powerful at his touch. As her back arched, her breasts lifted. He was making her display herself to him. Her heart pounded into her throat, body rippling with sheer need. *Yes.*

She stared upward. She could create a vision of his face, just the way she liked it. Strong, cruel and handsome.

"No," she said again. Flirtatious, with a smile that showed fangs, the threat of bloodletting. She had hungers, too.

She stomped on his foot, kicked, and he released her. She was off again. When he tried to block her with an invisible wing, she rolled against it and slid past. The feathers brushed her face with silken heat. His scent was all sex and conquering male predator, uncompromising and demanding.

Images swirled through her head. Him, this faceless being, pushing her into a mattress, into the earth, any surface he could find. He'd thrust into her again and again, make her dissolve into sensation, rise with the light of the moon, everything female in her responding to his male energy.

"No," she called over her shoulder. She put laughter in her voice to add to the provocation.

She swallowed a gasp as she was pulled into the air. One arm banded across her waist and chest, a bruising hand clasping her throat. The other arm speared between her thighs, his palm flat and fingers spread over her stomach. His forearm pressed against her throbbing sex.

He twirled them in the air. When a fang scraped against her neck, she elbowed him, snarled, struggled. Yet even as she pulled her head away from him, her body screamed to let him do it.

Let him bite her, drink from her.

He might not be a vampire, but he surely knew what would arouse one the most. If he was a sex demon, they had fangs as sharp as her own. Only his were thicker. The bite would be far more painful. A deeper penetration.

He was taking her up higher. It was exhilarating. Reaching back, she grasped a hip and found a garment like an ancient Roman soldier's battle wear, studded leatherlike straps over a linen skirt. No weapons in reach, though, except what he had pressed against her ass, a cock thick and ready for the woman who wouldn't shrink from its size or demands.

She didn't shrink from anything. And it would be on her terms. She redoubled her efforts against him.

"I'll drop you," he hissed.

"Don't hold back on my account," she challenged. "Asshole."

He let her go.

He hadn't taken her too high, because she hit the ground a blink after she oriented herself to mostly land on her feet. Well, after she crashed through a cage of small branches on the tree where she'd been taking her nap. He'd brought her back to where they'd started.

The tree helped cushion her from a bone-breaking impact. Bone-jarring was another matter, and several deep scratches from the branches burned. No time to nurse those. She rolled to her feet and spun around, looking for him. Waiting. When she felt his approach, he was still a few feet up in the air.

"What's with the Invisible Man routine?" she demanded. "Afraid I'll see you're ugly as dog shit?"

Her body was damp and shuddering. Everything throbbed, as if her heart was drum beating her from head to toe. She wanted to say *yes* to him. Worse, she wanted him not to take no for an answer. She wanted to give him the right to say what he'd said to her.

You never say no to me.

It could be spellcraft, or an innate power an incubus had, like vampire compulsion. Something not real. The thought helped her hold onto her own will, albeit by calling on every ounce of determination she had. Her own nature, chock full of deeply buried secret needs, could also be contributing to that power, feeding it. Which meant she had to stop this.

"You should have said yes." His tone still held a threat. Or was it a good-bye? She knew which one she liked least.

Deliberately, she lifted a middle finger, punctuating the gesture with a seductive tone that taunted him with what he was getting none of.

"No."

He swooped. Just like that whirlwind of air had done to the grass, it spun her about and knocked her off balance, no matter that she tried to counter it.

She ended up on the ground, flat on her back, his shimmering energy above her. Not touching her. Not physically. She had half a heartbeat to know what he was going to do, to manage a desperate, final, "No."

She felt his male satisfaction, that he'd gotten her to beg. His rough laughter danced over her mouth, teased her lips.

The erotic energy invaded her anew, far more powerfully than before.

He'd been holding back. *Holy fuck*.

It pinned her down, roared through every artery, every muscle and bundle of nerve endings, impossible to resist, to deny.

He wasn't...touching her. It was overwhelming. Nothing to grasp. She thought his breath whispered across her face, his lips again so close, which made the torment even worse.

Her breasts felt so tender, the nipples painfully hard. Her skin was gooseflesh, tingling, her thighs strumming with sensation. When the orgasm tore through her, her cunt convulsed, gushed. Her strangled cry pierced the night. She bowed up as if yanked on strings, caught in the grip of the worst, most intense, most incredible, most out-of-control thing she'd ever experienced.

The weight of his invisible gaze was another kind of penetration as those cries kept coming from her clogged throat. She clutched the earth, found it moist and rich in her hands, like crumbled chocolate cake. She wanted to touch him, hold onto him, yet even if she could have raised her hands, she wouldn't.

She could tell herself it was because she was being contrary, and yes, that was part of it. The other part was knowing he hadn't given her permission to touch him, and in this state, stripped down and vulnerable, she couldn't stop that part of her from coming forth.

But was it only one-way? Even through the chaos of her mind, she sensed his physical distance from her wasn't merely to enforce his mastery of the situation. Maybe he fought the same emotional dangers she did. Either way, it was the most connected and most isolated, lonely feeling of her life, tearing her apart, even as she wanted more.

Not more of it.

More of *him*.

When the orgasms—yes, multiple—left her, she was disoriented, shuddering and weak. Almost mindless.

He was gone.

It seemed like eons later when she rolled awkwardly to her side, her muscles protesting. When she did, she saw scraps of paper from the book Tau had shredded. Caught on one of them was a black and white feather. The white had a silver tint and a zigzag pattern. Like lightning.

She stared at it. Her brain weakly kicked back in and told her why she needed to pull herself together. If Tau came back, he'd decide she'd become something weak enough he could eat.

She needed to get up. She would. Any minute now.

As soon as she could convince herself a far more dangerous predator hadn't devoured her already.

CHAPTER TWO

"*S*he was asleep again. In the middle of the night."

Mal braced his hands on the split rail fence by the house, gazing at the field beyond it, dotted with purple wildflowers. Unlike other vegetation here, the resilient blossoms were native to the island.

The preserve was an amalgamation of environments, created by a sorcerer's spellcraft to provide optimal habitat for the animals Mal had rescued or brought here for rehabilitation. One-way portals, pieced together with fault lines between the protected areas here and the wild places where many of the cats would ultimately be returned, allowed that transition to happen less traumatically than a plane or boat trip.

So much that had once seemed impossible had become possible here. He didn't take any of that for granted. But there were days when he was filled with anger, because none of that could save his daughter from the dangers of the vampire world into which she'd been born.

Elisa stood next to him, her hip pressed against his thigh. Over eighty years ago, she'd come to him, and proven herself far more than a simple Irish maid from the household of another vampire, Lady Danny. Elisa was a woman who'd faced unimaginable loss with courage, not allowing it to stop her from caring for others. Or falling in love with him.

She'd become his third marked servant, which bound her to him forever. Three hundred years in this life, and whatever lay in the after-life, if vampire lore on the subject wasn't merely wishful thinking. He hoped it wasn't, because every day he spent with her told him no amount of time would ever be enough.

She'd also borne his children. Vampires rarely procreated, and if they did, and the child survived to adulthood, it was expected to be their one and only. Twins were an even rarer miracle. He'd only heard of it once before, so their children had received closer scrutiny.

For a mercifully brief timespan, they'd faced the threat of their removal. It was thought the children would be safer with a stronger, older vampire until they'd passed the age at which they were suscep-tible to kidnapping from the Trad sect, or other vampires who hungered for the status blood children could bring.

However, because of the island's special status, and whose direct protection it had—Lady Lyssa, last member of vampire royalty and currently the head of the Vampire Council; Lord Marshall, the Florida overlord; and Lady Danny, once a Region Master in Australia and now a Council member herself—Mal and Elisa had had the freedom to raise them here, and let them become as extraordinary and unique as Fate had planned.

Sometimes Mal wanted to punch Fate in the mouth.

At the young age of fifty, their son Adan had officially become apprenticed to an accomplished sorcerer. Through a trial no one had expected him to survive, he'd evolved from that into a Light Guardian. Thanks to his mating and vampire-servant bonding with a hamadryad, Catriona, who happened to be the ward of the powerful Fae Lord Keldwyn, Adan was also a valuable bridge between the Fae and vampire worlds.

Mal didn't have a problem with any of that. Well, not so much anymore. While it was unlikely he would ever fully trust the Fae, he didn't doubt Catriona's love and devotion to Adan. She'd been with them during the thirteen years when they weren't sure if Adan would make it through the grueling Light Guardian training.

Now the two of them traveled together on the many tasks that involved a Light Guardian, but Adan visited the island whenever he could. Since a vampire was immortal, what was a long time to a human wasn't much more of a blink to them.

Except when it came to the absence of their offspring.

Elisa curled her hand around Mal's braced forearm. "Ruth is safe on the preserve. None of the cats would be after hurting her. She has a way with them. It's one of her many gifts."

They were both aware of what traits *weren't* gifts. Elisa and Mal had recognized the differences between their two children early on, but the years Adan had been away from Ruth had made those things more noticeable. When they were together, they'd functioned almost as a unit, and made it easier for those issues to be overlooked.

Elisa's jewel-blue eyes lifted to his face. "It's all right, Master," she said softly. "I know it. These things work out."

"Usually if the people aware of the problem act before the worst can happen." He set his jaw. "It's time, Elisa. The Circus is the safest place for her."

Elisa tensed, but they'd had the discussion before. Argued about it, something she rarely did with him, but when it happened, it was always about protecting someone. Him, their children. Other children.

That was how their relationship had started all those years ago. She'd brought a half-dozen vampire children to his island. Not born vampires like theirs. These had been human children forcibly turned. Aberrations that most would have agreed needed a swift and humane end. She'd argued with him to save their lives. Argued, pleaded, cajoled. And prevailed. Four had survived and adapted.

They'd found places in the world for them, but Mal remembered the agony of those early days, when they didn't know how it would work out. If it would work out.

Now they visited William and Matthew in Florida frequently, where they lived with Lord Marshall and his servant, Nadia. Adan and Ruth considered the boys good friends. Same for the two females, Nerida and Miah, who resided at the Farida Sanctuary in Tennessee. They were thriving. As much as children forcibly converted to vampires by a monster and forever doomed to look like children could thrive. But yes, they were content and reasonably at peace, in the best scenario possible for them.

Still, their leaving had been hard for Elisa. Adan's thirteen-year separation had been awful, but before that, when he'd left to apprentice with Derek, another Light Guardian, she'd accepted it as what a boy did when he became a man.

Ruth was different. She was another fledgling leaving the nest, with weaknesses that made her far more vulnerable to a dangerous world.

But despite how often her soul had worried, suffered and grieved over her children, adopted and born, his servant was a strong female. And she trusted him. Mal valued that trust and worked hard to keep it.

"Adan says there's a member of the Circus with a threat against her," Mal continued. "She has a protector, but he has other commitments pressing upon him. Lady Yvette, the Circus's Mistress, has suggested a female vampire addition to their security team, one who can specifically watch out for her when he has to attend to those commitments."

"A bodyguard?" Elisa's brow furrowed. "But vampires might attend the Circus performances. They have before."

"Yes. But the Circus already has strong protections in place, even for performances watched by vampires and other races. Yvette is an accomplished sorceress, and Adan says she has additional help in that area. Plus, if Ruth is there, she's under Lady Yvette's protection, and all that entails.

"As far as the job itself, Ruth is well trained. She may not be as strong as other vampires, but she can fight. She's focused, intuitive to danger, and can stay ahead of threats, calling in stronger reinforcements as needed. It's what a good bodyguard does."

A small smile touched Elisa's lips. Her hand tightened on his arm. "A job that says she's capable of being a protector, where she'll have the protection she herself is needing."

"She could take it as a measure to placate her. Her brother is a respected free agent in the vampire world, and she's being offered the job of a security guard, where she'll be cushioned from most of the vampire world's demands."

"Ruth knows her limitations, better than anyone," Elisa noted. "We'll be honest with her, as we've always been."

Mal met her gaze. "We've never discussed the other issue straight out with her. We've waited for her to bring it up."

"Because it's a bloody sin in the vampire world." A rare bitterness edged Elisa's words. "It's ridiculous. They have their own pecking order, the stronger vampires taking the lead, the less strong agreeing to be ruled by them in their territories and regions. How is it so different?"

"You know why." He wrapped his arm around her hip, cupping it with strong fingers. "Vampires are dominant by nature. They submit only when someone proves themselves stronger than them, and only as long as they can hold onto that position. It doesn't indicate a change in their nature.

"Our daughter is a submissive," he stated. "And she's too strong-willed to be good at subterfuge. A vampire around her any length of time will pick up on it. So far the ones who have are family, or as good as. She won't be safe in normal vampire circles. Especially with her being behind the curve on the physical strength she should have by this age."

"Lord Brian said it would continue to develop," Elisa said.

"Yes. Much more slowly than anticipated, and it will reach a stopping point."

Lord Brian ran the research centers in Savannah and Berlin, studying the strengths and weaknesses of vampire kind, helping to contribute to their survival. Even so, he hadn't been able to predict when Ruth's development would cease. His best guess was during her second century. Most vampires continued to strengthen as they aged, enhancing their ability to survive and prosper.

"She is not the first to have the issue," Brian had told them. *"I will not tell you his identity, but there is one well-placed vampire, four centuries old, who has adapted and so far overcome the issue by developing his wits and intelligence. Cultivate those traits in her."*

"If only I hadn't been so determined not to tell anyone." Elisa's voice had that broken note Mal wouldn't tolerate.

He lifted her chin. Catriona had told Mal his servant's faceted eyes were the color of indicolite, a tourmaline. Adan's Fae servant and mate had given Elisa a necklace with them once as a birthday gift, proving it. Except Elisa's eyes had even more facets, thanks to all the emotions that brought them to life.

Her thick brown hair was clipped back, but it clustered in silken waves around her face, tempting him to pull the clip loose so he could spool those locks around his fingers, ease the tightness of her soft lips.

"No. That choice was mine," he told her. "I forbade you to tell anyone about the pregnancy, especially once we realized you were carrying two babies. I knew it would make you a target for other vampires. They would have tried to take you, cut the babies out of you when they were ready, so they could have them."

As he thought of such vampires, his grip tightened. If any of them had come after Elisa, Mal would have done anything to stop them. And it wouldn't have been enough.

The shadows that replaced the fire in his heart clung to his next words. "I could only protect you so much here. It was my decision, Elisa. Our daughter paid the price for it."

"No." Elisa pulled herself out of her own castigation. "You didn't know what would happen. And you *did* permit me to tell Lady Danny, when I became worried at what I was sensing."

Lady Danny was the only other vampire he'd known to have come from a twin birthing. As soon as she'd heard Elisa was carrying twins, she alerted them to the danger they'd never thought to consider.

Better late than never.

Ruth had been a frail child who'd given them a lot of harrowing moments during those first few years. But she'd pulled through.

Because they *were* honest with their children, Mal and Elisa had struggled with the decision they'd ultimately made, not to tell Adan and Ruth why Ruth had been born so much weaker than her brother. They saw no purpose to it.

His Irish flower, his *atsilusgi*, put a hand on Mal's arm. "Her Da looks after her and loves her," she said staunchly. "He would do anything to protect her. Just as your dear mother did for you, God rest her."

A sore point, but one that hit the right target. His mother had sacrificed her life for him on the Trail of Tears.

"Right, then." Elisa squared her shoulders. "So Ruth will be joining the Circus and protect a lass who needs protection. Sounds like a fine adventure."

Day to day, Elisa had educated Brit and a touch of Aussie in her accent, because that was how she'd been raised, as a house servant. However, over the years, she'd purposefully reclaimed even more of her Irish heritage, including in her speech. He understood that need.

Mal drew her close, putting his mouth on hers. He made the kiss the kind that took them deep inside one another, where they danced together in a night sky of stars and shared history, love and loss, laughter and tears. All theirs.

When he lifted his head, her hands were curled against his biceps, her fingers stroking the tattoo there of a lioness, batting at feathers inked over the contour of the muscle.

"Just like every cat brought here, we work with what we have and give them the best possible chance of a good outcome. We'll do the same for Ruth." He said it for his own benefit, as well as Elisa's. "I have faith in her. She has her mother's stubbornness and strength of will."

Elisa's eyes twinkled. "Aye. Her *mother's* stubborn will."

With a mock stern look, Mal lifted her onto the split rail and slid his hands under her skirt. Her knees parted for his demanding touch, her blue eyes darkening as he put himself against her. "I'm going to take you right here," he murmured. "I want to see your eyes reflect the stars, and hear you cry out for me. You are irresistible."

"That's what Kohana used to say about Ruth," Elisa spoke breathlessly as he stroked her clit, and slid several fingers inside her sweet cunt. Ready for him. Always ready for him.

Then there were those gorgeous, full breasts. He'd suckle them until she came for him again.

"Oh..."

"What did he say exactly? Tell me, Elisa."

He loved to watch her struggle to obey a command in such a moment. Her exasperated look was touched with desperate humor. Her nails dug into his biceps again. "He said the man whose heart Ruth captured would need all the help he could get, to resist her."

Kohana had been Mal's second marked servant, for decades the thorn in his side, and his closest friend. He could well imagine the big Lakota Sioux making that wry comment. Mal gave her a dark look. Plus an admonishing pinch for her barely suppressed smile. "One crisis to deal with at a time."

～

She was leaving the island.

Ruth's mind spun like an upended turtle on a busy highway. She needed it to slow down, but after the conversation she'd had with her father, there was little chance of that.

It was just before dawn, so she was in her room underground, where she'd be protected from the sun. Once dawn came, sleep would claim her, whether she wanted it to do so or not, but at least it would give her busy brain a break.

Ruth lay in her bed, studying the handful of black and white feathers she'd been able to find and collect in the vicinity of her wrestling match with the incubus. She'd put them in a clay pot on her dresser, one that Chumani, Kohana's wife, had made for Ruth when she was nine. Etchings of bounding bobcats formed a decorative collar below the rounded lip.

Before Ruth put the feathers in there, she'd laid them out on the dresser. Three wing feathers and a contour feather. She'd confirmed the jagged lightning pattern, the silver-tinged white intersecting gleaming black.

She'd gathered them up into one hand and stroked them through the channel formed by her half-curled fist. The contact made her shiver and recall the astounding force of his sexual energy. The demanding strength of his hands upon her.

He'd liked her resistance. She suspected he'd particularly liked it because she'd known she was overpowered and outmatched, and it didn't stop her from fighting.

The over-the-top climaxes had left a very pointed message. *I let you run from me, but when it comes time to take what I want, you* will *submit.*

She had an answer for him. *If we meet again, I don't plan to make it easy on you.*

Incubus was still her best guess on what her dangerous playmate was. But she knew of another winged race.

Angels.

Adan had told her there was one at the Circus. She'd thought he was messing with her, but he insisted he wasn't. She'd never had the chance to attend a Circus performance. That was about to change.

A woman needs protection there... The Circus travels to many places. As a Circus employee, you would be under the protection and rule of Lady Yvette. She would be your overlord while you're with them.

When Mal explained the situation to her, she'd heard all the unspoken messages. This was an option to broaden her world, with the best safeguards possible. But there were no guarantees. For the first time in her life, if she needed immediate protection, she would be out of range of the people and setting she trusted to provide it.

"Do you wish to go?" he'd asked, watching her closely.

When her father was experiencing strong emotions, his voice became flatter and harder, his expression freezing in lines that made him look almost cruel.

They'd been in his home office, dominated by a scarred giant desk that looked like an old sea chest. When Mal had asked her to join him there, Ruth had been sure it was because he knew about her earlier encounter. She'd braced herself for his censure for not alerting him, but that concern had vanished in the face of the unexpected topic.

Even so, she wasn't in the habit of lying to her father, or hiding information from him. For the first couple decades of a born vampire's life, it was impossible anyway. Vampire parents could scour their kids' minds if they suspected even a hint of evasion. They didn't hesitate to do so, since a pre-pubescent vampire's bloodlust, strength and lack of impulse control could take an adult human's life, and their island had a staff of a dozen humans. They were all first or second marked, but only a third mark "might" have the strength to fight off a born vampire child and prevail.

At that age, if she'd ever even thought about copping an attitude, demanding her parents "respect her privacy," her father's stare would have pushed the words right back down her throat, wisely blocking anything else from coming out. Other than the two words he'd expect.

Yes, Sgidoda.

Yes, Da.

She used the Cherokee and Irish terms interchangeably.

She was an adult now, but the respect was still there, and well-earned. Ruth circled the desk to sink to her knees beside him. She put her hand on his leg as she gazed up into his face.

"Yes, I want to go. I think I need to." Change was scary. But she was ready for it, and that would give her the courage to bear the uncertainty. "I won't forget just how precious home is."

Mal stroked her hair as she laid her head on his knee and wrapped her arms around his muscled calf to hold him close. He always smelled like earth, fur, forest. Wild things.

"I will miss you, *tlanistè*."

The affectionate, informal term for *daughter* was gentle in his deep voice.

She raised her head to gaze at him. She saw her father, but there was no denying his appeal as a man. All vampires were sexy and mesmerizing. Whenever Ruth accompanied her father to the mainland for a supply pickup he had to handle directly, human females stammered and blushed over his simplest question, like "Do you have half-inch PVC pipe?"

Elisa liked to tease him, saying he looked like a warrior from the set of *Dances With Wolves*. With the long hair he sometimes wore braided with feathers, beads and ribbons—when he didn't have to work close to the big cats—it was a pretty accurate comparison.

When Ruth was a child, he'd been strength and authority to her, the port in the storm. She'd watched him weather some awful ones and hold fast. As an adult, she wanted him to be proud of her. Wanted him not to think of her as a burden, a constant worry.

Aside from her own reasons for wanting to go, she hoped this was a path to do that.

Dawn was getting closer, and they'd discussed what was needed. As she rose to leave, she stopped at the office door and traced the knife marks alongside the frame. It was an idle habit, Mal testing his throwing accuracy from his desk.

When Kohana was alive, he'd come to Mal's office and brace his hand next to it as he informed Mal of important matters. Like when Mal had his head up his own ass. Some of those marks were Mal's answer to that assessment.

"Have you ever hit him, *Sgidoda*? By accident, or on purpose?"

Adan had asked the question when they were both much younger. Ruth remembered her brother's wide blue eyes.

"I never miss what I aim at," Mal had told him. "How do you think he lost his leg?"

They'd been in the living room, Elisa mending clothes, Mal whittling, Ruth and Adan playing a game on the rug. Kohana, peeling vegetables in the large kitchen, snorted and tapped his prosthetic leg with the butt of the peeler.

"Your father is telling tales," he told Adan. "He annoyed me one day and I lacked a proper weapon. So I cut off my leg to have something large enough to beat some sense into him." His mouth twitched. "Sadly, it was not large enough."

According to her father, Kohana had written his own job description as a second marked servant. Her father still missed his friend. They all did. She and Adan had called Kohana "uncle." When Kohana asked why, Adan told him, "Because you and father are brothers. Aren't you?"

The two men had been out in the barn, working together to fix a faulty pump for the rain barrels. Mal had lifted his head at the comment. Kohana said nothing, one of the few times Ruth remembered him showing the deference a vampire expected from a servant, but ever after she'd known Kohana honored those protocols, not because they existed, but because he respected her father.

"Yes," Mal said. "We are."

When Ruth emerged from Mal's office, she saw her mother sitting in the hallway. Elisa was rarely idle. Tonight, she was reviewing and making notes in her garden journal. Her curiosity, her desire to learn and her love of reading were things she'd given Ruth.

Unlike Mal, Elisa didn't have an expression that walled off what was going on behind it. Her mother was resilient as hell, but the wave of emotions she was feeling made Ruth grip the frame anew.

"I'll be okay." Looking over her shoulder, Ruth met her father's eyes, her back straight and chin set. "We knew I would eventually have to face the big, bad world of vampires on my own. I'm ready to take those risks. Just like Lil Sol."

Lil Sol had been a bobcat cub born with a deformed leg and a bad heart. He'd been found on a Florida highway and had two years on the preserve before his heart gave out. Initially, they'd thought to keep him away from the others to protect him, but he'd pined for the company of his brethren. With them, he managed many of the hunting and play behaviors they did.

"There's no sense in living a half-life to get twice as much time," she told her father.

His flat expression came back, which surrounded her heart with his love and held it tight. Ruth moved into the hallway to accept the warm strength of her mother's arms.

"Lil Sol was far tougher than those other cats expected," Elisa said, woman to woman. "'Tis the way of it, more often than not."

Returning to the present, Ruth curled her arms around her knees, drawing them up against the pillow she was holding, and gazed at the bouquet of feathers.

Was the male she'd encountered earlier tonight both angel and incubus? Was that possible? She couldn't ask Mal, not at this point. With the significant turn of events, she'd decided not to raise the issue she'd expected to have to discuss, why she hadn't called for him when she realized an intruder was on their island.

She couldn't give Mal an answer she didn't know herself.

In the few days before she left for the Circus, she'd wait and see if the winged male came back. If not, then it was a passing encounter, over and done. Nothing her father needed to know about.

The sun was starting to crest, because the lethargy she could never seem to shake or push past started to grip her. Other vampires her age could get in a couple hours more waking time in whatever burrow they found from the sun. Watch cable, write letters. Surf social media. Instead, she was comatose once it fully cleared the horizon, and started its slow ascent into the sky.

She wondered how it would be at the Circus. Adan had told her when they weren't doing a show, the Circus set up camp in the in-between places between worlds, and the daylight was a soft buttery gold that didn't burn vampires.

On an impulse, she shoved herself off the mattress and stumbled to the dresser. She brought the clay pot back to her nightstand and took one of the wing feathers into the bed with her. As she held it against her, the tip teased her collarbone like the male's fingertips.

Whether it made her sleep more or less restfully didn't matter. Whoever he was, she wanted him in her dreams with her.

CHAPTER THREE

Several nights later, she was ready to depart, and full of anticipation. Adan had called and said he'd be the one guiding Ruth through the portal. He'd handle her introduction to Lady Yvette personally.

The thirteen years he'd been in the bowels of the Underworld, with a slim-to-none chance of surviving Guardian training, had been agonizing, for all of them. Though he was out in the world doing Guardian work now, Ruth still treated a chance to see him like being handed water when on the brink of fatal dehydration.

She tried not to show it too obviously, because he *was* her brother, which meant she had to give him a lot of shit about things. With the Light Guardian mojo, he'd become way too insightful, aka "pretending to be a know-it-all."

Catriona, his mate and third marked servant, was visiting her adopted father, Lord Keldwyn, in the Fae world, so he'd be alone. However, on the call, he'd promised Mal and Elisa they'd both be at the next family holiday. If he managed it, Ruth would make sure Lady Yvette knew she'd need time off to join them.

She viewed Catriona as a sister-in-law, with a heavy emphasis on sister. Considering the first time they'd met, Ruth had done her best to kill the slim Fae, their relationship had progressed pretty well.

Last night, Ruth had attached a fastener to one of the feathers and strung a chain on it. Before that, she'd returned to the savanna environment to give the others back to the wind. And to give the male one more chance to return.

He didn't, but Tau had pounced on one of the released feathers, sniffing it suspiciously.

"Yeah. He was pure trouble." The remembrance of just how much trouble shivered over her skin.

Now she was headed for the creek portal, located in the mountain lions' habitat. Mal drove, Elisa in the back seat of the Jeep, her hand on the seat next to Ruth's shoulder.

Fragile humans climbed mountains and jumped out of airplanes. Ate bad food. They could be erased in an instant, and they did those things because their lives *were* so short and fragile. She wasn't going to be outdone by a mere mortal.

As they pulled up, Adan was already there, waiting.

Her twin had Mal's sculpted cheekbones and jaw, his build and a light bronze skin tone, but Elisa's captivating blue eyes and thick waves of molasses colored hair, though Adan kept his short. Ruth had her father's straight black hair and dark brown eyes with hints of gold, but her mother's barely five-foot height. However, while her mother was an ample-bosomed, tiny waisted hourglass, Ruth's leanness, taut as a steel cable, also came from her father. She'd enhanced it through refinement of her fighting skills and building as much strength as her body would let her have.

She possessed a vampire's usual arsenal of tools. Her compulsion ability allowed her to draw in a random human for blood needs. She could make their mind hazy enough to forget the event afterward. Most of her life, she'd had access to the blood of willing second marks on the island, making those abilities unnecessary, but she knew how to use them.

While she had a woman's curves and her sexual appeal was as distracting as her brother's and father's, she didn't give that much thought. Well, up until the other night, when the male's attentions said how much he desired her. His touch made her aware of every curve, the softness of her skin, the thick weight of her hair. She'd thought of how it would feel, caught in his hard fist as he shoved into her.

Stop thinking about that, right the hell now. Vampire families were open about sex. They had to be. Until she'd learned control, her father had to be within range to supervise, so she didn't kill the blood donor she was enjoying that way. It had been the same for Adan.

But they could detect arousal as readily as the smell of fresh blood, and her feeling worked up right now would draw curiosity and questions. Fortunately, the timing worked as a good distraction. Elisa was out of the Jeep almost before Mal parked it. Adan caught their mother in a warm and laughing embrace, lifting her off her feet.

Becoming a Light Guardian had made Adan look harder and stronger. Even as a young vampire, he hadn't been a pushover, but he was connected to powers that could create or destroy, and his serious eyes said he'd more than once faced the difficult decision of which to choose.

He clasped his father's hand, their elbows bending to pull one another in. Mal cupped his son's head briefly before drawing back. "You're looking well."

Adan smiled, a wry expression. "Don't tell Derek. He'll think he's not working me hard enough. I swear he goes out and starts cosmic trouble, just to make sure I don't have a day off."

In addition to being the Light Guardian who'd mentored Adan during his early magic-user training, Derek Stormwind had helped Mal set up the island's portal and fault line magic years ago. He'd also done what he could to ensure Adan survived Guardian school, when the Unseelie Fae Queen had drafted him into it far earlier than any other enrollee in history.

Yeah, Catriona was cool, but the Fae Queen fit Ruth's low opinion of most of the race.

Derek and his wife, Ruby, an accomplished witch, brought their son, Jem, to the island often. Elisa and Jem had a special bond; Elisa reacted to his presence the way Ruth expected a human would to a beloved grandchild. Which was good, because with the low vampire procreation stats, it was unlikely Adan or she would ever offer their mother that.

Their parents had stepped back so Ruth could have her turn to hug Adan. "Whine, whine, whine," she said, addressing Adan's complaint about Derek. "Don't pretend you don't love not having to shovel out the rehab enclosures."

"How long is it going to take Da to realize he'd be better off feeding you to the cats? Or is he worried you're so rotten, you'd give them fatal indigestion?"

She was going to punch him in the side, pull his hair or at least make a face, but instead she held onto him an extra moment. God, she missed him so much, so often.

Her other half.

Would there ever be a time when she didn't fear that emptiness she'd felt all those years, his soul beyond her reach? A vampire mind link only reached so far, but his life force was so intimately connected to hers that, as long as he was on the physical surface of the earth somewhere, she could feel that connection.

The Guardian school training was in the Underworld, so the bond awareness had vanished as soon as he was enrolled. The only thing that helped her hold the terror at bay, until Derek told her it didn't mean he was dead, was remembering it wasn't the first time it had happened. Adan had been kidnapped by the Fae as a child, and it had disappeared then, too.

When he returned from Guardian school, she'd had half a second to hold onto the hope she'd never have to feel that awful emptiness again. Then Adan had let her know whenever he and Derek went between worlds, dimensions, wherever the hell they were, it would likely happen again.

She'd mostly adjusted to it, knowing it was part of his job, but she would never like it. If he died, that was what it would feel like. Permanently.

Adan's arms were secure around her. *Don't be morbid, sis. I've proven how hard I am to kill. Twice now.*

Eavesdropper. And you're a cream puff. I could kill you with a sun lamp. On its lowest setting.

He drew back. When she goaded him like that, he rarely answered in kind. Instead, he insulted her prickly personality, barbed tongue, or music taste. Now, his eyes upon her, he didn't hide where his thoughts had gone. She'd asked him never to do so, and he'd promised.

"This is a good decision," he said quietly.

"Yeah. I hope so."

Adan glanced toward Mal and Elisa. "Lady Yvette has someone who wants to meet with Ruth, before she's officially accepted under her care."

"I didn't think I needed anyone's permission other than hers. She's ranked like an overlord, right?"

"Yes, but she does answer to the Council."

Mal's expression tightened. "Who?"

Adan paused, glancing at Ruth. *Don't lose your shit, sis. If you freak out, he will.*

"Lady Lyssa."

~

Mal respected Lady Lyssa, arguably the most powerful vampire in their world, and the current head of the Vampire Council. Many Council members and higher-ranking vampires had visited the island over the years. Most stayed a few days, and some even pitched in to help with the island's daily labor-intensive operations. Mal knew the value of having such influential patrons, while grumbling over the disruption of the sanctuary's routine and the need to hone diplomatic skills that didn't come naturally to him.

In the 1990s, Kohana had noted the vampires viewed the island as an "eco-vacation." A place to reconnect to the earth and slow life's pace. Mal had scowled at the term and inflicted another scar in the doorframe.

While Mal fortunately didn't seem too disturbed by Adan's announcement, he wanted to know why such an important vampire needed to sanction Ruth's presence.

"It has to do with the woman she's protecting," Adan told him. "Ruth's going to be fine, Da. Promise."

On that note, Ruth allowed herself one last hug from her parents and then stepped up beside Adan as he called the magic that would open the portal.

She'd never traveled that way before. Adan had told her how it would be, but he'd framed it in a context she would understand. Which wasn't accurate at all.

Her recent experience, being plucked off the ground effortlessly and accelerating through the air at a speed that made it impossible to have any thoughts at all, came far closer. Adrenaline, a dash of terror, and a heavy dose of *oh, that cup of blood for breakfast was a really bad idea.*

When her mind stopped spinning, she was kneeling on an unfamiliar forest path. Adan held her hair back as she coughed and bent over double. Thank the Great Father and Mother that Adan hadn't portaled her directly into the audience with Lady Yvette and Lady Lyssa.

When she straightened, Adan pulled a handkerchief out of the bag slung across his body. "Portal first aid supplies?" she rasped as she took it in a trembling hand. "Oh, fuck."

"What?"

She glared down at herself. She'd chosen her outfit carefully. Snug black jeans with a cream-colored tank, the jeans tucked into calf boots. Her belt had an ornate buckle Adan had brought her from a Cherokee festival. Around her neck was a collar of turquoise nugget ovals set in silver frames. Below it rested a bolo tie with a matching silver and turquoise pull on it.

Because Adan had warned her the Circus's current in-between portal campsite was in a colder climate, she'd donned her calf-length inner fleece and outer cowhide jacket. It had a rich camel color and was quilted, the squares edged with the same cream-colored fleece.

Some of her hair was pulled up in a top knot, the rest loose down her back, the strands Adan had held out of the way. Silver rings adorned the shells of her ears, and another turquoise and silver nugget adorned the top knot.

It was a stylish, sexy and professional outfit, now baptized with several drops of bloody vomit. No time to fix it; no one with any sense of self-preservation kept high-ranked vampires waiting.

"Here, stay still. Don't tell Derek I did this. He's anal about using magic for trivial purposes."

"I want to see Derek tell Lady Lyssa an audience with her is trivial. Double crap. Where's my case?"

"I found out where you'll be quartered before I came to get you. I sent it there as we came out of the portal. Another thing Derek would ping me for, but I figured it would be easier to stride through camp with a determined, badass bodyguard look if you weren't dragging a giant suitcase behind you."

"Good thinking." As he focused on the several drops, Ruth closed her eyes and tried to come up with an alternative plan if he couldn't fix it. A brush of heat and an amused voice broke into her mental scrambling.

"I can protect the world, but you think I can't get a bloodstain out of cloth. You're all set."

Opening her eyes, Ruth saw with relief her clothes were pristine. "I'm allowed reasonable doubt. *Sgidoda* built an entire bespelled sanctuary with Derek that connects to portals all over the world. Yet if he puts his Jeep keys down anywhere but the hook in the entryway, he can't find them without *Etsi's* help."

"You know why. She told us."

"'Women have the magic 'find-things' uterus. Men have the 'fix-anything' pecker.'"

When Elisa had made that proclamation, Kohana had laughed so hard he nearly fell off the bench at the dinner table. He roared even louder when Mal entered moments later to demand, "Where the hell are my pliers?"

Elisa had calmly found them on the railing by the porch swing. He'd laid them there a couple hours before, when the two of them had shared a glass of lemonade. She'd been curled up against his side, her hand resting on his thigh as he tasted the tartness of the fruit in the glass, then moved to sample it from her lips.

First a light brush, then deeper, his knuckles brushing the side of her ample breast, moving up to her shoulder and throat, where he put his own mouth to take a meal from the vein that pumped harder in response to his touch. Like every part of her, striving to please him and offer what he needed.

Whenever her father mislaid something, nine times out of ten it was because the pleasure he took in his servant had captured his attention to the exclusion of anything else.

Yep. There wasn't a species on the planet that could match the vampire sex drive. Except maybe the male Ruth hadn't physically seen.

Stop thinking about him.

Adan gave her a critical look. "You look dynamite, sis. Sexy as hell and twice as kickass, gotta say. You put thought into the look."

She had. She might have her issues, but she could protect a human female and wanted to look the part. The boots were flat, the soles thick rubber. Two knives were concealed within easy reach.

She knew several fight disciplines, and practiced the forms regularly. Plus sparred with anyone who could be trusted with the knowledge of the extent of her abilities. The vampire world was all about power. Who had it, who didn't, and who could take it from someone else.

The thought brought a wave of nerves and a reminder that she was really doing this. Leaving the shelter and protection of home.

She'd be fine. But still... She gripped Adan's biceps and touched her head to his chest, gratified when he dropped a kiss on her head. "Thanks," she said. "Thanks for reminding me you're still my dumbass brother, even if to the rest of the world you're an all-powerful Light Guardian."

He snorted. "I'm a bottom of the totem pole Light Guardian who Derek routinely kicks around to remind me of it. He says humility is the most important skill for me to learn right now. Except when I need my reservoir of 'I-can-save-the-world' arrogance to back him up in a firefight."

She grinned, linking her arm through his. "I'm available to spar with you whenever you need to hone those firefight skills. Just to make Derek happy, I'll include a full scoop of humility."

"Dream on." Adan rolled his eyes, but he gave her hand a squeeze and escorted her toward the forest line, beyond which she saw an open field populated by large tents.

He didn't need to give her any direction on the upcoming meeting. The flow of important visitors on the island meant they'd been coached as children on vampire etiquette.

But she did yank free from him, an involuntary reaction, as she noted what vomiting up her last meal had caused her to miss. It was daylight.

"It's all right," he told her, as she peered warily up at the sky through the interlaced tree branches. "Remember, I said the in-between portal space is a magically manufactured environment."

"There's a sun," she said.

"It's not our real sun," Adan said. "The light doesn't harm us here, just like in the Fae world, though we can't really explain why for either. You won't have to sleep underground here, but your body will remember the cycles of day and night. When the Circus comes out of the in-between spaces for a performance, Lady Yvette times the emergence for after dark. You and she will come back into a place like this for your daylight rest and rejoin the Circus at dusk."

"Okay. Sorry." She took his arm again.

"A lifetime of knowing sunlight is fatal to us isn't so easily discarded," he told her. "I get it."

As they stepped out of the tree's cover, she tried not to crane her neck to keep looking at the "fake" sun. It was chilly, as Adan had warned her, making Ruth glad for her coat, but she could *feel* the sun's mellow heat against her face and throat.

"The portal area where we emerged looked a lot like the island side," she noted. "With the creek and same trees."

"When the Circus is in an in-between location," Adan told her, "I structure the current portal on their end so it looks like where we came from. It helps me remember what the current setting is."

"Makes sense. Does Derek know you got lost on the island where you grew up?"

Teasing him helped steady her. She hoped he'd understand.

"I was a lot younger than I am now." Adan shot her a mock look of offense. "Pretend like you respect me in front of Lady Lyssa and Lady Yvette, and I'll give you candy afterward. If your mouth doesn't get you killed. In which case, I'll eat it all myself."

To uphold the sibling code, she offered no promises. But truthfully, she'd be on her very best behavior.

On Lady Lyssa's first visit to the island that Ruth remembered, the vampire queen had lifted Ruth onto her hip. Ruth had threaded small hands through the straight dark hair that looked like her own. It felt like strands of satin ribbon. Though Lyssa's jade green eyes were warm and smiling, Ruth had detected a vibration of power around the vampire queen, overwhelming enough she'd ducked her head shyly, making sure her father was near.

Lady Lyssa's servant at that time, Thomas, had played with her and Adan after dinner, a card game that taught them bible verses. He'd gravely asked them about the animals on the preserve and seemed suitably impressed with their knowledge. Before he came into Lyssa's service, he'd been a Franciscan monk.

As Ruth and Adan grew up, Lyssa returned to the island several times, often with Council members. The liberties a child could take gave way to an uber-respectful deference for the thousand-year-old plus vampire. She was slim and no taller than Ruth. Yet the still way she watched everyone and everything around her reminded Ruth of the big cats, if they were on the hunt...constantly.

Thomas had died some years ago. Jacob, her current servant, had a keen intelligence and gift for insight comparable to her monk, but he was a fighter, not a scholar. He was protective of his lady, but also amiable and level-headed. He'd sparred with Ruth to help improve her fight skills, and she'd tailored her speed and strength to make it an even match and learn everything she could.

Lady Lyssa and Lady Yvette were going to see a vampire female capable of being a bodyguard. Not the girl who fell asleep in trees with a book in her lap.

They'd entered the Circus campground, which distracted Ruth from the nerves the thought tried to poke to life. Colorfully painted wooden wagons, the 19th century ancestor of the modern RV, were scattered over several acres, arranged around large pavilion tents.

One of them had its flaps pinned up, revealing that it was a cook tent for the Circus troupe. A buffet was set out, and the picnic tables surrounding it were partially occupied. The buffet was attended by a handful of busy men and women wearing aprons. They moved between it and the prep area. Cooks monitored Dutch ovens and skillets on stovetops, chopped ingredients and stirred deep stockpots. She smelled some kind of chicken soup and fresh bread. Several camp dogs—possibly also performers, since one was a poodle doing an impressive, give-me-a-treat whirling dervish on his back legs—closely watched the goings-on.

"Why does it look like we stepped back in time?"

"In-between portal locations adapt better to less technology." Adan gave it all a fond look. "When the Circus emerges into our world to do a performance, the wagons become RVs, and the cooking appliances update to the latest in shiny outdoor equipment. Unless Yvette wants it to stay old-timey looking for the parades they do when the Circus first 'comes to town.'"

"That kind of set up takes a lot of work."

"Yvette's a damn good sorceress," Adan said.

"Is she more sorceress than vampire?"

Adan shot her that patented predatory look of their kind, showing her the gleaming point of a fang. It reminded her that when he'd returned from the grueling years of Light Guardian training, his first order of business had been claiming Catriona for his own, making her his third mark servant, bound to him forever.

Even before seeing Ruth or their parents.

"One doesn't exist without the other," he said.

"Oh...wow." Her attention was pulled to the sky. What her peripheral vision had suggested was a pair of large birds, maybe turkey vultures, turned out to not be that at all. Two young dragons, swooping and teasing one another, had changed course. They plunged toward the ground, on a straight line toward a plucked chicken sitting on a table, waiting for the cooking pot.

A screech cut the air, ten times louder and more ear-shattering than a hawk's. What appeared in the sky, as abruptly as if it had materialized there, had Ruth readying herself for the unwise decision to fight or, the more prudent one, to run for her life. Adan clamped a strong hand on her arm, keeping her still.

"It's best not to move," he advised.

The really, really large female dragon, with teeth that looked longer than Ruth's forearm—a lot of teeth—swooped downward, though not as precipitously as her young. She also didn't come as close to the ground.

It was enough, however. The young dragons banked so close to their target the move rippled the cooks' apron strings. They shot up into the air above the mother, then dropped like stones, landing on her back and hooking themselves to the layers of gleaming scales.

She grumbled at them, a sound that would make a pit bull's snarl sound like the yip of a teacup Pomeranian. As she rose back into the air, continuing on, Ruth noted she dipped her wings at the lead cook, who gave her a respectful bow and sign of gratitude.

"Holy shit."

Adan grinned. "Yeah. That's Jetana. Welcome to a normal day at the Circus. There are lots of species and races here, most with their own protocols. Be sure to learn them. I don't want to find out if a partially digested vampire sister can be restored."

"Will Derek consider *that* trivial?"

"Let's not test it." Adan elbowed her.

She noticed everyone had stopped their conversations and eating with the appearance of the big female. They didn't return to either until she was well on her way. An apparent sign of respect—and caution.

As they proceeded on, she took mental snapshots to consider or investigate later. Roustabouts sat on buckets, playing cards. A smithy, a muscular dwarf, worked under a smaller tent, shaping metal and offering advice to another man repairing a pulley system.

Acrobats practiced on open ground near jugglers. One woman was reading a book while in a Chinese split, her elbows on the ground between her spread thighs. She sucked on a Tootsie Pop, the purple wrapper creased in her fingers.

Ruth was getting her own interested glances. She didn't act too friendly, but offered courteous nods when eye contact was made. The responses were a mirror of her own. This was a place where she'd have to earn her spot. She didn't mind that. She preferred it.

When the hairs on the back of her neck rose, she glanced over her shoulder. She saw nothing but open ground between several of the wagons, but then a flock of starlings flushed out of a bank of long grass outside their perimeter. It reminded her of the warning signs when one of the big cats was in the area.

A shadow passed behind her, the brush of feathers against her thigh, sliding over her hip.

"Still say no?" A whisper in her ear, echoing inside her body.

Ruth spun, knocking against Adan as she did so. Her brother immediately went on alert, one hand on her arm, not to hold her, but to tell her where he was, like soldiers entering a battle zone. His other hand had lifted, ready to point a magical defense. "What?"

She paused, heart pounding. Gazed around her. The blacksmith was studying her with cool eyes. His companion was noting her exposed fangs and asking a low question of the dwarf, his brow lifted.

She saw nothing to explain her reaction. Damn it. But she knew she hadn't imagined it. "Just a voice," she said, low. "I thought I heard someone. Felt someone."

Adan gave her an odd look. "Do they have a version of hazing for newbies?" she asked.

"Yeah, but pretty good-natured stuff, for the most part. And they wouldn't do it before they know who you are or why you're here."

"Well, they sure as hell know *what* I am now." Embarrassingly, she'd not only bared her fangs, but triggered their defensive lengthening. She retracted them, and did her best to look at ease so everyone would go back to what they were doing.

Why did she feel like *he* was here, close by? Laughing at her.

Waiting to mess with her some more. She thought of a reason for it, and then cursed her own weakness. That damn feather she'd kept...

"I like it when you run away. It makes me want to catch you all the more."

How could Adan *not* hear that? She could tell he couldn't, because his concerned expression didn't change as the words slid along the side of her neck, shivering straight over her collar bone and the upper rise of her breast.

"Seriously, fuck off," she muttered. "Just getting my head on straight," she told Adan. She put her hand on the bolo tie. Not to grip it, but to press the point of her wrist against what lay beneath it, nestled between her breasts. The wing feather she'd tucked under the band of her bra, for fuck-all knew what reasons.

She'd ignored a basic tenet of magical practice. Direct contact with objects of power was one of the strongest ways to feel their influence. The incubus or whatever-he-was had had magic oozing out of his pores. And apparently from his feathers.

"Ruth..."

She shook her head. "It's okay. Let's go. I don't want to be late for my job interview."

Adan wasn't buying it, but with the Council head waiting, he didn't have much choice. Fortunately, there was no repeat of that weirdness as they arrived at Yvette's quarters. The yurt's frame was crafted of sturdy wood, the sloped circular roof larger than the circumference of an amusement park carousel. The fabric that created it was painted in a marble swirl of black and red.

The entryway to the yurt was an open archway. They could hear two female voices conversing within.

Jacob sat to the right of the opening. He was sanding a dagger, one of six blades on a small table before him.

"Gundar put you to work?" Adan asked.

Jacob's midnight blue eyes under dark brows showed amusement. "I admired his works-in-progress, and he told me if I sanded these, he'd give me one of the final products. Plus, Yvette prefers everyone enjoying the Circus to earn the privilege, no matter how short the visit."

"Everyone, including your lady?"

Ruth held her breath at the impertinence, but Jacob chuckled. The easy familiarity said Lyssa's bound servant considered Adan a friend. On the island, he was just her brother. Here he was a Light Guardian, treated on par with the company he was keeping.

"I leave that question between her and Lady Yvette," Jacob said. "A place I wisely stay clear of."

Jacob's thick brown hair had traces of russet and was long enough to reach his broad shoulders. His trained fighter's body moved with grace and deadly intent. Yet his face held a mild amiability—until something more dangerous was required. He coupled his intelligence with self-restraint, all elements vital to serving a queen. Particularly one who'd dealt with the cutthroat politics and violent tendencies of the vampire world for a *very* long time.

His attention moved to Ruth as he rose to give her a courteous bow, observing the required courtesies. In their world, the highest-ranked servant still fell below the lowest-ranked vampire.

Jacob had chosen strategic times to ignore such protocols, risking the ire of other vampires. Sometimes even his own formidable lady's. However, those incidents had only added to his reputation, ultimately on the side of respect, because such acts were *always* done in the name of protecting Lady Lyssa. Her well-being meant everything to him. *She* meant everything to him.

Such devotion from a servant was appropriate. A vampire feeling the same way toward their human servant? That was a sticky problem, one that plagued the Council and the vampire world.

For a long time, the accepted thinking—and arguably still the prevailing feeling among most vampires—was that a vampire didn't fall in love with their servant. Such "weakness" made the vampire vulnerable to dangerous influences from the human, and that would undermine the vampire world in unacceptable ways.

Depending on the rank of the "misguided vampire," their overlord, Region Master or the Council itself, would order the execution of the servant. The vampire would be placed under the direct supervision of a vampire who could "reinforce and reeducate" them as needed.

Then, over a decade ago, Lady Lyssa had declared her love for Jacob before the Vampire Council itself. Since then, Lord Mason, who also currently served on the Council, had made a similar declaration about his servant, Jessica.

While Ruth didn't know how she felt about the matter, she couldn't deny a twist of satisfaction over Lord Mason's announcement.

It had set back on their heels those who'd always claimed the "malady" was a female vampire problem. Because female vampires were more susceptible to emotional manipulation by male servants. Of course. Cue the eye roll.

Around the same time Lord Mason had made his declaration, Lord Brian had presented strong proof that vampires and servants with "closer" bonds had a more likely chance of successfully reproducing. With less than five thousand vampires in the world, and a disturbingly low percentage of those being born vampires—considered genetically stronger and more vital to the overall survival of their race—things that might aid their survival carried a lot of weight.

The proof had driven the framing of a comprehensive policy which would improve the standing of servants in the vampire world, giving them certain protections and rights they'd never held. Originally introduced by Lord Mason, it had been stalled ever since, as it was subjected to multiple revisions and "cooling off" periods, depending on what else Council was handling.

With immortal beings, debating a society-altering piece of legislation for over a decade wasn't unusual, but recently, a push to finish it, to call it to a vote, had been growing. Not just within the Council, but from Region Masters and overlords. It was hard to tell how it would go, because strong feelings existed for and against it.

Adan hadn't had much interest in vampire politics, except as needed to navigate the magical studies he wanted to pursue. Until Catriona, he hadn't even given any thought to being in love. And though Catriona had Fae and human blood, her Fae side was given far more weight, so the subject of vampire-human power dynamics didn't really apply to their relationship.

But Ruth thought about it. Some of the stories about Lady Lyssa and Jacob were probably exaggerated, but seeing them on the island, she knew many were not.

She'd wondered what it would be like to have that total bond of physical and mental intimacy, not just what could exist between a vampire and servant, but between two souls, as it obviously did for Catriona and Adan. His devotion, his fascination with his Fae, their protectiveness and love for one another, was evident. Undeniable.

Why the fuck did that bring the invisible male back to her head? It had been a chance meeting, a game, driven by healthy lust and the fun of a good fight. If he was lingering in her mind, it was because of the mystery attached to him. That was all.

Earth to Ruth. Wake the fuck up.

The mental jab from her brother snapped her attention back to her immediate surroundings. Jacob was giving her a puzzled but too keen look.

He asked you how your portal jump was.

"Dizzying," she said. "Apologies. I may still be a little disoriented."

Jacob dipped his head toward the yurt's interior. Ruth recognized Lyssa's even voice. Whatever she said caused a short burst of sensual laughter. It rolled over Ruth's skin even as it prickled, a warning of the power of its owner. Yvette, she assumed.

"Sometimes a portal jump can deplete your energy," Jacob told her. "If you carry a blood reserve with you, I recommend taking a couple swallows before going in. This isn't an audience where you want your attention to wander."

No kidding. She removed the flask she carried in the hip bag she wore. As Adan exchanged a few comments with Jacob about the daggers, she took a couple discreet swallows. Elisa had packed it, telling her daughter, *"I know, you don't think you'll need it, but just in case."*

Etsi never stops being Etsi. Are you all right? Adan asked.

He hadn't stopped talking to Jacob, but vampires learned to split their mental attention to communicate with servants or, in their case, a vampire with whom they had a mind link.

Yes, I'm fine. I'm ready to do this.

Whether it was true or not, a different expression crossed Jacob's face, indicating he'd received his own missive. He glanced at Adan, a telling look, before he spoke. "My lady and the Lady Yvette are ready for Ruth. Lady Yvette thanks you for bringing her, but assumes you have other matters to handle for Derek."

Adan's expression shuttered. Ruth put a hand on his arm. "Of course."

If I need a protector for a job interview, I'm not going to be much of a bodyguard, am I?

Adan met her gaze. *I'll check back in on you soon, sister.*

She felt love for him for his care, but also a slight resentment at the implication she needed the backup. She was going to prove herself here, damn it. Her brother might be the big, bad Light Guardian, but she had her own gifts.

"I'll be fine. Go away. We women have serious business to discuss."

Adan's eyes twinkled as Jacob chuckled. *Good.* That was the response she wanted from them both. Squaring her shoulders, she stepped inside the yurt.

And saw the male who'd left a handful of feathers in her grasp.

CHAPTER FOUR

H old it together.

Ripping off her own arm would have been easier than yanking her gaze from him, but she managed it before she had time to absorb anything except her certainty it was him. She should have registered that dense energy and inhaled his scent well outside the yurt, but she'd figure out why she hadn't later. First things first.

Lady Lyssa and Lady Yvette sat in two velvet-cushioned, polished wood chairs. A table holding one delicate teacup and one snifter sat between them. Lyssa's tea was jasmine; Yvette's half empty glass held an alcohol with the scent and color of bruised oranges.

Ruth dropped to one knee for Lady Lyssa, then rose and executed a respectful waist bend to Lady Yvette. "My ladies. It's an honor to be here."

She pushed confidence into her voice, building a wall around her and the women that excluded anything else.

If he started doing his sex-her-up whispering thing, she would stab him with *both* of her knives.

Lyssa's parentage had been a Japanese vampire mother and a High Fae father. Ruth assumed her long dark hair was from her mother's side of the family, as well as the piercing slant to her jade eyes, a narrow, vibrant view to a compelling yet hazardous world. Her dress looked like something Fae spirits might wear to dance in one of their magic circles. The deep purple color with hints of green showed off tiny sparkles on the close sleeves and nipped waist. The flowing skirt framed matching purple boots. Raw jade mounted in a beaten gold collar rested against her sternum, just above the hint of cleavage the dress's V-neck offered.

Ruth noted a ring on her left hand, a sapphire stone framed by a silver fairy. Her tiny hands were upon it as she lay in the clasp of her lover. Their intertwined bodies formed half of the band, as well as the setting for the stone. Because it was a simpler, more sentimental piece, Ruth wondered if it was a gift from Jacob.

Yvette wore sleek black leggings tucked into matching boots with a sturdy three-inch heel. Her blouse, made of a transparent gold fabric, had full sleeves and an unlaced neckline that exposed high, firm breasts in a lacy black bra. An array of silk corded pendants rested in their cleft. Garnet earrings brushed her long neck.

Her hair was plaited in slim golden braids, most wound around her head, but some spread over her shoulders. Those braids were threaded with bronze beads that picked up the luster of her skin. Her eyes, fixed on Ruth in a blatant assessment, were a mix of gold and gray. Before colored contacts, Ruth couldn't imagine how Lady Yvette would have passed as human. She reminded Ruth of a lion, born without the imposition of civility or the degradation of natural spirit that captivity could inflict. Such a creature could be as wild as the elements themselves.

Ruth liked her immediately.

Adan had said no one knew Yvette's exact age, but the Circus had first drawn notice in the 1700s.

A crop with metal-tipped tassels was tucked into Yvette's boot. She uncrossed her long legs, bracing both feet on the ground, and rose. Her gaze continued to travel over Ruth, examining every detail. Lyssa took another sip of tea.

Ruth had made her greeting. Further conversation would be invitation-only. She met Yvette's gaze. No matter that she often felt a nearly unbearable natural compulsion to do otherwise, Ruth had learned to do that with stronger vampires. Usually she countered that dangerous compulsion with bitch-face attitude, but that wasn't the best option for this scenario.

"What do you know of why you are here, Ruth?"

"You have a protection detail that needs reinforcement."

43

"No. Not reinforcement. Just an extra set of eyes."

She didn't recognize the male voice, but she'd been vaguely aware another male stood near the one she was so studiously pretending wasn't in the room.

"If only eyes were needed," she said, "A smartwatch could provide that."

Okay, she had grabbed for the snark. Regardless, it had been a mistake, because a distinct chill gripped the room, from the speaker's direction.

Biting back a curse, she pivoted toward him. She made sure she chose the direction that would keep her biggest distraction out of her direct view.

Holy fucking shit. Later, she'd knock her head against the wall for her preoccupation with her island tormentor, which had made her ignore who stood next to him.

A freaking angel.

He must be the one Adan had told her was with the Circus. Since she'd never been in the presence of one, she'd assumed she wouldn't know when she was. But facing him, taking in everything about him, there was no confusion about it. His existence spoke to something deep inside her, as if long before her current soul had inhabited this body, it had known his kind.

Her mother's stories said babies were guarded by angels in the Hall of Souls. Maybe they rocked the new souls in their cradles, carried them around.

Just as she had for Lyssa, she dropped to a knee and bowed her head. "My lord, forgive me. I spoke with the desire to assure my audience that I won't be intimidated in ways that endanger who I'm here to help protect."

Total silence. Then she heard a chuckle with an edge to it. A mean one. Scorn was in the tone.

Now that he was standing next to one, she couldn't believe she'd thought the incubus might be an angel. He was as far from being one as she was.

Even so, the tone of the laugh tightened her lower belly, sending a quake through her limbs. She squashed that reaction. She didn't know why the incubus was mocking her, but she didn't give a shit.

The angel stepped toward her. He wore sandals with straps that wrapped around his taut calves. "You deny pride factored into your reaction?"

His baritone told her he could bark out an order that would be heard halfway across the Circus's vast grounds.

"I do not, my lord. My apologies again."

Another pause. "Apology accepted."

"You can rise." Yvette's order held amusement. "Genuine deference annoys Marcellus. If you can't keep holding your own with him the way you just did, before you knew what he is, you might as well take your tough act back home."

Ruth rose to her feet and deliberately lifted her gaze to Marcellus's. What she saw startled her enough to drive her back a step.

His eyes had no whites. Darkness filled the area, framed by thick lashes. His square face was framed by thick brown hair to his shoulders. Dark green feathers layered his wings, arched over his broad shoulders. If he spread them out, the tips would brush the yurt walls.

Guards on his forearms were crafted of gold metal, etched with symbols and words in a language she didn't recognize. His biceps shimmered with similar markings, and then they were gone, like a hidden tattoo.

He wore the same kind of battle skirt the incubus had worn on the island, a crimson red linen skirt beneath the leatherlike straps. A sword harness crossed his bare chest, the weapon evident over his shoulder. Set in the hilt was a blazing red jewel, surrounded by black stones. A faint scar ran beneath the hold of the harness.

"My father said it's your woman I'm here to help protect." Again, she might be running her mouth without thought, but she went with her intuition. He didn't confirm or deny, so she continued. "I'll do whatever's needed. I have no experience in this kind of work, but I'm a good fighter. I pay attention to details, and I think things through before acting."

Mostly. When it was important to do so. And when her head wasn't clouded by psychotic winged incubi.

"Your desire to prove yourself, that kind of pride, can lead to mistakes. Most of being an effective protector is being smart. Anticipating before a problem can become a threat. Knowing when to call for backup."

Though Marcellus's eyes made it hard to know what was going on in his head, and he could obviously dice her into salad fixings, he reminded her of her father, when he was teaching her something he damn well expected her to learn on the very first pass.

"I won't let pride interfere with the most important thing. Keeping her safe, however you think I'm best suited to do it."

Marcellus studied her. "How you fight says a great deal about how you think. I will see your skills."

She was going to spar against an angel? Fucking hell.

"You'll spar with Merc."

Marcellus dipped his head toward the section of the tent she'd turned into a mental black hole, ordering all her senses away from who inhabited it.

Only her vision had successfully complied. Throughout the conversation with the others, she could smell his heated scent, hear the shift of his movements. She could feel him against her skin, like one of the sanctuary's housecats when they twined around her. Even that scornful laugh had sent shivers up her spine.

Danger and an insane level of sexual vibes had never been part of that feline attention, but the overwhelming insistence to be the center of it? He excelled at that.

"She hasn't noticed me, Marcellus. Before she can be trusted to watch your gypsy fortune teller, her observation skills need improvement."

You absolute prick. A cannonball of irritation knocked those ten pins of sexual attraction flat. Deliberately, Ruth pivoted toward him.

"I'm sorry," she said sweetly. "You seemed...invisible to me."

The exchanged glances between the others covered the several strong heartbeats where she lost awareness of anything but her first visual impression.

The irises were so dark red they were almost black, like dried blood. While not covering up all the whites like Marcellus's, they did take up more space than most humanlike species. Traces of silver bled into the white. Lightning.

His hair had thick waves and some curl on top, but was shorn at the nape and sides. The color reminded her of fallen leaves in the mountain habitat. Particularly once they'd been on the forest floor long enough to pick up deeper shades of brown. After rainstorms, the angles and tips gleamed.

His wings were folded close to his body, cloaking his shoulders. They weren't as broad as Marcellus's, but wherever skin was visible, he was smooth, touchable muscle.

Marcellus wore what she'd associate with a biblical angel. Maybe the authors of those texts actually *had* seen angels.

Though Merc had worn something similar on the island, today he had a different fashion statement. Grunge rockstar angel sex demon? A day or two's growth of beard added to the look.

A black tank shirt revealed distracting biceps and nestled close to his upper torso—she didn't blame it. She assumed it was altered in back to accommodate his wings. His jeans fit the way any man with a mouthwatering lower body to share with the female world should be required to wear them. Snug over hips and thighs. Creased around the groin area without being too tight, but suggesting what was there needed more room than it had.

No shoes. Long toes, elegant arches. The man had nice feet. *Jesus.*

When her gaze returned to his face, her attention was caught by something she'd missed on the first pass, because his wing had shadowed them. Four long scars disappeared over the curve of his shoulder.

She knew that wound pattern. One of their big cats had gotten him. Alarms went off, but if any of the cats had been harmed, she would have known before she left home. Every one of them was checked daily.

She hadn't forgotten she was in the middle of an interview, but she wanted to know who he'd wrangled with. As she opened her mouth to demand an answer, his gaze flashed, a warning.

He didn't want the others to know about their meeting. Interesting. For his benefit or hers?

Until she knew, she would stay silent. But they were going to discuss that smartass comment he'd made, too.

As he held her gaze, the pulsing need in her body increased. Perspiration brought coolness and heat both to her nape, planting the thought of having his mouth there.

Son of a bitch.

"Merc." The warning in Marcellus's tone drew Merc's gaze toward him. When that intensity was replaced with indifferent insolence, the feeling lessened.

47

"Can you handle this?" Marcellus asked curtly.

Merc's lip curled, showing the tip of one fang. "You trust me around harmless children. She's no different."

Anger spurted at the undisguised condescension, but Ruth was catching up. It was all a test. If she failed to learn the pride lesson after just being schooled on it, Yvette was right. She might as well go home.

Merc's provocation might be planned. Even if it wasn't, she adopted a flat calm, as impenetrable as a wall of black diamonds. Look at the pretty shiny stuff. The hardest substance on Earth. Whatever happening behind it was nobody's business but her own.

"Shall we take the fight outside?" Yvette's attention rested on her.

Lyssa rose, a tacit agreement. Ruth was tempted to lunge for the tent opening, to seek the hopeful lessening of Merc's effect on her in the open air. Fortunately, she had enough self-possession not to shove in front of the Council head, the Circus owner and an angel.

However, before she could follow them, Merc closed in on her. She could have bolted. Maybe he hoped for that. Instead she spun to face him.

"Going to run?" he murmured.

She went still as he slid a finger with sure intent under the slim chain at her throat, though it was buried beneath the bolo strap and turquoise rosettes.

She could slap his hand away. She was staring daggers at him, but her heart thudded under his touch. He followed the chain past the tank shirt's neckline, tracing one bra cup before finding the wing feather.

Merc stroked the feather's edge while her breath shortened, and her body vibrated.

She couldn't do this. Whether part of the plan or not, he'd taunted her in front of them. Questioned her ability. Did she want contempt from a man who could command her?

Not in this lifetime.

She stepped back and pulled the feather into the open between them. Yanking it free of the clasp, she let it fall.

"You're about to lose more of these," she said.

He smiled, showing both fangs this time. Most vampires avoided doing that, to maintain the appearance of civility. That didn't seem like a big priority for him.

"You're trembling," he said. "I'm not worried."

He didn't understand her reaction. If ever she gave herself to a Master, he would earn the right. He would fight her for it; otherwise she wouldn't respect him. She might be a submissive, but she would give that gift only to the Master who treated her as she deserved to be treated. She wanted the bond her parents had. And while it had to be with a being stronger than herself, he'd love and respect her. Even as he owned her in all the ways she desired.

There was nothing simple about her needs. But that lack of simplicity was her greatest protection from her own kind. And now possibly from a being she couldn't identify, except to know he was more powerful than she was, at least on every physical level.

"Stop fucking with my head or I'll tell them how we met," she said.

Bull's eye. His jaw tightened and he stepped back. After a brief staring contest, during which her trembling increased, but so did the jut of her jaw, he gestured to her with exaggerated courtesy. An invitation to precede him.

Not far from Yvette's tent, a large square had been marked out. A trio of acrobats were using it to practice some impressive gymnastics. When Yvette informed them the space was needed, they withdrew without complaint, but they didn't go away. Other Circus members not-so-subtly positioned themselves to watch the show.

Ruth moved into the sparring area as Marcellus stopped Merc outside it. As she stripped down to the essentials of leggings, tank and boots, she kept a peripheral eye on what they were doing. Perhaps discussing what tactics Marcellus wanted Merc to use, to prove her fight skills. Though in the yurt she'd noted a combative edge between the men, Merc's attitude here was attentive. Giving Marcellus a short nod, he turned toward her. He stretched out his wings in a quick snap, showing the lightning pattern. The air currents from the movement reached her, feathering over her skin.

She ignored them, and braided the loose waves of her hair. By the time she'd tucked the braids into the top knot, he'd folded the wings in again.

"No hair pulling?" he observed. "Shame."

He did a cartwheel from the outside of the arena into it, pausing on the palm of one hand and studying her from the upside-down position before he flexed his thighs into a split, bent his knees and brought one foot down into the sparring space, then the other, his body flowing back into an upright position, every muscle on rippling display. The feathers brushed against the jeans, his arms and shoulders, wings arching up and then settling again.

"I'll pull yours later, while I fuck you up the ass," she responded. "If you ask nicely. But we better do this first."

A murmur went through the observers, punctuated by a bark of laughter. She didn't know if the murmurs reflected disapproval of her trash talk, or shock at her taunting an opponent who could possibly do her real damage, but their reaction wasn't her concern.

This was one of those important forks in life's road. How she handled it would either take her forward or worse, leave her at the fork, with nowhere to go but back the way she already knew.

"You'll pay for that comment." His voice was calm. The still fix of his gaze told her he didn't mean here and now.

"Only if you have something to offer worth paying the price," she retorted.

The trash talk stopped when Marcellus brought a crate into a corner of their sparring space and sat down on it. He settled his dark green wings on either side of him. "I am the person you are protecting," he told Ruth. "Proceed as you would if you were dealing with Merc as an approaching attacker. Keep him from getting to me."

Ruth nodded. After considering how she would prepare her charge for such an event, she drew close to the angel and spoke to him in a low voice. "Go now. Follow the escape strategy you and I reviewed and tested a hundred ways before this moment, in case something like this happened. Find a place to hide where he can't find you, or seek help. I'll hold him as long as I can."

Marcellus's eerie eyes flickered. "So sure you will lose?"

"He's a stronger and faster opponent. I don't plan to lose, but I likely will. I can buy you time before he kills or disables me. If I beat him, we'll have agreed on where to meet."

Marcellus rose and stepped out of the marked space. "Good. I have left the area to do as you instructed. Show me your fight skills."

Ready set go. Ruth turned and moved forward.

Merc did the same.

He came at her fast. She dodged and slid under him, flipping around to kick his knee. He was already gone, but a slower opponent, a human one, would have been disabled, the fight over. But if they expected her to fight humans, she wouldn't be sparring with Merc.

Apparently some electronics worked in this in-between place, because someone nearby had cranked up their music. "Too Much Time On My Hands" by Styx. The beat worked.

She used it, even as she blocked her awareness of her audience, and the pressures associated with them. She was back on the preserve, where she'd gloried in any opportunity to fight and outmaneuver an opponent.

She took a blow to the face that somersaulted her backwards. She landed hard on her ass but rolled away, sweeping Merc's leg. He used the damn wings to counter, keep himself from falling next to her, but it was an awkward maneuver and she sprang from the ground, pouncing on the outstretched wing and jamming her fingers hard into the shoulder joint as she rammed a foot into his lower back.

He used the wings to flip them over. He would have crashed down on her, breaking her nose in the resulting face plant, but she twisted and took the impact on her shoulder. The mind-numbing bolt of pain announced dislocation, but that could be fixed. She had another arm.

She punched him in the abdomen. There was no give there, at all. Lightning fast, she adjusted her angle and hammered the solar plexus. The flurry of blows succeeded in driving him back a step, and giving her enough room to regain her feet, but he was on her again in an instant.

She'd been right. This fight wasn't about defeating him, but about the time she could give to her protectee. So she kept her full focus on keeping him occupied and not getting too quickly disabled.

Vampire speed was a boon, and she'd worked to be faster. Play with cats wasn't play at all, but hunting skills. That and the martial arts and other fighting skills she'd accumulated helped her now.

The fist she drove into his face was hard enough to crack his eye socket. The eye blazed with pain, but also rage and then...

A blast of pheromone-infused heat hit her, weakening her knees, making her shudder, jerk. Fucking hell. Was he really trying to make her orgasm in the middle of a fight?

Well, any weapon was fair game, and two of them could play it.

She dropped to a knee, rolled, and punched him between the legs. It was a shame, because the man had nice, heavy testicles. But if she did him permanent harm, he'd asked for it.

"Stop. Merc, stop."

The order lashed out from two directions, Yvette and Marcellus. As she tuned in to their surroundings, trying to control her breathing and stop her shuddering, she saw there was a literal whip around Merc's throat, digging into the skin aggressively enough to draw blood and constrict his breathing. Yvette was holding it, her other hand lifted toward the incubus. He'd dropped to a knee, but was fighting to stand, though an invisible force seemed to be holding him down.

He snarled, the light in his gaze promising hell to the sorceress, if he could get past her magic.

He was still battering Ruth with that energy, dragging her toward the precipice. She was barely keeping her feet, swaying, resisting the wave of sexual desire with everything she had.

You never say no to me.

Marcellus was next to him. "The fight is over, Merc. You have done as I asked."

A slight head shake. Merc's gaze didn't leave her. The power of the energy increased.

No. *No.*

"Don't touch me," she managed in a harsh rasp. Not to him, but to whoever had approached her on the left. She didn't look that way, because she couldn't chance losing this battle. She was *not* going to give the bastard the victory of a forced orgasm in the middle of a crowd.

"Back...the...fuck...off."

That *was* to him.

At long last, he gave a brusque nod. Whatever was driving her arousal, compelling her to release, started to ebb. She kept her gaze on his, fighting not to look away. If she did, she was sure he would ramp it back up, pushing what he was doing to its natural conclusion.

Marcellus had asked for a test of her skills. Physical, mental. Endurance, will. Merc had tested all of it in short order. Marcellus had said she'd passed.

She should be satisfied about that. But she was soaked with sweat and felt weak. The lightest touch would set her off. But then the reduction of sexual arousal brought back the pain in her shoulder.

"I can give you medical attention." The female voice to her left spoke. It pulled her attention away from Merc, the soothing tone an oasis in the storm of pain, laced with lightning bolts of unwanted pleasure.

"I'm all right. I'm a vampire. Everything heals on its own."

Well, most things. And not as fast as they should for her age. So if the woman could speed that along, that wasn't a bad thing.

Merc's focus had changed. She could tell he didn't want her to look at him. Not when they had him on his knees, pinned down like that, the whip collaring his throat. It was in his burning gaze.

It didn't make him look weak to her. He reminded her of the damaged cats they brought to the island. The ones who'd reached the limit of being told who and what to be, being forced to be what they weren't. They would kill without thought, because tearing, rending and destroying gave them a taste of freedom, experienced in the most destructive way possible. It matched the rage in them, the terrible fear of ever being that helpless again.

Everything else, even the results of their own savagery, was bearable.

Because she understood it, she dropped to one knee, her other hand pressed to the ground, and dipped her head. An acknowledgement to a worthy opponent.

She could see it startled him. It also helped to calm him, though Ruth was pretty sure he'd never lost control. Proving it, at least to her, Merc turned his head toward Yvette and put his hand on the whip, gripping it firmly, no matter that it looked as if the contact burned. Yvette nodded, and the bespelled whip, glowing with a flame-colored energy, fell away. It left angry marks at his throat, as well as on his palm. Marcellus offered him a hand up, but Merc refused it, raising himself to a standing position.

Feathers drifted against his bare feet, because she'd attacked his wings several times to keep him from using them as a lift advantage. As the wind took them away, she wondered if others in the Circus would collect and keep them as she unwisely had.

The four slashes on his shoulder had broken open. Blood was in his right eye, probably from that head shot she'd landed. A cracked eye socket didn't seem to bother him, and she wondered what his own healing abilities were.

He came toward her, ignoring how Yvette and Marcellus shifted, positioning themselves in case they needed to intervene. Lyssa sat on a chair someone had brought for her, no expression on her face. Jacob stood behind her. Ruth detected some anger in the servant, as if he thought they'd let the fight go too far. He was protective of women, she remembered. Even his Mistress, the strongest of all of them.

Ruth would reassure him later that she was fine. Right now, with the fight adrenaline draining away, it was hard to think past the dislocated shoulder.

The owner of the gentle voice was a woman so thin she made Catriona, whose core spirit tree was the willow, look like a voluptuous Mae West.

She was also barely five feet tall and human, but the energy she carried held...more. Her long reddish gold hair, freckles, and pale skin made her look young, but Ruth thought she was in her thirties. Her cloudy blue eyes and the way she tilted her head toward voices without eye contact said she was blind.

She was also someone's second marked servant. Vampires could detect that ownership, though not always the identity of the owner. She might be Yvette's. Ruth would figure it out once pain wasn't screaming through her collar bone, shoulder and all the connected muscles.

When Merc moved in her direction again, she was ready to fight, but he shook his head and closed his grip over the limp fingers of the arm that was dislocated. He put a surprisingly light hand on her shoulder, telling her what he was doing.

Her skin vibrated around the touch. He'd turned down the sexual energy, but she still responded to his presence as if he were a magnet, drawing that reaction back to skin level, pulling her toward him.

But again...sex and vampires. While obviously not immune to it, she was a drinker with an exceptionally high tolerance. For form's sake, she bared her fangs. "Stop doing that."

"I'm not doing anything. The fight is over."

"It's over for now," she corrected him.

She forced herself not to draw her hand out of his grasp as he dropped to his heels and supported the arm. When he slowly extended it, she fought not to throw up.

She wondered if he'd try to cause her more pain on purpose, since she'd kicked him in the balls and torn out more of his feathers.

"Charlie," he spoke to the redhead, "Tell me when."

"Let me give her something so it will be easier."

Merc's gaze rested on Ruth's. "She doesn't want easier. The muscles will heal."

Charlie sighed. "You fighting types. You make things so difficult." Her slim hand overlapped his, readjusted his grip, and she checked the position of Ruth's shoulder.

"This would be a good time to beg for mercy," Merc observed. His voice had that heavy rain quality, and the earthy need in Ruth drank it in.

"I'm listening," Ruth managed. "Whenever you want to start."

His mouth curved. Not a smile, but a promise of temptation held out of reach until need became a raw and bleeding open wound.

"What did Marcellus tell you right before the fight?" she said, not wanting to think about what was about to happen. Maybe some pain meds wouldn't be so bad.

"Not to kill you. Just to push you past your threshold, so he could see how you handled that."

"How do you know where that threshold is, other than seeing me on my ass on the ground?"

His lips pursed. "It's one of my many gifts."

"I call it pushing someone's buttons. You're pretty damn good at that. What are you?"

"Incubus. Angel. Human. The worst parts of all of them."

He said it without deprecation, owning it. His face showed her the monster. The meanness. But his hands on her weren't rough and he handled her carefully, attending to what Charlie was doing. She also noted that when he was feeling something strongly, or concocting some deviltry, the silver streaks around the black blood irises sparked.

As a result, she was partially braced for the renewed shot of sexual desire. A cry broke from her lips, body jerking back. At the same moment, he pulled and twisted the limb.

Ruth hadn't seen Charlie's nod, but it was better not to know it was coming.

Merc made it a smooth, easy move, the shoulder clicking back into place. White hot fire surged through her arm and upper body, but the anesthetic effect of the sexual compulsion had balanced it. It was done. Back in place, bringing the relief she'd expected. Also some terrible residual muscle pain, but he was right about that. As a vampire, in a couple hours she wouldn't feel it at all.

If it had been Adan or her father, that relief would have arrived in fifteen minutes, but she'd take what she could get.

Charlie's hand remained on her. Ruth noted a flush to her face, a moistness to her lips, that suggested Merc's act hadn't entirely contained itself to Ruth. Perhaps it wasn't something he could help when another woman was this close. But his gaze never left Ruth, absorbing everything, from the pain he'd caused, to the relief he'd offered, and the sexual desire she'd experienced.

Leaning forward, he put his head alongside hers. Not touching her, but his breath stirred her hair. "I can take or give. Your behavior determines which response I choose."

Having grown up understanding what vampire compulsion could and couldn't do, she realized her reaction to him wasn't wholly manufactured. She couldn't blame it all on the incubus thing.

And that sucked.

She turned her gaze to meet his. His physical proximity gave her no intimacy. Just enough of a taunting hint of it to tempt her onto the field of battle with him again. If he recognized that, then it was calculation, with motives she couldn't trust.

"Maybe you should be thinking the same about me," she said.

His arched brow made her want to smooth her fingers over it, feel the hard bone beneath. He drew back, tossing Charlie a look. She responded with a mildly reproving one, though Ruth noted it was brief, as if Charlie had difficulty meeting his gaze—or knew it was unwise. Which gave Ruth a weird spurt of jealousy.

Her mind was obviously scrambled. And not just because of that. The woman was blind. How could she...

"Well done," the healer said. Ruth wasn't sure if she meant her exchange with Merc, who was now headed back toward Marcellus, or how she'd handled the shoulder adjustment. "An ice pack will help, until your accelerated healing kicks in."

Ruth lifted a hand in front of Charlie. A corner of the woman's mouth twitched with good humor. "I can see. Just not in the traditional ways. I see auras. It gives me as much detail as a person who sees the way you expect. It's a different language of seeing, if that makes more sense to you. It's also how I see health and sickness."

Charlie had brought a cooler with her first aid kit. When she flipped open the top, Ruth saw the ice pack she'd mentioned. "After Yvette confirms the terms of your employment, you can share lunch with the other Circus staff. I'm pretty sure you've been hired."

CHAPTER FIVE

*M*erc had busted open her lip early in the fight, and her hands had been scraped from stopping her forward progress when he'd tossed her across the sparring area. Minor injuries, which healed with a reasonable approximation of a vampire's normal regeneration ability.

Which was good, because by the time Charlie offered Ruth a damp towel to clean the blood off her face and hands, Yvette and Marcellus were headed her way. Lady Lyssa and Jacob had already departed.

Charlie had insisted on taping the aforementioned ice pack around her shoulder. It did help as promised, but as she rose from the crate where Charlie had parked her, Ruth wished she had no lingering evidence of injury.

"Will you tell me how I can improve?"

She directed that question to Marcellus before she could remind herself they hadn't confirmed she had the job. Ruth bit her lip. "My apologies, my lord."

Though he still looked as serious as a gravedigger who needed a drink, she thought she saw his lips twitch. "Later today, we will go over your responsibilities and you will meet your charge."

He turned away, walked two steps, stopped. Spoke over his shoulder. "You will spar with me, Merc, Yvette and others I deem suitable here to elevate your skills. Daily."

His way of telling her she'd shown she could maybe do the job. Only time would prove if that was true.

He strode off toward Merc, who was perched on one of the wooden posts marking the corners of their sparring area. His bare feet overlapped the edge, his excellent ass resting on his heels. His wings were spread at quarter mast to hold the position, the layered feathers trailing his arms, drawing eyes to biceps, thigh and calf muscles.

While he appeared to be watching the acrobats who'd resumed their practice, whenever her gaze shifted to him, his eyes would land on hers after only a couple heartbeats, as if he was perpetually aware of her regard.

None of the Circus members had spoken to him as they dispersed. No "good fight, good job" kind of thing. Not even a "Hey, Merc, now that you're not busy, give me a hand with this," though it was obvious everyone here had more than enough to do. Just like on their island, she expected all staff members pitched in and helped if they finished their own tasks more quickly.

But she also noticed how his attention stayed on the acrobats. When one of the more complicated throws didn't go as planned, all those muscles tightened. But he didn't move, his eyes tracking the woman who landed heavily on the ground. She was all right, rolling out of it, but him letting her fall while seeming like he'd wanted to intercept, was curious to Ruth.

Yvette had been watching Marcellus depart. "Angels aren't big talkers," she noted. "But that was decent praise. Your father didn't oversell your skills, but I wouldn't have expected otherwise from Mal."

"Is there more to this, my lady?" Ruth heard the ice in the pack click as she adjusted her arm.

Yvette lifted a questioning brow. A reminder that Ruth could ask questions of a vampire more powerful than herself, but she'd best tread carefully, and with respect.

"I'm honored to be given a chance to help, but to do the job effectively, I should know what the threat is. Lady Lyssa's involvement, and an angel... Even if the woman is his, it doesn't explain why her well-being warrants this much interest."

"Appropriate questions." Yvette nodded. "They'll be answered. For now, go to the food tent for some blood. It's safe-sourced, from vetted and willing staff members. The cooks are excellent, so enjoy sampling the food as well. I've arranged to have a guide show you around, and deliver you to your quarters afterward."

Charlie had picked up her first aid kit and slipped away, Ruth assumed to alert that guide to join them.

"You'll share sleeping quarters with our security team members who are single," Yvette continued. "It's best for you to stay closely coordinated with one another. You work in shifts, so you'll have time off, and there are plenty of places at our in-between campsites to get time to yourself."

"Of course, my lady."

"Good. I'll take a swallow of your blood now. From here forward, I'm your overlord. You understand what that means?"

She did. It wasn't a minor thing. The sampling of blood by an overlord or Region Master confirmed a vampire's loyalties. It also allowed them to locate Ruth if needed, or sense if she was in fatal distress.

Up until now, Ruth's mind had been more occupied with getting the job than the consequences of doing so. She reminded herself that Yvette couldn't be in her mind; not unless during the sampling she injected the serum from her fangs that would make that possible.

Doing that to another vampire, without their knowledge or permission, was forbidden by Council. Technically. A Region Master or overlord had a certain amount of discretion to increase the binding on their territory's vampires if they felt a vampire required the additional layers to keep him or her in line.

In short, allowing a vampire to take one's blood was an act of trust and loyalty that often preceded the earning of either of those things. But Lady Lyssa supported Lady Yvette, and supported Ruth being here. And her father had suggested she come to the Circus.

That was enough to mostly overcome her trepidation about anyone illegitimately gaining access to everything in her head. Blood family members were born with the ability, which was why she, Adan and her father could talk to one another the way they did. Her mother as well. Despite being a human servant, not vampire, the parental blood link allowed it.

"Your wrist," Yvette said.

Observing the protocols, Ruth dropped to a knee and extended her arm. Even with him fifty yards away, she was aware of an abrupt sharpening of Merc's attention.

So was Yvette, because her golden gaze slid that way, touched Merc. Her lips tightened before her attention returned to Ruth.

"Be careful of him." She clasped Ruth's forearm. "You show no fear of him, and he finds that far too intriguing."

"Is he used to women being afraid of him?"

"Yes. Any woman, of any race, would be a fool not to be. He's not safe, Ruth. Handsome, arousing, interesting, yes. But not safe."

"He was in control," Ruth said thoughtfully. "No matter what it looked like."

Seeing Yvette's look, one an older vampire would give a naive fledgling, Ruth knew she should work harder on not blurting out everything in her head. One of the dangers of growing up in the comfort zone of the island. But now that she'd committed herself, she explained.

"Marcellus wanted me tested. Merc pushed me out of my comfort zone to show Marcellus how I'd handle it. He knew what he was doing."

While she was pretty sure there'd been a personal and intimate component to that pushing, he'd helped her seal the deal on the job. He'd taken it farther than Marcellus wanted, but not farther than he had wanted.

Or Ruth herself.

"Mind what I'm telling you, and don't be too sure of yourself when it comes to him." But a glimmer of dark humor touched Yvette's gaze. "You've been raised around wild predators. Treat him the way you treat them."

With respect, compassion and an abundance of caution. Never turn your back, and never show weakness, because in a blink, you will become prey.

Yes. With the possible exception of compassion, that fit her analysis of Merc.

Yvette cupped Ruth's knuckles in one hand, clasped Ruth's forearm in the other, then dipped her head to bite. A quick pain, followed by a swimming sensation of sensuality and power. Ruth steeled herself so she didn't sway toward the woman. Yvette's eyes remained on her, her full lips closed over the penetration point. When she retracted her fangs, her tongue caressed Ruth's skin to close the wounds. Ruth couldn't contain her shiver, but that reaction to a dose of a stronger vampire's pheromones wasn't considered unusual.

Yvette squeezed Ruth's hand and released it. "Welcome to our ranks, child. Work hard, do well, and you'll earn a place here."

Yvette pivoted to stride back toward her quarters. The blacksmith dwarf was at the opening, waiting on her. Ruth had been officially dismissed.

"Hi."

Ruth turned to find a human woman standing a few feet away from her. She was in her thirties and had copious amounts of brown hair with hints of red. Two braids kept the abundance out of her face, the braids dyed a lighter brown and threaded with ribbons and beads. Her eyes were a mix of green, gray, brown and gold. A henna tattoo formed a graceful crescent from her temple to her jaw.

Gold and silver bracelets, embedded with crystals in multiple shades of green, adorned her arms. Similar stones hung from the double piercings in her ears and a chain around her neck. They weren't merely for decoration. Because a great deal of crystal work anchored the sanctuary magic, Ruth recognized the pale color of green amethyst, the stronger statement of polished malachite, plus fluorite, moldavite, and the rare prehnite.

"Yvette asked me to take you to lunch and show you around, if that's okay. I'm Clara."

Clara extended a hand. The human greeting wasn't often used by vampires. They didn't make physical contact until power lines were established, but Ruth had been around enough humans to react appropriately.

Clara's grip had a firm calmness, though the lack of threat in it was too pronounced. Like Charlie, Clara was thin, but whereas it suited Charlie to look that way, Clara looked well below the weight she should carry. The wide neckline of her loose cotton top slipped off one shoulder. As she'd turned to gesture toward the cook tent, Ruth had noted a vaguely familiar symbol tattooed on the back of it. The shirt was split along the seams of its two sides, forming a petal shape over a brown calico skirt, which swished as she moved.

"Yvette said you'd need some blood. That was some fight. You're good. Merc looked like he was actually having to try."

Ruth glanced toward the sparring area, but she already knew he was gone. It was unsettling to know she knew that, much like how he'd known when she was looking at him.

Then she remembered how he had described her charge. *Gypsy fortune teller.*

"Yeah, I'm the one you're here to protect," Clara confirmed, reading her expression. "From all the crazies in the world who think I'm the key to their evil master plan. No matter how ridiculous that sounds."

It did sound ridiculous. She was lovely...cute. Unassuming, like a cub. Not the type of female who could win the heart of a powerful angel like Marcellus.

But she had, so there was more here than it seemed. A definition Ruth applied to herself, so she would respect it. "So, you tell fortunes?"

"It's mostly intuition and deduction, giving people a little thrill and good feeling. I don't push deeper unless something in me says that's needed. And I always hope it isn't."

Her face tightened. The gesture made her look shockingly gaunt, and Ruth drew a step closer, as if driving that look away should be part of her untested arsenal of bodyguard skills. "I won't try to read you," Clara promised. "I don't do that with people I know and spend time around. It's not just being nice. I see things I don't want to see, learn things I don't want to know. I get enough of that in my head from other places, bad places."

"I won't ask," Ruth assured her.

Clara nodded. "I used to laugh a lot more. Smiling's harder."

"Perhaps that's why I'm here. It's definitely not because I'm the biggest and strongest on your security team. I'll teach you to play the way big cats do. They learn to hunt through play. They learn to protect themselves through play. Most importantly, they learn to enjoy each moment through play."

Seeing Clara's intrigued look, Ruth decided to go further down that rabbit hole with her. "Albert Schweitzer said the creatures of the world are caught in the darkness of Nature, where there's cruelty and loss, and indifference to both. But smart as he was, he missed that the creatures of the world don't carry the heavy psychological weight of that knowledge. Which means they embrace the joy of living each day, which eludes those of us who think we're so much smarter."

Clara blinked. "I love *Reverence for Life*. I keep a copy by the bed.

There must be a good library on that cat sanctuary where you grew up."

So they'd told her a little bit about her newest bodyguard. Good. "My adopted uncle had shaman ancestors. He read other teachers' thoughts on life, death and everything in between. I like to read, and he encouraged the addiction."

The quick sparkle in Clara's gaze was a star on the twilight horizon. Holding the promise of growing brighter, if conditions allowed for it.

A woman in her thirties and a vampire in her eighties were roughly around the same age, maturity-wise, so Ruth felt an easy kinship with Clara she knew might or might not be beneficial for protecting her. Only time would tell. She had no comparable girlfriends, beyond Nerida and Miah, who lived at a women and children's sanctuary in Tennessee. Ruth saw them far too rarely, though they stayed in touch with the technology the world had available to them. She still wrote them letters sometimes, like she had well before the electronic age.

"A meal sounds good," Ruth said. "Then I'd love the tour. I've already seen a dragon. Will everything else be equally amazing?"

"Frequently." After a hesitation, Clara slid an arm through hers. "I feel like we're going to be friends, and I'm a very touchy-feely person with my friends. Is that okay?"

"If and when it's not, I'll break fingers to teach you to keep your hands to yourself."

Clara chuckled, a cautious sound. "Okay, you'll be a scary friend. That'll be all right, too."

Ruth had her worries about what she might screw up or where she might fall short. However, on this at least, she felt the same way.

Peak lunch time had passed, so the tables around the kitchen tent were less crowded. Clara secured Ruth the promised blood, plus herself a slice of angel food cake. The top and base were layered with thinly sliced fresh peaches. As Ruth sipped from the blood, Clara moved a couple bites of cake onto a saucer she put politely in front of her.

Vampires couldn't ingest great amounts of anything other than blood, but they enjoyed the tastes and textures of food. The cake and fruit were good.

"They do miracles in that kitchen." Clara chewed on her own light-as-air bite of cake. Ruth agreed, and gestured to the tattoo on Clara's shoulder and the henna on her face.

"What are these?"

"The henna reinforces the properties in the crystals. Healing, protection, balance. I do henna myself, for fun and decoration, but this is a special kind of application. One of the married couples does them. They work together, bringing feminine and masculine energy to the work for a stronger binding." She lifted the shoulder. "The tattoo is an angelic protection symbol. And tracker, in a sense. I like it because it's pretty. Marcellus likes it because it helps him do his job."

Clara's cheeks had flushed a fetching pink color. "So he put it on you himself?" Now Ruth realized why it seemed familiar. It looked like the work on Marcellus's arm guards.

"Yes. He puts his hand over the area, and chants the proper words. I could feel it marking my skin, but not like the sting of a tattoo. More like being the earth while a Creator carves it with rivers and streams. It hurts, but not in a bad way. And his voice put me in a dreamy state. He stroked my hair while he was doing it. It was one of the first times he initiated that kind of touching with me. Before that, it was mostly me throwing myself at him."

Ruth grinned and Clara answered in kind before glancing at the tattoo again. "Most the Legion angels carry similar marks, praises to the Goddess, promises to serve Her with their lives, that kind of thing. They're applied via the same method, but Marcellus says an angel acquires them from higher-ranking angels, as an honor or award. One of those soldier type rituals. They can let them be visible or keep them melted beneath the skin, but they usually come out full wattage during battle."

"I saw them, when I first met him."

"They're sexy, right? Like everything about him." Clara gave Ruth a wry look. "I know what you're thinking. Everyone does. Him and her? Really? An angel and a strange mortal girl, centuries younger than him?"

"I had the thought. But I expect I'll understand why before too long." Ruth took another swallow of the blood. They'd seasoned it, and the flavor was excellent. Her initial caution about taking prepared blood, instead of fresh from the vein, had eased. It was also restoring her, the aches and pains melting away. "Even if I didn't, love doesn't have to make sense to anyone but the people involved."

"Unless it hurts too many others."

Ruth shook her head. "I think that's a separate issue. The love exists. If it sucks for others, if the cost of pursuing it is too great, a person can stop acting on it, but they can't stop feeling it."

"And since Love is connected to the Divine, the question is why was it given to you if it wasn't meant to be pursued? It might be an act of will that serves a good yet unseen." Clara made a whimsical face. "I've done some spiritual soul searching between the covers of a book myself. Maybe we can trade libraries."

She put her chin on her hand. The bracelets slid down her arm with a pleasant chiming noise. "You sound like you have firsthand experience, though."

"No. My father did. My mother did. Others I've met. But my father told me once, 'Love can kill you. Hate can force you to live. But only the one that can kill you is worth living for.' I kind of took it from there."

Clara gave her an impenetrable look. "What?" Ruth asked.

"I'm starting to understand why they sent you here. So I'm going to apologize ahead of time, for when you hear how I threw a tantrum over having another 'goddamn babysitter I didn't ask for.' He has this infuriating way of listening to me like an adult listens to a raving child, until I honestly want to hack off his wings with a steak knife. But then he'll do something that tells me he was listening all along."

Clara's expression became more tender. "I used to be a pretty social person, but because of my gift, I didn't have many *close* girl-friends. The ones I did...I needed them, as in really needed them, to keep my sanity. As this ability expanded, it got down to one. Alexis. We used to be able to spend a lot more time together. She has some abilities that helped her relate to my struggle with mine. But she's also a merangel, and her mate is a seriously terrifying Dark Spawn vampire sorcerer. That's okay, he's the right person for her, and they love each other to pieces, but he's apprenticed to a Dark Guardian, so Alexis is often on adventures with him."

"Like Adan and Catriona."

Clara brightened. "That's right, I'd almost forgotten. You're Adan's sister. He's wonderful."

"Catriona is wonderful. He's a pain in the ass. For my thirtieth birthday, he ground up a Carolina Reaper pepper and mixed it into a glass of my dinner blood. He did stop me from taking more than one swallow, but I was hacking and wheezing for an hour. He told me it was to welcome me to vampire adulthood—thirtyish is the vampire version of that. My throat and tongue were raw for a day."

"A Carolina Reaper pepper?"

"Ranked one of the hottest in the world, and sold by the Pucker-butt Pepper Company. I think the name was part of the appeal to him." Ruth pointed a stern finger at the amused fortune teller. "Don't be fooled. The mature and serious Light Guardian is all an act. His core identity is obnoxious asshole older brother. He claims the 'older' shit only because he shoved me aside to come out first."

"You adore him, I can tell. But I won't rat you out. We have a couple performances in the Carolinas. Maybe we should get some of that pepper and return the favor."

Ruth scoffed. "I got even a week later. When you get a chance, ask him how, and watch him lose his shit."

Clara laughed out loud. The heads of the few people sitting nearby swiveled in their direction. From the pleased surprise they showed, touched with some concerning poignancy, Ruth determined Clara's mirth wasn't as common an event as it may once have been.

Though she'd have to guard against sentiment, she was already feeling drawn to the young woman herself. "I know Alexis," she told Clara. "She and Dante have come to the island a couple times."

While Adan and Dante talked magical sorcery stuff—obsessive workaholics—Ruth had shown Alexis around the sanctuary. They'd ended up hanging out in Ruth's tree for a couple hours, talking about Alexis's work with an ocean center in Florida and her travels with Dante. As well as her angel father and mermaid mother.

So often in their world, people were circumspect about their back-grounds, but Alexis had been refreshingly open. Ruth had liked her. She wouldn't mind getting to see her again.

"Your cat sanctuary sounds like supernatural species central," Clara noted.

Ruth chuckled. "You should hear my father complain about it.

So...how long do we have to know one another for you to tell me what sex with an angel is like? In great detail."

Clara had put a slice of peach in her mouth. Her startled reaction sent it down her windpipe and set off a burst of coughing. But the light in her eyes grew encouragingly more sparkly.

"Newest security hire lets VIP choke on peach and die," she wheezed. "That's going to suck on your resume."

"I will engineer a cover up," Ruth told her, though she shifted to tap Clara on the back until the peach was properly rerouted.

Clara sent her a watery-eyed look. "You're really not what I'm used to from a vampire."

"Impossibly scary or irritatingly stodgy?"

"You've met a few. Do all of them look at you like they're determining where you rank in the food chain? Literally."

"Well, it's hard not to. We're in the top ten in that chain."

"Who ranks above you?"

"Angels for sure." Ruth's mind moved to the incubus male who also had some angel blood. His fighting skills, his strength, were far superior to hers. If Merc had gone all out, he would have killed her. She didn't doubt that. But thinking about Yvette's warning, she decided to test it out on her new friend.

"What can you tell me about Merc?"

Clara's reaction was impossible to miss. Uneasiness and apprehension. Coldness gripped Ruth, the girl's emotions triggering a punitive response. Irresistible sexual beast he might be, but she'd figure out a way to chop off those relevant parts if he'd done something to warrant it. "He's harmed you?"

"Oh, no," Clara assured her, though her gaze remained sober. "Not exactly. Merc is...difficult around women. We all know not to be alone with him. Not ever. Incubi...most of them, the pure bloods, they don't live too long, not by human standards. The hunger for sexual energy drives them, and it keeps growing. Sometime around their thirties, it has a high chance of going from hunger to addiction. They start draining women for the high of it."

She shook her head. "While most of us might say dying of an excess of sexual pleasure is one of the better ways to go, at that point, Guardians have to execute them." Clara paused. "I'm not sure you could call whatever created incubi and succubi a loving deity, but I guess the clue is in what else they're called. Demons. Sex demons."

A different feeling gripped Ruth at the ominous words. "But Merc isn't a pure incubus."

"Marcellus doesn't say a lot about it, but he's told me Merc's incubus side is at constant war with his angel side. Don't get me wrong," Clara added. "He's way better at self-control than the first years I was here. Sometimes I think he enjoys making people think that grip is still far more of an iffy thing than it really is. But Marcellus warned me not to get complacent. He said though it might take a far stronger trigger than it once did, it can still be tripped."

A shadow crossed Clara's face. "There are those who say he wants to let it go. He doesn't want to resist it. That the self-control is just an act."

"Has he ever harmed anyone here?"

"No. The worst he did was before he came to the Circus, years ago, but it was pretty bad. Marcellus is in charge of him. Which also means in charge of his execution, if Merc crosses that line again. It makes their relationship complicated. Sometimes I think Merc likes yanking that chain. As if daring Marcellus to do it."

"You've read him," Ruth realized. "Merc."

Clara lifted her gaze. It had that haunted tightness again, telling Ruth the source of her gauntness. Her abilities took a toll. "Once. I didn't mean to, but something happened where he did scare me. It opened up the part that reads people. Really reads them, not what I do for the Circus. I saw..."

She stopped herself. "That's not for me to share. It's about him, and the things I see, yes, they come true a lot, maybe almost always, but sometimes I think, if there's even a chance it won't end that way or come to that, if I say it aloud, I destroy that chance. Does that make sense?"

It did. Though Ruth really wanted to know what she'd seen, she understood that feeling. Plus, she'd gained the information she needed.

Merc was trouble. Lots of trouble. Knowing he was a danger to Clara or other women pissed her off, and made her recall the meanness she'd detected in him in the yurt. Yet Marcellus was obviously devoted to Clara's well-being and protection, and Merc was part of her protection detail. If Marcellus thought Merc was a true danger to Clara, Merc would be nowhere near her.

More than that, she expected the incubus would be six feet under and worm food. The contradiction was puzzling.

"When you fought him, it didn't feel like you were afraid of him at all. Were you?"

She tuned back in to Clara's words. "No." At least not of what made Clara and the other women afraid. That just made her want to kick his ass, and get past what she was pretty sure was bullshit, even if it was genuinely dangerous bullshit. Her desire to pursue what lay behind it was what made Merc most dangerous to *her*.

She thought about what she'd seen after the sparring match. No one talking to him, no obvious friendships. And he'd been here well over a decade.

Seeing Clara regarding her pensively, Ruth realized the conversation was taking too dark a turn. She didn't want to pull Clara there, since the girl was already dealing with enough of that. Ruth tossed back the rest of the blood as Clara finished the cake. "Ready to show me around?"

"Sure." Clara tidily put their plates and cups in a wash bin. Before they left, she introduced Ruth to the few occupied tables. She received friendly acknowledgements, curious looks, and brief summaries of their roles she committed to memory.

"We'll do more introductions over the next few days," Clara told her as they exited the tent. "We have a pretty good-sized crew here, and that's just the humanlike races. Best to take it in stages. Yvette mainly wants you to know who and what to expect, so you don't offend someone by accident."

"Like large dragons?"

"Amazing, aren't they? Dragons have serious protocols, so until you learn them, it's best not to approach Jetana or her mate, Tragar. If you do surprise one of them, act like you've met Lady Lyssa in dragon form." Clara stopped to demonstrate. "Respectful bow, back away, apologize for disturbing, et cetera. Now, if the babies take a liking to you, and want to perch or nibble, there's no protocol for handling that. Just survive it the best you can."

On that alarming note, Clara pointed out the communal showers and sleeping areas, including the pavilion tent where Ruth would be quartered. It was on the western perimeter and looked roomy for the fifteen people Clara said shared the space, including Ruth.

They moved past the Big Top, set up for practices and meetings of the whole troupe. Beyond it were hilly open fields and patches of forest. From Adan's description, Ruth expected the in-between portal spaces drew in the real world environments they bordered, like the corner of a blanket pulled in under the crack beneath a door.

It was how the piecing of the island habitats to their real world counterparts worked. On the preserve, the "savanna" environment had a portal border to the actual African savanna. Though in their case, there were filters that allowed prey from the real savanna to wander in limited groups into the island savanna, offering the cats a chance to hunt.

Clara explained what other non-human races were with the troupe. Centaurs, unicorns, mermaids. A handful of common Fae, pixies and gnomes, were here. Their participation was permitted by King Tabor, the Seelie ruler, and Queen Rhoswen, the Unseelie one, Lady Lyssa's half-sister. The one Ruth would cheerfully have punched in the face, though Adan and the Queen got on tolerably well now. Her brother was far more forgiving than Ruth.

"So many different peoples work and live together here who aren't always friends outside of it," Clara said. "I like the hopefulness of that. Look over there."

Ruth followed Clara's pointing finger down the hill they were standing upon. The slope was populated by white, yellow, purple and orange wildflowers. At its base, a lake spread out in an irregular shape, its slate blue waters lapping at sandy banks. A lissome windsurfer, clad in a wetsuit, was taking advantage of a fresh wind to streak across the water's surface. She moved with her craft with grace and strength, anticipating its movements, gripping the bar on the sail.

"Oh." Ruth's eyes widened as two mermaids leaped out of the water, clearing the curved long line of the sail. It was a dramatic display of sparkling scales and bare skin, arched backs and throats. They circled the craft, came back and leaped again, one over the bow, the other over the stern, a choreographed dance.

"Sometimes we do water shows when we have performances on island resorts. That's Medusa they're practicing with. She and her man, John Pierce, have a house on an island off the Florida coast, a private artists' retreat. They go there during the Circus's off months. We do three months on, one month off. JP's a former special ops guy and totally hot."

"Like almost every person I've seen here," Ruth observed.

"Yeah. Everyone new is given a week to gawp and drool before they're expected to pull it together. As a vampire, you're so used to being around eye candy, it's probably nothing special."

"Yes. If we didn't come with the uber-charged libidos."

Clara chuckled. "I've noticed that. Whenever I've met a vampire here, I can tell they're doing the food chain evaluation, but they're assessing other things, too. It's unsettling, but most are decently polite about it."

"As in, 'I'm thinking about all the ways I could fuck you, but if you're off limits—and your winged boyfriend could turn me into meat shavings—all I'll be doing is thinking about it.'"

"Exactly." An enigmatic smile touched Clara's mouth. "She's coming in. Let me take you down to meet her."

When they reached the water, Ruth moved forward to help Medusa pull the craft onto the shore. A courtesy, since the woman looked more than capable of doing it on her own. However, as Ruth bent to grasp the board, she froze.

She was eye-to-eye with a bush viper.

A stuttered heartbeat later, she realized the snake was curled around Medusa's arm. He had lifted and extended his head from where it had rested on the top of her hand. Now he doubled back to slither up her arm and join another snake, a much smaller one. They tied themselves in a companionable knot, then the smaller one formed a loose necklace around the woman's throat and put his head on her shoulder, gazing out at the water as if he wanted her to return to windsurfing as soon as possible.

While Medusa looked young, Ruth sensed that impression wasn't accurate. The sea green eyes studying Ruth held a maturity beyond her apparent age, and she looked human, but wasn't fully, though Ruth couldn't determine her race.

"Medusa, this is Ruth, the newest member of the security team. And appointee to my private army."

"Welcome." Medusa measured her with a glance. "If you passed Marcellus and Yvette's inspection, you must be impressive."

"She sparred with Merc," Clara said. "And held her own."

"Really?" Medusa's interest increased. "If you need additional practice partners, count me in."

"Have you sparred with Merc?"

"In a way." Ruth noted the reserve in the response, similar to Clara's reaction. "We had a couple run-ins where I emerged unscathed. My snakes don't care for him, so we avoid one another."

Not really the answer she wanted to hear, but Ruth let it pass, since today wasn't about solving the mystery of the male she was supposed to have met here for the first time.

She'd handle that part of things with him soon. She didn't like deceiving her new employer. Even if it was information that hadn't been requested, she knew the dangers of a lie of omission. She *would* tell Yvette, but she'd discover the reason for Merc's strong aversion to that first.

"Good stage name," Ruth observed. "Are the snakes on the water part of your performance, or do they just like to tag along?"

Medusa glanced at Clara.

"No, I haven't told her yet." Clara turned to Ruth. "Medusa is *that* Medusa. The turning-to-stone eye thing, the snake hair-do. All of that was a curse. JP went through an alternate dimension time thing facilitated by Maddock—he's a sorcerer and Charlie's boo."

"Though it took them an eternity to admit it," Medusa put in with a female eye roll.

"Tell it, sister. You'll meet him eventually," Clara added. "Adan knows him, too. Maddock worked with Yvette on some of the later modifications to the Circus's way of traveling through portals. Anyway, Maddock helped JP and Medusa end the curse."

Medusa smiled at Ruth's expression. "The Circus's inhabitants all have their own stories. I suggest taking them one bite at a time."

"Maybe not the best way of putting it to a vampire," Ruth rallied. "It doesn't take much to encourage us to get fang-y."

Clara looped arms with Ruth. "I like her a lot already."

"I can see why."

The softening of Medusa's gaze as it touched Clara reinforced what Ruth was picking up. Everyone was worried about the fortune teller.

When they left Medusa to continue her practice, Ruth put aside her fascination with her new environment to focus on her charge. "How long have you been here, Clara?"

"Ever since I left college. Initially, it was a temporary gig. That was the first time my clairvoyance attracted the attention of a bad guy. It was scary, but compared to now, it was so much simpler. I saw something I shouldn't have seen, my cluelessness brought it to the attention of the wrong people, and they came after me. Thanks to Alexis and Dante's connection to the vampire and angel worlds, the Circus was determined to be a good safehouse. So I joined the troupe. By the time the danger was past, I'd decided I liked it here."

Clara lifted a shoulder. "Can't take the gypsy out of the blood. My great grandmother was a traveling fortune teller, too. I ran away from college to join the Circus. I never really got past the general curriculum to settle on a major, anyway."

She took a breath. "A few years ago, my abilities started changing. Theories differ. Some think it's because of all the energies of the Circus, but I don't think so, because I left it for a while to hang out on Medusa and JP's island, and it just kept expanding. I started to tap into bigger plans, from bigger bad guys. Things that affect the fabric of our world. Maddock believes it's a natural evolution of a gift the universe wanted me to have."

She grimaced. Her shrug looked like it was resisting a weight pressing down on her shoulders. "Gives me terrible headaches afterward. Like my head is going to explode. Charlie can put her hands on it, and not necessarily make it go away, but it's like some of the pain goes into her hands. It's even better when she has Marcellus do it and overlaps his hands with hers."

She managed a glimmer of that natural twinkling personality that Ruth was realizing wasn't gone, but it had taken a beating. Maybe a lot of beatings. "The first time she thought of having him do it, I told him she'd given me a great reason to have a headache. He didn't think it was funny, but that was when he was way more of a sourpuss. Plus... he doesn't like to see me in pain. Let's look at the sky."

She folded herself down among the wildflowers, her skirt billowing around her calves. As she stretched out, stacking her hands behind her head, her colorful outfit and jewelry made her a picture among the equally vibrant wildflowers. Ruth sat down cross-legged, but Clara pulled on her arm, so she stretched out next to her. "If you lie here long enough, quietly enough, sometimes the pixies will come land on you. They'll ignore you, talking among themselves, but they'll braid flowers in your hair, paint pictures on your skin, things like that."

Clara gazed up at the sky. "You know, when I first realized I was clairvoyant, which seems like a hundred years ago, I would see things that I couldn't change. People's deaths, terrible things that were going to happen to them. Sometimes good things, though. Now...I can make a difference. I pass the information on to Marcellus, Maddock and Yvette. Depending on what I've shared, they make sure the information gets into the right hands. It's like I'm an undercover spy. The problem is, it's not undercover enough. There's something that happens when I really lock into a vision, where my presence can be sensed. And tracked."

When Ruth sent her a sharp glance, Clara offered that grimace again. "It's like the universe wants to balance the advantage I didn't ask to be given, with a downside I really don't want. The way the Circus moves around, in and out of portals, makes it very difficult to pinpoint my location. If I stay out in the world too long, and whoever detects me hasn't been dealt with, they're looking for me. To use, or dispatch as a loose end. Since the Circus only does three-day bookings at a time, and to date, thanks to Maddock and Yvette's skills, no one has associated me with them—knock on wood—me sticking with them is a win-win. And we've taken other precautions."

She lifted a lock of her hair. "Like this. The consensus from the security squad was that I had 'far too noticeable' red hair. Yvette changed it for me. I miss it sometimes, but a least she left me a hint of the original color."

She gestured at Ruth. "Part of why you're here is I'm no longer Marcellus's sole responsibility. He was injured when he was initially assigned to me. That scar on his chest, and another on his back, beneath his left wing, are the only remaining evidence of it. It's taken a while, but thanks to Charlie and his own angelic powers, he's healed enough he can command a Legion battalion again."

"He definitely seems like someone who should be ordering troops around."

"Yeah. He rocks that sexy commander thing. But he deeply missed being part of them. It's a brotherhood. I'm glad he's able to do it again, though I miss and worry about him when he's not here. It's a lie, that nothing can kill an immortal. But you know that, don't you?"

Ruth nodded. Clara pressed her lips together. "Some of the things I've seen have increased the Legion's responsibilities, over and above what they were already doing in the universe. Sometimes he has to be with them. He doesn't like it, but we both know it's needed. So I agree to whatever protection measures he wants when he's gone, within reason." Her mouth set in a stubborn line. "Being reasonable isn't his biggest asset."

"Care to share what is?"

Clara swatted Ruth's thigh, but chuckled as she did. "I tell you threat-to-the-universe stuff, and you make dick jokes."

Ruth lifted a shoulder. "Humor's how I counter too-serious stuff. When I get overwhelmed by it, I can't live. Or think clearly about how to handle it."

Clara looked at Ruth thoughtfully. "We don't know one another well enough for you to trust me yet, but if we reach that point, I wouldn't mind knowing more about what can overwhelm you."

Ruth had lain down next to Clara at an angle, so it put their faces close, their shoulders almost brushing. The wistful tone behind the question, the way the hazel eyes darkened, told Ruth that Clara wasn't poking into someone else's business out of idle or uninvited curiosity.

"Okay." She leaned in and put her mouth on Clara's, a playful, teasing kiss with a touch of tongue, a scrape of fang over her full bottom lip. Clara stiffened in surprise, but then relaxed as Ruth kept it as she intended it. Light and easy, an exchange of female intimacy. She was smiling against Ruth's mouth as Ruth put her hand to the girl's throat, the pulse speeding up under her touch.

When Ruth settled back, lacing her hands on her stomach, Clara huffed out a breath. "Vampires," she said.

Ruth smiled. "Yes. I intend no disrespect to your angel. But it helps me to know more about you, and you needed the distraction."

"Glad you're looking out for me." Clara shot her a droll look.

While they took a break, going quiet to gaze at the sky and enjoy their surroundings, Ruth thought about what Clara had told her. Yvette had said she would be given the truth about the girl's need for protection, and now that she had what she suspected was the gist of it, she needed to consider what other questions she should ask.

Clara's hand was still close to hers, and a few moments later, her pinky tapped Ruth's knuckle, a signal to stay still. Ruth saw a pair of pixies hovering over her bent knee. One landed on it with dainty feet and used the perch to bend and adjust the hem of the skirt she wore, layered and shaped like a rose bud.

The other spoke to her impatiently. Ruth couldn't make out the language, but the whispery sound reminded her of the sound nodding flowers made when they bumped and slid against one another. Something most human ears couldn't pick up, not consciously. The other pixie dipped down, seized her friend's tiny hand and they were aloft again. They disappeared like hummingbirds.

"You weren't kidding about them ignoring you."

"Yeah. When they're practicing for a performance, they'll tune in and respond. Yvette has a universal translator spell over the Circus grounds, so we can understand one another, but everyone knows how to turn it off, if they want to talk to their own race without anyone listening in. So if you don't understand a conversation, that's why."

"Though they don't seem like it, usually they're hyperalert as house flies." Clara fluttered her fingers over her stomach. "If you'd lifted a hand toward them, they would have been gone before you could blink. But they'd mark the insult. Usually they'll raid your living quarters and take small items, make you think you're losing your mind."

"Has anyone threatened to go after them with a fly swatter?"

"Yvette. Numerous times. Though she doesn't mean it. She's very protective of them, of all of us. Leadership leads by example. We take care of one another here. It makes it hard to ever want to leave."

"Unless you have no other choice." Ruth met her new friend's gaze. "Does it feel like a prison sometimes?"

It was the worst thing about being at risk for whatever reason—being weaker, or having traits that put one at the edges of the herd, vulnerable to attack. Who you were, who you wanted to be, your options, your horizon, could become lost in all that.

"There was a time I felt that way," Clara said slowly, shadows in her gaze. "But we go everywhere, and I see so many amazing things. Maddock and Yvette's shielding of my identity have allowed me to keep interacting with the audience on the midway. Then there's Marcellus."

Her face softened in a way Ruth knew well. She'd seen Elisa look at Mal with that expression a million times. Since her father was hyperaware of Elisa's state of mind and whereabouts, he'd often turn and meet Elisa's gaze, giving her his own version of that expression. As Ruth had developed a woman's heart and mind, it had seeded the yearning to want a male like that. One who would look at her the same way, with all that it meant.

"Figuring things out with him," Clara said. "That was a big part of finding contentment with what and where I am. If I wasn't human, he could fly me up into the heavens so I'd be permanently out of harm's way, but he does take me flying. I mean, for a woman with 'limited' options, I've had a thousand more experiences than most ever get."

She sat up, brushing grass off the back of her shirt. Ruth helped her reach where she couldn't, and Clara did the same for her. As Ruth rose, she helped the girl all the way to her feet, clasping her hand.

She knew how to modulate her strength for handling a human, so her brow creased when Clara flinched, jerked. Then she swayed on her feet. Ruth slid a steadying arm around her.

"Clara, what's going on?"

Clara looked toward the lake, where Medusa was practicing with the mermaids. Only she wasn't seeing them. Her body went loose, wobbly, a puppet with cut strings.

As Ruth caught her before she could fall, the girl's pupils dilated. The black took over the way Marcellus's did, only they didn't stay dark. Instead the blackness was swallowed by a murky gray.

Clara began to convulse.

CHAPTER SIX

"*S*hit." Ruth eased her to the ground. "*Help*," she shouted, waving her arms to draw Medusa's attention.

As the woman swiftly turned the windsurfer toward the shore, Ruth knelt over Clara. Her body was doing a jittering dance like an epileptic. Ruth stripped off her belt to put between her teeth, but before she could do it, Clara went harrowingly still, eyes fixed vacantly on the sky. Her hands flopped to her sides, but they weren't relaxed. She was a soldier at attention, her body plank straight. The tightness to her mouth, her pale, tense face, said wherever she was, she didn't want to be there.

A spurt of relief replaced terror as Ruth put her hand on the girl's throat and felt the blood pulsing strongly.

Marcellus dropped out of the sky, landing on the other side of Clara's inert body. The ground vibrated from his impact, his arrival so swift the air disturbance from his wings blew against Ruth's hair and clothing.

"It just happened," Ruth told him. "Is this usually how it works?"

He nodded, kneeling beside his fortune teller. He brushed his fingertips over Clara's brow, lingered there. "When the veins start throbbing with the headache, it means the vision is almost at an end. It is the usual process."

Not one he liked, from the set of his jaw.

"So we just wait it out?"

"Yes. It's best not to move her when it's happening, because movement increases her agitation. It can be done, however, if she's in danger." His lips pressed together. "She was supposed to advise you of the risk of this, so you would be prepared."

"I expect she wanted to get to know me first. People dealing with something like this don't like to be defined by it." No matter how much it did. "Can I put my coat over her? She looks cold."

Marcellus's gaze slid to her, held a beat, then went back to Clara. "Yes. That would be kind."

Ruth laid the camel-colored fleece duster over the girl. "Does she give you any information during it?"

"Rarely. She remembers afterward, and gives us what the vision provides then. Despite the headache, she must do that immediately, or she can lose important details."

From his tense expression, Ruth suspected he had to watch her offer that information while she fought the pain. "Headache" was probably an understatement. What had Clara said? *Like my head is going to explode.*

Medusa had approached, but at a gesture from Marcellus, she retreated with a respectful bow. Ruth logged the information. Thanks to that tattoo or whatever other link they had, if Marcellus was on site, he could be at Clara's side within seconds of her distress. If he was elsewhere, that was when Ruth would call for reinforcements.

When a new employee was hired for the preserve, he or she had to work through a learning curve. It was the same for her responsibilities here, no matter how unusual.

"What can I do for her while she's like this?" She kept her voice low. She didn't know if it was necessary, but she didn't want to cause any distractions from what Clara was seeing or hearing, such that she had to stay in this state one second longer than necessary.

"Watch over her until it's done." He adjusted the coat to lift the hem of Clara's shirt and reveal a sheath hooked at her waistband. Marcellus tapped on the contents, a sleek black cylinder made of hard rubber. "This is to put between her teeth, if needed. Most times, though, she goes right into the vision state. The seizure symptoms disappear swiftly."

"It was like that this time."

After readjusting the shirt and coat, he put a hand on his bent knee, since he knelt on the other. The dark green wings spread out to either side of him, the feathers vibrating with the tension she saw in his curled fingers. Evidence of how much effort it took him not to touch Clara right now.

"So you can't go ahead and put your hands on her head to help reduce the impact of the headache on the front end? She said your touch makes it a lot better."

His mouth softened. "Unfortunately, no. We have tried it before. Touching her too early made the visions...worse."

She changed the subject. "How often does this happen?"

"Too much, of late. We do not yet have enough pieces on the current subject of her visions, not enough to put together a picture and address it. Their frequency will increase until we do."

The veins in Clara's temples were starting to noticeably pulse, and she shifted, a moan escaping her rigid lips. Her eyes remained vacant, far away, but the veins and moan were apparently the cues which allowed Marcellus to lay a hand on her forehead. As he did, Ruth saw those symbols and praises to the Goddess reappear over the curve of his biceps, a metallic gleam against tanned skin.

Ruth had thought it would be difficult to tell what he was thinking, with his eyes wholly dark. But the lines around his eyes and mouth spoke eloquently as his large hand rested on her pale brow, fingers framing her delicate temple and cheek. "I will return her to our quarters. Come there in a half hour. Clara will want to see you."

"All right. Take the coat with you to keep her comfortable. I'll get it then." Ruth had more questions, but she held them as Marcellus lifted Clara into his arms. He cradled her as if nothing in the universe could ever be as precious to him.

"Ruth?"

"Yes, my lord?"

"You are handling yourself well. But there is one very important rule you need to never break."

His dark gaze came to her and locked. That, and the tone of his voice, the flicker in his eyes, held her very, very still.

"If you wish to kiss her in the manner you did, you require permission. *My* permission. Do you understand?"

"I do. Sir. My lord." She cleared her throat. "My apologies."

"No apologies are needed. But if you do it again, far greater amends will be demanded." Without waiting for a response, the angel rose into the air, a gentle take-off that didn't jostle Clara.

Ruth watched the wings, the flex of Marcellus's shoulders, and drew in an unsteady breath as he disappeared over the hill. That quake in her lower belly was one of her favorite feelings, even if she had to hide it when it was caused by someone, instead of being manufactured by her own fantasies.

Concealing the reaction when she hadn't been expecting to be hit with such a powerful dose of it was difficult, but any evidence of it would pass under the not-untruthful guise of respect for a being powerful enough to obliterate all memory of her existence. And no one else was around to notice anyway.

Or so she thought.

"You respond to him."

Lack of situational awareness was an automatic fail for Bodyguard 101. She needed to do better.

Her irritation over that, her concern for Clara, and those worrisome lingering tingles, didn't put her in the best state. But she wasn't backing down from a challenge.

She turned to face Merc.

He leaned against one of the trees on the border of the forest. It was a deceptively casual pose, one wing folded forward, feathers brushing the shoulder and upper arm it was draped over. The other was tucked behind him to clear the tree trunk. He had his arms crossed over his chest, and had changed into a T-shirt. Same sinfully well-fitted jeans.

This shirt had artwork, a demon perched on a church. Intense dark eyes, forked tongue, horns, and a barbed tail wrapped around the steeple. A stone angel, sculpted on the roof edge, stared up at him in frozen horror. Had he bought it to annoy Marcellus?

"You didn't deny it," he said.

She forced herself to remain indifferent as he moved toward her. A lazy predator, ready to engage a burst of speed and take down his kill. She raised a brow.

"You didn't ask a question. But any female would respond to him. It's the tattoos," she offered blandly.

Ink appeared along Merc's arms, intricate art that picked up the theme of the shirt, showing a wrestling match between angels and demons. Then it was gone, his skin unmarked again. A deft piece of magic.

"No," he said. "It wasn't a physical trait that made you go still, made your knees weaken, ready to drop you to the ground if he bade you do so."

Several more steps. He didn't choose a straight line, instead moving to the right to gaze at the lake, where Medusa was again practicing with the mermaids.

"Mermaids and sirens are often confused as being the same, because they look the same," he noted. "The way most vampires are assumed to be the same, because they look and act the same. You try to act the same, but you fail at it."

"I'm done sparring for the day," she said. "I'm going to check on Clara."

"He said a half hour."

"I was being polite. My mistake. I don't want to be around you."

She pivoted and stopped as he landed in front of her, still in bare feet. "Do you ever wear shoes?"

"Yes. I didn't say you could go."

"I don't recall needing your permission."

"But you need his?"

"He's an angel, and projects that in a way hard to ignore." Her eyes narrowed. "The women here avoid being alone with you. Why is that, Merc? Would you hurt them?"

"Yes. Quite possibly." He blinked at her, like a hawk being asked if it would raid a bird nest and eat the fledglings.

Something was off about it. She wasn't buying the simple acceptance of his monster side, though she had no reason to doubt it. Nothing but her gut. Which could be her sexual response to him, fucking with her head.

Knowing she was playing with fire, she nevertheless took one measured step toward him. She noted the flaring of his nostrils, the kindling of his gaze. "How can you hurt them?"

"You are not afraid of me," he observed, instead of answering. "I want you to be."

"You're shit out of luck there. I refuse to fear anything. You're not answering the question."

"I don't answer to you. Would you like to fly?"

"You already took me off my feet at the preserve. You do it again, I'll stab you wherever I can reach. Won't really care about where. Only that it will hurt a lot."

"We were fighting then. Taking you in the air was an advantage. Would you like to fly? For fun?"

The word sounded odd on his lips. Like he wasn't entirely sure what it meant, but he would give it a go, see what it was like if she was game to try.

She'd wanted to know more about him. Was this his attempt to try to do the same with her? Nothing about him was aboveboard. Any assumptions would be a mistake.

"Which of the cats got you?" she nodded to his shoulder.

"The lion that was with you. He stalked me when I was... distracted by our encounter. I caused him no harm."

"I know. Why haven't they healed?" Everything she'd done to him at the fight already had.

"I wanted to keep them longer. A reminder."

He closed that last step. Her body tightened up at his proximity, all that maleness, his scent, his power, the threat of him. He put his mouth to the round part of her shoulder, the same place the scratches were on his. When his fangs scraped her skin, a passing tease, it made her shiver.

"Turn around, put your arms behind you and grip my belt with both hands. Never fear, little vampire. I'll have you back in time to meet with Marcellus. Wouldn't want you to be in trouble with him. You'd enjoy that too much."

The acid edge warned her, but if she showed fear or avoidance of him, it would only cause her more trouble with him down the road. Best to get this over with up front.

That was what she was telling herself.

"Shove the 'little vampire' shit up your condescending ass." Turning, she reached back, fingers finding his belt and the waistband of the jeans under his untucked shirt. She pushed behind them to grip, her knuckles against the bare, firm skin inside his hip bones. The man didn't wear underwear. At least not right now. Her thumbs brushed the buckle and tooth. "Don't mess with me on that. Promise me you'll get me on the ground in time to meet with Marcellus."

"I don't make promises to anyone."

"It does break the card-carrying dickhead code, doesn't it?"

A chuckle, that mean note to it, and one arm slid around her waist, the other over her chest, just above her breasts. His hand gripped her opposite shoulder.

She sensed him looking down at her, seeing the way her body fit against his, how her arms being behind her arched her back and pressed the tops of her breasts more firmly against his forearm. He moved the hand on her shoulder to her throat, curving his fingers around it. Her pulse hammered against his palm as her breath slowed, shortened. Stopped.

He was squeezing, yes, but that wasn't the only reason she reacted that way. She held still, holding everything in, though it was all there, crowding against the gate, so damn eager to come forward, to offer, to give. To serve.

To be with a male who deserved her submission.

He hadn't come close to proving he had those qualifications, but fuck, he knew all the buttons to push. But so did every vampire male she'd ever encountered. Though they didn't know she was a submissive, vampire dominance games weren't limited to human servants. Their whole world was built on a power hierarchy.

"Are we doing this or not?" She was behind that black diamond wall, the question fired at him in a flat tone. He might be able to detect her arousal, but he didn't command her responses.

"Say please."

His lips were near her ear, and her eyes half closed when he spoke. He slid his thumb along her carotid, his breath a touch of heat on her cheek. "Ask me to take you flying. I would hear you ask me for something."

She'd had a tart response for the 'say please,' but there was a note to the rest that pulled from a deeper level. His grip on her throat loosened, fingertips exploring the sensitive skin along her jaw. She moistened her lips. She almost dipped her head toward his touch, asking for more. She didn't do that, but allowed herself to indulge the other desire. To obey his demand to hear her ask.

"I'd like to fly. Will you take me?"

He moved his hand back to her shoulder. "I will."

He took off, stealing her breath at how fast they ascended. She felt no strain from holding on. The strength of his arms carried her, and once he was high enough, he rolled back at an angle where she reclined against him, staring at the sky and the horizon.

His wings were strong and sure, his chest muscles flexing in small movements beneath her, the adjustments he was making to hold them there. His feathers fluttered against her forearms. She wanted to let go of his belt, reach out and stroke them, turn around and face him. Wrap her legs around his body. See how he would respond to her disobedience. She wanted to fight, needed to fight him.

But she was flying. She'd always wanted to fly. On the island, she ran up trees, leaped over things. But that was different. She envied the birds their wings, the freedom it gave them to just fly away.

She shared that with him.

"It's a lie. There's always someone fast enough to catch up."

His tone was curiously flat. He turned them and dove. She sucked in a breath as he swept down toward the trees. He banked so close above the canopies, the leaves brushed her knees. When he shot back up, she laughed in delight. Her mind cut loose, soaring like her body.

It reminded her of a story her mother had told her, when Mal had taught Elisa how to ride a bicycle. Elisa's eyes had sparkled as she put her arms out to her sides. *It was like I was flying.*

The freedom. The weightlessness. A different way of traveling through the world. A different sensation, especially when provided by a male who'd captured her interest.

Merc rotated them back to that diagonal angle where she rested against his body, then stroked her throat, making her lift her chin. She propped her head on his shoulder. His hand slid down her stomach, deft fingers unhooking her belt then slipping the button of her jeans before they moved beneath.

Arousal surged, combining with the exhilaration of flight.

He explored the folds of her swelling sex, light strokes over her clit, firmer circles on the labia, finding the moisture between them and spreading it over her tissues, making her slicker.

She felt that sexual miasma he could use, a weapon with an irresistible promise.

"Don't," she whispered. "Don't use it. Let me feel it the way you want me to feel it."

He stilled, so abruptly they lost altitude. When his muscles and wings flexed, bringing them back up, she knew she'd stepped over a dangerous line with him, though she didn't know what had caused it. He ignored her request, that energy winding itself around her, tightening. She bucked, moaned as he stroked her with such devastating gentleness, even as the arousal yanked her in the direction he demanded she go.

Violence was more terrifying when it was iced with gentleness.

Her loose hair mixed with his feathers, black on black, with glimpses of the lightning bolt white. She clutched his belt, so aware of the heated muscle of his abdomen against her knuckles, but the rest of her was limp under his incubus compulsion. Her head was too heavy to lift. All of her wanted to just give herself over to him. Let the power of the desire he was drawing from her take over.

"Submit to me," he said. "Let me have you."

No. Not like this. But she couldn't get the rest of her to comply.

"You responded to the Master in Marcellus," he rumbled in her ear. "You are a submission slut. You don't care who the Master is. Just that he is willing to hold your leash."

Nothing like a male acting like a bastard to shock her will with a Taser.

She fought to the top of that tidal wave of pure lust and rode it, rotating her hips against him. "Sounds like that pisses you off," she rasped through taut lips. "Why would you care? I'm just a meal. Sex demon."

His hand closed on her throat again, and she shifted with him. It covered her movement, her hand leaving his belt to reach the knife holstered at her hip, hooked to the loosened waistband of her jeans. Before his grip started to constrict, she'd drawn the blade and brought it down, stabbing him in the thigh.

He ripped the knife from her grasp and tossed it away. Damn it, she loved that knife. But she had bigger problems. Merc let her go, shoving her out into the open air.

Fucking hell. This time, they were much higher off the ground. As her body hurtled downward, she knew this was going to hurt like hell. She only had a few seconds to orient herself in the way that would break the least bones. They'd heal up, but it would take time, and she sure as hell wouldn't be in any shape to meet Marcellus when he'd told her to.

Goddamn asshole. Now he was a liar, too. Or maybe not. She

wouldn't put it past him to deposit her broken and bloody body on Marcellus's doorstep, just to say he'd honored his promise.

The ground rushed up at her, and she tucked, hoping she could roll and remove some impact from her more vulnerable skull and spine.

Merc caught her inches from the ground, hard hands scooping her under the arms. Her body jerked, full body whiplash. When the weight hit her still sore shoulder, she couldn't bite back the cry of pain. She didn't care. That was just physical crap.

She squirmed, fought, tried to unhook herself from his hold. When he refused to let go, she swung herself out and tried to bring her legs over, planning a double-soled smash to his smug face. Or to crush his head between her knees. He shook her like a rag doll until she stopped trying to fight. Even after that, he held her long enough to prove she couldn't get loose without his say-so. Then he dropped her again.

This time she was only a couple feet off the ground. She whirled toward him, her second knife in hand. He knocked that away, too, and had her against him. Her top knot had come unpinned during their fight, so he seized a handful of her loosened hair. His expression was one of cold menace, the black blood eyes giving off heat like molten coal. The silver was in full-on heat lightning mode.

"Is that what pissed you off enough to be mean to me?" she spat, not caring to give him time to say anything. "Can't arouse a woman without using your magic? You're just a vibrator. You need to be plugged into your power to work."

Merc's lips curled away from his fangs. She knew—*she knew*—she was about to die. Clara had warned her to be cautious. So had Charlie.

She didn't care. He'd messed with her trust. She'd happily die rather than let someone think it was okay to treat her that way.

He held her gaze. Her eyes were watering, and she refused to blink. "You don't look down when I look at you," he said. "But you want to."

"I want to, yes. For the right Master. You aren't him. You aren't even close. You're not even trying to be."

He may have guessed it, but she'd just said aloud what she never had. But he didn't know that. She calmed the cold ball of apprehension. If he repeated it to anyone, it would be interpreted as an empty taunt. Not the actual truth. She had bigger problems. Like being dead, right here and now.

His mouth tightened, the fangs disappearing. So did he, taking flight so abruptly she stumbled backwards. Then she yelped and jumped back further. The knife he'd tossed out into the open air, way above the earth, landed before her, point embedded in the ground.

By the time she retrieved it and the other one he'd knocked away from her, he was hovering above her again. When she stared at him, a knife held at the ready in either fist, she felt it again. The strong desire to lower her gaze, be on her knees to him. The asshole.

It was the sex demon thing. Not the man behind it. Or was it? She might be being naïve about his ability, but her gut told her the compulsion magic couldn't have this kind of hold on her. Nothing about him, or her reaction to him, made sense.

She knew how to handle that. She held her position and waited for his next move.

His expression shuttered and he gave her a short nod. Almost courteous, if she hadn't sensed the inferno of want and need raging between them. He left her company, winging away across the mellow sunlit sky.

After she watched him go, she realized she was where he'd first picked her up. Medusa was onshore again, standing by the windsurfer as if she'd pulled in to be available if Ruth needed backup. As Ruth lifted a hand in thanks, Medusa's expression adopted the bemusement of someone who wasn't sure what exactly they'd witnessed, but it wasn't what they'd expected.

Though Medusa acknowledged the wave and returned to the water, Ruth knew Yvette would be informed of the interaction. Normal sexual wranglings between staff probably weren't considered worthy of anything more than gossip, but Ruth was a new variable, and Merc was obviously kept under close watch.

Ruth cleaned the dirt off her knives and returned both to their hiding places. She refastened her jeans and belt, and straightened her clothes. Then she headed for the camp. Maybe by the time she reached it, her nerves would be calmer and her sweaty palms would be dry.

Getting Merc out of her head was going to be a lot harder. She needed more information.

CHAPTER SEVEN

*S*hould she worry about the repercussions of stabbing a Circus staff member? She'd noted the blood was already coagulating when he'd hovered in the air above her. It seemed to confirm his healing properties were as decent as a vampire's. And he had mentioned that he'd "kept" Tau's slash marks on purpose.

He hadn't fed on her, though. Blood helped vampires heal faster. Did sexual energy do the same for him?

She'd figure out a way to check on him later. Not that he deserved it, but she was going to be the better person. The challenge would be finding out where his quarters were. Probably a dark hole in the ground, shared with roommates Gollum and Hannibal Lecter.

Marcellus and Clara had a yurt, too. It was the same size as Yvette's, which made sense, not just because of Marcellus's status, but for the practical amount of space his wings would need. The flaps were open, and she heard voices. Marcellus, Clara and Charlie. The healer stepped out as Ruth arrived.

The blind healer "looked" at her, her brow furrowing. "You need some chakra cleansing, my lady," she said. "And a deep tissue massage. You'll feel better. He has a contaminated energy."

"There's no privacy here," Ruth told her.

"Very little," Charlie agreed. "Too many insightful people, plus a handful like me, with intrusive reading powers. We have an agreement to keep it on the surface level, though. Only for detecting health and wellbeing issues we can resolve. Yvette has the right to dig deeper, but even she does it primarily for the Circus's interests."

Though Ruth had deduced a lot of that herself, she appreciated Charlie's friendly heads up. It also told her she'd be able to find out more about Merc if she asked the right people the right questions. "How's Clara?"

"Tired," came a weary voice from inside the tent. "But doing okay. Come on in, Ruth."

Charlie moved away as Ruth entered the yurt. A large bed was on her right. The sturdy wood frame looked capable of handling an angel. Did angels sleep? Even if they didn't, Clara did. Angels obviously also had interest in other things that could be done in a bed, another reason for overbuilding it. Vampire beds weren't spindly structures, either.

If she was dwelling on stuff like that, her body was still too worked up. *Memo to self; next time, pick a fight* after *getting the mind shattering orgasm.*

Clara was a small figure on the vast mattress, but she was propped up on pillows and looked more like herself than when last Ruth had seen her.

The yurt walls were collaged with hand painted pictures, photographs, flowers and postcards. A wardrobe probably contained Clara's colorful clothing. A coat rack next to it held Ruth's coat, a long knotty sweater, and a fedora with so many souvenir pins attached to it the black felt was barely visible. Other than that, a table and a couple of chairs, the area was clear.

"We don't keep much furniture in here," Clara said, watching Ruth take in her surroundings. "Marcellus's wingspan can clear every flat surface like a golden retriever's tail. I want him to feel this is his home away from home, so I do what I can to make it comfortable."

"Where is he? I thought I heard him."

"You did." Clara pointed toward another entrance to the yurt, the two accesses allowing a fresh breeze through the space. "He went to tell Yvette and Maddock about my latest vision. After that he'll report to Jonah. Jonah is Prime Legion Commander, which means he leads the angelic forces that protect the universe."

"So no one important. I feel like I've been blown off."

Clara's eyes warmed. "You wear the wiseass persona well."

"It's not clothing. It's an essential part of my charming personality."

"Noted. Marcellus told me to tell you to go see Gundar. He's Yvette's right-hand ringmaster and another of her second marks. We have a performance tomorrow night in Tennessee. He'll explain how the Circus security works during performances and how you'll blend, while still watching over me specifically. Marcellus and Dollar, who heads up the security team, will give you more specific guidance in the briefing with them tomorrow."

A tender smile touched Clara's lips. "He didn't leave until he heard you approaching. He's already decided he likes you being around me when he can't be, at least when I'm on my ass like this. You can take that as an encouraging sign of job security."

Ruth noted Clara was shivering. "Do you want the flaps closed?"

"No, I like the cooler air. But if you could bring me that sweater, that would be great. Your coat was wonderful, by the way."

Ruth retrieved the oversized and shapeless sweater and had Clara lean forward so she could wrap it around her shoulders. "The first time I wore this, Charlie told me I looked like I was wearing a bath-mat. In addition to being our healer, she's our costume designer and dressmaker. But even if it offends her fashion sensibilities, she understands comfort clothing is as important as comfort food."

Ruth sat on the bed, her hip against Clara's thigh, under the covers. "This is taking too much out of you. Isn't it?"

Charlie's expression had been worried, but it had also held a resignation Ruth didn't like at all.

"If it keeps on like this, it will kill me," Clara said simply. "Sooner rather than later. About a year ago, Maddock found a way to block the visions. I just have to agree to try it. But I've asked him to look for a way to filter it, instead of stopping them completely."

Ruth studied her. "You don't feel you have the right to be that selfish."

"Wouldn't you feel the same? Remember what I said, how when I first got my gift, I couldn't change anything? Back then, I asked the Powers-That-Be why would they give me an ability to look ahead, if there was nothing I could do to change a bad outcome. I realize now I was going through training steps. I had to learn the lesson of what could be changed, and what couldn't. Now I *can* save lives. I have the gift for a reason. If it takes my life, it takes it. Your boy Albert Schweitzer says we find the divine through service, suffering and eternal gratitude."

Clara glanced toward the little book on her side table. It was an old copy, the hardback a faded salmon color, the title in silver stamped lettering. "There's a part of me that understands that, now more than I ever have." She tilted her head toward Ruth, her gaze sparking with subdued mischief. "Charlie and Marcellus found it weird that a vampire would read this book."

"I've read a lot of things. It doesn't stop me from being blood-thirsty. And who are you to talk? You have *Reverence of Life* stacked on top of Anne Rice's *Sleeping Beauty* and the *Wonder Woman Golden Age Omnibus*. Which has some serious female Dominant imagery and themes."

"So you've read that, too. Of course you have." Clara smiled. "Jacob loaned me that one. Having met his Mistress, I'm not surprised he has it, and not just because he's passionate about comic books. I think he wanted to remind me of my inner female power. Whereas Sleeping Beauty..." She shot Ruth a devilish look. "Marcellus likes the way it affects me when I read it."

Ruth was glad to see the smile, though she knew the need to change their focus might make it disappear. "Should I know anything about your vision today? I don't want to put you through it all over again, but does it figure into what might come after you?"

Fear flashed through Clara's gaze. When Ruth clasped the fortune teller's hand, she didn't like the weakness of her grip.

"Whatever plan I'm tapping into, the one I think is in charge turned around and looked right at me. Spoke my name." Clara paused. "His face was blurry, but he's a vampire. He's not like you and Adan, or Yvette. You all...you dress nice, enhance all those sexy vampire vibes. He doesn't care about any of that. He reminds me of a wild animal, except most wild animals don't look like a homeless dictator about to launch a genocide campaign."

A knot cinched itself in Ruth's stomach. "A Trad."

The Trads were a vampire sect that lived outside the Council structure. They inhabited remote places, preferring to embrace the savage predator in their natures. They sneered at having human servants. Humans were food. Since reproduction was as much of a concern for Trads as all vampires, females were sometimes captured, serving as blood donors while the Trads attempted to plant their seed. When that didn't happen, as it mostly didn't, the women were used for blood until they died. Which Ruth hoped didn't take long.

They'd take a female vampire if the opportunity arose to create a "pure" born vampire, one with two vampire parents. A far rarer occurrence than vampire-human servant offspring, but scientific evidence didn't seem to figure into their obsession.

"The Trads are always planning some crackpot scheme to destroy all of us who don't believe the way they do."

"Yes, but I wouldn't receive a vision about those. Unfortunately, what I get are the things with decent odds of succeeding." Clara's face tightened. "I've been given forty pieces of a thousand-piece jigsaw puzzle. Yvette tells me it's forty more than we would have had, but it's still frustrating. Especially when the things I see…"

She swallowed. "No matter how it started for our bad guys, by the time it gets to me, pure hate has taken over. The desire to take, kill, destroy."

She gave Ruth a look of dull despair. "Beyond the practical details, I'm sucked into the worst parts of a person's soul. The more often the visions happen, the more I get hit with that side of it."

She'd lifted her hand to her temple and was massaging it, a firm pressure with thumb and forefinger, as if she could push those thoughts out. Ruth stroked her forearm. "That's all I need to know. No more. Give yourself a break."

Over the past few years, rumors and incidents suggested the Trads were getting more organized. The group that boasted of being off the grid, rejecting the Council's "pretense" of "acting like humans," might be using the same tactics for their own purposes. *Shocker.* Mal said hypocrisy was always in the arsenal of those who wanted to justify hurting or taking from someone else.

The Council balanced the vampire need for hierarchy imposed by power, with efforts to preserve the race. They didn't pretend vampires were anything different from what they were. Which meant Lady Lyssa, the Council, Region Masters and overlords weren't shy about using brutal methods, if they felt they were necessary.

Vampires not in the upper echelons, like Ruth or Mal, might debate whether the decisions made were right or wrong. However, most agreed that, as long as Lady Lyssa was in charge, her hand firmly on Council's tiller, the vampire race would be well served.

All that aside, Clara's current visions offered further explanation for why Ruth had been selected for this job. Though she wasn't the strongest vampire, she had vampire instincts, and could detect the presence of another one.

Because she planned to prove her usefulness, she'd been ready to accept the distasteful idea that she'd been offered this job as a favor to her father. A patronizing act to give her something "important" to do, while having more opportunity to be out in the world, in a place she'd be mostly protected.

She should have had more faith in her father. And her brother, since she had no doubt he'd had a hand in this.

Clara's visions had far-reaching, dangerous implications. A vampire world run by Trads would be a human bloodbath, with the even worse ramification of making the human world at large aware of the existence of vampires. Humans would use their superior weaponry to detect and exterminate vampires. Something the Trads had always absurdly refused to acknowledge, treating humans as if they had the brains of a McDonald's Big Mac.

On the flip side, that made it hard for Ruth to imagine them coming up with a plan that had far-reaching consequences, but she didn't doubt the chilling proof Clara had provided.

The fortune teller's eyes were drooping. "I'm going to get some sleep now. Don't forget to see Gundar before you settle into your quarters. Oh, Marcellus said to tell you it was okay for me to have another kiss. You have a really sweet kiss. Gentle even. Not like I'd expect a vampire's kiss to be. Would it be okay to ask for another?"

The sleepy hazel gaze was hopeful, impossible to deny. Ruth leaned in and cupped her nape, feeling the slim bones under her hand. Mal had told her the trust of a human, like the trust of the animals on their preserve, was a special gift. Particularly when both were aware of how easily a vampire could kill them.

Ruth put her lips on Clara's. There was a sweetness to her mouth too. Literally, a touch of chocolate mixed with vanilla, coconut, and cayenne pepper. Clara petted Ruth's hair, her upper arm, then gripped as Ruth deepened the kiss just enough to give the girl a bolstering shot of lust. When she drew back, Clara's eyes were laughing.

"A good reminder you're not tame. Just like Merc. Tell me something about him. Like a bedtime story."

"I just met him," Ruth answered, puzzled.

"Yeah. But you two had an after-fight meeting. Or after-fight fight."

"Grapevine moves fast around here."

"Faster than shit through a goose on a triple dose of laxative."

"And you're nosy," Ruth added, suppressing a smile.

"It's one of my most endearing traits. Tell me something about Merc I don't know."

"His scent. Do you recognize it?"

"I may be cute as a Pomeranian, but I don't have a dog's sense of smell."

Ruth chuckled. "It has a spice to it. Like wandering into an opium den. It's floral, but earthy too. You know how when you're aroused, what might seem like a bad smell when you're not aroused—heat, sweat, sex—is like perfume, drawing you in? It's like that all the time with him. Even when it's not turned on, so to speak."

Clara digested the words, but her eyes were almost closed. She was drifting off.

"He took me flying," Ruth said softly. That opened the eyes a wider crack.

"Really? He does that with the kids during the Promenade."

"What's the Promenade?"

"The Circus aftershow. The audience is allowed to come into the rings and talk to the players. Merc will take kids for short flights under the Big Top. After seeing him do it for years, it shouldn't still surprise me, but it always does. It's like the key to his better side, but no one can find that key outside of the Promenade. You can't hold onto it."

"Does Marcellus take the children for flights, too?"

"Yes, when he's here. I get to see it sometimes, but I work the midway and we're supposed to be at our stations for the blow off. That's when the guests exit the show and get engaged by the criers to check out the sideshows and souvenirs, if they didn't have time to do it on the way in. Or get a candied apple or bag of popcorn...for the road."

The last words were a mumble. Clara's head had sunk into the pillow. Ruth sat with her until she confirmed the fortune teller was sleeping easily, without pain. Then she brushed a kiss over the girl's forehead, adjusting the blankets before rising.

Clara refusing to back away from the torment and brutality she was witnessing in her visions, despite the fatal toll it was taking on her body and spirit? Marcellus's devotion to a "mere" mortal was making a whole hell of a lot more sense. Ruth was half in love with her already, and she'd known her less than a day.

When she turned, she already knew Marcellus was in the doorway. He said nothing, his gaze on Clara. His wings were pulled in so Ruth could get by him. Though his dark eyes were unreadable, it didn't matter. She could feel his anguish.

She touched his arm. The praises to the Goddess rippled with mild electric current under her fingertips. He glanced her way.

She would do everything she could not to let Clara down. When she let him see that in her expression, she was glad to see he understood, responding with a brief nod.

She left him reluctantly. Learning from a passing bearded lady in a satin dress and combat boots that Gundar was in the Big Top, she headed in that direction. As she strode toward it, she noted Charlie sitting at one of the picnic tables set randomly throughout the campground. The rough surface had been covered by a thick tablecloth, and she'd spread a shimmering length of fabric over it. From watching her mother make clothes, Ruth knew she was pinning and marking a pattern.

"Dressmaker *and* healer," Ruth remarked, stopping beside her. "Why do I expect that's only two of many jobs you do?"

"When you serve a vampire who's the Mistress of the Circus, you do whatever is required. My lady." Charlie spoke amiably, but she also started to straighten from her task to give Ruth her full attention.

She may have been raised in far more informal circumstances, but Ruth knew what the healer was doing. "It's Ruth," she said. "And while I'm here, treat me like other Circus employees. Unless we're around the stodgy vampires who get their knickers in a twist about it, you don't have to do the vampire-servant protocol thing."

"Thank you, my lady. Ruth." The second marked servant returned her attention to the fabric, feeling her way along the edge. "Cai tells me the same, when he is here."

97

Ruth propped a hip on an unoccupied corner of the table. She could see Gundar in the entryway to the Big Top, talking to six roustabouts in tool belts. She had a moment to kill. "Cai, as in the vampire who pisses off stodgy vampires, but hasn't been staked the way he deserves because he has the sexiest lupine servant in the world?"

Charlie smiled. "Yes, that Cai. You might get to see him and Rand while you're here. They don't perform with us anymore, but they stop in, as good friends and family will."

"They've been to our sanctuary quite a few times." The acid-tongued loner vampire preferred the wild spaces more than settled, urban ones. As a wolf shifter, his servant Rand's preferences walked the same lines. Though Rand appeared more amiable than his Master, if the moment called for it, he could be formidable and intimidating as hell. Whether in wolf or human form.

They'd let Ruth run with them, allowing her to test herself against their speed and strength. He might be edgy, but Cai was never cruel to her.

Not the way she could tell Merc wanted to be. Or struggled against, depending on whose story you believed.

"My father is keenly interested in the wolf shifters. Beyond his island family—blood born and acquired—he's always preferred the company of four-footed species."

"Sensible. The animals we have here are usually far easier to get along with than the humanlike races. That includes the dragons. If they exterminate you in a puff of flame, you know exactly why."

"No psychological analysis required?"

"None. Oh, I've left several shirts in your quarters. For performances, the security team wears black slacks or jeans, and a black golf shirt with the Circus logo in red embroidery on the pocket." Charlie paused. "I'm glad you're here, Ruth. Clara seems to like you."

"I like her, too. Everyone seems worried about her."

"Yes." Charlie's face reflected the added concern of a healer. "Seeing what she is seeing is traumatic, mentally and physically. Her gift has imposed an isolation upon her, no matter that she's surrounded by friends and those who would protect her. She's extraordinary, but we can all see she's reaching the end of what she can endure." Charlie's lips tightened. "She has accepted the inevitability of her death."

Ruth rejected that kind of thinking. She expected she wasn't the only one. "How does Marcellus feel about that?"

"He'll fight for her, even if his greatest opponent is Clara herself," Charlie confirmed. "However, because he loves her so deeply, if her pain becomes more than she can bear, and he cannot bear it for her, he won't hold her just to keep her with him."

"Makes sense. He's an angel. He can just visit her in a different neighborhood, right?"

Charlie's eyes filled with sadness. "It doesn't work that way. He'd see her again, but it would be a long, long time before it happened. The part of heaven where the Legion angels dwell is not where souls go to await reincarnation. When she assumes mortal form again, there are rules against him approaching her unless the Fates decree it. It interferes with her path to ultimate enlightenment, when she can be with him forever."

"That's bullshit. And even if it's not, it sucks."

"Yes, it does." Charlie cocked her head. "I assume she told you about Maddock's solution?"

"Yeah. And that she's not going to take it."

"They could force her, but self-determination is the one abiding rule here." Charlie gave her a look. "Much like for a vampire's second or third marked servant. One key choice is ours."

"To belong to the vampire or not." Ruth nodded.

After that all the choices belonged to the vampire. The dressmaker's behavior toward Yvette had already confirmed that she found the Circus owner a fair Mistress. Charlie was content with the binding.

Clara had said that Charlie and Maddock had a relationship, but most vampire masters or mistresses were open to that for permanent second marks, servants the vampire had no intention of taking to the soul-binding level of the third mark. If servants pursued such relationships, they were almost always with another marked servant, or someone vetted to have knowledge of vampire existence.

Even for a third mark, it was possible, because most vampires had the "approved" kind of relationship with their servants. Her father's reaction to that would be far different. As she suspected Lyssa's would be with Jacob. Nothing about the queen said she had any intention of sharing her servant's affections.

Gundar had finished his meet with the roustabouts. As Ruth bade Charlie good-bye and headed for the Big Top, she knew she'd find plenty to keep her engaged here.

Merc flitted through her mind, no help for it. Could she safely act on the insta-sexual attraction, let it burn out and move on? On such occasions in the past, she'd stifled her yearning for submission, never giving it enough room to determine if her reaction to a dominant male was an opportunity to exercise it. Too dangerous.

Merc was something different, though.

Gundar was the dwarf smithy she'd seen earlier. Aside from the muscled, compact body, he had coal-dark eyes set deep in a brick-strong face, and handsome, thick sandy hair. He provided her so much information about the security detail, she thought she should have brought a way to make notes. He assured her it would all be reviewed again at the briefing, but when she asked where she could find Merc, his reassuring demeanor vanished. When he gave her a hard look, she realized something she'd suspected but hadn't pinned down before that moment. He was a Dom himself.

Yvette's two primary second marks were a submissive healer and a Dominant smithy and ringmaster. More stories to learn, more mysteries to solve.

"Don't go looking for him by yourself, my lady." His voice had a gravel-rough authority that didn't brook argument. She had to remind herself he was just a human. As far as she could tell.

"Just Ruth."

His brow arched. "You're a born vampire."

"Just Ruth," she repeated.

She suspected he might have issued a stronger warning, as much as his status as a second mark allowed, but they were interrupted by a maintenance worker needing his input. So she gave him a cordial nod, and went in search of someone more willing to answer her question.

Buzz, a cook in the kitchen tent, drew the short straw. The male with frizzy blond hair pulled back in a ponytail had a lined, fifty-something face, brown eyes and tats on his arms and throat that suggested he'd once been in a gang or done prison time. Or both. He looked wary of her question, but at least he didn't warn her like Gundar had. He also didn't know where to find Merc.

"So he doesn't bunk in a communal tent, or have his own wagon?" she asked.

"No one really knows where he goes when he's not here." She heard a hint of Australia in his voice. "Except maybe Marcellus and Lady Yvette."

"No one's really curious," another cook put in, a lean black man with a gold front tooth and bristling moustache containing patches of gray. He laid a pan of brownies on the counter. Similar tattoos and comfortable body language suggested he and the blond man were friends with history. "They're just glad not to deal with him."

"Does he cause that much trouble?"

"Not so much as he did when he first came," Buzz admitted. "But he never stops looking at you like I look at a cut of meat."

"How he wants to cook it, and what recipe it'll work best in." The black man elbowed him with a half grin. Then he sobered as he looked Ruth over. "No offense, just some advice, ma'am, but..."

"Don't go looking for him by myself. Got it. Thanks."

Ruth moved off. As she did, she heard Buzz chide the other man in a low voice. He must not realize how acute vampire hearing was. "Cree, she's a fucking vampire, mate. Don't try to tell her what to do."

"She's not Lady Yvette. Merc is trouble she shouldn't try to handle on her own. She seems like a nice girl."

A nice girl. She'd never been called that before.

She spoke to one clown and two roustabouts. They didn't know, either, but she helped the roustabouts move some crates into storage. They seemed glad for the help, so as she moved through the campground, she took other opportunities to assist, introduce herself and chat. Getting the lay of the land and learning the people would be useful to her job. Recognizing who belonged, who didn't. Noticing what was out of place.

She didn't downplay her vampire side, though, knowing some healthy fear would gain her quick compliance to her direction when her job required it.

She catalogued further questions to ask Marcellus, Gundar, or

Dollar, who she expected she'd meet tomorrow, if he wasn't sharing her quarters.

At the sanctuary, she'd worked hard to prove herself an asset. With their strong work ethic, her parents had taught her the value of honest labor and pulling her weight early.

"The Council, Region Masters and overlords get a lot of attention," Kohana had told her and Adan when they were in their teens and understandably thinking of what that glamorous world would be like. *"But most vampires aren't that. They have to figure out how to earn a living, find a place where they can meet their blood needs and not attract attention. Enjoy their lives and find value in it.*

"Doesn't matter what race you are, pretty much all of them are set up like that. It's not a bad thing, because it's a balance. But I can promise you that your father has been far more content being what he is, doing what he does, than playing games of vampire politics, power and intrigue."

His gaze had slid between the two of them. *"Wherever life takes you, you'll be your father's offspring. And your mother's. You'll learn that's not just a good thing; it's the best thing you've got going for you."*

She'd reached the forest on the western edge of the Circus's campground, a much thicker and deeper terrain than the small patches of trees around the lake. This was like the mountain lion habitat on the preserve, where the barely marked paths were created by the animals who lived and hunted there.

When she discovered a similar faint trail, it was marked by hoofprints. Ruth detected an equine scent, mixed with human male, but muskier, heavier. The Circus had horses, but Clara said they also had unicorns and centaurs.

It had to be a centaur. She'd love to tell her father she'd met one and give him all the details. As she'd told Charlie, Mal was keenly interested in animal behavior, habitat, hunting skills and instincts.

"Nerds," her mother had murmured to her, during one of Adan's too rare but precious visits. "They're both nerds."

Her brother and Mal had been discussing magical theory, mixed with ecology and science. Ruth had closed her eyes, as the male voices overlapped, separated, lifted and fell, modulated by humor, intrigue, serious insights.

She'd been sitting next to her mother, working at her loom. The comfortable *clack, clack, clack* had been a fitting background for the conversation, Elisa's foot working the pedal while her hands moved the shuttle. The world was all good, as long as the four of them could hold the fabric of it taut between them.

A shift to her left, and shadows flitted through the forest, the light clomp of hooves reaching her ears. Because a vampire's scent was more earth-based, the forest was the environment in which she could most easily blend. So she approached the hoof owners without detection. As they materialized, she felt a thrill.

Centaurs. Three of them. Children, two boys and one girl.

If they'd been human, she'd estimate their ages at eight or nine years old. They had bows and arrows, and were practicing with a target they'd hung from a tree branch. The girl and one boy were damn good, consistently hitting the X they'd marked. The third was having more difficulties, but one arm wasn't as long as the other, the fingers curled and inflexible. A birth defect or old injury?

No one had discussed centaur protocol with her yet, but since they were part of the Circus, she assumed she shouldn't be hiding. They weren't wild animals she'd startle if she made her presence known. She liked being around children. Some of the married second marks on the island had children, so she'd enjoyed having them as playmates. After Mal taught her and Adan how not to break them.

She moved forward, purposefully making noise. When the girl turned and saw her, Ruth nodded. "Hello."

In a blink, all three had their bows up and aimed in her direction. The boy with the deformed arm lost his grip on the string and the arrow released.

She leaped out of its way, though the tip grazed her neck before the collar of her coat deflected the arrow's trajectory. It spun away and embedded itself in a tree.

"I come in peace." She lifted both hands. "I'm new to the Circus. I work with security."

Was that translation spell working? She sure as hell hoped so, because the ground was vibrating. She spun to see several more centaurs coming toward her, vaulting over foliage and dodging around the trees.

Not children. Three fully grown males, with enraged gazes, showing pure hostility and aggression. Shit.

She dodged behind the nearest sturdy tree with a half-baked

plan to call out her intentions and defuse the situation. Only they weren't slowing down to hear it. One of them had a much bigger bow, and he was drawing it, the lethal arrow tip gleaming. As she bolted, the arrow whizzed past her. If she hadn't run, she would have been hit.

Her coat snagged on the dense foliage so she left it behind. The centaurs were making angry whistling noises, like an enraged stallion protecting his herd. She'd seriously fucked up. She needed to get the hell out of here, make it back to camp and figure out how to fix her gaffe.

Except more centaurs were coming out of the woods to her right. Another flight of arrows streaked by her as she changed direction, again just in time. Wooden arrows. If one of them hit her in the chest, she'd be done.

Staked over a misunderstanding. Shit. Great.

She'd treated the centaur children like kids on a playground, and she knew better. Many species were rabidly protective of their young.

Being way-the-fuck bigger, at least the male centaurs had to navigate the forest accordingly. Though this wasn't her home ground, she knew forest terrain as well as they did. She should be able to use her vampire speed to slip away.

Nope. Reinforcements had arrived, and they worked together, keeping her hemmed in. The only way she'd break through their line was by going on the offensive, and she wasn't going to do harm if she could avoid it.

The universal message of surrender wasn't going to register before she was trampled, but maybe it would prevail against the arrows. She dropped to her knees and held up her hands, appealing for mercy before she became a pin cushion.

A weight hit her in the back, driving her to her stomach. Her chin bounced off the leaf-packed earth. While her instincts screamed at her to fight for her life, logic prevailed long enough to recognize what had shoved her down so forcefully, and it didn't have flesh-cutting, trampling hooves.

Merc. He closed his wings around her body, his feathers brushing her skin. A dubious but still appreciated shield. Were his wings arrow proof? She didn't want him hurt, either.

Guttural snorts and angry, piercing squeals surrounded them, along with the vibration of hooves. Merc snarled back, punctuating it with a hiss that would have sent most cats at the preserve scrambling.

When he spoke, his words became understandable mid-sentence. The translation spell must have glitches. Or maybe adrenaline blocked the spell's effectiveness, so that she had to calm her rapidly beating heart to let it penetrate.

"She's a new hire. Yeah, we should have told her before she wandered around, but she didn't know, Pholos. She's no threat. Look at her."

"Get off of her and we will."

"Not until you lower the fucking bows."

Some other time, she'd argue with the no threat shit, but occasionally she was smart enough to know when to hold her tongue. The edge to Merc's voice, the tension in his upper body, pressed over hers, his knees planted outside of her thighs, said things weren't close to okay.

She would have tried apologizing or explaining now, but the hard squeeze from his hand on her shoulder told her that she needed to be silent.

And show complete submission.

Ironically, not as difficult for her to pull off as it would have been for most vampires.

The shifting of the heavy hooves was settling, and the squeals weren't happening as often. The agitated snorts continued, but more as an expression of annoyance. The sound reminded her of bulls. Some of the lore about centaurs suggested it originated from men who fought battles on bulls.

"We will speak of this transgression to Yvette." The male she assumed was Pholos spoke. His voice could have competed with the rumble of a diesel engine. "It should not have happened."

"Maybe. But you could also ask someone who they are before you try to kill them. Fucking hell, man. She's a skinny vampire girl less than a hundred years old. Get a grip."

Ruth choked on a very inappropriate laugh, fueled by a little hysteria. A little while ago she'd been congratulating herself on how well she was adapting to her security job. Then she'd stumbled into a situation where she needed protection. Great confidence builder.

She didn't think the laugh had escaped, but the shudder as she contained it seemed to have an effect.

Pholos's voice was gruff, but held a more mollified note. "Get off her, Merc. She is safe. Lift your head, girl."

Ruth didn't play damsel-in-distress unless it made it easier to get close to an enemy. But when Merc rose and lifted her to her feet, he kept her against him, her shoulder blades brushing his chest. His hand went back to her shoulder. The strategic pressure of his thumb against the base of her throat told her she'd better capitulate with grace, so she didn't get them both shot. It was also damn distracting, but it had life-threatening competition.

If they showed their age the way humans did, Pholos looked in his forties. His hair was shaved on the sides, enhancing the horse's mane look of the thick line of it down the middle of his skull to his nape, where it narrowed into a line of silken hair that ended at his lower back. That was where his upper torso expanded into the horse's body, bearing a glossy black coat.

His hooves were silver tipped and sparked against roots and rocks as he shifted. Black tattoos on the bare sides of his skull and arms matched what was painted on his flanks. His tail was braided with ribbon and feathers. Having grown up well versed in Native American and Irish history, she recognized a tribal clan culture when she saw it.

She glanced up at Merc to make sure it was okay to speak. Though his gaze remained watchful on Pholos and his men, he gave her a slight nod.

Taking a measured half step forward, she executed a respectful half bow toward the centaur leader. "I apologize. I meant the children no harm. I was admiring their aim."

While still well-shielded from Ruth, the trio peered at her from around powerful hindquarters. Her gaze landed on the one with the deformed arm. "Your stationary target practice might need work, but your aim at a moving one is sound. I had to use speed to avoid your arrow, and it still made contact." She directed the boy's attention to her neck. The graze was healing, but the bloodstain proved her words weren't empty praise.

Pholos glanced at the youth, whose initial surprise at the compliment was quelled before the elder's severe gaze. But when Pholos returned his attention to Ruth, the other boy and girl nudged their companion with hidden smirks. Kids were kids.

"Your name." Pholos issued it as an order.

"Ruth," she responded, with another slight bow.

"Learn our ways so you do not come to harm at our hands," Pholos said. "You are lucky you are female. We would have killed a male without hesitation. Welcome to the Circus."

Sexism had saved her life. She could accept that.

Pholos issued a short command, and the centaurs wheeled as one unit. Within an impressively short span of time, they'd disappeared, taking the children with them. The only evidence of their presence was the foliage crushed by their intimidating advance, and their horse-human scent. Ruth let out a breath and turned to speak to Merc.

She was alone.

Seriously?

It was his fault she'd wanted him to hang around longer. She still had that surplus of sexual energy he'd stirred up in her earlier, and since he'd landed on her like a wheelbarrow of bricks, she'd registered the imprint of every muscle group, his pelvis and cock pushed against her tense ass. And then there was the sensual clasp of his wings around her.

Yep, even under the threat of imminent death, her sex drive kept ticking like a Timex. Too bad a couple arrows hadn't hit him. Nothing fatal. Just a shot or two lodged in his excellent ass.

Yes, it was a petty reaction. He *had* saved her life. But a sexually frustrated vampire could be a cranky vampire.

CHAPTER EIGHT

She retrieved her coat from the bush that had snagged it when she decided to leave it behind. Maybe Charlie could fix the five holes in it.

The arrows that had done the damage were gone. The centaurs had gathered them up, even the one the boy had shot. She wondered if they had unique feathering on them, so each archer knew which ones were his. She would have liked a closer look.

She'd also like to meet the female members of the clan. Find out how they handled their overbearing males.

As she emerged from the forest, she discovered the lake Medusa had been sailing upon had a shore here. Shedding her shoes, Ruth dug her toes into the cool mud. She'd return to the camp soon and explore her quarters, but she wanted to collect herself.

"*My lady*.'" Merc's voice came from above her. "Gundar and Charlie both called you that. Vampire aristocracy."

His sarcasm made it difficult not to respond in kind. But it was too soon for her to get into another fight with him, no matter how appealing the idea was. "When you're a born vampire, the title is bestowed at birth. My father isn't 'my lord,' because he's a made vampire, though he's earned that respect a hundred times over. I haven't."

Merc chuckled, a warmer sound that shivered up her spine. He landed a few feet from her. When he'd been pressing her to the ground, his clothing had felt different. He was back in the battle skirt. His wasn't crimson red like Marcellus's. It was black, with the leather-looking protective straps over it—pteruges were their official name; she'd looked them up. His belt was silver chain links hooked to a buckle and bearing a scabbard for a dagger with a spiral hilt. His upper body was bare. Her gaze climbed the terrain with pleasure. He wasn't as broad as the angel, but he was very... well-sculpted.

"I missed an opportunity," she noted. "If I'd turned around before you landed, I could have looked up your skirt. Boxers, briefs or commando?"

When he dropped to a knee beside her, she didn't draw back. He leaned in, nostrils flaring. Like a cat, he was assessing if the object of his interest was something to consume right away or play with, aka torment, first. His muscle tension showed the readiness to pounce.

"I don't recall giving you permission to stare at me like you wanted to eat me," he murmured.

"Don't recall giving you permission to treat me like a submissive."

Your submissive. She looked toward the water, pushing down the uncomfortable surge of feeling that came with the thought. Not about him specifically. Just the wish, always there, controlled by cold reality. No sense whipping herself into a frenzy over the Christmas gift she'd never get. Though Merc made her want to toss the desire into a blender and hit exactly that setting.

"I need to report that run-in to Yvette," she said, ignoring her internal idiocy. "I don't want her to think I'm trying to hide it when Pholos complains to her."

Merc settled onto his heels, his forearms resting on his knees. The wings adjusted out, and the left one brushed her back, an incidental contact. Or a presumptuous one. She decided not to comment on it.

"I doubt Pholos will mention it. Despite the posturing, he gets that it was an honest mistake, and you'll learn from it. Or his kids will have more live target practice. Works for him either way."

She curled a lip, but she wasn't going to let his obnoxious personality keep her from being courteous. "Thank you for keeping me from being impaled. It would be a poor first day on the job if I ended up dead. But I will tell her. And maybe not just that. Why don't you want Marcellus and Yvette to know you met me at the preserve?"

"They're in my business enough as it is. Didn't care to share." He shifted. "Can you smell my blood?"

The abrupt subject change told her there was more to it, but since she understood the desire to keep some things private, she went along with it. "Yes."

"Is it different from a human's?"

"Yes."

"Does that mean it would taste different?"

"I expect so." Her pulse started to thud. She reminded herself she'd had a recent meal, with dessert.

She was sure he wasn't offering her his blood. He liked to taunt, get a rise out of his prey, get them stirred up over something. Was it because he liked the spice of that emotion in *his* food?

He drank sexual energy. She drank blood. Neither source was divorced from the emotions, pleasures and agonies that went with them. Based on what she'd been repeatedly warned about when it came to Merc, she had a good idea what his favorite seasoning was.

Fear.

He wasn't getting that from her. He should know that by now. "So why are you dressed like that?" she asked.

"Marcellus wanted me to accompany him on some angel business. This is a more familiar and accepted look for that."

"Does he ever wear modern clothes like you do?" She couldn't imagine it on the austere and commanding male.

"On performance nights, for Yvette, he wears the security team uniform. He cloaks his wings so no one sees them. If he participates in the Promenade, he reveals the wings and changes back into Legion wear. That's been his uniform for hundreds of years. Anything else feels like playing dress-up to him."

She glanced over her shoulder as one of the feathers teased the nape of her neck, thanks to the light breeze. "I know you can do the invisibility thing, but can you cloak just your wings, too?"

"Yes. I wasn't aware I could do that until I met him. He's helped me look deeper into the abilities my angel blood gives me."

"You sound like that bothers you."

The black blood and silver eyes flickered. He had a straight, patrician nose. Thin, sensual lips. Cheekbones cut from smooth marble. "I'm an incubus. That blood holds the angel side in contempt."

"Maybe I'm contrary, but that would make me all the more determined to figure out what it doesn't want me to know about that side of myself."

He said nothing, but his expression shifted to something she couldn't interpret. "What?" she asked.

"I'm not used to having casual conversations. Not with a female like you."

"A vampire female?"

"No." He didn't elaborate, and she held his gaze, though it took effort.

"Is it less fun than trying to scare me?"

Merc reached out and placed his palm on her chest, the heel of his hand against the upper rise of her breast. Curious, she gave way to the pressure behind it and laid down on the grass. He stretched out next to her, bracing himself on his elbow, and leaned over her. His wing arched over the higher shoulder, and she reached out to brush the black and white filaments. He intercepted, clasping her wrist.

His thumb moved over her pulse, nostrils flaring anew at her sexual response. It shouldn't mean anything. She'd fucked males she cared nothing about. Sexual response was sexual response, though she'd matured enough to realize the cost of that attitude.

Most vampires were fine having sex with whomever they wanted, and walking away. Like visiting different restaurants. You might go back when you were in that neighborhood. You might not. It wasn't a two-way commitment. The restaurant's feelings didn't matter.

She wasn't wired that way. Maybe that was her raising. Every interaction with a living being mattered, leaving an imprint of some kind, on both sides. Whether they acknowledged it or not.

"Can you feed on that?" she asked, a little breathlessly.

"Yes. I can feed on any level of sexual response." The silver in the whites of his eyes were like glints of mica. He dipped his head over her midriff, a central point to inhale whatever was coming to him from all points of her body. "But some are more appetizer than meal."

He focused on her neck, where the arrow had grazed her. It had healed, but the blood was there. When he put his mouth on it, tasting her essence, she quivered. Hard. He spoke against her skin. "It's a pleasure, isn't it? Someone else enjoying your blood? Putting his mouth to your throat?"

Him in particular. She didn't respond, but he didn't seem to need her to answer.

"Who do you feed upon at home?" he asked.

"Members of the preserve staff."

His tongue moved slowly over her flesh, his fangs grazing her as she trembled harder. "Direct from their flesh, or bottled?"

"Usually bottled. Sometimes direct, if we're out on the preserve." If it had been a physically exerting morning, she'd weaken and need it right then, in order to keep working.

"Do you prefer the throat or somewhere else?"

"Depends on the person, the relationship."

"If it was me?"

Throat. No doubt at all. The idea of putting her mouth, her nose, close to that beating artery, having the opportunity to give him even a tenth of the sensation he was giving her, was irresistible. She would want his arms and wings around her, cradling her as she drank, seeking nourishment from him. The romantic fantasy was impossible to dismiss. Fortunately, so was the knowledge it was based on characteristics she wanted him to have, not ones he did.

"I don't drink from unknown sources. I don't know whether incubus or angel blood is okay for vampires."

"That's a deflection, Ruth. It was a hypothetical question."

"I'm not much on hypotheticals. Survival in the vampire world is literal, 24/7."

"Fair enough." He inflicted that derisive smile on her, but behind it she detected understanding. The kind that came from firsthand experience.

"Hypothetically, I would like to see you take it from my wrist," he said. "While kneeling before me, my fingers sliding along your face, your throat, the curve of your ear, into your hair. The movement of my fingers would increase the flow of blood, wouldn't it?"

She cleared her throat. "Yeah. I guess."

He still held her wrist in his grasp, but his ruffling feathers grazed her twitching fingertips. He'd told her she didn't have permission to actively stroke them. She could sense his attention sharpen, as if he anticipated her disobeying him.

She was tempted. So tempted. But when she didn't move, he drew back. Curving one wing so it dipped into his direct view, he pulled out one of his primaries with a sharp jerk.

"Ouch. Does that hurt?"

"Not badly. Another will grow in its place shortly." He drew the dagger from his belt and pressed a release on the hilt to reveal another, shorter knife nesting inside it.

"Wow, nice work." She propped herself up on her elbows. "Can I see the bigger one?"

He handed it over so she could examine the release mechanism. While she did that, he sharpened the quill. When he was done, he took back the longer knife and handed her the feather. "Hold onto that and lie back down."

When she complied, brushing the feather over her palm and testing the quill's sharpness on the pad of one finger, he put the smaller knife back into the sheath of the bigger one and set it aside. Her attention left the feather as he put his hands on her thighs, slid them up to the fastener of her jeans and unhooked it, pushing down the zipper and then the denim to expose her thighs to her knees. He left her panties in place, though his gaze touched on the black cotton, the lace waistband. "Give me back the feather."

When he reached for it, she switched hands, holding it playfully out of reach. "You took my other one."

"No I didn't. You threw it away. But despite that disrespect, you can have this one when I'm done." His expression held hers. "Give me back the feather, Ruth."

The words delivered a bouquet of quivering feathers inside her chest. As she gave him the one she had, he closed his hand over it and her fingers, gripping them firmly enough to send a brief pain through the joints. A warning that increased the tingling through her body.

"Hands behind your back, fists in a knot at the small of your back."

She should refuse and get up. Leave him. She wasn't that smart. Instead, she complied. He put his other hand over her mound, hidden beneath the cotton of her panties. His thumb caressed her clit through the fabric, then passed over the crotch below, a sure stroke with enough pressure to have her biting her lip. "Nice and wet," he observed.

He settled lower, his elbow on the ground, forearm across her pubic bone and upper thigh as he held the feather like a pen. The sharp tip scraped her before he punctured her thigh, making her jump and a sound catch in her throat. He did it a few times, with deliberate precision. Each penetration made her wetter, more needy, her body arching, breath clogging in her throat.

He bent and tasted the tiny drops of blood. Moving between her legs, he put his mouth on her cunt over her panties. A firm, sucking hold, tongue tasting her through the fabric. A moan tore from her, her fingers tightening in that knot he'd commanded her to make against the small of her back. Her grip on her own hands, the press of her knuckles in her back, was as painful as his bruising hold when she hadn't given him the quill right away.

He held the climax out of reach, tasting her thoroughly, inhaling her with nuzzling contact. Learning her scent, her responses. But more than that. She became aware he was drawing energy from her. He twined it around her, carrying her on it like she rode a cloud. A miasma with a fragrant perfume, her pure sexual response.

He was feeding on her.

Before she could decide how to react, he drew back. Sliding an arm beneath her, he lifted her enough to tug her jeans back up over her hips. Leaving them open, he tucked the feather marked with her blood under the waistband of the panties. The sharp quill pressed against the swollen flesh of her clit, the feather end teasing her flat stomach and tender indentation of her navel.

He rose, unsmiling. "Don't give yourself a release. I want you wanting."

Him standing over her, leaving her shuddering and aching for more, and worse, wanting to comply, snapped her into a different part of herself. She scooted away, rolled to her feet and snatched out the feather. She tossed it away, just as she had before, no matter the wailing protest from the part of her that wanted to do what he'd ordered.

"You don't command my pleasure," she told him.

He didn't move, but he didn't have to. His presence pushed against her, called to her. "But you want me to."

"Wanting is not the same as needing," she retorted. "And I know what happens when one gets mistaken for another. I'm no one's fast food lunch. So fuck off."

In a blink, he was close enough to haul her up to her toes with a clamp on one arm. She hit him in the face with her free fist, and twisted to break herself free.

He twisted with her, proving the move was ineffectual. But then he released her and shoved her back onto her heels. He could catapult her across the field, but he'd restrained himself so she stumbled but didn't fall. She planted her feet, fists clenched and ready.

"They don't know you can travel the portals by yourself, without detection," she guessed. "That's the problem. Isn't it?"

When his sneer showed the lethal shape of his fangs, she wondered why he hadn't used them to mark her flesh, instead of the feather. Maybe because incubi didn't drink blood. But he'd seemed to enjoy the taste of hers.

"You think your threats will keep me from doing whatever I wish to you? I can *feel* how much you want me to overpower you. Make you behave."

That mocking tone inspired reactions she detested. Uncertainty, guilt, anger, resentment. Confusion. But she was certain of one thing, and she had no trouble acting on it, no matter how much she might regret the things she had to abandon to do so. But if the choice was between that and her self-respect, her choice was made.

"They're right about you. You don't know how to treat a female you really want. Don't come near me again until you do."

She left him. Though she didn't look back, his regard was a weight on her back, like the target the centaur kids had fired upon. If he retaliated, she likely wouldn't have a chance to defend herself.

But the issue wasn't whether she could win the fight. It was the choice to fight. And she would. Because she preferred a fight over fear.

Plus, a traitorous part of her really wanted to fight with him again. She informed it that the incubus angel thing was a total ass.

It told her that she hoped he'd prove her wrong.

She told it to shut the fuck up.

CHAPTER NINE

For the next day and a half, Ruth pretended she was too busy to think about him. She *was* occupied enough to keep him tucked in the back of her mind. Even if he spent his time there caressing and teasing her, as if his wings were brushing her neurons.

Her roommates in Circus security were a level-headed, well-trained group. No egos would interfere with teaching her what she needed to know.

Their shared living space wasn't the army-styled barracks she'd imagined. The pavilion tent had comfortable cots positioned behind privacy screens, giving her a space to call her own. A communal area provided a kitchenette for basic food prep.

Quarters like these were transferred to new locations via magical means. Personal items were packed and transported the normal way. The Circus's Big Top and anything related to performances were taken through the portal in the wagons that became RVs, buses, flat beds and semi-trucks.

"Part of the fun for our audience is being able to see the Circus set up," Dollar told her. The head of security was a human with thirty years of special ops, Secret Service and private security experience. He looked the part, a tall black man with a shaved pate, trim goatee and perpetually narrowed eyes that his people believed could track a dandelion seed across snow-blanketed terrain. His clothes were crisp, dark and professional, showing a body in excellent fighting shape.

His team also joked that he slept standing up and fully dressed, so nothing was ever creased. He didn't deny it. His authoritative tone could bark, rumble or slice a person's legs out from under them, but she'd been told if she did her job a hundred and ten percent, he was a fair boss.

"We could do all of it magically, just appear where we're scheduled," he told Ruth. "But Lady Yvette has stuck with the tradition of hiring locals to help with the set-up, to involve the community, boost ticket sales and the town's economy. Though there are people who will drive from a bigger city to attend a show, we do smaller venues, since she limits audience capacity to one thousand."

She'd expected to be restless, not sleeping underground for the first time in her life. However, with how much she was learning and doing, plus the daily sparring Marcellus had promised with various skilled members of the staff, she face-planted in the mattress when it was time to go to bed.

Helo, one of the other security members, had to wake her up today. She first called Ruth's name from the other side of the screen. The alert pulled her slowly back toward consciousness, but to get her all the way there, the woman came in and shook the cot frame, staying well away from her.

When Ruth surfaced, Helo nodded. She had freckles, a lot of red hair, and the muscles of a Viking warrior. She was also an accomplished helicopter pilot who'd done medivac work in war zones. She and Ruth had talked about their respective flying experiences at one of the team's "jawing sessions," as Dollar called them, when they hung out in the main room, cleaning and checking weapons, or informally trading stories about threat scenarios.

"None of us react well to someone being right over us when we wake up," Helo said. "I figured a vampire might be similar. Or wake up hungry."

Ruth was flustered that she'd had to be woken, but Helo's follow-up comment helped. "When you first start having to flipflop between performance time zones and the weirdness of the portal in-between spots version of night and day, it takes time for your body to get acclimated. I've done it longer than most, so you're not the only one I roust."

"Yeah, she's our den mother," a voice called from the main area. Ruth smelled coffee brewing.

"Fuck off, Burt," Helo said, without missing a beat. "His crappy coffee will be ready in a minute," she added to Ruth. "If you drink it."

The Circus would be leaving the portal for a performance venue today, so after the standard start-of-day briefing, the security members were encouraged to help with that process wherever needed. Their security duties would take up more of their time once they were "back in the world."

On her way to check in with Clara, she saw Merc, albeit at a distance. As she approached the fortune teller's quarters, Marcellus and he were standing outside the yurt. Before she reached them, their discussion concluded. Merc gave the angel a short nod and went into the air. He was wearing jeans with the black and red security team shirt.

Thinking of what he'd said about cloaking his wings on the midway, she wondered if she'd still be able to feel them if she reached out to touch. She thought of how he'd closed his hand on her wrist, prohibiting her from doing that.

As Ruth reached Marcellus, Clara emerged. She slid her hand around Marcellus's biceps and laid her head on it. Ruth melted a little as his wing slid around her, offering her warmth from the chill. She was in a nightgown, a shawl wrapped around her.

"Wow. It usually takes me longer to repel people enough that they fly away when I approach," Ruth said, winning a smile from the hollow-eyed girl.

"He and Marcellus have a pre-move checklist, relating to the adjustment of magical properties as the Circus moves, how it changes our perimeter and its protections. Merc is an accomplished magic user. He can also move pretty fast, so if he'd been in a big hurry, he would have looked like he vanished. Vampires can do that, too, can't they?"

"Yeah, but our speed usually only fools humans. You *homo sapiens* got the short end of the evolutionary stick."

"There is good reason for that," Marcellus observed. "The talents they do possess are used for destructive purposes."

Clara nudged him. "No human bashing. My optimism charge to counter your grumpiness isn't 100% until I've had coffee."

He kissed her head, his large hand moving gently over her shoulder. "Go get dressed. I want to make sure you are where I expect before I get involved in the chaos this day will bring. And yes," he added before Ruth could volunteer to stay with her, "sometimes you will take over escort duties with her. But Dollar, Gundar and I want you to see the full move process. Today you will not carry the same responsibility as the others. Everyone goes through this training, so they can be as effective as needed."

He hadn't had to add that, but perhaps he saw her desire to be as useful as anyone else. "Yes, my lord."

A few hours later, after having helped lift, pack, move and direct, she passed through the portal with the rest of the troupe into a mild Tennessee night. They were in the hills, the air full of the scents of pine forest and oaks. The Circus had emerged onto a rural highway, their train of wagons now a convoy of motorized vehicles, following a curving road into the town.

Ruth expected some of those details Clara had mentioned included making sure that transition happened without a collision with traffic on the "real world" side, and at a spot where the convoy's appearance wouldn't seem like it had happened out of thin air.

Helo told her that was a less pressing concern these days, thanks to the likes of David Copperfield and Chris Angel. Humans could explain it as an extraordinary illusion act, especially once they saw the current Circus logo on the vehicles, a trumpeting elephant and roaring dragon flanking a blood red rose. "The Circus" was printed across the rose in gold, and a black ring of thorns formed an oblong border around the picture.

Their destination was an open flat field. In preparation for their arrival, it had been mowed by the county's maintenance crews. The handful of locals who'd been hired to help were ready and waiting. Despite the evening hour, many had brought their kids, at Yvette's invitation.

It quickly became apparent how much the Circus people enjoyed the kids and their parents, meeting them with true affection and good spirits, no matter the many set-up tasks awaiting them.

She *really* liked being part of the Circus world.

On opening night, Ruth was assigned to the midway. When Adan had described the Circus to her, she had inhaled the stories like candy. The reality was even better. The prep of vending wagons, sideshow tents and the Big Top, the creative arrangement of props, the players getting into their jaw-dropping costumes, the last-minute practices. All while the teasing scents of popcorn, cotton candy and peanut brittle started to permeate the midway.

When she patrolled the perimeter, she kept potential vulnerabilities specific to the fortune teller in mind, and marked Clara's tent. It was draped in gold and blue parachute fabric that created silken waves whenever the wind picked up. The open flaps were hemmed with sparkling beads and tassels. A wooden painted banner, *Fortune and Joy Foretold,* was mounted over the opening.

Prior to the gate opening, part of Ruth's job was checking the interior of the tents on her assigned route, to see that all was well and ensure the occupants had no issues or new security concerns. With that in mind, she entered one of the tents where smaller scale preshow acrobatics and skits would be performed.

Sarita, Karl and Nikolai were going over a new routine and Sarita was nervous about it. She was the least experienced acrobat, an apprentice to the two veterans. Ruth had picked up that backstory from Clara, but also learned more from what she witnessed now.

Sarita was balanced on one foot on a large ball. Karl stood in front of her, Nikolai behind. As Nikolai watched, Karl's touch slid up the inside of one braced thigh, his fingertips moving against the thin crotch of the sparkling leotard she wore.

"Hold," he said. "You will hold that pose for your Masters forever if we require it. Won't you?"

"Yes," she managed, offering a slight smile at the tease but also showing the strain as her arousal grew. A tiny moan, a little whimper, escaped as he put his fingers inside her, under the crotch panel, and began to do a slow in and out thrust. His fingers were slick with her response.

Sarita shuddered and the leg buckled. Even Ruth's vampire speed couldn't have matched the response of the two Masters, who caught her in ready arms.

"You will perform beautifully for us." Karl brushed her hair from her face. "You always do. If there are any mistakes, we will be there to catch you."

"And correct you later," Nikolai noted with the right touch of sternness. "In ways that will make you long to do much better."

The care made Ruth's chest hurt. As she glanced around, she saw Charlie on the top row of the fixed tiered benches, the audience seating. She was sewing flowers on a hat. However, her unique way of seeing had noted Ruth. She lifted a hand at her regard. When she bit the thread to finish up the repair and rose, Ruth moved to her aid, but Charlie came down the graduated steps easily.

"You're kind," the healer said quietly. "I admit, I do have more trouble in unfamiliar environments, but I know the Circus like I know my own bedroom."

Slipping outside with her, Charlie showed Ruth the hat. "It's Buella's, one of our clowns. She adopted a stray cat a few months ago. The little terror shredded the flower, so I put on some new ones. I like this trio of forsythia, nodding over the brim. I've added a couple beads and some wire so they'll bounce around like bug antenna."

"She better hide it from the cat. But I love it. The kids are going to want one."

Charlie chuckled. "Yvette will order me to send the pattern to our vendor supplier for small batch production, I'm sure." They fell into step together, since Ruth's perimeter check was taking her near the entrance, where the clowns were gathering. They would spread out when the gate opened, to mingle and entertain the ticket holders as they made their way toward the Big Top.

"So why did you choose that tent to repair the hat?"

"It was closest when Buella gave the hat to me. I carry scraps and a sewing kit for the things I have to do on the go." Charlie patted the bag on her hip. "Karl, Sarita and Niko have wonderful sexual energy, even when they're in work mode. You should see them on Play Night."

"Play Night?"

"Many of our members are in power exchange relationships." Charlie nudged her. "I'm sure you've noticed."

With the Circus being owned and run by a vampire, it was practically expected. The Circus offered two types of performances, one for families, and one for erotic, more sensual venues, such as Club

Atlantis. The Atlanta BDSM club was owned and run by Anwyn, a made vampire whose servant was Jacob's brother, Gideon.

When Adan had apprenticed with Derek, he'd helped set up the portal at Club Atlantis that facilitated the Circus's first performance for an exclusive audience that included the Fae court and Vampire Council. The Circus had returned there at least once a year ever since. Ruth hoped she'd be with them long enough to see that.

"So, once a month, there's a staff Play Night in the Big Top," Charlie continued. "Since we use the same props, Yvette says she gets new ideas for the erotic shows."

They were reaching the clowns, and Charlie pressed her arm in a brief, affectionate grip. "You should plan on coming to the next one. You don't have to play. Voyeurism is entirely encouraged. It's just all of us, the Circus family. No outsiders allowed."

"Sounds like fun. Thanks."

Charlie nodded and headed toward the clowns. Buella came toward her, hands out for the hat. Her pleased smile said she liked Charlie's efforts. After she put it on, adjusting the chin strap, she bounced in a circle like a waddling penguin, jumped into a handstand and followed it with a somersault, seeing what the antenna would do.

While vastly entertaining, Ruth reminded herself she was on the job and moved on. She did think about Charlie's invitation, though. Hell yes, she'd go, even if she'd be eager to watch but afraid to participate.

Story of her life.

The parking lot was filling up fast. Gundar had told her that most of their performances were sold out before the Circus arrived.

Local hires were handling the parking process, though Burt floated among them. Dollar said their presence, employed proactively, in the right way and at the right times, headed off most situations before they became a problem. The team members who were physically imposing had an obvious leg up, but a calm and authoritative attitude was the best tool any security member could employ.

The challenge for Ruth grew as the gates opened and the midway became clogged with people, filtering into the sideshow tents or moving toward the Big Top. She didn't spend much time in busy urban environments, so she had less practice at sorting this much sensory input.

However, the humans on the security team managed to stay as vigilant and situationally aware as was required. She had far more acute senses, so with effort and patience, she could do the same.

She'd learned from the feline preserve inhabitants. They knew how to filter their surroundings, so neither the scratch of a rat moving across dry ground, or the shadow from the dip of a hawk's wings far above their heads escaped their notice.

As she made a circuit of the midway, moving with the tide of people, she paused outside Clara's tent. A man was sitting at her table while she listened. When she asked a question, her expression was warm and inviting. She wore a head scarf, her abundant hair tumbling around her face, her velvet dress matching the gold and blue colors of the tent. Makeup pulled color into her cheeks, and admirably managed to make her hollow eyes seem more deep set and mysterious. The shawl draped on her shoulders obscured the thinness of her upper body, but she looked lovely.

As she'd told Ruth, most of "fortune telling" was listening and intuition. "But I don't fake it," she'd added. "I make sure what they get for their money is sincere and real. I'm just not doing a deep dive into what's ahead of them. I don't think most people really need to know that. They just need to be pointed toward the ways to handle it. Or embrace it."

Ruth finished her second trip around the midway and outside perimeter of the Big Top, coming back to the front gate. Showtime was in five minutes. They'd already blinked the strung lights along the midway as a warning.

Late people, exiting their cars at the far end of the full parking lot, hurried at the attendants' urging, carrying shorter-legged children toward the gate.

The wind had picked up and, as it did, it brought Ruth a scent. Just a hint of something, brief enough she couldn't quite catch it, but it brought her to a halt. She was near the popcorn vendor's cart, and changed her position so the food smells drifted away from her.

She increased the reach of her senses, a pack of hunting hounds let loose. Her attention moved over the parked cars. Moonlight gleamed off the various colors and sizes. Beyond them was a pine forest. Burt, who'd been helping the attendants shepherd in the last groups of families, had moved to the gate and was speaking to the ticket vendor.

Ruth melted into the shadowed area between two tents and used the parked Circus trucks behind them as cover to gain a different vantage point of the lot and pine forest.

She waited. Studied the trees, the cars. Two minutes. Three. There. A slight movement between two trees. Then it was gone, but she caught it again thirty seconds later, between two vehicles at the back end of the parking lot.

The ticket gate was an artificial barrier. The only physical impediment to coming into the Circus was the chain link fence around the outer fairgrounds, a six-foot climbable structure, and the vigilance of the security team. Every ticket holder had a glow-in-the-dark hand stamp, two and a half inches in diameter, so they looked for it on all attendees.

Whatever this was, it wouldn't be coming to the gate to get a handstamp. She didn't want to be an alarmist, the newest member of the team trying to prove herself, but something was off.

"What do you see?"

She'd felt him come up behind her, that light flutter of air and arousing scent. While the shiver of sexual reaction was automatic, she ignored it, also putting aside the question of whether Marcellus had assigned him to babysit her.

"East side, behind the red pickup truck. Gone now. Whatever it is, it's on the move. My gut says it's trying to approach without detection. It's not human."

Merc curved a hand over her shoulder, thumb sliding along her collar bone. An intimate touch, but a brief one. "I'll go that way. Act casual. See if we can flush it out. Watch the midway and the gate."

"Got it."

He was gone. Clara was right. He was fast. Was he as fast as a full blood angel, like Marcellus? And how fast was that? Another question for later.

Waiting for the interloper to make itself known again was like watching for a diving cormorant to surface in a parking lot sized body of water. She changed position and increased the range and depth of all her senses, including her intuition, to determine where that bird's head might pop up.

Merc hadn't questioned her instincts. A nice thought.

Another whiff of that obscure scent, and she tried to isolate what it was. So faint, so faint...

Shit, it was past the gate. She made her way along the midway, feeling for whatever it was. It was close.

And it was getting closer to Clara's tent.

Unease shot up the base of her spine. This threat might have a target.

A roar came from the Big Top as the show kicked off, the reaction thrumming through her feet. Colorful lights speared the sky through the roof opening in the giant tent, a kaleidoscope of color.

No matter the limited audience size Yvette preferred, it was more than enough noise to cover someone who'd planned their incursion well.

If they weren't being tracked by a vampire on one side and an incubus angel on another.

It was taking a circuitous route, but she'd locked onto its trail and was sure of its goal. Yep. The fortune teller's tent.

It was cloaking itself in more than one way. When she finally had enough sensory input to identify it, she realized why. He knew he would be recognized.

A vampire.

Not just any vampire. Trad vampires had an unmistakable smell, like how dogs and wolves smelled differently. She'd never met one, but her father had described them in detail to her in her teens, because of the threat they posed to young female vampires.

Unease became cold anger, and her predator instincts went into killing mode. Within seconds, he would be aware of her presence, if he wasn't already. Her only advantage was if he thought his cloaking had kept him shielded. Even so, he was too close to his goal. Abandoning any pretense, she bolted toward Clara's tent.

It was a good decision.

Because the show had started, Clara was in the tent alone. When Ruth entered the front, a blade flashed as the vampire sliced an opening in the back and shoved through.

The fortune teller surged up from her table, trying to put it between her and the attacker.

The vampire threw a bolas at her. It whipped through the air, wrapping around her calves. When the balls hit her ankle bones, Clara

---

cried out. As she fell, she grabbed at the table, clutching the blue cloth draped over it. A heavy crystal ball swirling with lights came tumbling off of the surface.

The move wasn't uncalculated. When she flipped over, despite the bolas's restraint, Clara had the crystal ball in her hands. She flung it at her unwelcome visitor.

Not enough force or speed behind it to do real damage, but he had to deflect it, which provided Ruth a vital distraction.

She noted a human-sized burlap sack at his belt, ready to conceal his human prisoner. Not happening.

Ruth launched herself, hitting the Trad with enough force to shove them back out the slit in the tent. When hard blue eyes turned her way, the Trad evaluated her age and strength in a heartbeat. He wasn't old, but he knew she was outmatched.

She didn't mind being underestimated. She dodged the strike of his fist at her throat, leaping back from the knife he drew. While the one she clutched was razor sharp steel, his was wooden. His thin-lipped smile showed dirty teeth and big fangs.

"Fledgling," he said, whipping the knife at her. She deflected it enough that it only grazed her shoulder, and spun under his guard to hit him mid body again. It rolled them farther from the tent. She stabbed him twice with her knife before he hit a pressure point and the weapon fell from nerveless fingers.

Fuck, she needed backup. If the Trad wasn't alone, a cohort could take Clara while Ruth was fighting him. She hadn't detected one, but with that cloaking spell, she couldn't rule it out.

The Trad lunged at her. Ruth blocked his next kick, turning into it and pushing him off balance. It was a sound tactic, but he regained his feet, clamped his hand on her forearm and thrust it at an awkward angle back toward her. His knife was rushing toward her chest. Ruth twisted hard to break his hold. Her bone snapped, but it saved her life, the wooden knife shoving into the right side of her chest, instead of into her heart.

She'd screamed when the bone gave, but rage was mixed with the pain. Despite having only one functional arm, she struck at the Trad with the other. She had no problem fighting in ways other vampires considered beneath their dignity. She stabbed a finger into his eye, rupturing it, and hooked a thumb into his mouth, trying to wrench his jaw loose from its hinge.

Now he was the one shrieking. He tried to pull back, get the knife loose and stab her again. She wouldn't be able to stop him, so she focused on breaking his jaw, wrapping her legs over his thighs, refusing to let him get away from her. The problem was him realizing the advantage that tactic gave him. He could crush her ribcage inside the band of his arms.

"Let go."

The snarled command didn't come from him. It penetrated her fury-filled mind, and she released her opponent, rolling away. The Trad was pulled off of her, a sweep of black and white wings obscuring her pain-blurred vision as Merc tossed him across the ground.

The Trad had taken the knife with him, the blade ripping more flesh, but leaving her heart intact. Before he stopped rolling, Merc was on him again. The Trad spat a curse, but then went curiously inert, holding the knife out to his side. He shot a contemptuous look at Ruth. Then smirked.

The Trad's arm shot up, and he jammed the wooden knife into his own chest. Merc hadn't anticipated a self-inflicted attack. Pale green smoke wafted from the Trad's open mouth, like fogged breath on a cold day.

"*Merc, move back*," she shouted. "Everyone keep away."

That was for the other security personnel who'd arrived, It relieved Ruth of the worry about backup eyes on Clara, but not of her fear for Merc.

She struggled up, lunged across the ground, stumbling, but when she reached Merc, grasping his arm, trying to pull him back, it was too late.

Confusion gripped Merc's features. Then the whites of his eyes went full silver and he stiffened. His fangs shot forth, large, gleaming and deadly, and his attention locked upon her. Wild, hungry. Homici-dal. She'd fallen onto her knees while gripping his arm, her other hand pressed to the wound in her chest.

Though she was far too close, no hope of outrunning him, she sat back on her ass, tried to stay non-threatening and move back from him slowly. His lip curled, a smirk way too close to the Trad's. He knew he had her and was just letting her think she could get away.

Nothing but violent, hungry predator was in his gaze. No empathy or awareness of her beyond something to tear apart and consume. Nothing she did or said would penetrate. But while he was tracking her futile retreat, he wasn't focused on anything else.

A familiar tremor went through the ground, a small earthquake. Her head whipped toward Marcellus. Since she knew where his attention would immediately go, she screamed to pull it toward her.

Just as the incubus charged for her.

Marcellus conjured a sword from the air. Fear spiked in Ruth's chest, giving extra strength to what she shrieked next.

"Hallucinogen."

Thank the Great Father, Marcellus understood. The sword disappeared. "Take care of Clara," he ordered, already in motion.

He and Merc met with an impact that should have broken bones. Merc had almost reached her, so that she covered her head and curled into a ball to protect herself as Marcellus straddled her, hanging onto the snarling, thrashing incubus. Their wings beat at one another like enraged roosters in a yard, the feathers whipping across her back and neck.

Then they were in the air. As she lifted her head, she saw Marcellus had his arms banded around Merc in a wrestling hold. A blink later, they were both gone.

Please don't hurt him. A crazy thought, with all the other things Ruth had to think about, but it was as strong as any other impulse she was having.

Dollar knelt by her. "Christ, what the hell was that? Has Merc finally lost it? Or was he working with them?"

She stared at him. No matter the years he'd been here, no one trusted Merc. Which meant it wasn't his home. Did he have any place that was?

"No," she said. "The Trad had an airborne hallucinogen capsule behind his fang. It's designed to fuck up whoever is right over them. It dissipates pretty fast, but I'd still wrap him up and let the sunlight have him after you examine his corpse."

"Fuck." Dollar barked a warning at the team members approaching the Trad. "Get something impermeable to put him in and stow him somewhere safe until the show is over. What are you doing?"

Ruth was struggling to her feet. She grabbed his arm to push herself to her feet. "Clara," she said.

Dollar didn't argue, a good sign for their future working relationship. He did keep his arm out to help her get back into Clara's tent faster, which Ruth supposed was evidence she looked a little rough at the moment.

The fortune teller was sitting with Zee, another woman on the security team. The bolas had been removed and Clara was sitting in her chair, rubbing her ankles. She gave Ruth a wan thumbs up. "Thank goodness my last client had left."

Ruth didn't think that was luck. This had been too well planned. Clara's expression was pale and tight, but also angry, a good sign. Her attention slid to Ruth's blood-soaked shirt. "Dollar, why the hell is she standing? Has Charlie been called?"

"I'm fine," Ruth told her. "I'm not human. Remember?"

"Yeah, but you still don't look so good," Dollar said. "An arm is not supposed to point that way. We should probably get it fixed, because it's making mine hurt just to look at it."

"Big baby," Ruth said between gritted teeth. The jibe earned a startled look, followed by grudging approval. "If I can get someone to set it, it will heal," she told him and Clara. "Did you ever have one of those dolls with moveable joints? It's like that."

"Yeah, but those dolls aren't in agonizing pain while their bones are shifted back into their proper place." Another member of the team had arrived, a man as big as Dollar. She'd met him during the security briefing. John Pierce, Medusa's mate. Like Dollar, the male was former special ops, and looked every inch of the warrior he was. He glanced at Zee. "Go get Charlie."

"No. I mean it." Ruth waved at him. "It's not the first time I've broken a bone. If Dollar's not going to bother Yvette about a Trad attack during the performance, I'm sure as hell not pulling away one of her key people to do something I can do for myself. One of you big, strong types can help me set the bone. If someone else can go grab me some blood, that would be great."

Dollar and JP exchanged a glance. "Do you two want to do rock, paper and scissors to see who has the balls to do it?" Ruth asked.

Zee hid a smile as Dollar cleared his throat. "I'm in charge, I'll handle it," he told JP. "Go take care of the body."

JP gave Ruth a steady look—another Dom, of course—but it was tinged with respect. When he departed, Dollar pointed Ruth to Clara's guest chair, which Zee set upright. As Ruth sat down, she told him how to set the bone.

At his dubious look, she added, "Have you ever done one of those online puzzles, where if you get the pieces lined up close enough, they pull together the right way? That's what vampire bones do. If I did absolutely nothing, one piece of the bone would eventually gravitate back toward the other one, until they met and fused on their own. It's excruciating, but vampires injured with no one around to help, their spines broken, have talked about how it happens."

"All I'm hearing is that it's going to hurt like a son of a bitch."

"It hurts that way right now. The smoother and quicker you do it, the better. If you stop and ask me if I'm okay, I might rip out your throat. Speaking of which, it would be *really* good to have that blood on the way."

Zee disappeared on that errand. Ruth could control her blood hunger to a certain point, but it was increasing, her body seeking the nourishment to augment the healing process.

Clara sat down next to her and gripped Ruth's hand, a kind offer of moral support, if entirely inadvisable.

"You okay?" Ruth asked. "I'm sorry I wasn't in time to keep him from getting into the tent. Stop looking at my arm or you're going to faint."

Clara gave her an exasperated look, though it was overshadowed with other concerns. "Marcellus?"

"Dealing with Merc." Ruth explained what had happened, and then disengaged her hand with a reassuring squeeze. "When Dollar does this, I might break all your fingers. Marcellus will kill the Circus's newest security hire."

"Oh. Forgot about that."

Ruth winked at her, then gripped the edge of the table. "Please stop dicking around and do it," she said in Dollar's general direction, as politely as possible.

He complied. It was like being struck by lightning, without the mercy of being knocked unconscious. Biting back the undignified scream didn't work, but she kept it to a muffled shriek behind clenched teeth—the enamel might have cracked—until she "felt" when the bones were aligned properly and could tell Dollar he was done.

He was sweating, a slight tremor in his hands. When she gave him a questioning look, he grunted. "First time I've had to do that to a slip of a girl."

"I can bench press you," she coughed. "Then hurl you halfway across the Big Top."

Crap. She shouldn't have said that word. She barely had time to grab a cauldron she sincerely hoped was a decorative prop before she threw up into it.

When she was done, Zee had returned. The woman sat two packets of blood on the table and withdrew a cloth rectangle from her slacks pocket. It was a tissue holder. As she offered Ruth one to wipe her mouth, Ruth noted the fabric was printed with cheerful ladybugs.

"I have allergies," she told Ruth. "Charlie made me the tissue holder. I like ladybugs." Her gaze shifted to Dollar. "I'd pay good money to see her do that bench press thing, boss."

Dollar had recovered enough of his aplomb to shoot her a *you wish* look. He watched Ruth closely as she probed the stab wound in her chest. It had clotted, and its healing would accelerate moderately when she had the blood.

When she started to reach for it, Dollar pushed it closer so she didn't have to aggravate her shoulder. "Do you want a sling for that?"

"I'm good. After I drink this, I can finish my shift tonight."

"There's such a thing as overkill when it comes to proving yourself," he noted grimly.

"I did ask for your help setting the fucking thing. See? I can be girly."

Though the residual pain was pounding through her body like the drum section of a high school band, she grinned at him. Having the arm back in its proper healing spot reduced the pain considerably, and being able to prove it with her banter, no matter how weak the delivery, eased some of his tension.

She was really worried about Merc. It would take time for the hallucinogen to wear off, but she reminded herself it would do so, and Marcellus was more than capable of looking after him. It replayed in her mind, the Trad coming back for that killing blow, Merc pulling him off of her just in time. Yes, that was his job. They worked together as a team to protect the Circus and each other's backs. But what stuck in her mind was what he'd snarled when he'd pulled the Trad off of her.

She wondered if he was aware he'd said it. It had been a guttural hiss, barely recognizable as speech, but her sensitive ears could detect the nuances of a cat's purr. Happy purr, sad purr, angry purr.

"She's mine."

"That's Charlie and Gundar's blood," Zee told Ruth. It made Ruth stop mid-swallow.

"Tell me you didn't take it from Yvette's stock without asking?"

Zee gave her an amused look. "Do I look like I have a death wish?"

"We had permission," Dollar interjected. "I sent Lady Yvette a brief status update over my second mark. She had Gundar intercept Zee with these packets."

The honor of the Circus owner's gesture was as rejuvenating as the blood itself. Ruth straightened in her chair.

"Yvette's still doing the Promenade at the end of the show, right?" Clara asked.

"Yeah, far as I know. I told her we had the situation contained for now, though there'll be a hell of a briefing after close-down tonight."

"Good. The Promenade's my favorite part. Will you feel up to it, Ruth? After you drink the blood?"

Ruth exchanged a look with Dollar. "If my boss is okay with me taking a few minutes, you can count on it." But she had a more serious question for Clara. "Was the Trad the one you saw in your vision?"

"No." Clara shook his head. "Probably someone doing his bidding."

"I believe there was more than one," Ruth told Dollar. "Fortunately, the second one was just a spotter. Kept his distance. Probably long gone." And returning to villain central to report a vampire was now active on the security team. *Shit.* But at least they knew it would be far harder to access Clara here.

Maddock or Yvette might be able to retool the spellwork that helped "hide" Clara at the Circus, but it wasn't likely they could fix the vision Trad's awareness of her presence here now.

"We have the rest of the team scouring the area around the Circus," Dollar said.

"After I finish the blood, I'll do the same. In case I detect something they can't." As Dollar looked undecided, Ruth pushed. "That's my job. Right? Let me do my job."

"That's my job if I say it's your job. Right?" When his gaze hardened on her, she swallowed back a kneejerk retort. "I have to assume you know your own limits, Ruth. A security team member who doesn't becomes the weakest link in a crisis. Understand?"

"I do."

"All right, then. Once you finish the blood, check the perimeter."

"Thank you. Seriously, Dollar, in the vampire world this is just Tuesday night. That's why we have accelerated healing and a high threshold for violence and stress."

"Like comic book characters," Clara said.

"Yeah, but are we the ones with lots of sex and pretty people, or the gritty, life sucks and then you die kind?" Zee asked wryly. "You know, the perpetually tortured and broody hero?"

"Ooh, those are usually the sexiest ones. Can we be both?" Clara asked.

Ruth chuckled, but her mind went back to Merc, her broody, sexy incubus. *Please be all right.*

CHAPTER TEN

*T*he blood would keep her going, but she knew her exhaustion would catch up and pass it well before dawn. Sooner than she'd like, she'd be forced to seek sleep and full recuperation inside the portal's shelter. She was determined to make it through closing on her first show night, though.

It wasn't just pride. They were down two major team members, Marcellus and Merc. Dollar needed all hands on deck. While no one thought a follow-up attack was going to happen tonight, there were other things to watch out for.

Like the trio of boys who'd decided they were running away to the Circus and hidden in a large crate. Because her senses told her she was dealing with human children, she hadn't descended on them in full attack mode. Her normal ability to scare the bejesus out of a mortal worked just fine.

Under her stern gaze, the boys stammered out that they'd intended to hide there, living on the food supplies they'd brought, until the Circus packed up. Once they were in another town, they'd emerge and wheedle their way into being a new sideshow offering.

They had a juggling act, incorporating decent boy band dancing and singing. Ruth made them show her, and accepted a snack-sized Almond Joy from their "supplies" before she sent them home. She told them to graduate high school, then come back and apply for a job.

The incident lightened her mood and distracted her from far more sobering aspects of the evening. And the uncertainty about Merc.

Where the hell were he and Marcellus?

She'd only had a moment to tell Marcellus what was going on. But surely if he'd needed more info to help Merc, he would have been back to get that. Right?

When at last she heard from Dollar that Marcellus had returned and was at Clara's tent, she headed in that direction. Before she'd made it halfway there, she saw Merc. He stood at the entrance to the acrobat tent she'd visited earlier in the evening.

His eyes were back to normal, but they were like a snake's gaze, forbidding in its emotional opaqueness. His wings were at a tight half mast, joints looming over his shoulders, the feathers ruffling in the light breeze. His shirt was gone, and he wore only black jeans. No shoes.

All Fae were associated with an element. Catriona, as a tree spirit, was earth. While incubi weren't Fae, with their overwhelming sexuality, she expected they were associated with the earth as well. And possibly fire.

Hellfire.

Perhaps that was why Merc preferred bare sole contact with the earth, no matter the terrain or weather.

He disappeared into the tent, a clear invitation. She followed, pausing at the entrance. It was empty, since all the acrobats participated in the main show. Merc prowled around the large ball Sarita had balanced upon earlier. He glanced up as a trapeze twitched from the air currents.

"Are you okay?" Ruth asked.

He turned toward her. She wondered if he was masking any lingering effects from the hallucinogen, like fatigue. But maybe it didn't have that effect on an incubus or an angel. Or a combination of both.

"Yes. Are you?"

"Good to go. That's why I'm patrolling." She pulled the radio from her belt. "Dollar, can I get a few minutes off duty? Merc is back and I want to check on him."

"Yeah, we're covered. Marcellus is with Clara, same reason. Your juveniles have been perp-walked to a responding mother's car."

135

She pressed her lips against a smile. "Glad that threat has been contained." When she clicked off, Merc was still looking at her. She couldn't tell if he was curious about the exchange, but she explained it to him.

A nod. No smile.

Okay. She thought about moving to the bottom row of the audience seating and encouraging him to join her, but if she sat down, she wasn't getting back up. Best to avoid temptation.

"You taunted me at the lake," he said. "Challenged me."

She wasn't expecting him to go there, thinking tonight's drama would have made the argument water under the bridge. "You were being pushy. And mean."

He continued as if she hadn't spoken. "You said I couldn't arouse a woman without my incubus...powers. But it isn't separate from me. It's who I am, and yet it's what makes me dangerous, out of control."

The red in his irises glinted, thanks to the yellow safety lights mounted in the rafters. "Do you consider your bloodlust part of who you are? How would you feel, having something that's so much a part of you, that you ache to let it loose, be the thing you have to contain? All the time. Otherwise, you incur a death sentence for the crime of being who you are."

The words struck a chord, targeting her heart, her sense of herself.

"I can tell you understand. But there's a difference. If I set my desires free, I kill indiscriminately. I take pleasure in it. I relish feeling their life force slipping away. When the drug was in my system, I felt that rise up, what I am required to hold down. All the fucking time."

The surge of black rage in his gaze almost had her stepping back, but she resisted the urge. She suspected he saw that struggle. But he also saw her contain it.

"When I looked at you," he continued, his voice soft with menace, "Feeling that way, about you, made me very angry. What kind of cruel god makes a creature like that? Like me?"

Another question she'd asked about herself, though perhaps with less, "I'd burn down the universe if I could" emotion than she heard in his voice. She answered carefully, but with sincere curiosity.

"Is it that you feel pleasure in their life force slipping away, or you feel pleasure in the feeding, the fulfillment of it, that sacrifice? The

136

giving to you of everything, taking in who they are, a way of connecting. In that moment, you *are* together. It's not separate."

He studied her a long moment. "Except I'm taking their life."

"Vampires have an annual kill. You're aware?"

"I've heard of it."

"The purity of the blood, the spiritual component is important, because vampires already walk too closely to darkness. It's required to be a good person, not an evil one. We have to make our peace with that."

Even now, after having done it so many times, it wasn't the easiest thing to talk about, but it answered his frustration with something meaningful, not pointless platitudes. She would look at it without flinching.

"The first couple times I had to do it, my father was with me. He told me we have to survive, and if something made us this way, made it impossible to survive without it, then our obligation is to be humane about it, even while taking what we need to live."

She took a breath. "I try to give pleasure during it, to provide an anesthetic so the human never sees it coming. Never feel it, except maybe at that very last moment. A blink of fear and pain before it's over. And there's a moment where...I try to connect with them. So they don't feel alone."

Her mother had sat with her after her first one. "*Say a prayer for his soul, and ask forgiveness. Because though the annual kill is necessary for you to live, his desire to live was no different from yours. You took his life, which connects you to him forever. You will meet again, because that's the way of it.*"

"It's different for me. For the incubus part of my blood," Merc said. "What I see in their eyes, in the end, yes, they are experiencing physical pleasure, but deep inside, a part of them is screaming. That excites me, too. In a way that makes me want to do it again. Sooner than is necessary. Tonight...reopened that craving to an unacceptable level."

She understood the drive of bloodlust, but what he was talking about...it *was* different. He was like an alcoholic who'd fallen off the wagon. All the effort to live a sober life was suddenly in jeopardy.

She swallowed as his gaze got flatter. "Have you ever fed on a vampire?" she asked. "An immortal being? Does it have to be human?"

"I haven't considered it."

Not until recently.

She read that from his unsettling gaze, but she wasn't going to cut and run. "We still have to have a human annual kill, but vampires can exist day-to-day on other blood, as long as it's from a humanlike species. My brother feeds exclusively on Catriona. Since she's part human, everyone pretends that's why she can meet his needs, but that's because Queen Rhoswen gets very prickly about vampires nourishing themselves on Fae blood."

"You're inferior to them." Merc shrugged.

She refused to be goaded, though she did roll her eyes before she made her point. "Maybe we should try it sometime. Feed on me, the way it's obvious you want to do. Not just a taste, like earlier. All the way."

She made the offer with a casualness she didn't feel, especially when his expression went from flat to full-on, in-her-face, hungry predator. Her knees quivered.

He hadn't moved, but he felt a lot closer. Still, his response was unequivocal. "No."

Which foolishly encouraged her to press the case. "Vampires can be killed by very specific things. Beheading. Burned to ash by the sun. Staking our heart with a hardwood."

"So plywood would be ineffective."

He was making a joke, but his tone didn't change. It was eerie, but also a full-blown warning that he was fighting a war for control inside of him.

She was perverse enough to keep pushing. "Point being, I've heard nothing about vampires dying from a sex demon's powers."

"It could still weaken you. Harm you. You are proposing an experiment with no guarantees or safeguards."

"Maybe on the guarantees. But there is a safeguard."

"What would that be?"

"You. You have control. You know how to use it."

"Within limits. Stop."

She'd started to move toward him, but halted at the tone of command. At least for now. "I think the idea intrigues you. It does me." Another step. "What would happen if you found you could have that limitless feed on another being and not take their life? For one thing, you could test whether what gives you the charge is actually killing them, or just having been given everything from them. Making that connection I mentioned. We all have a hunger for something deeper than food, Merc. We can pretend we don't, but it doesn't make it true."

"If you do not stop moving forward, I will leave."

"You do that a lot. Retreat when you don't want to have a conversation."

His gaze narrowed. "This isn't a retreat. It's a refusal to allow you to direct me in the way you wish."

Had he just suggested she was topping from the bottom? Okay, she probably was. But she had no problem with that. Not if it gave her the fight she craved. She was pretty sure it was right in front of her, a hair's breadth from taking up that gauntlet.

"Some kinds of questions are best left unanswered," he said. "It allows one to hold onto the idea that he might be better than he really is."

A fist closed around her heart. She remembered how Dollar had assumed Merc might have betrayed them. In a wrong-ass way, it made sense. He held himself away from the others, and no one seemed interested in changing that. Most of all Merc.

Don't offer friendship, and the question of whether anyone wants to be your friend, if anyone trusts you enough for that, is left unanswered.

"Females act like prey around you," she said. "Submissive females."

"You don't."

Was that what he'd meant, during that earlier conversation? *"I'm not used to having casual conversations...with a female like you."*

"A vampire female?"

"No."

Her submission, coupled with her lack of fear—despite his best efforts—was what had drawn his attention?

She pressed for more. "You encourage their fear."

"They lose it when I compel them. It only remains deep within, the unconscious part of them that recognizes the danger. That kernel of fear is the seasoning among the sexual desire. You have it, too, but it's a different...flavor." He shook his head. "So it's better for them to consciously fear me."

Bingo. He *was* aware of what he was doing with the *keep away* vibes.

She started to move forward again. This time he didn't tell her not to. When she stood before him, she tilted her head to look up into his forbidding expression. His hands were curled at his sides, tense. Waiting. "I want to touch you," she said softly. "May I?"

"Humans get fascinated with vampires," he said. "Like rock band groupies. Sex demons have the same problem."

She gave him a cool stare. "If you want me to stab you in the groin, you can suggest that's what this is. I'm happy to cut your ego down to size."

His lips twitched, but she could still tell nothing from his expression. Until he reached out and touched her face. Slid his fingertips along her brow.

"It's sometimes necessary to lie to those around us. So they do not know our thoughts, our condition. How we feel. You won't lie to me. Not ever. You're tired, Ruth. The Trad hurt you."

"I'm all right. I had some blood. I'll keep until the show is over." Yet she was still hungry. Maybe that was what was making her so unwise. One of many reasons. She started to lift a hand toward him.

"I didn't say yes." he said quietly. "Keep your hands to yourself. Or I will tie them behind your back."

"What will you do after you do that?" The growl in her voice was an invitation. Merc leaned in, his wings curving forward. They tempted her to defy him and touch. Maybe he'd clasp her wrist like he'd done earlier. She'd rubbed it before her latest sleep, thinking of that restraint, the heat in his hold.

"I don't think you'd like what I'd do, little vampire."

She curled a lip. "You're calling me that to piss me off."

"You're aroused."

"I can be turned on and angry at the same time. Most times, I prefer it that way."

Something eased between them, though that only increased the flow of erotic tension, making it nearly unbearable to resist the desire to come further within that wingspan, within reach of his tempting mouth. Tease her fangs against his, prick his mouth, see if he'd score her flesh with his.

"You haven't had a Master's firm hand," he observed, studying her, seeing it all.

"I haven't had a Master who knows how to handle me."

140

She hadn't had a Master at all, but she wanted to put it out there, what her expectations were.

The red disappeared back into the black, leaving only a mysterious hint of the blood color in his eyes.

Her radio beeped, startling her out of the lock with his gaze. "Fifteen minutes to the finale." Gundar's voice. "Line up for Promenade."

When she looked down to adjust the radio, wings brushed her face and her shoulders. Closing around her body, a cocoon. That was new. Then his hands slid down her back to give her ass a squeeze, so hard it made her gasp and shot arousal to her core.

Then his touch and presence were gone.

He was making a habit of that. She wondered if clipping his wings would help. Next time, she'd bring shears.

The Circus ended as it began, with a dramatic, thundering centaur race around the rings. They blew curved horns, leaped barriers with a flash of decorated hooves, reared high in the air and split the air with shrill, piercing calls that shivered down the audience's spines. Pholos led them, his fierce expression and brandished spear causing the crowd to draw back then cheer as he passed.

After that, the rest of the performers emerged and paraded along the same track. They strode within reach of the front row of audience members, only the short wall in front of their swinging feet separating them.

Children crowded that barrier, trying to touch sparkly costumes, as well as the unicorns, dogs and horses. The adult dragons perched in the rafters and called out to their young when they swooped too close to the audience, but allowed them to dance in the open space over the rings.

After three clockwise circles, the performers broke into clusters in the rings. Yvette gave the audience permission to come down to meet with them. Her command to do that in an orderly fashion was obeyed, helped by security members like Ruth, positioned to help enforce it.

Some performers had a personal bodyguard. Medusa sat on a tall crate, her snakes wrapped around her arms and neck, one or two poking their heads out from beneath the curtain of her thick curling hair. John Pierce was at her side. While he was kind to the children and curious parents, he projected a firmness that said all ages were expected to be respectful and restrained.

Medusa was good at that herself, encouraging the children to be gentle with the snakes and take turns asking questions. Ruth could see why the performers enjoyed this part. They could share their love of the Circus with the appreciative fans, and interact with the wider world in a way they might not be able to do otherwise.

Yvette understood the value of reminding her troupe they *were* part of that wider world. That way, nobody forgot how to be civilized. A thought that made Ruth look for Merc.

He and Marcellus were absent, so no flights around the Big Top with the kids. She understood; it had been a crazy night, but she was sorry to miss that. Hopefully she'd get to see it another time.

Yvette was demonstrating her single tail to wide-eyed children. They jumped at the sharp crack, then curiously fingered the fall and popper. The female vampire wasn't warm and fuzzy like Medusa or Clara, but the children were drawn to her, a fascinating but stern Goddess. When one shyly asked to touch her golden braids, Yvette gave her a measured look, then bent and allowed her a brief touch. Her gaze lifted as if she felt Ruth's regard, and a slight curve came to her lips, followed by a simple nod.

Approval, reassuring her that she'd done well tonight. But Ruth also saw simmering anger in the vampire female's gaze. Not at her, but at what had happened.

An hour after the last ticket holder had gone home and the Circus was closed for the night, the briefing happened. Ruth was glad to have experienced the pleasure of the Promenade. As Dollar had predicted, this was the polar opposite to it.

Yvette was pissed. And an angry female vampire sorceress her age was nothing fun to be around. She had no patience for speculation. She wanted the hard facts of what had happened.

Ruth and Dollar provided the information they could. Merc had taken a spot near the back of the acrobat tent where the meeting was convened. As Ruth was speaking her piece, she turned toward him. "I went down the midway while Merc tracked him from the parking lot. He may have more information on what the Trad did during that time period."

VAMPIRE'S CHOICE

"Your senses did you credit," Gundar told her. "You did well."

"Yet the Trad still breached our perimeter," Yvette snapped at him. "With a seasoned and veteran security team in place. Congratulations can wait. For anyone. Merc?"

"He knew where he was going," Merc said. "It made more sense to allow him within the perimeter instead of killing him in the parking lot, because if we killed him there, we had no information on why he was here or who he was targeting. Clara is not the only one here with enemies."

Yvette stared at him, but Merc didn't flinch. His expression was a stone wall. It gave the energy between them a different charge, and not necessarily a good one.

"It's a good analysis," Marcellus said, breaking that look with a pointed emphasis that drew Yvette's gaze back to him.

"It all happened fast, and the show was in process," Dollar noted. "Up until he released the hallucinogen on Merc, we had it under control. Marcellus arrived in time to take care of that. Everyone's training was up to snuff, my lady."

"I see. Is that evaluation your call, Dollar?"

Dollar stiffened, braced for her ire, but he also proved he wasn't a coward. "You pay for my experience, my lady. And my honesty. I meant no offense or presumption. Just wanted you to know that everyone performed to the best of their ability. If you feel the training's lacking, I'll get on whatever you think needs to be improved."

"So why did he kill himself?" John Pierce asked. He stood next to Marcellus, arms crossed over his broad chest.

"Trads are zealots," Yvette said. "He was outnumbered, and he wasn't going to give up any info."

"All of it was planned too well, though," Ruth noted. "He knew she'd be alone. Knew their best chance to grab her was during the opening. They've scoped this with human help, probably hired help, so there was no Trad stench on them."

"Trads despise humans," Yvette said.

"Yes, but younger Trads see the benefit of using them as tools for their purposes," Ruth responded. "Several years ago, Lord Brian discovered a Trad in his lab who'd assumed the guise of a "normal" vampire to get the information Brian had on vampire fertility."

143

"Can we find one of these humans they used to recon the Circus?" Burt asked. "Get more info out of them?"

Ruth met Yvette's gaze. The sorceress was giving her a speculative look, but at Burt's question she gave Ruth permission to continue. "To stay consistent to their culture, if you want to call it that, when a human is done serving them, they kill them. But my guess is they wouldn't know much even if you could find them. They were hired to scope out the Circus schedule. They wouldn't be given access to any other part of the plan."

"You know a great deal about them," Dollar noted.

"I've heard them discussed at length by visitors to my father's island. My father has collected what info there is, from Lord Brian's science institute and other sources."

At Yvette's raised brow, Ruth qualified. "He has no desire to join them. But the Trads are like a different sect of vampires, living off the grid, refusing to have any interaction with humans except as food. My father was interested in their community, their social behavior, how they hunt and live." She paused. "He also had a young daughter on an isolated island. He did everything possible to protect and inform me of their tactics."

"Monsters." Gundar spat on the ground. Yvette arched a brow at him, but the simmering sparks in her eyes said she didn't disagree.

Dollar's gaze shifted to Marcellus. "It may be time to revisit the idea of relocating Clara."

"No." Clara sat in a chair near Marcellus. She was tired, her makeup no longer successfully covering it, but her chin was set in a resolute jut. She laid a hand on the etched metal on Marcellus's forearm.

"As long as Yvette agrees, this is where I stay. They can grab me anywhere, and this is the hardest place to pin down. It's also where I have the most reinforcement. As Merc said, many of us here have enemies. We stand together against them. All of them."

Marcellus's expression was as forbidding as Ruth had ever seen it, but he touched Clara's face with a gentle fingertip. "They can *try* to grab you anywhere," he corrected.

A slight smile. "Yeah. They can try." Clara turned toward Merc, and included Ruth in the sweep of her gaze. "Thank you both. I'm sorry either of you were harmed, but I'm very glad you were there and that all of you," she gestured to the full security team, "do what you do as well as you do."

She looked toward Yvette. "My lady, I know you have the last say on this. But as the target, I can say they did their job. I'm here, the bad guy is dead, and we have some more information."

As Yvette inclined her head, several gold braids fell forward over her breasts, lifted in a black satin corset. "I'm glad you're fine. But we evaluate every incursion into the Circus, beyond its success or failure. It's how we remain as effective as possible at repelling them. If I determine someone needs a punishment for it getting as far as it did, that is my call."

"Yes, my lady. But I hope that won't be the case." Clara paused. "It took a long time for me to believe what I just said, that this is the best place for me. I know it means people I care about are put in positions where they have to risk their lives on my behalf. Since I'm in danger no matter who I'm around, I've had to accept that being around those most equipped to handle it is the best scenario. It doesn't mean I sleep well over it."

"It's our job, miss." Dollar's voice held a strong and determined note. "If you weren't worth protecting with our lives, you wouldn't be here. That's how the Circus works."

His gaze slid to Yvette, a check to make sure he hadn't overstepped, but the slight incline of her regal head told him he hadn't caused offense.

Clara's eyes filled with tears, though she brushed them away. "Thank you, all of you. I'm going to bed. I should stay, but..."

Abruptly, she rose, turned and left the tent. Ruth's gaze slid to Yvette and Marcellus. He looked torn, his rigid expression telling her how much he wanted to follow her, even knowing they had more strategy to discuss.

She was the low person on the totem pole, and she'd shared the information she had. Ruth would get briefed by Dollar later. "My lady, may I..."

"You may." Yvette picked up on her thought.

"I'll watch over her until you come, my lord," Ruth told Marcellus. He gave her a slight bow.

"Thank you, Ruth."

She glanced toward Merc, feeling his shadowed expression resting on her. She gave him a nod, too, before she slid out of the tent.

Clara wasn't hard to track. She'd returned to her fortune telling tent, and was trying to clean it up, putting the broken things on her round table. As Ruth came in, the girl was sinking down against a post holding up the back tent wall.

She stared at the broken glass and chipped candles. Then her shoulders buckled, her hands covered her face, and she leaned forward into them to stifle the sobs.

Tenderness didn't come naturally to Ruth, but with Elisa as her mother, she'd had the best example of how to offer it. Kneeling next to Clara, she slid an arm over her back. The girl leaned against her, folding down to press her face to Ruth's knee.

Clara didn't say anything, ask any questions, or demand answers from the universe. She'd already proven to Ruth she had accepted its designation for her life. If Marcellus was here, Ruth suspected Clara would contain the tears, because most men felt helpless before such distress, wanting to fix it. Whereas women knew tears were their best way of finding the strength to take up arms against the world again. This was how Clara would work through it, so she could keep honoring the path Fate had chosen for her.

So Ruth sat with her, stroking her hair, being present. Standing with her new friend against an unbearable world.

When Charlie arrived, either because Marcellus or Yvette had requested her, or she simply knew where she was needed, Ruth relinquished her spot. Charlie stroked Clara's thick hair back behind one ear. "This earring is pretty," she noted, fingers tracing the strand of beads looped in an infinity knot. "That's from that Colorado craft fair, isn't it?"

Clara sniffled. "You should have let me buy you a pair."

"They fit you best. How about we get you to your quarters?" The blind healer rubbed her back. "I want to give you a good energy treatment, help you build up your strength."

As Charlie rose, drawing Clara to her feet, she staggered, because her patient's knees gave way. Ruth moved in and picked Clara up, cradling her in her arms. "Lead the way," she said.

Clara closed her eyes and put her face against Ruth's neck. "You smell like a forest. And wild things. The right kind of wild things."

146

She left Clara in Charlie's care once she felt Marcellus drawing near. Outside the RV that was their current quarters, Ruth paused before him. "She's all right," she said.

There was nothing else to say, because he knew what that meant. And didn't mean. When he moved toward the door, his right wing brushed her, an unspoken thanks. She ached for him. For them both.

"If she dies too soon, she had the chance to love someone with everything she is, and be loved back, the same way. That's worth anything, Marcellus. Even immortality."

She was a silly young vampire, saying things to an angel who'd stared into cosmic wonders she couldn't even imagine. But she wanted to help, to ease the pain she felt from him, and it was all she had.

Marcellus glanced over his shoulder. Then he nodded and went into the RV.

Loss was as much a part of life as anything else. But did it have to hurt so damn much?

She wandered through the camp. Once dawn approached, she'd meet Yvette at the portal so the two of them could sleep out of reach of the sun. Many of the non-human troupe members, like the centaurs, unicorns and dragons, returned to the in-between campsite as well. But she had a little time before she'd have to do that.

Though she was exhausted from the overly eventful night, she didn't want to go to bed just yet.

Roustabouts were playing cards and hanging out with performers, discussing the show. Many had plates of food. The cooks provided a generous post-showtime meal.

It had taken a while for all the ticket holders to leave, because they were encouraged to stay and spend their money on souvenirs and the midway attractions as long as they wished. But she'd been able to tell when they were all gone, because the environment was more like the in-between portal space. After showtime, Yvette's magical cloaking was put in place, an effective alarm system allowing for a skeleton security crew. Ruth had offered to take another shift, but was told she'd done her part for the night.

She saw Medusa sharing a plate with John Pierce. They were bent toward one another, bodies brushing. When he gave her food from his fingertips, Ruth's body tightened at the energy that sparked between them, a Dom caring for his sub, enjoying her reactions to his attentions. One of the snakes, coiled around her wrist, grabbed something off the plate, taking advantage of their distraction.

She picked up some blood. No one questioned why she needed more after having had Gundar and Charlie's. Maybe they didn't know about that.

Regardless, the cook on duty, Estella, gave it to her in one of the high-end souvenirs, a thermal travel mug with the Circus's elephant-dragon-rose logo engraved on it. "To celebrate your first performance night," she told Ruth. "And a gift for watching after our Clara. Bring it back for free refills anytime. You should go over to the Big Top. Fun stuff is usually happening there this time of night."

Ruth smiled, pleased at the gift, and headed in that direction. When she arrived, it was far busier than she would have expected. In the center ring, several performers were practicing moves they didn't feel they'd gotten quite right, or working out new routines. Choosing a section of the tiered benches with a good view, she took a seat along the top row and leaned against the guard rail behind it. At a squawk, she looked up to see one of the young dragons on a beam above her, eyeing her with measured intent.

"You're not big enough to eat me yet," she told him. "Give it a couple years."

Ruth looked around. Yep. There. Jetana was tucked up into the shadows, not more than a hundred feet away. Unsettlingly hard to see. Her large body was draped over crisscrossed scaffolding, able to hold her weight without much creaking complaint or danger of buckling the tent. The Circus had gifted maintenance workers.

Ruth wouldn't have thought it a comfortable bed, but the dragon was as motionless as the moon on a cloudless night, her half-closed eyes gleaming and nostrils flaring as she took in Ruth's scent.

Ruth immediately stood to give her a courteous bow. "I'll move if you prefer me not to be so close to your child," she said.

When Jetana lifted a formidable back claw to scratch her ear and yawn, showing teeth capable of eating everyone in the tent, Ruth decided to take that as an *all's good*.

As she drank her blood, she noted the meticulous way the workers were resetting things for tomorrow's performance. They would double check it then as well, to protect the performers and the audience. Despite the familiarity of the routine, they weren't careless about it. Everyone was fully charged, alert, fully involved.

The complexity, the beauty of all of it, gave her a sense of wonder. She was really part of this.

Now that the briefing was over and Clara was safely under Charlie's care, Ruth realized she was feeling a little giddy and wild. She wanted to run and play, celebrate, no matter how inappropriate that might seem. They'd dealt with serious shit tonight, but she'd been a part of the team that had dealt with it. She'd protected someone important, and had earned their respect.

"Busy?"

She tilted her head toward her shoulder. Where she sat, there was a seam in the tent, giving her a two-inch wide view of the outside. A familiar presence hovered at eye level with her. She inhaled him the way the mother dragon had. And considered what he would taste like.

"It depends. Is there a better offer than what I'm watching in here?"

"Very few things are better than being a Circus insider after a show. But I can give you a different view. Come to the storage tent, second one on the left outside of this one."

CHAPTER ELEVEN

*S*he left her bench, giving the mother dragon another respectful nod and the disgruntled younger dragon a wave. If he had a cell phone like most teenagers, she expected he'd be using Google Earth to find the nearest flock of Tennessee sheep.

The storage tent flap was closed, and when she lifted it, the interior was dark. Vampires could see in the dark, though. Supply crates were stacked in here, and a couple carts holding folding chairs. As she moved down the aisle they formed, she could sense Merc was here. Was this a familiar hangout for him, in the dark and quiet?

That bothered her, but then her pensiveness over that slipped away. He was behind her.

"Are you afraid of the dark?"

"Not of you, or the dark. But I can see."

"Close your eyes."

He put his hand over them, fingers caressing her cheekbones. As she complied, lashes brushing his palm, he expanded his exploration of her face, her throat, her sternum. As he trailed fingertips down it, the lack of sight increased her sensitivity to his touch, that lovely tingling sensation that tightened her nipples and made her breasts ache to be cupped, kneaded. Held.

Then she stiffened as he returned his hand to her cheek and pushed her face toward his shoulder, exposing her neck. She fought him, but his other arm curled around her waist, and she couldn't dislodge him. He was too powerful. It wasn't even a contest.

This time, he wasn't tolerating a fight. He demanded her submission. Called it forth from her with his inflexibility. Proving it, he spoke against her neck.

"Remember what I said. You don't say no to me. Not now, not ever."

"I won't just give in to you."

"That's different. I like it when you fight me. I like the smell of your hair, your smile. The vulnerable look in your eyes, around your mouth. Your beautiful mouth..."

She paused at the shimmer of energy that came from him. Sexual, but also yearning. Want. Something she hadn't felt from him before. His voice had roughened, suggesting it wasn't something he normally projected.

Or it could be a ruse. She hadn't known him long enough to trust his emotions.

She started to open her eyes, turn her head toward him, but he held her in place. "Keep them closed, Ruth. I won't tell you again. A vampire can heal from having her eyes put out. Don't make me be mean to earn your obedience."

His words were cruel, and yet his touch was tender. The contrast was terrifying. Touch gliding, stroking, undoing things inside her. Letting her draw a deep breath, even as he stole it away.

She rolled her hips against him, playing. Like she was dancing. In answer, he pulled her back against his body and opened her black jeans. He slid his hand into them, under her panties, between her legs, taking over.

He gripped, weighed, stroked. He pressed against her labia, caught and squeezed the petals of flesh. A man hungry for land to call his own, who'd claimed a property and was exploring its terrain, imagining all the potential it would yield to him.

She was already moaning out her pleasure, helpless to do otherwise. "You don't control the pleasure," he whispered, admonishing her for her tease. "I do."

He wasn't using any incubus vibes. She thought about what he'd said earlier, about how it was a part of him. Was he proving he could do this to her without it, even when he wanted to add it into the mix? Or was he saving it for the right moment, to blow her mind?

His fingers targeted the left side of her labia at the base of her clit. Answering her question, an energy slipped off his fingertips, strumming that area. That one limited area, making her undulate against him. He refused to move anywhere else, building the need, making her crazy.

"A woman's cunt has different zones. Focusing on each, one at a time, can give her so many orgasms. Give her so much pleasure...a feast."

"For me or you?" she managed, dropping her head back against his shoulder.

"For both."

The climax rolled up and he pinched her, hard enough to hold her on that shuddering edge. "Ask me for it, Ruth," he growled in her ear. "Ask me to give you pleasure."

She scored her lip with her fang, thrashing against him, against that one pinching hold, which only increased her response, the blood pulsing against his fingers. "No."

"Still trying to say no."

He returned to playing with and stroking the left labia, bringing her up, stopping her short, bringing her back down.

At Lord Marshall's, during vampire dinners with William and Matthew, she'd watched human servants endure forced orgasm torture from their vampire masters before dessert, then prolonged orgasm denial afterward.

Merc was a master of those torments as well.

As he kept cutting her on that edge, he kept a tight band around her with his muscled arm, his hand clamped over her shoulder, forearm pressed between her breasts. Like a seatbelt, holding her in place, refusing to let her get out or escape the need building higher and higher. She was moaning, pleading without words.

"I can do this all night. You are...delicious."

He was taking small sips of her energy, absorbing it, but he wasn't taking a meal. But she suspected if he decided to do so, the longer she delayed the climax, the more of a meal she would give him.

He was holding back for her, because of what she'd said. She was almost sure of it. A dilemma, because she found she liked the idea of nourishing him. Her choice.

"Please."

He stilled. "Please, what?"

"Please...take. Feed."

He didn't respond to that. Not immediately. Instead he put her through another hundred close calls, yanking her back from the edge every time she was about to topple over it.

"Will you hold back your climax until I have drunk enough from you to be satisfied?"

That could be hours, days. She heard the threat of it in his voice. He wanted to test her, wanted to know how deep she'd tear into herself to obey him. He wanted to know what kind of submissive she was.

She wanted to know, too.

"Yes." Tears were on her face. She knew if he took her down that road, she'd work harder than she'd ever worked to resist the pleasure her body was screaming for.

Because he wanted her to do it.

Merc closed his hand fully on her labia and clit, squeezing them in his large hand with proprietary intent. She cried out, startled, as he whispered in her ear.

"Come for me. Right now. Don't refuse me."

The unexpected change in direction broke her control. The climax slammed through her, her body jerking against him. His hand covered her mouth so she could scream out her pleasure without worry the entire Circus would hear.

Then his other wrist was against her mouth.

Do not refuse me.

She sank her fangs into the artery, and took a marvelous swallow of his blood, rich and different. Maybe it would make her sick, like too much human food, but she'd risk that consequence, because it had been a long night and her mind said it was nourishment. It had a heat, a sizzle of magic in it, a metallic blend.

Though her sore body felt the impact of the climax, the pleasure overrode it. She bucked violently in its embrace. Merc's hold shifted, one arm diagonally across her chest, holding her securely, keeping her sore shoulder immobilized.

When at last the climax started to ebb, she was still pulling on his wrist, though she was taking sips now instead of greedy swallows. She was just reluctant to stop, especially when he was stroking her hair.

He eased them to the ground, him on one knee, her legs folded under her, her body in the shelter of his as she drank. When she made herself be done, she licked his wrist, closing the wound for him with the anti-coagulants she had in her tongue. Her body was still vibrating, as if it knew there were plenty more "zones" for him to explore.

She settled though, quiet under his hand. He'd given her what he was going to give her, and she'd done what he'd required. It was unusual, the contentment of this moment. Nothing to do but sit there while he petted her.

"Would you like to fly with me?" he said at last.

"Yes."

"Take off your clothes."

"Are people going to see me naked?"

"No. We'll go too high and fast for that."

She rose. As she removed her shirt, he clasped her waist, caressing her navel, the arch of her rib cage. She liked his hands upon her, large, slightly rough palms, long fingers gripping her. Only when he removed his touch did she take off her shoes and socks and remove the jeans. Bra and panties followed. She could feel his attention on every curve and crevice revealed.

After she had a neat pile of clothes beside her, she reached a tentative hand toward his face. When he closed his hand on it and lifted it for her, allowing it under his control, she touched his lips, his cheekbone, his jaw.

"You've impressed me, Ruth. You haven't opened your eyes. Do so now."

When her lids lifted, his gaze was on her breasts, watching his fingertips trace the curves. It was unsettling, how he did it.

"You act...as if you've never seen a woman's breasts before."

He didn't say anything right away. His slow gliding touches were making her tremble again.

"It's...different," he said. Before she could respond to that, he drew her attention to a small cut on her ring finger. "What's this?"

"I caught it on a burr, on the metal scaffolding in the Big Top."

"You don't heal the way other vampires do."

"No. But I *do* heal. Just a little slower. It was much deeper when I did it, earlier today."

He stood, tall and strong, before her. "Arms around my neck and waist."

When she complied, caressing the short hair at his nape and the heated skin at his waist, fingers playing beneath the waistband of his jeans, his arms closed around her. He slid them out the back flap of the tent and, before she had to be self-conscious about who might be watching, they were in the air, shooting upward like gravity wasn't a thing.

"How much do you trust me?" he whispered.

"Not a damn bit."

Dark laughter twined around her as he let her go. She was falling, spinning and spinning. When the velocity had compressed her lungs and scrambled her mind, he swooped up beneath her and absorbed the impact of catching her so she felt like a feather landing in the palm of his hand. As soon as she could speak, she was laughing, too. "Let's do that again," she said.

His eyes were on her face, her smiling mouth.

"We do this first. Hold on."

He shifted her so her arms and legs were wrapped around his body. He opened the jeans, and then, her bare breasts pressed to his chest, he drove her still slick tissues down upon his cock. In that same slow, crazy, excruciating way he'd touched her.

He stretched and filled her, held her impaled as she arched back and a cry tore from her throat. As he started to ascend again, every pump of his wings shoved him deeper inside her, a thrusting and retreat that was bliss and torment. When they were so high she thought there was no more oxygen, he dove downward and spun. She tightened her legs over his flexing, taut backside, held on and cried out with every stroke inside her body.

His energy shimmered around her. Though he'd just fed, she could tell he wanted more. More and more. Maybe that wasn't a good idea, but she had a problem. She kept saying no to him primarily because she didn't want to say no. She didn't want to deny him anything, which was beyond stupid. But oh, Great Father, to feel this free, above the earth, with an ocean of pleasure engulfing them, it was heaven. Everything heaven should be.

Take all of it. Take it all.

She didn't think she'd been crazy enough to say it out loud, but suddenly he pulled out of her. Her heart twisted in her chest, as if she'd been denied something vital, something she could never get back and would never stop wanting. She clawed at his hips, trying to pull him back, and he shoved her away, sending her free falling again. She snarled and cursed him, tumbling through the air. The heavy compression of gravity descended upon her again.

He caught her a few feet from a bone-crushing reunion with the ground. She shoved away from him, toppling from his arms and landing on grass. They were in a field populated by sleeping cows, who blinked at the intruders who'd landed unceremoniously near them.

She rose on weak legs and stared at him. Merc stood a few feet away, with hard eyes and tight mouth. His chest rose and fell, betraying his exertion, but it wasn't from flying. It was from keeping himself from doing what he wanted to do.

Take from her until there was nothing left.

Though he'd refastened the jeans, he was still erect, hard and aching. She deliberately licked her lips, moistening them. "If I help with that, with my mouth, will it carry the same risk?"

His dark eyes burned. "Yes. But...it might be less difficult to restrain myself."

She bared her sharp fangs. "Because you know I could bite the shit out of you?"

Wry humor returned to his gaze, mixing with the fire. "No."

"Do you trust *me*?" She threw his question back to him, and his more unpredictable side gave further ground, this time to a sinful smile.

"Not a damn bit. But come here."

Good. She was aching and angry, but they were still in this game, this sparring match of wits, needs and wants. Neither of them was going to let female pique or male broodiness interfere with it.

When she stood before him, that fight rose in her, but it warred with other things, too. Something she could let herself give into, just this once, if he would do what was needed to let it happen. She thought he might.

Behind his stare she saw his awareness of it, which was maybe why he drew it out, increasing her anticipation for several bated moments.

A cow lowed. Mist rose on a nearby pond. The moonlight reflected on her skin was marked by the shadow of a passing cloud. His gaze followed its passage over her flesh.

"Kneel, Ruth. Serve me."

Yes. Her knees gave way, that twist in her chest a different kind, but no less painful, responding to the conflict between what she was supposed to be, what she actually was, and all it meant in her world. But he wasn't of her world, and this field was far away from all that.

Close up, his cock was as impressive as it had felt. As she opened the jeans and closed her hand over it, she stroked smooth, stretched skin over the shaft, the ridge of the head, and found the moisture at the tip. She sampled that moisture first, ran her tongue around it. She tasted herself on him, which she liked with a territoriality that was all animal.

All vampire.

She pushed her tongue against the slit, then sucked on the ridge, getting familiar. He tolerated it at first, his hand resting on her hair, but then his grip constricted, and he pushed her down onto him. All the way down. She had only a second to adjust, relax her throat, before he was fully in, no mercy or quarter. She choked, but he didn't let up. She was going to adjust or gag as she sucked him off. Her body tightened, her cunt getting slicker against her calves as he issued his next order.

"Hands clasped behind your back. I control this. Not you."

She complied, a whimper in her throat as she gave herself to it. For the very first time in her life, she was fully serving a Dom. The joy and agony could break her heart into a million pieces, because this confirmed what she had always known. She wanted a Master. Needed one. Even if she couldn't have one. Not and survive her world.

Sometimes taking a drink of the best tasting wine was a mistake. Because the longing to have it would last for an eternity.

She let that jagged ache become part of the fierce passion to serve him. Lick, nip, scrape, suck. She tried not to score him with her fangs, but it was her first time doing it like this, with no hands. When she took sexual pleasure on the island, with the second mark servants who gave her blood, she had to pretend she wanted to be in charge. Make her willing donor keep his hands behind his back, like this, or tie him, so he wouldn't touch her. So he'd believe she was teasing him to emphasize she was in control. All while she was really imagining doing this for a Dom, to increase the arousal for herself in a backhanded way.

Merc's body tightened, and her sob of pleasure, of satisfaction, vibrated against his shaft as he released into her mouth. His grasp was painful on her scalp, still not allowing her any retreat. His thigh muscles became rigid, a harsh groan tearing from his throat, telling her the pleasure she was giving him.

Though she was choking on the hot flood of his release, she fought to swallow him down. She also lifted tearing eyes to gaze hungrily upon his arched throat, the movement of his Adam's apple as he dropped his head back on his shoulders.

His taste differed from the salty musk of a human. There was a sweetness to it, like honey and biscuits. Floury and sweet, musky and male. With a tingling edge of magic and electricity.

When he finished, his head lifted, and his eyes were upon her again. His thumb passed over her cheekbone, over the wetness the strain had caused her. Then he shifted his touch to her shoulder to ease her back. He adjusted the jeans.

"You can move your arms."

She kept her head down, trying to steady herself, bring everything back under control. It felt impossible, after letting her desires run so free.

"Ruth..."

She shook her head and rose on shaky legs. She moved a few steps and turned away. She collected the words in her head, arranged them in a way he'd understand. And reinforced it for herself. It was necessary.

"I can have a Dom, but only in moments like this. I can't have a Master. I can't commit to that. There's no room in my world for it. But it's okay. You and I are the perfect match. You have enough shit going on with you; you're not really looking for commitment either. So this will work until it doesn't. I'm good with that. Just so you know. It's fine. It's fine."

Merc watched her have the conversation with herself. She was pulling herself back together, rubbing her face ferociously, pulling her hair back to redo her braid. She wasn't aware of what that did to him, her slim arms raised, the delicate line of her neck and naked back and curve of her ass, the tense set of her shoulders.

He was used to women's tears. When the survival instinct buried beneath the overwhelming weight of their arousal had recognized they were giving their lives to sate his hunger, his need for nourishment, they cried. Even as they were swept away on an ocean of pleasure.

Her tears were different. Self-contained, directed at herself, not an appeal to anyone. He knew about the vampire world's hierarchy, knew none of them were naturally submissive. A female vampire was as dominant as a male one. They capitulated based on proven power rankings, not because they wished to do so.

Ruth was different. He'd picked up on it immediately because what he was gave him an in-depth awareness of the sexual core of every female who crossed his path, the unique shape and nature of it, and all the things connected to that core. He didn't often follow those connections, not wanting that level of intimacy with his food, but, again...she was different.

Over the past few days, he'd listened and watched. From conversations he'd overheard, he'd picked up that she'd spent her life on her family's big cat sanctuary, making only limited forays into the wider world. Which explained how she'd masked what would put her at risk of exploitation and harm in the vampire world. Until now.

She would have been safer if she'd stayed there, but it would deny what was equally a part of who she was. She might be vulnerable, but Ruth was not weak. And she had courage. With no hesitation, she'd protected Clara against a Trad who easily could have killed the younger female vampire.

He hadn't found it so easy. The thought almost made Merc smile.

"Can you take me back to the Circus?" Her voice was calmer. She turned toward him, her expression quiet.

"Yes."

She offered a tight smile. "Thanks for the flight. It was everything I wanted it to be."

159

Merc moved to stand before her. Her fingers twitched at her sides. "We've covered this. You don't lie to me."

Her look became touched with despair. "It's the best way I know to lie to myself."

He stroked a fingertip along her sculpted cheekbone. The energy vibrating off her was so distracting. She had no idea the temptation she presented to him, to pull all that life energy to him, woven with her sexual desire.

Always before, his restraint had to do with self-preservation. An incubus who couldn't control his hungers was marked for death. He'd carried that mark for some time.

This... He had a desire to protect her. Not to protect himself, but to keep her safe.

"You said you can't have a Master. But here's a thought to consider." He touched her chin, drawing her gaze up to his.

"When you meet the Master who wants you, the right one, he won't give you a choice. You'll be his, no matter your fears."

CHAPTER TWELVE

*S*he would not become obsessive, an addict desiring more from him. Everything he'd done, she could do for herself, after all. With or without electronics. Except...

You don't control the pleasure. I do. She could interpret that as an indirect command. *Don't give yourself pleasure. That's my job.*

A Master could require that. She'd told him he wasn't her Master. Couldn't be. She just had to tell herself not to act like he was, pathetically because she'd gotten her first taste of what she'd wanted for so long.

It was bad enough, how her mind dwelled on the ways he'd touched her, his unforgettable attention to detail. But then there were other things.

The very next night, she'd passed through the Big Top and noted a roustabout sanding the pipe where she'd cut herself.

"What are you doing?"

"There was a burr on it," he said. "Merc pointed it out to me, and suggested I get it fixed."

His expression said that "suggestion" had been delivered in a manner that catapulted it to the top of the to-do list.

How had Merc found the spot, in a maze of scaffolding? A trace of her blood would have been left on it. Of course.

The scary sex demon who enjoyed women's fear had been bothered about her simple cut. She thought of that glimpse of yearning she'd seen in his face while they were together.

He'd had her take his blood. Normally she had to fight the urge to take a nap halfway through her waking hours. An extra draught of human blood and self-discipline pushed her through it, but tonight, she didn't experience it. She even had an extra spring to her step, though there could be several reasons for that.

She needed the energy, though. Marcellus and Dollar had doubled up on everything security-related for the second night of the Circus's three-day performance run. Clara was determined to work. She didn't want anything to keep her from doing what she normally did. Ruth planned to stop by her tent frequently. She'd make it seem less like hovering by sharing some titillating details of her flight with Merc, to distract the girl and make her smile.

Ruth passed the popcorn vendor's cart. It wasn't yet open, but the aroma of popped kernels, butter and salt lingered around it. As well as another pleasing scent she recognized. Even before the owner of it spoke, she was grinning and turning his way.

"Don't tell me they're so hard up for security at this outfit they're hiring skinny little girls now."

Gideon Green, Jacob's brother, was sitting on a sturdy crate and applying a wicked knife to sharpening a wooden stake. A half dozen of them were piled at his feet.

She affected a disapproving look. "I see you still lack respect for your betters, servant."

His shrug was unapologetically insolent. "Haven't had anyone beat it into me yet. Want to give it a go?"

He tossed the stake in the pile and rose, assuming a sparring stance. She went in under his guard, but Gideon compensated, countered, blocked her. She kept their strength on an even par, making the fight about skill. When she saw her opening, she spun, kicked and knocked him back a few steps. He rallied in a heartbeat, but she'd winded him.

Gideon was the one who'd told her not to avoid those "undignified" moves she'd used on the Trad. He'd informed her there was no such thing in a fight to the death. He'd also taught her never to take herself too seriously. "If you and an opponent walk away from a fight together, share a beer," he'd told her. "Finding common ground means he or she might be your ally down the road."

Gideon kept the match going long enough to test her range before she got him on his back and sat on his muscled abdomen, crossing her arms and giving him a look of triumph.

"So there."

He chuckled, patting her thigh. "Work on the leg sweep."

"It knocked you on your ass."

"But a vampire with greater speed and strength would have had you on *your* ass. And put a stake in your heart." He thumped her chest with a light finger. "So work on it."

"Got it." She offered him a hand up, nodding to the stakes. "Used up your current stock?" she asked.

A smile warmed his midnight blue eyes. His unruly dark hair reached his broad shoulders. The jeans and plain black T-shirt were as much of a fashion statement as Gideon Green ever made, unless his vampire Master and Mistress wanted to dress him up.

"Always good to have extra on hand."

"Then there's the added benefit of pissing off Lady Yvette if she sees you doing it."

"I get my joy where I can find it."

She laughed and jumped into his arms, accepting the firm hug. "You ever going to grow up and act like a properly uptight, stick-up-your-ass vampire?" he asked.

"Soon as you learn how to act like a proper servant."

She returned to her feet and slipped her hands into her back jeans pockets before cocking a hip. "What are you doing here?"

"Lyssa wants us to stay in the loop with what Clara has told Yvette and Maddock. If we can ever get some concrete idea of where these Trads are, Daegan and I can go on the hunt. Last night's attack was too aggressive to let pass."

"Yeah."

He gave her a considering look. "I understand you got in a Trad's way."

"I had some help."

"Yeah. Eventually. You took first blood. That's pretty tough, as well as stupid." He grinned. "My preferred MO."

"You stole my line."

"That's why I said it." He sheathed his knife and tucked a stake in behind it, adding the others to a bag he shouldered. "Do you have time to see a good sword fight?"

"Who?"

"Merc and Daegan."

Her eyes widened. "Does Merc have a death wish?"

"Absolutely. But not for this. Merc's pretty damn good. A blade is one of his favorite weapons. Daegan considers him a decent opponent, and that's saying something."

She'd learned something new about her incubus. She should try to push past the tidal wave of sexual power he emanated to find out other things about him. Did he have hobbies beyond sword play? Favorite foods?

Other than the life energy he could summon from a woman when he aroused her.

In addition to being the servant of Anwyn, Mistress of Club Atlantis, Gideon was also bound to Daegan, the Council's hunter and enforcer. Over the years, the three had been to the island several times to spend a few days, helping out while taking a break from work. Unless a vampire was personally invited by Mal, usually that was a privilege reserved for higher ranking vampires. As a young, made vampire, Anwyn didn't really qualify.

Daegan was a different matter.

While initially his identity had been a closely guarded secret in the vampire world, it was now generally known how he served the Council. If a vampire stepped out of line, or a threat to the vampire world required a hunter who could track it down and take it out, he was their choice.

Watching Daegan practice with his katana on the island, Ruth had witnessed a warrior's integration with the weapon he wielded.

"Calling him a hunter suggests the prey might have a chance," Mal had murmured to her. "He's more like an exterminator."

Daegan had not only occasionally observed her sparring with Gideon, he'd helped enhance the knife skills Mal had taught her.

She might not have been given the strength of other vampires, but they hadn't had the opportunity to learn their fight skills from the very best. She'd survived the fight with the Trad, and done him damage, because of those skills.

She fell into step with Gideon as they went down the midway, headed for the Big Top. "Yvette considered giving Merc an act that uses his sword skills," Gideon told her. "But at the time, Marcellus said he might decapitate someone if they pissed him off."

"They should re-evaluate that. His control seems pretty good."

"You've been here what, less than a week?"

She stiffened, but it was a valid point, and her defensive reaction was too telling. She covered it with a question. "I don't know much about him, just impressions. Do you know his background?"

Gideon gave her a studied look. "He was young when a Dark Guardian found him, living in a sparsely populated area of Russia. He was near a fault line portal, so the theory is something thrust him through it and left him, like dumping a dog out of a car and driving off. They couldn't bring themselves to kill him, but they didn't want any association, either. Probably thought leaving him as a kid in the wilderness in the middle of winter would do the job."

Ruth came to a full stop. "How young?"

"Maybe eight or nine years old, best guess. He was taken down to Hell, Lucifer's domain, because it was safest to have him there." Gideon grimaced. "Sounds bad, but they couldn't treat him like a child. There was nothing childlike about him. They made zero headway with him until someone realized how much he liked to fight, and wanted to do it even better. So as Lucifer taught him, that became an avenue for Merc to learn other things. Like language and reading, wearing clothes, learning about the modern world. And how not to act like a stray, draining every female in reach because every meal might be his last."

Gideon paused. "I'm not sure if I should be telling you this, but it's not a secret. And maybe you need to hear it."

She shot him an even look. "I'm not a child. Tell me."

Gideon sighed. "He made them believe he was on board with all their plans to 'civilize' him, until he'd increased his skills enough to make him think he could handle being on his own again. Then he escaped. Hid out for about three decades before he was located again. Thanks to the trail of bodies he left behind."

Gideon glanced at her. "The same Guardian was sent to track and execute him, which is what they do to any sex demon when their hungers take control. Because they weren't sure what kind of abilities his angel blood gave him, they sent a Prime Legion captain as backup."

Though that "trail of bodies" comment tightened the fist in her lower belly, another light dawned. "Marcellus."

"Yeah, Marcellus."

"So what happened?"

"Marcellus said any other incubus in that state would have been as mad as a rabid dog. When they found him, Merc wasn't. They didn't know if that was because of the angel blood, or because supposedly there was some black magic involved in his conception that changed the makeup of his incubus side. Regardless, he was brought back to Hell, where Marcellus recommended he be evaluated by a witch who's more than a witch, and not just because she's mated to an angel.

"She concurred with Marcellus, that there was a slim possibility of redemption. Under her guidance, he was kept in the Underworld for a while and 'rehabilitated.' Fuck all knows what was involved with that, but he did okay enough that eventually he was deemed ready to try the world again, under close supervision. And with the understanding there are no more free passes. He fucks up again, he's done."

She remembered what he'd said. *Otherwise, you incur a death sentence for the crime of being who you are.*

"Marcellus wasn't fighting with the Legion at the time, thanks to an injury. He'd been assigned temporary guard duty over a clairvoyant who was deemed important to the angelic realms."

"Clara."

"Yep. He brought Merc along with him, after they got Yvette on board with it, which took some convincing. Merc doesn't go out of his way to be charming."

At her arch look, Gideon made a face. "Yeah, Miss Smartass, I know I'm one to talk."

"There are still plenty of vampires who want you dead." She gave him a nudge. Before being bound to Daegan and Anwyn, Gideon had been the most successful *human* vampire hunter their world had ever encountered. If not for the binding with his two vampires, he would still be on the most wanted list. Or already executed.

"What can I say? I have a devoted anti-fan club." Gideon shrugged, then sobered. "Even after all these years, jury's still out on him, Ruth. Don't get too attached."

She understood. Even so, she thought about the child Merc, being dumped like trash, and anger surged within her. As well as gratitude toward Marcellus and the others Gideon had mentioned, who'd recognized such desolate circumstances had earned that "child" a second chance.

What were Merc's feelings on all of it? And was he "rehabilitated," or merely toeing the line to stay alive? The word smacked of turning him into something he wasn't, but in her world, it meant other things, too. Teaching new and better survival skills, while healing an injury, whether to the soul or body.

Gideon quickened his steps. "They're about to start."

His eagerness was more than a desire to view the competition. He didn't want his Master without backup. Which reinforced what he'd said about Merc.

Jury's still out on him.

The match was taking place in the Big Top's center ring. Daegan was a tall, lean vampire with dark eyes and close-cropped hair. He wore a tank shirt and *gi* pants, appropriate for a workout. As he moved in a series of muscle-rippling warmups, his katana was still sheathed.

Merc had chosen the same kind of blade. She didn't know if it was his or if it had been borrowed from Daegan, but he looked exceptionally comfortable with it.

A few roustabouts and performers were scattered at safe distances to watch. With a spurt of happiness, Ruth saw Adan sitting on the low wall in front of audience seating. As she and Gideon joined him there, she sat down between them and gave her brother a fond nudge. "Didn't expect to see you back so soon."

"It's not too often I get to be in the same area for more than a few days, so I'm taking advantage of it. Thought I'd check in." He did the obligatory tug of her braid and she responded in kind with a side punch. "Heard you held your own yesterday pretty damn well."

"I did okay."

I'm all right, big brother. This is what I'm here to do. And I kicked ass.

Adan draped an arm around her, a quick, hard squeeze. "I don't doubt it."

Merc had noted her arrival. His gaze touched hers, then it

returned to Daegan. She squelched a shiver, hoping the distraction of the fight would keep Adan from noticing.

Nope. His blue eyes narrowed on Merc before they turned toward her again.

You know you don't want to mess with him.

He's all right. He pulled the Trad off of me yesterday. After *I kicked his ass,* she repeated.

Merc was stripped down to jeans and his bare feet. An outfit that differed from the other day only in that the jeans were faded blue, thinner and more worn. She approved, the denim creasing in all sorts of distracting ways.

As he limbered up with his own blade, she saw the mental stillness and controlled movements of a trained fighter, comparable to Daegan's, though each man had his own style. She forgot to be self-conscious about staring. Fortunately, the rest of their audience was equally involved.

A warrior practices endlessly. When he drills down into the heart of the forms he learns, he finds their spiritual essence. The end intent is to protect, defend, and yes, to kill if necessary. But there is an art to fighting, just as there is to living and dying. All of it is part of creation.

When Daegan had told her that, he'd been showing her the beauty among the brutality. He'd given her a stick to use as a practice sword. They'd stood on a rocky crest and he'd put her through several simple forms while the moon shone on the gazelle herd grazing on the wide plain below them. "If you can't stop the blade a hair's breadth from your opponent's throat," he said, "then you haven't trained enough."

"So I'll never be good enough," she'd complained.

He rapped her on the head with his own stick. "None of us is ever good enough."

Daegan was mirroring Merc now. Lights in the Big Top touched the blades, making them look like silvery water as the flashes advanced and receded.

They started to draw closer to one another.

Ruth leaned forward. Gideon was right. Merc's form was almost as flawless as Daegan's. When the two men at last engaged, a roomful of held breath released, blending into the sound of blades meeting, a chime of metal, a sliding together that drew sparks.

Extraordinary footwork took over. The katanas could decapitate,

168

slice through flesh and bone as if it were nothing. But the dance and control were the thing here. They weren't seeking the kill or a decisive win. Anticipating and countering the other man's movements, *that* was the competition.

It was awe-inspiring to watch. Forward, back, a leap from Daegan, a lift from Merc, using his wings. Spinning, and now they brought more hand-to-hand into it, incorporating kicks, strikes with a free fist, the hilt of the sword. The dust they put on the Big Top floor for traction was kicked up in small plumes.

Above them, in the upper levels of the Big Top, the bright, glittery motes of pixies darted about like hyperactive fireflies, excited by the match. Since Clara had told Ruth how alert the tiny Fae were to the bigger life forms occupying their space, what happened next took everyone by surprise.

One of those frenetic sparkles shot downward, right into the path of Daegan's blade. Proving his words to Ruth, he was able to check the sweep, but seeing the pixie barreling right at the katana's edge, no time to change course, Daegan knocked the creature off track with as gentle a strike from the back of his hand as he could manage.

It still sent the pixie spinning through the air. He plunged downward and thumped to a halt against the base of the wall near where Gideon, Ruth and Adan were sitting.

A gasp snapped Ruth's gaze back to the center ring. Merc, in the middle of a spin, wasn't expecting Daegan to be where he was. There was no avoiding the contact, perhaps the rare exception to Daegan's rule. Merc's sword sliced across Daegan's shoulder. Blood spurted and Daegan staggered, causing another exclamation from those watching.

Yvette's piercing gaze shot to the cloud of pixies above the center ring. In a heartbeat, the bulk of them vanished, slipping out the nearest tent seams.

All except two young male pixies, who zoomed down to check on their fallen comrade. As Gideon surged to his feet to go to Daegan, Ruth grabbed and pushed him, to make him sidestep. At his startled gaze, she directed his attention to the fallen pixie who would have been trampled under his boot.

"I've got this. Check on Daegan."

Ruth knelt over the pixie, aware of the other two chattering. They were on her shoulders, grabbing her hair. The pixie blinked blearily.

Seeing he was conscious, the other two crowed and bounced up and down on her collarbone, hanging onto her hair.

Even without interpreting the language, she could tell his friends had dared him to "dash" between the blades. Ruth barely resisted the urge to swat them.

Fortunately, someone else was willing to do the honors. An older female pixie with a stern matronly air descended upon them. She flitted in front of Ruth's face as if she wasn't there. Her focus was on the dazed male she hovered over, her fussing also requiring no translation. She landed next to him to do a closer check.

"Is he all right?"

Ruth looked up. Daegan stood a couple feet away. He appeared unconcerned about the blood soaking the towel Gideon held against his shoulder, but his arm hung at his side, suggesting some muscle tissue had been cut.

With his strength and age, he'd heal fast. Especially with Gideon providing him whatever extra blood he needed. It still spoke well of the male vampire that, instead of being angry with the tiny creature, he was worried he'd done him irreparable harm.

Ruth looked back down to see the male pixie get to his feet. He was testing his wings and stretching all his limbs, likely to reassure his mother. With a smug smile, he gave a thumbs up to his friends.

The mother rolled her eyes and slapped his head, evoking an indignant retort. Ignoring it, she pulled him airborne by a wing and fired a machine gun of words at the other two, ordering them along in her wake as they exited the tent.

"Right now, yes," she told Daegan. "Maybe not after his mother and Lady Yvette are done with him."

"Better bisected by her tongue than my blade," the vampire responded.

Gideon touched his arm, still holding the towel in place. He tilted his head toward an empty section of the tiered seating behind the wall. "Let's get you the blood you need. Anwyn is having a conniption in my head. Next time you get clipped, do it out of range of Atlanta."

Daegan gave him a half smile and nodded, allowing himself to be guided by his worried servant.

Though it was considered rude to stare at a senior vampire feeding for functional purposes, versus ceremonial ones or public sexual play,

Ruth watched out of the corner of her eye as Daegan took a seat and Gideon sat beside him, offering a wrist. Daegan slid a hand behind his nape, caressing his servant's shoulder and hair, while he lifted the wrist to his mouth and bit.

Even knowing the same thing she knew about Daegan's healing abilities, Gideon's eyes never left him, and he kept holding the towel to his Master's shoulder, helping the blood to clot.

Gideon wasn't unaffected by the contact, aroused by it as servants inevitably were. Just like vampires. She didn't look toward her brother or Yvette, knowing they'd have their own response. It was how they were made, no shame to it, but it was why the courtesies were observed.

She could look toward Merc, though. He'd sheathed the blade after cleaning it and set it aside, and was watching Daegan feed off Gideon with undisguised attention. He wasn't a vampire, and any sexual energy would capture his interest, whether or not it was meant for him.

When his gaze slid to her, she thought of the way he'd fed off her. That pull hadn't only affected the obvious erogenous zones. All of her, her whole body, had been his to command, to take, to use for his needs, and she'd only wanted to give him more.

Maybe it was hazardous, her encouraging him down that road, but his longing to feed fully from her had been so obvious, and called to the part of her that wanted to satisfy him. She'd told him it shouldn't be fatal to her, but he'd resisted.

Was he more concerned about the consequences of her being wrong, or of her being right?

Daegan closed the wound in Gideon's wrist, leaning in to brush his mouth over his servant's, the hair on their brows brushing as Daegan nuzzled his nose and cheekbone. When he rose, he stripped off the bloody shirt and put it in a trash barrel, along with the towel he'd used.

Merc had moved to the middle of the ring and now faced the vampire, drawing Daegan's attention. He'd picked up the sheathed katana and held it before him. As Daegan approached him, he executed a bow, and the enforcer responded with the same, as well as a compliment.

"A good match."

Merc handed over the blade, confirming it was borrowed. He then drew his own dagger, removing the smaller blade from the hilt and offering it to Daegan. "Take an equal measure," Merc said.

"There's no need," Daegan said.

"A good swordsman is prepared for any eventuality," Merc said. "I should have been prepared to pull back."

He said nothing more. He simply waited.

The tent had gone silent. Daegan glanced at Gideon, a mind message spoken and received. His servant stepped back.

Daegan took the shorter blade with a courteous nod. Merc dropped to a knee, offering the same shoulder. Daegan swept the blade over it, a cut Ruth had no doubt was identical in length and depth, within a hair's breadth. Merc didn't flinch, but something eased in his expression.

Ruth moved to the stack of towels Gideon had found, placed next to the ladder leading up to the trapezes and high wire. As she picked up another one and came to Merc, she was aware of her brother and Gideon's attention.

Merc rose to his feet. After the barest of pauses—not so much to be noticeable to others, but meaning a great deal to her—he nodded. Permission. She put the towel over the wound, applying pressure.

He would heal as Daegan did. She'd wanted to help, regardless, but now she had another problem. She kept her lips pressed firmly together, so no one saw her fangs elongate as she inhaled the scent of his blood and remembered its rich taste.

"A good bout," Yvette said, breaking the silence. "Lord Daegan, if you will join me in my quarters, Marcellus will meet us there and I can update you on the Trad attack. Lord Adan, you are welcome to sit in if you feel it's relevant to Guardian business."

Daegan gave Merc a nod and turned, taking his leave with Gideon. Adan had joined her and Merc in the ring. She hadn't moved, holding the towel on Merc's shoulder.

"How could it not be relevant to Guardian business?" she asked.

"Guardians, like angels, have boundaries on what they can be involved in," Adan said, but he didn't clarify if this situation fell outside of it. "Regardless, you should go, too."

"She would have invited me if she wanted me there. I'm part of the security detail. Dollar will tell me what I'm supposed to know."

She wouldn't overstep her role because of family connections. She wanted to work her way up the ladder. "Plus, this way you can ask Yvette if I'm really all right, without me there to tell you to kiss my ass."

She said it mildly, a gentle tease, but Adan's gaze had shifted to Merc. Before she could figure out what that was about, she felt a vibration under her hand and looked up, startled to see Merc expose his own fangs in a decidedly unfriendly way.

The aggressive testosterone surge wasn't helping her manage the rising bloodlust.

I'm fine, Adan, she added, with a touch of urgency. *Really. I'm safe with him. I promise. Males get him riled up. That's all. Go see Yvette. Please.*

Adan's gaze narrowed, but he offered a curt nod. "I'll be close," he told her. "Call if you need me."

When he departed, they were alone, the roustabouts and performers having drifted out of the tent to other duties. Covering her hand with his, Merc moved the towel out of the way. "Clean the wound in the way you wish," he said.

His arm slid around her waist, fingers dipping into the pocket of her jeans to grip her buttock as she put her mouth on the still wet blood.

When she was younger, she'd experienced the "crush" born vampires sometimes developed toward their donors, a result of first discovering the intimacy of the act. Infatuation, not to be equated with "real" love.

With him, the desire to drink deeper, consume more, was strong. It nourished far more than the physical body. Watching Daegan drinking from his servant had been arousing. Merc's blood, the taste of it, actually *was* arousing, as if his ability to command sexual desire permeated his blood, bones, muscle...all of him.

Merc's head dipped as he lifted her off her feet. He moved his mouth to her shoulder, teasing her collar bone. He explored her throat as she licked his shoulder, his flesh, taking every drop of blood she could, coming back to his wound and tracing the cut with the tip of her tongue.

She wrapped her leg around his hip, the contact of his stiff cock against her core making her moan, which he answered with a growl. He tightened his hold on her waist, keeping her where she was. When she drove her fangs into either side of the wound, blood spurted into her mouth again.

Could someone get addicted to an incubus's blood?

She was close to orgasm, her body quivering. She'd learned her lesson the previous night and restrained herself, even as she could feel the desire to beg rise within her.

He didn't give her the option or opportunity.

Spreading his wings, he carried them up over one section of tiered seating and dropped them behind it. The area beneath was screened because they kept extra props there, shielded from audience view. He pushed her into that space, turned her toward a waist-high cabinet and shoved her down on it, opening her jeans and pulling them to her knees. He didn't ask, didn't prepare her, but she needed no preparation. She was drenched with need as he thrust into her.

"Come now," he hissed.

The orgasm detonated through her. When he braced his hand by her shoulder, she sank her teeth back into his forearm to muffle her cries. He worked himself in her, a smooth yet forceful taking that had her losing awareness of anything but him and this moment.

She'd been in control for so long. Had to be. He'd taken it away from her. Reminding her of what he'd told her.

If a Master decides he wants you, he won't give you a choice.

He released with a groan, his wings draping over her, over them both, a cloak that held them in darkness. She gathered them to her, holding the feathers against her face.

"You haven't even properly kissed me yet," she said at last. Softly. Breathless.

"I don't kiss women," he said.

That hurt, but she refused to let the implication that she was nothing different from other females take away from the moment. "Why not?" she asked instead.

A dozen heartbeats, breaths slowing, synchronizing. "This isn't a time for talking," he said. "Be still, Ruth."

She would have pursued it further, maybe even lashed out, but he laid his forehead against her back, between her shoulder blades. The moistness of his breath through her shirt, the heat, had a strange vulnerability to it.

"Okay," she said. Held the feathers closer. *Okay.*

CHAPTER THIRTEEN

Over the next week, those pursuing leads, like the Vampire Council and Daegan, had no new developments. And Clara had no new visions.

Maybe the failed kidnapping attempt had sent the bad guys back to the drawing board. Whatever diabolical plan they'd been hatching had been put on the shelf, for now.

"The Trads aren't known for their complicated political strategies," Yvette had pointed out. "And since they'll stab one another in the back in a heartbeat, whoever perceives himself in charge can change just as fast."

In the meantime, it gave Clara a respite, something everyone welcomed, even if the silence was worrisome. Yvette briskly directed everyone, including her fortune-teller, to focus on the upcoming show schedule. They had three-day bookings in four different towns. Circus season was in high gear.

Ruth reveled in the chance to be part of the routine. They were some of the best days she'd had as an adult vampire.

It lacked only in one area. Merc.

The few times she saw him, he was in the company of others, and he made no attempt to change that. So fine. She let him have the space. She wasn't going to chase him.

Which didn't mean he wasn't constantly on her mind, the things they'd shared re-living themselves in her mind, way too often. As a petty act of vengeance—known only to herself—she classified him as the most distracting *crush* she'd had to date, and refused to treat it as more than that. She excelled at channeling her desires in more useful directions.

Like today. Passing one of the staff workout areas, she saw Caleb, the Circus's "strongman," frowning at a formidable set of weights. Caleb was extraordinarily strong for a human. Rather than have him demonstrate it in the expected ways, Yvette used his strength and perpetually somber manner in the clown skits, in ways that made him an audience favorite.

For instance, in one of them, he leaned against the Big Top's center pole, looking startled when the whole thing began to shake. As he valiantly tried to steady it, the clowns piled on him to help. But when an errant breeze took his cap, spinning it onto a platform far above him, Caleb forgot why the tent had started to shake and started up after it.

Since the implication was that he would bring the tent down by climbing the pole, the clowns used elaborate sign language to stop him, three hanging onto his arms. As he tried to dislodge them, one let out a shrill whistle, making everyone freeze. He pantomimed a comical series of gestures. When Caleb finally understood, he braced himself stoically as one clown after another climbed onto his shoulders. They came up one clown short, all of them making frustrated motions.

That was when Jojo ran out, one of the Circus poodles. He climbed nimbly up the tower of bodies, jumped and grabbed the hat. As he did, he launched himself into the air, inciting audience cries of alarm. Jojo was of course caught in the capable hands of the dog handler, standing in the right spot for that purpose.

The dragons left the poodles alone, no matter how much they looked like sheep, because Yvette had mandated it in her usual warm and fuzzy way. "They're the most reliable performers I have," she informed her staff. "And the cheapest. I'll sacrifice one of you to the dragons first."

The silent act for Caleb wasn't an act. He could speak, but he rarely did unprompted. His communications were mostly reserved courtesies. Ruth detected a deep turbulence in him, one that inspired a desire to soothe. But he kept everything behind a wall, unavailable.

Everyone in the Circus had a story, and protocol said you waited for them to share when they desired to do so. Charlie had noted many were here specifically so they didn't have to.

"Does anyone know them all?" Ruth had asked her.

"Yvette, of course. No one comes into the Circus without her knowing their backstory."

An unsettling thought, one Ruth didn't think about too much.

While she might not have an invitation to solve Caleb's deeper problems, she could maybe assist with his current one. She approached the strongman.

"Can I help?" she asked.

Caleb didn't lift his eyes from the weights. "When Greygirl is okay with it, I can stand beneath her, put my hands on her belly and lift her. Mostly she prefers to wander up to the audience and take offered peanuts. Yvette believes she'll turn the color of a peanut eventually and her name will be confusing."

He was referring to the one elephant in the show, who'd been rescued from a sideshow zoo. Born and raised in captivity, she had health issues that prohibited any rehab and release options. They'd intended to place her at a sanctuary, but she liked the conditions provided for her at the Circus. She wasn't required to be in the show, but she traveled with the troupe. She showed no interest in leaving the Circus grounds, except when they were in the in-between spaces. She explored the green spaces there, usually with a cloud of pixie Fae perched upon her. Or the young dragons.

She contributed to the show in her own way, however, wandering the midway, surprising and delighting the attendees. Trip, her primary caretaker, stayed with her, making sure no one did something unwise, like allow their toddler to sidle close enough to have toes pulverized by Greygirl's feet.

Ruth had been warned Caleb didn't follow a linear track in communication. But from the time he could talk, Adan had had his head up the ass of the universe, firing great cosmic magical questions at it, so she understood what the strongman was saying, half of it in his mind, half of it said aloud.

"You're bored. You want more of a challenge today."

He lifted his gaze and studied her thoughtfully. "Yvette tells me I'm not as strong as a vampire, but she's never arm wrestled me."

Ruth offered a deliberately fangy grin. "That sounds intriguing, but I have a different idea. Game to try it?"

At his nod, she came closer. He wore a workout tank and shorts that did little to hide how startlingly well-endowed he was. The man had a horse's cock. She expected that attribute made him equally popular with the adult-only shows. "Lift me above your head, arms fully extended, me stretched out like a plank."

His gaze covered her. "You weigh far less than I can lift. Even if you have that vampire no-buoyancy thing."

"Wait for it, big guy."

He shrugged. "I'm going to lift you to my shoulder and adjust you from there. Is that all right? Are you afraid of heights?"

Her mind went to her flight with Merc. A big *no* on that one, but she teased Caleb. "You're tall and strong, but not *that* tall. And I don't break easily, so I won't be worried about being dropped."

"I won't drop you." He looked appalled that she would think it was a possibility.

"Good." As she put her hand on his shoulder, she noted it twitched under her touch, his eyes going to it.

It surprised her that casual contact outside a performance bothered him, but instinct had her injecting a gentle note to the question. "Is this okay?"

"Yes. Thank you for asking, my lady." His voice was oddly formal.

"Just Ruth." At a flicker of his expression, she amended, "Unless you're more comfortable with *my lady*."

He didn't respond to that, but at her nod, he picked her up, shifting her over his shoulders. She crossed her arms over her chest, a la Dracula going to bed in his coffin, as he adjusted his palms beneath her.

"Lift me as high as you can," she directed. "And brace yourself."

Adan had shown her the "trick" after he'd used it to play games of strength with William and Matthew. When she chanted the words and focused the energy, she heard Caleb's surprised grunt. Because she didn't have Adan's abilities or control, and she wasn't a total sadist, she made sure her weight increased gradually.

Showing off, Adan had accelerated his so it was like a piano had been dropped from a great height. He'd enjoyed squashing Matthew beneath him like a bug. *Boys.* Just like the male pixie Fae and his friends.

She felt a fizzy sensation on her skin, a soda right as it was opened. To Caleb, it would feel like her weight was doubling, tripling, and so on and so forth...

As the obvious strain for his grip and shoulders increased, he braced himself, letting out a breath. A satisfied one. She was giving him the challenge he wanted. She'd crossed her ankles, so he wrapped his fingers around her leg between her closed thighs. His other hand was flat between her shoulder blades.

"When you take a knee, I'll stop," she said.

She heard whistles and catcalls, performers and workers encouraging the show. Caleb answered them by straightening elbows that had started to bend, thrusting her upward in a determined fashion.

"Can you river dance while you do that?" she taunted.

Hearing her joke, two of the clowns, wearing street clothes right now, jumped in on either side of him. They coaxed the serious Caleb into doing the Electric Slide with them. A radio was turned up, the Foundations' "Build Me Up Buttercup."

She noted the telltale quiver of Caleb's arms, a reaction that swept through his body. It was time to dial it back. No matter his strength of will or abilities, he *was* human, and she didn't want to hurt him. She wasn't going to have Yvette after her for damaging one of her performers.

"Take a knee, Caleb," she said, and murmured the reversal chant so her weight would reduce as gradually as it had increased.

He was reluctant, but no matter his pride, he was as conscious of his responsibility to protect himself as she was. He took the knee carefully, then brought her back to a sitting position on his shoulder, her hand braced on the other slick, bare one, her thumb against his racing pulse.

When she was standing on her own two feet again, Caleb put his hands to her waist and lifted her, verifying she was her normal weight again.

"My brother Adan taught me that spell," she told him. "It's really just a parlor trick."

She'd surprised him enough to gain a brief window into his head. His expression was one she recognized. Now she knew why he preferred her title instead of a first name basis. That, and what he said next.

"Thank you. And if you need blood at any point, my lady...from the vein, you're welcome to take from mine."

He believed as everyone did, that all vampires were dominant. But when it came to the relationship between vampires and humans, she actually had no problem holding that upper hand. Even if she had some troubles with her own issues around the more dominant human servants, like Jacob or Gideon, knowing they were human made it far easier for her to dismiss that feeling and behave as she should. As she did now.

She placed a hand on his shoulder, showing appreciation of the offer. "And if you need help working out again, let me know."

"I just got a delightful skit idea," Buella told him. "You can be holding a barbell above your head while we do a line dance. Audiences love dance routines. As you turn, you could pretend to hit a clown on the head with the barbell, knocking him off his feet—"

"And we could modify the line dance, make it something people could do sitting down," the clown on his other side said. "Using hands, stomping their feet. Yvette would love it."

Ruth left them discussing the matter. Caleb looked as if his mind was far away from what they were telling him, but she'd seen that same distant look when another complicated routine was being reviewed. On its first run-through, he'd done it perfectly.

Gods create universes while eating spaghetti and reading spy novels.

Adan had said that to her. He'd been absorbed in one of his books while they sat with the bobcat kits in the rehab area. Since she'd been complaining they needed more rabbits on the island, and he hadn't responded, she told him he was ignoring her. He'd continued to read, but he'd picked up a handful of long grasses and woven them through his fingers, a seemingly idle task while studying his text.

A few minutes later, a rabbit made of grass hopped across the ground to her. Adan had put aside his book then and they'd made a game out of trying to get the rabbit to move fast enough to evade the kits.

Adan had eventually allowed them to capture and shred the doppelganger, hunting practice that prepared them for release. But that night, there'd been another one on her dresser in her room. Not animated, but that was okay. The memory would always be animated.

She knew Caleb's gaze followed her as she left them. Thinking of other things she'd noticed about him, she recognized he was a submissive who would serve a Dominant of either gender as a matter of pleasure, and to meet mutual needs, but his preference was male. His attention lingered on acrobats like Nikolai and Karl in their form-fitting costumes with a different intensity, but when they looked in his direction, his gaze cut away.

Had he ever found a male Dom to top him the way he craved? Or did he fear that volcano inside him too much?

She'd been on her way to another smaller workout area for her own training, a spot located near Gundar's smithy, the communal showers and cooking tent. When she started lifting, she used her earbuds and music player to keep her company.

She could easily lift hundred-pound weights, but strength only served her in a fight if she had the right control over it. As she did her reps with that precision, she hummed along to the music. The words made her smile, with a touch of more complicated feelings.

As if summoned, the cause of those feelings arrived to send a shiver across her skin. She tilted her head in Merc's direction as he touched her damp nape, the shell of her ear, and plucked the bud from it.

"What's making you smile?"

She knew he watched her, all the damn time. It had helped her feel somewhat better about him keeping his distance. If he was watching, he wasn't disinterested. Just the opposite.

Lurking was a thing for him. When he wasn't needed for anything, she'd deduced he regularly observed the Circus goings-on from his perches in different unseen spots. It was how he knew so much about so many things.

Putting down the weights, she turned and took the earbud from his hands, brushing his hair with her fingertips as she started to put it in his ear. When he drew back, his expression perplexed, she paused.

"Haven't you worn earbuds before?"

He shook his head.

"Any moral objections to them?"

His lips pursed as he realized he was being teased, but he bent down and let her tuck it into his ear. "Listen to the lyrics," she said. "They remind me of you. That was why I was smiling." While at the same time feeling that sad twist at its potential truth.

As she started the song over, she put her hand on his forearm, half-closing her eyes to listen to Tim McGraw sing through the other bud she'd kept.

Wondering why he acted the way he did, being his own worst enemy, waking up so fighting mad...

"'Guess it's just the cowboy in me,'" she sang softly. *The restlessness, the heart of stone...* The smile left her as her hands tightened on him.

Merc listened. By the time the last note finished, he had a faint frown on his face, and an unexpected opinion. "It's you, too."

He cupped his hand behind her neck, drawing her up onto her toes, making everything tighten. Her hands landed on his chest and hip to steady herself. His body twitched under her touch. "How so?" she managed.

"There's not a line I haven't drawn that you haven't crossed."

"That one applies as much to you as to me. Just ask Marcellus and Yvette."

She'd made a mistake. He didn't like being reminded he had a keeper. He let her go and stepped back. Maybe she'd be compounding the mistake with her next question, but fuck it.

"Did you seek me out because you're hungry, and you thought about what I said?"

His expression darkened. "You think that's the only reason I'd come to you?"

"You tell me. I haven't seen you much."

"No." He stepped closer again, though this time he didn't touch her. She wanted him to, and she knew he could tell. He liked making her want. Not to be pointlessly mean. But to be pointedly mean, holding out of reach what was his to decide to give. "But you've felt me, haven't you?"

"Yes." They stared at one another.

"Would you like to sit in one of the places where I watch you?"

At her nod, he slipped an arm around her waist, letting her put hers around his neck. As she did whenever he gave her the opportunity, she played with the short hair there, liking the brush of it against her knuckles. Her eyes half closed in bliss at that lovely lift feeling, the wind from his wings brushing tendrils of her hair back from her brow. A few moments later, they were perched in a longleaf pine located in a cluster of them on the southwestern side of the camp. The tree offered a panoramic view of the Circus compound, the road leading into the small Georgian town nearest them, and the hills it disappeared into. "Wow. Good line of sight."

"One of my jobs is to monitor the area from the high ground."

So not just a lurker. He was a scout and camp guard. Marcellus and Yvette were good at employing their people's strengths.

Merc sat against the trunk, one leg resting along a substantial branch, his other foot braced against another, a triangle of stability. It allowed her to settle on his thigh and prop her feet against his opposite leg. His wings had folded behind him, cushioning his back, the tips trailing down either side of the trunk.

He slid a finger into the V of her T-shirt, tracing her breast above the hold of her bra. "You don't sample human food as much as other vampires do."

"A lot of vampires like the sampling thing. I don't do as much of it, unless it's a formal dinner where the host has prepared something. Don't want to be rude."

"Blood tastes better?"

"Yeah. But I really like certain things, and I can only have a little of them. Having a little can be as bad as having none, if you know what I mean."

He studied her. "Perhaps. What things?"

"Well, Kohana... He was my father's right hand, a second mark who was like a human uncle to me and Adan. He made this stone-ground corn bread and added stuff to it. He'd make it for me when I was sad, or to celebrate, or just for the hell of it. He'd cut it into little heart-shaped cubes. He bought the cutter special for me."

She paused, cleared her throat. "After he passed... If I ever sat down to a loaf of it again, I wouldn't be able to stop myself. I'd eat all of it, and be sick for days. Which is a moot point, because if he isn't the one making it, it wouldn't be the same."

"Vampires can get sick from human food?"

She gave him a curious look. "How do you not know that? You said you've watched vampires sample food."

"Yes. I didn't know that was why. I assumed it was because vampires simply prefer blood."

He hadn't asked anyone. Did he feel questions made him vulnerable, by exposing ignorance? Or was his focus primarily on the information necessary to safeguard his own survival or respect the boundaries that would keep him from becoming a further target?

He'd already revealed enough about why he didn't want them to know about his visit to the island to suggest his presence here was like being under house arrest. If he wanted to leave Marcellus and the Circus, could he? Or was that death sentence his only other option?

"I'll figure out what other favorites you might have," he decided. "I like the idea of feeding you and leaving you wanting more."

Without warning, he flipped their positions, setting her against the trunk as he stood. His wings spread and he launched himself, rocking the branch. She grabbed at the trunk with a yelp, and gasped as he returned, almost as quickly. When he restored their original position, her perched on his lap between his braced thighs, she shot him a cranky look. "An 'excuse me, I'll be right back' is more polite than leaving me flailing like a fledgling about to fall out of nest."

Ignoring her complaint, he extended his hand, revealing a tiny square of white cake. "Charlie made these for Maddock. He's coming to visit her tonight, after the show."

"Did you steal one?"

"She's made him plenty. He enjoys them, but it will be her body he wants to sample and devour when he gets here."

"That isn't a no." Ruth gave Merc a severe look, though the cake's aroma was heavenly.

He shrugged. "I want to see you taste something from my hand. Open your mouth."

When he got that tone, that look, her scruples wavered. It was just a bite of cake, after all. She'd apologize to Charlie.

She parted her lips, and he put the cake to them. "Slowly," he said, the look in his eyes intensifying. When she took it on her tongue, she closed her mouth and began to chew, gradually breaking into all the flavors the cake had. A shudder rose from her core because he shifted his hand back to her throat, closing fully around it.

When she swallowed, it was because he allowed it.

After she was done, he didn't ease his hold. He moved his other hand to her hair, taking the clip out of it so her hair fell to her shoulders, straight long strands fluttering around her face and over his forearm. His thumb moved to her lips, then his grip on her neck constricted.

"Vampires don't need to breathe, do they?"

She shook her head. The feeling of not being able to breathe could panic a younger vampire, but she knew how to work through it. Breath was mainly needed to speak, and to add strength to physical effort, but right now he wanted silent submission and held her still.

"Lower your gaze, Ruth."

When she obeyed, the grip tightened further. He had the strength to crush everything he held, but she didn't think he would damage her throat. She let her hands, resting on his abdomen, relax and curl into the waistband of his jeans through the loose T-shirt he wore. This one bore a print of Michael Parkes' famous *Gargoyle* painting, a child blowing a bubble over the side of a building as the stone gargoyle on its corner burst loose to chase the floating sphere.

"Who gave you this?"

"Clara, some years ago. She was returning from a visit with her friend Alexis, and brought gifts back for everyone. Including me."

The shirt was faded and soft. He wore it often.

He could be such a frustrating mystery; despite that, sometimes she felt she could see inside his soul as easily as her own. She held that thought, her attention moving to his feathers, gleaming black and traces of silver white against a broken pattern of brown bark.

He drew her closer, so her mouth almost touched his. Almost, not quite. "It disappointed you, that I don't kiss women. I'll have to think about that."

His glance moved down, a brow arching. She'd drawn her blade from its hidden scabbard and pushed the point against his abdomen. His lips curved, eyes glinting. "You don't want me to speak of 'women' in your presence, as if you are one of many."

Quicker than she could follow, he'd grasped her hand with the knife and pressed it under her ear. She drew in a breath as the tip cut several inches above her pounding artery. He leaned in, inhaling her blood with flared nostrils, and sampled it with his clever, teasing tongue. She moaned, a futile oath on her lips as he took her blood into him.

What if she had given him the first mark the other night, when she'd bitten him? She had no idea if that would even take on Merc's incubus and angel blood, though Catriona had accepted all three marks from Adan. She had some human blood, though.

The bond meant a lot of deeper things than what it seemed on the surface. But it was an absurd, crazy thought. One she should put away. Merc was definitely not servant material.

Merc eased back. "I get what you mean, about the more you take, the more you want."

He slid the knife into the scabbard, his touch intimate. Firm. "If you draw that against me again, I'll put it inside you. You'll have to hold still so it doesn't cut you more deeply than the shallow cuts I'll make upon the first thrust, so I can taste your blood and your cunt at the same time."

She managed to link a bland look to her hard quiver, a look that promised nothing. But she did settle her feet anew against his thigh and clasp her hands around her knees.

"Gideon said you were found in the Russian wilderness."

She wasn't sure how sensitive he'd be about it. Fortunately Merc seemed unconcerned, but he was also disinterested in the topic. He twitched the cord of her earbuds. "Let me listen to more music you like."

Ruth knew he'd once participated in Circus performances, before moving more fully into the security end of the Circus. He and Medusa had even had a flight sequence together, when Medusa and JP had first arrived. Merc had helped choose more instrumental pieces as a score for it. But had he never dipped his toe into pop culture, modern music, TV? The Trads viewed it with contempt, feeling vampires should be wholly savage. She wondered if it was like that for Merc. Had it been easier to be savage and objectify the world that didn't want him?

He'd said his incubus nature fought his angel side. Was it a choice, him purposefully avoiding exploring that side of himself, for whatever reason?

"You threaten me with my knife again, I'll knock you out of this tree," she told him.

"You can try. I'm not worried about the fall." His lip curled.

"Wasn't that also in the song? We don't worry about the fall... 'because of the cowboy in us all?'"

～

Lady Yvette leaned against the pillar outside her yurt. Small metal squares covered the wood. Each one represented a troupe member. When they were fully accepted as part of the Circus family, he or she could add their seal to the post, telling Gundar what they wanted on it. He was as accomplished with metal engraving as he was crafting weapons.

When it was put in place, she wove its energy with the others, pulling that member even deeper into the bonds of the Circus.

Only one long-term resident had never gone through that ritual. He didn't see himself as part of them. Many of the Circus members didn't see him that way, either. Though it had been some time since Merc had fully broken the parameters that allowed him to be here, Yvette had never issued the invitation. An essential ingredient had always been missing. For both of them.

Trust.

As she absorbed the camp activity, she confirmed all was well. A usually pleasurable task, drinking in the emotions. Excitement, flirting, friendship. The good kind of weariness. Effort and concentration, as someone practiced their Circus skills. Sexual pleasure, mostly explored inside the RVs, since they weren't inside a portal space. Amiable competition at card games, or companionship over meals.

Her scan paused over the silhouette of the pine tree grove at the far end of their encampment. Eavesdropping wasn't part of this, unless it was warranted. It was the energy that came to her that held her focus.

She opened her mind to share what she was experiencing with Gundar. He stood by her side, "listening," arms crossed over his chest. She touched his shoulder, his neck, tracing the artery with a sharp nail. Felt the pump of reaction.

He didn't move, though he was ready for her command. If she wanted blood and his body, he would go into the yurt and wait by her bed. When she bid him do so, he would get up onto it and prop his back upon the pillows, his boots courteously left on the floor.

She would lie in the curve of his strong arm—those who thought length mattered in the estimation of that were incorrect—put her mouth to his throat and sink in. Her Dom servant liked her to give him pain, not be gentle. Unlike Charlie, whom she treated like an egg when she drew blood from the slim healer.

People's differences held their secrets. Yvette's attention turned toward Maddock. The sorcerer sat on a chair he'd brought out of Yvette's yurt, to enjoy the night air. He'd remained quiet while she did her status check, but he had a distraction. Charlie knelt at his feet, leaning against his leg. His hand was in her hair, his thumb teasing the bra strap on her shoulder, bared by the scooped neckline of her dress.

Some of Yvette's second marks, like Dollar, were marked merely for operational needs, to provide the close communication Yvette required. Charlie and Gundar were different. She fed from them, and they shared her bed when she had that desire. Both carried a symbol of that more intimate commitment, a ruby that reflected the red hues in the Circus logo. Charlie, wore it on a necklace that nestled between her collar bones, whereas Gundar wore it worked into the metalcraft of his belt buckle.

When Maddock was here, Charlie was his. Volatile negotiations over the years had worked that out between them. Yvette still reserved the right to revoke his privileges when he was an idiot. Well, specifically related to his behavior toward Charlie, since Maddock was generally an idiot. Even if he was an outstanding sorcerer and a friend.

"It's like a courtship between two wild animals," Maddock said. His gaze was trained in the same direction as hers. "The male bringing the female prizes while displaying plumage. In this case, stealing my cake and showing off those panty-dropping wings. Should have spelled the food to zap his fingers."

"I can make more," Charlie assured him, propping her chin on his knee, amusement in her voice. "I think it's sweet."

"Yeah. Merc being sweet. That trips my freak-o-meter right off the charts."

"Ruth is a different experience for Merc," Yvette noted thought-fully. "Though she has no physical advantages over him, she's not afraid of him, like most females are, unless he uses his compulsion abilities to draw them in."

"You're not afraid of him," Maddock pointed out.

"I'm a Dominant."

Maddock's expression flickered with surprise, but before he could ask the question, an annoyed male voice intervened.

"I thought I made it clear that Merc playing with my sister isn't a good idea."

Adan strode around the curve of Yvette's yurt. He'd been working on a minor glitch to the protection spell for the Big Top. Maddock could have fixed it, too, but Adan was Yvette's backup for problems Maddock might not be available to resolve. She liked giving both males the opportunity to stay familiar with Circus magic.

"You knew he was close enough to hear," Maddock observed.

"It's best we have this out." Yvette gave Adan an impatient look. "You told me your opinion. I didn't say I was going to act on it. You could see what was happening at the sparring match. It's not just him playing with her. She's playing with him."

"But we understand your concern," Charlie put in before the two vampires—one a sorceress and one a Light Guardian—could get snappish and put body parts and inanimate objects at risk. "My lady is letting things take their natural course, but keeping an eye on things for the same reason it concerns you. To make sure he doesn't harm her."

Maddock gestured the tense Adan to another chair he'd brought out. "You know your sister better than any of us. You know she's tough."

"Yeah, but not always tough enough. When we were growing up, she let me take the lead, but she was right there at my side, ready to provide back up with a ferocity that rabid badgers wish they had. If someone tries to corner her, no matter how strong they are, she'll fight." His jaw flexed. "She won't win. She'll get bloody. And even if she knows her opponent can kill her, she won't back down."

"It makes you afraid for her, even as you wouldn't want her to be any other way," Maddock said.

"Letting fear rule you destroys everything you hope for yourself," Adan said. "So, yeah. Doesn't mean I want to throw her in the path of danger."

Yvette glanced toward the pines. "This is the Circus, Adan. The rules here are different than in the vampire world, as much as I can manage it. It's a large part of why she's here, right?"

When her golden eyes came back to him, his expression had shuttered. "Yes."

"Merc's incubus side was in control from the beginning, because demon blood doesn't miss an opportunity to take the lead, particularly if nothing else is nurtured," Maddock noted. At Adan's censorious look, he raised a quelling hand. "However, Marcellus has often believed the angel is stronger within Merc than Merc has accessed. Over the years, he's encouraged him to explore that. With how much success, it's hard to determine. Merc doesn't reveal much."

Charlie lifted her head from Maddock's thigh. He shifted his hand to her back, tracing the bumps of her spine under her thin shirt. "Most people's energy changes as they interact with others," she said. "Over the years, his has always gone opaque around Yvette, Marcellus and Maddock. As Maddock says, there may be a great deal going on behind it, but the impression is he's being what he's required to be, to stay alive. What lies behind the wall... My gut says something has changed for him, these past few years, but I'm not sure."

"Have you noticed what his energy and auras are like around Ruth?" Yvette asked.

A slight smile touched Charlie's face. "Chaotic. A little frightening, but beautiful too, like a storm. I don't think he knows what to make of her, but she brings out the Master in him, something I've never seen him overtly exercise, though it's always been there."

"Really?" Maddock tugged her hair. "You've never mentioned that to me. How do you know?"

She shrugged. "How does any submissive know? We feel it, from the way you conduct yourself, the way you talk and act. Even though he's suppressed it, it's there."

Maddock glanced between Adan and Yvette. "Is that what all the subtext between you and Adan is about? You're saying Ruth is a natural submissive?"

"Goddess help us, he finally catches up," Yvette murmured, shooting him a look.

"Give me a break. I'm not around here as much as I'd like to be." His glance went to Charlie, lingered. Then he glanced at Adan, who had stiffened. He locked gazes with the wizard.

Maddock rose, his respect for the other male evident in the formal gesture. His hand stayed on Charlie's shoulder, conveying his understanding of the drive to protect and care for one he loved. "What's discussed here goes no further, Adan. You have my word."

"Marcellus is already aware," Yvette added. "He and I have discussed the need for discretion. He knew the first time he met her." She arched a pointed brow at Maddock. "How can such a smart male be so clueless?"

"I will put lice in your mattress."

"I will remove your testicles with barely a thought."

Charlie interjected a distracting thought, still aimed at reassuring Adan's concerns. "Merc isn't a vampire, and he's far stronger than one. In terms of your world's acceptance of the situation, doesn't that help?"

"Yes and no. It has to do with her, not him. A vampire *capitulating* to a stronger being because they're stronger is an accepted part of our natural order. A vampire *wanting* to be topped, wanting to submit, isn't."

"Your concern is if it gets revealed by her relationship with Merc, but the relationship ends..."

"She's been outted," Adan said tersely.

"She has allies here already." Charlie accepted Maddock's hand to stand at his side. "We'll do all we can to protect her, Adan. The same as we do for all the Circus family."

Yvette met Adan's gaze. "She's already proven herself willing to work hard and be a contributing member of this troupe. She's a good fit. We recognized what she is, Adan, because we're all misfits here. Aren't we?"

Adan couldn't summon a smile, but he inclined his head. "She's... she's in my soul, my lady. Don't hide anything from me that will help me protect her."

"I have not and will not. But I will respect her independence. As you and your father have done, by facilitating her job here. Life is not safe, Adan. Not if you're doing it right."

"Yeah." After a silent moment, Adan nodded to the Circus Mistress. "Glitch is fixed. Let me know if you have any other problems. With anything."

When he strode away, Maddock looked at Yvette. "I'm not sure we helped."

"Because he knows the vampire world too well," Yvette said, her expression grim. "But my primary concern is Merc. To have a submissive female trust him, not afraid, curious, willing to play and test him, is entirely new. It remains to be seen how he will handle that." She glanced toward Charlie. "And what will be revealed behind that wall."

～

"Motown is a treasure chest," Ruth told Merc. "The Temptations, the Supremes, the Jackson 5..."

They'd been in the tree for an hour, sharing music through her earbuds. "'I'm gonna make you love me,'" she sang. "I like the part where he says he's going to shower her with love and affection. I used to tease my brother with that song when he claimed to like me less than shoveling cat dung. Mum liked that song. When it first came out and was always on the radio, she and Da would dance to it."

She swung her feet, brushing her bare toes through the trailing ends of his feathers. She'd toed off her shoes and let them drop down to the forest floor. "Do you sing?" she asked him. "Dance? Tap your feet?"

So far, he hadn't engaged that way with the music, but his eyes flickered with intrigue on every song she chose.

He touched her mouth, sending a shimmer of pleasure through her lips. "Play another."

"Okay." She already knew which one she wanted, and scrolled through her vast library for it. "But you have to answer another question for me. Do female and male sex demons mate?"

"I haven't spent much time with my kind, but what I know is they breed, but rarely mate. The sexual hunger, the drive to feed, isn't conducive to permanent attachments."

"But you belong to another race as well. How about angel kind?"

"I don't feel I'm part of that race. Not enough to be influenced by it." He assumed an impassive look she was starting to suspect was a cover, when his answer wasn't entirely true, or didn't cover all the relevant information.

She didn't press him on it. "Most vampires don't mate with other vampires, either. Hard to commit to someone for that long. Some might be together for a few decades or even a century, but then they'll go their separate ways. Sometimes they get back together, years later, but not that often."

She paused. "The longest continuous relationship in a vampire's life is usually with their third marked human servant. Servants live for three hundred years, and the vampire holds all the power, in theory."

"In theory?"

"My father is my mother's Master, but he'd do pretty much anything for her happiness and wellbeing." Her gaze shadowed. "My world has requirements that sometimes don't gel with what you'd prefer your priorities to be. So you have to fight for whatever space you can give them, if that makes sense."

She frowned. "I think it's hard for vampires to fully trust one another. Their nature is either to fight for dominance, or look for the opportunities to take control. With servants, there's more room for that trust to develop, because a third mark is a full soul bond. There's nothing they can hide from their vampire. Oh, this is a good one."

Removing her own earbud and putting both in his ears—giving her the chance to incidentally stroke his hair and brush her fingertips along his sexily stubbled jaw—she stood up on the branch to dance. She could pick up enough of the beat through her vampire hearing. She gave the song the full hip action treatment, incorporating a hair-brush move as she rocked down to her heels and back up again. "'There's nothing holding me back...' Shawn Mendez. It's hard not to dance to this one. Listen to the lyrics."

He was obviously doing that, while watching her in a way that had her skin prickling with heat. She spun to the drumbeat, working around his outstretched leg. Then he held out a hand and she took it. He rose, put one earbud back in her ear...and launched them.

She wondered how Shawn would feel if he could have the chance to spin through the sky and clouds to the upbeat drum beat and guitar plucking in the song.

Nothing holding me back...

Merc gave her that feeling. When he landed at the base of the tree, she was breathless, laughing. She'd noted he hadn't smiled, not once. When they'd started the music marathon, he'd told her he wanted her to talk and act how she would if he was actively engaging with her—without him actually doing so.

At first, she thought it would feel like she was on a stage, but she'd realized how much it pleased him, not needing to give her anything... but his absolute attention.

She leaned against the trunk and looked up at him. He had his wing curved over his shoulder, close to her right side. She stopped herself from touching it, because it was different from brushing her feet against the trailing wing tips. He projected a certain reserve when he wanted her to ask permission to do it.

"Since we don't have a performance tonight, a few of the troupe are going into town," she said. "There's a club with live music. If you're not interested, we could explore a couple parks I heard about. One has a waterfall. If you don't mind flying us there, so we can get in after closing."

"You prefer to be with me rather than going with them?"

"Well, yeah."

"Because I can give you powerful orgasms."

"Don't be a jerk. Because I want to spend more time with you. Isn't that why you're with me right now?" She shrugged. "The orgasms are a nice bonus."

"I might join you in town," he said. "I have some other things to handle for Marcellus first."

She noted a tight look around his mouth, suggesting a problem, but the look also said he didn't want to talk about it. "Okay. But you might miss karaoke."

After she explained what that was, his look of horror had her stifling a giggle. "What? Can't sing?" she asked.

Her smile faded as he put his hand to her mouth again, tracing the shape. "You say you don't kiss, but everything about you says you might like to try it," she whispered. She thought about lifting on her toes, just that slight amount to close the distance, but he put a hand on her shoulder.

"No," he said. "And don't let Caleb touch you again. I don't like it."

Then he was gone, leaving her blinking with shock.

CHAPTER FOURTEEN

*A*fter Merc left her, Ruth wondered if that tight look was caused by what she'd suspected? Was he not allowed to leave the Circus without Marcellus's express say-so?

As sensitive as he was about the topic, she wasn't going to push him to confirm it. However, finding someone else to ask might be okay.

That ended up being Gundar. He was at his smithy. He'd been making metal roses lately, tinting them with hints of color. She admired a bouquet of them, noting the stems were flexible enough to deliver a stinging bite to soft flesh, thanks to their metal thorns.

Intentional, she was sure. Gundar confirmed it by showing her the roses' other uses in that realm. He had her put out her arm and pressed the metal rose against her flesh. When he took it away, there were tiny marks.

"You can heat one and apply it like a temporary brand."

"I better place my order before everyone else does."

Gundar grinned beneath his dark beard and patted the bench next to him. "What do you want to ask? You have that expectant look."

"Can Merc leave the grounds by himself? Without Marcellus or Yvette saying it's okay?"

"Technically, no, but he's been with us long enough to earn some slack to that leash. Yvette doesn't ping him if he's gone for a couple hours. More than that would be a problem. And he's definitely not supposed to navigate the portals on his own."

"How did he learn to do that? It takes a lot of training."

"Apparently angels just know how."

She filed that away, another piece of information suggesting Merc might have more angelic abilities than he claimed. Or maybe knew.

"Shouldn't you be asking him these questions?" Gundar gave her a steady look.

It was a Dom-to-sub kind of question, and Gundar had major Dom vibes, even as Yvette's servant. A human servant, she reminded herself, and made herself react as a vampire was expected to do.

"I'm asking you," she said evenly. However, keeping in mind he was also indirectly her boss, she relented with honesty. "I don't want him to see me as another babysitter."

Gundar snorted. "I don't think you have to worry about that. You're capable and a good fighter, so don't take the next part the wrong way. Merc is way above your league when it comes to strength, speed and power. It would be like making a mouse the housecat's babysitter. And the housecat is a saber tooth tiger."

She knew that, but it did offend her, enough that she couldn't stop the retort. "I was using the word babysitter to be diplomatic. I meant spy or snitch."

Gundar's coal-black eyes sharpened, reminding her he was also connected to Yvette, mind-to-mind. She shut her mouth before she said more inadvisable things.

"Does the Circus seem like a place that wants to curtail someone's freedom?" he asked.

"No," she admitted.

"You've seen his intensity. If he's having to work his ass off to keep himself from sucking away a female's life energy, it's probably good that someone's keeping tabs on that. Right?"

She thought of Merc's close regard as they listened to music. If he was fighting that hunger, it wasn't obvious. But if people she respected kept warning her not to make assumptions about him, she knew she should give those warnings the weight they deserved. Even so...

"The death sentence hanging over him. That's from when he was a lot younger, right?"

"Yes," Gundar said soberly. "Some people believed he should have been consigned to Hell for a much longer redemption period, rather than getting the second chance Circus option."

She thought of Merc offering her a bite of cake. The yearning in his expression when their bodies were joined. "Some people don't know shit."

Gundar's coal-colored eyes glinted. "You like him."

"I find him interesting. And I think there's a lot more to him, though I get that I haven't been here long enough to know shit, either. I appreciate you answering my questions."

The dwarf picked out one of the roses, tinted in red and silver, the petal tips scorched with black smoke color, and handed it to her. "Don't assume he needs a champion, Ruth. He has more of them than you think. Else he'd have been dead long ago. His champions just don't ride white horses and kiss his ass. They kick it, as often as he needs it, because they want him to succeed."

"Why?" she asked bluntly. "No one seems to like him."

"You said you like him. Why do you think that is?"

She twirled the rose, pressing her finger against one of the sharp metal thorns for the kiss of pain. She was pretty sure Yvette was listening in, maybe feeding Gundar the questions she wanted Ruth to answer. So her response was for both of them. "Because he's trying. He's trying hard, even if it doesn't look like it. I think he's trying to find his way out of a swamp no one but him knows how to navigate."

Gundar pursed his lips. "Interesting. Keep using your brain, woman. It's serving you well. You might be careful of the tongue, though. No disrespect."

That was a warning for her about his listening Mistress, she was sure.

"Okay." She rose. "I've asked him to join me in town tonight. If he shows, is there anything I should worry about? Watch out for, to help him?"

"He's learned how to control himself. He'll leave if he encounters a temptation he can't shake. With one exception." Gundar gave her a deadly serious look. "If he finds a pizza parlor where he can watch the guy make the dough, you know, on the fist," Gundar emulated the spinning, "He'll stay and watch for hours. That shit fascinates him."

~

There were a dozen troupe members on the outing, a mix of performers and roustabouts. The live music wasn't bad, and she enjoyed watching the others flirt and banter. They shared anecdotes with her about Circus life.

She looked like them. Young, ready to play and party. She didn't mind indulging the idea. But after a while, the beat of arteries got louder than the bass line, and the aromas of sweat, sexual interest and alcohol-induced loss of inhibitions became too distracting, goading her bloodlust. A reminder of her age and unfamiliarity with this environment. She thought she'd done well enough, though. It was the first time she'd ever done something like this on her own.

She excused herself, telling her companions she was going to explore the downtown riverfront. They knew she was with the security detail, and a vampire, so they were less concerned about her going off on her own. She told them she'd meet them back at the Circus.

The riverwalk had plenty of green space and sidewalks, populated by late dog walkers and lovers walking hand in hand. She wandered that area for a while, and leaned on the rail, watching nighttime commercial boat traffic.

Her senses tracked everything around her; humans, their pets, the water, the surrounding businesses and distant road traffic. For so long, she'd stuck close to the preserve, only traveling to and from the places she knew were protected. The Circus was a gift her father had given her. How could she ever have thought Mal hadn't noticed her need for this?

Guess she needed to come up with a really good Father's Day gift this year. Since her mother was involved in any of his decisions related to her and Adan, a good Mother's Day gift wouldn't be amiss, either.

Her mind snapped back from its meanderings, her fingers tightening on the rail. Another vampire was close by. Maybe more than one.

Some years ago, Yvette had earned the Council stamp of approval she needed for the Circus to operate in and travel through different territories, without applying for the time-consuming permissions other vampires had to have. As a part of the Circus, that protection would extend to Ruth, but when it came to a random crossing of paths, vampires didn't necessarily consider that approval at odds with establishing a pecking order with the vampire in question. By what-ever methods best suited them.

She couldn't head back to the others. That could put them in danger. She didn't know these vampires. But she also didn't have any other direction to go, because they had detected her first and were hemming her in, coming from two different directions, nothing but the river in front of her.

Okay, a bluff then. She straightened from the rail and turned, leaning against it and waiting for their arrival with an expression of casual indifference. Willing to be friendly if they were. Telling herself she was ready to handle it if they weren't.

They were both over a century, both made. They had her overpow-ered in strength and speed. Fight skills, too, if they'd spent the last century working on those. But on rare occasions, vampires were lazy about that.

She weighed playing the status card, introducing herself as Lady Ruth instead of Ruth. But that could backfire as easily as it could give her points. Made vampires could be touchy, especially if the born vampire couldn't back up the title with greater strength and power.

She looked good tonight, in her fleece jacket, silk blouse and jeans. She had on a couple strands of earth-colored crystals, and a medicine bag strung on a silk cord. Kohana had made it for her when she was a teenager. It contained a bit of tiger fur, a lion's tooth. A dash of earth from the island, and a few other ingredients Kohana said were a secret. Elisa had added beadwork to the fringe.

She wished she wore one of Merc's feathers. Whether wishful thinking or not, it would feel like an additional layer of protection.

The oncoming vampires were male and female. The energy vibrating off them told her they were in a cruel mood, and ready to play. Which meant they could detect her strength level, and thought she was younger than she was. A common mistake, though it didn't make any difference.

She wasn't challenged on the island. Didn't have to abide this terrible feeling in her gut, of falling short, of being overpowered, her decisions taken away from her.

Hell, one trial and she was ready to tuck her tail and retreat. *Suck it up and deal, bitch.*

The female vampire was blonde and tall, with deceptively pleasant green eyes. Her attractive dress would draw a human male's attention, making it easy for her to secure blood for dinner. The male was working the grunge band look, with long hair, ripped jeans, and a T-shirt that showed off tattoos and muscles. He had a nose stud. The brown eyes locked on Ruth belied the young rocker look. He was the older of the two, probably around a hundred and fifty.

"I'm Ruth," she said with a courteous nod. "Working security with the Circus, under the protection of Lady Yvette."

"Trinidad and Parva." Trinidad nodded to his companion. "We weren't advised a new vampire was traveling with the Circus. Lady Yvette is supposed to let the overlords know that, isn't she?"

"I'm sure it's in process. I'm a very recent addition."

"Or you're passing through, heard about the Circus and are using it for cover."

"That's not what I'm doing," Ruth told him. He was getting too close, leaning in. Parva was on the other side, and reached toward Ruth's straight hair. Ruth slapped her hand away and bared her fangs. She slipped away from the rail and faced them. Trinidad shot Parva an amused look.

"Jumpy, isn't she?"

"Weak." Parva flared her nostrils. "Like a tempting little human morsel."

Ruth chuckled. "Nice try to get a rise out of me. Pretty public place to pick a fight."

"Easy enough to fix."

Parva seized one side of her, Trinidad the other, and before she could orient herself for a decent defense, they were outside a shed in a junkyard. She could hear the riverfront beyond the high fence. Vertigo from the launch over the fence hit her on the back end, but she wrenched away from them, her knives out, and took a fight stance. "You're making a mistake."

"The fledgling has some spirit," Trinidad observed. "I like that. But if you weren't strong enough to be on your own, you shouldn't have been. Maybe we teach you that lesson and Yvette realizes the mistake in hiring you."

Parva lifted a brow. "Want to cry? Want to whine about why everyone won't leave you alone?"

"That's Lady Yvette to you. And no," Ruth said, though the ache in her throat was pricked by the pathetic thought. Which made her angry enough to tighten her grip on the knives. "I want *you* to cry. If I mess up that pretentious outfit you're trying to pull off, that's just a bonus."

Parva's eyes narrowed, and she was in motion. Ruth ducked left and took a glancing hit on the shoulder as Parva grabbed for her and missed. She jammed the knife into the vampire's side as she passed. Ruth moved with her, using Parva's momentum, the howl of pain, as fuel to spin and kick at Trinidad as he closed in. He took the blow rather than dodging it, which thwarted her next move.

He struck her in the face, snapping her head back and putting her on her ass. If she'd been human, the blow would have broken her neck. One of the knives clattered away. The other was still in her fist, and when he swooped in, she went full-on blitz, slashing before her, catching his shirt front, a portion of chest, and twisting upward, aiming for the throat.

Against a comparable opponent, one who wanted to test themselves against her, she could have gained herself more time. But Trinidad fought her the way a vampire who'd gauged the strength of his opponent fought. Like he was fighting a child, shoving into her, knocking her off balance, disarming her because he had the superior speed and strength to do just that.

Parva, the less experienced fighter, had been more concerned about Ruth's sparring abilities. Trinidad wasn't.

As Ruth scrambled across the floor, she noted they had two humans here. They were sprawled in a near unconscious state, next to a table bearing a tin can of wildflowers and an open bottle of wine. Parva and Trinidad had had a romantic dinner. The humans were like dishes knocked to the floor after the meal had been eaten.

Ruth closed her hand on her knife, even as her cold gut told her Trinidad had waited for her to grab it. He kicked the weapon out of her hand to prove the point.

He retrieved it and was back beside her in a blink. When he grabbed a handful of her hair, Ruth shoved at him, rolled, kicked at his leg. His overconfidence and her training worked in her favor, because this time she was at the right angle. She made solid contact with his knee, cracking bone.

He let her go with a hiss, but plunged the knife toward her face.

She ducked her head enough that it missed the vulnerable eye and jugular, but the blade scored her cheek and shoulder. Parva pounced on her, grabbing her from behind and arching Ruth back so forcefully, her spine complained. Ruth shoved backward and knocked them both to the ground, Ruth landing on top of Parva.

"Stop fucking fighting," Trinidad snapped, tossing the knife on the table. "If you just give in, we can enjoy the evening and send you back to the Circus."

"I was enjoying my evening before you arrived," Ruth snarled. "I don't care to enjoy it...with...you."

Parva locked her arm around Ruth's head. "Another move and I will break your neck," she said. "You can lie here like a dead fish while we play. Like them."

She turned Ruth toward the two humans, giving her a closer look. The couple were naked, enjoyed by the vampires sexually as well as for food, because vampires didn't mind putting the two together when the opportunity presented itself. Though usually it was a one-on-one seduction, and the vampire left his or her meal with a hazy memory of pleasure, like a dream. No worse off than before.

There is an important difference between treating a random human source as a meal, and turning them into a victim. Though many vampires would not agree with me, the latter has a cost to your soul as well. We don't have to be the monsters we are believed to be, but we are well capable of it.

Mal, teaching her how to find a blood source when she was away from the island and not somewhere like William and Matthew's, where there were servants to provide sustenance.

The two vampires had overfed. Not fatally, but the humans would definitely be out of it for a while. When they shook off the compulsion, they'd believe they'd been mugged. And raped. The latter would be true. They'd tried to hold onto one another, their limp hands still loosely laced together. Their wedding bands matched. A married couple. She felt sick to her stomach.

"We don't want to treat you like them. Don't be a bitch. You're pretty. We like you. We just want to play."

Parva's tone had become soothing, seductive. They wanted to prove they were in charge and could overpower her, but once she accepted that, they'd probably get along just fine. As long as she did what they wanted.

Almost every vampire in every territory faced such "games." She'd been protected from them, but she knew they existed. What's more, dealing with it, accepting it, was part of being an adult vampire, "independent" within that structure.

"I think we could keep her," Trinidad said. "She's so young. Why did her parents let her out of their sight? Maybe they didn't want her."

"That's all right. We want her." Parva wound Ruth's dark straight hair around her fingers. Ruth had gone still, pretending that she was considering compliance—as she fought the chilling knowledge that it might have to move from pretense to reality. "If Yvette would let you go, you could become our pet. I could put you on a lovely little leash, get you a collar sewn in these beads you like. Oh, look at this."

Ruth grabbed for it, but Parva had already snapped the cord of the medicine bag and was examining the beadwork. She shoved Ruth at Trinidad, and he held her as his companion tied the medicine bag around her own neck.

"No, it doesn't go with the dress." Parva took it back off and opened the bag, dumping the contents in her hands. Her nose wrinkled and she tossed the bits of fur and dirt away from her distastefully.

Ruth had cherished it since Kohana had died, feeling like it was infused with the spirit of the stern Sioux, everything she'd loved about him.

They were within arm's reach of the table where Trinidad had left her knife. With a scream of rage, Ruth seized it and turned on him. She slashed the blade across his thigh, cutting through denim, flesh and the femoral artery. Blood spurted and gushed over his jeans. He cursed, letting her go to put his hands on the wound.

She didn't try to get away. She was right on him, making him pedal back into the table. It scraped across the floor as he landed on it. When she stabbed his face, she hit an eye, rupturing it. Roaring in pain, he shoved her away and rolled to the floor, landing on the limp doll humans.

She pivoted and went after Parva.

Parva's face had gone blank with shock. Ruth only had seconds to take advantage of it. She stabbed the knife into Parva's heart as many times as her vampire speed would allow her, which was about eight before Trinidad was back on her.

He yanked her away from his blood-soaked comrade and disarmed Ruth again. His arms locked around her throat and upper body as he lifted her off her feet.

"You're going to die, little bitch. No one is going to miss you."

"That...is...not...true." She caught a glimpse of his gleaming fangs, extended to full length. Her struggles increased, but to no avail. His fangs tore into her throat, and blood gushed as he ripped open the carotid and shredded the muscle and tissue around it. Then he dropped her, shoving her to the ground onto her hands and knees.

She'd made a good accounting of herself. Gideon would be proud of her.

The fuck he would. He'd say, *"You're not dead. Why aren't you still fighting?"* She wasn't done until she had no other options. She could still move, so she had them.

Ruth scrambled across the ground, headed for the knife. When she grabbed it and turned, she tried to keep pressure on her neck with her other hand.

She'd assumed Trinidad was fucking with her again, giving her a moment to let her think she could win, but then she saw he had bigger concerns.

His feet were off the floor, Merc's ruthless grip on his throat. Her incubus's black and white wings were spread, showing her all those lightning bolts. They matched the hellfire in his eyes.

Despite the stabbing, Parva was back up. Ruth gave the female vampire props for loyalty as she made a clumsy attempt to rush Merc. Merc lifted a hand in her direction. Magic crackled from his fingers, spinning out like a thrown net. It covered Parva and dropped her to the ground, where she writhed in agony. Ruth smelled burning flesh.

She also heard the crunch when Trinidad's cervical vertebrae broke under Merc's grip. When he dropped the male, both vampires could barely move, but they were doing their best to crawl away.

Merc moved to Ruth, who was still on her ass, trying to contain the wound in her throat. Removing her destroyed shirt, he tore it into strips and tied them around the damage, then cupped his hand over the makeshift pressure bandage.

"You should not have gone off on your own." His expression was cold as a glacier.

"Story of my life," was what she felt like saying. Instead she rasped, "Need blood. Human. Not Circus. Not...them."

She dipped her head toward the couple. They'd already had too much taken from them. She also didn't want anyone at the Circus to see her like this. She was fighting anger, shame, a whole trashcan of emotions, all bad.

Merc picked her up. That toxic mix made her angry about that, too, but his arms tightened, and he gave her a look that settled her. Then he was aloft. He must have cloaked both of them somehow, because no one freaked as he passed over the riverfront. It took her thirty long seconds to find what she wanted. She pointed with a trembling, bloodstained finger.

He landed in the alley next to the Dumpster where a homeless man slept by himself, camouflaged by blankets and shadows. His blood was going to be a little boozy, but he would do, and he was sleeping deep. Merc eased her down to the ground next to him.

"This first." Though she made a noise of protest, Merc wasn't tolerating any refusal. He sliced open his wrist and put it to her mouth.

"My blood rejuvenated you last time. Let it do so again, then you can use this man to supplement it."

The allure of it was too much to resist. She latched on, trying not to use her fangs on him, and swallowed several rich gulps. Thank heavens Trinidad hadn't damaged her throat so badly she couldn't swallow. Great Father, what was it in Merc's blood? She could feel it rushing through her within the first few seconds, telling her its healing properties were going to get right to work.

She made herself stop. "Please go...move humans." She didn't want Parva and Trinidad to recover and take it out on them. Reading his face, she added, "Don't kill...vampires."

"I can do as I please." He touched her bent knee. "I've not wanted to kill someone so much in a very long time. It's difficult to resist."

He meant it. With the least word of encouragement from her, they'd be gone. It would be nothing to him. But he'd told her the dangers of that to his control.

She also understood it. Over and above the annual kill, the Vampire Council allowed a vampire to take up to twelve human lives a year—geographically dispersed and with a reasonable time lapse between kills. It was considered a compromise between a vampire's "natural" urges and the need to keep a low profile in the human world.

At territory meetings at Lord Marshall's, she'd met vampires who took full advantage of that rule, and she understood why her father had taught her to be wary of them. When lives were treated like the number of cookies one could indulge from the cookie jar, something got broken in the head.

One annual kill was more than enough for her. She dreaded it every year.

"What they did was not...prohibited." A whisper was the best she could do right now, but he could hear her. "Me defending myself, you helping me, also okay. Killing them, not okay. Yvette has to tell overlord...then Region Master. It's a whole thing. Merc...please. Take care of the humans."

"I will be back." He brushed his knuckles along her cheek, then took off, his wingbeats sending a welcome breeze across her clammy forehead.

She put her hand on the homeless man's shoulder, summoning as much of a push as she could to keep him asleep. She went right for the throat, because she needed the rush of blood into her mouth, the gulping swallows. She felt his heartbeat accelerate as his brain registered the threat. She soothed it with her compulsion. *I won't cause lasting harm. I just need a meal...*

When she had what she needed, she fell back onto her backside next to him. She petted him absently, a *thank you*, even as she fished out a twenty and tucked it into one of his pockets to find later. Maybe he'd buy himself a night or two in a shelter. Or more booze. She wouldn't judge. It took a lot to get through any life, let alone one that had taken the unfortunate turns his obviously had. Whether from his own choices or others, everybody was capable of fucking up.

The alley smelled of noxious things, but the homeless man's shirt was mostly clean. He must have been able to wash his clothes recently.

The wound was mending. She stayed still, helping her body focus on that most important priority. Merc's blood tingled through her, along with the human donor's. Would Merc's alone have been enough? An interesting thought.

One she shouldn't dwell upon. He'd overridden her protest to give her blood, but with the effect it was proving itself to have on her, it would be too easy to take advantage. Their relationship was way too tenuous, and if he had one of his mean moments, where he accused her of using him for that...that might hurt worse than anything Trinidad and Parva had done to her.

When feathers brushed her ankles, she opened her eyes to find her angel incubus resting on his heels in front of her, his wings angled forward on the outside of her knees and hips, offering her a shield. He wasn't just using his wings to do that. The noxious fumes in the alley had been replaced by that interesting musk he could put out. There were hints of flowers in it, chocolate, sunshine, soft rains.

"Wow." She cleared her throat. "You can turn that on or off at will. Without the sexual component."

"It's there. You're just not in a condition to appreciate it."

"I must be almost dead then."

He didn't smile. She didn't either. A rage was waiting on the other side of this, and a despair and sadness that would swamp her. She couldn't avoid the truth she'd faced tonight.

She needed to go home.

She thought of the preserve, her tree in the lion's habitat. Her books. The daily routine. The safety. Her father's protection.

No, damn it. Stop that shit. Her weak ass was staying at the Circus. She had to learn how to handle this. How could she protect and defend all her father had built, if she couldn't protect and defend herself?

She couldn't. That was the beginning and end of it. She pulled herself out of her head. "Are Parva and Trinidad alive?"

"Yes. Not because they deserve it. I put the humans at a hospital ER entrance."

"Thank you." She laid her hand on top of his, still clasping her knee. She traced the dips between his knuckles, the veins his grip raised. He watched her touch him, his expression like when he'd looked at her breasts. Simply for pleasure, to enjoy affection. That was why it had seemed new to him. She'd bet on it.

"So you came to find me. Thanks."

"I was joining you for live music, food. And karaoke."

"I'd picked out a duet for us. 'Just Give Me the Reason,' Pink and Nate Ruess. We're bent, not broken. Appropriate, right?"

For the first time, she noticed the alley had graffiti art sprayed across the brick wall. *Sunlight is married to darkness.* The tagger had signed it *H2O.*

"I get so tired. Does that happen to you, Merc? Do you ever get so very tired that you just want to lie down and not get up?" Let life turn her into a road that others traveled, while she just laid there and felt their passage. Endured their passage.

Merc grip tightened on her. He could use crushing strength on someone like Trinidad, but he wasn't using it on her. "When I was a boy, in Russia. There was a songbird I would see in the trees, during the warmer months. He had a red spot on his head that helped me recognize him. He offended me. How weak and fragile he was, yet he survived, thrived. Sang.

"But then I saw his beauty. It helped me, the way he lived, no matter that his life was so short. His presence added to what was inside my soul. Changed it. Very little, then. But when Marcellus found me, the memory...it changed me more. Because I *could* change then."

She gazed at their linked fingers, afraid if she lifted her eyes, he would stop talking to her. Giving her what was deep inside of him. Only when the silence drew out did she speak. "My father told me those we think are weak and fragile, but who affect us, always deserve a second look."

She expected Mal had been trying to reassure her about being weak in the vampire world. But when he said it, he'd been looking at Elisa, and Ruth had understood the message. Nothing that could get inside you and stay like that could really be weak or fragile.

It shares the same existence with us. Which binds us together.

She wanted to tell Merc that, and maybe she would, later. If they shared a mind link, she could say it in his head.

At times, though, Merc had an uncanny understanding of what she was thinking, where her head was at. He also seemed to be able to find her, the way a vampire could find a first marked servant. She thought of the day she'd met with Yvette and Lyssa. When she'd "heard" him, it had been in her head, and Adan couldn't hear it.

"Merc...can you talk in my mind?"

"Yes," he said simply. "Sometimes. When I focus the right way. The ability comes and goes."

The shock of the confirmation was a welcome distraction from the other things she was dealing with. "How about my thoughts? Can you hear them?"

"No." He frowned. "But I can feel them, in a sense. And I can follow that feeling to where you are. Again, when I focus. It seems like something I have to practice, and I haven't had much interest in that. Until recently."

Her toes curled in her shoes. *Stop being stupid and romantic,* she told herself. *Near death experiences make you mushy.*

"You're *not* tired. You don't allow yourself to be tired." He took her back to her earlier admission, and lifted his free hand to touch her face. "You fought well and you're strong. But if you need a moment to recoup your strength, I'll carry you."

"How long is a moment?"

The silver in his sclera glinted, sending a ripple of light over the black blood irises. Rather than answering, he picked her up off the alley floor, cradling her in his arms. "You smell like human urine."

"You could have been chivalrous and put your shirt down for me to sit on."

"I like this shirt."

She wouldn't chuckle. It would hurt. She rested her head on his chest as he took to the air. Looking down, she saw the homeless man rouse. He lifted a tentative hand and she smiled at him. She imagined what he was seeing, Merc's wings against a city-lit sky, her hair streaming over her shoulders and Merc's arm.

"You didn't cloak."

"A person like him deserves hope. I may not be an angel, but he can look at me and believe they exist."

Then they were high above everything. Up here she could hold onto better emotions, but the despairing feelings were chasing her. As the blood restored her, the frustration welled up, needing an outlet.

She curled her fingers into a claw against his chest. "Can you find us a place where I can do some screaming? Maybe beat my fists against something I can't hurt?" A dead tree, a big rock buried halfway in the ground. She'd broken her knuckles against several at home when this anger came upon her. The boon of vampirism was the agonizing pain could swallow up the emotions and make them manageable, before the injury conveniently healed itself.

Merc landed them in an empty field, nothing around but patches of wood and distant houses. As he let her move away from him, Ruth stripped her ruined shirt from her throat, and stretched her arms out to the sky. Looking at the stars, she turned in circles, making them wheel above her, or seem that way, even though she was the one turning. She didn't run, scream, punch and hurt things like she'd expected. That was probably good. Her throat wasn't pretty, but it wasn't open and bleeding. She didn't want to reverse that.

She wanted something different. A challenge, something that reinforced what Merc had told her. That she was strong. Mighty. Not just in the ways that her world thought mattered.

She knew what would do it. But she'd think it through for a few minutes. She didn't want him to think it was an impulsive gesture. Plus, he would take some convincing. He'd already proven that when they'd broached the topic before.

"Going bra-only will draw some attention at the Circus." Plus it was stained with her blood. She'd worn a flesh-colored one tonight with her outfit. "I might have to dash through a store, grab a top and leave some money on the counter."

In answer, he took off his shirt, pulling it free of his wings in a practiced move, and handed it to her. "No more urine and garbage stains around," he noted.   .

She suppressed a smile, enjoying the ripple of muscles. Studying the hemmed slits in the shirt's back, she wondered if Charlie handled the alteration. Picturing Merc with a needle and thread, or curled over a sewing machine, was too mindboggling. She'd ask another time. "Why do you and Marcellus bother with a shirt at all?"

"One less thing to conjure when we have to make the wings disappear from public view. But it's an annoyance and another reason he prefers Legion wear. When I'm alone, I tend not to wear a shirt, either."

"Can't say I object." She saw the surprise in his eyes. "No one flirts with you, do they?"

"Most consider it inadvisable."

She held the shirt in her hands, feeling his warmth. When she pulled it on, she liked the teasing touch of air where the wing slits were. Maybe he'd let her keep it, even if he liked it.

Time to throw it out there and see what happened. "You're always hungry, Merc. That's got to be kind of miserable. I want you to feed on me. The way we discussed."

She'd startled him, but he recovered, his eyes narrowing. "Hunger is not as miserable as the alternative. Many go through life hungry without letting it change their course, their goals or ambitions."

"Like who?"

"Super models."

She rolled her eyes. "I mean it, Merc. Please. I need...I want something that reinforced what you said. What I know inside me. I *am* fucking strong. I'm capable of not just being cared for. I can care for someone else, in a way that most can't. I do have that strength."

"And if you're wrong? If it drains you? You were badly wounded only moments ago."

"Your blood is healing me." Remarkably fast, compared to her normal healing rate, what she would have expected with only the homeless man's blood. "Worst case scenario, I'm weak and tired for a little while. I'll double up on blood packs at the Circus. It's not going to kill me. You don't have to worry about that."

"You believe it can't kill you because a vampire has never tried it before."

"The things that can kill us aren't subtle. Fire. Decapitation. Wooden stake."

"Delilah virus. Ennui."

She was surprised he knew about those, but he checked into things that interested him. He'd made it clear that vampires had recently made the list. A thought which brought on another surge of unwise feelings.

"Ennui is a disease that leads to a vampire taking their own life. Not even related. And Lord Brian found a cure to the Delilah virus that mostly works."

If one was okay with sacrificing their servant. Most vampires were. You could get another servant, after all.

The sarcasm didn't make it any less true or terrible.

"You're missing the most important point," Merc said.

"What's that?"

"The decision isn't yours."

"I'm not missing it," she grated. "It's why we're having the discussion. I'm asking you to have that fuck-the-world moment where we embrace something that others believe can't happen, shouldn't happen. Defy the odds. Believe things can be different. I need that."

Her voice faltered, her fists clenching. "Will you go down that road with me? Will you be my friend tonight, the one who joins me in that last inadvisable tequila shot because we believe we can handle what comes after, even if we can't? Or are you going to be fucking sensible and responsible?" She shot him a look. "That's not what brought you to my island. It's not why you're still standing there now. Is it?"

CHAPTER FIFTEEN

*R*uth's need pushed upon Merc. He knew what she wanted, and she'd fired the arrow as if she could see the center target of what he himself wanted. He still wanted to kill the two vampires in the most painful way possible. He was feeling possessive and strongly protective of her. Vulnerable to her desires.

He hadn't been feeding the way he should. He was supposed to take measured, evenly spaced amounts from what local prey was available, to manage his hunger and protect their lives.

However, he'd learned that projecting the demeanor that made others fear him, then pushing enough incubus vibes their way to get an airborne mix of sex-fear energy, resulted in an approximation of nourishment that patched him through. Snacks, so to speak. Sometimes he preferred that to the fight for self-restraint he had to call upon when actually feeding.

Yes, Ruth. I do get tired, too.

He wasn't in the mood to pull on the focusing effort to put that in her head, like he'd described, but he thought she could read it from him. It was probably why she asked the questions she did, as if they knew one another more intimately than they did. Technically.

With a normal incubus, the struggle to restrain oneself eventually reached a point where the incubus lost. The need to kill and feed, kill and feed, never stop, won out. And they were executed.

However, he wasn't a normal incubus. Perhaps because of that angel blood, his hunger war could conceivably stretch into infinity.

No, it wouldn't. He wasn't at that fatalistic decision yet, but one day, he would be. He could already foresee that his rebellion against having anything dictate terms to him, even his own body, would start to seem like a pointless exercise. His interest in the world wouldn't disappear, but the endlessness of the struggle, the way it kept him from trusting or making any meaningful connections with others, would take its toll.

There were days he thought he'd been better off as a feral child, who didn't have time to think or feel those kinds of things.

The hunger was both worse and more manageable around her. She was challenging his restraint. She wanted him to let go. Feed fully. Sate himself. For a few blessed moments, she wanted him not to feel hungry.

It was a trap, the wrong move. Even if it didn't go badly, it would have to be a one-time thing. And in the short term, the hunger would be far worse, because he'd have to rein it back in and teach himself to do without satiation again. He'd had that experience too recently, with the Trad's green smoke.

But would it be the same? Somehow, it felt like maybe it wouldn't.

Before she'd put on his shirt, she'd put it to her face, rubbed her cheek against it, stirring him. Now, she took it off again and set it aside before facing him. She was going to push the issue, because that was what she did, his disobedient, willful, beautiful vampire.

The possessive told him how close he was to losing the battle to her.

Her breasts quivered in the hold of her bloodstained bra, her dark hair rippling over her bare shoulders, the jeans sitting below her hip bones. Her dark eyes were upon him. Challenging, no fear. Wanting.

He saw her wounds were healing, faster than her normal rate. Because of his blood. He understood why she was reluctant to take it, even when he insisted. But if he were her Master, he'd want her to do so. Would require it of her, to let him care for her.

She was upset about the attack, feeling out of control of things, daring the world to knock her down. Would he let her take the risk, just to help her feel more in control? A foolish, foolish decision, but one he understood too well.

He had an unreadable face to most, but there were those who'd spent enough time around him, like Yvette and Marcellus, who could read some of the hidden pages of the book.

She shouldn't have that ability. As she came closer, she shed the shoes and jeans, and stood before him in her bra and panties. Thin garments that showed curves and points, intimate crevices. Her toes curled against the ground. She kept her hands at her sides, not reaching for him.

She was offering herself as a submissive would. Waiting on his decision. She didn't lower her eyes, though, letting him see the need, the desire, the belief that this would soothe the ache, the storm inside her. Inside them both.

She submitted and challenged him at once, a rare combination. An alpha female in certain circumstances, a submissive in others. Both for him, at least in this instance.

He knew how to read mindless desire, knew if the woman he faced was beyond sensible inhibition. Ruth was, and yet her sharp intelligence hadn't abandoned her. She'd brought this up before, the offer to feed him fully. Since then, she'd been pondering it. It wasn't a passing impulse.

He'd been pondering it, too.

He put a hand on her shoulder, thumb caressing her collar bone. He knew she could hear the rush of blood in his arteries. Did she know that sexual energy had a similar pulse? Even at rest, he could call it forth from any female within his range. She wouldn't be able to resist its pull. She'd cling to him, beg him for more as he drank from her, until life slipped away, leaving the physical scent of her desires in his nose, the evidence of it bathing his cock.

Her hard, final shudder would find an echo inside him, rippling through his blood, muscles and something deeper. A soul-deep reaction to her giving him everything.

Hadn't Ruth suggested the true drug might not be her death, but the female's full surrender to him? An incubus delighted in taking every drop of life energy, the kill. But was Merc seeking something deeper?

He didn't have to use compulsion with Ruth. He could feed until he was sated while she stayed fully conscious of how deeply he was drinking. She wouldn't fear it. Which would prove if fear really was the drug it had once been to him.

The homeless man's blood, as well as his own, was restoring her. She hadn't lied about that. Her trauma wouldn't make her weaker than normal. Sensing it, feeling the strength of her heartbeat, seeing the color in her skin, the determination in her eyes, peeled away his final resistance.

He removed his jeans. Her eyes were lowered, and her lips pressed together as he revealed his erection.

"Lift your chin."

As she did, he felt her gaze on the shift of muscle across his upper torso. He leaned in, putting his mouth to her throat. The skin was tender and pink, but able to receive his ministrations. He tasted the blood that had stained her skin, and felt her reaction.

From her, he'd learned how sensitive the area was to vampires. He explored that, tracing the veins and soft female flesh with his tongue, the edge of his teeth. Whenever he scraped her, she shuddered, but she held still, fighting back the obvious desire to sway toward him.

"Try to get away from me, Ruth. Do your best to fight me."

He wove the magic around her, drawing out her arousal. A woman's body was a sexual instrument from head to toe, and he'd played every note, explored every melody and arrangement. When he'd had to learn to feed without killing, he'd forced himself to focus on the same tedious pattern, so the lure of something new and wondrous didn't pull him in and risk his food's life.

He'd stopped looking for a new song to hear, but this vampire female was offering one. Hadn't she played her own music for him, through the earbuds? Sharing it with him.

Ruth broke away and made it several steps. He grabbed her around the waist, and she turned in his grip, sinuous as a snake. Her feet found his thigh, kicked the corded muscle, shoved off. She landed on her back with a thud, and he let her scramble up and take a fighting stance again. He circled her, dove in, spun her around, took her punches, her kicks, slid away from them, caressing her body as he did it. Testing her strength, how restored she actually was. Not as much as she claimed, of course. But enough.

He brought her to the ground, putting her on her knees, his body pressed behind her.

"Spread your thighs for me."

When she resisted, he knocked them apart and took her all the way to the ground, pinning her down, his wings spread over them. "Fight me," he said harshly. "Don't accept."

She did fight. Not as tactically well as she normally would have, but she made up for it in persistence. She fought and fought, until tears were on her face and breath sobbed in her throat. It did things to him, seeing those tears, feeling that pain.

He leaned in, put his mouth to her cheek, sliding along to her ear, her neck. Then down, between her shoulder blades, where her wings would be, if she was like him. He pressed his cock against her ass, played in the seam, reached under her and found her damp cunt. She whimpered as he slid his fingers into her, caressing her perineum with a thumb, an easy stroke that had her struggling even more, the sensations rolling over her.

"You can't get away from me, can you?"

She shook her head.

"I'm completely in control. Aren't I?"

A pause. Then slowly, a nod.

"That's something they couldn't do, those two vampires. For them to be completely in control, you had to *want* them to be. Even if they overpowered you, put you in chains, what you are giving me... it is a giving. It can't be taken. Lift your hips. Rub yourself against me."

She complied, her fingers curled into the earth on either side of her. She still had anger. But he had an outlet for that.

"Push yourself down on me. You'll have to work for your pleasure. For your request. You serve me. I don't serve you."

The force behind the words, the message it sent, had a powerful effect. He felt it through her trembling torso and thighs as she positioned the mouth of her sex on his cock. He angled it for her with a hand curled around the base, and then she was pushing down on him, those lovely buttocks flexing, quivering, as she made it to the hilt. She had a gorgeous ass, smooth, tight, with the right sweetheart shape. She paused, gasping, shuddering.

His voice was thick. "I didn't tell you to stop. Fuck me, Ruth. Earn your pleasure. You get no free passes from me."

That little whimper in her throat again, a curl of her lip, an

217

intriguing half snarl. Then she was moving again. Up, down, up, down. The bliss of it worked through him. It was time. No more hesitation.

Either he was being unbelievably stupid, or they were doing something meant to be.

He opened himself to it, the sexual energy spiraling from her, that had spiked as he commanded her. The first touch of it was indescribable, the unique, pure uncompelled taste of the woman he was using for nourishment.

Who was *offering* herself for his nourishment. He gathered it in, watching her spine arch, her buttocks tuck in, lift, her breasts pushed against the forest floor, fingers still seeking purchase. Putting his hands on her waist, he took over, bringing her down on him, lifting her up the length of his cock and bringing her down again. Increasing speed and force, once again showing her just how helpless she was against his strength. The right kind of helpless. She'd offered, wanting that, and he'd taken. Given.

As he expected, the lesson increased her sexual arousal, her desire to serve. He wanted a full, fucking Thanksgiving feast, as other Circus members celebrated it, while he stood on the periphery, his hungers never abating. Never full.

"Tell me what I am, Ruth. What do you want me to be?"

A pause. This was a stumbling block, so he said what also needed to be said.

"If you could trust me, if you could have what you wanted, if I could be what you wanted, what would I be?"

He leaned over her, bringing her up against his chest with an arm banded over her breasts as he thrust into her. Pushing against her slim thighs, he spread them wider, taking her deeper, higher. Her energy was feeding him through his very pores, and when she spoke, it was dessert and the main entrée in the same shot, the best possible wine accompanying them.

"Master."

"Whose Master?"

"M-mine."

"Yours. I would own you, Ruth. Every thought and feeling mine to know. Every beat of your heart."

Every moment of her life his to enjoy. Honor. Protect.

He didn't say it out loud, but just like him making her say the words that increased her sexual energy to that feast level he sought, him thinking the words increased his intent to feed from her very soul.

He was in new territory, and he wasn't sensible enough not to drown himself in it. In her.

"Yes," she whispered, and tears were trickling over his knuckles, her curtain of hair brushing them.

He took her back to the ground, pressing her there while pushing himself deeper. He was causing discomfort, but drawing pain from her in service to his pleasure motivated her. She could handle pain. She'd proven it for the wrong reasons. He'd have her prove it for the right ones.

"Take, my lord," she whispered. "Take everything you need. Take... it all. Please don't stop. Please."

She'd added the please. Remembering she couldn't command him.

He could feel her body drawing on deeper reserves. Physical reserves to serve his hunger, and his hunger was spreading out, growing, taking every grain from the field, every apple from the tree, everything he'd denied himself for far too long.

The normal alarm bells went off, but instead of reining them in, he took the risk and ignored them, pushed past. Brought her up close to climax, again and again, not letting her go over, feeding on that energy as it grew richer, denser. When he finally tipped up the glass and found the bottom, she was still with him. Her cries weak, her body limp in his grasp.

But she was alive.

He let himself release, clasping her against his body, taking them into the air and pumping into her with the use of his wings. She'd seemed to love that before, and as she rested in his arms, her head dropped back against his. "Please..." she begged in a near whisper.

"Please what?"

"Please...Master."

He put his hand on her clitoris, and gave it the heated, electric energy that made the massage even more intense. Her tissues were drenched under his manipulation.

"Oh God...I can't."

"You are mine," he told her. "You will. Come for me."

Her climax exploded in her at last, and her scream vibrated

through the forest, spooking several roosting birds to fly in a confused spin around them. With shaky fingers, she reached out to brush their wings, the way she liked to touch his.

She liked to fly. He wished he could give her a set of wings of her own, but he'd give her the next best thing. He'd take her flying whenever she wished.

For the first time in a very, very long time, he was not...as hungry. Being in her company, feeling that way, only made what they'd just experienced together more potent.

The climax was still coming through her in waves, but she had no more strength to cry out. He treasured the whimpers as much. Only when he was certain she'd experienced every last spasm of the release did he bring them back to earth.

Easing out of her, he sat them down against a tree, holding her between his legs. He lifted her face to see her condition, and found she was pale, her cheeks drawn, eyes dazed. But there was a vague smile on her lips.

He stroked her, traced her mouth and throat. His possessiveness had a new level, more complicated. More...permanent.

Committed.

The significance had him pausing, because it connected to something he'd downplayed, denied. Scoffed at. He suspected he was being delusional, caught up in the euphoria of the moment. Making more of it than it was.

He could speak to Marcellus about it if he was willing to be more... open, than he usually was with the angel. It would take some thinking about.

First, he had to tend to her. Because several minutes later, they found she couldn't stand.

At all.

⁓

"So I guess beyond the utter stupidity of the risk you took with her, you didn't think that we have a show tomorrow night and she's a member of the security team and Clara's protection detail? Dollar will be minus a team member."

"I'll be fine by then." Ruth was sitting in a chair in Yvette's tent, where Merc had placed her. His hand rested on the top of the chair next to her shoulder. "I'm healing faster than it looks like I am."

Lady Yvette gave her a censorious look. "Be quiet. That's an order. Do you understand?"

Ruth's lips tightened, but she did respond appropriately. "Yes, my lady."

Merc spoke before Yvette could continue to tear into him. "I made a decision, based on Ruth's request and a measured evaluation of the situation. She may appear physically worse for wear, but she's correct. She'll heal. It's something we won't do regularly."

The look he shot at Ruth held the same warning Yvette's had. She pressed her lips together, with enough rebellion in the expression to intrigue him, but he turned back to his current priority.

Marcellus was standing a few paces away. The angel had so far remained silent.

"She's a smart female and convinced me of the acceptable risks," Merc continued. "If I have someone I can feed upon, to ease my hungers, without causing irreparable harm..." He locked gazes with Yvette. "If you'd had to endure blood hunger for centuries, how would that have impacted what you have learned and accomplished?"

A muscle twitched in her jaw. She looked toward Marcellus. "Are you going to weigh in on this, or are you playing statue?"

His eyes glinted with a warning of his own, but the Legion captain lifted a shoulder. "I will speak to Merc alone." He tilted his head toward the yurt opening. "We will be back."

As he moved past Yvette, Marcellus stopped and spoke to her. He was using sound interference, because even with his sharpened senses, Merc couldn't hear the low volume exchange. Surprise flitted through Yvette's eyes. Then the angel exited.

Merc drew Ruth's gaze to him. "Rest and do what Yvette and Charlie tell you to do. I have things I want to discuss with Marcellus as well."

The healer had been waiting outside, but when Marcellus left, she stepped inside, her attention going to Ruth.

"I would stick my tongue out at you," Ruth said to Merc, "but I'm too tired to argue. I'll punch you in the face later."

As he gripped her arm, her fingers curled into a fist. He put his hand over it. "You won't raise a hand to me without suffering the consequences."

"Or enjoying them," she said unrepentantly. She tried to lift her other hand and put it to his face. It didn't work. She was too weak. He helped her do it. She stroked his face, an almost tender gesture. Before her, it had been easy to count up the number of times a woman had touched him that way.

Zero.

"I'm all right," she said. "You know that, right? It was amazing."

He was aware of Yvette and Charlie's attention, but in this moment, all that mattered was the truth between them. "Yes. I do. Thank you, Ruth. I'm grateful."

She blinked at the formal response. He squeezed her hand, returning it to her lap, and looked toward Yvette, his gaze moving between her and Charlie. "Care for her." Then he pivoted and followed Marcellus.

"Did that little bastard just order me to do something?" Yvette noted, her brow arching.

"He's not that little," Ruth muttered.

The healer suppressed a smile as Yvette shot Ruth another reproving look. Ruth closed her eyes, dipping her head. "Sorry, my lady."

"Hmm." Yvette snorted.

"So I'm okay, but I'm thinking it will make Lady Yvette feel better if she hears you say it, Charlie."

Charlie gazed at her with that intent, focused look that seemed at odds with her physical blindness. "She was severely weakened," she told her Mistress, "but with more blood and a prolonged sleep, she'll be restored. He did her no permanent damage."

"Look at me, Ruth."

Ruth wanted to ooze to the floor and embrace her post-dawn coma a couple hours early. However, at the Circus Mistress's sharp command, her eyes snapped open and her spine straightened.

"It seems your experience with the Georgia territory vampires earlier in the evening didn't make an impression. So let me point out what should be all the more obvious. Being as vulnerable as you are right now, even for a short time, could be catastrophic around other vampires."

Ruth pressed her lips together. "It was an in-the-moment thing, as risks like this sometimes have to be. Now that we know the results, we can plan better. And when I'm with him, I'm as safe as I could possibly be. What did Marcellus say to you?" she asked, an attempt to change the subject.

The Circus Mistress gave her a neutral look. "If he'd wanted you to know that, he would have addressed all of us. I'll leave you in Charlie's hands. While I take issue with Merc's delivery, I don't disagree with the order. Follow her direction and restore your strength. We don't employ shirkers around here."

She marched out of the tent.

This time Charlie didn't hide a smile. "You should see the face you just made in auric form."

Ruth sighed. "It sucks to be the youngest immortal in the room."

She wondered what Marcellus wanted to talk to Merc about. And vice versa. But she didn't feel like she had to worry about him. The others might think Merc's behavior today was a big change, but Ruth was beginning to believe that shift had happened well before today. In his rare moment of vulnerability, Merc had as much as said so. Today was the day that change became manifest to the world around him. And she was a part of it. She had to believe that.

Even if she was falling for an immortal whose mind and plans were still mostly a mystery to her.

~

Marcellus took flight when Merc emerged from the tent. Merc had to maintain a swift but not insane pace to keep up with him, but they were still moving faster than a mortal eye could track.

He'd always assumed Marcellus, being pure angel, could move faster than him, since Merc stubbornly asserted he wasn't much of an angel at all. But that didn't feel as true today, not with the revelations he was having simmering in his mind.

He needed to stop calling them that. *Revelation* was too dramatic. Too biblical. *Jumble of thoughts*. That was better.

When they kept ascending, far past the clouds, Merc realized where they were going. When Merc banked, uncertain, Marcellus paused and gestured him forward until they hovered together, looking toward their destination.

The silver and ivory spires of the Citadel pierced the seven layers of heaven. It was headquarters for the Legion angels, the warrior class who fought the enemies of the Goddess. Right now, they were in third heaven, Machanon, which overlooked the Garden of Eden. At this distance it was a green valley cut by a glittering river, the two trees of lore arched over it, branches intertwined like lovers.

While battle strategy and other Legion work was done in Shamain, the level closest to Earth, Machanon was an oasis of sorts, a place for the angels who regularly had to fight the Dark Ones to take their ease.

Merc had had to accompany Marcellus here in the past, but he'd taken up a post on one of the available turrets, keeping his distance from the other occupants.

Fortunately, Marcellus turned them toward Eden. Merc followed him to the bank of the river. Marcellus crouched by the gurgling water, his dark green glossy wings unfurled as he dipped in a hand. A small school of fish leaped out, sliding across his forearm, and continuing with the current.

Merc stayed standing. "This has never felt like home. Nothing has ever felt like home."

"You have never set foot in the Citadel. Perching in the spires like a wary vulture does not count."

"You think putting my feet on the flagstones would make it feel like home to me?"

"I think when you are born without one, home is what you build throughout your life. Even when you are born with one, a soul may find it has to move and find another home, better suited to what life and experience bring."

"Why did you bring me here?"

"It felt right for whatever words, whatever truth, you wish to speak to me." Marcellus glanced at him. Waiting.

"You said you had something to discuss with me first."

Marcellus raised a brow. "Do you want to play games with me today, Merc? Your vampire would feel better having you near while she recovers."

Merc pressed his lips together. "What you call games, I view differently."

"Yes." Marcellus gazed at him. "Survival behavior. But for a while now, there's been something going on behind it. Do you trust me enough to show it to me? Come down here. You are giving me a crick in my neck."

"You could always stand back up." But Merc dropped to his heels next to him and, emulating Marcellus, he dipped his hands into the water. It wasn't every day one touched the waters in the Garden of Eden. It tingled over his skin, telegraphing its healing and regenerative properties. Maybe that helped him say the words that had been inside him a while. A wary act of trust.

"For years you have championed me, not just with others, but against myself, when I only wanted to embrace the darkest part of my incubus nature. In the first years, I hoped to do something that would force your hand, make you kill me."

"That was a difficult time. You almost accomplished it."

"No," Merc said. "I don't think you ever lost sight of who I was. Who I could be. You gave me responsibilities. Opportunities. Lately, you've been giving me more of them, things that rely on my angel blood to fulfill them."

He paused, made himself say it. "The blood no one else thought mattered inside me, because I myself rejected it."

Marcellus's gaze flickered. "Demon blood will always try to reject angel blood."

Merc stiffened, but he knew Marcellus wasn't insulting that side of him, just acknowledging the dichotomy within Merc. But when he'd fed on Ruth without killing her, responding to her trust and following that path to its natural conclusion, he'd realized he was master of both parts of himself. Something he'd sensed but not really known, not to the level needed. Angel blood, incubus blood, they were all him. *He* held the upper hand on both. The choices were his.

Maybe they hadn't always been, but the things Marcellus had cultivated in him, the things Merc had explored himself, had brought him to this moment.

"Why did you agree to be responsible for me, Marcellus?"

Because of his age and power, Marcellus might answer a question or he might not. This time, however, he did.

"Because of Mina, the seawitch, but not for the reasons you think."

Witch seemed a very limited term for what Mina was. Bonded to an angel herself, her power seemed more demi-goddess in scope. When she'd evaluated Merc in Hell, determining his Fate after he was dragged back there, her bi-colored eyes, one dark blue, one crimson red, saw every shadow in his soul. Under that gaze, he could hear the helpless cries of everyone he'd fed upon as their life was pulled from them. He'd had to see her a couple times since then, but he always hoped it would be the last, no matter that her assessment was why he hadn't been summarily executed.

If he owed her a thanks, which he grudgingly assumed he did, he'd send her a fruit basket.

Marcellus's expression was touched with grim humor. "She is not easy to be around. Once, I wanted her dead. She is half Dark Spawn, and the Legion has fought their kind for centuries, seeing nothing redeeming in them, creatures of pure evil. Yet she saved this world, and likely others, not in spite of that blood, but because of the way her own will blended her mermaid blood with it.

"We are far more than our birth. To consider our origins a mistake, rather than accepting them as part of us...we limit our path."

He gazed at Merc. "Things that come from darkness, they often see and know things that we need, and what *they* need is someone in their corner. I believe the universe sent me to you for a reason, after I learned my lesson about Mina. But I had to wait to see if you would see it yourself, because accepting that truth is up to you."

Merc could feel his heart beating in his ears. "I can speak it, Marcellus, but I would ask a favor. That you say what you believe."

He needed to hear it said by a male...he respected.

Merc saw he had surprised the older angel. They rose to their feet together, and Marcellus faced him with gravity, giving him the rare straight answer. "I believe the angel blood is stronger than your incubus blood. Far stronger. I think it is your core. And would have been from the beginning, if you had not been so shamefully abandoned."

As Merc stared at him, Marcellus continued. "When you were young, I think the more you gave yourself to the incubus abilities, the less obvious the angel ones were. Angels automatically protect the universe from unbalanced demon influence. Your angel side went

VAMPIRE'S CHOICE

dormant because it would not hand your incubus side the arsenal that being an angel would give you."

"I don't want to deny my incubus side. It isn't evil."

"No, it is not. No more than humans are evil. But it is believed whatever created them came from darkness. It was the Goddess who had compassion and gave humankind Her spark of creation, the fighting chance against the darkness."

Marcellus's eyes were even more unfathomable than usual. "When there is time and opportunity for it to make itself known, the will can decide, Merc. And I think, like Mina, time and circumstances have given you that opportunity to determine your full potential and however the Goddess means you to serve. She has been there, too, has she not? Her influence inside you. You can feel the connection to Her."

When he was alone in one of his perches, listening to the forest, watching the stars in the sky, all the elements pressing against him... yes, he had felt Her. A whisper in his mind, in his heart and soul. At first, it had frightened him, but lately, not so much. When he was with Ruth, tapping into the deep feelings between them... She was there, too.

"The incubus has to have room to be, too," he said, rather than answering.

Marcellus lifted a shoulder. "As it should. That side of you will always be there, making those sensitive to those energies wary, but as they get to know you, they will realize how much control you have over it. Much as Mina has proven. You respect it, but refuse to let it dictate to you. It is a battle that has been won. You desire the full freedom to choose your path. That is what you wanted to say to me today. Correct?"

Because Merc had to be contrary when Marcellus was being a know-it-all, he scowled. "You know how to spoil the punch line of a joke."

Marcellus didn't smile. "You are not a joke, Merc."

He sat back down, and Merc sat next to him. For a while they didn't speak. Their wings were adjusted so they didn't touch, but they were close enough Merc felt the heat and energy in Marcellus's. Merc put his bare feet in the water and watched the fish jump over them.

"You had things to say to me, too."

227

"It seems we covered them. There is no need to discuss the matter about Ruth. I have my concerns, but I will ponder it. Along with what we have discussed here. There is something else, though. Yes?"

It was more personal. Yet Marcellus's encouragement made the desire to talk about it unsettlingly strong. Merc didn't confide in others.

But he thought of the angel's gentleness with Clara, his fierce protectiveness. Marcellus was more than an angel. He was a male who loved a female.

"I saw Ruth watching the acrobats." In brief terms, Merc described the exchange between Nikolai, Karl and Sarita, particularly the way that the two men called an emotional response from Sarita as part of their Mastery. A vital enhancement for it.

"Ruth was as drawn into and aroused by that, as she was the physical part. My experience in controlling a woman, her pleasure, is with the sexual side."

When he'd imposed compulsion upon his prey, the physical had flooded the emotional, keeping it at a distance, where he didn't have to deal with it. "I have no experience in that. I don't know what it feels like."

"Bullshit." Marcellus arched a brow at Merc's surprised look. "Yes, I do know how to curse. Selectively, for maximum impact. Asking about her emotional wellbeing suggests you do. It is just new terrain. You want to give her something, and not because it provides measurable benefit to you. How she feels, what she wants, matters."

Merc pressed his lips together. "Is that how you feel about Clara?"

Marcellus didn't talk about that with anyone, though those closest to him, like Jonah, his Commander, knew. But he could see Merc struggling with this, and Marcellus wouldn't deny him the knowledge he needed. Particularly after stating he believed Merc was more angel than anything else. And an angel was a brother.

Even one still trying to figure out what being an angel meant to him.

"There is nothing I would not do to see her happy. And protect

228

her. I am proud of her strength, her will, to help us identify threats against this world and others."

"Even as you see it killing her," Merc said bluntly. "Maddock has a solution. Why don't you make her do it?"

Marcellus wanted more than anything to follow that path, and that impulse had overcome him several times. Fortunately, Jonah had talked him off that perilous ledge. Still, hearing Merc say it aloud, evidence of how new the younger male was to the relationship quagmire, had Marcellus biting back a grim smile. "You do not like it when choices are taken from you, when we control your path."

"I do not." Merc's eyes flashed, but he added, "Though I acknowledge I have more justification for that reaction now, than when you first found me."

Marcellus nodded. "Taking choice away from anyone, just because you have the power to do so, is as serious a decision, and as much a potential crime, as taking a life. It should always be considered carefully, particularly your motives. To take that choice from Clara, overriding her desire to help, would destroy her spirit. I would be taking away her right to be who she is."

Marcellus met Merc's gaze, the odd mix of dark red and black, those always intriguing hints of silver. "Protecting who she is might require the sacrifice of her physical wellbeing."

"That's a shit choice."

"Yes. It is. I do not always succeed at it, and I make her angry when I fail." His lips twitched. "So if I am going to incur her wrath, I make sure it is for good reason. If you care about Ruth, make sure whatever you demand of her is what you both wish. What brings you both pleasure."

Marcellus met Merc's gaze. "Clara and I have what is between us and have not given it names. However, with vampires, it manifests itself more as it does in the Circus world, so I'll use those terms.

"A Master can be demanding, strict. He can impose pain and punishment. But he does so knowing that is what his submissive truly desires and needs from him. And he watches her carefully to be sure it doesn't cross a line where it no longer is good for her or what she needs."

"So if a male is acting as he should, he is serving her, as much as she is serving him. Even if he is Master."

Marcellus had given Merc as much stroking as he felt was wise for one day, but pride surged in him at the younger male's intelligent conclusion. "Yes. Moreover, that is one of the definitions of love."

Merc's startled expression, bordering on terror, made throwing the comment out entirely worth it. Marcellus hid his grin, swiftly changing the subject.

"I would go to Machanon for a few minutes to speak to some friends. I want you to accompany me."

"I'm not prepared for that."

"You have a place here, Merc," Marcellus said seriously. "It will be different, because you are different. But it does not make it any less true. We can continue to develop that connection, if you wish it."

"I think I do, but I'm not sure if I'm ready now."

"It is not an official visit. I won at cards, and am going to collect the debt. The debt is small; the joy is in ribbing Bartolomew about the win. We will be there only a few minutes." Marcellus put a hand on Merc's shoulder. Merc wasn't used to physical contact from another male that wasn't a threat, so Marcellus didn't keep his hand there long.

"If I have earned a measure of your trust, let me provide a bridge to a place you might one day feel more comfortable calling home." A slight smile touched his lips. "In addition to the one you might find in the arms of your vampire."

Merc considered, his gaze resting on the hand Marcellus had returned to brace on his own thigh. "You said you thought as long as the incubus held the upper hand, that my angel abilities held themselves outside my reach, to ensure balance. But you told me of a time when Jonah was taken over by darkness, and it almost destroyed everything."

"Yes. But there were other forces at work then, and he was emotionally compromised when it happened. He missed the warning signs."

"Have you ever worried an angel will turn rogue from within? No sorcery involved?" Merc asked.

"No. That connection to the Goddess you feel growing as you accept your angel side? It is a constant for all of us. Deep within you is a love for your Mother. For creation. For female energy. For its strengths and vulnerabilities. It is what draws you to Ruth."

Marcellus paused. "There were times, early on, when Yvette would make you submit to her in key ways, to learn obedience and control. Though you resisted and it is not your core nature, there were moments of yearning where you recognized what you are feeling now. When your heart is right, your mind, it all makes a great deal of sense, even as it is the most profound of mysteries. Like love itself."

Merc's eyes narrowed. "You're trying to freak me out by bringing up love again."

Marcellus smiled, neither confirming nor denying. Merc snorted. "Fine. But tell me the truth. I'm not going to wake up one morning and forget how to use contractions, am I?"

"Wiseass." Marcellus spread his wings, batting Merc smartly as he prepared to head for Machanon. With satisfaction, he could tell Merc was going to follow him. No matter how uncertain he felt about it.

Merc exploring his feelings with Ruth was opening up key pathways that had reached the right time to be traveled. The Goddess made herself known in such ways.

And truth? Over the past few years, Marcellus had transitioned from championing Merc as the debt owed for his earlier behavior toward Mina, and moved into territory he was sure would unsettle the male even more.

Marcellus had begun to care for him, protect him as he did his younger brethren in the Legion. If Merc allowed himself to become part of their world, he would find he had the family he should always have had. Then his journey forward would expand into places he never thought possible.

Just like letting Ruth into his heart and soul would do.

Which meant it was time to broach the other idea percolating in Marcellus's mind. And really "freak out" his angel incubus companion.

He needed to meet with Yvette and Adan.

CHAPTER SIXTEEN

*Y*vette hadn't said what Marcellus wanted, but when a Legion angel asked for a meeting, it was wise to respond. When Adan entered Yvette's tent, the male was waiting on him. And sitting. Marcellus hardly ever sat. But there he was, perched on a sturdy wooden stool, his back straight, wings brushing the ground on either side, like a dark green cloak elegantly swirled around him. His head was dipped down, as if he were in deep contemplation.

Yvette sat in the carved wooden chair she preferred. She was doing the eerie motionless vampire thing, as Kohana used to call it, with the exception of two fingers. Her wicked long nails were tapping the wood in a rhythm like uneven footsteps. Click, clock. Click, clock.

Their stillness was permeated by the powerful energies they were both capable of unleashing.

"I feel like I should back out and hope you didn't notice me. What's going on?"

Marcellus raised his head, those dark eyes with no whites focusing on Adan. "Your sister should third mark Merc."

Adan was trained for the unexpected. He could regroup fast when what was thrown at him changed radically. If an army of demons had erupted from the floor of Yvette's yurt, armed with water balloons and maniacal clown masks, he would have taken it in stride. This?

"Have you lost your fucking minds?"

When Marcellus's brows lifted, he added, "Respectfully."

232

Yvette's lips twitched, but she said nothing. For the moment, she was letting Marcellus take the lead.

"Guardian training plumbs the depths of the souls of its students. Uncovers everything, leaves no fault, no mistake, no weakness of character hidden. Is that not correct?"

Marcellus's tone told Adan he was being addressed by a Legion captain, one who'd fought battles against the world's enemies eons before the spark of his own existence had come into being. He reined in his emotional response, his answer appropriately formal.

"That is correct, my lord."

"So you are aware of why your sister is weaker than most vampires."

Adan froze. That knowledge had come to him after the Guardian teachers stripped away every ounce of ego or confidence, leaving nothing but a shivering soul, standing under the ice-cold surge of truth about themselves, all the potential and desolation. No chance to lie or hide.

It was the make-or-break point, where students would prefer death, if death was an option. It wasn't. Not in a school held in the Underworld itself.

"Speak it," Marcellus said.

He was a Light Guardian. No one but Divinity Itself could command him to do anything. Not even an angel. Technically. But if the command was just, that was a different matter.

"I fed off of her in the womb."

"Yes. But your mother sensed her weakening, her distress, and your father permitted her to reach out to Lady Danny, who had been a vampire twin herself. She was able to identify the danger, because she had killed her own brother, though it happened in a shared crib, rather than in their mother's body."

Silence reigned in the tent.

"Ruth didn't fight you," Yvette said quietly. "She gave you what you needed."

"I wish to God she had fought me."

"But she wouldn't. You've known all your life she has a submissive soul, a strong, steady light that serves those she loves. She will fight to her very death for them, but never against them."

"Yes." Adan turned toward the female vampire and spoke what

he'd always known about Ruth, what made him both proud as hell and scared as shit for her. "Her soul is as strong as they come." His gaze shifted back to Marcellus. "Where is this going, my lord? How does it connect to her marking an incubus sociopath?"

"Your evaluation is clouded by emotion," Marcellus noted.

"This is my sister. You're damn straight."

"Adan." Yvette's tone held the reproof. "Hear him out. He has some points you will understand."

"Of course. Please continue, my lord." He sounded reasonable. Even between gritted teeth.

A glint went through Marcellus's dark gaze, but he continued. "Merc has a problem he has fought his entire life. When he did not resist it, he earned a death sentence. But when he was captured so that sentence could be carried out, it was recognized he had never had a valid chance to choose. Never had the space to do so. His father was an angel, his mother a succubus with a quarter human blood.

"A child should not have occurred, but she used black magic to make it happen, thinking she would produce offspring capable of protecting the sex demons from the retribution of the Guardians when they lost control of their impulses. She was obviously already well down that road herself. The judgment of the angel was lacking, so the angels felt the fault of his creation was theirs, and the innocent should not be punished."

A Light Guardian had an enhanced ability to see patterns, the ways puzzle pieces could fit together, in this case two beings, two souls. Adan didn't want to see it, but he did. Which he assumed was the angel's intent.

Marcellus's expression became wry. "Though innocent is not a word typically applied to Merc, it applies to the truth of his circumstances.

"We have recognized improvements in Merc's level of control over the years, but in focusing on that, the side that posed a risk to others, we did not always dedicate as much effort to healing or building up his character. Some part of that had to do with his own unwillingness to engage with others. He protected himself with a hypervigilance he assumed he had to have, with everyone as strong or stronger than himself."

"The level of self-restraint he had to exercise toward those weaker

234

than himself, especially females," Yvette put in, "also kept him even more closed off. It was easier not to risk misunderstanding or missteps. Especially knowing it could lead to his own execution."

"Yeah. That's a hell of an obstacle to personal development," Adan said dryly.

"You have an unusual vampire-servant relationship," Yvette noted. "A vampire-Fae pairing, which at one time was illegal for both Fae and vampire, but now is not, thanks to King Tabor and Queen Rhoswen's agreement to permit it, under certain circumstances."

"Yeah. Like Catriona not being bound by human servant rules, where a high-ranking vampire can command her over my direction." Adan lifted a shoulder, "But it doesn't hurt that I'm no longer considered fully vampire. As a Light Guardian, I'm a different rank."

"Is Catriona stronger than you?"

"Before I became a Light Guardian? It was a fairly even match at times." He remembered some of those times with sensual pleasure. "Honestly, she could kick my ass with her dryad stuff."

"But you are her Master. She wanted to surrender to you."

"Yes. She's a born submissive."

Like Ruth. He was starting to figure out where this was going, even if he wasn't sure he liked it. "The vampire-servant relationship is linear Dom-sub. Merc isn't going to be topped by anyone."

"No. We wouldn't expect that," Yvette said. "The point is the precedent for an expanded definition of the vampire-servant relationship, in a situation where the "servant" isn't human. It doesn't come with the same biases that still pervade our world on the vampire-human servant relationship."

"That the acceptable level of affection a vampire should feel for their human servant excludes true romantic feelings, because the human is inferior, and the vampire holds all the power?" Adan shook his head, thinking of his parents. "Even though, when they pursue those feelings, it expands their understanding, and things change for the better, for both vampire and servant. No matter what our law says on it."

Yvette sighed. "The law they have been trying to change for over a decade, while they endlessly tweak and massage a new one, which is just an excuse for one side trying to give it more protections and the other to weaken or scrap it all together."

"Politics," Adan said grimly. He nodded to Marcellus, patiently listening to the sidebar on vampire issues. "So okay, I get your point, that there's a window that could allow a marking to happen between Merc and Ruth. You still haven't said why you think it should."

"Because he's strong enough to protect her," Marcellus said bluntly. "And the vampire world has no power over him. Just as it has no power over your and Catriona's relationship, except what you are willing to give it."

"He's also strong enough to destroy her."

"No matter what unsettling vibes he puts out, Merc has learned to control his impulses." Yvette met Adan's gaze. "It's impossible to miss, when we are directed to look at it. We've had no incident of concern for years. I believe I overreacted to his sparring match with Ruth based on the past, not the present. But that is because of what we just discussed. He's never been viewed as part of the Circus; more as a model inmate. One who chafes at the restriction. Understands it, while resenting it, while remaining isolated, untrusted. Friendless, because he resists any bonds."

"And you want my sister to be the guinea pig relationship to let him out of the cell?"

"No." Marcellus met his gaze. "I'm saying the cell became unnecessary some time ago. I want you to trust what we are saying, that what they are becoming to one another makes this potentially the best next step for both of them."

"So at what point do I or Merc get to be part of this monumental decision that impacts us both?"

Adan turned toward the archway. Ruth stood there, with an expression he recognized. She was pissed. She also looked...wan.

He came to her. "What happened?"

"Nothing I didn't ask to have happen. And don't change the subject. You shouldn't be making decisions without me." She pushed past him, sending Yvette a courteous but stiff nod. "Thanks for having Gundar come get me."

Yvette gave Marcellus and his arched brow an even look. "She *should* have input into this. So should Merc, but the first level of discussion belongs here. She must agree. If she does, you'll broach it with him, I'm sure, but I believe you would agree the final say will be between the two of them."

Despite Ruth's raised hackles, Adan directed her to a chair and pushed her into it. "Be mad while sitting," he told her. "So you don't fall down."

She gave him an annoyed look, but complied, an encouraging sign her anger wasn't full blown. He saw no evidence of wounds, though those might have healed, depending on their severity and when they occurred.

"She asked Merc to feed from her. Fully," Yvette noted. "After an attack by two vampires in town. Nothing outside the bounds of our world's typical power plays. But Merc intervened."

At Ruth's annoyed look, Yvette pinned her with a *stow-it-or-else* look. "This is a conversation that requires your brother's full focus. No point in having his attention divided, trying to figure out what is going on."

"Ruth, what the hell..."

"I am *fine*," she repeated. "And he gave me blood of his own free will before I asked him to feed from me. His blood is about three times as potent as human blood." She paused, met her brother's gaze. "Adan, it accelerates my healing ability and improves my energy."

The surprise of that revelation stopped him mid-tirade. Marcellus turned things back to the subject at hand. "While Merc has already embraced the control he needs to keep his demon blood yoked and channeled for the right purposes, when Ruth started spending time with him, she showed him another reason to live that life. To protect and be worthy of a woman who matters to him."

Ruth's expression went still. This was news to her. Adan saw the feelings for Merc were there, but Marcellus had given her more information, a perspective Merc hadn't put out there yet. At least not that baldly. If Merc was dealing with the confusion of falling in love with a female, Adan grudgingly acknowledged it tended to stifle and eradicate communication skills, regardless of species.

Damn Light Guardian training, which helped him see patterns that served the greater good. Thanks to it, Adan might be feeling less opposed to the idea, but only if he got to the bottom of the two most important points. Ruth had her own question first, though.

"Why does the servant choice of a low-ranking vampire matter to the owner of the Circus and an angel?" she asked.

"Because Clara has dreamed of you two being bound," Marcellus said.

Ruth's eyes widened. "It was a dream, not necessarily a vision," the sorceress explained. "Which means the free will of the parties involved and changing variables can alter the picture. But it turned our thoughts in that direction, which led to a consideration of how it might benefit you both, if you chose to go down that road."

"If Merc fully embraces his angel side, he will be yet another warrior on the side of the Goddess," Marcellus noted. "While you, Ruth, will be protected and able to live your life fully. That is a separate matter from your relationship. If you two end up not wishing to be together, I do not foresee Merc turning his back on his protection for you. Ever. Even if it is ultimately in the service of honor and friendship, instead of love."

Her expression held mixed emotions at that evaluation. She was already pretty gone over the guy. Adan would have classified it as infatuation, except he knew his sister. She didn't give her affections lightly.

"But you said it was a dream. Not a prophetic vision that can impact our races. So it could be a glimpse of a possible future that has no particular significance beyond Clara's interest in and friendship with me."

"Correct," Marcellus said. "But I have learned, with Clara, small matters can figure into bigger ones. She would not have shared it with me otherwise."

"It's a vision, not a manual," Yvette said.

"It doesn't matter. The bigger stuff doesn't matter." Adan shook his head. "There's only one thing that does."

Dropping to a knee in front of Ruth, he met her gaze. Those dark eyes, the set mouth. The strength and resilience. The beauty. His twin, who'd done her best to hold up her parents when Fate had thrown him outside their reach. Even as that uncertainty had torn her up inside. Under those circumstances, the twin bond became a shredder, planted inside the internal organs and turned on high.

His hand was on hers, holding tight. "If he agreed to be your third mark, if that would work, for whatever your relationship is, is that something you want? Do you want him? Yeah, you're scrawny compared to most vampires," he added, "but you're a shining light. You have the right to love, to live. That's what's important in the cosmic scheme of things. That helps the fabric of the universe in ways you can't imagine. I promise. It's not just romantic bullshit."

"Scrawny," she said at length. But her eyes were full of the same emotions he was feeling.

He smiled. "Scrawny as an underfed chicken."

"You're a dickhead."

"Yeah. But all that said, if you do want him, and he gives you the chance to live a freer, longer and happier life, then that's what you can count on me supporting. Because I need you to be in this world, Ruth."

His voice faltered, surprising him as much as her. "I nearly killed you before you could be born, beloved twin," he murmured. "One half of my soul. I wouldn't be whole without you."

She disengaged her hands immediately, leaning forward to put them on his face. It was in moments like this she almost looked older than him, that concern and love so much like their mother's. "Mum and Da think you don't know."

"They don't know you know, either."

A half chuckle answered him. "Sounds like we need to have a family discussion."

She put her forehead against his, and he felt her love pour into him. It was as he'd said. She'd do anything needed to serve and care for those she loved. Including being the warrior he knew she was. No matter how often her ass got kicked. It didn't matter that the gods hadn't been smart enough to give her the physical strength to match her force of will; that wasn't going to slow her down.

Her example, being willing to fight when the odds were so against her, could inspire those of them who did have the power to put it in the service of the right thing. He needed to tell her that sometime.

A pointedly cleared throat, and Adan drew back, rising to stand at Ruth's side. "Apologies, my lady, my lord," he said.

"No apology needed," Yvette's expression looked just a tad softer than usual. At least for a blink, then the miracle was gone. "It appears we've reached the point we need to reach. We just need to know her answer. Do you want him, Ruth?"

"Yes," Ruth said. "But we haven't known one another that long."

"I've seen third markings happen within several days of a vampire and human's first encounter, and last for three hundred years without incident."

"I've also heard about the ones that are huge mistakes," Ruth returned. "The vampire kills the servant, rather than risk the embarrassment of asking for a chemical separation. I don't see that as an issue for us, but the mortality link is. If the vampire dies, the third marked servant dies. I don't want to...it's not likely I'll be the vampire that breaks our race's records on longevity."

"Don't underestimate yourself," Adan said, pushing down the pang her matter-of-factness gave him. "You're mean as a mad snake and twice as determined."

Marcellus shook his head. "His angel blood will override the mortality bond. You can rest easy on that."

"All right." Ruth sent Adan a faint smile for his snake comment. "But if the marking works the way it normally does, will his angel or demon side have a dangerous reaction to what I could do to him?"

At Marcellus's curious look, Yvette explained. "The third mark is a soul binding that permits the vampire to take over the servant's soul. Nowhere to hide any feeling or thought, even the ones out of conscious reach of the human himself. If the vampire so desires, she can use that access to break that human's mind and spirit."

"Even if it's not likely that I'd have the ability to break his mind and spirit," Ruth said, "there's the question of how his soul will react to that kind of invasion. Could it unleash the side of him that left a trail of bodies when he was younger? Or what happened when the hallucinogen was released from the Trad? Unlike most vampires with their servants, I won't be able to control or contain that kind of reaction."

"You have spent a lifetime learning not to rely on brute strength to accomplish things," Marcellus said. "And I believe serving and protecting you will be more effective than any punitive bindings that could be put upon him. But your point is well noted. I will check with the Thrones and Memory Keepers in Zebul, our sixth heaven, to be sure, before we proceed."

He paused. "Earlier today, Merc and I had a discussion. I told him

I believe it is his angel side that now forms his core. Except under extreme circumstances that would tax most of us, it will continue to do so."

His gaze met Ruth's. "In short, he will hold the upper hand with you in the ways that matter."

Had Marcellus intended the provocative message resting in that statement? While it sent prickles of anticipation through her, she did her best to conceal them. Adan noticed, though, shooting her a side-long look that made her want to poke him in the side.

"If I discover no obstacles to the marking," Marcellus said, shifting the focus, "including Merc's consent to it, then we can also monitor the process."

Ruth's reaction to that was immediate, but her brother spoke before she could. "No."

It surprised the angel, as did Yvette's emphatic agreement. "The third marking is a sacred act, my lord," the sorceress explained. "Very intimate, a coming together between the vampire and servant. While I have the same concerns about things that could go 'awry,' I think we let that call be Ruth and Merc's. Merc can speak in your mind, can he not?"

Marcellus nodded, and the sorceress continued. "Perhaps when it is about to be done, he can let you know so you can be alert, from a distance, where it won't disrupt the process."

Marcellus looked toward Ruth. "If the marking does set off something in the demon side, I might not be able to get to you in time to prevent harm."

Ruth glanced at Adan. He was letting it be her call. "I'm going to trust in what's behind the marking to get us through it."

Marcellus's gaze showed interest in her response. "Very well. I will speak to him of it."

"Shouldn't that be my call as well?" she said.

"No." Marcellus knew how to play dirty. He met her gaze with an expression that had her fighting not to do the gaze lowering thing, because he went right for the Master-sub vibe. "As you yourself pointed out, he has the right to make his own decision. Since you say you desire the marking, it is his call to bring it up with you. Correct?"

Yeah, yeah, whatever. She ignored Adan's and Yvette's amused looks. Damn Doms. So she was pushy and tried to top sometime. But how Marcellus realized that, besides the obvious qualities in her personality...she had to voice the suspicion. "Did he tell you that I pushed him to do the feeding thing? My lord." She softened the demanding tone with the grudging addition of the title.

"He did not." Marcellus's dark gaze gleamed. "Merc has a formidable will. But if you did 'push' him to do the feeding, even if he capitulated for his own reasons, you might end up facing an interesting discussion about that as well."

Shortly after that equally provocative statement, the conversation reached a natural end. It turned to portal and fault line matters between her brother and Yvette. A few minutes into it, the Circus owner dismissed Ruth with a subtle gesture.

As she exited the tent, Marcellus's point stayed with her. Facing the possibility of that "discussion" created an unsettling, not entirely awful feeling in her.

She'd told Merc she didn't mind a fight. With his blood and the homeless man's helping her, it wouldn't be too long before she'd have the strength to give him a fair one.

For the next several days, she didn't get the chance to make that decision. Or hear how the third mark discussion had gone between Merc and Marcellus, though she did receive confirmation through Charlie that the Thrones and Keepers didn't have any concerns.

She was busy doing security, this time in Alabama. Marcellus and Dollar made sure she was strong enough to work that first night—she was, though she was glad for her bed at dawn, and the bubble bath in healing oils Charlie blissfully arranged for her.

Both were lonely, though. What would it be like to share them with Merc? Be twined around him in slippery soap, then later in the bed, sheets pulled over their bodies, naked, still a little damp from having each other ten different ways before dawn claimed her. How would water affect his wings? Would he fluff them out like a stately heron? Or beat them powerfully in the air, sending water droplets everywhere? The thought gave her a smile, even as all of her thoughts made her ache for his touch.

When Merc did see her, even at a distance, his gaze lingered, telling her she was in his mind. His reasons for keeping away might be his own, but she didn't feel ignored. Those brief looks could warm her for several hours. He didn't speak in her head, but she remembered what he'd said about "feeling" her state of mind.

Occasionally, she instructed herself to discard the whole third mark discussion. In her weakened state, after the euphoria of him feeding on her, all sorts of things that had seemed possible seemed illogical and ridiculous. If he didn't bring it up, she wouldn't.

Wherever she and Merc were taking this thing between them, the vampire shit didn't have to be part of it. He wasn't in that world, and it was far better that he wasn't. He had issues of his own to deal with, without taking that on.

It wasn't as easy to discard Clara's "dream," especially when Yvette and Marcellus had felt it was important enough to discuss the possibility. When Ruth had gone to bed at dawn, after that meeting, Adan's question stuck with her.

She hadn't thought about taking a third marked servant, because she feared a servant would know she wasn't a Dominant. Plus, a servant, by nature, wanted to serve. It wouldn't have been fair. Ruth knew what being denied that outlet felt like. She also wasn't ready to make herself vulnerable to a human that way. When it came to mortals, she had zero submissive inclinations.

Lord Brian could separate marked servants and vampires, usually without complications when the bond didn't exceed a certain time period. If the servant was returning to the human world, their mind was wiped of the years they had spent in the vampire one. But it wasn't foolproof. If Ruth's submissive orientation was known, the only way to ensure that info was expunged would be to kill the servant. An act that was still tacitly okay in the vampire world, and left to the vampire's discretion, but Ruth wasn't geared that way.

Long and short, she put all of it away. Whether intended or not, Marcellus had given her an instruction that relieved her of the burden of it, because Merc didn't seem inclined to initiate the discussion.

To counter her frustration with his elusiveness—an entirely

different issue—in her off time, she hung out with Clara, Charlie and other females. Usually in Charlie's tent, a female haven where the furniture was mostly cushions, which could be moved around to accommodate the racks of costumes and her sewing tables. They played dress-up, painted toenails and exchanged fashion tips.

Tonight was special, however. When Ruth arrived, her hair had been in the tight knot she employed to keep it out of her way for her job. Charlie had immediately taken it down and started working on Ruth's look for the evening.

It was the Circus's "Play Night."

Since last night had been the final performance in Alabama, they'd shut down the Circus and moved it back into the in-between portal location, with even more speed and efficiency than usual. Everyone liked Play Night.

Charlie braided Ruth's hair, threading it with ribbons and flowers. She'd done a lot of that this week, because the Circus had performed with a Renaissance Faire theme, flavored with medieval legends and lore. The audience had roared its approval of the dramatic George and the Dragon fight in the center ring. Fortunately, the combatants finished on a respectful bow with one another, rather than the dragon being skewered, or George being eaten.

Caleb had played George, having the strength to handle the grappling moments with Tragar, and the unexpected speed and grace to avoid the strike of the lethal tail or grasp of a taloned claw. So impressive was their coordination, Caleb appeared as if he were barely escaping those dire fates.

"Are we sure Caleb's fully human?" she asked Clara.

"Yes. Just an incredibly strong one. Maybe he has giant blood. You know, one of the ancient, long-gone races."

Clara's perky optimism tonight was the real thing, not a costume she'd had to reach for. The recent lack of visions was giving her back some strength. She was painting Charlie's toenails as the blind woman worked on Ruth's hair. "I'm so glad you're going with us, Ruth," she added.

"I'm a vampire. Our internal GPS identifies any kink event within twenty-five miles of our current location, and we show up, invited or not. So will Marcellus and Maddock be there?" Ruth half closed her eyes as Charlie worked on her hair. She loved having it brushed and stroked. Would Merc ever do such a thing?

"Not Marcellus. Not his scene. I like to go watch, and he's okay with that. Long as I look and don't touch. He comes to me afterwards, though." Clara chuckled, delicately applying the soft pink polish. "So I don't have to worry about finding an outlet for all that sexual energy."

"Or he doesn't have to worry about you finding one," Charlie put in with a smile.

"Maddock?" Ruth asked.

"Sometimes, when he's in the area, but not this time. His work has him traveling a great deal." Longing and loneliness crossed Charlie's face, and Clara paused to grip her shin, a reassuring caress.

"I don't want anyone but him," Charlie said. "But it can be difficult, to want someone so much and only get to see them a few days at a time, with too long absences in between."

"Would Yvette let you travel with him?" Ruth asked.

Clara looked up with an expression that made her regret asking the question, but Charlie answered in a normal tone.

"It's difficult, with my gifts. They have to be managed in an environment like this, to keep them from overwhelming me. Maddock could probably work out some kind of buffering if we were together elsewhere, but I wouldn't want his energy to be divided, because he often works in dangerous situations."

She sighed. "So maybe it will always be this way. But I know our love will only grow stronger. That's the balance. The gift with the sacrifice. He's good about visiting me in my dreams. I feel his touch there often. And his words. Sometimes I think he holds me in my sleep, from wherever he is. I wake with the sense of his arms around me. He's a complicated man, but his love for me is simple and deep. When I can start my day with that feeling around me, I know it's as it should be. All will be well, no matter what we face."

Clara had paused, listening the way Ruth was. Charlie was lost in the strength of her feelings. Ruth was so used to proving herself capable of handling things, but could she trust Merc with her feelings like that? If she simply reached out, tried to find him because she needed his company, would he respond? Merely because she wanted to spend time with him?

She didn't expect she'd ever stop fighting and challenging. But there was room for caring and romance, right? Was he capable of it?

Charlie gestured around her. "My life is amazing. At one time, I thought it was hell on earth, thinking I'd never make sense out of it, make sense out of who and what I am. But I ended up here, with Yvette and a family, and then Maddock..."

Clara dipped a knowing look toward Ruth. "Back to Schweitzer again. Life's true joy is only found through suffering. We have to live and learn a lot of hard things to understand that." Changing the tone, she shot Ruth a mischievous glance. "Will you play tonight?"

"Probably not. I'm more of a watcher." The Circus might be a "safe" place, where the troupe would never reveal one another's secrets, but it was too ingrained in her, to hide that part of herself. There was only one reason she might consider doing otherwise. "Does Merc...attend?"

"Never. Which to be honest, has been a relief. It would be hard to relax, knowing he was strolling around a place saturated with sexual energy." Clara made a conciliatory gesture. "No offense. I know Marcellus says he's doing better, but that vibe he puts out...it's not that I doubt Marcellus, but it's like Merc wants us to stay scared. It's mixed messages, and I err on the side of caution."

"He does attend," Charlie corrected. "He watches from where no one can see him. I've felt him."

"You've never told me that," Clara said.

"He never ventures into the rings, and after a time, he leaves. I was respecting his privacy, while helping you and other women who are uncomfortable with him feel safe in that space."

Ruth imagined feeling Merc's hidden presence as she wandered through the play sessions, watching and reacting, at least internally, to what she was seeing. Her response to that was much different than what Clara was expressing.

She touched the flowers and ribbons in her hair. Even if she defaulted to "play it safe" mode, she was ready to immerse herself in the scenes, populated by beautiful bodies and the intensity of the power exchanges, the Dominance and submission. Her body was fairly humming.

With Clara's enthusiastic input and Charlie's expert opinions, they shifted to a discussion of Ruth's outfit choice for the night. Charlie had helped her put it together, and it was in Ruth's quarters, concealed in a garment bag. Based on what Charlie had suggested, Ruth had a feeling the healer knew her hopes for the evening.

"I'll meet you outside the Big Top in thirty minutes." Ruth directed that to Clara as she rose, because Charlie had informed them she needed to drop in later. "If that gives you enough time."

"Oh yeah. I'm ready to go." Clara wore one of her colorful dresses with intricate embroidery and tiny mirrors worked into the bodice. A wide belt and soft boots enhanced the skirt that swished around her calves. "Without my man there, I'm not trying to get anyone to salivate over me. Unlike one hot and sexy female vampire."

"I don't have to try," Ruth informed her, and departed with catcalls and chuckles following her.

She grabbed a quick shot of blood from the kitchen tent and headed for her quarters. She was passing between two storage tents when hands settled on her shoulders. Merc's wings closed over her. The feathers had an electrical energy that created tiny bursts of sensation wherever they made contact with her flesh.

She stored up so much anticipation for his touch, experiencing it often felt like the first time. The thought jolted her further.

"You have one rule to remember tonight." When Merc spoke against her ear, his voice just added to the impact. "Tell me what it is."

"Nice to see you. Hope you've had a good week." She rubbed her hips against him. "I wouldn't presume to know. You tell me."

"No one touches you. No Master, no Mistress."

"If you're there, it won't be a problem."

His warning growl didn't stop her from reaching back to caress his hip. He gripped her wrist, pulling her arm high up against her back. Discomfort bolted through the joint. Unless she wanted it to get worse, she better not move. He slid his hand down her front, into her jeans, cupping her sex. No hesitation or warning, but none was needed. When she arched against him with a hiss and he pushed fingers into her, her cunt had gone slick and wet in the mere seconds it had taken for him to detain her.

"Do you seek to be bound to me, Ruth? Never be rid of me, your Master into eternity? That's what your third mark does, doesn't it?"

Her eyes closed. All her rationales about letting it go, pretending it had never been suggested, vanished. It was back in her mind, large and

247

possible and not absurd at all. But it wasn't her nature to make things easy. "It makes me your Mistress."

She taunted him with words they both knew she didn't want to be true. He called her on it. The electric energy sparked from his fingertips, his thumb, exploring her labia and clit. She shuddered against his body, everything inside trembling, her body damp and aching. Tight. When she tilted her head up, she saw him draw in her response, nostrils flaring. A rumble came from his chest. "Keep challenging me, *little* vampire. I want to punish you. Make you beg for mercy."

She tried to hit him for the *little vampire* bullshit, but her free arm had no coordination. Which was what happened when a climax as strong as Caleb's grip seized her.

"Oh...God..." The reaction was entirely his design, his pace, pulled from her before any part of her could brace against it. She screamed against his palm, dampened it with her tongue, scored it with her fangs. He worked her through the orgasm, but when it ebbed, he wasn't done. He manipulated that energy and the angle of his touch on her sex, his stroke, the pace, until another gripped her.

His diabolical patience, as if he had all night to do this, only enhanced the torture. When he at last *allowed* her to be done, she was limp in his hold, his voice in her ear.

"You know who your Master is, Ruth. You already carry *my* mark. Keep fighting me. It will give me more opportunities to prove it."

It took forty-five minutes to get dressed and meet Clara. Ten minutes to unscramble her brain, and the rest to make sure if he was going to lurk, she was going to give him an eyeful. His threat lingered on her skin, in her mind, like his touch. She wanted both back, up close and personal, and was happy to challenge him to get it. The disappearing act was getting damned old.

When she rejoined Clara, the fortune teller's eyes widened. "Wow. I'm torn between saying something like 'you're almost wearing that dress' and 'you're wearing the hell out of that dress.' Charlie knows her stuff."

"You had key input as well."

The neckline of the dark red dress was low and draped. Creative underwear pushed her small curves up and together to make that view 3D, rather than a flat glimpse of her sternum. The skirt had a tight tulip bulb fit, a split up the left leg to the waistline. What was beneath—and what wasn't, since panties weren't possible—was tantalizingly hinted at by a trio of glittering beaded straps across her upper thigh. A choker with the same sparkling embellishment had a strap that ran vertically down her sternum, between her curves, to disappear under the lowest part of the draped neckline. It attached to the band that cinched in the waist. She'd paired the dress with high heels.

Though she had loved the flowers and ribbons, she took them all out, so her black hair was loose and flowing, giving her a wilder, more sexually dangerous look.

The dress was an invitation any Dom would recognize, if he didn't know she was a vampire and a top herself. Supposedly.

Merc knew better.

As she and Clara moved toward the Big Top, he was all she could think about. However, once stepping inside, she found other astounding distractions.

Angled mirrors hung over the rings, slender rectangles that turned with the air currents. They reflected light and slices of what was going on below. Other mirrors were anchored panels on the ground inside the rings, creating informal divisions between stations and groups of players.

The pixie Fae flitted everywhere, like fireflies on a summer night. A flock landed on the back of a bound sub, digging their tiny nails into his flesh before lifting off, right before a whip strike from his Mistress.

Tragar was here, sitting in a stately upright position just outside a ring. Near him, a Master stood beside a woman bound on a metal table, her face and neck covered with a wet towel. When the male stood back and glanced at the dragon, a courteous request, flame swept over the woman, shot from the dragon's maw. Her skin was glistening as if coated with oil, some type of alcohol buffer, Ruth assumed.

Her Master moved swiftly, dousing her with a wet blanket, but the fire bottom's ecstatic cry reached Ruth's sharp ears, even over the music pounding through the speakers, a sultry mix with lots of bass and drums. She suspected it had been put together by the Circus composers who did all the score work for the performances.

Unlike most circuses, where fire was of paramount concern, Yvette had fire protection spells on the tent, so no flame could misbehave.

"Ever seen fire play like *that?*" Clara asked.

"Never." Ruth shot her a grin.

The knife throwing wheel was in use. The Circus's knife performer was a woman, a Mistress who looked pleased with her current "volunteer." It was Caleb, wearing only a tight pair of black shorts. His presence there worried Ruth a little. He was far heavier than Zanath's usual assistant, Tink, who stood to the right of the wheel. The slim, pretty male was rubbing his cock through his tights as Caleb's eyes clung to the motion.

With the wheel rotating, would Zanath be able to accommodate the assumed change in timing from his weight?

Ruth and Clara slid to one of the audience seats to watch. Other people stood closer to the scene, inside the ring, but they had a decent view here.

As each knife thunked into the board around him, Ruth noted Caleb's body quivered in response. His erection strained against the shorts as Tink moved toward the wheel and locked it in place. While Caleb's dark eyes followed his every move, the man stripped off his tights. Putting his foot on Caleb's thigh, a hand to his shoulder, Tink climbed him. Then he turned over and grasped the hilts of the embedded knives so his elbows were bent on the outside of Caleb's hips. Though he was slim, Tink's fitness was evident, his biceps and thighs flexing. The assistant spread his legs in an impressive split and rubbed his cock and testicles against Caleb's face until Caleb's lips parted. Then Tink angled himself to push in between them.

As Caleb sucked, Tink brought his legs back up and hooked his ankles on the top of the wheel so he could pull down Caleb's shorts and return the favor.

The Mistress picked up a remote and started the wheel turning at a moderate pace. She threw another dozen knives, outlining their bodies without once hitting flesh, though she came close enough Ruth thought they felt the burn of the metal.

"I love Play Night," Clara murmured.

When Zanath issued a command, her assistant gracefully removed his cock from Caleb's mouth. Executing a backbend off the wheel, he returned to a standing position, removed the knives, and offered one to his Mistress. She approached Caleb and drew the flat of the blade over his bared cock, still slick from Tink's mouth. She leaned in to bite his nipple, play her tongue over it. His fists clenched, his sizeable organ convulsing.

He groaned when she cut the surface skin layer in a diagonal line over his ridged abdomen muscles. Blood trickled down to the waistband of the shorts. Tink had left the front folded down below his cock. When Zanath cupped his erection, the hilt of the knife pressed against his shaft. Caleb pushed into the pain and earned a slap that left a handprint on his face. He snapped at the blow, cursed her.

Tink moved in and kissed him with lots of tongue, lowering his hand to work Caleb's shaft until he was groaning again. Then Tink moved back so his Mistress could do some more throwing. Caleb looked perilously near release, but even with all the physical pleasure he was experiencing, Ruth could tell he was keeping that volcano contained. Separate.

"Why won't he play with a Master?" Ruth asked.

"Caleb won't say, and no one pushes him. However, if I had to guess, and I don't think this is my romantic side talking, I think he had one in his old life. He remains loyal to him, even though they're not together."

"What kind of idiot Master would let him get away?"

"Maybe he didn't. Maybe it was Caleb's decision."

"Right. I forgot. In your world, humans who bind themselves to a Master or Mistress are given that annoying ability to walk away."

Clara offered her an amused look. "Yeah. Forced servitude is such a better idea."

"See? I knew you were civilized." Ruth nudged her. On the trapezes, a female submissive bound in silks was being swung between two Doms, a man and a woman. When the Mistress wrapped a single tail around the silks, holding the sub in one dangling spot, the Master used another whip to lash at exposed skin. Their captive danced in the silken bindings, crying out.

When the single tail was jerked loose, she swung back toward the Master, who caught the tail of the silks between her thighs, and hauled her up so her legs were over his shoulders. Her body arched over space, arms still bound as the Master put a hungry mouth between her legs. His eyes lifted to the Mistress, who swung lazily, sitting on the bar of her trapeze. Her top was at her waist as she taunted him with large breasts, toying with pierced nipples.

"Let's see what's happening at the left ring," Clara said.

Karl, Nikolai and Sarita were here, only it was Karl's turn to be tormented. While the two men were Masters, Nikolai topped both. Karl stood on one hand, his legs spread shoulder width apart above him. As Sarita strapped a cock cage on him at Nikolai's direction, that arm trembled. It increased as Nikolai put a lubricated phallus into his ass.

When Sarita was done with the cock cage, Nikolai closed her hand over the dildo, showing her the pace at which he wanted her to slide it in and out of Karl's ass. Then he applied a violet wand to the thin metal bars of the cock cage.

Ruth was impressed by Karl's one-armed balance under such duress, though he did start to plead with his Master for the right to put a second hand down. Nikolai took his time with that permission, but granted it at last. When both arms were shaking, Nikolai and Sarita attached chains to Karl's ankles, drawing the slack up so his weight was partially carried by the chains. Sarita stayed close, her hands on her bound Master, stroking him. Her face was suffused with sweet concern for her Master's suffering, at the hands of the one who topped them both.

Had Adan and Catriona ever strolled through Play Night? Ruth expected they had, probably for voyeurism purposes.

A vampire liked showing that a servant was his, and what she would do for him. That inclination was part of why D/s play with servants was so popular at vampire gatherings. But with vampires being insatiably curious about testing limits of pain and endurance, Adan likely played the Light Guardian and Fae card and kept them out of the most extreme stuff. Her brother struck her as more private and protective with his Fae servant than he'd been with the second marked human servants they'd shared with William and Matthew.

Lightning flashed across the upper reaches of the Big Top, as did a drifting and luminous cloud of light, imitating an aurora borealis. When done during performances, attendees would attribute it to visual effects, and some of it was. Here inside the portal realm, it was the manipulation of energy, done by the same troupe members who handled the electric visuals.

She saw an example of it with another Master using a wand. He was applying a comb attachment over the nipple and testicle area of his bound sub. However, the crackling power to fuel the wand came through his hand, not from batteries or an outlet.

Same for another electrical play quartet. A Mistress had three subs on their knees in front of her. She held out a wand fitted with a two-headed metal dildo. At her order, two of her subs faced one another, each one taking a phallus in their mouths until they were close enough for their lips to touch. As the electricity passed through the toy, their lips and faces quivered, their bodies jerking. They were naked, their wrists tied behind their backs, but she brought them together so chests and genitalia were pressed together. Her assistant began to run what looked like steel cable around them.

The Mistress turned to the third kneeling sub. A bit pressed down his tongue. The straps holding it, also conductive metal, were strapped around his jaw and head. When she touched the bit with current, the sub jerked against his bonds, his eyes streaming with tears. Yet his body language begged for more.

"Most electrical play is done below the waist," Clara murmured. "Heart and brain issues. But here, when people have different abilities, or magical protections are in place, everyone can be more adventurous."

Clara's information was intended to ease human-related concerns, but vampire play could get way more dangerous than this. Third marks were far more resilient.

The creases of Ruth's palms were moist. It was second nature, staying aware of her reactions to such scenes, reshaping her body language so that any vampire watching would interpret them as an attitude of vampire dominance, arousal at seeing humans topped.

Ruth drank in the heady intensity, feeling it in the places she usually kept walled off. Here at the Circus, could she dare reveal her true feelings, show what really fascinated her about the scenes?

She'd keep thinking about it. Tonight wasn't the night to take that risk. There were plenty of things Ruth did impulsively. This wasn't one of them. But Great Father and Mother, she was aching.

She blamed that on Merc. He had eroded her resistance. Which didn't mean she didn't want him right here, right now, so he could keep grinding it down.

They moved to a suspension scene. A flexible Asian Indian woman was tied so her back was bowed in a U-shape, her arms bound securely to her sides. The rope Dom had used green and black rope and attached a line of fringe beneath it. He'd turned her into a human caterpillar. Her hair was tied in two high ponytails, giving her antenna. A rope over her forehead kept her head raised to show the henna tattoo around her neck and sparkling studs along the shells of her ears. Her Master rotated her on a hook to display her to an apprecia-tive audience.

A sharp clap pulled Ruth's attention to another couple. The Dom was applying a paddle to the reddened bare ass of the female he had stretched over one of the balls the clowns used to roll across the ring for their acts.

The woman was one of those clowns, but she didn't wear her colorful silks and bright blue wig tonight. Her face was painted, but differently. Her cheekbones were sharp slashes, her mouth a pursed bow. A track of golden stars followed one cheek bone, outlined her eye socket, then arched over her brow.

She wore only an upper body harness and collar, her pussy and breasts exposed. Her nipple clamps were threaded with a thin rope her top had taken through her collar and three D-links in the back of the harness. Because of that, she had to keep her upper body lifted and balanced on the ball, or the pull against the nipples would become painful.

As the paddle hit her buttocks, she jerked, a strangled shriek coming from her, but she stayed in the arched position. Which Ruth knew only spiked the arousal. The dampness in her own palms became slicker.

The Big Top was a dungeon tonight, populated by athletic, flexible people capable of turning every scene into an erotic art performance. Stills could be captured on film, put in a gallery and cherished by those who understood how to interpret them. Ruth would slip into such a gallery, past closing, and walk past each one. Alone but safe to gaze her fill, fantasize about feeling the way each of those submissives did. Serving their Masters and Mistresses.

She'd known what Merc meant about his unsated hunger, even as she understood the key differences. If he didn't control his desires, he would kill. If she released hers, the only one that would die would be her—emotionally at first, and then physically, because she wouldn't accept being treated as someone's slave.

She inhaled the scent of the woman's desire. Her body twitched every time the paddle hit, her sex contracting between her tightening thighs.

"Do you want to play?" asked an unfamiliar male voice.

CHAPTER SEVENTEEN

*P*lenty of troupe members enjoyed just watching, like she and Clara did. But some were seeking a playmate.

The man who'd asked Ruth the question was one of the newer roustabout hires, so either he didn't know she was a vampire, or that vampires were all dominants.

The muscular and tanned male had a handsome mix of Malaysian and English features. Dark, penetrating eyes, thick hair, and he was on the tall and broad-shouldered side, flattered by the jeans, boots, and long-sleeved snug shirt he wore. His calm assessment gave her that unsettling jolt that a Master's regard always did.

Fortunately, he was human, so it melted away after the first flush.

"We can talk about your preferences." His teeth flashed, his expression honest and straightforward. "I play anywhere from beginner to extreme. I just like having a beautiful woman responding to my hand."

Ruth opened her mouth to answer, but was stopped by a feeling that wrapped around her, a binding so cold it burned the skin at first touch.

It was to keep her from interfering. The main blast of that energy had a target, and it wasn't her.

The Dom took a step back as if pushed. His gaze darted around her. No matter how new he was, if he was part of the Circus, he was aware of how many of its members might express their displeasure using magical means.

She gave him credit. He didn't cut and run. He held his ground long enough for a courteous nod. "My apologies. To you and your Master." Then he moved away.

"I don't believe it."

The frozen rope feeling dissipated, but Ruth still felt its hold in her churning reaction. She did her best to focus on Clara's comment, laced with quiet astonishment. The girl had stayed at the suspension scene while Ruth wandered over to the impact play, but had now rejoined her with the incredulous comment. She hadn't noticed Ruth's predicament, which was probably a good thing.

The fortune teller glanced meaningfully toward the far end of the Big Top. Merc was perched in the scaffolding. He had one fist pressed against a beam, his muscled arm taut as he crouched, balanced by fully outspread wings. The traces of white and gleaming ends flickered with the lightning flashes. Though his expression was shadowed, she could feel his gaze upon her. The echo of his message to the Dom was reverberating inside of her still.

Hands off.

It had caused ripples through the tent. Players and onlookers shifted uneasily and looked around for an imminent threat. Fortunately, after only a puzzled pause, that feeling melted away and they returned to their play.

For Ruth, there was no abatement. It had embedded itself in her pounding heart and trembling lower belly. Maybe because she was holding onto it with both hands.

"As you can tell from our conversation earlier, I've never noticed him here before. He doesn't make his presence known. Apparently, he felt the need tonight."

A slight smile touched Clara's lips, a mix of companionable female humor and concern as her gaze slid over Ruth. "You want me to stay close or make myself scarce?"

"I doubt he's going to leave his perch. But..."

Clara's eyes shifted to her left, and that twinkle in her gaze increased. Ruth's eyes briefly closed.

Merc had landed a few feet behind Ruth.

A very different energy wave happened then. Instead of his

incubus vibes ensnaring everyone like a net, it was wafting outward, elevating the sexual play, increasing its pleasure, its intensity, whatever element the players wanted to augment.

An offering they recognized, albeit with surprise toward the offeree. She noted gazes moving toward Merc to warily acknowledge it. One Mistress even nodded her thanks to him before returning to her electrical play. Ruth noticed the sparks from her wand temporarily shifted from a white-blue color to a brilliant flare of silver-limned red. Like Merc's eyes.

Clara swayed at the saturation of sexual energy. "It's like a bubble machine, where the bubbles are full of pheromones. Every pop is like a mini-orgasm. Nice." She shivered. "I'm going to mosey back to my quarters, in case Marcellus gets back earlier. Unless you need me to stay."

She gave Ruth a direct look, then shifted it to Merc. A challenge. Clara had her back if Ruth didn't want to be left alone.

When Ruth felt the gathering of his response, along the lines of what he'd unleashed toward that Master who'd asked if she wanted to play, she turned, her hand landing on his bare chest. "Don't," she said.

A brow twitched, as did a muscle along his throat and shoulder. Ruth had felt a range of emotions in his burst of energy, but his mien was as flat and forbidding as usual.

"Do you consider a friend looking after my welfare an enemy?"

That look dialed down. Offering not just an acknowledgment, but a certain level of acceptance.

Clara let out the breath Ruth expected she hadn't known she was holding. Ruth clasped her hand. "I'm good. But thank you."

Clara withdrew with a tentative smile. Ruth watched her join Charlie at the suspension scene, then dipped her head toward her shoulder. When she lifted a hand to her side, she smiled when she encountered feathers, and Merc didn't tell her she couldn't touch. His wings curved forward, his body close enough he formed that shelter around her she liked.

He was also wearing the jeans she favored on him, frayed and worn so thin they clung to him in distracting ways. She stayed in place, thinking if his feet were bare as usual, she wouldn't want to step on them with the spike heels.

Unless he gave her cause.

When he closed his hands over her wrist, she shivered at the relentless pressure in his grip.

She tightened her muscles to see if she could withdraw, and when he didn't allow it, the bolt of pleasure went straight to every erogenous zone, plus some other less physical places. She drank in the ripples of incubus energy, and the unique essence of Merc that flavored them.

"Trust is a difficult thing," he said. "It comes in increments. Bite-sized. It's difficult to change the habit of self-protection."

He'd noticed her struggle. If Merc hadn't disrupted the conversation, the Master noticing her desires would have startled her enough to withdraw. Maybe even shut him down with a display of vampire dominance that made him question what he "thought" he'd noticed. Even if she had to be rude and offensive about it.

"The desires and needs shown here don't get revealed outside this tent, when that's the wish of the one exercising them. Yvette implements a particular spell to reinforce it. If anyone here would do harm to another with their knowledge, no matter how inadvertently, when they leave the tent, that piece of knowledge leaves their mind. They don't recall it."

"She didn't tell me that."

"It's not widely known, except from those who can detect the shape of the magic, and those who need to know. It also works well as a vetting test for newer employees, or those whose hearts might have changed. Yvette will have Gundar or Charlie ask them a casual question later, and if they don't know the answer because they've forgotten, it tells her they are less trustworthy than she'd hoped. Soon after, they'll be dismissed with a week's pay and find themselves back in the world with no memory of having worked for the Circus."

"She never relaxes her vigilance." All highly placed vampires possessed a certain level of reserve, but Yvette's made more sense than most.

"The Circus is her 24/7 job. Her passion, her home, and her place in the world. And not just for her. She never underestimates the importance of that."

Yvette didn't consider Merc a confidante, so what he was telling her came from those observation skills he'd honed so keenly. "So why do you think she didn't let me know?"

"Perhaps she thought it better to let you decide on your own how much you wished to trust this environment."

She hoped the roustabout would prove trustworthy. Though not what she was seeking, there were other submissives here tonight who would welcome his attentions.

Merc tipped up her chin. The opaqueness in his eyes seemed to be taking up more of the whites, the silver a glimmer on the edges of the dark irises.

"Tell me what you would do, if there was no fear of discovery. Tell me what you fantasize about, in this tent full of fantasies."

She moistened her lips and began to shift her gaze. His grip tightened. "I didn't tell you to look away. Answer the question."

Nerves warred with defensive anger, but her gut told her he wasn't going to tolerate a fight. He was threatening a decisive and quick ass kicking if she didn't answer.

"I don't know. There's so much. And I can't... Even knowing what you told me, my brain freezes. I'm too used to protecting myself. Everything shuts down."

"All right." He let her go.

Irrational and frustrating disappointment flooded her like a caustic poison, but before she could push past that to make a graceful retreat—or say something mean to him to vent her spleen—he'd drawn her against his side, an adjustment, not a withdrawal, and they were aloft.

He landed them in the audience's seating area on the uppermost bench, which had the most shadows. He'd chosen a center ring section, for optimal view of everything happening below. Merc guided her to sit, but he didn't sit next to her. Instead, he took the bench one row below hers and faced her. He clasped his hands between spread knees. "Back straight," he murmured. "Hands braced on either side of the bench. Knees spread. Do it."

A submissive posture, open to her Dom. When she complied, with a brief, quivery hesitation, he touched her knee, making her spread it out another couple inches, which pushed her hips back and her chest out. The dress stretched, but it also slid higher up her legs. If he chose, he could dip his head and see what she didn't wear beneath it.

Instead, his gaze rested on the curves of her breasts in the low neckline before it lifted back to her face. "That dress isn't going to survive the night," he promised. "Start to your left, and look at each scene. You have to watch it until I tell you to move on to the next one. Do you understand?"

"Yes."

"Start now."

In the left ring, a new suspension scene had started. Depending on the form chosen, the bottom would often feel pain at first, even if the right kind of pain. The key was settling into it, because beyond that pain, euphoria could wait. She'd learned that by talking to one of William's go-to servants who enjoyed suspension play at his hands.

The bottom for this scene was a contortionist, and the Dom wanted to push her beyond her normal threshold to that ecstatic level. He'd drawn her backwards like a hairpin, her head touching her buttocks, arms stretched toward her ankles and tied there. It put her in a teardrop shape.

Multiple ropes created a fan shape above her prominent rib cage, like a hemp bloom balanced on the curve of the teardrop. As he surveyed his work, the Dom caressed the jut of her hip bones and stretched lengths of her thighs. Her sex was pressed against the crotch of the pink leotard she was wearing, the damp labia clearly defined. When the Dom put her in a slow spin, his hand trailing over her, the sub moaned at his touch.

"Move to the next."

Reluctantly, her gaze went to an electric play scene. An arc of white-blue power moved from the top's fingers to the sub laid out on a board, wrapped against it with thin silver cord. His body danced, caught up in a river of shocks being applied along his naked torso.

"Next."

His close regard had her wanting Merc's hands. The posture he was making her maintain didn't allow her that. It was all dependent upon him. Her body shuddered, and he wasn't even touching her. Just watching her watch all of this.

Just as she'd imagined.

Impact play was next. The Dom who'd spoken to her had found a playmate, an equestrian performer. She did acrobatics on the Percherons, plus skits with the unicorns.

They also had a Pegasus in the troupe. Ruth imagined Merc riding

Pegasus, the two sets of wings aligned. Had he ever done that? Or were the animals as leery of him as Medusa's snakes?

The Dom had put the rider's hands against one of the steel tent poles and bound them there. He stripped his belt out of his jeans and doubled it. She was clothed, but only in a thin dress with nothing beneath. As the male gathered up the filmy cloth, he revealed neat, firm buttocks. His fingers played over the seam, stroked the curves and her upper thighs. Warming her with his touch, readying her for what would come next, while enjoying the intimate contact.

When the first slap of the belt came, she had her bottom lip in her teeth. Ruth was emulating her, digging into plump flesh, her tongue tasting the moisture against her teeth.

The simplest of scenes so far, and it captivated her.

Merc was gathering intel on what excited her, uncovering those deep desires she couldn't show anyone.

The score music had given way to someone's play list. "Goodbye's Been Good To You" by Teddy Swims. The rough voice and insistent beat matched the insistent sexual percussion throbbing through the Big Top. The Dom matched the beat in his strikes.

"Next," Merc said, after the Dom had administered twenty blows. Her own buttocks throbbed. Her nipples ached. If Merc had touched them, she would have whimpered from the sensation.

"I can't see the next station. There are people in the way. It seems popular."

Merc put his hands to her waist, and they were aloft again. He took her up into the scaffolding, giving her a direct downward view of what she hadn't been able to see.

Those who loved D/s play could be endlessly creative. And the Circus had access to toys and equipment that most didn't. In this case, the claw machine had been brought into the Big Top. On performance days, it was on the midway. A guest inserted a ticket, activated the claw inside, and tried to capture the stuffed toy or trinket they wanted.

In mundane carnivals, the toys were packed down, making it difficult for that to happen. The carnival received far more profit than gave away toys.

At the Circus, the toys were tossed in loosely. Almost everyone won, with less than two tries. The Circus made their nut from sold out shows, special engagements and performances, like with BDSM clubs such as Club Atlantis. Being indulgent with their games meant happy attendees and more return business.

The claw machine had a very different use tonight. The toys had been removed, except for a layer on the bottom. A woman was inside the box, bound to a pole that had been added to the space. Her feet and ankles were buried in that layer of colorful plush toys, but a spreader bar held her thighs apart. Straps bound her hips and waist to the pole, while another was cinched above her breasts, emphasizing the lush curves and tight nipples. Another strap was over her forehead.

Her upper arms were held to her sides at the elbows. Her wrists were cuffed securely together, no slack, and her hands were folded and tied around the handle of a vibrator, the tennis-ball sized head pointing downward.

Those watching were using tokens to move the "arm," a control rod attached to the wrist cuffs. Ruth deduced it must have a dozen settings, because they could apparently rotate it against her sex, make it pump up and down, rub against her clit, or brush and tap it.

The woman had no control. They had it all. To keep going, the participants merely had to keep feeding the machine tokens. If they chose to have merely a "turn," the length of that seemed designed to leave the sub panting and aching for what the next in line would do to tease her.

"There are different contests involved," Merc said. He shifted their positions, so Ruth sat on his knee, his arm around her waist. He slid his fingertips along her breast, brushing her taut nipple. Ruth bit back that cry she'd known would come from his touch.

"Who keeps her on the edge the longest," he continued, his eyes reflecting that intense, predator-in-the-dark gleam. "Or makes her climax the hardest. Or the most quickly."

As she watched the girl writhe, scream and plead through the marathon of erratic stimulation, Ruth's mind locked up. She couldn't speak her needs, but her shaking body told him. He was watching her, but his stillness told her things would move at his pace. When he finally rose and turned her around, a crazy sob caught in her throat.

His hand clamped over her ass, his fingertips probing the sensitive seam between her buttocks.

"Hold onto me."

He exited through the open top of the tent. The smooth and sinuous way he angled through the metal frame pieces made her tighten her arms around him. Her smile over it landed on the sharp edge of other things she was feeling.

Vampires should have the ability to fly. Would a child born of an angel and vampire have that ability? Would it be the first of a new race, or had it happened before?

The thought was random insanity caused by an excess of arousal. Vampires were notoriously bad breeders, within their own race or with their human servants, let alone with other races. She didn't know of any successful offspring, except for Dante, Alexis's mate, Clara's merangel friend. Dante was a half-breed vampire crossed with a terrible race from a different world, the Dark Spawn. Though she didn't know all the details, she expected the pregnancy hadn't been a natural thing. Dante, like Merc, had struggled with his volatile nature.

Merc wouldn't have harmed Clara, but he wasn't above using intimidation to take over the moment. She should talk to him about that. Even if she did feel a guilty surge of pleasure when he did it to assert a territorial claim over her.

They were coming in for a landing at that storage tent Ruth was starting to realize was the closest thing Merc claimed as his own quarters on Circus grounds.

"Where do you sleep?" she asked.

"Often the forest. I prefer the trees. Or I anchor myself to a cloud bank and drift with it."

"You can sleep in the clouds?"

"It requires some energy manipulation, which has to be maintained while I sleep. Marcellus showed me how."

A slight smile touched his lips as he read her expression. "Yes, you could sleep with me there. If you behave and I decide you're worth the extra trouble."

She made a face at him. "Me behaving—what you would call behaving—would bore you to death."

Instead of answering that, he put her down, opened the tent flap and gestured her inside. The interior had changed, and the differences had her heart skipping a beat.

The crates were in a semi-circle around a wooden chair, similar to what Yvette had in her tent to "hold court," as Gundar dryly put it. A side table was behind the chair. She could see its edge, but not what might be on it. A mat was on the floor in front of the chair, as were a scattering of white petals that emitted a haunting, hard-to-place fragrance, a wistful memory. Increasing the yearning.

"No one will disturb us here without my knowledge," Merc said, "and I'll be aware of it before they can see us." He met her gaze. "You're safe to be who you are, Ruth."

She reached for flippancy, her true reaction too strong. It would spill over and embarrass her. "So whatever female you planned all this for wasn't available tonight?"

"Stop." His gaze seared her, a stripe of fire across her heart, painful enough to have her stepping back. She wondered if it was made worse by the clash between her ragged emotions and his implacable ones. He wouldn't release her hand, so she had to halt when she reached the end of that tether.

"You don't get to hide. You won't protect yourself here. I won't put up with it. Say the truth."

"You prepared this for me tonight." A million reactions spiked as she forced out the words. They terrified her. "Why?"

"Because I wanted you here, to myself. To have you as I desire. The longer you were in the Big Top, the more painful your yearning for what you want to do, to be, became. I won't put up with that, either. So we explore it here."

She moistened her lips. "What did you have in mind?"

"First we deal with your punishment."

"Punishment for what?"

When his gaze moved over the dress, she made a guess. "Wearing this outfit?"

"No. You wore that for me. There is no punishment for trying to please me and drive me insane at the same time." His attention lifted from it. "You'll earn a worse punishment if you pretend not to know."

"Talking you into feeding fully from me." Yes, the choice had been his, but she had pushed, hard.

Merc dropped her hand and crossed to the table behind the chair.

The item he lifted was a ball gag. One with a screw through the ball, a crank on the outside. "After I put this in your mouth and strap it on your head, I turn the screw. It pushes the ball into your throat. Up to three inches. Good training for teaching a sub to take her Master's cock as deep as he wants it to go. You did well the other night, but you could do better."

"You think three inches is far enough?" She tossed out the challenging sass, even as her insides quaked.

He draped his forearms on the top of the chair, the gag dangling in his right hand. His look was a shuddering caress of her exposed skin. The energy drifting off of him was closing around her. "Enough to shut you and that mouth of yours up. Take off that dress that attracted far too many male eyes." His eyes gleamed. "Leave the shoes. Then turn around, your hands clasped and resting on your ass."

She wanted this. Wanted it badly, but suddenly she was frozen, teetering over an abyss containing every worst fear she'd had about making it a reality.

He didn't admonish her, which might have made her get pissy, letting her fear start a fight. Instead, he went for a more devastating tactic.

"Once a servant is bound to the vampire, all choices belong to the vampire. Isn't that correct?"

She managed a nod.

"You can choose me as your Master, make it the rule between us for tonight, but if you want a different choice, you would be wise to run from me."

She didn't run. Not from anyone. And she suspected, no matter what he said, if she ran from him...

She bolted. Proving that whenever they'd played this game, it *was* a game, him indulging her, he caught her almost before she began to move. He pinned her back against him, his wings brushing her sides. When she tried to stab his feet with the heels, he lifted her and pressed his erection against her ass, through the thin cloth, a reminder that it was just her beneath.

"So you didn't mean it," she said. "I don't get to choose."

"No. You don't." His breath passed over her cheek. She smelled vanilla cake, and wondered if Charlie made extra this time, to plan for his pilfering. "You've taunted, defied and insulted me. All because you knew there were consequences, and that twisted, hot place inside you longed to see what those consequences would be. Kick off the shoes. Now."

When she did, he put her down. "Lift your hair and stand still."

As she raised her arms, holding the weight of her hair in her damp palms, he released the clasp of the slim and sparkling choker, sending it tumbling down with the sternum strap. Then he pushed the dress down, over her ass and thighs, letting it fall around her ankles.

"I thought you promised to shred it," she said, trying to hold onto a bit of humor among the nerves.

"Charlie loaned it to you. I won't cause you the wrong kind of trouble." His touch followed the bumps of her spine. She could feel him staring down at her breasts, lifted and displayed in the satin demi bra. "I knew from how it clung to your ass you had no panties under it. I almost claimed you then. Brought you here. But I wanted to see your reaction to everything, because it would make my cock harder and thicker, and I could demand more from that pretty mouth and tight cunt."

He unclasped the bra and let it fall. He trailed his knuckles along the sides of her breasts, making her skin prickle, her nipples tighten further.

"They don't look as impressive without it."

"Your breasts are everything I want them to be. There is nothing about you that disappoints me."

Her heart stuttered, then went back into full hammer mode. He caressed her arms, still lifted and holding the mass of her dark hair. Until he closed his grip around her wrists and pulled them away. The strands untwisted and tumbled, some falling forward over her breast and nipple.

Stepping back, he adjusted her arms so they were behind her, her wrists in one hand. A gasp escaped her as he pushed against her knee and dropped her to a kneeling position. Then he let her wrists go and put her on all fours, crouching over her, his breath again on her nape. "Show me what your animal instincts are telling you, Ruth," he said.

Trembling all over, she went to her elbows, dropping her head to her forearms, tilting her chin to the left, so he could see her eyes were lowered. She spread out her knees. Lifted her hips.

His breath left him, a harsh whisper that hit the edge of a growl and made her tremble more.

"Good." He gathered up her hair, twisted it in his fist and brought her back up, standing on her knees. He stepped in front of her. When she dared to look at him from beneath her lashes, he was staring at her body even more intently, taking in every inch of flesh, every quiver.

She felt like every emotion was equally exposed. She couldn't handle it. She had to fight.

"No." His grip tightened. "There will be no fighting me tonight, Ruth. Give yourself this. Stay where I put you. Hands behind you again. Knuckles on your beautiful ass."

He eased his grip until she stood on her knees on her own. When he returned to that table, he bypassed the gag he'd left in the seat of the chair when she bolted, but she was sure he hadn't forgotten it.

Then her worry about that was replaced by horror at what he produced this time. "Oh, hell no."

Merc chuckled, dropped to his heels and nipped her shoulder, pricking her sharply enough a drop of blood welled up. The breast harness he carried was pink. *My princess was* stamped on it in silver.

"It was a last-minute decision from the available toy stock. I'm fine with my tough sub looking girly tonight."

"What if she's not fine with it?" she muttered.

"Refer back to the clause on who owns all the choices tonight." The harness buckled around the throat, the straps running between and beneath her breasts, separating them as he buckled it in the center of her back. Snugly. The look of it didn't matter so much after he did that. The restraint's internal impact was powerful. To save face, she still threw out a warning.

"You call me an Indian princess, and I will neuter you."

He scoffed. Another strap went around her biceps and over her breasts. When he attached it to the harness in the back and tightened it, it arched her back and made her breasts jut out beneath the horizontal hold of the strap. After he spread her thighs out even wider with a shove from his knee, he put a cuff around each, then put cuffs on her wrists and attached them to the thigh restraints.

Except for a very awkward ability to run, she was well and truly caught. He moved to face her, holding her with that fist in the hair again, exerting pressure so she stared up at him. He pressed his erection, still behind denim, against her sternum and throat, her chin on the waistband of his jeans. It was a position meant to intimidate, emphasize the difference in the power they held in this minute.

She wasn't ready for this. She wasn't. She'd fantasized, but had only imagined this in stages...and yet her body couldn't do anything but respond to everything he was doing to her. She was melting from the heat.

"When you give me your fear, your uncertainty, I feel it. Recognize it. Your shaking tells me everything. But if you third mark me, or even second mark me, I could hear your exact words in my mind when you beg me for mercy."

He inhaled, his hand tightening, and she watched him feed on the arousal pumping from her. Now he retrieved the screw gag from the seat of the chair and brought it in front of her face. "Open up, my Indian princess."

She fought him. Tried to jerk away, overbalanced, but used what limited mobility she had to roll, put her face to the ground, away from that gag. He yanked her back up on her knees by the hair, and used her yelp to shove the gag between her lips, his thumb wrenching her mouth open wider so he didn't push her teeth in with his strength.

When he had it strapped around her head, he swung her up in his arms and carried her to the wooden chair. He sat down on it, then put her on the mat, on her knees facing him. He'd thought of her knees, her comfort. To make up for the ways he would be deliberately ignoring her comfort.

"Assume a submissive position, Ruth. Show me how lovely you can be."

His voice had changed to a purr, his eyes glittering. He was proud of her for fighting him. Liked it. She'd given him an appetizer for the full meal she'd offer him tonight. He wouldn't take as much this time, she was sure. Too many things going on in the next few days, plus the third mark question hanging out there.

But she could feed him enough to hold him. He wouldn't be hurting for more, having to take it from a random source where he had to restrain himself far more than he had to do with her.

Beneath that benevolent thought was her aversion to him seeking anything from another female. And the killing rage it inspired. Those thoughts, at least in this moment, made her find her pride and exercise it as he was demanding.

Her back was already bowed back from the harness, but she tightened her core to add to her erect carriage. She lifted her chin, mouth stretched by the gag. Almost tenderly, he cupped the back of her head, then pinched the small crank between his forefinger and thumb. And began to turn it.

She could taste the metal against her tongue as the screw started to lengthen and push the ball into her throat. Her gaze dropped to the erection straining against his jeans. He wasn't a small man. She fully expected he would push the gag in as far as it could go. Training, just as he'd said.

Training her to serve him.

The thought alone could have made her explode into full release. Was it because this was the first time she'd been with someone strong enough to put her in this position? A male she *wanted* to put her in this position.

A male that she trusted, enough for this. Maybe for more than this. When it came to him, her subconscious was a mystery to her.

He took his time. She could tell he liked watching her expression change, her eyes get a little wider, her body shake more as the ball pushed deeper into her throat. She worked to relax it, to take it, to not panic at the feeling. She didn't have to breathe, she was a vampire, but that air hunger feeling was there when the ability was restricted or taken away. It had to be managed, because the gut would produce the desire to struggle.

His hand tightened on her skull, anticipating it, but she watched his sensual mouth, the set showing his approval, and refused to give in to that false anxiety. Her chest heaved once, resulting in an excruciatingly painful cough against the block in her throat. He held onto her as her body was wracked by it, but then she was past it, and the gag was as far as it would go.

"Nicely quiet," he said. He put his hands on the chair and gazed at her. "You're mine, Ruth. If I want you like this for the next three hours, just to look at you, you would stay still. Wouldn't you?"

This time the choke came from a near sob that surprised her. His eyes darkened and he leaned forward, ran the tip of his finger down her throat. "Answer me, Ruth," he said softly.

She nodded.

He moved his clever fingers down to play with her jutting nipples, trace the harness's outline around them. She swayed at the sensations that speared through her. "I wonder how you would handle climaxing with that in your throat. Even if vampires don't need to breathe, I think you might pass out."

He lifted her onto the chair, changing her position so her legs were wrapped around him, folded behind his hips. Her hands were still bound to her thighs, so he had to steady her, handle all of it.

He opened his jeans, pushed them down enough to free his cock. He fisted it, rubbing the shaft against her clit and lower belly. A whimper vibrated in her chest.

She watched, entirely helpless, as he lifted her and lowered her slick sex down upon him. He went slow, so the discomfort from his size, taking him at that angle, was manageable. When she was seated, her clit spread over him, every inch of her cunt in contact with his velvet heat.

"Your face is so flushed, lips so glossy."

He didn't kiss women. She remembered that, longed for it to change, as he leaned in. He did take a small sip of moisture from the corner of her mouth. He cruised up to her ear and down to her neck. His hands were on her hips, then over her ass, kneading it, which made him move inside and against her in increments that had her needing to pant.

He inhaled more of her energy, then sat back, fingers on her biceps, over the straps holding her arms to her sides. The heels of his hands were against her rib cage. "Lift and lower yourself on me. Do the work while I watch."

His grasp upon her kept her from toppling backwards or disengaging their bodies, because her normal vampire balance and grace seemed to have deserted her. He rubbed his thumbs over her nipples, another nearly unbearable pressure, as she lifted and lowered herself on him.

"All the way down, all the way up to the tip. Milk me hard. Don't shirk, or I'll put you over my lap and spank your ass bloody. I'll probably do that anyway. Punishment for a vampire needs to be something severe."

He put his arm behind him, to that table of diabolical toys, and brought back a strap the length of a ruler and studded with uncut gems. When he turned it she saw they'd been fitted into holes in the strap, so the cutting potential existed on either side.

"These represent the chakras," he said. "Balance is important, right? Charlie chooses interesting toys for the Circus members' use, and for her Mistress's."

He slapped the strap against her thigh, and Ruth jerked as the gems bit into her flesh. He rubbed his palm over the marks they left.

"Keep fucking me, Ruth. I didn't say stop."

Her body was so close to climax, and she saw that was his plan... until it wasn't. When she was so close a bare word would have sent her over, he stopped her and slowly lifted her off. She had tears running down her face, emphasizing how little control she had over...anything.

He turned her over, still wearing that gag and the harness. "While I think even a hundred strikes wouldn't change your stubborn will, we'll do something a little less tonight. Maybe. It's hard to resist marking this."

He rubbed her ass, played in the crease, teasing her rim. She screamed against the gag as his thumb went lower and pushed into a heated ocean of arousal. She felt the shudder from him, that crazy electrical energy as he drew it in, nourished himself.

"Sometimes small meals *are* best. Especially when every bite can be savored like this. Every sip."

He slapped her backside with the strap. Fuck, it hurt. He hooked his thumb in the harness's collar strap, holding her fast as he started to whip her. Quick repetitions, a pause, an out-of-nowhere hard strike. Again and again.

By the time he reached whatever number he deemed fitting, she was strangling her scream against the gag. The effort sent her into a faint, only to have the pain rouse her again, the demand, the insane, pounding level of arousal. When he harshly ordered her to do so, she climaxed harder than she ever had in her life. Again blacked out, roused by three more strikes against a raw ass that had to be bleeding, or at least would bear a quilted pattern of those gems.

From the thought, she climaxed once more.

When she surfaced from that one, he'd unscrewed the gag and let it fall free, though he kept her other bindings in place. He had one palm wrapped over her face, his fingers against her eyes and cheeks.

272

She sank her fangs into the heel of his hand, and blood flooded her mouth. He rubbed her ass with his hand, pinching her with strong fingers, before he lifted her and shoved her tender pussy back down on him.

He wasn't asking her to do the work this time. He took over, thrusting into her. While his climax built toward its pinnacle, he released the wrist cuffs from her thighs and the strap on her biceps. Only the breast harness held her. And his sure hands.

When the orgasm gripped him, his arms slid all the way around her. She didn't question the intimacy, or have any wariness about it. There was no room for distrust right now. She wrapped her arms around him, too, his head against her breasts, her jaw against his hair.

She held onto him through the storm of reaction that carried them beyond the climax, into a dark and drifting place where everything was known and nothing was certain.

It was the way of the world. And what gave it its unbearable sweetness.

CHAPTER EIGHTEEN

$\mathcal{H}$e flew her up into the sky, and Ruth slept in the clouds, in the arms of an incubus angel. Going forward, if he wanted to taunt her, or she pissed him off, he might drop her again. But now he'd always catch her before she hit the ground.

She was pretty sure of it. Mostly.

Resting in the clouds was like being in a drifting boat on calm waters. Sometime during that sleep, he roused her to have her again, doing that wonderful thing with his wings where every thrust took them higher into the sky, penetrated her deeper, made her shriek her pleasure to the whole universe. Then they floated back into their cloud bank and she slept once more.

She woke in her quarters in the security team's tent. He'd put her there without being noticed, because there were no speculative looks or amused smirks. She would have worried it was all a dream, but her body told her in a hundred ways it most definitely hadn't been.

She grabbed a shower, a blood meal, then headed for the security briefing for the upcoming performance. She was pleased to be early, but then she saw Marcellus standing between two tents. His head was down, arms crossed and wings folded tight against his body.

He could be praying. But that wasn't the vibe she was getting, so she changed course and drew closer.

"Is she okay?"

He lifted his head. He'd been somewhere deep inside it, but she didn't feel like her question was an intrusion. She wouldn't presume to know what a being like him was thinking, but everyone needed a break from their worries, especially when they were standing-room-only in their minds.

"She had another vision a few hours ago. It was...difficult for her."

A pang hit her mid-chest. "Is Charlie with her?"

"Yes."

She suppressed the immediate urge to go to Clara. In this moment, that wasn't her job. "Any new information come out of it you can share?"

"It still revolves around the Trad vampires. New variables have entered the vision."

He wouldn't tell her anything above her pay grade. A moment later, she wished this had been one of those times. "She saw Lady Lyssa...and signs of a death connected to her. It was not clear what kind of death."

At Ruth's curious look, he elaborated. "There can be a physical death or a metaphorical one."

Like the death of a queen's reign. Which, in Lyssa's case, could result in a lot of physical deaths. Most vampires knew her strength, her stabilizing power as Council head, kept restless vampire factions and other potential opponents contained. The potential enemies of the current status quo were limitless.

Marcellus confirmed her sobering thoughts. "It could herald a far wider conflict in the vampire world. Which would impact the human one."

"How about the angels?"

Marcellus shook his head. "We stand apart from conflicts the Fates and Goddess deem should be left to the decisions of others."

"So if the vampire world tears itself apart, you'll do nothing?" She tried, unsuccessfully, to pose it as a neutral question.

"You have many influential players. It is not our fight."

In theory, she understood. She could tell it didn't necessarily sit well with him, either, though.

"It is often recommended that angels stay detached from the worlds and peoples we protect so we don't get overly involved," he added.

"A personal relationship with one of those people screws mightily with that," she observed.

"Yes."

"But it's not prohibited."

"No. Not usually. The Goddess respects free will and the evolution and growth it can support. No matter how painful those processes can be."

"Freedom's never easy," Ruth said. "My father has had to fight a lot of battles on the political front to keep his sanctuary operating the way he wants to run it. Some days he says physical combat would be less exhausting."

Marcellus nodded. Seeing he might need a distraction, she chose a different direction. "Marcellus, what do you eat?"

He blinked those solidly dark eyes. "Manna is what sustains angel kind."

"Have you ever offered any to Merc?"

"Yes." Marcellus's lips quirked. "He did not like the taste."

"Has he ever tried eating it right before he feeds the way his incubus side prefers?"

Marcellus raised a brow. "Not to my knowledge." He shifted his gaze to her right. "Am I correct?"

"Yes."

She turned to Merc. It had to be intentional, his ability to full-on sneak up on her, since other times she could close her eyes and feel how close he was.

His wings were pulled in close around his shoulders, enhancing the black. He wore his security garb, black jeans and short sleeved shirt with the embroidered security logo. Black shoes with thick soles. Marcellus was in his usual Legion wear.

When last she'd seen Merc, in his faded jeans and bare feet, she'd realized why each man looked more comfortable in his preferred garb. Marcellus's square cut jaw and formal stance smacked of military command. Merc was the rogue anti-hero, with the stubbled jaw and devil-screw-it look.

Two different styles of eye candy.

She held that thought to herself, but would share it with a more appreciative audience later. Like Clara and Charlie. Clara would welcome the chance to smile.

Marcellus's gaze shifted between them. "So Clara said you two were together last night."

Merc's eyes narrowed, but Ruth nodded. "We were. I'm in top condition today. If needed, I'll scale a few trees to prove it to Dollar."

"So he did not feed from you?"

Merc stepped forward. It put him between her and Marcellus, though he wasn't blocking her view. "I did. But not fully. As I said, that will be a rare occurrence. I'll seek other sources as needed to protect her strength."

Ruth's temper flared, but not so hot she didn't notice how the men's gazes had locked, or the tension in Merc's shoulders. It wasn't her job to defuse his reaction to the babysitter treatment, but Marcellus was already out of sorts over Clara, and Merc didn't know that. Testosterone could be a mine field.

But she had her own territorial reactions. So, despite those warning thoughts, she put a hand on Merc's arm. "The person you're talking about happens to be right here. You won't be feeding on someone else to spare me."

She'd successfully captured his attention—and his ire. "Your tone with me is unacceptable."

"Your feeding on someone else is unacceptable."

"Incubi are not monogamous."

It was a cruel shot, forcing her back a step. He registered the hit, his own expression tightening in a way she couldn't interpret. But before she could retort, her brother spoke.

"They can be."

They turned toward Adan, joining the impromptu meeting. His arrival, so soon after his last visit, raised her hackles further. Merc wasn't the only one who didn't appreciate babysitting. Did Adan really feel she needed this much checking up on?

Okay, yes, the first time he'd visited, she'd been attacked by a Trad. Second time, a pair of vampires had attacked her, and she'd been drained for a full feeding by Merc, so...

She scowled. Fine. But *his* job was incredibly dangerous, and she didn't pop up at his workplace every day. Never mind she had no way of knowing where that would be, and it was often frustratingly out of range of their twin bond or the mind link.

A lone voice of reason reminded her he was also supposed to be keeping tabs on Clara's visions and their impact on the wider world, aka Guardian jurisdiction, and Clara had just had a pretty significant one.

"Sex demons may not always be sexually exclusive, but they can be emotionally monogamous," Adan continued. "Raina is both. She's a succubus witch who runs a bordello populated by sex demons. And she's bonded with a Dark Guardian both of you know." He indicated Marcellus and Merc. "Mikhael."

Marcellus's brow lifted. "Mikhael is fully monogamous. Emotionally and physically."

"Yeah. She's the same," Adan said. "By choice I might add, but if she had any thoughts otherwise, Mikhael would just incinerate the poor bastard with a thought and keep reading his morning paper."

"I really want to visit her place sometime," Ruth mused. At Merc's lifted brow, she added, "It's been on my bucket list since Adan first told me about it." But she had a more pressing question. "How does she feel about it?"

Surprising her, it was Marcellus who answered the question. "She's devoted to him. It's a True bond."

At her puzzled look, he explained, "Angels only mate once in their eternal lifetime. If their mate is not in the life cycle intended for the relationship, the angel will keep his distance, leave them to live their lives, until he or she reaches the point of readiness."

"Wait." She was picking up a lot of information on the back end as she digested all the implications from the front. "Mikhael, a Dark Guardian, is an angel?"

"Yes." Marcellus said. "Partly. He has enough angel blood to carry that characteristic."

When the angel looked at Merc, a sudden silence descended. As the implication hit Ruth, it freaked her out, more than a little. It appeared to unsettle her brother, too.

Merc's expression darkened. "My angel blood might have a greater impact than I have accepted or considered before now, but that doesn't mean it fully defines who I am. Most incubi are *not* monogamous physically. For obvious reasons. Sexual energy is still my primary food source."

Ruth's temper flared hot, telling logic to take a hike. "I wasn't asking to set up house. I don't give a damn what your angel blood does or doesn't tell you about soulmates. But while we're together, I'm not going to share you. Period. You want that, then find someone else's head and heart *and* body to fuck with."

She should match her tone to her audience, but she was no longer in a giving mood. She looked toward Marcellus as she pointed at Merc. "I want him to take from me what I want to give. I'm aware of the cost, so that's my choice. Mine. If it impacts my work for the security team, I'll be the first to identify it before it causes a problem. Serving the Circus and protecting Clara is important to me."

Her gaze moved to her brother. "I love you, but if the primary reason you keep coming back this often is to check on me, I want you to stop. It might be an illusion, me being able to protect someone for once, rather than having everyone bend over backwards to protect me, but let me have that illusion as long as I can. All right?"

Her volume had risen enough to draw attention. She checked herself, but pivoted and stalked away. She'd made it almost to the end of the line of tents and the open field beyond, the lake where the mermaids swam, when Merc landed near it.

He gripped her arm and she tried to throw him off. When he refused to let her go, she swung, snarling. He took the punch when he could have blocked it, his head snapping back, but then he turned them, her back against his body. She did her best to bite him and kick his shins as he lifted her off her feet, but his wings folded around her, enclosing her in that soft darkness.

He didn't use his incubus power to arouse and distract her, which would have turned her anger into full blown rage. Instead, he offered a wave of genuine emotion, surprising her enough to check her anger.

Regret. Agitation. Confusion.

That, and his next words, saved him from the cutting edge of her tongue. "When I was first assigned to him, Marcellus would throw out comments and questions that tipped over everything I believed. It annoyed me then. It annoys me now, though he does it less often. Your points were valid, and my answer was...unkind. But your tone with me *was* unacceptable. Fix it, if you wish me to consider your wishes."

Did he realize when he acted all in charge, he was more like Marcellus than he realized? Acting like...an angel?

Probably not the best time to point it out. She couldn't manage a totally civil response, but she did force out a raw and honest one. "I'm a vampire. Sexual play with servants, in the company of other vampires, it's part of our damn social structure. But what we share with someone...who matters, that has boundaries. It would hurt me to know you'd fed from another female because you prefer that to feeding from me."

His grip on her eased, though he still held her close, his mouth next to her temple. "If I choose to do so, it'll be because I'm protecting you. Not because I prefer another female. I can promise you that. While we're together, in whatever we are in right now, that will be the truth. I want to feed off you every time, Ruth. When hunger stirs, you're who I'm thinking of. Whether the hunger is merely a need for a sip, or to consume all of you."

"You can take that from any woman."

"Yes." His gaze met hers. "But I can't make them give me what you give me. What you offer. Freely. Willingly. And more importantly, I don't wish to take from them what I want to take from you."

That mollified—quite a bit—but she wasn't going to back away from the point. "I want you to have everything you wish from me. No limits. Maybe that's stupid and crazy, but it's the way I feel."

"And why I'll be the one to determine the limits. To protect you," he repeated. "That's the job of a Master, isn't it? The submissive feels a natural desire to give him everything, when she opens herself up to that need. So he needs to protect her, even as he cherishes the gift."

He backed off. As she turned his way, he folded his wings over his back, the tips overlapping near his ankles. His expression was still, waiting on her response.

"Have you been reading a Dom how-to manual?" she asked. "Because that sounded pretty impressive." And had hit the mark of what she admitted was true about herself and her desire to submit, dead on. Not that she was going to tell him that.

His eyes showed humor, but the set of his mouth, his silence, said she wasn't entirely off the hook.

"I was a bit mouthy," she allowed. "I'm sorry. It's just...I get a little crazy when I imagine you touching anyone else to feed. I can't change that. Not while I feel the way I feel."

His expression eased. "It's how I feel about you as well. I'm all right with you taking blood from the cook tent, but if you wanted to draw it straight from someone...I would want it to be me. It also helps you, doesn't it? Makes you stronger."

"Yeah," she allowed. "But I don't want to use you that way."

"Why? If you had a servant, that would be one of my primary jobs, wouldn't it? If I'm also your Master, caring for you, for your needs... that falls under the same answer." At her wry look, he pressed his lips together. "No, I haven't been reading a book, but I pay attention on Play Night. I hear the discussions. I've learned without doing."

Much as she had, up until meeting him. They were finding their way. She sighed and let the anger go. Then blanched. "Oh fuck, I practically dictated terms to Marcellus. I need to apologize."

"But not to the Light Guardian?"

"That's my brother. That's different." Though she probably did owe him a follow-up conversation. "I'm worried about Marcellus. He was worked up over Clara."

After she explained, Merc offered her a hand. "It's time for the security meeting. Let's go support him the way he needs. That's likely all the apology necessary. Clara is his mate."

Merc's hand was warm and firm on hers. They walked back, and he didn't let her go. As they passed through the populated areas, she noted the startled looks, but also some tentative smiles. Maybe they were starting to see Merc as something different, more a part of the Circus.

If she'd had a hand in that, as Yvette and Marcellus had implied earlier, then she'd made as useful a contribution as helping with Clara's protection, in her opinion. No matter how she and Merc ended up.

When they arrived at the tent where Dollar and the other team members were assembling, Adan was sitting on a stool, his heel hooked on a rung, arms crossed over his chest. His gaze touched their clasped hands.

You two are so cute. The incubus angel who can suck the life out of someone through their gonads, and the rip-your-throat-out-if-you-annoy-me vampire.

She narrowed her eyes at him. *Eat shit.*

Their version of an apology. He was trying to trust her judgment against his protective brother, alpha male, Dom concerns. She was telling him she understood and appreciated the love.

After a brief squeeze, Merc dropped her hand and moved to his normal spot, a few feet to Marcellus' left. As he passed Adan, they exchanged a neutral look that held some of that same testosterone exercise he and Marcellus had had, but it stayed on low boil.

Ruth joined the security personnel, standing beside Helo and Burt and behind Zee. "Someone had a wild night," Helo murmured. "Any interesting scars to show?"

"A lady never tells."

The chuckles settled as Yvette joined them. The Circus owner was an unexpected addition to the meeting, but as Dollar moved out of the center position to give her the floor, she explained her presence.

"Lady Lyssa has contacted me. The California overlord, Lady Kaela, informed her that a Trad in her area has requested a meeting. He wants to discuss plans he's heard hinted about among his kind. Things he feels won't benefit Trads or vampires as a whole."

"Setup," Dollar noted. "Gotta be."

"It's possible. But Lady Kaela won a measure of his respect during an encounter a few years ago. Though she would not call him a friend, she believes his concern is genuine. He mentioned a recent failed attempt to secure 'the seer who sees too much.'"

Marcellus's mouth tightened. "Bring him here so we may question him."

Merc shifted closer to the Legion captain's shoulder, a show of agreement.

Yvette shook her head. "Trads embrace the savage predator that lies at the core of all vampire kind. What we've controlled with civilized trappings and our ritual protocols, they rarely restrain. If you force him here or to Council headquarters, he'll refuse to offer anything more specific."

"Or take his own life, like the one the other night," Adan added.

Yvette's gaze shifted to Marcellus. "He says he'll only meet with Lady Kaela, but he's asked for the presence of a Truth Vessel, so his word isn't questioned. Another reason Kaela is treating his request as credible."

"What's a Truth Vessel?" Dollar asked.

Marcellus glanced at Merc, then spoke. "Angels. We know a lie, even obscure ones told to oneself."

Maddock stepped into the tent. "Like I swear I'm going to lose those ten unsightly pounds, right *after* I polish off a stuffed crust pizza."

Yvette rolled her eyes. "I keep forgetting to reconfigure the portal to burn your DNA to ash upon re-entry."

"You never forget anything," he said. "You love me."

"You continue to be moderately useful. And Charlie loves you, for incomprehensible reasons."

It was the first time Ruth had seen the sorcerer close up. Today he wore jeans and T-shirt, a tall and angular male with black hair, raggedly cut, and cat-intense hazel eyes. With the exception of his trimmed beard and moustache, he looked like a cross between a particularly handsome homeless man and dangerous hitchhiker. But his vibration of power was the same that Ruth detected in different doses from Adan, Yvette, Marcellus and yes, Merc.

Maddock carried a carved staff embedded with crystals. Since it was worn smooth beneath his palm, she expected he'd had it for a while.

"On the incomprehensible reasons part, we're in rare but total agreement." Despite the teasing, the sorcerer's gaze sobered. "Don't let me interrupt. I'm just here because I was informed my moderate usefulness was needed."

At Yvette's curious look, Marcellus filled in the blank. "Clara feels some additional protections or cloaking might enhance the safeguards for those she cares about."

The look he and Maddock exchanged didn't take much interpretation. The protections were already pretty damn good. The strain on Clara's nerves was making her jumpy.

"Definitely a discussion we can have," Maddock said neutrally. He glanced at Adan. "You can be my wingman on that meet, if you want."

"Bullshit. You can be mine."

"*Top Gun*? Really?"

"You opened the door, man. I just stepped through it."

Maddock snorted and returned his attention to Lady Yvette. "So the Trads know there are angels here?"

She shrugged. "It's not a hard thing for preternatural beings to figure out. Even if Trads can't breach the grounds without our knowledge, they'll have heard about the Circus. What humans believe are miraculous special effects and feats of makeup, they would know are real. Though it's interesting they didn't assume our 'winged members'

283

were Fae. It confirms they've had magic-trained human spies in our audiences we didn't detect."

Dollar's expression hardened. "Maybe we can figure out better ways for our team to detect that."

Marcellus glanced at Merc. "In the meantime, you will visit Lady Kaela and hear the Trad's story."

If the angel had sprouted bunny ears, he couldn't have startled the tent occupants more. Including Merc.

"I have spoken to Jonah. It is a chance to prove what I already know. You are being offered the invitation to serve as an angel. Will you accept?"

Most of the people in the tent didn't understand how significant an offer Marcellus was making, but Ruth did. Merc's gaze moved to her. Her hands curled as she realized he was looking at her because it was a significant issue. Something that would impact both of them, if they were moving forward together.

Merc's gaze returned to Marcellus's. His answer was cautious, but positive. "How I perform this task...it will tell me more about whether serving the Goddess is my destiny. The blood of the incubus is strong and has its say, too."

"The formal vampire world has protocols," Yvette said. "It would be wise for a vampire to accompany you."

"I'll go with him," Ruth said.

She'd jumped to the front of that line before Adan could do more than open his mouth. But it didn't make him close it. "That's not a great idea."

Merc faced her brother. "No harm will come to her. You have my word."

"No offense, but there are things required of her in our society that you can't influence. Not without damaging her standing in it, and ironically making her even more vulnerable when you're not around."

Merc inclined his head. "Which is why she'll do as Marcellus suggested. She'll third mark me."

She managed to hold her tongue as Dollar resumed the security briefing. She was proud of herself for not telling everyone making foregone conclusions about her life and her decisions—including one overbearing angel incubus—to go fuck themselves.

When they were done, Maddock cleared his throat, glancing between her and Merc. "Marcellus, you, Adan and I can meet with Clara now, if that suits her. Yvette, should we cast a protection spell on the immediate area so no permanent property damage is done in our absence?"

"You are not helping." Yvette's attention shifted to Ruth. "A human servant must choose to become one. But taking a servant is also a vampire's choice. One never to be treated lightly. Especially when the relationship will be far different than one with a human servant. I trust the discussion about it will be civil. Or at least won't damage anything I paid good money for."

"I'll do my best, my lady," Ruth said courteously. "But breaking through a skull shellacked with testosterone often requires Newton's Third Rule."

Yvette's golden eyes gleamed. "Your honesty is appreciated."

"I think you should take Merc to the sanctuary," Adan said unexpectedly. "Let him meet *Etsi* and *Sgidoda*. Have your discussion there."

In the place you feel most balanced, in control of who and what you want to be. Home.

He understood her too well. Ruth met his gaze. "Is there time?"

"Yes," Yvette said. "Lady Kaela is finishing up a quarterly meeting with the vampires in her territory. The Trad will not come back to Lady Kaela's home until it is over, no earlier than the day after tomorrow."

"There's a portal route to California," Adan said. "I'll make sure it's configured for you so you can take it from the sanctuary, when it's time to go."

Impressive use of Newton reference, he noted. *You were paying attention when we were home schooled.*

Don't get too impressed. It's something Etsi said about Da. And Kohana agreed.

"Won't you need..." She'd intended to ask Yvette if her and Merc's absence would leave the Circus and Clara short on security needs, but the answer to that question, at least as it concerned her, was crushingly obvious. There were plenty of assets to protect Clara.

"You talking to that Trad sounds important," Dollar said. "So it's best to get yourself in the right headspace for it. You're not going to lose your spot. You've proven yourself valuable to the team. Watch your ass, so it can get back here in one piece."

It moved her, more than she could say. "Before you leave, I'm sure Clara would appreciate seeing you," Marcellus added.

"Okay. I'll do that, and then we'll go to my home. Agreed?" She directed that to Merc. He nodded.

"See how that worked?" she said sweetly. "I suggested a plan of action and sought your input."

She stalked up to him, close enough to poke a finger against his chest, her eyes snapping with the temper she'd kept banked. "It's like Lady Yvette said. When it comes to a third mark, no one is making that decision for me. Period. That's different from...the other things between us. A Trad isn't the only one who has a line they won't be pulled across."

She was aware of her brother's regard, and those in the tent, but what mattered was the male who stared down at her. "I will break myself in pieces first, and all you'll get is the meat of what's left. If that matters to you, then meet me at the portal in about thirty minutes. If not, take Adan to see Kaela and do what needs to be done. I'll stay here."

Turning on the ball of her foot, she exited the tent.

If Yvette and Marcellus hadn't had more things to go over with him, Ruth suspected that Merc might have had a response beyond a curt nod. Adan had remained in the tent, so later she might ask him how Merc reacted.

For now, she forcibly shifted her mood into a better place to visit Clara. Charlie had finished one of her bolstering energy infusions, because the tingling remains of it filled the yurt and vibrated out from the fortune teller.

The brief respite from visions had helped Clara add weight, and strengthened her mentally. For Play Night, she'd looked almost healthy.

The toll this vision had taken shocked Ruth. No wonder Marcellus had seemed so out of sorts. It had stripped all progress away and taken even more, as if punishing Clara for the hope her recovering health had instilled. Ruth wasn't sure how she was sitting up on her own. Her face was so drawn it looked skeletal, and Ruth could have fitted three fingers into the pockets of her collarbones.

"Marcellus says enough. That even a gift from the gods has limits for what it can ask." Clara gave Ruth a tired smile and gestured, so Ruth sat on the bed with her. "I need to see this thing with the Trad through, though, before I make any decisions."

Ruth wondered if she'd live long enough to do so.

"Maddock thinks he might be able to reinforce my life energy and give me more strength. Yvette even proposed turning me, sending a request for it into the Council." Clara gave Ruth a lopsided smile, baring her human canines. "Since my visions are proving to be as much of an asset to your people as to the universe. I don't know what to do."

She sighed, rubbing her face. "I don't know how Maddock's spells, or vampirism or whatever will impact the visions. They seem to be getting a little vindictive. I don't know what it will do if I mess with them. I'll decide after we figure this Trad thing out," she repeated. "It feels like it's a really important one. I don't want to block something that will help save the world. And I don't want to stop being me."

Clara's hand tightened on Ruth's like a vise. Her focus sharpened, a laser point ripping through the universe. Ruth was already surging forward to hold her as the fortune teller bucked in the grip of the first convulsion. "Charlie..."

Charlie held onto Clara from the other side. "Just let it pass through," she instructed, her eyes full of pain.

As before, after only seconds, Clara went corpse still. No need to protect her tongue. Ruth thought she might prefer to see her have a full seizure.

The twitching started. Tiny moans. Ruth gritted her teeth, and at one point, she and Charlie clasped hands over top of Clara's, a knot to hold her to this earth.

"Oh fuck, Charlie..."

Clara's face was becoming even more drawn, her body shaking. Charlie's grip tightened. "Hold fast," she said. "We can only wait it out."

When the telltale veins finally began to throb in her forehead, blood trickled from the tender shell of Clara's ear, and from her nose. It didn't rouse Ruth's blood hunger in the slightest. Her fear and anguish for Clara far eclipsed it.

She held Clara in her arms as Charlie found a towel to blot the blood.

"I've barely begun to know and enjoy you," Ruth whispered. "Become a vampire. You'll be eternally beautiful and can eat anything you want."

Clara's eyes rose, and her quivering lips curved. She managed a chuckle, though the head resting on Ruth's shoulder was too weak to lift.

"You're an important key, Ruth," she murmured. "No matter what you and Merc decide about the marking, you have to go see Kaela. Your experience, what you see and feel, what you know, will help you see something the others miss. You might not be in time to stop... whatever it is, but it will give them more of a chance to counter it. Whatever the plan is."

Hair rose on the back of Ruth's neck as Clara's fixed gaze locked on her. As she'd spoken, her hand had latched onto the hem of Ruth's shirt with a strength her body didn't seem to possess. The force of the message planted a foreboding impossible to shake.

"It would be so much easier if these visions would just spit it out," Ruth muttered to Charlie. "The Fates may be the worst communicators *ever*."

Charlie folded the towel and set it aside. Putting her hands on Clara's, she started humming, in a rhythm that reminded Ruth of Kohana and other staff members, doing a ritual drumming on moonlit nights. Rise and fall. Rise and fall. Connecting to the earth's heartbeat.

The harsh intensity in Clara's gaze melted away, leaving the normal light in her hazel eyes. She slowly came back to them, one hand lifting to touch Charlie's face, then Ruth's. "I'm all right," she rasped, when she obviously wasn't. But that wasn't what she meant. She held onto them as she looked at Ruth. "I'm glad I got to meet you, too."

Ruth took a firmer hold on the girl. "Screw that fatalistic bullshit. Figure out a way to live until we can take care of this, whatever it is. Once that's done, do what Marcellus wants. Let Maddock block the visions. You've said you're going to die if you don't stop. Maybe *that's* the Fates' way of saying 'Okay, you've done enough.'"

Clara's startled look suggested she'd hit a point the girl hadn't considered before. When her expression turned inward, pensive, Ruth shot Charlie a subtle look of triumph, and hope, however slim it might be.

"You can go back to being a normal fortune teller," Ruth continued. "One people think has offered amazing insights into their lives. The stuff that would be obvious if they'd get the hell out of their own way."

The lines around Clara's eyes crinkled. "Like that you're falling in love with Merc, but you're terrified of the binding of a third mark, and what that will mean for the two of you."

At Ruth's surprised look, Clara lifted a shoulder. "It's not just cosmic visions I stay on top of, you know."

Ruth pinched her gently. "Even if I agree to it, it might not take. I don't think a vampire has ever tried to mark an angel. Or an incubus."

"If it doesn't work, but it gives you an advantage, them believing you've marked him, pretend it did around the vampires. Yvette says she can't detect Catriona's marks, and she thinks it's because she's Fae. So it has a precedent."

Whether intentional or not, Clara had given Ruth an out, or rather, more time to adjust to the marking idea. Or discard it entirely.

Ruth placed a gentle kiss on Clara's mouth. Totally platonic, so she wouldn't ruffle Marcellus's feathers. "Do not die. I will be *really* mad if you do."

CHAPTER NINETEEN

$\mathcal{T}$he surge of anger she'd felt toward Merc earlier couldn't hold. When she reached the portal exit and saw him there, he sensed where her mind was. Rather than saying anything, he offered her a hand. When she took it, he pulled her to him and put his arms around her. And his wings.

She hadn't looked for tenderness from him, or compassion. He gave her both, plus a needed silence. When she finally drew back, she wiped at her face self-consciously. "Let's go."

She was braced for the usual alarming, organ-jarring portal experience, punctuated by another blood vomiting episode. She still didn't travel well on the longer jumps.

However, this time the transition was like stepping out of one room and into another. She looked at an open field around her. It was an unfamiliar place, but obviously far closer to the in-between space they'd just left.

"I can get us there without the longer portal trip," Merc told her. "If you will trust me to do so."

Mutely, she put her arms around his neck, and he hefted her up so she could wrap her legs over his hips. "It will be fast, but less jarring. Have you ever wanted to travel at the speed of a rocket ship?"

She tipped her head back up to look into his face. His close, intent face. Before she thought about what she was doing, she'd brushed her lips against his mouth. "Yes," she said simply.

He stared down at her.

"Oh. I—sorry. I didn't think. I know you don't kiss...women."

He didn't say anything. Instead, after a long moment, he cupped her head and brought her back to his mouth. His eyes stayed open, staring into hers.

Her heart pounded, her mind scrambled by the knowledge something momentous was about to happen. Or maybe it would just be a kiss. Nothing special. Because he had avoided the intimacy, any potency would simply be from the anticipation, the previous denial. *Yeah, right.*

Slowly, her eyes dropped to half mast, then fully, a sound caught in her throat as he molded his mouth over hers, learning her shape. When he parted her lips, his arms tightened around her. His tongue came inside to explore the tender insides of her mouth, follow the length of her fangs, tease the tips. She shuddered, that sound becoming a moan.

She let him take the lead on the exploration, curbing her desire to do the same. For once, she surrendered without any resistance, telling him how much she fucking loved to be kissed by him.

Then she was in a tornado, spinning, shooting like a star—or a rocket. She was in his arms, held securely, her head tucked against his chest, the wind from his wings like ocean currents. Her mind couldn't hold onto anything but that kiss and the feel of his arms around her.

Just as she thought her internal organs were about to be squeezed to a pulp, and she'd need vampire healing ability to reinflate or reassemble them, he slowed down.

She didn't have the ability to turn her head to look below until they were gliding like a bird would, descending in lazy circles. "Oh," she said softly.

She was much higher than the altitude at which she flew the supply plane. Being in the thinner night air was a cool contrast to the heat of his arms around her.

But as they at last dropped below the clouds, she saw the island. Then the tiny silhouettes of lions prowling the savanna. A cougar in the mountain habitat, perched on a rock. From the angle of her head, Ruth imagined her glittering eyes were tracking their descent with curious interest. As they circled the island's perimeter, she saw the rehab area, the figures of the staff. With it being nighttime, her father was probably with them. Which reminded her she needed to announce their arrival.

Sgidoda, I'm arriving by air. With a guest. He's an angel. And an incubus.

The wordless mental acknowledgement included a rewarding deep pleasure that she was home. Two shots of it, her father's welcome reinforced by her mother's as he shared Ruth's arrival.

Her father's reaction to her announcement was in the mix as well. Though he didn't voice it, the emotion was easy enough to pick up, and made her smile.

An angel incubus. What the fuck?

By the time she directed Merc to touch down on a hill near the house, and they walked over that crest and down into the valley where her childhood home nested, her parents were on the porch.

She'd felt self-conscious about landing before them, wrapped around Merc. It didn't matter that they'd seen her in plenty of sexual situations with human servants. It wasn't about sex, but she wasn't going to dissect that right now.

Mal was sitting in his preferred chair, made of woven branches. Chumani had crafted plenty of them for the staff quarters and their home. Elisa was on the steps.

Ruth wasn't surprised that Mal had returned to the house to greet them personally. *Hey, Da. Bringing a sex demon to the island. Is that cool?*

She guessed every parent had to deal with who—and what—their offspring might bring home.

When Mal met them in the yard, Elisa was at his side, both of them studying Merc. His wings were folded along his back, the arches visible over his broad shoulders, the crossed tips brushing his calves. The moonlight made the white gleam and gave the black glimmers of silver, which touched his hair as well.

The incubus emanations were there, the sexual and more unsettling ones that alerted fight-or-flight instincts. She hadn't been able to have the talk with him yet, about toning that down.

When Mal angled himself so her mother was mostly behind him, she wished she'd thought to do that. Ruth put her hand on Merc's arm, a nonverbal reassurance to them. Her mother rallied quickly.

"A real angel," she murmured. "What a rare and fine thing that is."

"Part angel." Merc's attention covered her from head to toe, lingering on the canvas sneakers visible under the knee length hem of her skirt. Leopard faces were hand-painted on the shoes. Her dress was blue, with a satin ribbon edged scoop neckline. The color brought out the same hue in Elisa's eyes.

She and Mal were very hands-on with the never-ending sanctuary work, so she must have done a quick change before their arrival. Her thick hair was pulled up and clipped with a comb, curls falling to her shoulders.

Merc's scrutiny, coupled with the incubus vibes, started to cause a problem for Mal, but before Ruth could think how to defuse it, Merc spoke.

"Ruth has your physical features, but her mother's beauty comes from the inside and shines through. She also has her smile and voice." He extended a hand to Mal. "Thank you for allowing me to visit your island."

Ruth managed, barely, not to let her jaw hit the ground. Of course Merc knew the courtesies of the different races he encountered, but she'd yet to see him observe any of them.

Mal accepted the hand. The firm shake made it clear the two men were taking one another's measure. Ruth glanced at her mother, and saw a suppressed smile.

No way to deny it. She was witnessing the unpredictable power dynamics of a father-suitor encounter. Which made Ruth feel even more ridiculously self-conscious. She was glad Adan wasn't here to make fun of her.

"The invitation came from Ruth, but my children's guests are our guests," Mal said. "I need to finish the wellness evaluation of the reha-bilitating cats. If you join me, you can see more of the sanctuary. We'll sit down to a meal afterward. Ruth, stay and help your mother."

Mal's gaze never left Merc. Merc held it long enough to make a point before he shifted his attention to Ruth. "Is that what you wish?" he asked her.

"Yes, that's fine." After a light touch of his arm, she moved to her father, and gave him a welcoming hug. "Please don't start a fight with him," she murmured. "He's still figuring us out."

JOEY W. HILL

Mal shot her one of his patented inscrutable looks that promised nothing, but his arms around her were strong. "It's good to have you home."

"You've barely had time to get used to me not being here."

Mal's gaze flickered, a mixed reaction which tightened her heart in her chest. He touched her face, caressing a strand of hair that had loosened from her braid, thanks to the wild flight with Merc. Then he moved away, jerking his head at Merc and leading the way to the Jeep.

Ruth managed what she hoped was an encouraging look at Merc. She'd never been so uncertain of what was going on or what she was supposed to do. Feeling this foolish could make her irritable, but that wouldn't help. Fortunately, it was balanced by another feeling, though one just as mystifying. She wanted him to meet her parents. She was glad to show him her home. Officially.

When they reached the Jeep, Merc spoke to her father, and Mal nodded. He got in and turned over the ignition. As he put it in gear and gassed it for the climb out of the valley, Merc waited a few seconds, then took to the air, following. Probably a good decision. If Merc stood in the back holding the bar so his wings weren't mashed against a car seat, Mal wouldn't appreciate having him so close behind him.

Merc flying was always something to see. "Hmm," her mother said. "Would that feeling be coming all from the incubus part of him?"

"You mean the continuous sex vibes? Part of it is. The other part is just him." Ruth gave her a nudge and a smile. "Just like Da. Part of it is the vampire, part of it is him."

Elisa grinned, looping her arm with Ruth's. "Don't worry about them. Your father hasn't murdered a guest yet."

"He did let the leopards chase that one vampire's servant up a tree."

"Because he wasn't listening to your father's direction. It solved the problem, and the vampire agreed the lesson was needed." Elisa's eyes twinkled. "The two of them will figure it out. Nothing is required from us."

Her mother's knack for reading her mind was still effective. "Why do I feel like it is?"

"Because you're not in control of the situation, and you dislike that feeling intensely. Most of the time." Elisa winked. "It's a bit of

294

time until staff meal. I don't have to start the pastry rollout for the meat pies right away. Let me stage it, then we'll sit and you'll tell me how it's going."

As they went up the stairs, Elisa's questions prompted easy conversation about the Circus, allowing Ruth to stay away from the more intense elements for now. And yet, maybe because of the marking question, and all it meant, her mind landed on a topic her gut refused to let her leave alone. She needed to ask. There'd be no better time to broach it.

"*Etsi*...is *Sgidoda* disappointed...in how I am?"

It came out awkwardly, but she'd never thought about how she'd put the question out there.

Elisa had circled the kitchen island, an area big enough to allow her and the staff who rotated kitchen duty to work together. When the weather was rainy or there wasn't time for a meal at the picnic tables under the sprawling canopy of the oak tree in the yard, sometimes the staff grabbed a quick standing bite around it as well.

Ruth's question brought Elisa to a full stop. She pivoted, came back around the island and took Ruth's hands, pulling her onto a stool. Elisa faced her on the one next to it. Her blue eyes were somber, and she didn't immediately reply. No instant reassurances. It put an ache in Ruth's throat and dropped her stomach into her knees.

"He fears for you," Elisa said. "Deeply. Because he knows the vampire world. You should be asking him this yourself. His answer would bring ease to you both. But disappointed?"

Elisa's gaze brightened, bringing sunlight back to Ruth's heart, something her mother had always been able to do. She'd said that when she was nine. *We don't need to see it. Mum gives us the sun, Adan.*

"Never. You are him, Ruth, in so many ways. You carve your own path, no matter the obstacles."

Ruth gripped her mother's hands tighter. "I have to be sure. Are we talking about more than my...physical differences, with other vampires my age?"

Elisa's gaze softened. "We're talking about your desire to surrender to a Master worthy of the gift."

Ruth instinctively looked around her. "It's safe to say it here, just the two of us," Elisa assured her. "I wish you lived in a world where you didn't have to be that cautious. But maybe if it was handed to you, it wouldn't have the same value. Earning that gift, the ability to be who you are, openly, is important."

"So, even that, he's...okay with it?" The age-old desire for a parent's approval. Even when the "child" was over eighty years old.

"He fears what dangers that may bring to you. But when he looks at you and Adan, he knows you're exactly as God intended you to be. He's also glad he can't get gray hair, because his 'would look like rain-pregnant clouds all the time.' Unquote."

Elisa sat back and patted her knee. "So tell me about your angel incubus. Or incubus angel."

"The proper order depends on the day," Ruth admitted wryly. "He's scary, *Etsi*. And wonderful. Wild like lashing rain and tornadoes and earthquakes that reshape the ground. He's fought his own darkness and won, even though he still deals with the distrust of those around him."

"Perhaps that's why he's met you. When you have someone who can reflect who you truly are by what they're willing to give you, it can change your world—and the world's view of you—in good ways."

Ruth paused. "Is Da...in your head right now? Hearing this conversation?"

Elisa's expression went soft. "Aye. I feel him when he's there, even if he doesn't say anything."

"Having a third mark, it helps a lot of things, doesn't it?"

"Yes, it does. If it's the right third mark."

"They think I should mark him."

Elisa's brows rose to her hairline. "Do they think that it will take? And why do they want you to do that?"

"They don't know. As to why..." Ruth explained the other side of her job, the more-than-a-security-detail things, with Clara, and the visit to Lady Kaela. When she was done, she was glad Mal was in Elisa's head, so she wouldn't have to explain that twice. She'd thought about skipping the attack by the two vampires, rationalizing that Adan might have already told them. Or would tell them. Then she realized it might help Merc's case with her father, so added it in.

Elisa immediately rose and put her arms around her. Ruth told herself she didn't need the reassurance, but the strength of her mother's embrace was a balm to the part of Ruth still a little raw over the experience.

When she drew back, Elisa dropped her voice to a humorous stage whisper, since they both knew Mal could hear her. "Well played, adding pieces to Merc's side of the board."

"I guess I wanted to offer definitive proof of what Marcellus and the others think. That Merc can protect me in the vampire world. But if I decide to do the marking, it won't be because of that. I'm not going to let fear make the decision for me."

"I'd expect nothing less of you. What *is* worrying your head about it?"

"I don't know what the shape of it will be. It won't be a traditional relationship like yours and Da's. He may not be with me all the time. He has other responsibilities. And we haven't known one another for long. Lady Yvette says that really doesn't matter, not when it comes to vampires and servants. When I look at you and Da, and other pairings, like Lady Lyssa and Jacob, or Cai and Rand, all the different ones we've met here who are...really close, most didn't know one another for long. It was circumstances that pointed them toward the binding."

"Yes." Memories crowded in behind Elisa's eyes, good and far more painful ones. Though mostly good.

"I guess if it turns out to be a mistake, he'd just go back to his life and me to mine. The vampire world has no hold on him. There aren't any repercussions, like a human servant a vampire wants to cut loose. Or who wants to be cut loose."

"Hmph."

Ruth snorted. "You're getting better at Da's cryptic grunt. The one that has all the 'I am Groot' meanings."

Her mother understood the *Guardians of the Galaxy* reference, because Elisa liked movies and music. Though he would deny it, Ruth and Adan were sure that was why Mal had such a good generator for the house. He'd given Elisa her first record player in the 1950s. Over the years, he'd upgraded accordingly so she could enjoy each new decade of music—and then cinema.

Reliable wi-fi was a no-go on the island, thanks to all the magic in play, which suited Mal just fine. In his opinion, Cerberus had vomited cell phones straight up from the Underworld. Adan and Ruth had them; they just didn't work well on the island, if at all.

"He says Kohana taught him that grunt, and it's contagious." Elisa tapped Ruth's knee again. "The vampire-servant bond. Plenty of vampires think it can be defined, and every pairing will fit inside those boundaries. I admit, those boundaries, that definition, has worked reasonably well for the survival of the vampire world, and for many vampire-servant relationships. But there's no one set definition for it."

Elisa shrugged. "Lord Mason proposed a document on servants' rights, not only because of what his servant Jessica went through before she became his, but because of what he himself knows about it, how deep that relationship can go and what it affects."

"How do you feel about it, *Etsi*? Do you think it should be passed?" It was the first time she'd ever asked her mother the question. With a spurt of shame, Ruth realized she'd never considered a human servant's input about it relevant. And most of the vampire world held the same opinion.

Elisa's expression became pensive. She pulled over a jar on the counter and lifted the lid. "Biscuit?"

Oatmeal raisin, one of her mother's specialties. Since it fell in the category of Kohana's cornbread, something she wanted far more of than she could have, Ruth shook her head. But that wasn't the only reason she refused it. She leaned forward, putting her hand over her mother's. "I've upset you, Mum. I'm sorry."

Elisa gave her a sad smile. "No, you haven't, love. You know, Adan calls me Elisa most of the time now. You remember to do it when we're around the vampire visitors who expect you to view me as a human servant more than as a mother. However, when we're alone, you *always* call me Mum or *Etsi*. You're protective in different ways. Adan is protecting my physical wellbeing; you're protecting my feelings."

"*Etsi*..."

Elisa shook her head, squeezed her hand. "Your father made sure you two *always* saw me as your mother first, his servant second. There are other human servant parents who aren't as fortunate. They're sent away soon after the babe is born, because it's the vampire parent's blood the newborn most needs. They aren't brought back until the child is fully bonded with the vampire parent, to ensure the human servant is always viewed the 'proper' way."

"Oh, Mum. Da would never. Not in a million years."

"I know." Elisa's expression reflected the love and trust she had in her vampire Master. "When you're first together, learning one another, you have more fears and insecurities. It's a terrible thing, knowing your fate rests entirely in the hands of another, Ruth. Being a servant is an unimaginable act of faith in the vampire who binds you. Because only time will give you that knowledge of one another."

Ruth remembered when they'd learned the news about Lady Lyssa declaring her love for Jacob. They'd been visiting Lord Marshall. Elisa had risen from the floor where she'd been sitting, playing a game of chess with Matthew. She'd gone to Mal and done something peculiar. She'd knelt, kissed Mal's hand and rested her face against it. He'd bent over her and murmured something that had her fingers tightening around his calf. Words of reassurance...flavored with a sliver of hope.

"When I've thought about it, and I have, a great deal, I've realized I can't speak decisively on whether it should be passed or not. I made the decision I made, the leap of faith, for Mal. For my vampire, because that's the core of what makes the vampire-servant bond so strong."

Elisa shifted their grips, her hand tight on Ruth's. "I stood before him and said 'I will belong to you' in every conceivable and inconceivable way, in a world many think makes it impossible for love to thrive between vampire and servant. But power inequities don't kill love. They might make them harder to understand for those who only focus on the inequity, but a flower can grow out of a crack in the sidewalk. Why wouldn't love exist in environments equally as challenging? Love doesn't fit in any box, or single way of thinking."

Her gaze had taken on an intensity Ruth had rarely seen, and she wondered if, wherever her father was, he'd stopped to give his servant's words his full attention. Elisa said them with such conviction, it was as if she was etching them on his heart, one letter at a time.

"Love has no boundaries, Ruth. None. No matter what laws are passed, for or against servants, no matter if no one ever says it out loud, the vampire world survives with the vital help of that vampire-servant bond, the strength, protection and connection it provides the vampire."

Nodding, the matter settled for herself, Elisa took a bite of her cookie. "When it's finally voted upon, it might well be a fine thing. I hope so. But for me, it will have no relevance. I have what I need.

Now I just want you and Adan to find that kind of happiness. I think your brother has, with Catriona."

"I do, too. Though they're kind of sickening to watch together." Which wasn't at all true, but she had to be a sister first and foremost, rather than a female who adored seeing the tender bond between her brother and his delicate dryad. "Oh, and *Etsi?* Whatever Adan calls you when he's around you, when he talks about you to me, or in his head, it's *always* Mum or *Etsi.*"

Elisa smiled and handed Ruth a piece of the cookie. "Eat a bit. Just because you can't have everything you wish of it, don't deny yourself something you want. Find a different way to appreciate it."

Ruth gave in, putting the piece of heaven in her mouth, flavored with brown sugar and cinnamon. As they chewed companionably together, she had another question for her mother. "What did it feel like? The third mark? I've asked Adan a lot of questions about his side of it. I could talk to Catriona, but Da is always saying you and I have a lot in common. So I thought, even though you're human..."

"My experience would be somewhat relevant." Elisa chuckled at Ruth's obvious discomfort. "Vampire superiority over humans is embedded in you, but I appreciate the efforts you and your brother have made to recognize it, even if you don't always resist it."

Before Ruth could object to that—or acknowledge it—Elisa's gaze turned thoughtful again. "Once it happened...I was never alone again. But it's terrifying, Ruth, because with the wrong Master, loneliness can take on a depth and pain even Hell cannot match. Be very sure before you take that step. But over the years, as I've watched vampires make right choices, wrong choices, I've decided it's like love itself. You take the leap and see where it takes you."

Elisa stroked Ruth's hair from her brow. "But no matter where that leap takes you, *a chuisle mo chroí,* remember we're here. You have a family. We're the net at the bottom. Always."

~

Merc noted that Mal seemed distracted as he went through the rehab wellness checks, though he answered whatever casual questions Merc posed about the fascinating process. Merc had cloaked his wings, deciding it was easier to present himself as a visitor of indeterminate origins. Even so, the other staff members maintained a wide berth. He wondered if Mal had requested that, or if it was the vibe he put off. He'd meant to tone it down around her parents, but something about meeting her father had made him...he was *not* going to use the word nervous, but the end result was he'd stuck with what he knew. Being intimidating.

He could have saved himself the effort, since the male was obviously Ruth's father. He didn't intimidate. And while Merc would have to be tortured to admit it, Mal could be pretty damn intimidating himself, with that steady stare and expressionless face.

It didn't stop Merc from asking the question he'd wanted to ask for a while. Having the staff members at a safe distance helped make that happen. "Why is she weaker than other vampires? She sleeps more often, and goes to bed earlier, gets up later, than the ones I know."

The male vampire turned to lock gazes with him. "You've done nothing to earn my trust, and yet you ask me questions like that."

Merc inclined his head. "My apologies. I intended no offense. I sought information because...I want to know more about her."

"Then you should ask her."

"It's a question that might hurt her, or make her uncomfortable. I prefer to avoid that."

That dark gaze could have shaved rock. Merc held fast against it, though not without unexpected effort. At length, the vampire male grunted and moved to the next enclosure. Pointedly without giving him an answer.

"It's not tall enough, Mal," one of his staff members said, pointing to the step ladder lying on the ground. "If we make a scaffold, we can get up there and repair it."

Merc noted this enclosure had netting over the top, twenty-plus feet above the ground. He expected the tear near the center was what the conversation was about.

The animals within, sleek golden cats with long ears and pointed faces, watched the gathering outside their enclosure with intense slanted eyes.

"I think we have this," Mal told his staff member. "Return the ladder to storage." As the man gave him a curious nod but headed off to perform the task, Merc noticed Mal was studying the space his wings inhabited, though the cloaking made them invisible. "Do you know how to mend a net?"

With the edge in his tone, he might as well have asked, *"Can you walk and chew food at the same time?"*

"You could direct me," Merc said evenly. "Why doesn't your injured tiger have a covering over his area?"

"Tigers aren't climbers or jumpers the way caracals are. Too heavy. They're the only cat species that likes to swim, though." Mal's eyes flickered. "Ruth learned many lessons here. Even the most powerful creature has an unexpected weakness. And the smallest can be more resourceful than expected."

"Her ability to keep her wits about her in the most terrifying of circumstances proves she learned those lessons well. But I think they worked with what was already there."

"Hmph." Mal picked up the coil of rope and snips next to the ladder and handed them to Merc. "Weave this through the torn opening," he pointed to it, "draw the hole closed, and knot it securely."

"You aren't concerned about your staff seeing my wings?"

"We've had Fae here."

Fine. if Mal wasn't worried about it, neither was Merc.

Merc let the cloaking vanish, aware of the staff's indrawn breaths, their sudden attention. Intrigued but not astonished. The unexpected *was* the expected thing around here. Well, except for one young male who had the air of a newer hire. He went stock still and watched Merc like he'd never seen such a sight before.

Merc took the rope and went aloft. With his dagger, he didn't need the snips. As he hovered above the torn spot, he was amused to see the caracals tracking him. "You will catch far more than you can handle with this bird," he informed them.

They didn't look convinced, but since he was outside the netting, they settled and watched as he followed Mal's direction to repair the opening. Mal handled other matters as Merc worked, but Merc was on his radar, because when he finished, Mal had returned. Merc waited until the male vampire gave him an approving nod. "That'll work."

When Merc landed, the newer staff member had drawn closer. He reached out toward Merc's wings, but Merc's warning hiss, the flash of sharp teeth, had him snapping to attention as if he'd been woken from a sound sleep.

"I wouldn't advise it," Merc said.

"My apologies, sir," the man said hastily. "I forgot myself."

"Don't let it happen again, Shane," Mal told him. "Many of our visitors are as dangerous as the cats."

"I know. I mean, I...thought I knew." Shane looked hard at Merc. "You just...it's a feeling..."

"I suggest suppressing it," Merc said.

The male offered another apologetic nod, almost a bow, and retreated, though his gaze kept stealing back to Merc.

Mal had watched the exchange with an impassive look. "I expect you have to deal with that at the Circus, too."

Merc chose to interpret the comment more narrowly. "I cloak the wings when I'm doing security work. But I allow the children to touch them during the Promenade, the aftershow."

"You like children."

Incubus energy had no effect on them until they passed puberty. So their reactions to him were honest. He liked that. "Yes. That male doesn't seem the same as your other staff members."

Mal led him toward the next enclosure. "He's a seasonal hire. Half Irish, half Cherokee. His mother is a second mark in Lord Marshall's household, our Florida overlord. He's studying to be a minister."

With Marcellus, even if they thought they'd never met an angel, some core part of a person's soul recognized him as such. As Ruth had when she first met the senior angel. They didn't have that issue with Merc. Or rather, they hadn't ever done so before.

The idea that they could, that the male might be picking that up from him... The thought was uncomfortable. Merc wasn't sure how to react to it. He put it aside, because he had more important things to pursue than whether or not Shane had actually detected the angel instead of the incubus blood.

Merc met Mal's gaze. "What would you ask of a man who wants to be with your daughter?"

~

The winged male was an unknown quantity, but Ruth had brought him here, and she had good judgment. Still, Mal wasn't going to abandon a father's automatic suspicion. Taking Merc with him to work the sanctuary was a way to gather evidence, for or against.

Throughout the tour, he'd been attentive, followed Mal's direction, and asked intelligent questions. Until he'd tried to pick Mal's brain about Ruth. But in fairness, Mal had poked him a couple times himself, to assess his temperament.

In Merc's question now, Mal heard an uncertainty he recognized. A male trying to figure out what a woman needed. Even if Ruth hadn't given him the heads up on it, Mal could tell that was still new territory for Merc.

While he wasn't going to make exploring that ground easier, he would be honest. Because the honest answer wasn't going to map things out any better for the male.

"That he cares about her wellbeing more than his own. That he sees her, sees who she is. And, if it is the best thing for her, even if it destroys him to do it, he will walk away from her."

Merc's jaw went tight, caught between annoyance and a deeper internal struggle. Mal had to hide an unexpected smile at the answer that reaction provided him. Even before Merc spoke and confirmed it.

"You think that's what would be best for her?"

"That's not for me to answer. That's for you and her. And truthfully, Merc? I have no concerns about Ruth choosing a male who's wrong for her. When it comes to her will and self-respect, she's as well armed as her mother and I could possibly wish."

After they finished up in the rehab area, Mal indicated they should head back to the house. This time Merc took the offer to ride in back, standing and holding onto the bar. He stretched his wings straight out behind him, as if he enjoyed the feel of the wind passing over them that way. Mal checked them out in the side mirror. They were impressive, no arguing that, but he wasn't going to be caught staring.

The discussion between Elisa and Ruth had astounded him. Broken his heart and restored it. He'd never thought his daughter worried about him being disappointed in her. He and Elisa had given her as much responsibility on the island as she could handle, and pushed her out of her comfort zone whenever it made sense to do so. He didn't have to push much. Most times, he had to stop himself from reining her back.

Disappointed? Her even having the thought had been a gut punch, making him wonder if he'd done or missed something over the years that had instilled that worry.

No. It comes from her own heart. Her great love for you, her desire to make sure she lives up to your expectations, even as she meets her own for herself.

It was second nature to share concerns about their children, mind-to-mind. Elisa's staunch reply eased his tension.

Mal didn't shield his children from challenges; there was certainly no room for it in the vampire world, but it was idiotic for any species to do it. A parent's job was to prepare their offspring to stand on their own two feet in the world, not shield them from it. A parent who did that was the actual child. A selfish child, protecting a favorite toy.

It didn't mean he grieved any less for the pain his children had to endure to get through those challenges. But because Elisa shared that burden with him, it kept them from interfering, taking choices and opportunities away that they shouldn't. Which had certainly been a danger, given the challenges they'd faced when the children were much younger.

She's falling in love, Elisa noted. *What do you think of him?*

He's feeling the same. Far less familiar territory for him, though. And he's damn scary.

That's not a bad thing for her. Not if his desire is to protect her.

Mal shot another glance at the spread wings, the male's braced legs, the way his attention moved around them, taking in everything.

Perhaps not. But I'm not sure how well he'll protect her heart.

When they reached the house, Merc had to fold his wings tight around his shoulders to get through the front door, but it was a practiced, almost unconscious move. Elisa and Ruth sat in the kitchen, comfortably chatting in the way of women.

Elisa's blue eyes brightened as she rose and came to Mal. She was brushing back a chestnut brown lock of hair that had escaped from her barrette. It tried and failed daily to hold the entirety of her mane, which Mal didn't mind at all.

He put his arms around her, held her close. *I heard your words,* atsilusgi. *How is it you make me love you more every day?*

I've been with you for eighty years. I've never made you do a single thing you didn't want to do.

He smiled at the tart reply, held her closer. *What Kohana said about Ruth being irresistible? I think he said it about you first.*

She pushed at him, giving him her soft smile, then his practical maid was back, leveling an intent gaze on Merc. Elisa had everything laid out for the staff meal. Normally, she'd have it cooking by now, but the delay was quickly explained.

"Merc," she said. "I'm glad you're back. I need help with the pastry dough for these Scotch pies. Your fingers are just the right size for pinching the sides. Mal," her gaze turned innocently toward him. "You and Ruth should go see the east field. Those purple wildflowers are in full bloom and you know Ruth loves those. She can show you later," Elisa told Merc.

Ruth had a droll expression on her face. *Tell me again who's boss on this island, Da?*

Mal shot her a look, but since Elisa was still in reach, he tucked the lock back into the barrette, his thumb passing over the cushion of her lips. While he gave her buttock a reproving squeeze, he knew her intent, and agreed with it.

A good servant anticipates her Master's needs and desires, he told his grinning daughter.

Merc's mystified expression made Mal want to chuckle. He expected the male wasn't used to being told to help in the kitchen. In a million years, he might never again meet someone brave enough to do so. But his servant was one in a million.

He brushed his mouth over Elisa's, savoring her sweet lips. *Be careful with him*, atsilusgi. *He's not entirely house trained.*

Her fingers rested on his chest, brushing the straight black hair that had fallen forward over his shoulder. *I'm well used to that kind.*

Now was not the time to follow up on his desire to put her beautiful mouth and hands where he wanted them. His daughter was giving him the '*Really, Da? We have a guest*' look.

She was one to talk. Whenever her gaze turned to the male, the heat between them was obvious.

Mal gave her a *don't disrespect your father* look, but left Elisa with a heated thought that put a flush in her cheeks and planted the promise they'd return to the feeling later.

Yet when he gestured to Ruth to precede him to the door, Mal's mind shifted into a far different mode. He met Merc's gaze with a hard stare. And waited.

Earning points, Merc responded without the question being put out there. "She will come to no harm from me."

Mal inclined his head. "Don't ruin the meat pies," he said.

As he and Ruth left the house and walked toward the field Elisa had mentioned, Ruth leaned against him. Mal put his arm around her shoulders, pulling her close to kiss her forehead, her hair, wrapping both arms around her for a moment. Then she spun away and jumped on his back with a laugh that still held a touch of the child she'd once been. He piggy backed her to the field as she wrapped both arms around his chest.

"I need to take a picture," she said. "No one will believe that Merc helped out in the kitchen. What's got into *Etsi?* She's never drafted Lady Lyssa to help prepare dinner."

Mal chuckled. "She knows the protocols with vampires. Plus Merc is more than a guest. You've made that clear. Your mother has her own vetting process."

Ruth jumped down and walked beside him. When they reached the fence and she took a seat on the top rail, him resting his elbows on it next to her, he asked her some follow-up questions about her Circus experiences, things Elisa's own conversation hadn't already covered.

He could tell his daughter liked being there. Really liked it. Despite the more harrowing experiences she'd had, it reassured him anew that the decision had been a good one. She would guess, but he didn't need to detail, that Adan had made routine reports to Mal about how she was doing.

He hadn't told them about the two vampires attacking her, but his son hadn't hidden the information. Adan hadn't had a chance to touch base with Mal since then. Being a Light Guardian didn't always let him get within range of Mal's mind or, even better, have a face-to-face visit.

When the conversation reached a natural pause, Mal decided it was time to say what he knew needed to be said. "You know I love you, Ruth."

Her gaze flickered. "I know, Da. I've always known."

"Yes. But here's what you need to know, beyond the shadow of a doubt. I honor your strength, your will, your independence. And I admire it."

As she went still, he had to take a beat. What he was about to broach wasn't something he spoke of often. It had taken him years to accept the knowledge for himself.

"I was born Cherokee. I was made into a vampire. Being born of one race and evolving into another, one that integrates with and remolds your original self, isn't easy. It took me a while to learn to be proud of who I am. It took time for me to accept that being different doesn't make me any less of a vampire.

"You were born a vampire," he told her, "but you have traits that make the vampire world more challenging for you. If ever those traits become common knowledge, it will be even more difficult. But if anyone can do it, I expect you'll be the vampire who shows them natural submission in our kind is not weakness."

Her eyes widened. He'd never said it aloud, but he would do it now, showing her that she should carry no shame about it. Just caution, to protect herself.

"No more than it is in the people we claim as our servants, our greatest strength." He thought of Elisa, and the other servants he'd known. Kohana. Chumani. "That form of submission has honor to it. It's a choice, made from a position of strength that most who are Dominant may never truly understand. But I do. You're as much a warrior as your brother.

"There are always going to be people who want to put who you are, what you do, in a box, in a cage, and say you can't step outside that definition or expand it. You have to be the one to find the key and unlock the door, break down the walls and make them bigger. Turn it into a home you're comfortable in, and give that house light and space."

"I think Merc understands that struggle, Da," she said slowly, digesting his words. "Between being an incubus and an angel. I think it's part of what draws us to one another."

"Good. But whoever you choose, whether him or another, make sure he helps you strengthen that foundation in yourself. I hope we've helped with that, in all the right ways, which can also be some of the hardest ones. We often stood back when all we wanted to do was catch you, stand between you and pain, disappointment."

Her eyes went luminous, full of emotions. "A long time ago, Da, you boiled it down to three things that always seem to work for me."

"I did? Enlighten me on my own wisdom."

Her smile eased the ache of the emotions, for both of them. "Be respectful to all. Be kind where possible. Use whatever strengths I have to resist doing something I don't think is right, or being someone I'm not." Her face shadowed. "Even if I have to hide and protect that definition of myself deep inside my soul."

"Did I say that last part?" he asked.

"No. But it's a strength. Being able to do that, hold onto it, along with the hope that one day I won't *have* to hide it."

"I rarely repeat myself, but I'm going to do so again. I couldn't be prouder of you, Ruth. Don't ever doubt that."

Slipping off the fence rail, she came into his open arms. She put her face to his shoulder, a brief tender exchange, then straightened and stepped back. "So...do you like him?"

He lifted a brow, feigning ignorance. "Who?"

She made a face. "*Sgidoda.*"

"I'm not prepared to make a judgment yet."

"Good." Her eyes sparkled.

"How is that good?"

"You haven't *passed* judgment yet."

He made one of his neutral grunts and she laughed. "I like him, Da. I really do. He's dangerous and yet honorable. Confusing and mean and tender all at once. In the right ways. He's like us."

"He's like the cats you love."

"Maybe so." She gazed around her. "I love it here so much. Right now, I'm glad I'm seeing more of the world, but my heart knows *this* is my place." Her attention returned to him. "Thank you for creating it, Da. For telling the vampire world to piss off and doing the impossible."

That little smile came back to her lips. "And I'm glad you don't disapprove of him."

"I don't yet approve of him. I might. Once he proves himself."

"In a hundred years or so?"

"That's a little hasty. Perhaps two hundred."

She laughed and changed the subject to more mundane things, giving their deeper emotions time to even out. "You have a crazy couple days dead ahead. Lord Mason and Farida. I wish we could stay."

"If your business concludes early in California, swing back and catch the tail end. Your mother is excited. She's already baking their favorites."

Ruth chuckled. "For Mum, the visit is all about the kids. Lord Mason's just an afterthought. Is Kane still coming with Farida?"

"Yes. Though that information is as confidential as confidential gets," he reminded her. "Lady Lyssa is letting Lord Mason bring him while she handles other matters. His servant Jessica will join us, once she stops in Atlanta to have a shopping visit with Anwyn. Mason wanted to give her a few days' respite from servant duties, since being a Council member's servant can be," he paused, obviously recalling Mason's exact words, "'Almost worse than the hell of *being* a Council member.'"

"I think only his friendship and regard for Lady Lyssa keeps him serving. He likes politics as much as you do, Da." Ruth nudged him. "And I haven't been gone long enough to forget the all-important rule about our visitor schedule. Top secret, need-to-know basis. Always."

Especially when it included the young progeny of Council members. Normally the importance of the guests had an inverse relationship with Mal's desire for them to visit. However, in the case of Farida, Mason's daughter, and Kane, Lyssa's son, the teenagers loved the island and the cats, and were such appealing, intelligent youngsters that he welcomed them as much as Elisa did.

For form's sake, though, he grimaced. "At least they've been here before. I shouldn't have to go over the rules again. Much."

"*Etsi* will remind them while she feeds them."

On that note, while they'd talked, Mal had kept his mind inside Elisa's. With a half smile, he shared what he was seeing with Ruth.

Elisa was instructing Merc on how to pinch the dough around the meat filling. She placed her hands on his to show him the right way of it, and when a timer went off, she ducked under one of his wings, brushing it away like a curtain as she grabbed her potholders.

He admittedly liked that Merc tried to help, moving to take the boiling stock pot off the burner for her. She stopped him with a quick admonition. *Here now, you'll burn yourself, grabbing them bare handed. Use these potholders.*

The unlikely picture of Merc using quilted potholders with bright flowers had Ruth smiling, but her eyes were soft. Yes, his daughter was falling in love. As a woman did, not a girl.

Elisa had felt his watchful presence. *I do like him, Mal. Yes, he's scary and maybe cruel at times, but he's also vulnerable and wants to be kind. I think he's besotted with Ruth. And confused by her.*

Almost an echo of what Ruth herself had said.

His daughter was looking up at him and shaking her head. "Only Mum."

Mal brushed a strand of hair from her cheek. "When it comes to your mother, I think the universe is like me. It just stands back, shakes its head and smiles."

CHAPTER TWENTY

*a*fter Merc demolished four of the Scotch pies, and Ruth enjoyed a few bites herself, he asked her to take him to her favorite places on the sanctuary. He already knew about her tree in the savanna area, so she started with the mountain habitat. She and Adan had played in the creeks, scaled the trees. Run with the different cougars who'd inhabited it over the years.

She showed him the preserve's most impressive view, which was located there. For the magic user or person with the proper permissions, the rock ledge offered even more; a panoramic view of the whole island, all the magical fault lines that connected the different habitats, and provided portal access to similar terrains in other countries. When she looked at that view, she felt even more connected to the island, knowing she belonged here. The magic told her she did.

"Is this where you come when you need to feel better or more balanced?"

It was an unexpected question, but he didn't usually ask the expected things. "I love it, but no."

"Take me there."

It was back near the lions' habitat, on a grassy slope that melted into a rolling plain. That plain met the blue line of the African portal, a mirror of what lay behind it, more grassy slopes, and beyond that, the sea. When it was opened to release a rehabilitated cat, she could smell the salt air, a different scent from the ocean surrounding their island.

The first time her father had found her here, she'd explained why she liked the spot, in mostly the same words she gave Merc now.

"What I felt here, it was a mix of my mother and someone else, a love so strong...it was comforting, a cocoon. When things were worrying me, I'd come here and know, no matter how bad things could get, it would be all right, because something was stronger than all of it. A place that says hold on and have faith."

An indecipherable emotion had gripped Mal's features. He'd assured her it was a safe place, and she wasn't in trouble, but he'd waited until she was older to explain his expression.

"Did you continue to feel it as you got older?" Merc asked.

"It became more of an echo. Still comforting, but like a familiar childhood marker. Do you have any of those?"

"The first stability I had in my life was Marcellus." He said it in such a matter-of-fact way, she wondered if Merc understood its significance.

"Have you told him that?"

"I expect he knows."

"I'm sure he knows, but he might like hearing it. I think he cares and worries for you. Like my parents do for me."

Merc seemed surprised by the comparison. A little discomfited. "Our relationship is different."

Maybe less so than he was willing to admit, but she left it alone. Merc was like her father; neither easily explored or expressed deeper emotions. She was still reeling a little bit from how open Mal had been with her out by the field. Even as she knew she'd never forget what he'd said to her.

Proud of you...beyond the shadow of a doubt.

He said what he meant, which meant she'd earned it. She would keep earning it.

"I understand why you see yourself spending most of your life here," Merc said. They sat side by side on the slope, his arm braced behind her back, his wing curved over that. He was warm against her side, and she had her hand resting on his thigh, drawing figure eights on denim. "Even as I can see you want to see more of the world first. Travel."

"What about you? If you decide to serve the angels, I'm guessing your world will become much wider. Do you like being with the Circus?"

"I do. Particularly these past few days. My relationships with the others are changing shape. Thanks in large part I think to you. Or them seeing me with you." A frown crossed his face. "But...what if they all want to be friendly? Desire company and endless conversation?"

His obvious horror had her grinning. "Trust me, the ogre vibes are still there." She lifted a brow. "They were set a little high when you first met my parents."

"I was unsettled," he told her with dignity. "I haven't ever been introduced to someone's family. Not like that."

He stretched out his wings, letting the wind move through the primaries as he tipped his head back to look into the night sky. When he yawned, it reminded her of someone stretching out their arms at the dinner table after a full meal.

"Mum is a serious feeder. Do you need a nap?"

"No. I can sleep, but don't need to do so. However, if I ate at your mother's table too often, that might change."

He pulled her into his lap, so she was the center of his attention. She didn't object, a fizzing of nerves happening at the look in his eyes. Lurking among all those emotions and thoughts behind his eyes, the incubus watched and waited. Seeing if the angel side of him would ever weaken enough for it to take control.

The eternal war between Id and the Super Ego, Merc the Ego holding the balance in between. Only for him, there was nothing theoretical about it. It was an actual battlefield, a war he'd had to decide how to fight, since Marcellus and Mikhael had found him.

Merc wouldn't let that side of himself take control from him again. She knew it. Just as she knew he'd never reject his incubus blood, never abandon or leave it out in the cold, because he knew what that felt like.

"The third mark," he said abruptly. "You're concerned I don't understand its meaning."

"I understand you want to protect me. And I appreciate that. But it can't be the only reason."

She wasn't entirely sure how to explain what reasons would be enough, but Merc stopped her from saying more. He cupped her throat, thumb moving over it.

"I've watched Yvette with Charlie and Gundar. Just through a second mark, her ability to speak in their minds, her way of knowing them, has a closeness to it I found intriguing. But I've also spent time around Adan and Catriona. It's deeper. A soul connection, where the vampire can come inside, not just the mind of the servant, but their soul."

"You've paid attention." Her heart thumped a little harder.

"I've always paid attention, but lately the knowledge has more context."

She couldn't smile. "I don't know how the mark will work with you. Angels are more powerful than vampires. Catriona is Fae, and High Fae are way more powerful than vampires, but she's a lesser Fae, and the Light Guardian thing might have weighted it on his side. Or not. It doesn't matter. Not really. They love each other."

"Yes. They've found a home in one another." His expression became thoughtful. "A different kind of home from this place, though it's still home to him. I overheard Charlie speaking to a troupe member. His wife left him a couple years ago, and he's still having difficulty. She said when a relationship dissolves, it's like the home it created has been wrecked. Leaving one feeling homeless and adrift."

"You think...the third mark is a form of home." Her hand was resting on his chest, his heart thudding beneath it.

"Isn't it?" Those dark eyes held her. "I heard the conversation you and your mother had, after dinner."

~

"I like this." Ruth stroked the wood's texture. The family picture had been mounted in the living room for years, but as a thank you for letting her and her children visit the island, one of the Farida Sanctuary mothers who did woodworking had sent Elisa and Mal a new frame for it. Small rectangles of reclaimed antique wood in multiple earth hues had created it.

The painting had been done by Evan, a vampire artist sired by Lord Uthe, a former Council member. It had been his gift to Mal and Elisa, shortly after Adan and Ruth turned fifty. In the portrait, the four of them sat on the porch steps. Elisa's gaze and hands were on her children, Mal's on her shoulder and Adan's. Ruth sat between Mal's knees, her hand on the left one, closest to Adan. All of them linked.

Many born vampires didn't make it to fifty, but if they did, their chances of doubling that life span or making it to full maturity increased considerably. It was considered the "take your first deep breath" point for most born vampire parents.

Elisa touched the frame, just below Mal's braced foot in the picture. "Ruth, I want you and Adan to have your lives. I know you've told us you want to come back here, but your father and I want that to be your choice. Understand? Life is long. Especially for a vampire."

"Of course, *Etsi*."

Merc and Mal were discussing the history of the sanctuary, so she assumed her and her mother's conversation was mostly private. "Are you all right?"

"Yes." But Elisa's gaze was thoughtful when she looked upon her daughter. "A servant lives to be three hundred, if God is merciful. But Mal can live so much longer. My hope is that you and Adan, the families you build for yourself, will be part of his life, so when that happens, as it will," the Irish increased in her voice, "he'll never be alone. He's a strong man, that he is. But his soul...his soul will need you, the both of you."

"Mum." Ruth put an arm around her. "Of course. Adan and I...we love you both so much. We'd never..."

"I know. And don't fret. I'm not being morbid. I just want to say it, because loss is a part of life, and we don't get to choose when loss happens, no matter our plans. Or how immortal we think we are."

The gemstone blue eyes touched Ruth's, held. "Whenever that end comes, for you or one you bind yourself to, the best you can do is hope that you didn't take anything for granted. You tried to be your best self, which means you gave far more than you took. And you loved with your whole heart."

Elisa turned toward the men. Mal had put a sheet of paper on the coffee table. The top of the table was a horizontal slice from the trunk of a giant tree, fallen by a hurricane that had hit the island a decade ago. The golden stain and polish highlighted the age rings. Mal was sketching out a point about the fault lines to Merc.

"Lord above, he's not an easy man, but who of them are?" A small smile played on Elisa's lips, then she nudged Ruth. "And who wants easy? We all know the difficult ones make up for it in other ways."

As Ruth rolled her eyes, Elisa's narrowed. "Those are a little close to the fire," she murmured, and casually moved in that direction to close the fire screen. As she did, she used the toe of one of her canvas sneakers to nudge Merc's wing tip a few inches further from the range of sparks.

Merc's lips twitched, showing he was aware of the movement, though he didn't fluster her mother by turning his head toward her to draw attention to it.

In that moment, Ruth realized the greatest danger she'd risked in bringing Merc home to meet the family. Seeing him with her parents, her ability to think sensibly about him, resist the desire to bind herself to him in every possible way, had only moved farther out of her grasp.

~

Merc touched her lips. "If the third mark is a home, it's one I want to share with you. I've made my choice, as a 'servant' must before a vampire takes that step." He drew them both to their feet and put his hands on her shoulders. His expression held her still.

"I won't be ruled by your mark, Ruth. But I'll serve you with it. Protect you, care for you. Learn how to build a home with it." He paused. "I'm not sure what love is, but if it's required to build a home that lasts, I'll learn how to do that as well."

She managed a half smile, impressive considering how his words overwhelmed her. "Just another skill. Like riding a bike or using a power saw."

"Exactly," he said, with conviction. "Though I don't know how to do either of those things."

She chuckled, pressing her forehead to his chest. Thinking.

The two of them faced one another, the sea and worlds beyond this one laid out around them. The home she'd always known, counted on. While he offered her another one.

"Tell me more about how it works. It will help you to stop shaking." Drawing back to take her hand, he pulled them into a walk. Just a stroll through the sanctuary on a moonlit night, as they contemplated an eternal bond with one another.

"First mark is a geographical locater." She cleared her throat. "The second allows mind-to-mind communication. We usually do them one at a time, with a little break in between. All at once tends to burn through the servant like acid, so I'm told. But even if that wasn't true, I'd want to take it one step at a time. See the effect. If the first one doesn't take, none of them will."

If it didn't, she'd struggle with the absurd feeling that it was an omen, for how long their relationship would last. Total nonsense. It would simply mean angel blood was too powerful for a vampire to bind it.

"If that's the case, it doesn't matter. I'll bind you to me in my own way, Ruth. Be your Master however you need. As long as you desire me to." His lips curled, showing a hint of fang. "Or as long as I desire it. Whichever is longer."

She attempted another smile, but stronger feelings were pushing forward. Merc turned the subject in a seemingly different direction. "You said your father eventually explained to you why you felt as you did, on the slope overlooking the lion habitat."

"Yes. My mother had to say good-bye to a child she loved here. A made vampire, turned far too young. He chose to end his life, and she held him in his last few moments."

Which was terrible, but the two messages that had remained in that spot, impressing themselves upon her well before she knew what had happened there, weren't.

Love survives everything, and there were worse things than death. Like living a life she didn't choose.

I choose him. I choose you.

She didn't say it, but she didn't have to do so. He'd said he could "feel" things from her. His hand on hers tightened, and the silver in his eyes glittered. He turned to face her.

It might be a stupid impulse that merely felt like Fate, but she was doing it. "I think we should go back to my room to do this. If you're all right with that. Dawn's not too far off."

"Agreed. Would you like to fly or walk?"

"Will that be a perk of our vampire-servant bond? A permanent flight option?"

He gave her an imperious look. "Didn't we just discuss that I won't be a traditional servant?"

"You did say you'll care for me in the ways I need."

"The desire to fly isn't a need."

"How would you feel if you couldn't do it?"

His answer was a grunt. Elisa might be right about the expression being contagious. But Merc did step closer, encouraging her to put her arms around him before he lifted her in cradle fashion. The trip wasn't long, and he didn't go fast. During the easy glide, he held her close, her arms around his shoulders, the two of them gazing down as she told him different things about the sanctuary. As he dipped his head closer, she brushed her lips over his ear, nuzzling it. His hair feathered across her cheek and brow.

She'd wait for him to initiate the next kiss, since she'd done it for the first one. It was as he'd said. This wasn't going to be a typical vampire-servant bond. He wouldn't be hers to demand what she wanted from him.

But she thought he would be hers. And that worked.

They landed in front of the house. Elisa and Mal were out doing the final checks before Mal came in for dawn. Usually Elisa joined him for a little while in their room. Once he was fully asleep, she'd rise and do the things she handled during daylight, but she'd go back to him a couple hours before sundown to take her ease beside him and be there for what he desired from her when he woke. Blood, or other things.

Servants didn't need much sleep. Their vampire's blood kept them running like a train.

Even if her blood didn't feed Merc the way her sexual energy did, she hoped he'd still take it from her, beyond the requirements of the marking. The intimacy to it was a different form of nourishment, for them both.

The house was empty, except for the current pair of housecats who were always on the porch, lounging on the dining table, or sleeping in Mal's office, sprawled over his desk paperwork or on the worn couch cushions. She stroked the head of one on the kitchen counter before guiding Merc down the steps to the underground sleeping quarters.

Her bedroom was the furthest and deepest. The most protected. She hadn't recognized the significance of that until she was in her teens, perhaps because Adan's was next to hers. Her parents kept them in the best place to protect them from encroaching enemies and the sun. When Farida and Kane came, their guestrooms would be the ones right across the hall from Ruth's, for the same reason.

As Merc entered her room with her, he took in his surroundings. While it had an adult décor, she'd kept a few nostalgic vestiges of her youth on the shelves. Like Adan's grass bunny, now brown and dry, but kept intact under a glass shade so the house cats couldn't shred it.

There was also a beaded bracelet, woven from her twin's hair. Before he'd gone to the Underworld, she'd cut his hair and made four of them. One for herself, Mal, Elisa, and even Catriona, though at the time Ruth had had far more ambivalent feelings about the Fae who'd captured her brother's heart. Ruth had worn the bracelet until Adan's return, though she'd touched it so often, it was a wonder it hadn't fallen apart before she carefully placed it there to preserve it.

"No mirrors," Merc commented. "A tell, for vampires."

"If the vampire's not worried about anyone noticing the lack of reflection, you'll still see them, because they make a space look bigger, and we're as susceptible to decorating trends as anyone."

She shot him a smile. "Vampires who live among unsuspecting humans usually have them where visitors would expect, like a bathroom, to blend better. They have to stay conscious of not getting caught in front of one, but most humans aren't that observant, or they don't acknowledge what that subconscious part of them doesn't want to know."

Paintings of the cats were on her walls. The canopy over her bed was strung with beads, feathers and bits of fur. It hummed with the energy of the protective spell that intensified when she was in the room. As her fingers trailed over one of the strands, her heart tightened over the loss of the medicine bag again. But it was all right. Kohana lived inside her, and in her home here.

So did his kin. Kohana's grandson, Hanska, was Mal's right hand on the staff. Showing the shamanic aptitude Kohana always claimed was in his ancestry, he assisted Mal on maintaining the magical protections, another apprentice.

Merc touched the bed post, absorbing the energy, and turned toward her. Ruth wasn't a shy person, but what they'd come here to do had her at a loss. She'd second marked human staff members growing up, those who assisted Mal and Elisa with her care. Yes, she'd thought of them as extended family, but unapologetically also subordinates.

"Have you ever given anyone the marks?"

He'd tapped into the direction of her thoughts again. "I've done a couple second marks. A lot of born female vampires wait until close to their first century mark to do a third mark. My father...a few years ago he suggested I bind one of the men here. I never reached a decision."

"Did I meet him tonight?"

"Maybe at the rehab center. Hanska. He's like Kohana, his grandfather. Unexpectedly tall for an Indian. That's what Hanska means. One of the meanings. Tall."

She pressed her lips together, and thought of other things to say. Before she could, Merc shook his head. Keeping his eyes upon her, he removed his shirt, folding his wings back to slide it free of the openings cut for them. He hadn't changed out of the security shirt before coming here.

"I thought it would be good to show your father I'm employed."

She laughed. Then her attention slid down his chest, to the hip bones revealed by his jeans as he stretched upward for the movement. The gleaming layer of dark chest hair that narrowed over his navel and disappeared under the waistband drew her gaze to what was below it.

Merc took off his shoes and socks, then unbuttoned the jeans and opened the zipper with a casual pull on the tab. When he removed the pants, he revealed dark shorts beneath. His cock was a smooth, tempting curve beneath their stretched hold.

Staying in place, he extended a hand, making her come to him, which helped steady her. When she reached him, he grasped the hem of her shirt. She lifted her arms as he took it off, then turned her, releasing the clasp of her bra and sliding that off her arms. He trailed his fingertips down her back, over her shoulder blades and spine, exploring the small of her back. He slipped a finger in the waistband of her jeans.

"Take them off. And what is beneath them."

When she did, leaving her naked before him, he turned her back around and tipped up her chin. "You do this with no barriers."

"Clothes aren't a barrier."

"They're a symbol of deeper, more significant barriers."

He put a hand on her shoulder. Just a slight pressure, but she knelt, resting her palm on his knee. Then, following her instincts, she put her forehead against his thigh. She could hear the rush of blood from his femoral artery. Her fangs started to lengthen, saliva gathering in her mouth.

His hand was in her hair, stroking her scalp, slow, but not easy. The weight to his touch promised he was about to be demanding. She waited on it, glad to recognize it.

He gathered her hair in his fist in that way that made her mind stumble over its own thoughts. As Merc twisted it around his knuckles, his fingertips caressed her nape. "Where can you give this mark?"

"Anywhere really, though major arteries tend to be the best. Carotid, femoral..."

His grip shifted enough so she could move her head, gaze up at him. "Use the femoral for the first mark," he said. "I like looking at you like this."

A wave of his incubus energy enveloped her. When she leaned forward, she had to pull against his hold, a tug on her scalp. "You can use one hand to steady yourself, but put the other on the floor, next to my foot."

When she complied, he shifted, holding her fingers there with the pressure of his toes. She molded her other hand around his calf. Pinning her hand to the floor, gripping her hair, were the needed reminders of who was in control. She was moving toward a dangerous bliss, a tumultuous sea of things to come, things she wouldn't be able to control at all. She wouldn't let fear of that control her.

He was the only one she'd give the right to control her.

She put her mouth on his thigh and found the artery. Her lips and tongue caressed his flesh, savoring the moment, and he allowed that, too. The evidence of his arousal was increasing, just as hers was, anticipating the bond between them.

When she bit, his grip constricted, but it wasn't a flinch. It was approval. She tasted his blood, that unique incubus-angel-Merc flavor. Mindful perhaps of what Adan and Yvette had said, about how third marking was supposed to be a sacred act, he didn't order her to get to it. Or maybe that was because he was experiencing it as well. She'd expected him to respect the significance of this step for her. Allowing himself to feel it as well was less expected...and increased the power of it.

She released the first serum from behind her fangs.

If it worked, no matter where he was, she could find him. As long as he was within range. But she wondered if, as an angel, his range would be even greater than hers, such that he could find her anywhere. In any part of the world. Or the universe. They had a lot to explore and discover.

"Don't withdraw. I don't care about the pain." His voice was rough. "I want the second mark now."

She wanted that, too. The second serum came quickly. She swayed, because it had been a really long time since that last second mark to a staff member, and she'd forgotten the disorienting rush as channels opened between two minds.

Lord Brian, the vampire who headed up the various research centers that delved into vampire biology, had pinpointed a lot of the chemical reactions associated with marking. But there was still a significant area he acknowledged fell under "unknown" or "magical and spiritual properties." In their world, those influences carried equal weight in Brian's research, no matter their resistance to scientific methods and measurements.

She didn't want to think about practical things like that, but they helped her find an anchor to pause and think about Merc. This was a servant marking, but he was a male she was accepting as her Master, her job to serve him. When she drew back, closing the wounds with the coagulants in her tongue, she noted his hand had left her hair and moved to her shoulder.

Looking up, she saw his fascinated internal focus on a jumble of thoughts that weren't his own, and what they revealed as they sorted themselves out.

With effort, she pulled herself back into her own head, to give him room to adjust to the connection, follow the paths to her without her thoughts cluttering those passageways.

When he stepped back, she was concerned, but he wasn't leaving her. He lifted her to her feet and moved them to the bed, where he sat down on the edge, guiding her between his spread knees. She put a hand on his shoulder as he met her gaze. When he spoke, she let out a little gasp. Because his lips didn't move.

There is a great deal going on in here.

It made her laugh, and also choked her up some. He touched her cheek, coming away with moisture. She held his hand, pressed her face against it, and answered him.

Human servants can't prevent a vampire from reading their minds.

"But vampires can prevent the servant from reading theirs, when they don't wish to share."

He'd heard her. She nodded. "I don't know how it will work with us, but I won't read your mind unless I have your permission."

It was why she'd withdrawn, resisting that temptation. She wanted to honor what they were to one another, what he was supposed to be to her, even more than she desired to do that. Which she guessed was irrefutable confirmation of what *she* was.

Come inside my mind, Ruth.

Joy filled her as she obeyed, letting herself be swept back inside his mind. Nonverbal communication was a big part of actual communication, and that held true for communication in the mind. So many feelings and hints of deeper things.

I want her. She's beautiful. Simple, basic need thoughts. It made sense those came through as words. But what lay behind those was a cave with endless twists and turns. It could narrow down, squeeze in on her, make her breathless. Or widen out and pitch her forward to tumble into open space, populated with thought, currents of sensation, emotion, images. It held her, carried her along, all parts of his language.

She had her hands resting on his chest. Her head dropped forward, too. He put his hand on her nape, his palm large enough to cover the base of her skull. Slow strokes as their minds met, explored. And this was just the second mark.

Do you need a moment before you do the third?

That was usually the vampire's line. She lifted her head and found his gaze upon her. Watching. Energy sparked off of him, telling her he wasn't calm, but he was in control. And he wanted that mark. If anything, the first two had made him even more intent upon it.

"With the third mark, you can look through my eyes, see what I see," she said.

"Not with the second mark?"

"Yes...if I work at it. It's easier for older vampires." Stronger vampires. She didn't feel like saying that, though. Instead she thought of her father, showing her Merc in the kitchen with her mother, and the negative feeling eased.

"You're strong enough for me, Ruth," Merc's gaze sharpened on her. "That makes you very strong. You haven't answered my question."

"Yes, I'm ready." In his head, where feeling was far more powerful than thought, there was only one answer. "You need to take some of my blood for the third mark."

He grasped her forearm, lifting it so her wrist was brought to his mouth. Her fingers quivered, then rested against his cheek and jaw. "Did I give you permission to touch me?" he said.

His mood had shifted, and her fingers pulled back like a startled bird. His gaze glittered at her through their frame, her arm still held in his grasp.

I would like to. Please.

You will wait on my command. Yes?

Yes. She swallowed. Whispered it. "Yes. Merc..."

This was new and strange, even for them. The natural way he was taking over, as if he knew just how much she wanted to be pushed this way. Had fantasized about it. Feared it. Feared where it would take her.

Maybe he'd been able to explore those corners of her mind far faster than a human servant could. But she'd seen how fast he could fly, with her as a passenger. Maybe it was the same in their minds.

"Do you fear me?"

She lifted a lip to show a fang, her automatic defiant response. "Do you want me to?"

His challenge helped steady and reassure her. Had he intended that?

"Would I be disappointed if the answer is yes?" he asked with deceptive mildness.

"Probably."

The intensity of his gaze didn't lessen. He put his mouth over her rushing pulse, and she saw the tips of his fangs. He could cloak them the way he did his wings, and often did so during the performances. When he let them show, like now, they were intimidating and large, like a leopard's.

When she was younger, Adan had told her that hers were the size of a house cat's. When she'd bitten him hard enough to make him

325

snarl, she'd smugly noted that size didn't matter. It was the pointiness. And how much time a person had to twist that pointiness around and rip flesh.

Don't bite your brother. She remembered Kohana's admonishment from the kitchen, the threatening wave of a wooden spoon.

This was a very different moment, but when Merc's gaze glinted with momentary humor, she knew he'd heard the details of the memory and caught flashes of it.

With the third mark, such a recollection would be much clearer, like watching movies in her head. Would he show her the same about his life, his memories? She hoped so. The good and the bad. She wanted to know him. All of him.

He leaned forward, putting off the decisive moment. "Part your lips and stay still."

When she did, he scraped his fangs over hers, his lips and tongue tracing their shape, making her feel the difference in size. As he caressed them, other feelings swirled among the unsettling ones.

"I want you to fear me in the right ways, Ruth. Do you? I like your defiance, but this isn't the moment for it. Only truth, if your own heart will reveal it to you."

"Yes. I do." Her breath was erratic against his skin. His grip tightened on her arm. The soul could hide things, things too difficult for the heart and mind to process. It was the guardian of both, the last defense, taking the blows to keep the others from being crushed. Because they were far more fragile.

She had no doubt the third mark would put Merc inside her soul.

He drew back, positioning his mouth over her wrist again. His lashes lowered, and she watched his fangs sink into her flesh. She shuddered, caught between pain and ecstasy at the powerfully intimate act between vampire and servant. Or in her case...Master.

He tasted her, tongue against her flesh, collecting the blood.

Please, please let me touch you.

He picked up on her inexplicable urgency, and was merciful. *Yes.*

Her hand flew to his throat, to put her fingers there so she felt his very first swallow. And stayed, as he did it three times.

That should be enough to accomplish the first part of the binding. It wasn't a directive. She wouldn't tell him what to do. Only give him the information to make the decision.

Merc lifted his head, sliding his thumb over the punctures to hold pressure on them. He brought her close to him, flush against his body, arm around her waist, and let her taste herself on his mouth, his tongue. With a satisfied sound, he deepened the kiss, rediscovering the pleasure of it all over again. She got lost in it, barely aware as he stretched them out on the bed. He spread out his wings as he turned onto his back. He put her between his spread thighs, his straining cock against her stomach, her upper body on his chest.

Use my neck for the third mark.

His grasp returned to her hair, holding her fast as she put her mouth against his corded throat. Urgency and a desire to savor the moment fought for the upper hand, and her Master told her which he wanted.

Do it now. I want your soul, Ruth. I want all of you.

She bit. Not like the adult vampire she considered herself, but with the hunger of a fledgling willing to tear through any barrier to get what she wanted. She was letting herself be out of control, because she could be. Merc's strength held her fast, keeping her bite controlled. He was in charge.

She released the third mark, a yearning sound coming from her as she crossed a barrier to an unknown world, no turning back. She might have other third marks in her life, depending on how long Merc would be willing to share this path with her, but it would likely never again be with a Master. It would be someone she'd have to take on to protect herself, to give the illusion of what she would never be.

She told herself to stop thinking about what lay ahead. This was not that moment.

A rush of male approval followed the thought, a reinforcement flavored with admonishment. He knew the value of staying in the present, too.

A heartbeat later, there was no room for anything but what happened next.

Every vampire saw third marked relationships around them. Every vampire was told there was nothing that fully explained the marking experience itself.

Elisa's words were in her head. *I was never alone again. But it's terrifying, Ruth, because with the wrong Master, loneliness can take on a depth and pain even Hell cannot match.*

"Tell me how it normally works." As she finished the mark, savoring the blood she'd taken as part of it, he spoke aloud. Perhaps because he was struggling with what was going on inside of him like she was.

"The vampire can move through the mind, into the heart, past the heart. Into the soul. If the human...the servant, is open to that, it's a startling feeling, but not painful."

"And if he's not open to that?"

"If he's human, the vampire can push in anyway. Take over. They can...destroy the human from the soul outward if they so desire."

"Would you wish me to try to resist your entry? See if I can keep you out? You like a fight."

"Not for this. No. Please." Her hands were on his biceps, as she pushed up enough to look at him. The black blood red in his eyes had gotten notably larger, only a small amount of silver and white visible. When she told him, he looked surprised, then thoughtful, but the energy vibrating off his taut muscles said that was one of many things he was processing.

"Does it work in the other direction? Can I come into your soul?"

Only a heartbeat ago, she'd felt that was a very real possibility. "I don't know."

Merc held her gaze. She felt him there inside her mind, as she was in his. Together, of one accord, they started to descend, on parallel tracks. Their bodies responded to the mental effort, pushing against one another, sinking into a closer embrace.

She saw so many images in his head. As she reached the heart level, she saw flashes of the child he'd been, the dark, cold world where he'd been abandoned. Then the adult male he was now, the journeys of heart and mind, the lessons learned, tragedies felt...

His discovery of a world that wasn't about fighting, killing, surviving. Flashes of Marcellus, the angelic Legion. An amazing glimpse of a sky full of winged warriors, the silver spires of a place beyond them.

Machanon. Where the Prime Legion gathers for leisure.

When he'd first seen Machanon, some part of him had recognized it as a place he belonged. He'd rejected that. Angrily, fiercely. He'd spent his life walling himself off from rejection, hurt, refusing to deceive himself.

Then she saw the recent memory, Marcellus speaking to him, giving him a different view of it, a place where he would be accepted. Such thoughts weren't like flashbacks. They were experiences that had made such a strong impression they were in his heart. Having someone believe in him...he'd never had that. Never acknowledged it.

A tear touched her lips as she wondered at the things he was feeling in her own heart, finding his way within her, two beings twining into one. She could focus on his journey, find out, but it was too much. She stayed where she was, inside him.

His hands were on her hips. He'd removed the shorts, and was easing her down upon his cock, adding another explosion of sensation to what was happening to them both. Bringing them as close physically as they could possibly be.

She'd reached the soul level, but when she leaned into it, it didn't let her through the way his heart had. Guided by embedded instinct, she exerted more pressure.

He stiffened, and she jerked back, but it was too late for defense. An urgency seized him. She gasped as he gripped her under the arms, fingers spreading over her rib cage, bringing her up closer to his face so he could latch onto one breast, suckle her hard. His cock drove up into her. It was an abrupt contrast, but it didn't disrupt the connection. It widened the universe of possibilities inside themselves into a raw, rougher world. A scarier one.

The power he could wield as an incubus wrapped around her, a full body cocoon. The first climax hit with the brutal impact of a car crash. It took away every choice she had, planting a seed of fear, even as she drowned in the pleasure, two climaxes, three climaxes...

"Merc..."

She couldn't capture what was going on outside their bodies, except for a brief glimpse of his dark gaze. He was pulling in her sexual energy, and this time he'd roped her life force to it. He was intending to kill her.

No, not Merc. The incubus inside him, the demon. It had taken her attempt to enter his soul as an invasion. A threat to be eradicated. Merc was right. She was about to discover another way a vampire could die.

She tried to fight it, to fight him, crying out in his mind, because her throat was strangled with passionate cries, begging for more. She was experiencing what his victims had, their fear, their realization they were about to die. He'd told her all of that with flat dispassion, though she'd sensed far more beneath it.

But she wasn't them. She wasn't human. She was a vampire. This conflict was merely a different version of one she'd dealt with all her life. The conflict between what she wanted and what she had to be. The strengths that didn't seem to outweigh the weaknesses.

But they did. Even in moments when it didn't seem like that was true.

That form of submission has honor to it. It's a choice, made from a position of strength that most who are Dominant may never truly understand. But I do. You're as much a warrior as your brother.

Merc had asked her if the third mark was two-way, and if she trusted him that much. Trust had to be earned, but sometimes it also had to be taken on faith. If she chose wrongly...

If she chose wrongly, Mal would do his best to kill him. He'd fail. But it wouldn't matter. And then Adan would go after Merc. Or a Dark Guardian would be sent to execute him, with Marcellus.

With her mind inundated by the storm of responses, she let go of everything but what she needed.

Merc, I'm afraid. I'm alone. Help me.

Then she had no strength left to hold onto her own mind. Like everything else, it was pulled away, something he could take, leaving her lost in a passionate storm, her body rigid, caught in an endless, excruciating climax, funneling a gluttonous feast to him as she weakened, and weakened further.

She dropped through a trapdoor, right into his soul.

CHAPTER TWENTY-ONE

*S*he was in darkness. Total darkness, but things in that black watched her. Waiting. Silent. She considered the possibility she was dead, but she had some sense of connection to her physical body. She just couldn't see it, or orient herself.

This wasn't a place about the physical senses. This was Merc. She could feel his presence all around her. His soul. A place that had blocked her entry, but not because he'd wanted to prove she couldn't get in there if he didn't want her there.

He didn't come here. He knew what was here, he'd told her. But somewhere along the way, he'd shut the door and locked it, refusing to visit it. And now she was locked in with it. Alone.

The incubus. No. Merc had insisted from the beginning that the incubus was part of him, and he wouldn't turn his back on it. But the demon part, the hungry part that would only take, that was what was here. Because that was where Merc had put it.

But it wasn't the thing to fear.

As she put her hands out, or what she was thinking of as her hands, she started to hear them. Voices like a choked gurgle beneath water, then they broke the surface, an army of cries becoming mournful wails, chilling her all the way through. Squirming tendrils of energy pulled her arms out to her sides, then her legs, wrapping around and around her, turning her, disorienting her, making her feel sick.

The voices begged for sexual release, moaning their passion, but a cry which should have been arousing, drawing her own response, couldn't quite get there. Then the darkness showed her why.

Out of the black, a woman rose up in the straining arch caused by a climax, but a giant barbed fishhook shoved through her upper torso held her in that position. Her head was tipped back, mouth open on a scream, a plea, while her body shuddered in ecstasy.

A subconscious image that reflected the terrible reality, the memories stored here. *Oh Great Father and Mother.* This was where they were. All the ones whose lives he'd taken.

She flailed for a way to process, and found her own memories, the annual kill.

"Say a prayer for his soul, and ask forgiveness. You took his life, which connects you to him forever. You will meet again, because that's the way of it."

She understood the price of those souls, the weight of carrying them. But she'd had her father and mother to guide her. Merc had had no one. When he finally did, when he had Marcellus, that same side of him had to learn to live with this. These lives could never be restored. Maybe his unconscious had helped the demon side keep the door closed to her, because it was somewhere he didn't want her to be.

But she did. She wanted to be here.

Merc. It's all right. Please...come be with me here.

Her soul was inside his soul. She just needed him to join her. She had her fingers stretched out beyond the bindings, and she gripped hands. Female hands. She accepted the fear and pain, the loss, brought it inside her, cried for all of them. And they became part of her. Living inside her soul as they lived inside his. Because that was part of the third mark, when it was two-way.

Everything shared, every pain, every mistake and disappointment, every tragedy. Every joy, every moment of life given to them.

A familiar touch slid over her arm, and the bonds loosened. He could hold her, wings covering her, then the bonds were around them both, spinning them, the tears and cries turning into something else. Sounds like a forest, of life and death, all the cycles turning as they should.

They were together. That was all that mattered.

He had her. That was what she needed. He'd returned control to her, but she offered it back to him, freely surrendering, submitting.

Slowly, slowly, the world came back to her room, the physical awareness of his body against hers. He was above her now, one wing shad-
owing his face because it curved sharply over his shoulder. He had a
hand on her cheek.

"Ruth."

She was weaker than that first time. She couldn't form words yet,
her body an empty husk. He put his wrist to her mouth, but she was
too weak to bite, so he punctured the artery with his own fangs, then
returned it to her lips.

He curled his arm around her back, his wings closing over them,
holding her inside that cocoon as his head rested against her temple,
his harsh breath against her. As she managed to swallow his blood, he
put his mouth to her throat, her shoulder, teased her collar bone with
his tongue, caressed.

Nerves rippled, a sweet sensation. He moved to the rise of her
breast, and a quiet gasp escaped her as he closed his mouth over her
nipple and suckled. Gently, calling her back to life with the blood
offering and sensual demand, the things a vampire was most likely to
answer.

As the blood returned a measure of strength to her, she lifted a
hand and clasped his wrist, holding it to her as she drew on it, biting
and licking his flesh. His other hand moved to her waist, fingers gripping her buttock, lifting her up as he pushed inside her again,
stretching sore but accepting flesh.

*You surrendered to me, Ruth. I honor that surrender now by giving you
back the life you offered to me.*

She felt that overpowering incubus energy swirling around her, but
this time, instead of drawing energy away, it was sinking into her,
joining with her blood, restoring her.

He was feeding her with what nourished *him*.

He was stroking inside of her, slow. She licked the puncture
wounds on his wrist until they closed, then slid her arms around his
shoulders, fingers against his feathers. When she wrapped her legs
over his hips, his buttocks flexed beneath them, the slow thrust and
withdrawal that had her body lifting to him, asking for more.

She dug in her nails, giving him the fight he liked, and his expression changed. Became fiercer. There was a quality to it that twisted
her heart, because it wasn't just the warrior she saw. It was everything

333

else she'd seen in his soul, every face he'd had to wear, created by the experiences he'd had, the weight of the lives he'd taken to survive. The embedded emotions all of those things had given him.

The sensations expanded, taking over until she thought they would kill her, this time in a way she welcomed. He shuddered, telling her he felt it, too. She held on, giving him whatever strength she could, but knowing he could carry them as far as they needed to go. Then she made it official and formal.

You honored my trust, Master. I give you my submission.

They climaxed together, explosive, intense, mind-scrambling, but not life-threatening. When they came down, he was braced on one arm, and his wings were fully spread over either side of the bed, a feathered tent that delighted her. She ran her fingers over the arch and the primaries she could reach, as her body trembled in the aftermath.

"Do you want to lie down?" She offered a small smile, her voice a whisper. "Vampires are known to wear out their sexual partners."

He wasn't ready to smile yet. He settled onto one elbow, but still held most of his weight on the other arm as he traced her face. "You said a vampire coming into a servant's soul could be excruciating. It was. I didn't expect that. I reacted wrongly."

"I'm all right. You made sure of it. I don't care about having a safe life. Just an interesting one. Would you...would you kiss me again?"

The glimmer of his usual expression reassured her. Amused, exasperated and ready to admonish her. But at her request, he leaned in, giving her what she'd asked. She murmured against his lips, and his hand cupped her cheek, fingers on her temple as they sank into it together.

Her fingertips drifted over his shoulder, under his arm, feeling the brush of feathers against her knuckles. And then something else.

He felt the difference when she did, and they both drew back to exchange a look.

So uncertain if the marks themselves would take, she hadn't considered the possibility that one of their effects would happen.

"Um...all fully bound servants get a mark somewhere on them. It looks like a cross between a brand and a tattoo. It never fades."

It might not be that. But what else could it be? If he'd sustained an injury from earlier events, it would have already healed. And if she'd scratched him in the heat of passion, that would feel different. He would know it was a wound.

Sliding back from her, his gaze resting on hers, he shifted, putting himself on his stomach. He lifted his wings to remove them from her field of vision. When the wings jangled the strings of feathers and beads in her canopy, he glanced up and adjusted them outward to avoid tangling them.

"I guess I might have to rethink that setup, if I share my bed with an angel incubus." She pushed herself up on an elbow and looked. He definitely had a mark on his back, below the joining point of his left wing, above the small of his back. It was a good size, nearly the length and width of his own hand. Larger than hers.

"What do you see?" he asked, his voice hard to read.

"I'm not sure. Hold on." She sat up and scooted down the bed, turning so that she was looking at the mark from the opposite direction. A small smile touched her lips. "Now it makes sense."

The mark had the silhouette of a type of cat she recognized, but she didn't know if he would.

"Show me in your head, Ruth."

It was a thrill, doing that for the first time, and knowing from his response it was successful.

"A caracal," he said, surprising her. "Your father and I tended to them."

The caracal was leaping for a bird. Not the caracal's usual prey. It was a much larger bird. Rather than seeming to be attempting to escape, the bird's talon was outstretched, making contact with the caracal's reaching claws. Connecting.

"It's always something that makes sense to the two people." She traced the outline. "Even if not at first."

Reaching back, he gripped her hand. "It makes sense."

He turned and brought her to him, resting her against his chest, folding an arm around her and a wing over her. She traced both with her fingertips, her eyes half closing, thinking of what it all meant. They drifted for a while that way, then he spoke against her ear. Reluctantly.

"Marcellus reached out to me earlier, when you were with your father. Lady Kaela has completed her territory business, and the Trad is due to meet us at her home at eleven o'clock tonight. Pacific Time."

It was too close to dawn to leave. But she remembered how fast Merc could travel. Or they could use the portal Adan had arranged.

"Sleep. When you rise, I'll get us there in time. You'll have time to speak to your parents before you leave. Your mother said she was making corned beef hash and biscuits."

"If she wasn't making breakfast, would I have time to say good-bye?" she teased him.

"An irrelevant question, since she is."

"Will you stay with me while I sleep?"

"Is that what you wish?"

Yes. If that is what you wish.

It is. "I'll get up at dusk to speak to your father, but I'll stay for now. To ensure you do as you're told and rest. Fully recuperate."

She pinched his leg. "Don't treat me like an egg. What are you going to talk to Da about?"

I'll treat you as I wish. I'm your Master. You've said so.

Don't let it go to your head. Or I'll cut it off. You didn't answer the question.

Manly things. Don't worry your pretty head about it.

She did her best to find more sensitive appendages to pinch, hard, but he thwarted her, gripping her wrists and holding them across her breasts, his thumbs teasing her nipples. She halfheartedly hissed at him as she enjoyed the sensation. He chuckled at her, but when his grip on her wrists constricted, it was a little harder than expected. *I mean it, Ruth. Sleep. Regain your strength.*

She obeyed, because she had no real choice. Dawn and the night's events were pulling her under. His blood and sexual energy reversal had restored her to herself, but only to herself. It hadn't made her a stronger vampire. Wishful thinking, she guessed.

Your will more than makes up for that. And you don't need to be stronger. You have me.

She drifted off on that thought. Merc watched—and listened—to her do so. He expected that Mal, as a stronger and older vampire, would be up as soon as dusk arrived. It would give Merc time to have the discussion he wanted to have with him, while not leaving her alone for long.

He'd done a lot of shitty things. Far more awful than risking the life of a female vampire who attracted him. Yet he'd never had the strength of feelings he had for her, and rather than blaming that as the cause of how he was feeling now, all he could think was that he never, *ever* wanted to feel how he'd felt when he'd regained control of his demon side and seen how close he'd come to taking her life essence.

She might not have died, physically, but he would have left her mind and soul an empty vessel. He'd been sure of it.

The third mark...it was indescribable. He was bound inside her and she was bound inside him. From exploring the shape of it, yes, he had the power to push her out, reject the marks. Close down the gateways she could pass through to reach his body, mind or soul. He couldn't think of anything he desired less. He felt reunited with parts of himself he'd been away from for so long, they were new and strange. Some of them he wasn't sure he'd ever met before.

Something to explore, like the third mark between them.

Marcellus had suggested the mark as a way to protect her in her world. Merc would make sure of it. He would be the servant no one in the vampire world would fuck with. Not if they wanted to live.

He stayed in her room as the hours passed, examining the things from her childhood and items collected from her present, filing away questions to ask her about them later. Eventually he lay next to her again and let himself have the pleasure of doing nothing but holding her, of gazing down at her when she shifted and turned, curling herself against him. She had no idea that no woman had ever done that with him. He'd never allowed it. Never wanted to allow it.

Now he considered demanding it from her at every sunset.

When dusk arrived, he rose, he settled her under the covers and left a feather in her hand, curled under her chin. His tough vampire female, who looked like a child when she slept. He'd tease her with that, next time he wanted her in a fighting mood.

As he emerged from below, Elisa was coming through the side kitchen door with a handful of herbs and a smile. "Can I make you some coffee? I'll have breakfast ready when Ruth rises, but I can get you something now."

"No, but thank you. I've interrupted your gardening."

"Just gathering some seasonings for the meal."

He noted the dirt on her gloves and the garden apron she wore over jeans that fit her curvy body well. "I was looking for Mal." He dipped his head toward the hallway leading from the living room, where he could sense the vampire.

"He's in his office," Elisa confirmed. "He'll call me if you need anything."

Ruth's father was leaning back in a squeaky and ancient-looking metal office chair. He had the tip of a lethal-looking and sizeable knife balanced on the desk blotter and was turning it in meditative circles, obviously a routine habit while thinking. Though if it did double duty as a warning for his daughter's chosen, all the better.

Merc could respect that.

"Did you sleep well?" Mal asked courteously.

"Your daughter gave me three marks," Merc said.

He had no patience for small talk. Mal gestured him to a dilapidated sofa across from the giant desk that looked like a sea chest.

"We thought she might. What's on your mind?"

He asked Mal to explain vampire overlord protocols and "expected" servant behavior, so he could support Ruth as needed. Much of it wouldn't apply to him, but Merc was thinking of what Adan had said. Mal confirmed the line Ruth needed to straddle. "They won't expect you to act as a typical servant, but they also won't expect her to act submissive. If she does, or you dominate her before them, she'll lose any respect they have for her."

"I can fix that attitude," Merc said darkly.

Mal appeared to appreciate Merc's opinion, but he shook his head. "That would end her ability to be part of the vampire world in any meaningful way."

"I don't understand."

"When the two vampires tried to take advantage of her," Mal's jaw tightened, telling Merc his feelings about that, "she was seen as a vampire, one of us. If you take violent action as you describe and she encounters vampires on her own, without you, she won't be seen as one of us. She'll be prey.

"And if you do encounter vampires when you're together, they'll respect and deal with you. She'll be dismissed, as if she's the servant. Titles in our world are a front. The vampire that holds them always has to back them with the appropriate power. It's the only thing a vampire's nature truly respects. It's a hard bias to overcome, no matter how conscious we are of it. Even Ruth, for all of her challenges, has her share of it."

"You're a confusing race, full of contradictions."

Mal lifted a brow. "Do you know of one that isn't? I expect angels and incubi have their own challenges. And we all know how confusing humans can be."

"Including your servant."

Mal's lips quirked. "A female of any race is confusing. Human or vampire."

Ruth was up. Merc could feel her leaving the bed, figuring out what she was going to wear. She also reached out to him. She didn't interrupt his conversation, but the touch of her mind was almost as pleasant as the touch of her hand. He "touched" her back and her pleasure flooded him. She liked being connected to him.

As Mal had just dryly pointed out, he'd likely have to put some work into keeping it that way. Merc rose. "I understand her desire to stand on her own two feet in her own world, and ask for nothing that she didn't earn. I'll do my best to respect that."

Mal's eyes glinted. "Did you just share that with her, or did you keep it between us?"

Merc pressed his lips together. "I think it's better if she just assumes I'll always step in when she's at risk. Whether she wants me to or not. Because if it comes to a conflict between vampire protocol and that, there's no question as to what choice I'll make."

"I don't necessarily disagree. Just make sure you think it through, before you make that choice for her."

Merc could tell Mal understood. Because it was male logic.

Simple and straightforward.

～

Lady Kaela's home was in Monterey, perched on cliffs overlooking the slate-blue Pacific surf. When they landed in the driveway, Ruth had a question for her angel incubus.

"So do angels have built-in GPS? You're given an address and you just know where it is?"

"You scoured my soul a few hours ago. I choose to keep some things a mystery, so you don't tire of me and cast me aside too soon."

339

"Is that your way of saying you have no fucking clue?"

She dodged his attempt to grab her, laughing. However, when the front door opened, she had the somber mien appropriate for meeting an overlord. Years of adopting the habit for their many vampire island visitors made the transition seamless. Locking down the trepidation vampires she didn't know provoked within her was part of the same process.

When Garron, Lady Kaela's servant, stepped out, it didn't relax her guard. An overlord wouldn't meet a lower echelon vampire at the door, and Lady Kaela could still tap into her servant's head to see Ruth's behavior.

If Caleb ever moved on, Garron could step into the strongman's role. Their height and muscle mass were comparable. Garron's shaved head gleamed in the evening moonlight, and the exposed scalp was scarred. So was his face, a mark running from his cheekbone, across his straight nose, to the hinge of his jaw. Another formed a groove from his left ear to his throat, disappearing into the collar of his dress shirt, tailored for his massive body.

The damage must have predated his marking, far enough back the transition hadn't been able to erase it. He was a charismatic male, his sexual appeal undiminished by the old wounds. He was also a Dominant. She recognized it like a favorite perfume.

When the opportunity presented itself, many vampires preferred bonding with a human Dominant. There were bottomless pleasures involved in topping a human used to being the one holding the reins. Though they'd never have the chance to exercise it on their vampire, it was also a useful trait for the entertainments involving other servants.

Plus, the higher the vampire's rank, the more administrative demands were placed upon the servant. He or she needed to be courteous and deferential, yet know when and how to stand up for and represent their vampire's interests among a world of aggressive and volatile personalities.

Plenty of power submissives could ably handle those responsibilities as a vampire's servant, but there was an extra punch to it when the servant was a Dominant. Like with Lyssa's servant, Jacob.

Kaela's success as an overlord had predated her marking Garron.

However, because of the female overlord's reputed savvy and political nature, Ruth expected Garron was well suited to the role.

Garron executed a short bow to Ruth before allowing his eyes, dark with hints of blue, to shift to her companion. Merc's wings were cloaked.

While Lady Kaela had been read in, so she knew a Truth Vessel was an angel, Merc had decided it made more tactical sense to conceal his most attention-grabbing feature. Let those who didn't need to know guess at what he was, even if they could tell he wasn't human.

On a normal day, he was pretty attention-grabbing, even without the wings. Today he'd gone the extra mile.

After breakfast, he'd excused himself, telling Ruth he was going to change before they headed for Lady Kaela's home. When he met her outside the house, he wore black slacks and a crisp white dress shirt, open at the collar and the sleeves folded back from his forearms. His dagger was on his slim black belt. Though she expected it would still have that sandpaper rasp she liked, his jaw was clean of stubble.

"Wow," she said. "You clean up nice."

"Your father said a more formal appearance is advisable. Though I outrank her considerably on the food chain, if we choose to reveal our marking, I wish her to respect you as well."

She cocked her head. "You're sort of talking like Marcellus."

He blinked. "If I stop using contractions, cut off my head and burn my body. Make sure the virus can't spread."

She chuckled. "Does he never use them?"

"They slip through now and then. He used to use them more. Apparently, as angels get older, they tend to speak more formally. Or maybe it just happens when they lose their sense of humor."

Noting his gaze sweeping over her as well, Ruth straightened accordingly, wanting him to get the full effect.

Her white cotton blouse was edged with lace at the off-the-shoulder neckline. The shirt had a gathered waist and a lace hem that draped over her hips. The broad turquoise stripes of her wrap-around skirt were divided by thinner ones in brick red and sand colors. She'd worn the skirt over her tooled Shepler boots.

The silver and turquoise conch shell belt completed the look, with matching ropes of turquoise at her neck and ears. She'd pulled up her hair. Merc drew closer and toyed with one earring, his fingers stroking the sensitive flesh beneath it. They were alone, because she'd made her good-byes to her parents after breakfast, before they headed out for the night's work.

Merc found her breast, the heat of his hand warm through the cotton. Ruth's body swayed toward him as he teased a nipple to a point with his thumb. Her bra was thin, the shirt even more so.

When she rose on her toes to put her nose to his throat, he slid his arm around her. He tilted his head to peer down at her. "What are you doing?"

"Just inhaling." Suddenly uncertain of what was moving through her, she tilted her head back. "Is that okay? To just enjoy you?"

He blinked. "I can't think of a reason to object. But I expect we need to get going."

"Yes." She gripped his collar and steeled herself for what was ahead. "Okay. Let's go."

⁓

The nice clothes didn't diminish Merc's always dangerous demeanor. So Garron took the extra moment to gauge her companion in the way a protective servant and fighter did.

"The requested Truth Vessel," Merc said, inclining his head without smiling.

"Yes." Garron executed another bow toward him. "Is 'my lord' the appropriate address?"

"Merc is fine."

"Very well. My lady welcomes you both. If you can follow me, I'll take you to her office."

"Has the Trad arrived?" Ruth asked.

Garron's jaw tightened, a less-than-subtle expression of his displeasure at having a Trad in his Mistress's home. Ruth didn't blame him.

"Stating a need for extra precautions, he has moved his arrival time to tomorrow at dusk. However, my lady thought it wise to have you here at the original time, in case he changes his plans again. She also thought it would be wise to discuss a coordinated strategy in handling his visit."

Inside, the house was open and airy, with lots of windows to show off the impressive view of ocean and Monterey landscape. The lower part of the home was built into the cliff, and Garron pointed out a descending staircase.

"The quarters for vampire guests are that way. There's a separate staircase to my lady's quarters, to ensure privacy."

Garron didn't reveal the access point to Kaela's quarters. A wise choice for a cautious overlord. Kaela's promotion had come about due to a corrupt overlord removed by Council. She'd been a member of his territory, selected and charged by Lady Lyssa to clean house. Kaela had personally dispatched several vampires too loyal to the overlord, when they unwisely challenged the Council's decision to make a change.

Vampires could be brutal in such matters, but the best overlords, like Florida's Lord Marshall, or Lady Lyssa, knew how to follow it up with wise leadership. After swiftly handling the executions, Kaela had restored balance and brought prosperity to the previously subjugated vampires in the territory, earning their respect. They no longer lived in fear of unpredictable and sadistic leadership.

Meeting a more powerful vampire always made Ruth nervous, but this time it was tempered by a genuine interest in the vampire who'd done what most had thought would require a more imposing male vampire to do. Lady Lyssa's decision had been questioned— quietly of course—but Kaela had quickly reinforced the queen's judgment.

After all, our Council head is a female, and no one doubts her *power.* Those who'd doubted Kaela had sagely pointed that out afterward, as if they'd known all along it would turn out fine. *Yeah, right.*

Admittedly, Kaela was nowhere near as old and powerful as Lyssa, and she was a made vampire, not a born one. So gender aside, the question and concern had been valid. She'd proven it unfounded, regardless.

Kaela's office had more of those windows, creating a vista of dark sky and darker ocean behind her desk, the demarcation flanked by sparkling stars above and white caps below.

Kaela had shimmering thick waves of red hair, held back from her face by bronze combs. Her golden-brown eyes, with a dark ring around the iris and fringed with reddish-gold lashes, focused on Ruth with the usual piercing vampire regard. Though the California over-lord could pass as human, it was helpful she was in an area populated by Hollywood celebrities. Even for a vampire, Kaela had exceptional looks.

Ruth liked learning history from vampires who'd lived far longer than herself, and wondered if she'd get the opportunity with Kaela. Lady Yvette said she'd been a Confederate spy before she'd been turned.

One had to step carefully toward such memories, though. Kaela had lost a husband in the War Between the States, and years didn't always dull the pain of such a loss.

When Ruth was a child, long before Lady Lyssa was blessed with Kane, Ruth had asked the queen if she had any children. Lyssa had been sitting at the kitchen table, Ruth on her knee as they played a puzzle game. Born vampire children were cherished, because births were rare. So during their growing up years, all vampire visitors, regardless of rank, showed them tender protectiveness and kindness. Even playfulness. But this had not been a playful moment.

Ruth still remembered the flash of anguish in Lyssa's jade green gaze. "No," she'd said, her tone suggesting that hadn't always been the case.

Ruth had tentatively touched the queen's hand. "I'm sorry." She might not know much, but she knew sorry and a touch helped fix a hurt.

Ruth returned to the present. Kaela had risen from her desk and nodded her greeting to Ruth before turning her attention to Merc. After a brief assessment, she executed a short bow. "My lord."

She would have heard Merc's preference through Garron's mind, but the overlord had made her own decision on it. Merc was measuring her just as circumspectly, so perhaps not correcting her was a tactical decision of his own.

When Kaela gestured Ruth into the guest chair, Garron moved behind his Mistress, crossing his arms. Though it was a standard position when the vampire wanted their servant in attendance, the bodyguard vibe to it was obvious. When Ruth tuned in to Merc, trying to determine if it was because of his usual incubus vibes, she realized he had re-channeled and reworked them, creating a comfortable hands-off buffer around Ruth herself.

His vigilance is not entirely because of that, Merc told her. *He can't think I'm a threat.*

I'm not certain what it is. But remain on guard.

Since that was her usual operating mode for vampire meet and greets, she didn't disagree.

Kaela's gaze was moving between her and Merc, the silence lengthening.

"Is there a problem, Lady Kaela?" Ruth asked. Courteous, but with an edge that asserted her own rights in this situation.

"No, Lady Ruth. I apologize. Your relationship with the...Truth Vessel, seems to be more than that of a vampire escort from Lady Yvette's Circus. Would you care to satisfy my curiosity on its nature?"

Since she had no desire to hide her attraction to Merc, and vice versa, Ruth had been prepared for the question, somewhat. She'd run it by Merc before they arrived.

I'm fine with however you wish to define it, Ruth, he confirmed again. *I know what lies between us.*

His response could also be translated another way. *I'm fine with however you wish to define it, because I'll be carving my own definition, no matter how I scar up vampire protocols to do it.*

The thought provided mild terror and amusement. Plus an unexpected relief that he refused any attempt to mold his behavior. She didn't have to be responsible for it.

No, you don't. Just guide me on the protocols that make sense. I'll ignore the rest.

She suppressed a smile. "Since I'm here to assist him with vampire cultural norms, it was deemed a good idea for him to carry my marks. It helps our coordination and provides me protection as I navigate waters that may rub the Trad the wrong way. Since I'm barely an adult to most vampires."

"Yes. A second mark would handle that adequately." The question hung there. Kaela had a good stare, but maybe because of Merc's reinforcement, Ruth held the Dominant female's gaze with far less difficulty than she usually did. Also a relief.

Unless Kaela asked the question, *"Is he third marked?"* Ruth wasn't going to volunteer the information. Before she left, she'd confirmed with Mal that he couldn't detect the marks on Merc. But the body language projected during the mind-to-mind communication was a giveaway most vampires recognized, and had probably sparked Kaela's interest.

"What can you tell us about the Trad?" Merc said. He'd chosen a cushioned bench instead of another guest chair. His knees were spread and feet braced. If they'd been visible, his wings would have likely been folded over one another, the tips crossed.

A servant entered with refreshments, a dish of chocolates and dried fruits, and crystal glasses of clear water with ice shaped like crescent moons. When Merc's gaze turned to her, she faltered and would have dropped the water pitcher if he hadn't closed his hand on it and moved it to the desk.

"My apologies, my lady," she stammered.

Ruth gave Merc a narrow look as Kaela reassured the servant with a brief word and sent her on her way. He shrugged.

"It's a hard energy to overlook," Kaela said wryly. "I've attended the Circus and seen an angel there, but at a distance. No offense, my lord, but are all angels this arousing in close proximity?"

"I'm not full angel," Merc said. "The other part is incubus. Sex demon. With a smattering of human blood."

"Ancestry dot com is still trying to work it out," Ruth said.

The overlord chuckled, but her eyes stayed thoughtful. Garron didn't smile. Merc gave him a bland look.

Don't pick a fight with the human servant, Ruth advised. *It's bad manners. He's just protective of her.*

Very.

Kaela laced elegant fingers on the desk and answered Merc's question. "Are you familiar with Trads, my lord?"

"Ruth and Yvette have told me what little they know."

"The Trads are very secretive. While we know some about their beliefs and how they live their lives, they're very individual in their pursuit of that. We know of no coordinated efforts among them, beyond the acts of small clans. There are vampires in our ranks, like Lord Uthe, or Cai," she glanced at Ruth, "who were raised by or among them, and they've confirmed that. It's best not to extrapolate from one and place that belief upon all.

"We do know they live in forests, mountains, and other remote places. Many are nomadic. Even if they have what approximates a permanent home, they likely have several of them. They'll stay at one for a while if they have a captured human they're 'storing' as a food source." Her lips tightened. "Or if they're making a breeding attempt."

"No female Trads?" Merc asked.

"None to date. We know of female vampires they've captured, for those same breeding attempts. When it's discovered, the Trads holding them are hunted down, and punishment is meted out. The females are retrieved. If they are still alive. Some take their own lives."

Her eyes flashed. "However, vampires can disappear for reasons of their own choosing, so it's possible there are captive females who have been with them long enough to adapt and accept that life, as worn-down prisoners might. However, Cai and Lord Uthe never encountered any during their time among them."

Ruth's brow creased. "So the Trad meeting with us. How is he different?"

"I wouldn't assume he is. Asva doesn't preach the worst of their nonsense to me, though he supports their rejection of human society. For the most part, he keeps his thoughts to himself. Which is why him contacting me and asking for this meeting got my attention. That, and him asking for a Truth Vessel to be present. Why do that if you're going to attempt deception?"

"He could have spellcraft that he believes can get him past Merc's detection skills. My brother says anything can be hacked with the right magic," Ruth glanced at Merc. "But I think this would be a pretty tough one."

"Agreed." Kaela nodded. "Let's discuss our approach to the meet, to ensure we're all on the same page and he can't take advantage of our lack of familiarity with one another."

Lady Kaela had put a great deal of thought into the possible issues that could arise at the meeting with the Trad, increasing Ruth's confidence in her leadership. She encouraged Ruth and Merc to provide their own input, raising questions that tweaked tactics to extract as much information as possible out of Asva, if he chose to be cagey.

Garron's contributions, many addressing the possibility of it being a trap, confirmed Ruth's guess that he'd once been part of a special ops military unit. He also pointed out a target Ruth hadn't considered.

"You're an angel," he told Merc. "If Asva's working for someone, who's to say they didn't tell him to ask for a Truth Vessel? They draw you here, away from the protections at the Circus, and try to capture you."

"To what end?" Ruth asked.

"If an angel has greater magic and power than the rest of us, he could get vampire females to conceive, right? Or destroy the vampire world you hate so much?"

"They think they could capture and control an angel?"

"It wouldn't be far afield of many of their outlandish ideas," Kaela said.

Merc glanced at Ruth. *If any race tried to capture an angel, the Legion would descend upon them. Not so much because they value a half-breed like me, but for the principle of the matter.*

I'm going to tell Marcellus you said that, and let him smack you upside your stubborn head.

Merc showed her the tip of a fang, but then their attention was drawn back to Kaela, who'd sat back in her chair. "I think we've prepared as much as we can. My cook has prepared an excellent dinner."

She glanced at Merc. "She'll be delighted to feed a guest who can eat a full plate, but Lady Ruth, I think you'll enjoy the artistry of our vampire portions. She likes being creative with her presentations. I also have two second marked household staff who can mix their blood with selections from my wine cellar, if you need that."

"She does not," Merc said.

Him stating baldly that he was providing her sustenance surprised Ruth, but she concealed it. There was something else she needed to address. A vampire meal with guests wasn't simply a meal. It was a ritual, a demonstration and testing of power, unless the vampire hosting it, or those who outranked her at the meal, indicated otherwise.

"This may be on the obvious side, my lady, but while Merc is carrying my marks, he's not a marked servant. As we're both familiar with the protocols at a vampire dinner, I want to make it clear that they do not fit his situation."

"That's evident, never fear." Kaela's gaze took on a peculiar intensity. "It's not the proper fit for you, either. Is it?"

CHAPTER TWENTY-TWO

*R*uth stiffened. "My lady, I'm in the company of an ambassador from Lady Lyssa. Both of them outrank me, just as you do. Are you suggesting I'm acting improperly?"

"Not at all. I meant only that our normal dinner protocols would not apply in this scenario."

The words were spoken smoothly, but it was a change in direction, driven by Ruth's reaction. A test. Ruth needed to settle down, because she'd put Merc on alert, his body language far less friendly. Which in turn did the same to Garron's.

I'm okay. I just get tense meeting with new vampires. Don't feed off my paranoia.

Merc placed his hand upon hers on the chair arm, a clear warning to Kaela. Because Merc wasn't the nurturing type, Ruth took it that way, but his thought carried enough reassurance to surprise her.

I'm here for Lady Lyssa, yes. But I'm also here for you. You don't need to be afraid of anything.

Kaela's shoulders held tension of her own. She dipped her head toward Garron, acknowledging whatever he was saying to her. The male's eyes were on the contact between Ruth and Merc, but Ruth didn't pull away. Everything she was doing was perfectly acceptable.

"Merc." Kaela turned her gaze to him. "Are you familiar with the sexual entertainments vampires offer at our mealtimes?"

"I have witnessed some at the Circus, when Lady Yvette entertains important vampire guests. They're memorable."

"I would expect so. Would that be of interest to one of your race, your incubus blood? If not, I'll ensure there are no such provocations at our meal."

Kaela's tone suggested nothing but a vampire overlord's intent to care for her guests, in a way appropriate to their respective ranks. Ruth was feeling like an idiot.

Merc's hand tightened on hers. *You're cautious. There's nothing wrong with that. Would you enjoy observing the entertainments she provides?*

Ruth thought of Play Night, how he'd had her watch the scenes and then had taken her to a private space to make demands of her. The memory made her vibrate with pleasure.

Kaela rose, coming around the desk and propping her hips against the front of the desk. Garron watched his Mistress carefully. Ruth was picking up something else from him now. He wasn't entirely on board with the direction Kaela was choosing.

Not unusual for a Dominant servant. A servant was normally the center of whatever sexual entertainments a vampire host and guests chose to indulge, during or after a dinner. With him already wary of Merc, he might be fighting his natural aversion to being put in a vulnerable position in front of him.

But Garron had been a servant long enough to quell such a reaction. Vampires fed on such reluctance, aroused by the chance to show the servant the depths of what their service required.

Submissive to Merc she might be, but Ruth was also a vampire. Watching Kaela top her powerful human servant, imagining how Merc could go down that road with Ruth later, when the two of them were together?

I like how you react to this idea. Tell her yes.

Is that a command?

If it was, would you defy me just to enjoy my reaction?

She could let herself have the spike of desire his response gave her. The arousal another vampire could detect didn't have an orientation attached to it. Ruth nodded.

"Thank you, my lady. You honor us."

Kaela smiled, seemingly easy again. "Would you like to have some time to yourselves before the meal? You're welcome to wander the house and grounds. The beach is beautiful this time of night. For a meal with the three of us, you can change into more comfortable clothing if you prefer. Let's be less on guard and formal, if that's possible for our kind. You're welcome to call me Kaela."

The words seemed honest. Even more perplexing, in Kaela's gaze there was a strange...vulnerability? Ruth felt a pull toward the woman, as if a hand was being offered, and all she had to do was clasp it before...what?

The thought made Ruth want to bolt for the door. She had to put effort into keeping her ass in the chair.

Ruth.

It's okay. Don't react.

Kaela had Lady Lyssa's support, but she was also an overlord. One of their jobs was identifying and punishing any breach of vampire law.

What's the concern, Ruth?

I think she knows, Merc. Knows what I am. And I don't know why she's calling it out.

Lady Lyssa sent you here to gather information. Do you think she was setting you up to expose that secret?

The idea was painful and shocking, and it didn't match what she knew of Lady Lyssa. But was her view colored by her memories of the most powerful vampire in the world bouncing Ruth on her knee?

Still, the Trad issue was far more important. Ruth couldn't see Lyssa getting sidetracked by something as insignificant as outing a weaker vampire with submission tendencies.

This was why Mal hated dealing with vampire politics. *Their games give me fucking migraines.*

Ruth steadied herself. Even if Kaela knew something, Ruth's behavior would confirm or deny it. She needed to pull her shit together and remember every lesson she'd learned to prepare for being in the company of vampires like this.

Plus, the Trad issue was a more important issue to *her* as well. Once they got past it, Clara might consider the solution that could save her life. That took priority over Ruth's crazy fears.

"Of course. Thank you," Ruth said courteously. "Though your rank doesn't require the invitation, you're welcome to call me Ruth. The 'Lady' thing has never felt like a good fit. My father deserves a title far more, though he would be horrified if anyone gave him one."

"From the pleasure of my few meetings with your father, I would agree." Kaela's expression softened a blink before it held polite reserve, with the right touch of courtesy and warmth. "Lady Yvette mentioned you had some interest in my background, my human years? I can answer questions at dinner, if you like."

"I like history," Ruth said. "Vampires carry around a lot of it. But I don't want to stir up bad memories. It took my father a long time to share his experiences, during and after the Trail of Tears."

But he had. Including how his mother sacrificed her life for him. *I forgot the name my mother gave me, Ruth. Don't ever let anyone take something that precious from you.*

Kaela's expression had shadowed, her eyes thoughtful. "Your kindness is appreciated. There are things too painful to recount for a pleasant dinner, but so much happened then, there are plenty of other topics to explore." Her attention returned to Merc. "I'd be interested in your history as well, my lord. Whatever you are willing to share."

Merc didn't speak right away, though his gaze held hers in a lock. As the silence drew out, a slight flush tinged Kaela's cheeks and her lips tightened. "I apologize if I offended you by asking."

"You didn't. I just haven't decided. Let's see what answers dinner provides."

Merc rose and offered Ruth his hand. Bemused, she put hers in it and let him draw her to her feet. "We'll go check out the beach."

Merc took them to the nearest exit, a set of glass doors leading into a side garden. It had an iron bench and he stepped up on it, sliding an arm around Ruth's waist. It was getting easier to anticipate the liftoff and move with him. As he flew out over the cliff face, she thought it was a spectacular way to experience that view, the salt-laden ocean air lifting her hair and touching her face, his arms around her.

When he landed, he'd chosen a stretch of beach out of sight of the house. The moon had gone behind clouds, leaving the tumultuous surf a dark and heaving living thing. She wouldn't have minded if he kept flying all the way to the Mexican border, because she didn't want to address what he'd gone away from the house to handle. She was starting to feel foolish. She'd overreacted.

"I'm okay," she insisted. "I don't need coddling."

Is that why you think I've brought you here?

The silky touch of his mind voice had her startled gaze snapping to him. He stood a few feet away, his muscular body loose but not relaxed, that roaring ocean the perfect backdrop for a night creature about to pounce on its prey.

Oh. Well, that put a different spin on things. She backpedaled, anticipation building as he began to stalk, the wings at half mast, adding to his looming, powerful presence.

"With what we both know about vampire dinners, I think it would be wise if I feed well beforehand," he said conversationally. "And if your wish that I don't use other sources still stands…"

"It does." Her gaze flicked down, then up. "Like a stone erection."

His gaze gleamed. "I'm hungry, Ruth. You'll feed your Master in whatever manner I desire."

She considered that. Bent and pulled off one boot, then the other, placing them out of range of the surf. "Don't get my clothes dirty."

"That depends on you. If you submit to me without a fight, you will stay clean."

"Not a chance."

She bolted. He cut her off, and she spun away on her bare foot to lithely head for the surf, kicking up salt spray. Kaela had said they could change into more informal clothing, after all, and Ruth had brought an overnight bag with some options. Though from the perfect appearance of the California overlord, her idea of informal might be Oscar de la Renta versus Versace.

She feinted when Merc grabbed for her, keeping out of his grasp. But he used his speed, his wings for lift, to counter her moves and corral her. Him playing the game heightened her response. When he finally made contact, she twisted, trying to throw off his grip. He moved with her, vaulting through the air, carrying her with him in a somersault of limbs. When he brought her back down, he dropped her onto her feet, and flashed her a challenging grin. She answered with the same and was off again.

More hand-to-hand. She got in a kick, but he slid away from the contact and turned, obscuring her vision with the slap of a wing—*ow, asshole*—then he had her around the waist, feet lifted off the ground, her body back against his.

When he put her down on one knee, he pushed the blouse off her shoulders, exposing the jut of her aroused nipples through her thin bra. She struggled, but he closed a hand over her nape, holding her still as he unclasped the back. The strapless garment tumbled free, and he divested her of the shirt, belt and skirt, tossing them above the tideline so they landed near her boots. Her two daggers, concealed under the skirt, joined the pile.

To do all that, he had to let her go, so she ran again.

This time he brought her down on the wet sand, rubbing it against her nipples, pushing it into the valleys created by her rib cage. She kicked, tried to hit pressure points with her flailing arms. He yanked her hips up against his groin, that rock hard erection, and rubbed aggressively against her.

"You would deny me."

"Never. I just want to make you earn it."

A chuckle, and he pushed his fingers under her panties, sliding them into her cunt, adding the pressure of his hips behind it. As he rubbed her perineum with her thumb, his cock pressed against all his digits, carrying the promise of what he planned to thrust into her next. "You make me do nothing, vampire. It's all about what I want. Isn't it? You have no power against me."

He knew the words that would cut her loose in her own head. "Fuck you," she managed, and groaned as he captured her clit in two fingers and pinched. Then he'd released her, set her on her feet and pushed her away.

She was disheveled, aroused, panting, off balance. He stripped off shirt and slacks and placed them next to her boots and clothes before they faced off again. The roaring surf had an undercurrent, a whisper that teased her ears and rippled over her skin. The darkness held a wildness, no light on the beach. Just the two of them.

"You'll come to me now," Merc said. "Kneel before me and take my cock in your mouth. You'll serve your Master, and I'll feed off of you."

I'll protect you. You have nothing to fear, from anyone.

She stared across the few feet separating them. "No one can protect someone from everything. Like you breaking my heart."

"What I can't protect you from, you'll protect yourself from." His belief turned it into a command. "You'd figure out a way to cut my

VAMPIRE'S CHOICE

heart out if I broke yours. I might be willing to let you do it. Is it your desire to serve me, Ruth? To treat me as your Master? You've said it is. Has that changed, just because we're in an overlord's home?"

She shook her head.

"Then do as I order."

Her knees quivered, but they both knew what she would do. Wanted to do. As she moved toward him, she took in the breathtaking sight of his wings, the muscled chest and thighs, the erect cock. But especially his eyes, the set of his mouth, the luster the moonlight gave the brown locks of hair over his high brow.

There'd been times when Merc had held very little power over his decisions, or his life. His Dominance had always been there, but it had to be dormant, unexpressed. Controlling prey wasn't the same thing.

She expected the Circus had provided him ample visuals to learn the mechanics, but when it had the space to surface, how had he explored the natural Dominant desire that had been there for so long?

Ask the real question, Ruth.

"Am I the first you've done this with?"

"Yes," he told her. "Stay in the now, Ruth."

She came to him, but wouldn't kneel. His lip curled and he gripped her hair, using that hold to pull her to her knees and put her face against his cock. He'd pushed the shorts out of the way, so the heat and steel of it brushed her mouth, her cheek. She inhaled a musky, earth and rain scent.

"If you bite me, I'll put a fistful of sand up your stubborn backside."

"Just the sand, or does the fist come with it?"

His thumb slid into the corner of her mouth, wrenching it open, and his cock came in behind it, thrusting deep. She choked, adjusted as he'd taught her with the screw gag, and that was all it took. Her body slid into a blissful pool where there was nothing but serving her Master, a place she'd so rarely had the chance to go, she thought she'd never take the privilege for granted.

She gripped his taut thighs, her eyes closing. His energy reached for her as her arousal built. Its feathered touch slid over her skin, then down between her legs, in between her buttocks, over her throat and shoulders, against her breasts, a firm, squeezing, kneading, stroking hold that immobilized her.

Literally. She made a startled noise. She was frozen on her knees, caught in the miasma of sexual energy, unable to move. She was helpless.

Terror, bliss, wonder. They tied together in a needy knot. He took over, pumping into her mouth, feeding off her rocketing sexual arousal, tangled with the trepidation.

The fear was part of the meal, too. He'd told her that. But this wasn't the terrible fear of dying she'd experienced during the third mark, channeling his victims. This was the right kind of fear. No decision to make about giving him control, because he simply took it.

Had she thought sexual arousal had a limit or definition, that it reached a certain ceiling before it peaked? If so, she'd been wrong. With an incubus who not only had access to her body, but to her soul, fully marked, all of it his, there were no limits.

You may fight me, struggle, but you belong to me in every way.

She couldn't speak to argue, but she didn't know that she would have. *I'm frightened.*

It's not the wrong kind of fear. He confirmed her thoughts. *That has a different taste. Yours...is better.*

Her eyes could move. She found his attention upon her face. "I like that. Keep looking at me. Beautiful vampire, with her mouth full of my cock, taking care of her Master."

At least you didn't say little vampire.

His mouth twisted in that sinful grin, and he leaned down, whispered against her ear as he nipped it, teased the shell with his tongue. "Little vampire. Sweet, bite-sized morsel I will devour, over and over and over."

His power feathered against her labia, a targeted stroke that vibrated through the rest of her cunt. When mewls were humming in her throat, tiny pleas, he built the reaction, an ever-climbing spiral of response that targeted erogenous zones until the throbbing reactions spread out, collided and consumed all of her.

She moaned his name against his cock, another plea. He drove in harder, and she choked, then steadied. He was telling her to keep her mind on her job, even as he took her apart in every other way.

The more helpless and crazy she became, the more she recognized how bound she was. He would take her as high as he desired. His sharp gaze pierced her heart like that barbed hook in the dark place in his soul, a spear through her torso. All the contrasts, the resistance and yearning together, were unbearable.

But she had to bear it. Because that was his will.

Yes. I would hear you call me Master in a sweet, female voice, all your armor and warrior nature stripped away. I want the little girl deep inside, Ruth. The woman, the maiden, the Goddess. I want them all to belong to me.

His gaze flickered, as if he'd tapped into something deeper in himself than he'd expected, but he grasped it, took ownership of it, the way he did her.

From her side, she knew this lay at the heart of him, the part that had an answer in her, no matter how crazy such a bond could be, no matter what destructive path it could take them down.

Or maybe it wouldn't be destructive at all.

The climax arrived like the weight of the entire ocean, crashing through her. It kept coming and coming and coming, over and through her body, pushing her under, holding her down. But it stopped short of letting her go over that final peak, where full bliss awaited. He had her on a tether, holding her back, denying her that fulfillment.

Her moan became strangled screams. He put his fingers under her chin, stroked her working throat. Then he tipped his head back and released, fluids flooding her mouth, thigh muscles rock hard and flexing under her fingertips. Though she couldn't move, she savored the sensation of his skin brushing against them. Every touch, every friction was up to him. She was surrounded by all of it, and her strength was flagging, her body caught in a vise of need and want, but it didn't matter. He held her up.

He continued to feed from her, measured portions that wouldn't drain her but made it clear she provided him what he needed. She was his sustenance.

When he withdrew from her mouth, she was shuddering. He put his lips against hers and gave her a gift, the ability to move her mouth over his, the way she had over his cock. The gift made her sob.

Her scream became raw as he put his thumb against her clit, two fingers sliding inside her to stroke the upper wall behind it, that explosive and responsive point within.

He let the tether go, just enough.

Come now, Ruth.

The Goddess must have created the stars in the wheeling dark sky during a climax like this. Ruth lost time and sense of anything but the pounding sensations, his touch, his scent, his closeness, and all those showers of light against the insides of her eyelids. When she was done, she was hanging limp in his arms, her upper body bent over one, head pressed to his biceps as he stroked the curve of her spine with the other. His lips were against her hair.

"Good girl," he murmured. "Very good girl. You've pleased me, Ruth. You've done well. I have you."

Her body was still not under her own control. He'd released her from the spellcraft, yes, but she had no bones or muscles.

She felt his smile against her hair. *They're still there. You are just relying on me for now, giving your body a moment because you can. Thank you for the meal.*

"Will it keep you from sucking the life out of Lady Kaela, Garron, and the household staff?"

"I believe so."

When she was able to tip her head back, reach up to touch his face, his eye twitched, just a little, as her hand rested on his cheek. "It's still new to me, a woman's willing touch," he said. "Uncompelled."

"Is that part of my appeal?"

"It's part of it, yes. There are other parts."

He carried her back to their clothes. After they donned them, he circled her to brush off any sand. Amused, she did the same. He gave her a sidelong glance.

"I don't think there was that much sand on the back of my slacks."

She shot him an impish smile, but then had a serious question to ask. "You said my fear has a different taste. Is it a substitute, for what it used to be?"

"You mean, am I settling for it, rather than having the kind I really want?" At her cautious nod, he considered. "When I was younger, their fear added...flavoring. But now, I don't feel like...I don't miss it the same way."

He seemed as if he was figuring his way through his own answer, and when he met her gaze, a wry smile tilted up one side of his mouth in an appealing way. "So, no. I'm not settling."

He glanced up the cliff, toward Kaela's home. "I could use a drink, and Lady Kaela has a well-stocked bar."

He didn't want to dwell in the past, not after having an experience that was all the right things. She understood that. "Well, she said to make ourselves at home. I've never seen you drink."

"Alcohol doesn't affect my blood, any more than it does a vampire's. Though your father didn't offer me any."

"It has a bad history with Native Americans, and a good number of his human staff are from the tribes. He prohibits it on the island. Only time I've ever seen it in his hand is when he shared a Guinness with my mother at Lord Marshall's." She smiled at the memory, his horrified expression at the thick texture and strong taste, her mother's laughter.

"So what does he like to drink?"

"Duh. Blood."

"Smartass." He took her hand, and they strolled along the beach.

"We're not walking the whole way, right? I'm not putting my pretty boots through two miles of scratchy sand. I worked hard for them."

"Your father pays you for your work?"

"When I'm working for him, I'm staff, so yeah." She paused to lift a foot in front of her, admiring the stitched embroidery. "But these were a birthday gift. *Etsi* asked what I wanted. I paid for half. *Etsi* and *Sgidoda* paid the other."

At his curious look, she raised a brow. "What?"

"Except for Cai, my experience has been limited to more highly placed vampires. And he steals what he needs. I've never thought about there being working class vampires."

"Plenty of us are, especially the made ones under a century old. Becoming a vampire doesn't include a kit with a manual and a billionaire's bank account. Though it would be really nice if the Council would arrange for that."

"You should speak to Lyssa about it."

"Yeah," she said dryly. "I'll get right on that. But seriously, most vampires who see the north side of two or three hundred years have accumulated wealth for themselves, if they have any brains or ambition at all. Sometimes by legal means, sometimes not. Most pay lip service to human laws and have no problem using their strength, speed and compulsion abilities to get them ahead in the material gain department."

"Like Cai."

"Eh." She shook her head. "He's a little different. He could care less for material gain. He just steals the basic supplies and clothes he needs to get along, so he doesn't have to be pinned down by a job and a paycheck."

She thought of what Kaela had mentioned, Cai's beginnings among the Trads. Though he despised them, one thing he'd kept from their culture was his indifference to possessions.

With the exception of his servant Rand. Cai was very possessive about his wolf shifter. And the feeling was mutual.

Seeing that in her head, Merc nodded his agreement. "Their bond is strong. But as far as those who do accumulate wealth in such ways, your father didn't choose that path."

"No. He crossed those lines when he was younger, because he had a crap beginning, both as a human and as a vampire, but either because of that or in spite of it, his moral compass steadied. When we were kids, if we took advantage of staff members, he came down on us like a ton of bricks."

"Give me an example. Involving you."

She made a face. "I have so many better examples involving Adan."

"I prefer the ones where you are punished."

"Of course you do. Perv." She punched him in the side, a blow he took without flinching, though his eyes flashed in pleasurable warning. "When I was much younger, I overpowered and took a knife from Pearce, one of the staff members. I wanted it."

"You do like your blades. How did your father react?"

The memory brought a little shiver. "Da never punished us in a violent way, but his expression when we were in trouble made us certain he had a dungeon hidden on the island, set up for torturing his offspring.

"He told me to pack an overnight bag. Next night, we flew to Tennessee, to the Farida Sanctuary where our friends Nerida and Miah live. It's an artist's commune, but also a sanctuary for domestic abuse victims."

"Nerida and Miah are vampires?"

"Yes. Turned as children, too young, so they're forever trapped, physically, in that age. It's the safest place for them, and where they can have as full a life as possible. Mal won protection for them from the Council. William and Matthew, who live with Lord Marshall, the Florida overlord, have the same protection. My mother brought all of them to the island back in the 1950s," she added. "It's how she and my father met. Because of his skill in rehabilitating predators, it was hoped he could figure out how to help them adapt and survive. He did."

She returned to her story. "At the sanctuary, Da had the director show us around and tell us about the people staying there." Her lips tightened as she remembered the stories she'd heard. The scars and haunted eyes of those who'd escaped abusive situations.

"When *Sgidoda* and I were alone, he scoffed. 'This is a useless place,' he said. 'Why give them sanctuary? If they're less powerful, they should have no rights. Correct? The more powerful should be allowed to diminish them, beat them. Kill them. Steal from them.'"

At Merc's expression, she nodded. "Yeah. Da knows how to make a point. His disappointment is the propulsion that drives it into your heart like a wooden stake."

What you did to Pearce had no purpose but to serve your own selfishness and darker impulses. In a vampire, in any situation where you hold the greater power, you must always stay aware of that. Because just as important as the results of your actions, how it impacts the one you have harmed, is what it does to yourself. Corruption and darkness can take over a soul.

Just when she thought she couldn't bear the look on her father's face any longer, it had softened enough to remind her he loved her, even as the sternness stayed in place. *You'll meet those stronger than you in life, Ruth. Just as Pearce did with you. Someone who can treat you as abominably as these people have been treated. When they don't, when they respect you, you'll understand that's not only a gift they're bestowing, but a right they are acknowledging."*

Merc's expression was thoughtful. "It's an interesting philosophy. He lives in a world that often believes and acts on brutal principles, particularly toward those weaker."

"Yes," she said slowly. "He knew what I would face. Not that day, but on another, he told me the most important thing to do if I get overwhelmed by someone stronger."

Merc faced her, his expression inscrutable. "What was that?"

She rested her hand on his forearm, her grip for both of them. "Hold onto yourself, who you are. If they end up taking your life, you meet their eyes at that last moment, and show them they've only taken what they can. Not what's important."

"Your father is an interesting male."

"He lives close to nature, and he knows it can be cruel and unfair. Even the animals he helps can have those qualities. He taught us to weigh our actions, always think about why we're exercising our power and strength over another."

It took her mind back to her discussion with her mother, about vampires and servants, and the contradiction there. Though she could never see her father crossing that line with her mother, Elisa had made it clear that many vampires didn't feel that way.

Merc touched her shoulder, pulling her back from that conflicting mix of thoughts. "What are my motives, exercising my power and strength over you?"

She quivered. "I think we both understand it, without having to explain it. Which is all the better, because I'm not sure there are words for it."

He slid his arms under her, lifted her. "I like this outfit. You look lovely in it."

At her look, he arched a brow. "Have I said something wrong?"

"No. I'm just...courtship hasn't really been our thing."

"I don't believe that's true. I've been courting you all along. We've just been doing it in a more violent fashion. But you do like romantic gestures, at least when we're alone."

"Don't let anyone know. Particularly Adan. I'll never live it down."

Merc flashed her his *no-promises* smile, with the sexy touch of demon to it, and they were in the air. When they landed, they came through the door into the living area, where the bar was located.

As Merc moved behind it and scanned the options, she slid onto a stool and watched him, bemused. He pulled two bottles off of the well-stocked shelves, rummaged through the mini fridge and retrieved a bucket of ice, a bottle of sparkling rose wine, and a small tub of raspberries.

"Did you moonlight as a bartender? I know you can cloak your wings, but how do you keep them from knocking glassware off the shelves?"

"There are different cloaking methods. One simply hides the wings. The other dissipates them materially, so that if you passed your hand behind me, you would feel a sense of energy, but not actual matter. Right now, they're not cloaked for you, but no one else can see them, and I have made them immaterial."

He showed her, sweeping his wing across a shelf. The feathers passed through the glass like a ghost wing. "Cool," she said. "And I like that 'cloaking for thee and not for me' thing. Can you do that at the Circus, on performance nights? I would prefer to be able to see them all the time."

"I'll try to remember. If I don't have more pressing matters than spoiling you."

She shot him a rude gesture, but he caught her wrist and kissed the tip of the finger with heated lips. She shifted on the bar stool. "Can you still feel them when they're...not material to others?"

"Yes. I have to act and move as if they are not there. It takes practice."

The bottles he'd chosen were Chambord and chocolate liqueur. He put one of the crystal glasses on the bar, added the liqueur and the Chambord, and removed the smaller knife from its hidden scabbard to make a shallow cut on his forearm.

In the aftermath of the violent climax, she'd forgotten her need to feed, but he hadn't. Hunger surged through her, but she stayed still as he positioned his wrist over the glass, the heel of his hand resting on the lip. The blood trickled into the glass, mingling with the two alcohols.

"You've fed your Master," he said. "I'll feed you now."

Ice went in next, and he splashed the wine over it, filling the glass and adding the raspberries, speared on a long toothpick. He slid the drink across to her. "This is called a Bachelor Rose. It's an older drink. Yvette had Gundar make it for her one night. She has a fondness for them."

Ruth inhaled the scent before she sipped. Her eyes brightened with appreciation. "The different tastes don't overpower one another. They mix the right way." His blood also gave it the richness and fortification she needed.

He removed an import beer from the fridge, twisting off the top and taking a swallow from the bottle. "Too girly for you?" She gestured with her drink.

"Too sweet. I like some bitterness and bite."

She smiled against the glass's rim. "Explaining your attraction to prickly female vampires. Did Yvette have Gundar make one of these for you?"

"No. I saw him do it. From a distance."

She tapped his hand, braced on the bar. "I think it's time to let more people at the Circus get to know you."

"There's a benefit to being on the outside."

"Less expectations of good behavior."

"Perhaps." He gave her that wicked smile, but she could tell he was thinking about what she said. Considering it.

"I would prefer it if...Medusa's snakes didn't dislike me. They try to bite me when I get too close to her."

"If she feels she can trust you, I'm betting that will change."

"I see you found the bar."

At Garron's comment, Ruth turned and lifted a glass. "He made me a Bachelor Rose. Do you want one?"

Though a slight smile touched the servant's lips, the watchfulness was still there. Probably because as soon as they'd detected him approaching, that Merc danger feeling had increased.

It's a general broadcast, so you can worry less about the political machinations of vampires.

His explanation was surprising. She'd simply assigned it to irrepressible testosterone surges.

I will *take the drink away from you.*

Turning her face away from Garron, she stuck out her tongue and earned another lovely shiver from the look on Merc's face.

Garron declined the drink politely. "Thank you. Dinner is ready, if you want to follow me."

As Ruth slipped off the stool, drink in hand, and followed Garron toward the dining room, her mind went to what was to come. Especially as her gaze lingered on the tense set of the male's broad shoulders.

Normally the only negative she had toward vampire social gatherings involved the effort to mask the direction of her interests during the sexual play. Other than that, she enjoyed the creativity and intense vibes as much as any other fanged attendee.

But thanks to her discussion with Merc, her mind once again went to Elisa, and how she and Mal handled those vampire social gatherings where Mal's rank meant he would have to subject his servant to other vampires' creative sexual games upon demand.

Whenever that topic had been broached, Elisa's response seemed rote, but truthful. *"I'm pleased to serve however my Master desires."* She'd add something to the effect of, *"However is needed to have our life together."*

Two pieces of a puzzle that went together, but seemed like a forced fit. Her mother never spoke further on it, and if the issue was pressed, Mal would intervene in the conversation, changing the topic.

But Ruth and Adan weren't blind. Before the required overlord and Region Master formal gatherings, Mal was perilously short-tempered, and Elisa would get really quiet or painfully perky.

The vampire-human servant relationship was never simple. She glanced at Merc. Case in point.

They weren't eating in the formal dining room. Garron led them to the cliff-embedded level, which held more than guest quarters. There was a luxurious private dungeon playroom.

Candles were arranged on iron stands and wall sconces. They threw flickering natural light on the room's main attractions. A dark red cushioned spanking bench, outfitted with silver and black restraints. A versatile St. Andrews cross. Plus a throne chair, forced orgasm tower, and a wall of toys and restraints.

A table for six had been set up, angled toward a grid of TV screens, covering the wall like the bank of windows in Kaela's office. The screens showed the beach and cliffs from outside cameras.

There were equally pleasant views inside the room. Two household servants knelt at opposite ends of the dungeon, waiting. A male and a female, naked except for collars on their throats and cuffs on their wrists and ankles. The female straddled a saddle outfitted with a vibrating phallus, her cunt wet with arousal. The male was on all fours, a fucking machine slowly moving in and out of his backside. Both servants were doing their best to remain still, Ruth assumed as they'd been commanded to do.

Another machine was in front of the male, thrusting its phallus into his mouth at the same pace as the one behind him. The female had been gagged with a rubber cock, held in place with straps around her head. The two people were blindfolded and wore muffling headphones, so they could only feel the pleasure and not know what was coming next. Or hear what their audience was discussing.

Knowing what was expected, and not finding it an unpleasant task, Ruth wandered around each servant, enjoying the full view. She detected nothing but helpless pleasure and a devoted desire to serve their Mistress. Both household servants were second marked.

Merc stood behind one of the six chairs around the table, his attention fixed upon Ruth, upon the third mark link that thrummed with information coming from her. His incubus energy responded, twining around her like it had on the beach. While this time it left her the ability to move, its velvet hold cuffed her wrists, her waist, her legs, tendrils spiraling under her skirt. As those bonds tightened and stroked, she stopped, closing her eyes. The sensation circled her throat, caressing her jaw and cheeks. Her ears.

Merc. Don't go overboard. I can't resist you. I need to be a certain way here.

Then ask for that consideration from me. You do not command me, Ruth.

She had naturally rebellious instincts, but he wasn't in a lenient mood. Her briefest hesitation to consider resistance had immediate repercussions. Those tendrils climbed two inches higher, brushing her already spasming cunt. He was more than capable of leaving her writhing on the floor, moaning.

Please.

The sensation eased, enough to maintain a reasonable outward decorum, but making her have to work for it. An intentional balance, she was sure. His expression of satisfaction confirmed it.

While it goaded her fight instincts, she couldn't deny the flood of exhilaration. She was in an overlord's dining room, being commanded. Mastered. With no one knowing, no one the wiser. Under Merc's command, control and protection. He wasn't asking her to be less than the fighter she was.

The thrill of it was far too dangerous.

She turned toward Kaela. The overlord stood at the head of the table, slim, manicured hands resting on the wooden arch of the chair back. Her golden eyes glinted. The table's centerpiece was a spiral of iron holding a dozen candles. It rested in a bed of seashells and interesting coral pieces.

"You offer an optimal setting for dinner, my lady. Kaela."

The woman inclined her head. "I'm delighted to hear that. And to know you are enjoying it."

She gestured to them to take a seat, and Garron stepped forward to pull out his lady's chair. As she sat down, Kaela overlapped his hand, her fingers caressing his larger ones. Her gaze rested on the two servants, drinking in their sensual distress. When she dropped her hand down to caress Garron's hip, his upper thigh, his covered hers, giving it a hard squeeze.

Ruth studied the gesture, the intertwined fingers, until Kaela took her hand away.

Merc had settled on a cushioned bench next to Ruth's chair. "Though you might prefer to keep your wings cloaked," Kaela said, "I thought you might appreciate that seating option, my lord."

"I do. Thank you."

"Garron and the household staff deserve the credit," she added. "They tend to anticipate my needs."

"The sign of well-trained and devoted servants," Merc noted. "Yvette has two in the Circus who know what she wants, almost before she has the thought. She has the same ability toward them. Anticipatory behavior isn't limited to one side or the other."

Ruth blinked. Her normally brusque companion had discovered a diplomat's double-edged tongue. *Merc, what are you doing?*

He didn't respond. His gaze had met Garron's. The look between the two males held a variety of things. Speculation. Readiness. Aggression. Things Garron would never show toward a visiting vampire.

"Is there a problem with my servant, my lord?" Kaela asked in a neutral tone.

"If there was, would you dismiss him from our presence?" Though the question startled Ruth, Merc's tone held only a mild curiosity.

"It depends on the reason. You're guests, and though I will show you hospitality, I expect courtesy in return." Kaela's expression was frosty.

"There's no problem, my lady. My apologies. You and Ruth were going to speak of history."

"Will you speak of your own?"

"No," Merc said. "I'll listen."

The servants brought in the first course, a pomegranate salad with pecans, goat cheese and pear tidbits. Merc's was served on a medium-sized plate with a gold rim. The two vampires had a much smaller portion, in a condiment dish with the same embellishment. A small pumpkin muffin was placed on top. Merc had a trio of them arranged along the curve of his plate.

After a weighted pause, Kaela directed her attention to Ruth. "What would you like to know?"

Since Merc only seemed interested in his salad, Ruth grabbed for the redirect. "Can you tell me about your life during the Civil War period?"

"Of course. My husband and I had a modest farm that covered our needs, if we worked the land and watched our funds. Like most Southerners, we weren't wealthy plantation owners."

As Kaela painted the setting for her past life, it helped ease some of the tension Merc and Garron's behavior had caused. Though the overlord glanced toward Merc often, including him in the conversation, she didn't ask questions about angels. Even if, like anyone else, she was rabidly curious. Fortunately, the setting provided useful distractions.

Having dinner in an environment saturated with sexual promise was the norm for vampires. When the two servants reached climax, the conversation was paused to enjoy, to watch the struggle, the helpless convulsions of their toned and lovely bodies.

As they were still twitching, now with the discomfort that came from the continued, relentless friction of the vibrating toys on flesh made overly sensitive from the release, Garron went to the male servant. He removed the ear protection and spoke in a hard voice. "Your Mistress didn't give you permission to come. Did she?"

"No. Forgive me, my lady." The words were muffled, because Garron had stopped the front machine's movement but left the phallus partially in the male's mouth. The servant had long blond hair, pulled into a queue so the contortions of his face couldn't be hidden, or how his lips were stretched by the girth of the toy.

Garron moved to the wall and returned with a quirt. When he landed the first blow on the blond's buttock, the male curved in on himself, his breath sucking in.

"You'll ask for the pain, not shrink from it."

Garron's command had a snap like Yvette's single tail. It yanked

Ruth's attention from the servant to the male in control of him. At his Mistress's order, she reminded herself. *Don't lose focus.*

Kaela might be watching the display with erotic absorption, her fingers caressing the stem of her wineglass, but Ruth was sure she was monitoring her guests' enjoyment. On the next blow, the male complied, lifting his hips to reach for the blow. Asking for more.

Merc was a statue on the outside. But he was hip deep in Ruth's mind.

She was doing as she always did at such things. Staring at the display, visibly enjoying it the way she was supposed to be doing, while inside she imagined the roles reversed. Only this time she had someone to share it with. She was imagining herself on all fours, serving Merc's cock like she had on the beach, as the fucking machine brought her to climax.

She felt the brush of his power inside her, an intimate caress, and barely controlled the tremble.

"Would you care to administer Embla's punishment, Ruth?" Kaela yanked her out of her head, nodding to the female servant, then gesturing to the wall of toys. "Choose whatever you prefer."

It wasn't a request. Ruth knew it wasn't. At such events, it never was.

"I think it's your servant who should receive the punishment," Merc commented. "He doesn't act like a servant. I expect you have to put him in his place fairly often. Is that how he got the scars?"

Ruth expected her stunned look matched Kaela's, though the overlord exercised the same credible effort to bring it under control.

"Unless I don't have the right to make my own requests for our mutual enjoyment, as your vampire guests do," Merc added. "He *is* yours to command. Isn't he?"

Kaela's face was smooth as glass. "Yes. He is."

Garron stepped forward. "Stop fucking with her head," he said. "Or I will cut your goddamn wings off. Even if I can't see them."

Ruth was speechless. Merc held the other man's gaze for a long moment, then shifted his attention to Kaela, who kept that brittle glass expression.

If you don't tell me what's going on, Ruth said, *I may help him.*
Give it a moment to play out.

"Vampires only detect sexual desire," Merc said conversationally. "Not the shape of it. For an incubus, desire is a detailed language, specific to our prey."

"That must give your meals a great deal of variety," Kaela said coolly. Garron had resumed his place behind her. His anger hadn't abated, but he seemed to be following his Mistress's direction again.

"Dismiss the other two," Merc said. "The sexual desire in this room is sufficient to serve us. Agreed?"

Since she had no idea what the hell was happening, Ruth chose a neutral poker face. Garron and Kaela were sharing a silent moment, a conversation Ruth would have given a lot to hear, but they were both accomplished at masking the tone of that discussion.

Merc reached out a hand and laid it on hers, tapping her fingers, giving them idle strokes. A cue to wait. To be patient. Not one of her award-winning traits, but his sidelong glance gave it the punch she needed. Making it an order.

Garron at last moved. He freed the two servants, helping them to their feet, but kept the blindfold and ear protection in place. The servers assisted them from the room, since they were understandably wobbly.

They returned with dessert. Tiny cheesecakes drizzled with chocolate, caramel, fruit and nuts. Kaela explained they were made locally, and discussed culinary offerings in the Monterey area. Though she behaved as if nothing untoward had happened, Ruth noted a broken glass look in the overlord's eyes.

After the servers left, Garron moved to the doors. He locked the deadbolt and punched a code into a keypad. Ruth was aware of a low-level buzzing. Some kind of forcefield outside the door, adding to the security of the entry?

Also a noise buffer. No one knows what's going on in this room until it is deactivated.

Should we get ready to fight our way out of here?

No. Everything is fine. Merc's eyes followed Garron back to his spot behind Kaela.

Kaela nudged the plate toward Ruth. "Have the one with nuts and chocolate. It's excellent."

Ruth transferred it to her dessert plate, another gold-rimmed piece, a saucer with thin scalloped edges. "I expect you had to learn as a child what a made vampire learns as an adult," the overlord noted. "How to handle something delicately, so it won't break from a normal vampire touch."

"My mother didn't let us touch glass until we were in our teens, for just that reason."

Merc took a cheesecake bite with a pineapple caramel drizzle. It was topped with a dark cherry. As her angel incubus put it in his mouth, the flavor spread across her own tongue, giving her a start. She hadn't known he could do that.

Merc still had Ruth's hand. He stroked her wrist, the individual fingers, as he watched her experience the taste. Then his focus moved back toward Kaela.

Crap. He was about to start doing...whatever he was doing...again.

"It's an interesting challenge, having a human servant who's a Dominant. But you're stronger than him. Faster. He can't top you. Unless you want that."

Garron laid a hand on Kaela's shoulder. She was staring into space, as if her mind was churning with so many thoughts, she couldn't be present in the room.

"My lord." Garron's voice was dry ice cold. "I'll ask one more time, with respect, that you stop with the games."

Merc dipped his head at Kaela. "You first."

Kaela's head tilted left, then down. She reached up and stroked her servant's fingers. When her gaze lifted to meet Ruth's, with relief, Ruth saw she was fully present. Fully herself again, even if there seemed to be a different quality to that.

"It's difficult to watch someone struggle with the same thing you do yourself, and not offer them a line of connection," the overlord said in a calm voice. "Everyone's life is a mix of lies and truth. It's how we live, survive and find happiness."

Ruth's mind froze. She wanted to deny what she was hearing, stop it from happening. But Merc wouldn't let it.

"I expect," Merc mused, "if a servant is a Master, service-oriented in a very special way, he can be what his vampire needs him to be, when she is being what the vampire world expects her to be."

His gaze lifted to Garron. "Submitting to his vampire at the right moments, if that's what's needed to protect and care for her—to be her Master—that's what he'll do."

Garron leaned over his lady and murmured to her. She shook her head and he straightened. With another glance at Ruth, she rose.

As she moved to an open stretch of the large Persian carpet, Garron turned to watch her. A few heartbeats of silent communication, and she nodded. An answer to him, and perhaps to herself as well.

In her elegant heels and fashionable dress—Ruth had been right about what Kaela considered informal—the powerful California overlord sank to her knees, clasped her hands behind her straight back and bowed her head.

Waiting for her Master's command.

CHAPTER TWENTY-THREE

*W*hat gripped Ruth was so beyond shock, there wasn't a word for it. How had she missed it?

Because Ruth was a submissive, but an alpha as well. And a vampire. She'd only submit for a male physically stronger than she was, and maybe on other levels as well. Emotionally, spiritually, and at the key moments when it mattered.

Not to a human. *Never* to a human. Humans had no right to command a vampire. Ever.

Look at him, Ruth. Look at him, and look at her.

She couldn't refuse Merc's demand. Reluctantly, her gaze slid to Garron. His expression on Kaela was fierce, protective. Proud. Worried. Now she understood his reluctance. Kaela had planned for this, because she'd recognized what Ruth was. Garron, his mind on her protection, had worried it exposed too much about her, a dangerous and wrong course.

He'd been right.

Ruth rose from the table, so abruptly her knee bumped the wooden edge, bruising her flesh. "Lady Kaela." She addressed the opposite wall. Where she wasn't looking at the kneeling woman. "Your meal and company have been...lovely."

The fake sound of her voice was acid in her mouth. "If you'll forgive me, I need to rest before the Trad's arrival tonight. And it appears you have other...business. With your leave, I'll retire."

Ruth hated herself as Kaela's head remained in that lowered position. A hard quiver ran through the woman, and before Ruth could look away again, she saw Kaela swallow, a convulsive movement of her slim neck. Garron moved toward her, but Kaela's hand came up, a sharp movement.

Garron stopped, with obvious reluctance and great effort, and his lady rose to her feet on her own and faced her guests.

Inside, Ruth suspected Kaela was shaking from head to toe. Outwardly, if Ruth hadn't seen what she'd just seen, Kaela looked like the vampire who had Lady Lyssa's full confidence and had brought order to the region. "Very well, Lady Ruth. Thank you for your company." Her eyes had that brassy shine, but her voice was even and courteous.

Ruth pressed her lips together. "I think...does Garron have to deactivate the security?"

"Yes."

Garron didn't move in that direction. Kaela sent him a look easy to decipher. *What can we do? Keep a Truth Vessel and a born vampire imprisoned to hide our secret?*

Ruth was no stranger to the risks of having her nature discovered. She'd learned how to contain and conquer the anxiety, the hated fear, but it didn't stop them from plaguing her, whenever she was put in situations where it could be revealed to other vampires. The unpleasant coldness in her gut and vigilance accompanied her every time.

Her mind might be rejecting this, messed up over all of it, but on one thing she was sure.

"Lady Kaela, you provided fine entertainment with your servants, and your chef's food and presentation are exceptional. If anyone asks me about your hospitality, I will report that the Council themselves couldn't do better."

Message received. Kaela's subtle nod said so, but the dull light in her gaze didn't bring Ruth any relief. "Thank you, Lady Ruth. If you or Merc need anything before the Trad's arrival, please advise Garron or the household staff."

Garron had deactivated the panel. As Ruth moved for the door, she purposefully didn't look at him. A servant. A human servant. All the trumped-up stories of human male servants taking advantage of

374

female vampires...she'd scoffed at them as ridiculous chauvinism on the part of male vampires, possibly some jealousy.

Having that idea trying to take root inside her now was like swallowing poison. She had to get out of here. That was all. She had to think about this.

Merc was following her, but she didn't reach out to his mind. She had too much buzzing around her own.

As she moved into the corridor, one of the house staff was coming their way. She addressed Garron. "Lady Kaela has a return call from Mr. Shalimar, regarding the insurance on her waterfront businesses," she said.

"I'll take it." Kaela passed Ruth with a courteous nod, and strode down the corridor, heels clicking, head up, the silk of her dress rippling across her narrow back. Garron's gaze followed her. He didn't look at Ruth, either to keep himself from shooting a look on her that would be entirely inappropriate from a servant, or because he was communicating so intently with Kaela he had no room to spare for the pretense of doing otherwise.

Ruth didn't care about that. She just had to go.

I'll find you, Merc told her. *Go where you need to go. I need to speak to Garron first.*

As Ruth went up the stairs and took the direction opposite from Kaela's, Merc didn't want to let her go, but her mind was blasting her need for space. He would give her that for a few minutes, just as he suspected Garron would for Lady Kaela.

Though the man's tension suggested how difficult that decision was, the one thing they'd proven in this sealed chamber was how much self-discipline Kaela and her servant/Master had to exercise, to maintain a successful façade for the true dynamic of their relationship.

Garron gave him a rigid nod. His gesture to Merc, to come back into the protected room, might as well have been the thrust of a middle finger. However, he didn't say anything until he secured the door, so they couldn't be heard by anyone else, unless Kaela chose to listen in on their mind link. Garron wouldn't be able to keep her out, but if Garron truly was her Master, perhaps they'd agreed she'd only do that when he permitted it.

When Garron turned toward him, Merc faced a human male who'd served as a warrior, who had a Dominant personality, and whose submissive had been hurt. A woman he loved enough to give her what most men like him wouldn't consider possible to ask of themselves.

"I want to punch you in the face. If you punch me back, I know I'll land somewhere on the eastern coast, but if you have a fair bone in your body, you owe me that one. You knew. You wouldn't leave it alone."

"She had a great desire to reveal it," Merc said. "She knew about Ruth. So did you. I merely brought the game to an end."

"It's *not* a game. Ruth has your protection. You could stand against ten vampires and come out the winner. I'm Kaela's emotional armor, keeping her balanced, giving her a way to submit. But I can't protect her physically worth shit and we both know it."

Garron stopped and steadied himself. "She accepts it. I have to live with it. It's a crappy way to live, but there are worse ones."

"Perhaps you should have thought of that before you committed to be her servant," Merc observed.

The male looked like he really would hit Merc. Instead he went for a different blow. "Okay. Tomorrow, someone bigger and more powerful than you—I'm sure there's someone out there that qualifies, because there always is—tells you to walk away from Ruth for her *physical* wellbeing, leaving her needs unmet, and all alone with that shit in her head. What's your response?"

Merc's jaw tightened. "I'm from a more powerful race, and there's no prohibition against our bond, in her world or mine. I can protect her, unlike you. I'm not trying to be unkind. I'm merely pointing out what you did yourself."

Garron's expression went to stone. "You don't know Kaela's heart. What she wants and needs. I'm her Master, and there are two sides to that coin. Actually, probably limitless sides, but the point is, the more I learned about her heart, her soul, and her incredibly intelligent mind, I knew I would never deny her what she wants and needs. No true Master can. Not one who loves his submissive down to that level of the soul."

The words effectively turned a mirror on himself, on his still new and uncharted feelings for Ruth. When Merc said nothing, Garron made a grim, satisfied nod and moved toward the door.

When he reached it, before he deactivated the security, Garron paused. "Everyone dies. Living is something most of us spend our lives struggling with, how to do it the best way we can," he said. "Maybe we get it right, maybe we fuck it up, but there are things we know we did right. However Kaela and I end up in this fucked-up vampire world that can't see beyond its narrow view and prejudices, we're both sure of that."

Merc knew the words weren't directed only toward him. Garron's gaze flickered as if he'd received some kind of acknowledgement, but sadness and pain came with it. The urgency with which he started to plug in the security code said their conversation was at an end. His lady needed him.

Merc put his hand on the door before he could open it. Garron shot him a warning and impatient look, but Merc held up a hand.

"She's lonely. Ruth. She's fearless, but she longs for another like herself. I forced the matter into the open so she could make that connection. I didn't consider Kaela, the pacing, as I perhaps should have. I also didn't anticipate Ruth's reaction to a human servant being your lady's Master."

"Neither did Kaela." Garron's expression eased a fraction and he sighed. "In fairness, the whole dinner setup was for her to take the opportunity if the optimal opening came. But your opening was not optimal."

"Perhaps we should have coordinated before dinner, since we both knew our ladies' hearts."

"Yeah, maybe. But I don't know you. And my loyalty is to her."

"Understood." Merc met the man's gaze. "Is she going to be all right?"

"She's always all right. She's the strongest, smartest woman I know. But every time she's hurt, I feel the wound here." Garron tapped a fist against his chest. He paused, and while the set of his jaw showed his anger with Ruth, his question showed his understanding of where her head might be at. "And yours?"

"Ruth's reaction was honest, but she'll be upset with herself. She wouldn't willingly hurt someone she respects."

"Submissives are pretty universal in how they handle thinking they fucked up, or actually fucking up. They need their Masters to help them deal with it."

"Will your lady allow you to do that?"

"If she doesn't put my head through a wall. She does have a temper."

Merc's lips tightened against a smile. "Your relationship is more of a mine field than most."

"Only physically." Garron glanced pointedly at the palm Merc had kept braced on the door. "Something else?"

Putting out his chin, Merc tapped his jaw. "It's a fair demand. One punch."

~

Beneath the house was a spacious patio, decorated with fairy lights, comfortable outdoor furniture, and offering the never-tiresome view of the ocean. Ruth watched the lights of distant boats, and thought about going to the beach. There was an access, a boardwalk she could see from here.

Why hadn't Merc just told her his suspicions—okay, realizations— in the privacy of their room, instead of revealing them in such an awkward way?

It offended me, her having to pretend to be something she isn't. She's an honorable woman. Like you. It offends me that you have to pretend, that your people consider it a weakness and it makes you a target. But there's something else that offends me.

What's that?

Your behavior toward her.

Merc swooped down and caught her around the waist. Before Ruth could break free, they were aloft. He held her against him and groped under her skirt, ripping her panties away with one yank. Even wrestling while shooting through the air, he bent her over his arm, pulled her hips up and sheathed himself in a strong single thrust.

Total shock gripped her as she cried out. The large dose of lust that flooded her had nowhere to go, the emotions she was experiencing unable to accommodate it. A giant, ruthless fist clutched her aching heart and churning stomach.

Merc didn't care. His palm pressed against her stomach, her legs hooked back over his calves as he fucked her in the air from behind, using his wings to shove in harder, deeper. It hurt. That wasn't all, though. He slapped her clit, giving it a spanking that stung and had her writhing on his cock, struggling to get away. It wasn't fun, but he wasn't in a fun mood.

Neither was she. But it was a punishment, and his overpowering strength required her to do the only thing she could. Submit. She clung to his arm, an iron band around her waist. Every slap, every thrust, brought an even worse pain. Kaela's gaze, that brittle, bright-eyed look Ruth had put there.

When Merc stopped spanking her clit and thrusting, he'd done it long enough she would have begged for forgiveness from whoever he wanted. But she also noticed, when he landed on their isolated stretch of beach and withdrew from her, her sex was sore, but she was strung less tight.

The ache was still in her throat, though. Which was probably why he wasn't done. He put her on her knees and clamped a hand on her throat, making her stare up into his implacable face. An avenging angel, here to punish her for her sins.

"Apologize."

"I'm sorry. I didn't mean to hurt her."

"Or Garron."

She snarled as he twisted a nipple. "Stop it."

He did it harder. "Yes, Garron. I'm sorry, I apologize to him, too."

When he released her and moved back, she charged him with a howl. He deflected her punches and stumbling kicks. She was unbalanced by what he'd done to her body. Then he caught her, took them both down to the wet sand and shoved her face-down over his knees.

"Don't you fucking dare…"

This spanking hurt like hell, with the additional dose of humiliation, being treated like a misbehaving child. However, he kept her legs open with a knee between her thighs, holding her ass up so he could spank her cunt some more, this time with a hand roughened by sand. She would have to rinse the grains out or walk around with them grating between her tender folds.

"That's what you'll do until I tell you to clean yourself," he told her. "Which will not be until you speak to Kaela."

"Fuck you."

Her defiance earned her more of the same. This time he rubbed the sand into her cunt himself, the sadistic prick bastard.

Shit. I didn't mean...

When he'd punished her to the point she was strangling back the sobs, furiously refusing to acknowledge the tears bathing her face, or what was causing them, he put her back on her feet and stepped away from her, arms crossed. Waiting to see if she had a next move.

She wasn't that stupid, though she did eye him with intense dislike and a desire for retaliation.

"It's different, Merc." She bared her fangs. Everything hurt, but what hurt most was her heart. "You know it is. Vampires are supposed to be dominant. That's the way it's supposed to work."

"Isn't she an overlord?"

"Her accomplishments aren't the problem."

"They don't seem to carry any weight with you. Perhaps a human, one she's bound to with the vampire-servant bond, is the only one she can trust enough to offer her submission."

Ruth shook her head, wanting to back away, but Merc's uncompromising look kept her where he'd put her. "She can't offer it to vampires, who might take advantage of her position. You haven't had any success finding such a male yourself among your people. As far as seeking someone from another race to fulfill her needs, the relationship between the Fae and vampires is still very touchy. With angels..." He spread out his arms. "There's only so much of this to go around."

"You are such an ass." She collapsed on the beach, wincing at the sand grating in sensitive places. In the aftermath of the punishment, which assuaged some of her inexplicable guilt, she couldn't argue with his logic. But it didn't change her feelings on it, which made it worse.

"I just...I wish she hadn't shown us that. I wish she didn't know about me."

"It's as she said. She didn't want you to feel alone in the vampire world, a unique oddity."

"A freak. You can say it."

"So now you are two freaks who know of one another." Merc drew closer, with a slight wariness that mollified her. She wasn't entirely unthreatening.

"You fight dirty, that's all." When he dropped to his heels, he put his hand to his jaw, testing it, and added, "It doesn't mean I'm afraid to be near you. Ever."

"Why are you doing that? I didn't land a face punch." Though it hadn't been for lack of trying.

"Garron has a very strong fist."

Her eyes widened, then she smiled. And chuckled. Feeling better. Sort of.

He'd...spanked her. And while it had been terrible, humiliating, a part of her had wanted it. Wishing it could make it all better. She also couldn't deny the flood of arousal it had caused. She didn't know how to feel about that.

I do. It makes me want to do it all over again.

Ruth pressed her fingertips over the bridge of her nose. "I need to apologize. Not because you said I had to." When he gave her a very Master look, she sighed. "I mean, yes, but...fuck it, you know what I mean."

His lips pressed against a near smile, but it didn't lessen the intensity. "I do."

～

She'd told Merc she wanted to do this alone. Agreeably, he said he'd stay in the bar area to make himself a Jack and Coke, and maybe peruse Kaela's library.

Fabulous. Glad he could have a cocktail and chill while she went to eat a huge helping of crow.

She hissed when he swatted her ass on the way to the bar. "I bet hair remover works on feathers," she threatened. She wanted to rub her stinging posterior—the male could deliver a smack, and she was still hurting from the beach pummeling—but refused to lose her dignity. She'd do it when she was out of his sight and hope he didn't tune in to snicker at her.

Merc caught her wrist before she could flounce away. Miserable, she closed her eyes and allowed him to touch his forehead to hers. It helped. "You'll feel better after you speak to Kaela," he told her. "And I'm in your head whenever you need me."

She dipped her head into his touch. Lifted it to meet his gaze. "Thanks."

She wondered if his acts of care surprised him as much as they did her. But they were definitely welcome.

When she reached Kaela's office, Garron was stepping over the threshold, about to pull the door closed behind him. She could tell he was set to say his lady wasn't taking any visitors. Then his jaw flexed. "You're welcome to go in."

Kaela's desire, not his. He left the door ajar, as much courtesy as he'd extend. When he headed down the hallway, Ruth could tell he didn't want to leave Kaela alone with her.

What would it be like, to be a Master who had to pretend to be a servant, to have to step back, get out of the way, when his submissive needed him?

"I didn't mean to hurt her."

He didn't turn toward her, but Garron paused, his chin turning toward his shoulder. A brief acknowledgment. Then he kept going.

Her mind in turmoil, she stepped inside the office. She was prepared to see Kaela as she'd been ever since they arrived. Tastefully dressed, every hair in place. Instead, she realized why Garron had been prepared to turn her away.

Kaela had a blanket around her bare shoulders, her legs bent and feet curved over the edge of the chair where she sat by one of the large windows. She gazed out at the picturesque Monterey surf, the scattering of stars. As far as Ruth could tell, she wore nothing under the blanket. Her red hair tumbled over her pale shoulders.

"Long ago, I sat at a small window in my small home, looking over fields stripped by a foraging Union army. They were so hungry. It was the war where both sides learned the terrible effort of keeping thousands on the march fed, clothed, the wounded and dead tended. An awful time. My husband was already dead by then. I didn't know that."

"I'm sorry."

"You're young, Ruth. I don't mean that in a condescending way." Kaela gestured to the chair across from her. "Will you sit? Or does my presence offend you?"

"No. Of course not." Ruth perched on the chair, uncomfortable. "I don't know exactly how to begin, except to say I know I owe you an apology.

"You understand submission to someone more powerful than you. But to a human, that you don't understand." Kaela gave a bitter half laugh. "Garron knew I was acting too precipitously. When I recognized it in you, I couldn't contain myself, the desire to connect to another vampire that...was like me. Only you're not like me. And I'm far old enough to know better. Your desires are a different shape from my own."

Kaela's gaze became flint. "Garron's life is in your hands, because of my foolishness. He submits, when there is no submission in him. As Merc noted, he has a great deal of 'service Dom' to him, which is what makes this work, but there is enough pretense to it, for both of us, to make it...difficult. He does it for me. Because he loves me."

Kaela took a breath. "I like being an overlord, and I'm damn good at it. But in our world, it's incomprehensible that I could also desire submission, when I'm not holding those reins. They don't see how a submissive soul can wield power, hold her own, and determine her own path. Not and equally desire someone I can trust, who will let me surrender to his care, his attention and demands, and find peace in myself."

Kaela's words echoed inside Ruth's soul, matching the thoughts she'd struggled with ever since she'd felt the first stirrings of a desire to submit.

"My lady..." Ruth spoke slowly, "I'm not sure if that's true. What you said about us...being different. But I just...I'm just not sure."

Kaela's gaze flickered. "You want me to explain why I submit to a human."

"I do. If you can forgive my unkindness enough to tell me."

Kaela studied her another long moment. "You like to fight, Ruth. Perhaps as an alternative to fear or uncertainty, but you also enjoy it. It's evident in your manner. I've been fighting all my life. Before I was turned, I saw war and bloodshed. Death, in extremes no one can imagine unless they experience it. Even then, it defied comprehension, the horror of it. To be who I need to be now, I need a place to go where there is no fight required, nothing to prove, except my devotion to my Master."

Clouds passing in the sky outside the window shadowed her face. "We live in a world where power is used to take whatever is wanted, including a servant's submission. What my heart craved was a Master who took what I needed him to take. Gave me what I needed to be given. Who I could serve because my service answered something for both of us, not just him or me. I found that in a human."

Which was what Merc had pretty much suggested to Ruth, hadn't he?

I'm always right. You should just accept that.

Eavesdropper. Go away. But hearing him in her head helped that raw feeling in her stomach, she had to admit.

"You would tell me you submit to Merc because he's stronger," Kaela continued. "I don't question that you have that need. But it's more than that. He can overpower you, but he doesn't overpower those things you need him to respect. To recognize, trust and honor." Her luminous gaze rested on Ruth's. "And eventually, to cherish, as something vital to your relationship with one another."

Hadn't Ruth always told herself a Master would have to deserve her submission? And that was a list far longer than just his ability to physically overpower her.

Her mother had good-naturedly chided her for her vampire-human bias. No secret there, something they laughed about. But right now, it wasn't a laughing matter. Ruth realized how that bias had blinded her, creating a wall between her and a woman who knew exactly how Ruth felt.

Neither of them was alone in those feelings.

"Ah, to hell with all of it." Kaela shook her head and stared out at the night again. Ruth saw her eyes glisten as the overlord revealed her woman's heart. "When I took Garron as my servant, knowing he was my Master, it was a step I never thought I'd get the opportunity to have, so for a little while, it was everything. Then, over time, knowing that you can't have more, that that's the limit... It wears you down. It wears us both down."

The slight break in her voice made Ruth want to reach out in comfort, surely not a wise move, but then it was gone, and Kaela was in control once again. "I think Lady Lyssa knows," she said abruptly. "I think she's always known."

Kaela didn't dwell on the shocking declaration. Instead, her lips curved in that sad smile as her eyes came back to Ruth. "Does my explanation help you, or simply make you more confused?"

Some of both. But while a lifetime of viewing things the way Ruth viewed them didn't change in a single moment, it could start her down that road. And she knew what the first step was.

Ruth shifted. "Everything you just said, it may look different, the way I pursue it, but I think what's inside of me isn't that different from what's inside of you. I also think you know that."

She managed a tight smile for Lady Kaela. "I wish our world was a different place. Or parts of it. I wish I hadn't reacted the way I had, but I hadn't seen the possibility for this in a human and vampire relationship. Now I do."

As Kaela's gaze flashed with surprise and myriad emotions, Ruth held out a hand. "You gave me the gift of your trust, and I didn't respond well. I apologize to you and to your Master. Perhaps when the business that brought me here is done, we could plan to get together again. Here, or at my family's island. Get to know one another better. Find out if we could become friends, my lady."

A slight smile appeared on Kaela's face. Less sad. She freed a hand from the blanket and clasped Ruth's.

"Just Kaela," she reminded her.

The following sunset, after Ruth rose, Kaela invited her and Merc to breakfast with her and Garron in the upper dining room. They enjoyed coffee and relaxed conversation, a new ease to it. Ruth entertained Kaela with stories of the Circus and encouraged her and Garron to attend another show.

While she was mindful not to treat Garron as anything more than a servant before other staff, Ruth included him in the conversation when it worked to do so. The subtle hints of appreciation from him and Kaela gave her even more to think about. Merc watched it all in his usual impassive way, but the approval in his mind was undeniably uplifting.

She hadn't thought of him as her teacher. But he could be.

Just as you are for me. Marcellus tells me that's the way this is supposed to work.

She met his gaze with a spark of humor. *Did he get that from the latest women's magazine poll on relationships?*

He never misses an issue.

Kaela stopped mid-sentence, only a beat before Ruth felt it herself. Another vampire was approaching the house.

"He's a couple hours early," Garron noted grimly. He apparently said something to Kaela, mind-to-mind, because she shook her head.

"As I did last time, I'll meet him alone at the door," she said. For Ruth and Merc, she added, "Trads see our bonds with humans as weakness. And they have no regard for human life."

"Ironic, since most of them are made," Garron said, with an edge.

"I will accompany you to the door, Lady Kaela." Merc met Garron's gaze. His lady would have backup. And she wouldn't have to risk her servant.

Garron gave him a stiff nod of thanks.

"Thank you, my lord." Kaela glanced at Ruth. "If you'll go to my office with Garron, we'll meet you there. It's better to assess his mood in my driveway, and not appear as if we're overwhelming him with numbers."

Ruth wasn't sure she liked being left behind any more than Garron, but the logic was sound. As Kaela and Merc left, Merc gave her a brief look.

If I need backup, I'll call.

Keep being a smartass. I'll dye those feathers neon orange.

A brief touch of humor from his mind, plus a reassurance, then they were gone.

Ruth turned to Garron. "If either of us sense a problem, we'll go help them."

"Yeah. We will."

In accord on it, they proceeded to the office. However, they didn't have long to wait before Merc and Kaela returned.

The vampire overlord came in first, followed by the Trad, then Merc. Asva was compact, and wound like a steel cable. His hair was shaved so she could see scalp through the light-colored fuzz. He wore cargo pants and a camouflage shirt with hiking boots. She was sure they concealed a variety of weapons. Blades, maybe even wooden stakes.

His most potent weapon was his stench, however. Ruth resisted the desire to cover her nose. Trads rarely bathed, which suited their off-the-grid lifestyle but not the olfactory senses of those who liked soap, deodorant and toothpaste. All vampires might be striking, even without access to toiletries, but they were no more immune to body odor than anyone else. Kaela would have to fumigate her chairs if he chose one.

He didn't. Instead, he nodded toward the door that led to Kaela's office balcony. "I would prefer being outside for our conversation. If it's secure."

"It's over a cliff. Only the birds should hear us. This is Lady Ruth, Merc's companion."

Asva's gaze had already moved to Ruth, and clung to her. His eyes were nearly colorless. "I am quite aware of her presence."

Merc shifted, blocking his view. "Become less aware."

The Trad held up his hands. "I meant no offense," he said. "If she's yours, may your union and her womb bear fruit. Even if it's not a pure-blood, it would strengthen our race."

Ruth didn't appreciate the Trad discounting her presence as nothing more than Merc's shadow. She stepped to his side, correcting that, and pinned the Trad with her gaze. "My womb is none of your fucking business. And Lady Kaela said companion. Make no assumptions from that."

"Of course." His eyes held hers. Hungry.

With that atavistic attention, any impact his Dominant nature could have on her held no power. Ruth held his gaze with no problem. Moving them away from dangerous waters, Kaela gestured toward the balcony door.

The wind was strong this morning. Merc tucked his wings in closer to his body, creating a wind break. He gestured Ruth into the chair in front of him.

Her hackles were up, but the chair put her in the conversation circle with Kaela and the Trad. Garron stood silently behind his Mistress's chair. It held a different message than Merc's decision to stand behind Ruth, though the men were in mirror positions.

"Asva, should I send for refreshments?"

"No." Asva's contemptuous gaze passed over Garron. "I don't need a human to wait upon me. I'll say what I wish to say and go. If I don't wish to answer questions, I won't."

"You requested the Truth Vessel," Kaela noted.

"To verify what I tell you isn't a lie."

"Very well. Say your peace."

"Not long ago, I shared a campfire with a fellow Trad. Grollner. He's a clever male. He sometimes speaks in riddles to discern the sharpness of others around him, to test their mettle. To play games."

Once settled into his discourse, Asva's cadence was like a college professor's, an odd contrast to the rest of him. He glanced around and shifted, as if gauging what would happen if he had to vault off the balcony and fling himself toward the rocks below. He wasn't at ease here, but Ruth couldn't tell if it was the company, or concern about his own kind finding out he'd met with the California overlord.

Some of both, I think. Merc shifted closer behind her. The strands of hair blowing in front of her face settled. She'd been giving thought to braiding it, but she didn't want the creepy vampire's eyes on her while she lifted her arms to do the personal task, so the block was appreciated.

"There were several others there that night," Asva continued. "I joined them while they were discussing a matter of common interest. They stopped talking about it, but Grollner wanted to throw me hints. He said we often fight like wild animals, a clean fight, for territory or food. While he said that's as it should be, if we want more room to live that life, we'll have to also become chess players. Working when needed with enemies, and choosing more complicated strategies."

"You believe he's allied himself with someone in my world?" Kaela asked.

"Trads do not ally ourselves with anyone outside of Trads. If we choose a partnership with vampires who like their comforts," his gaze traveled the room, exuding that scorn, "it is because of a temporary benefit to us, and because the partner has the power to serve our purposes."

"Are other races out of the question?" Kaela pressed for more.

"No one with power is out of the question, but a vampire alliance is the most likely scenario. You at least share our blood."

Garron was watching the Trad, and the Trad noticed. "He offends me with his stare. If he does not wish to lose his eyes, he should exhibit the proper respect I assume you have trained into him."

Tension thrummed across the balcony, but after a long moment, Garron gave his lady a slight bow and lowered his gaze. Making it clear he'd done it at her behest, not out of respect for the Trad.

"You came here because something worried you, vampire," Merc said. "Something that will affect the Trad world, because you don't give a fuck about Lady Kaela's. Do I need to reduce your brain matter to soup and sort through it to get the information she needs?"

Merc's willingness to deliver on the threat was obvious. The vampire's cheeks paled, and that furtive, jump-off-the-balcony look increased.

Can you do that?

Technically it would be more Jell-O than soup, but I didn't know if he'd get the cultural reference.

Ruth was *not* going to laugh. For one thing, no matter the outward calm, everyone on the balcony, including herself, was ready for a fight if the Trad made a wrong move.

"Grollner said the player who sees past the limits of the chess board has the advantage." Asva dropped the scornful posturing. "The board is a false perimeter. Beyond it are the pieces already in play. A two-opponent game might be three, two against one, with one unaware."

"So there *is* an alliance." Kaela leaned forward, her expression intent. "What else did he say?"

"He asked if I'd ever wondered why there was a king and queen on the board, but no prince or princess. I told him the king and queen are too busy with their battles. They have no time to procreate. He laughed, and said, 'They keep them off the board, hidden, so they are protected. But that puts them out of reach of the army. Ironically, the closer they are to danger, the further they are from harm."

A modified *Lord of the Rings* movie quote. Grollner was apparently hiding a DVD player in his off-the-grid treehouse.

Merc's hand tightened on her shoulder. "How do you know he's not just fucking with you?" he asked.

"After he shared it, he sat back and said, 'Let the dying fortune teller figure that one out. It will be too late when she does. And that will be the end of her.'"

Asva smiled.

Ruth's chair scraped over the concrete, tumbling to its side with the force of her ejection from it. She lifted Asva by the shirt front and slammed him against the wall of the house. She'd wanted to dangle him over the rail, but the force of her anger might have broken it loose, plunging them both into the sea. After they bounced off all the sharp rocks along the way.

Kaela pulled her off the Trad as Merc held Asva back, keeping him from retaliating. Garron stood between the two women and the Trad, additional reinforcement for Merc.

"She is *not* dying," Ruth snapped over Kaela's shoulder. "She'll be alive long after you're rotting worm food."

"Such fire," the Trad said. "You'd be a good breeder. The human I fed upon that night, one of Grollner's food slaves, failed in that task, as so many do. But she fed me well before she expired. Her last meal."

He looked ready to snicker over the joke, but Merc's grip on his throat captured and held it. The vampire tried to fight the hold, which only constricted further. Asva flailed, beating Merc's arm.

"Pinching off a tick's head is more difficult than me pinching off yours," Merc informed the Trad impassively.

Youthful bloodlust rarely gripped Ruth. It mortified her that it had crept up on her like that, but seeing someone smirk over Clara's death had broken her strained nerves. "Sorry, my lady," Ruth muttered, as Merc occupied the Trad.

"It's fine," Kaela said low, releasing her. "Trads are rarely good houseguests."

Asva gagged. His feet were no longer touching the balcony floor.

Merc, I'm under control. I promise. He didn't hurt me.

He wants to. It's all over him.

Yes, but bigger things are at stake.

Merc dropped him. As Asva sagged against the wall, Merc gave him a pointed look of disgust. "You'll mind your manners here. If you don't have any, pretend you do."

Asva straightened, eying Merc with dislike, but also a healthy amount of fear and respect. When Merc stepped back, taking up position next to Garron, his relief was evident. "If you are here to help your own kind, Asva, what purpose does goading us serve?" Kaela demanded.

"None, my lady." He sent Merc a sidelong glance. "It is...habit. I would apologize, but it's all I can do to be around your kind and your... servant, without either vomiting or attempting to kill you."

"The feeling is mutual," Ruth said. "All this chess bullshit aside, what do you think is going on? What's he planning? You probably have a guess."

"I don't know. But it gave me a terrible feeling. The dreams she has," Asva rasped. "The fortune teller. I've had them, too. We have... shared them, at times. That's how I felt her presence."

"So you're a seer. Did you lead them to her?"

When Ruth posed the question, and Asva nodded, her bloodlust screamed anew at her to rip out his throat. This time she felt a push from Merc, a small burst of energy that helped her control it.

"But that was before the conversation with Grollner," Asva admitted. "What I have felt and seen since then, it does not bode well for the Trads. I know my feelings are not specific, but they are rarely wrong."

"When will his plan happen?"

"He would not reveal that to me." Asva paused. "But if he was teasing us with it, my guess is it is already in process. He wouldn't risk tipping his hand too soon. Grollner longs for the destruction of your way of life. The Council is in his crosshairs. Honestly, I would not mourn their loss. But the more he spoke, the more I felt as if it were the Trads facing annihilation.

"And...no matter how much I revile how you choose to live, you are vampires. There is a hope, no matter how slim, that your world will come to the wild places and find the roots we have found. You would be the better for it, I am sure."

While Ruth was sure Asva wished to put her in a burlap sack and carry her off in a windowless van, she didn't doubt his honesty. Merc's slight nod confirmed it.

"Maybe you should consider that a two-way street," Kaela said. "The species that refuses to change often ensures its own extinction."

"So does the species that changes too much. Too many compromises, turning your back on who you are and what you were created to be." Asva rubbed his throat and eyed the door. "I have nothing further, and I do not wish to linger."

Kaela glanced at Merc and Ruth. Just a cryptic chess match and an anxious feeling. Yet that didn't reassure Ruth, because his worry was real, and he wouldn't have met with them if he didn't feel it was worth the great risk to himself.

His words were a puzzle planted in her head. Like Clara had said, each vision brought them missing pieces, and Ruth felt like he'd just handed them several key ones. That foreboding, coupled with Clara's specific warning to her—or guidance—had Ruth in a hold as ruthless as Merc's.

You're an important key, Ruth... Your experience, what you see and feel, what you know, will help you see...

Asva's words, while cryptic, weren't meaningless. If Ruth could just figure out what the fucking meaning *was*.

"I'll escort you to the door," Kaela told Asva.

Merc accompanied the overlord as before. After they left the balcony, Garron invited Ruth back inside the office. "So, from your reaction, Clara isn't doing well."

"No."

"I'm sorry to hear it. When we attended the Circus, she read my lady's palm. She was truthful, kind and hopeful."

"That's a good way to describe her." Ruth rubbed her forehead, pressed her fingertips against it. Chess...

When Kaela returned, she reached for her phone, putting it on speaker. "I told Yvette I'd contact her after our meeting."

Merc stood beside Ruth's chair, his hand resting on her tense shoulder. *What is it?*

I don't know. Just...going over what he said. She shook her head. Creepy, goddamn Trads.

The troupe was outside the portal for another three-day performance, and it was fortunately past nightfall in that time zone. When Yvette answered, she was in Clara and Marcellus's quarters. Maddock and Charlie were also there.

After they provided a report on Asva's visit, Yvette sighed and echoed Ruth's own thoughts. "I could wish for something a little less cryptic."

"Does it suggest anything to you, Clara?" Ruth asked.

The hacking cough that preceded the answer tightened Ruth's stomach muscles. She could tell the weakness of Clara's voice visibly startled Kaela and Garron. "The whole chess conversation makes me feel worried. An anxiety... Something..."

"Something right there in front of us," Ruth said.

Clara paused. "Yes, exactly. And I can't explain why, but my instincts tell me we should contact Lady Lyssa. Relay every bit of the conversation to her."

Lady Lyssa... No. It wouldn't make sense. Trads didn't have the strength or planning skills to pull that kind of ballsy move. But Asva thought they'd struck an alliance.

An alliance with someone who maybe *would* pull a move that ballsy.

Ruth bolted to her feet. "'No prince and princess on the chess board,'" she repeated. "Kane and Farida are visiting my father's island. With Lord Mason."

Mason was probably the third strongest vampire in their ranks, but depending on how many—and what—would come against him, he could be overwhelmed. Especially if his daughter and godson could be used as leverage against him.

Mal had plenty of magical defenses on the island, but they weren't designed for an offensive, pitched battle. Ruth had a very bad feeling that was what was about to happen.

If it hadn't already.

Damn it, she was out of range. No mind link. Kaela was talking urgently to Yvette as Ruth pulled out her cell phone and dialed. She bit back a curse as the answering machine picked up on her father's office landline.

Ruth turned to Kaela. As she did, she could hear Clara's tearing cough continuing over the line. "It may not mean anything," she told the overlord.

"Trust your instincts. What are they telling you, Ruth?"

She looked at Merc. "We need to get to the island. Now."

CHAPTER TWENTY-FOUR

The ominous feeling crammed into every corner of her mind, even as she told herself logical things. Like that it was totally normal for her father not to answer the phone. He was probably out on the sanctuary, working with the cats.

Adan was with Derek, doing Guardian things in another realm, out of Ruth's range. Out of anyone's. Yvette and Maddock would head for the island, but it would take time to reach a portal in their current location and configure it for the jump to the island.

No one could get there any faster than she could. She had an angel. And if all was well, Ruth could call off the cavalry.

She was glad she'd worn jeans and a T-shirt at breakfast, casual wear. Battle wear. When she and Merc moved back out to the balcony, there was only time for a quick nod to a worried-looking Kaela and Garron. Kaela had the phone set to her ear, trying Mal's number again.

Merc went as fast as he could go without damaging her. Even so, she willed him to go faster, faster. When he stopped, the sudden inertia made her gorge rise. She vomited everything in her stomach, trying to miss his supporting arm, not entirely successfully. Struggling through the haze on her vision the dizziness caused, she attempted to reinflate her lungs. "Where are we?" she wheezed. "Why are we stopped?"

"We're over the island. There's a shield over it, Ruth."

"Over the entire island?" Thank God for Adan's tweaking. Then her gaze cleared enough to see Merc's grim face. "Yes. It's not your father's magic. It's not a defense."

She reached out for Mal and Elisa. Nothing. Nothing from them, or the cats, that brush of feline presence in her mind. She tried the two or three servants on the island she'd second marked. Hanska. Again, nothing. It was as if the shield were a concrete wall, blocking anything behind it.

The power of a being who could do that, impose a field over an expanse that large, one she couldn't penetrate with her family blood link...

That alliance hadn't been with another vampire. She was getting a really bad feeling about who it had been, though that made no sense at all.

"Can you get through?" she asked Merc.

"Yes. But I don't know what I will trigger, or who else that could harm. I need a Guardian or a sorcerer to aid me."

Coldness spread into every corner of her being. She wished Adan was here.

As Merc descended, carefully, the shield's energy became so strong it hummed in her ears like a high voltage fence. The signature had been masked with as much reinforcement as the field itself. Despite her suspicions, she couldn't tell it if had been cast by human, vampire, Fae, or a being unknown to her.

"There's a rock formation on the island's west side," she told Merc. "It's a mile from shore. Drop me there and go get a sorcerer."

"I'm not leaving you here."

"You can travel faster without me. Please, Merc. Please." Her heart was beating wildly. "I'll be fine until you get back."

With a muttered curse, he took her to where she'd indicated. Seabirds squawked as the shadow of his wings passed over them. They scattered from the rocks as he landed.

"I don't like this," he said, his expression grim. "I can go slower and still make haste."

"We know who they're after. Putting this kind of shield in place gives them the cover to take them, but also time to cover their getaway. They may no longer be here." Her jaw hardened. "Like Asva said. Do we really think that Grollner asshole would have been so loose-lipped, if the plan wasn't in the advanced stages?"

She'd so wanted to be wrong about her chess theory. She'd have gladly accepted the embarrassment of overreacting, being a drama queen.

But she couldn't feel her father's magic or the sanctuary's magic. Some evil force stood between her and her parents, and all those they cared for and protected.

Ruth pointed to the rock behind her. "There's a cave up there, about ten feet deep. If for any reason you're delayed, it won't be comfortable, but I'll be safe from the sun."

"That's three hours from now. I'll be back."

"I know you will. I'm just saying. They come first." She gripped his shirt. "Help them, Merc. Please."

Despite her impatience, he lifted and deposited her in that cave, checking it out for himself. She could be offended that he hadn't trusted her, but he knew as well as she did that she would have lied through her teeth to get him to go.

He gripped her nape and kissed her, hard. "Never lie to me. Even if I can hear you do it. Stay here, out of sight, or I'll beat your ass black and blue."

Then he was gone, so fast she stumbled at the loss of his supporting touch.

Ruth squatted on her heels, lacing her hands behind her head, fighting for calm. Fighting to think. Panic served no purpose. She wasn't a child. There was no one to pick her up and tell her this was going to be okay.

A field strong enough to block mind links and blanket the entire island. That meant a sorcerer as powerful as Maddock or Adan.

Or a Fae.

A Fae would work with a Trad only if there was something to be gained on their side of things, and she couldn't imagine what that would be. She was too far outside of vampire or Fae politics. But a plan this complicated, and risky, taking Lady Lyssa's son and Lord Mason's daughter, required coordination and cooperation.

Kane and Farida. Their faces flashed in her mind. *Your mother is excited. She's already baking their favorites.*

Ruth squeezed her eyes shut. It wouldn't be a Guardian. Their loyalty couldn't be bought, manipulated or overwhelmed. Adan had told her so, not as a boast, but as a simple fact, related to their link to the Lord and Lady.

She stood up and paced. Back and forth, back and forth. She kept reaching out, trying to push through. Nothing. It was a wall. *Etsi, Sgidoda.* All the staff, Hanska, the cats...

When Adan had been kidnapped by the Fae as a child, she'd been unhinged. Inconsolable, nearly mad with grief at the loss of one-half of her mind, her heart. Mal and Elisa had done what they could, but they had all they could do, trying to retrieve their son and hold it together themselves.

Kohana and Chumani had taken over her care during those terrible months. He'd taught her how to calm her mind, hold her heart and soul together.

Ruth dropped to her heels again. Though everything in her rebelled against it, wanting to shriek, rail and fight her way through that field that would likely fry her brain, she started the chant, rocking back and forth, lifting her hands. Each word and gesture possessed meaning. She pulled on the power within her, of family. Her mother, her father, her brother, always with her, always tied to her.

It doesn't matter what world they're in. They're with you. Nothing severs that bond. You ride in the same hunt, side by side, always...

As her heart slowed and mind cleared, she focused on the lap of the water on the shore, the noises of the birds who had once again landed on the rocks. Her calmer energy must be helping them, too. Then she became aware of something else.

Someone was reaching out to her.

Someone beneath the water.

The voice...there were no intelligible words, but she could feel the insistent pull on her mind. It drew her to the mouth of the cave.

Merc's logic was sound. If someone powerful enough to impose that field was still around and saw her, she'd have no chance.

But this wasn't that. She was sure of it. *Fuck it.* Ruth picked her way down the rocks, slipping and sliding in her haste, cutting her hands and ripping a hole in her jeans.

She ignored that, scrambling to the water's edge and forcing herself to embrace that calm center again. Then she reached out with every sense she had.

Vampire. It was vampire.

Calling for help, with a savage urgency. No trickery. A trickster would be cajoling, pleading. There was nothing here but rage.

Definitely male energy. Not her father. She squelched her disappointment and considered what was below. An artificial coral reef, formed by several freighter containers and a shipwreck, an old fishing vessel. He had to somehow be trapped within them.

Vampires had no buoyancy. Swimming was like pulling a body-sized boulder through the water. But since who was calling to her so insistently was beneath the water, buoyancy wouldn't have been in her favor anyway. She removed all her clothes except for her underwear and entered the water.

It got deep quickly, and she used her arms to push herself downward, holding her own against the current. The pressure got uncomfortable, but a vampire didn't get the bends. She supposed at a certain depth they could still be crushed, but she didn't have to go that deep. She saw the wreck and the containers, half buried in the sand, claimed by the sea, coated with seaweed, barnacles and other ocean life.

But there was a newer container, and that deadly fury was coming from within it. The metal box was wrapped up in spellcraft that had the same signature as the field over the island, which explained why she hadn't immediately detected him. As she stroked closer, she reached out toward the latch.

An electrified bear trap closed on her arm. Fortunately, she shoved herself backward at its first touch, sheer luck allowing her to escape its range. If it had succeeded in knocking her unconscious with its voltage, she would have been drawn off by the current, her body headed for the Gulf Stream.

Then Merc would have really been pissed.

She planted herself on top of one of the other containers. Hooking her foot under a rusted bolt kept her there, and she did the centering exercise again to manage the air hunger her lungs didn't need to feed.

She stared at the container. There was definitely a vampire in there. The container should have exploded from the wrath of its occupant. He was pounding on it, loudly enough to echo through the water and inside her head.

It had to be Lord Mason.

The name matched the energy so precisely she knew she was right.

But that terrifying coldness returned. Who had the ability to contain a Council vampire that powerful?

Focus on the positive. They couldn't kill him, so they'd had to settle for containing him.

Unless there was a more important reason for leaving him alive.

She had no mind connection with Lord Mason, but he'd been able to reach out to her, so she hoped the concentrated feeling she sent back to him penetrated, in spirit if not in the actual words attached to the feeling.

I'm getting help. Hang in there.

She fought back to the surface and pulled herself onto the rocks. *Merc, Lord Mason is locked in a metal container under the water. I can't get him free.*

She didn't know what her range was with an angel. They hadn't yet tested it. She wished they had. She didn't get a response, but in case his range was better than hers, she repeated the message several times, in the hopes one iteration would get through so he could communicate it to the others.

Mason's pounding, that kind of urgency, meant really bad things. Things they needed to be handling. Not sitting here waiting for help.

Fucking hell, this was going to make her crazy. She thought again of Lord Mason's prison, the shape and look of it. When Adan was still young enough he did his magic lessons with Derek on the island, she'd trailed along and paid close attention.

There's always a key. It doesn't always take a sorcerer to unlock it. Especially if no one expects a sorcerer to be there.

What if they do?

Well, then they'll leave some kind of counterspell or trap to annihilate him. You won't even know what hit you.

Terrific. But back down she went. Being underwater put an unpleasant pressure on her chest, much like traveling with Merc at supersonic speeds. But she could handle it. Thanks to the spell, the container was wrapped in a faint blue light. She cautiously moved around it, staying clear of that defense field. Had the container been dropped here under the cover of darkness weeks ago, carried by a passing freighter? Had it been made ready for its prisoner then, well outside the sanctuary's detection perimeter?

Clara had suffered from the Trad visions long enough for that to be plausible. They'd spent time setting this all up.

Ruth picked up a piece of concrete and tossed it at the binding. It jittered upon contact, became the same blue for a blink, then floated unevenly down to the murky bottom.

Could balanced energy become unbalanced? Like putting water into a cup, and then tipping it until the weight inside took it all the way over?

Pumping her arms and kicking her legs with purpose, she scoured the coral reef and found what she was looking for. A bar of steel, crusted with barnacles, but solid, and long enough to keep her just out of range of the spellcraft preventing a powerful vampire's escape.

She wasn't as strong as a lot of vampires, but with the right leverage, she could do this. *Don't be afraid to use tools, daughter.*

Mal's advice, when teaching her to fortify her strength.

Plunging the bar into the sand beneath the container, she shoved it in, then jumped back as it made contact. A slight vibration went through the bar, but the blue light stayed around the freighter. Her lever wasn't electrified or hammered out of shape. She closed back in and pushed the end further beneath the container, then pulled down on it.

Her muscles groaned in complaint, but the container shifted. Triumph surged as she saw the energy vibrate, like water in a cup, showing it had been disturbed.

As the pounding continued inside the container, she left that bar in place, and moved to examine the door latch, without reaching out to touch it.

There will be an anchor point, where the magic will be arranged in the pattern needed to keep it running...

The door would make sense, right? She considered ways to test it and went in search of another steel bar. A shorter one that she bent into a hook at one end.

Returning to the door latch, she braced herself, then shoved the bar behind the latch, driving the hook down upon it in the same motion.

She hadn't let go fast enough, getting a fierce zap for her troubles, but her guess had been right. The energy shimmered, showing a series of symbols spinning around a hub before they disappeared in the flow of the water. They also warped her hook and dissolved it, making the water around it flash with heat.

So the spellcraft on the latch was what she had to "unbalance." Returning to the lever under the container, she went at it. Pushing on it, again and again, pausing only as briefly as needed to surface, cough water out of her lungs, and go back down again.

Fuck, this would be so much easier with an angel incubus. But he had a more important task. This one was hers.

She refused to let herself think of giving up, and at last the container was sliding away from the shelf where it had been placed. It wasn't much of a drop, the ocean contour behind it just a short hill. But she only needed it to tip. She heaved one more time, hard, shouting her frustration and demand for it to do her bidding. The gurgled sound of the yell hummed in her ears.

Triumph surged as the container started to topple over.

The energy stuttered at the latch site, like a lamp reacting to a cord coming halfway out of the socket. Hoping she wasn't wrong, Ruth darted in, grabbed the latch and shoved against it as hard as she could.

The magical energy that somersaulted her backwards felt like a lighting strike. When she slammed into the coral reef crusting an older container, she received an up close and personal snapshot of the insides of her eyelids and her skull, plus annoyed commentary from all the nerve endings in her teeth.

When she could shake it off, she snarled as she saw the latch hadn't completely given way. However, the energy also didn't have the same cohesiveness. The blue rippled and sparked, as if an important component of the spell had been knocked out of place. Before she had time to figure out how to take advantage of it, she was forcibly reminded she wasn't the only one working the problem.

The door exploded off its hinges, like a cannon had been fired at it from the inside.

It flipped away on the ocean current, bouncing off the shipwreck and getting caught against the stump of the mast.

The projectile that had broken the door loose wasn't a cannonball. It was a bowling ball, which arced down once it felt the pull of gravity and disappeared into the ocean bottom.

Cautiously, she approached the opening of the container, feeling some residual electrical ripples, but nothing debilitating. The spell around the container had been dismantled.

A man was struggling through the debris of the container's ruined contents. She assumed the bowling ball had come from one of the broken crates she saw.

Getting near an enraged male vampire was never a great idea, but he'd been underwater long enough to be disoriented, and she didn't know how else they'd weakened him. However, when Lord Mason's eyes found her, an amber color that reminded her of tiger eyes, she saw recognition. She stretched out her hand, and he caught it with a much larger one. His grip hurt, showing he was still less aware than normal, but she didn't let him go.

She helped him get free of his prison and start toward the surface. By the time they reached the rock formation, he was able to drag himself onto it, where he coughed out an ocean's worth of sea water.

He wore no shirt, soaked black trousers clinging to his muscled backside and thighs. Lord Mason was a big male, his long, copper-colored hair lying sleek against his broad back. It partially covered the tattoo there, a tiger looking as if it was ready to leap free of the skin. With his age and his amber eyes, it was difficult for Mason to pass as human. At this moment he had no interest in trying.

Almost before he stopped coughing, he was stumbling to his feet and spinning around to find the island. Ruth put a steadying hand on his biceps before he could plunge back into the water to get to it.

"It's shielded. We can't get through. Merc, an angel friend, went to get help. We don't know if they're still there, Farida and Kane."

Mason's chest and shoulders shuddered. He sat down heavily on one of the rocks, putting his hands on his knees. Carefully, Ruth rested her palm on his back. He'd closed his eyes, either to pull it together or keep himself from going mad. She wanted to reassure, but she knew as well as he did all the possibilities.

No. He knew more than that. When the centuries-older vampire straightened, opened his eyes and turned toward her, she saw his bleak look. It didn't dilute his urgency, or his killing rage, but it wasn't either of those things that made her draw back, avoiding the hand he reached out to her.

"Our children are no longer there," he said.

And she knew. In her faltering heart, her terrified mind, her frozen soul, she knew.

~

When Merc landed on the rocks, Marcellus was with him. Almost before their feet touched, the field over the island was dissipating, the energy fading, though the sky had the sickly green and yellow look it had before a lethal storm.

"Marcellus and I transported Yvette and Maddock. They dismantled it from the air. We put them down near the portal it was spun from so they could cleanse and reinforce its protections again. They're also evaluating the condition of the island's fault line and portal interfaces. They'll meet us at your house."

She was numb, but nodded. Fists opening, closing. *Please, please, please...*

Merc moved close enough to put a hand on her, but she moved back, shook her head, a short snap. His brow creased, but he turned to Lord Mason. Whatever he saw in Mason's face sent a tension through his shoulders and the arcs of his wings. A moment of silence, then Merc spoke, his voice flat.

"Marcellus is going to take you back to Council headquarters in Savannah. Lyssa is already there with other Council members so you can plan your next step, to get your children back."

Lord Mason's jaw flexed, and he looked toward Ruth.

"I've got her," Merc said. "You're needed in Savannah, my lord."

Ruth turned away from them and spoke through stiff lips. "Get me there," she said. "To the house. I need to see if my parents are all right."

She twitched when Merc touched her, but didn't resist when he picked her up. She didn't look at him, putting her face against the side of his neck, and staring over his shoulder.

It was a short flight, so she had her arms around his shoulders, her legs around his hips. The way he'd brought her to the island the day he'd met her parents. When she hadn't wanted them to see her in such an intimate pose, because of a silly self-consciousness.

Ruth.

As soon as he touched down, Ruth wrenched away and ran toward the house. She could feel the energy of the cats now. They were upset, riled up. The island was unsettled, unbalanced. Someone had fucked with it. Fucked with the magic. That had to be why she still couldn't access the mind link, but Mal and Elisa would be in the house. Or where the cats most needed them. She'd find them.

No. She'd found them. They were in the house. She could feel them. But no mind link. Just emptiness. A lack of...anything.

She smelled blood. Human, vampire. Death.

Yvette was inside. She would be with them. It would be all right.

Several railings of the porch had been busted, as if something had landed on them or kicked the boards so hard they split.

Merc landed in front of Ruth before she reached the steps. She tried to get around him, but then she was in the air, his arms around her again.

She struck at him, not caring if he dropped her. She landed a couple good hits before he brought them to the place she'd shown him, her place to find faith, when her faith was floundering. She saw the wavering energy lines between the African habitat and the sanctuary, but she didn't see any cats. They were hiding. Watchful. Too much violent energy, too disruptive. Everything was in fight or flight survival mode.

"Why did you bring me here? I have to get home, to see..."

She wouldn't let him speak, wouldn't let him say anything to her. She shouted at him, pushed, attacked. She didn't care if she hurt him. She would destroy anything in her path. He let her run away, toward the road that led back to the house. He retrieved her multiple times, until she collapsed on the grassy slope.

Then she started screaming, a voiceless wail.

She screamed and screamed her heartbreak, so it echoed through the sanctuary, imprinted and embedded itself there.

Merc was over her, holding her now, his wings covering her. He'd done that before, to give her sanctuary, rest. Now he did it to let her stay hidden from the world when she couldn't bear to show her face to it.

It seemed a lifetime before she could speak, and yet there'd never be enough time in the universe before she'd be prepared to say the words she said now.

"How..." she said, her face still buried in his feathers.

"You don't need to know that."

"You know I do."

"It was quick."

"His body is still there?"

"Yes."

She swallowed noisily. "No one would have gotten close enough to stake him."

"No."

She squeezed her eyes shut. Decapitation. Horrible, but a quick death, as Merc said.

"Your mother is next to him. It appears she was able to crawl to him before she succumbed."

The third mark bond between vampire and servant meant if the vampire died, the servant died with him, within minutes.

"My brother..."

"Mikhael, the Dark Guardian, is trying to locate them. Catriona is at Club Atlantis. She will continue to try her mind link with your brother until he's in range."

"I need to see them. I have to see them. So when he comes, I can tell him."

"All right. I'll take you to them now."

She lifted her head, stared at him with a swollen face and glassy eyes. He slid a strand of hair away from her damp mouth, his hands as gentle as they'd ever been. She didn't want him to be gentle, but she couldn't bring herself to reject the touch. "Why now, and not a few moments ago?"

"Yvette made some adjustments. She said there were some things no one should see. She was making it..."

Easier? Better? She saw him roll over the different words, none of them right. Not even close. She shook her head, relieving him of the need to try.

Merc took her back to the house. When they landed at the steps again, she stared at the wreckage. There was blood spatter on the porch boards. The chair Chumani had made was twisted out of shape and hanging on the jagged teeth of a shattered front window.

Ruth started up the steps and stumbled. When Merc would have lifted her again, she held him at arm's length. With dull despair, she knew if it became too much, he would take her away.

I'm begging you. Stand with me, so it doesn't become too much. I need to do this.

He touched her face, and wouldn't let her move until she looked up at him. He wouldn't let her shut him out. *I'll honor that request. I promise.*

It helped, in a terrible way she'd never be able to explain. Maybe the closest attempt would be what Kaela had said. *He can overpower you, but he doesn't overpower those things you need him to respect.*

Ruth moved into the house. The smell of blood, death and violence became stronger. It was so silent. The house was never silent. The grandfather clock had been knocked over in the struggle, so its ticking was missing. The house cats...she reached out and found their life energy. Still here. Hiding. She would help them shortly.

Furniture was destroyed, more windows shattered. Some of the glass was inside, crunching under her shoes. The fight had moved to the porch and back inside again, combatants breaking through both sets of front windows.

As she approached the kitchen, knowing that was where they were, her gaze dropped to the bloodstained floor. Her father's feet jutted out from behind the island. The frayed cuffs of his jeans, his work shoes. The tread was worn at the toe and heel. He'd mentioned needing to order some more.

She didn't know how long she stood there, but she was aware of Merc by her side. His hand rested on the small of her back, fingers curled in her waistband, under her T-shirt. She was shaking, yet under that, she'd turned to stone.

She felt like she could hear the echo of her mother's anguished scream. She imagined that last moment. Had her father had a chance to fix his gaze upon Elisa? Remind her in that last second the bond would never end, that they would go into eternity together?

She lurched forward, around the island. The blood smears marked where her mother had pulled herself across the floor to reach Mal's side. Ruth didn't want her eyes to reach the end of that journey, but they went there anyway.

Up her father's legs, to his knees. Her mother's feet were tucked partially under his calf. She'd been wearing a pair of her canvas sneakers with the cat faces. Mal painted them on every new pair she bought. Different types of cats, different expressions.

A sob hit her in the chest, like Mason's bowling ball had hit that container door. Merc's arm tightened around her, but he honored his promise. He didn't take her away. He was deep in her mind, in her soul. He knew what she needed.

Steeling herself, she let her eyes travel up their inert bodies to discover what Yvette had done.

The sorceress had left the area mostly unaltered, knowing Ruth needed to see it. For Adan, and for herself, she needed to see evidence of her father's heroic fight to defend Kane and Farida, Elisa and their home. Her mother's agonizing journey to reach his side before they crossed the Veil. But Yvette had decided there was one key thing Ruth did not need to see.

To her eyes, her father was intact, his head tilted down toward Elisa. Elisa had managed to pull one of his arms around her, their hands clasped.

In this position, they looked almost the way they did when they were on the couch. Elisa curled up next to him, Mal's arm around her as they spoke in low, affectionate murmurs, punctuated with the occasional soft laugh or wry comment.

The only evidence that what Ruth was seeing wasn't reality was the pendant Mal always wore, a carved cat's head on a silk cord. It connected to the bespelled energies of the island, helped him monitor them wherever he was. It was on the ground a few feet away. That, with more spurted blood patterns, told her where his head actually was.

Seeing her gaze move in that direction, Merc picked up the pendant. He had to step away and bend over to do it, but he kept his fingertips resting on her hip. He grasped Ruth's wrist, lifted her limp hand and put it in her palm. Her fingers convulsively closed over it, and the reality of it under her hand, the polished stone, told her all of it was real. There was no escaping this, no chance it was a bad dream.

She was Mal and Elisa's daughter. She needed to do what they'd expect her to do. Holding onto that as tenaciously as she held the pendant, she moved forward. While her bones felt ancient, she managed to kneel by them. Laying her hand on Elisa's was another terrible moment, the feel of her mother's soft skin and slim bones, the well-worn cloth of her father's shirt and solidness of his chest beneath it. All of it devoid of the life that made them...them.

After she choked back another sob, she began the chant to give peace to the dead, and wish them a safe journey.

For the living...she didn't want peace. She wanted death. Horrible, horrible death. For everyone responsible for this.

~

After she completed the chant, she rose, swaying, not sure what to do next.

"Lady Yvette is on the porch," Merc prompted her. "She needs to talk to you."

Ruth moved that way, mostly because Merc took her hand and led her in that direction. Her feet dragged, then stopped.

"It's all right," he said, reading the confusion in her mind. "No one is going to bother them."

Yvette stood against an unbroken part of the rail. There was a tightness to her mouth, an anger in her eyes, a deep well of emotion.

"Thank you," Ruth whispered.

Yvette nodded. "Lady Lyssa wants you at Council headquarters," she said quietly. "Maddock has already headed that way. You met with the Trad. There may be things you can offer that will help them find Farida and Kane."

Ruth stared at the Circus Mistress. "I can't leave them."

"Ruth." Merc touched her face.

She saw the knowledge in his eyes, felt it in her own self, but she savagely rejected it. She didn't want to go anywhere.

But Farida and Kane were in danger. Mal and Elisa would tell her that took priority over everything else. Especially the dead, who didn't need her help.

"There's some disruption to the sanctuary spell work, but the cats are safe," Yvette said carefully. "They're just very spooked. I patched it enough, and Derek can fully right it, once he and Adan return."

"The staff..."

"Three were killed. Two men, one woman. They were at the house when the attack happened, and joined your parents in trying to resist the invaders. The rest were at various places on the sanctuary, and found they couldn't approach the house. An additional blocking field was brought down around it. A man named Hanska said Farida and Kane were with your parents when it happened."

Hanska was alive. A relief, since he knew how to manage the sanctuary. A detestably practical thought, but it kept her from having to think about the three staff members who *had* been killed.

"I expect that's why they used the additional field," Yvette added, "to contain their target and keep out any other attempts to come to their aid. Not because they felt they were a threat, but to minimize the nuisance of having to deal with them. It saved most of their lives."

Yvette's gaze flickered with suppressed fury. "The humans were taken out far more easily than your parents were. Which did not make them any less brave for trying."

"No." Just the opposite. During visits by more contentious vampires, Da would firmly tell Hanska and the others not to interfere in any conflicts between him and them, because a human would have no chance against those vampires, and he didn't want them harmed. Their focus was the care of the cats.

But if they'd been close enough to help, they wouldn't have listened. Just as the three whose names she didn't want to know yet hadn't. Because they were family.

"Wolf, a vampire who works for Anwyn at Club Atlantis, is on the way to provide Hanska backup if they need a vampire's help with the cats. His servant Ella is with him."

Ruth must have been kneeling over her parents' bodies for a while, for Yvette to have time to communicate with Council and arrange for all that. And not just that.

The Circus Mistress met her gaze. "Your people have asked for the honor of preparing their bodies, Ruth. They said they'll hold vigil on them until we return."

No. I can't leave.

Farida and Kane are in danger.

Two sides fought a bitter war inside her, trampling her heart, overrunning her mind, tearing gouges in her soul. Then Merc tipped up her chin to lock gazes with him. *Call on the warrior, Ruth, not the child, and tell me what you really want.*

She stared into his eyes. *I want whoever did this to be eviscerated. I want them to suffer in ways hell hasn't even thought up. I want to do it myself. I want to laugh at their screams. I want to...*

Tears came with the hatred. The warrior couldn't separate itself entirely from the grief. *I want them back.*

Yvette's hand was on her, a comforting pressure, but also carrying the reminder that they had to go. There were things to handle. The rest would have to wait.

"It's perhaps good your brother is out of touch with Derek," The reluctance in Yvette's voice said she didn't want to say the words, but felt Ruth needed to know. "Guardians, like angels, have strict rules on interference in matters...like this. Mikhael said this is one of them. The angels are the same. Marcellus was instructed to report to his Legion duties, after he delivers Mason to Council."

Ruth stared at her. Even after what Marcellus had told her earlier, she'd assumed this would be different. It should be different. She couldn't grasp that he couldn't help. Or Derek. Light Guardian neutrality or not, if Adan was here, he would say fuck Guardian rules, right up the ass.

Which was why Yvette had said it was better he was not here. Though she doubted he would feel that way. She certainly didn't.

"Though you risked a great deal by making contact with the binding holding him, you did well on freeing Lord Mason," Yvette added. "That kind of intelligence, determination and insight is what we need from you now."

Lord Mason was alive. Her parents weren't. Why couldn't one of the most powerful vampires in the world stand against their enemies and save her parents? Why was he alive and they were dead?

It was a child's question. The adult knew the answer, and Lord Mason, as well as Lady Lyssa, needed the help of everyone who could give it. She would be the warrior that Merc had called upon. The grieving child would have to wait.

She met Yvette's gaze. "Yes. We'll go."

~

She'd heard of the formality that governed an audience with the currently nine-member Vampire Council. How intimidating it could be to stand before them.

She was too shut down to care about any of that, but when they arrived at the Savannah estate, Council headquarters, she noticed a distinct lack of that reputed formality. She'd arrived at a war room, where communication was straightforward, no wasted time with posturing or pretenses.

They were gathered around a large table in a big hallway, servants swiftly coming and going with information being cultivated from the network of assets throughout their world, anything that might be of use to locate the two young vampires.

Lady Lyssa and Lord Mason were shoulder to shoulder over the information laid out before them. Though Ruth was sure the mother in Lyssa and the father in Mason were suffering dreadful levels of worry, the only evidence was the flat, lethal sharpness of their eyes and the tension in their shoulders. They had lived through enough crises, protected enough of their own kind, to know calm planning and decisive action were the only tenable options.

Their servants were the same. Jacob stood at Lyssa's side. Jessica watched nearby. Anwyn was next to her, her hand resting on Jessica's back. Jessica being at Club Atlantis at the time of the kidnapping may have saved the life of Mason's servant. Though Ruth expected the thought brought the mother little comfort.

Gideon was beside her and Anwyn, his hips propped on a side table, arms crossed over his chest. He observed the strategy session with the stillness a weapon had, waiting to be pointed in a firing direction. Ruth didn't see Daegan, but he might be gleaning information directly from his own sources.

When Ruth's arrival was noticed, she was almost grateful that the Council dove right into an interrogation, rather than asking her about...anything else. Relaying what happened with the Trad, recalling every detail, kept her mind occupied. Merc stood at her shoulder while she did so. However, when more probing questions about what she'd seen on the island were asked, her voice faltered.

He drew closer, his wing curving around her shoulder as he picked up the information from her mind and spoke it aloud for her. Surprised gazes shifted to him, suggesting Lady Lyssa hadn't yet informed the Council of the possibility of the marking. Let alone that it had actually happened, but no one had known that. No one except Kaela and Garron and...

She pushed her mind away from that. She shouldn't need Merc to speak for her, but emotions kept surging up,. Keeping her head up, not letting what was hammering against her walls get through, was all she could do.

Huff and puff and blow your house down...

Not now. Not today. She imagined her father's will holding her up, and her mother's. And then she thought of why she was here. Why it was important to hold it together.

Ruth had held Kane when he was a baby, a great honor. He'd latched onto her hair with a small fist, his eyes so still and sharp, his mouth so sweet. She'd brushed and curled Farida's hair when she was ten. Stood at her side outside the rehab enclosure when the young girl asked Ruth if kissing the hurt on the leopard's paw would help. "It's what Daddy does for me," she confided.

The powerful Lord Mason. He and Lady Lyssa were both capable of terrifying and bringing the vampire world to heel when it needed that. Ruth had seen a different side, the proud and loving parents. During informal dinners on the island, they'd bonded with Mal and Elisa over the challenges and fears of raising vampire children.

Her gaze moved back to Jessica. Mason's servant had curly brown long hair, gray eyes and the build of a gymnast. While she wore jeans and a casual T-shirt, she also had on a choker of copper, bronze and gray metals in a tiger stripe pattern. The choker's lock looked like a talon. Ruth remembered a silver key hanging on a chain on Mason's wet neck, and made the connection. Her Master's collar.

Jessica's expression was frozen in a mask Ruth recognized. When Adan had been taken by the Fae as a child, her parents had worn that mask for months. Holding it together, doing whatever could be done, while behind it the primal cry of rage never ended, the grip of terror never eased.

Though Mason was focused on the strategy being discussed, she could feel the energy between the two, giving one another strength. But if the children were lost, it would be an immeasurable blow to two Council members. Which in turn would strike at the heart of the vampire world.

"Can we find him again?" Lady Lyssa demanded. "This Asva?"

"Cai and Rand are on it," Lord Belizar said. The big Russian male had cold gray eyes, and his thick, swept back hair was streaked with silver. He looked as if he'd been spawned by the brutal winters and wilderness Merc had endured. His fitted black dress shirt and belted slacks didn't soften the impression. When he spoke, his voice reminded Ruth of a general whose vocal cords had been permanently roughened by the roar to charge and give no quarter.

He'd been Council head before Lyssa deposed him, a decisive move that removed all debate about her strength and ability to hold the reins on the vampire world. And renewed his loyalty to her, which had been wavering before that power move. *Vampires.*

"Maddock portaled them to a spot close to Lady Kaela's home. Rand is on the scent," he added.

Ruth thought of their visits to the island, Rand shifting to run with Ruth at night, the giant black wolf wrestling with her. The cats had viewed him with great suspicion and animosity, except for one of the female mountain lions, who Cai had teased him was ready to break interspecies boundaries to become the first wolf-mountain cat mating.

Your children would be so adorable. Wolf-kittens.

Rand was an exceptional tracker, in human or wolf form, and Cai was no slouch at it, either. They would find Asva, if they hadn't already.

"Have we heard from the Fae Queen yet, my lady?" Lady Helga sat in a chair on the other side of the table. She had intelligent and concerned brown eyes, framed by thick blond hair she had pulled back in a chignon. "With this level of magic use, the Fae's involvement needs to be ruled out. I find it very difficult to believe the Trads have achieved the magical capability to fortress the island the way they did. And wipe your memory on top of that, Lord Mason."

Despite Mason's preoccupation, Ruth's confused look caught his attention. Probably because of her situation, he took the time to tersely explain, his voice laden with frustration. "I remember little before I was imprisoned in the container, except the children being taken and Mal...falling."

Tense silence descended. It was as if they suddenly realized Ruth was not just a vampire with information, but also Mal's daughter. A few expressions flickered, warning her she was about to be offered condolences. Ruth shook her head, almost violently, stepping back into Merc as if warding off an attack.

Fortunately the message in her reaction was heeded. Lyssa's eyes touched Ruth's, but then she spoke to Helga's question. "My half-sister, Queen Rhoswen, says it's impossible to know what every Fae might be up to. The machinations of their two courts are even more political than ours. But she is doing her own research, as is Lord Keldwyn, our Fae liaison."

"The children's visit to the island was known to very few," Lady Carola said. She had a dark bob around thick-lashed gray eyes. Her sharp cheekbones and chin gave her a perpetually intent look. Her face held little warmth, and Ruth suspected that was its normal temperature. "Isn't that correct?"

"Yes," Mason said. "Beyond Ruth, Mal and Elisa, no one except myself, Lyssa and our servants knew. Mal doesn't even inform his staff until we arrive. He also doesn't schedule other visitors Lyssa and I haven't vetted."

"Would your children have mentioned it to someone?" Lord Walton posed the practical question. "At a café, a discussion in a taxi, anything. It's expected that your children are watched by unfriendly eyes, and though you do all you can to protect them, information can be used and ferreted out, if the one seeking it is determined."

Lyssa and Mason accepted the idea with an exchanged tight look. Then Lyssa's gaze turned inward. "Lord Uthe has arrived with an update. Maddock is with him."

At one time Lord Uthe had been Belizar's and then Lyssa's right hand, respectively. He'd officially stepped down from Council some time ago, leaving the current nine-member count, but was bound to Lord Keldwyn, one of the first approved Fae-vampire pairings, something that still drove as much controversy in the Fae world as vampire-servant open declarations of love did in theirs.

If he was bringing a missive of support from the Fae world, it would be welcome news. Especially after Yvette's crushing news that the angels and Guardians weren't allowed to take sides. It was good Marcellus wasn't here right now. Ruth screaming curses at him wouldn't do much good for anyone.

Uthe strode into the hallway. His clothing was well made but functional and unadorned. He'd once been a Templar Knight, and still adhered to many of its warrior-monk tenets. On earlier visits to the island, before bonding with Lord Keldwyn, he'd kept his hair military short. Now he'd grown it out, a gleaming brown mane, but he kept it tied back. Except for the Fae Lord who liked it longer.

Just before he reached the tense knot of those waiting for him, Uthe stopped and closed his eyes. He looked as if he might be gathering his thoughts. Or praying. But then his eyes opened again, and he moved forward, executing a bow to Lyssa.

"Cai and Rand found Asva," he told her. "He was staked and burned, no more than an hour after he left Kaela. Rand sniffed out the ash residue."

"So someone found out he had betrayed them," Lord Stewart noted flatly. His olive-skinned face looked set in a permanent expression of disapproval, his brows lowered over intense green eyes. "Perhaps they were watching him, and executed him after he left Kaela's home."

"Or they fed him the information before then, watched him to confirm delivery, and then tied up loose ends. Which means the information itself is suspect." Mason's gaze was hard. "We need to know where the chess-playing Trad bastard is."

"We believe we do." Uthe slid a paper from his front breast pocket, glanced at it as if to remind himself of what was on it, then handed it to Lyssa. "Cai and I still have enough of a network in the Trad world to secure a high probability on his location. If we're correct, this might be where your children are being held."

His brown eyes met Lyssa's. "Our advantage is they won't have expected us to locate them this quickly. They also don't know the travel resources we have." His attention moved to Maddock. "Maddock said a portal route is possible that will deliver you within a few miles of the location. He's willing to be the conductor for that transport."

"Good." Lyssa nodded to Maddock.

"All that said," Uthe added, his expression grim, "I do believe they assume you will find them. Which means they will be prepared for that."

"So will we," Lyssa said.

CHAPTER TWENTY-FIVE

*L*yssa's jade green eyes swept the assembled. "I need hunters and warriors. Lord Belizar, you will handle Council matters in my stead."

The Russian vampire accepted the honor with a nod. "You are aware you leave a hammer in charge."

"A hammer may be needed if we require assistance." Grim humor touched her frigid gaze. "Lady Danny is also on her way from Australia. She's cutting short the leave she took to attend to sheep shearing at her station."

When her gaze moved toward Gideon, Ruth saw that Daegan had appeared beside him, the sheathed katana over his shoulder. "I am always prepared, my lady," the enforcer said. "My servant should come, too. He may be of some small assistance."

Gideon gave him an *eat shit* look, but the banter didn't interfere with the grimness around his mouth. He was Kane's uncle, after all.

"I'm with you," Maddock said. "Not just as a portal conductor. You may need another magic user in the fighter category, my lady."

"No chance you're leaving me behind," Lord Mason said to the queen.

"I wouldn't dream of trying," she responded. "We go get our children together."

"I should go," Yvette said. "To reinforce Maddock." The tips of her fangs showed. ""I don't tolerate those who use the young to fight their battles. They're monsters that require putting down."

"No." Merc spoke, unexpectedly. "Your position with the Circus is too important. You're the most powerful protection for Clara and others there. I'll go with Lady Lyssa."

Yvette's brow lifted. "Though you question the blood, you may have enough angel to fall under the neutrality requirement, Merc. Marcellus—"

"Today that is not the part of my blood that's important, except as it can be called upon to help against our enemies."

"Ruth needs you," Yvette pointed out.

"I am whatever she needs." Merc turned toward Ruth. "What do you need, Ruth?"

The Council members watched, but she knew their opinion wouldn't matter to him. "I need you to go after them. Get Kane and Farida back. And tear apart those who...dared to do what they did."

She stopped there, but he could read it from her heart. From every corner inside her.

"You will stay here," he told her. "I know you wish to fight, but..."

"I'm not powerful enough. You'd have to focus on protecting me. I get it." It hurt, but she was used to that kind of hurt. "Bring me bodies," she said. "I'll feed them to the cats."

If it wouldn't risk their digestive systems, she'd be dead serious. Some tribes ate the hearts of their enemies, to absorb their strength and establish their victory over them. She had no desire to touch any part of someone who'd murdered her parents. But she wanted to let the cats tear their earthly bodies to pieces.

"Lady Ruth." Belizar drew her attention. "Since Merc can speak in your head, you will remain in Council chambers with us, as will Jessica and Anwyn. If Mason, Gideon, Daegan or Merc can communicate their status, you will be able to relay that information to us."

"Is your ability to speak in her mind an angelic ability, or have you accepted her marks?" Lord Stewart's eyes had narrowed.

"I accepted her marks. All three of them. She belongs to me." Merc met the male's gaze. Though his expression was impassive, the menace was impossible to miss.

No violence against Council members, she reminded him. *Not until we get them back.*

The ache expanded in her chest, because she so passionately wanted those words to apply to someone else, not just Farida and Kane. The crippling wave of pain turned Merc's attention back to her. That cocoon in her mind steadied her. Helped her stay upright, inside and out.

"It's not the time to debate whether Council permission should have been sought first," Helga said shortly. "Save it for another day, Stewart."

"I was aware of the possibility of the marking, but it was a recent discussion," Lyssa added, her tone brusque. "It was a tactical decision, to assist in learning more about the Trad situation. I'll explain later. Now it's not relevant."

Lyssa moved on, addressing Uthe. "I know you'd stand with me. The battle I need you to fight is at Keldwyn's side, with Rhoswen. If this does not go well, if we did not anticipate our foe well enough, I need your clever tongue and wits to join with his and convince her to help her godson."

"Kel's currently with her at a High Fae event," Uthe said, "but I can send him a thought and he'll respond immediately."

"I know." Lyssa's gaze slid over the room again. "Those of you joining me, go prepare. Dress for a fight. We leave shortly."

"You'll be in the deep woods," Uthe added. "Up in the mountains."

"Shocker," Gideon said. "Maybe we can bring them a case of toothpaste. And soap."

"They won't be needing it," Mason promised.

As Lyssa moved for the door, the others fell in behind her. Jacob, at her shoulder, followed by his brother, Daegan, Lord Mason and Maddock. Mason paused next to Jessica, gripped her hand and brought her close. Ruth heard the rumble of his voice. "I will bring her back, *habiba.*"

"Bring both of you back." Jessica's delicate face was strained but held a fierceness that matched her next words. "I wish I could take down those bastards with you."

"They are the ones who will have to watch their backs." Squeezing her hip, he looked toward Ruth. Paused. Ruth braced herself. *Just go. Please just go.*

"It's said a certain type of memory spell can't hold once its owner is dead," he told her. "Or a certain amount of time has passed. When I return, I hope to have my memory back, so I can share better things with you. It feels...important."

Ruth fought off the ache in her throat to respond. "Come back safely, my lord, with Kane and Farida. That's what's important. The rest...we'll deal with the rest later."

"Yes." Mason looked back down at Jessica, pressed a kiss to her mouth, his hands cupping her skull, fingers in her hair. They touched foreheads, eyes briefly closed, then he released her and turned, striding away. Anwyn gripped Jessica's hand as Jessica watched his broad shoulders. Her face was pale, her composure holding by a thread.

Sometimes waiting was the hardest thing to endure.

Merc touched Ruth's face, his arm around her, a wing folded over her back. He'd gotten pretty touchy-feely of late, her angel incubus. She was okay with that. She desperately needed it. She drew on that energy, the strength of his body, and his thoughts.

You are strong, Ruth. So very strong. You hold fast, and when I come back, when the children are safe, I will take you back to the island to grieve. Until then, put it away.

He made it an order, made it a command she could hear vibrating through every muscle, every nerve. He knew she needed that order to reinforce her sense of self, to keep her from falling apart.

You will need your wits about you in this group, he reminded her.

That part she knew. No matter their sympathy for her grief, vampires respected strength above all else. She would be strong. She would be so fucking strong, like her parents were.

Had been.

Merc tipped up her chin and kissed her, a heated brand that jolted her. When he drew back and her eyes were open, he met them with one purpose. "Tell me you will do as I've said."

"I will. Just like I'll kick your ass later for trying to order me around."

He leaned in and moved his lips against her ear, even though the words came through her mind. *I will use a belt to beat your pretty ass for trying. Gundar has some nice thick ones. I will borrow one from his closet.*

The sexual ripple wasn't much against the other emotions she was feeling, but it reinforced what he'd said. *Put it away for now.* Wait until she could let it all loose, give it all to him, and figure out how to survive a pain too unbearable to contemplate.

She had her own directive for him. *Merc? Let the Trads think you're an incubus. Vampires have really strong libidos. It may muddle them. And not knowing about your angel side gives you an advantage.*

That was based on the hope that Asva hadn't revealed the identity of the "Truth Vessel" before dying. But if it couldn't be used as an advantage, Merc would adapt.

His thumb passed over her lips, his eyes very close. So close they chilled her, because they were more pitiless than Lady Lyssa's.

Remember I said I learned how to make it painless? I've never forgotten how to do it the other way. Make sexual pleasure the most agonizing thing someone has experienced. Purposefully crack open that subconscious layer, let them understand, at every level, their life is slowly leaving them, and there's not a fucking thing they can do except watch me rip it away.

Her savage instincts responded in kind. She embraced the surge of bloodlust, the desire to take life and cause suffering. Her nails dug into his biceps. *Good. If you can make it hurt, do. But mostly, just make them dead. So I know they're no longer in this world.*

There won't be enough left of their souls to cross the Veil. That is the gift I will give my vampire.

~

After the rescue team departed, the rest of the Council adjourned to their usual chamber, a spacious chamber with a high ceiling, criss-crossed with beams. They were wrapped with night blooming flowers that received sunlight through the sky light during the day, while the vampires slept.

Torrence, Helga's servant, showed Ruth to a chair set up in a quiet corner of the carpeted room. The Council seats were behind a horse-shoe-shaped table, a dark polished wood with giant carved feet like a griffin's. The chairs matched. Tapestries of past battles and historic moments in the vampire history hung behind them and on the left and right walls. In the opposite corner from Ruth, a koi pond had been constructed, the fish swimming lazily among the rocks and under the overhang of the fountain that kept up a low rush of sound.

Someone had instructed the headquarters staff to tend to her. She was brought a tea to soothe her nerves, according to the kind-eyed Inherited Servant who brought it. InhServs were the elite of the servant class, humans contracted from birth to be trained when they came of age to serve Council and the higher ranks. The arrangement was made with their families because of bonds they had with, or debts they owed to, the vampire world.

This InhServ also brought a blood-laced concoction from the Council's secured stores of second mark blood, to fortify her strength. Inherited Servants would be solicitous of any vampire. However, Ruth wished they'd treat her with the dismissive indifference more powerful vampires usually treated a far lower ranking one. Too much kindness would break her.

She held onto Merc's order, though, and mumbled her thanks. When her link to him vanished, it jolted her, but it meant they were in the portal. When it didn't resurface, it told her the destination might be beyond her range. Maybe Merc could amplify it from his end, but there'd been no time to suggest trying that option.

A bitter pill, but there was a lot of bitter to choke on right now. He would be in contact as soon as he could. She kept reaching out for Adan as well. Nothing. Damn Guardian business.

She needed her twin, but a separate part of her dreaded taking away his ignorant bliss. She wanted him to have that gift as long as possible, before he learned the foundation of their world had dissolved like a sandcastle before water.

Her numbness was a precarious glue. Sitting upright in the chair seemed almost more than she could do.

Pull it together. She gave herself that savage instruction, even as the vulnerable part of her cried for Merc, for her brother, for dawn, so the sun could knock her unconscious. She hoped she wouldn't dream, though it was probably a futile wish.

Jessica sat to her right, Anwyn on her left. Ruth wished the three of them had been told to sit outside chambers unless they received information from their mind links. She didn't want to hear the Council handling business as if life was supposed to go on the way it always did.

Anwyn was so close her shoulder almost brushed Ruth's, a show of support. She didn't want it. She wanted Merc. She wanted Adan.

She wanted her mother and father.

A tiny whimper caught in her throat, and her fists clenched. When Anwyn looked her way, Ruth snapped her spine straight, and gave her a nod. She was okay.

She was going to be fucking okay if it killed her.

"It is a difficult day, but before we received the news of the kidnapping, we had a full agenda," Lord Belizar was saying brusquely. "As Lady Lyssa noted, Lady Danny will be here shortly, but we have a majority of Council present. We can handle many things to lighten the load. There may be far more difficult challenges ahead."

Like the queen dealing with the loss of her son. Or Lord Mason his daughter. Ruth gripped the mug of tea, and her stomach heaved. She set it back down on the small round table between her and Jessica.

"Lady Carola," Lord Belizar said. "You have the first agenda item."

"Yes. It is a straightforward matter. Conveniently, Lady Kaela was already en route to this location, and arrived a short time ago."

Stewart frowned. "She was questioned extensively by phone. Why did Lady Lyssa request a personal audience?"

"She didn't," Lady Helga put in. "Lady Kaela's loyalty to our queen inspired her to come and offer her in-person support, if she needed another powerful ally at her back."

"Commendable," Lord Walton noted.

"Yes. But unfortunately bearing little support for the agenda item to be addressed." Lady Carola motioned to her servant, Wilhelm, standing at the door. "Have Lady Kaela and her servant brought before us."

The words jerked Ruth out of her numbness. When the Council chamber doors opened a few moments later, her stomach, already in a precarious state, bucked painfully.

Kaela wasn't escorted in as a dignified overlord bringing business before Council. She was hauled in, by the four vampires who served as honor guard when Council was in session. Guarding the door, or doing work like this.

Bringing a vampire prisoner before them.

Kaela's clothes were torn and bloody, hair snarled, makeup smeared from sweat and tears. The blood and the pallor of her skin said she'd sustained injuries, though she was strong enough they were no longer apparent, except from the location of the bloodstains.

The odd angle of Garron's right arm told Ruth it was broken. When he was shoved to his knees, the way he guarded his right hand, catching himself with the left, told her the fingers and wrist were also out of commission. The rattle of his breath said his ribs were damaged.

A third mark could heal from most things, just like a vampire, if they had each other's blood. He'd not been allowed to draw blood from his Mistress, or her from him.

If their battered state was an indication, the four guards hadn't had an easy time of it, either. Their wary stance toward Kaela said they were braced for more of the same. Kaela's attention had turned to Garron, though, as she tried to get him to stay down. He was having none of it. With great difficulty, he rose and positioned himself behind her and to her left. As a servant would in such circumstances.

"You continue to pretend." Carola's voice dripped with contempt. "As if your deceit is to be admired."

"Why are they in this condition, Borgas?" Lady Helga demanded.

Borgas had long dark hair and a mix of Asian and Anglo facial features. His eyes were frost blue. "They resisted when we brought the order to confine them to quarters," he said. "They didn't respond well to the charge."

"*They* didn't respond well to it," Kaela snapped. "They attacked my servant."

"You were quick to defend him, weren't you, my lady?" he responded, the title marinated in venom.

"Enough." Lady Carola's expression locked on the guard. "We will address your misconduct later. While your disgust is justified, you are required to act with restraint, until you are ordered otherwise."

"Yes, my lady." Borgas set his jaw.

"Take up your position at the door."

Until the guards complied, Kaela watched them with a sword in her gaze and tight lips on the verge of a snarl. Then she saw Ruth. That sword sliced down with an accusing heat, telling Ruth what the charge was.

Kaela thought Ruth had betrayed them.

Agony bled into Ruth's heart, a place with no room for more agony.

Ruth.

She grabbed onto Merc's voice. They were out of the portal, and they weren't out of range. *I'm all right. It's not related. Where are you?*

We're hiking through the mountains, heading for the Trad compound. Nothing yet to report. You're very distressed.

I'm okay. The shittiest day in the world has just become the shittiest one in the universe. Something happening at Council, with Kaela and Garron.

She gave it to him in a nutshell and added, *Lyssa needs to know. I think she's always known about Kaela.*

The time isn't appropriate, but as soon as it is, I will inform her. Help them however you can in the meantime.

Yeah, because she could stand against Council.

Yes, you can.

His certainty of it, no matter how misplaced, helped.

Kaela's lip curled away from a fang, a scornful sneer, before she dismissed Ruth and faced the Council. She drew herself up as if she wore a queen's robes. Ruth thought of her history as a spy, where she'd known she could end up in front of a tribunal like this and sentenced to hang.

"Lady Kaela, you know the charge brought before you," Lady Carola said. "You have an unnatural relationship with your servant, where you submit to him as your Master. Proof has been provided to us by a member of your territory who recorded you in the privacy of your rooms. Do I need to play it?"

It was a rhetorical question, because she'd already pressed the button of the small device.

Garron's voice. *"How will your serve your Master tonight, my lady?"*

"However you desire. Please..." Kaela's voice. Trembling with yearning.

"You need me to be strict with you? Use you hard? Bring you peace? Open your mouth, my lady, stretch those beautiful lips around my cock. You know where they're supposed to be. Put yourself to work for your Master."

What two people shared in sexual intimacy, aired this way, made it tawdry and humiliating. Especially under the shocked and condemning eyes of the Council members.

Kaela was being subjected to the worst part of Ruth's nightmares.

The overlord had proven she could control her emotions.

However, blood hunger and stress put a crack in her armor. A quiver passed through Kaela, and she became even paler. Garron's expression was murderous.

"Turn it off," Helga said, and Carola complied. The Councilwoman who'd brought the accusation stared at Kaela.

"I'm disappointed. The tiresome assumptions that a female vampire's more 'emotional' constitution makes her vulnerable to a male servant will once again be given weight. Your weakness has set us back, Lady Kaela."

"She is a made vampire," Lord Stewart pointed out. "Her craving for submission survived her transition."

"Which makes it a rare birth defect." Lord Walton dipped his head toward Carola and Helga. He had the slim, muscled body of a dancer and the level gaze of a tactician. "Not a reflection on our vampire females who are exemplary leaders of our race. It does not have to be perceived as a step backward, Lady Carola. We have progressed that much, I think."

Kaela's fists had clenched. Garron's eyes were now lowered, but Ruth was sure it wasn't an attitude of submission. It was so the killing light in his gaze wasn't as obvious. She expected there was a great deal of conversation going on between him and Kaela. He would keep his focus there, on what would strengthen and support his lady.

The way Merc had done for her, ever since she walked into her family home only a few hours ago.

"The accused is allowed to speak on her own behalf," Lady Helga noted. "Lady Kaela?"

"I've been an exceptional overlord," Kaela said. "You know this."

"It's what we have believed." Carola tapped the folder under her hand. "This member of your territory has many complaints. Perhaps you've just been clever at concealing the things you're not doing well."

"A resentful and ambitious vampire." Kaela's voice dripped with disbelief. "That's who you consider a valid witness?"

Lord Belizar drummed his large fingers on the table. "A valid point. Lady Carola, our kind will take advantage of opportunities to undermine and rise higher in our ranks. A vampire can manipulate voice recordings as easily as any human. Have you had the tape verified?"

"No," Carola admitted. "I had not thought of it, Lord Belizar."

"Understandable." Lord Walton spoke. "We older vampires have a tendency to forget the technological tools at our fingertips." At Carola's searing look, he lifted a hand and added, "I'm not insulting you, my lady. Merely pointing out what I know to be true of many of us at this table, including our absent queen."

"It took an act of God for Lord Mason to agree to use a cell phone," Helga said, "and he still views them with great suspicion."

Kaela's expression remained blank during the hatefully wry exchange. Ruth swallowed the ache in her throat, remembering her father's aversion to technology. And how she and Adan liked to tease him about it.

"You are correct." Lord Belizar spoke to Kaela. "We do not generally take the word of vampires of lower rank over the word of our overlords, unless far more compelling proof than this is presented. So...does this tape lie? Has this vampire manipulated the information to defame you?"

He'd just given her a chance to refute the relationship. Deny Garron was her Master. At the least, she could ask that the tape be tested, which would buy her time. Time for the matter to be settled when Lord Mason, Lady Lyssa and Lady Danny were present, all of whom were known to have closer relationships with their servants "than comfortable."

But none of them were submissive to those servants.

Ruth's gaze slid between Garron and Kaela. As Kaela's stoic mask started to slip, Ruth remembered the tired despair in her gaze in the study.

It wears you down. It wears us both down.

Ruth knew what her answer would be, even as she willed Kaela not to say it. Just as she was sure Garron was doing furiously in her mind, every muscle of his big body rigid.

But Kaela was done with lying.

She met Lord Belizar's gaze. "I submit to Garron for my personal needs. When I was human, I was submissive to my husband, and cherished him as my Master. As I cherish Garron now."

Her gaze slid to Lord Walton, and the edge to her voice was unmistakable. "It is no birth defect, my lord. Garron serves me as a vampire's servant, credibly, extraordinarily. He also serves me, the woman, as my Master."

Dismay gripped several faces, but the Council did not appear moved beyond that. Lord Welles addressed the Council as if Kaela had offered only one word.

Guilty.

"There are two choices in such cases. We can give Lady Kaela the option of dying with her servant, or require that she be put under the direct supervision of a Region Master who can recondition her to serve a useful purpose in our society."

"Which she has done up until now," Lord Walton noted. "On that point at least, I am inclined to doubt the vampire who maligns her. She has been an excellent overlord."

"Reconditioning is prolonged torture and blood hunger to reset the mind," Lady Helga said. "Don't dress it up, Lord Welles."

Lord Welles's brown eyes sparked at the challenge. He was as tall as Belizar, though not as broad. He wore an Armani suit, the dress shirt open at the throat, the silky tips of his ash brown hair brushing his collar. Since the rest of the Council was in what humans would call business casual, he must have joined the Council from another engagement. "The two choices are laid out, Lady Helga. You can choose the former if you don't have the stomach for the latter."

Helga tapped a finger bearing a ruby ring on the table. "I might rip yours out first. You can apologize to me as you're pushing your intestines back in. It would ruin that expensive suit."

Lady Carola waved a dismissive hand. "Stop this. His words were poorly chosen, but the situation can't stand, Helga. It's against everything that a vampire is."

"How am I different?"

Every head swung toward Ruth as she erupted from her seat. Anwyn caught the tea before it could tumble off the table.

Challenging the Council would have scared her shitless, if not for what had happened tonight, hundreds of miles from here. This was senseless. It was all senseless. She wasn't steady enough, level-headed enough to do what she was doing, but she couldn't let it stand, what Kaela was thinking about her. Or what Council was considering.

Anwyn's hand was on her wrist, a warning squeeze. Lord Belizar shot Ruth a ball-breaking look. "Lady Ruth, heed Anwyn and take your seat. You have no leave to speak unless you are communicating matters related to the rescue party. But in answer, you gave your marks —albeit without seeking proper permission—to a being far stronger

427

than yourself. Much as Lord Uthe..." He cleared his throat. "Much as we have acknowledged there is a component of that in Lord Uthe's relationship with the Fae Lord Keldwyn."

"Speak truly," Lord Stewart put in. "Would you countenance bowing to a being weaker than yourself? A human?" He cast a pitying look at Kaela, then an unfriendly one toward Garron. "I know your father. Your brother. It would be against your nature."

Ruth didn't resist Anwyn's touch, but she wouldn't let her pull her back into her seat. "Did you dispute the bond between my brother and his Fae servant?" she demanded. "Did you oppose the Fae sentence that was intended to kill him?"

No. They hadn't. Adan had survived the Guardian training that no one had thought he would survive. In so doing, he proved that things didn't have to be what people expected them to be.

But still, they persisted in acting like they did.

Lady Carola and Lord Belizar's expressions said Ruth was about to get a more strident set-down, though for Belizar she thought her offense was the protocol breach. The color in Carola's cheeks, the thinness of her lips, said Ruth was disagreeing with what was beyond dispute, and that wouldn't be tolerated.

"She's endured enough today to earn some latitude, I believe," Lady Helga interjected smoothly, drawing attention away from her. "She's young, but she's correct on one thing. It's not the first time we've had to come to grips with different relationships. Lady Lyssa herself set the precedent with an open declaration of her love for Jacob, her bond with him."

Lady Carola and Lord Stewart gave her a frosty look. Apparently, it wasn't something they wished to be reminded of.

"That's a far different matter, as Lady Lyssa herself has proven," Carola said. "She holds the upper hand with Jacob and never allows his influence to change the decisions she makes as queen and member of this Council. To suggest otherwise would imply the Council needs to take a further look at it."

Helga's eyes narrowed. "We didn't always believe that, Carola, or do you not remember? And do not threaten our queen. You've seen how well that turns out for Council members. She has not hesitated to deliver that lesson, even during a meeting. You were there, I believe?"

Carola blew out a ferocious breath. "What point are you trying to make?"

"Anyone we bond with has the opportunity to help us see things differently. In the right way." Helga glanced toward the opposite end of the chamber. The servants of the Council members stood in silent formation along that wall. A straight line could be drawn between each servant and their seated Master or Mistress. Helga's gaze lingered on her own servant, Torrence, before it returned to Kaela, then came back to the rest of the Council.

"As Lady Kaela said, she has proven herself an exemplary overlord. Brutal when needed, fair always. We've heard from many in her territory supporting that. Voices that far outweigh one malcontent who leaves recorders where they might document incriminating information."

"The matter with Lady Kaela is written into our law," Lord Stewart said impatiently. "The evidence has been provided, and it only requires a Council majority to pass sentence."

"You've brought up an interesting philosophical debate, Helga," Welles noted, "But Stewart is correct. The law stands as it stands. I support sending her to Lord Zixin in China. She's too valuable and intelligent to lose, and he has the right disposition to handle the matter."

Ruth's trembling knees couldn't hold her any longer. She'd sunk back down into the chair, Jessica's hand on her back, Anwyn's still resting on her arm. She felt their sympathy, saw in their faces they didn't agree with what was happening. But none of them had any standing to impact it. If she spoke again, she would be removed. She knew it.

Maybe that would be preferable.

The Council voted in favor of Welles' motion, with only one dissenting vote, Lady Helga. "You would vote for the first option, for her to die with her servant?" Lord Belizar asked. "It should be clarified for the minutes."

He nodded toward a scribe, an Inherited Servant at a small desk to the right of the Council horseshoe.

Lady Helga gazed at Kaela as she spoke. "Yes. I also think we should change the law going forward, to give the vampire the choice to refuse conditioning."

Kaela was so pale Ruth wasn't sure how she was standing, except Garron stood close enough that her back brushed his chest. She wasn't leaning, but the contact said she was aware of the support. The servant's eyes lifted and locked with Belizar's. "For being this goddamn stupid, your race *will* eventually be annihilated. And no one will fucking miss it."

Kaela's head had bowed in an attitude of defeat. Of exhaustion. Garron's undamaged hand went to her shoulder, holding. Ruth couldn't speak, the lump in her throat too large. *Oh, Great Father...*

Lord Belizar's expression had gone flat. Emotionless. He motioned to Borgas. "Escort her servant to the courtyard. We will adjourn there for his execution. Which will be handled quickly and painlessly," he added, giving Borgas a look that said he'd be heeded, or there'd be hell to pay.

Kaela's head snapped up, her anguished eyes meeting the Russian's. Lord Belizar's jaw tightened. "I will grant you a mercy, Lady Kaela. You may choose to carry out the sentence according to our laws, or return to your rooms to prepare for the journey to China. The honor guard will handle it. *That* choice is yours."

CHAPTER TWENTY-SIX

*T*he five miles between the portal exit and the location where Uthe believed Lyssa's son and Mason's daughter might be held were heavily forested. Tree branches and foliage pressed in on them as they emerged. There was no path.

"I miss Adan's mapping ability," Maddock said with a grunt, holding the branch that had smacked him in the face away from Lady Lyssa's as she stepped past it. "He could have gotten us closer."

"Stealth is probably a good call," Merc observed.

"Yeah. So was yours on Yvette. I'm not seeing latex and stiletto boots working here. Though she might have been able to use that whip of hers like a machete."

Merc offered a grim half-smile. Maddock and Yvette routinely goaded one another to justify their magical sparring matches, bouts that risked severe injury but both enjoyed too much to give them up. Merc was sure Maddock was hoping he'd pass the comment on to the Circus Mistress to draw her wrath.

Just as Yvette would have done, Merc was sure, Lady Lyssa had changed into hunter gear; black tank, brown cargo pants, thick soled boots, her hair braided and coiled on her neck. She was used to being prepared to fight, a reassuring thought.

Her head was up, eyes searching the thick canopy above them. "This forest is old. The type of place a Fae would seek, if they were in our world."

Maddock and she exchanged a look, and Lyssa shook her head. "I don't sense any. Not yet. But the warning sign should be heeded."

"Agreed."

Thanks to Daegan's tracking abilities, they did find a deer trail in short order. They could have used magic to open up a path, but such signatures were like sending smoke into a daylight sky. With the level that had been in play on the island, there was no way of knowing if eyes were already upon them or not, but playing it safe made sense. While Merc was tempted to take to the air, he kept his wing cloaking in place, mindful of Ruth's suggestion.

When they were within a mile of the proposed location, Mason and Lyssa came to an abrupt stop. One of Lyssa's hands landed on Jacob's arm, the other on Mason's. Their fingers twined together.

"What?" Maddock whispered.

"We can feel Kane and Farida," Lyssa said, her voice tight. "But we're being blocked from communicating. Both of us."

"I can feel Kane like he's next to me," Jacob added, "but it's like his mind is gagged."

"Trads can't do this," Lyssa said, low. Her eyes took on a killer's flatness. "Let's keep going."

Mason and Lyssa continued, side by side, Jacob to Lyssa's left. Without direction, the rest spread out. Being experienced hunters or fighters, they knew what was required.

At the half-mile mark, Merc detected the Trad vampires, as well as other aromas associated with a camp. Maddock had cloaked all of them, but when they were within a hundred yards and starting to see buildings through the thinning trees, a tinny voice echoed through them. Someone was using a megaphone.

"Lady Lyssa, is that you? Did you accept our hospitality, or did you and Lord Mason send lackeys? For your children's sake, I hope you came yourselves."

"Only a magic user like me could have detected the cloak," Maddock muttered to Merc. But obviously the speaker didn't know how many—or who—it contained.

Maddock moved to Lyssa and murmured to her. She glanced at Mason and Jacob, and the three of them proceeded forward. Merc, Maddock, Daegan and Gideon melted into the forest again, taking different points of the perimeter.

VAMPIRE'S CHOICE

By the time Lyssa, Mason and Jacob came out of the trees, Merc had found a tall pine with an optimal view of the camp. He also Lyssa stiffen and pause, and followed her gaze to the cause.

A fucking guillotine. It had been set up in the center of the small compound, which included a cabin and several tents. The frame of the guillotine was polished wood, the blade new and sharp, gleaming from the camp lights that illuminated the night.

Kane, Lyssa's son, was suspended from a frame of recently cut wood, positioned several feet above a bed of wooden stakes. His arms and legs were pulled out to either side. Farida was next to him on the same type of device.

Merc studied the cables and weights holding them in place. Being familiar with the Circus's methods of taking things quickly into the air or dropping them in front of a surprised audience, he recognized the far more diabolical purpose. A lever would activate the system, which would drop counterweights, aiding gravity by increasing the speed and force at which the frame would drop. With its vampire occupant.

Two vampires wearing cargo pants, T-shirts and hiking boots stood by those levers, gripping them firmly. If they were attacked, the levers would go down with them.

The guillotine may have been the first thing she'd seen, but as soon as their children came into view, Lyssa and Mason's attention locked upon them.

The teens had been suspended for far too long, weight pulling against shoulders, back and hips. One of Kane's shoulders had dislocated, probably because he'd struggled against his bonds. The joint was swollen, his face taut with pain. Farida's long hair cloaked her countenance, but when she lifted her head, it was drawn from lack of blood, her gaze feverish. But also feral. The fight hadn't left these two.

As their parents stepped out of the forest, Merc saw longing, rage and fear flash through their offspring's eyes, but they said nothing. Vampires were closer to wild animals than humans, their young trained early on how to react to threats. They wouldn't reveal anything which would give an enemy an advantage. Just like Ruth, the first time he'd encountered her, in the tall grass with the lion.

The mind link was still absent, evident from the flash of distress that crossed the young faces as they'd reached for the one comfort they'd thought might be in their grasp. If they were under less duress,

433

they would have anticipated it, because no way their parents could have been approaching, this close to them, and not have the mind link reactivate long before they appeared, unless someone had imposed spell work to continue blocking it.

He saw the rage in the parents, but Mason and Lyssa were old enough to control such reactions. They had one focus; take any opportunity to get their children to safety. And annihilate the ones who'd dared threaten them.

Jacob, for all that he was a human servant, showed he was truly his mistress's mate, because he was a deadly presence at her side, watching for that same opportunity.

A half dozen vampires were positioned throughout the clearing with crossbows. Loaded with wooden stakes with metal tips to ensure they penetrated skin and muscle swiftly, the shaft would bring death to the vampire target.

"They will not be pleased," the Trad with the megaphone informed Lyssa. "You're early." The megaphone made a staticky, whistling noise as he lowered it.

Merc assumed this was Grollner, and not just because the stump he stood near held a chess set, where he'd apparently been playing himself. Maybe his lackeys weren't smart enough to present him a challenge. He was built bullish, with thick shoulders and powerful thighs. His brown hair was snarled down his back, his pale blue eyes overflowing with keen intelligence and zealotry. The worst combination when trying to find a weak spot.

"It throws a wrench in their plans," Grollner noted. "But I'm glad. The waiting was getting tedious. Fortunately, your son is a pain in the ass, so he inspired us to get our axes out and build a better mousetrap to keep him subdued." He gestured to the pulley system. "We were so pleased with the results, we put the girl up there with him. He gets a little pissy when she's out of his sight. They're a true credit to you both."

He nodded to Mason and Lyssa. "Not a plea for mercy out of either of them. But he has a very creative vocabulary."

Chatty bastard. But Merc wasn't fooled, and neither was anyone else. Lyssa's green eyes were polar frost. "What's the purpose of the guillotine?"

"To kill you and Lord Mason. One of our more well-heeled members fondly remembers the French Revolution. He had this reproduction made a couple years back and has been using it to finish off his food sources when he's depleted them. He says it's so they don't suffer needlessly." Grollner's lips lifted in a grim smile. "But we all know that's bullshit. He likes to use the damn thing. Likes its efficiency."

"So you choose to use our children to achieve your objectives, instead of fighting us with honor."

Grollner shrugged. "There's too much emphasis on noble battles to the death. Different times call for different measures. We can return to the honorable ways afterward. No one calls a knight to exterminate rats."

"Once you choose dishonor, there is no path back," Jacob said quietly.

"A human's opinion is worth nothing," Grollner said to Lyssa, not deigning to look in Jacob's direction. His smirk vanished, his lips tightening. "You have backup in the woods. Our friends say four of them. There's a price for trickery, my lady."

The vampire holding the lever on Farida shoved it to the halfway mark. The frame dropped like it was on greased rails.

With a roar of rage, Mason leaped forward. The bows came up, but Lyssa was faster. She put herself in his path, using a deftly wielded combination of strength and magic to hold the much larger male vampire at bay, though he snarled and his heels dug into the ground, trying to push past.

It took a moment before Lyssa's murmured insistence, her restraining hands upon him, brought Mason back to himself, letting him see his daughter had *not* been impaled.

The frame had screeched to a stop, inches from the stakes. Even if Lyssa hadn't tried to "trick" Grollner, there would have been some excuse concocted to do it, because he wanted them to see how rapidly the sentence could be carried out. To ensure obedience. Compliance.

Merc's gaze narrowed. They *had* proven how rapidly it could happen.

Now he could calculate.

Lyssa glanced toward the forest and made a *come out* gesture.

"A wise decision, my lady. And impressive magic use. I thought we'd have the pleasure of seeing Lord Mason's daughter weep after my vampires staked him with a half dozen arrows. Not as satisfying as the guillotine, but I wouldn't want to lose any of my men to his pointless rage."

Mason had regained control of himself, but his amber eyes on Grollner were the timer of a nuclear bomb, marking the seconds. His daughter's rasping breaths as she controlled her own adrenaline surge punctuated the clearing. Merc suspected Mason felt every ragged breath as if it were cut glass in his own lungs.

Responding to Lyssa's bidding, Maddock emerged from the south, Daegan and Gideon coming from the west. Merc slid out of his tree and moved into view on the eastern side of the camp. As Grollner examined all of them, Merc allowed a fog of his incubus power to roll out and drift through the campground, surrounding Grollner's vampires. Getting their cocks hard, testing how open to distraction they were.

"A *human* sorcerer." Grollner's contempt toward Maddock was obvious. "A vampire warrior and his servant. And you...incubus." His gaze flicked toward Merc. "Did you hope he could compel us to fuck each other to death, Lady Lyssa?"

"He's a capable fighter," Lyssa said, her expression flat.

"There's nothing to fight. You could have left them at home." Grollner was done with the preliminaries. His gaze latched onto Mason. "You first. Go to the guillotine, kneel and put your head into it. Lady Lyssa will follow."

"You could have killed him on the island," Lyssa said. "Why now?"

Grollner shrugged. "Our invisible friends wished to avoid being directly involved in the killing of a Council vampire."

"They had no problem killing the owner of the island."

"He was of low rank. Of no consequence."

If Ruth had been here, Merc would have had to peel her off Grollner's face. She would have come away with his clawed-out eyeballs in her clutched hands.

He thought of Mal's love for his daughter, the straightforward intelligence and strength of the male. Of Elisa, the woman who'd nurtured Ruth and given her the courage to embrace her softer qualities, her submissive nature. Given *him* that gift.

Yes, someone *was* going to die here.

Grollner glanced back toward Mason. "Since we needed your blood, fresh, it was also important that you come to us, as you have done. The plan has had its hitching points, but it has succeeded."

Lyssa's lips thinned, but her jade eyes gleamed with a decisive light. "Your Fae allies can't lie. It's far easier to work around the question, 'were you involved' than 'did you do it?'" She spat on the ground, an impressive act of contempt.

The Trad's eyes glittered. "A distasteful alliance, but it was necessary to achieve our objective."

Confirmed. Lyssa's bluff had proven useful. Merc saw the brief flash of it in her gaze before it was gone. Too quick for Grollner to note it.

"And what is that objective?" she asked. "I'm sure you've practiced a speech about it to impress us."

Grollner's gaze narrowed. "I'm happy to have you go first. You can put your fucking arrogant neck in the guillotine right now."

"I personally enjoy diabolical scheme speeches," Gideon spoke up. "So if you're in a sharing mood, we're all listening."

Grollner shot him another look of contempt. "You will be dead in a few moments, human."

"It's not a long speech, then?"

Daegan shoved Gideon out of the way as one of the vampires released an arrow. It would have punched the former vampire hunter in the chest, but Daegan deflected it with a turn of his body, Gideon rolling to his feet on the other side of him, knife and stake out and ready.

"Hold," Grollner snarled. "Unless you want your children to die."

That had been directed to Mason and Lyssa, who had sought to take advantage of the distraction, but the Trad and his company had vampire speed as well. Even if not a match for Mason and Lyssa, it was enough. The crossbow holders had closed ranks in a solid line between the vampire parents and their children. Mason or Lyssa might get through them, but the delay would cost them precious time.

"If they die, you lose your leverage to control us," Mason said.

"If they die, it is regrettable, because we have plans for them. But if they must be sacrificed to protect ourselves for our overall objective, it will be done." Grollner's lip curled. "My allies are far more powerful than you, Lady Lyssa. Make no mistake, you will not be able to cut me down, no matter how fast you are."

"So your overall objective is to destroy vampires like us." Lyssa gave him a disdainful look. "Same shit, different day."

"With some more clever twists than my past Trad brethren. Without its two most powerful advocates for the changes that turn vampires away from what they should be, the Council majority remaining will likely revert to more traditional, less human-centric ways. There are those on your Council who have entertained having a Trad representative. We will make that happen."

"I think you underestimate their intelligence," Lyssa said. "Which is what happens when you isolate yourself, create your own echo chamber and feed it only with the information that supports your view of the world."

As she engaged with the Trad, Merc was scanning the area, his senses wide open. If their allies were watching from close by, they were damn powerful Fae, their cloaking making them impossible to locate.

"Your son will live, Lady Lyssa." Grollner's eyes flashed at Lyssa's words, but he had the bit in his teeth. "He'll be raised properly, learning how vampires are supposed to live. Your daughter," his gaze moved to Mason, "has a promising lineage. She might spawn a child to expand our ranks, if enough of us try to plant the seed."

Lyssa's hand tightened on Mason's arm once again, but this time the male vampire only grew more still. Like a snake getting ready to strike at the rat obliviously walking over his coils.

"As they grow and adhere to our culture," Grollner continued, "our way of doing things, they will teach others, bring a different way of thinking to the 'civilized' vampire world."

"I will fucking die first."

Despite the quivering that spoke of the agony of his physical state, Kane glared at his captors. And Farida wasn't going to be outdone. She hissed and spat on her handler, punctuating Kane's declaration.

When the vampire backhanded her, the force of the blow snapped her head to the left, and blood spurted from her nose and lip. It made her cry out, but when she sent him another look of murderous fury, it was an echo of what was on her father's face.

"No matter what else happens today, you will die."

Even though the Trads seemed to have the tactical advantage, Mason's menace was so palpable, Merc saw uncertainty flicker in the face of the vampire who had struck Farida. A reaction that could be contagious, at least among Grollner's backup. Lyssa and her group weren't acting like the outmatched force they were supposed to be.

"They do not have the advantage here," Grollner said sharply. "Remember our allies." He looked at Kane. "Allies powerful enough to wash everything out of your mind, except the memory of *this* place as your home, your world. And me, your father."

"My father stands over there," Kane told him.

"No. He is the human sperm donor." Grollner sent Jacob a contemptuous look. "Who never should have been involved in your raising. The scant few times our human cattle have borne us children, the females are killed shortly thereafter to remove their weakening influence."

His unpleasant smile moved to Lady Lyssa, then to Mason. "You were spared until now because the fresh blood of the parent is necessary for the memory wipe spellwork."

"I find it interesting these allies are here, even if hidden from sight." Lyssa's gaze moved over the forest. "As if they don't trust you to get the job done. They know you are not strong enough to stand against us on your own."

"You think I can be baited into doing something foolish, Lady Lyssa?"

"No." Her frank honesty caught Grollner's attention. "It's a question I think you should be asking yourself. They helped you kidnap the children to get us here. You need us for the blood, because the children, keeping them, is your prize. But also the bait."

"Yes," he said. "And you are here."

"Not for us. For you." Her half laugh was a blade being drawn. "As distasteful as you find your alliance, I can promise you it is ten times more so to a powerful Fae. If I do not finish you off here, they will. I guarantee it."

"Your children will still be dead," he said tightly. "If what you say is true, they will not allow any of us to live."

"Correct," she said quietly. "So why don't they want us to see them? What is their objective? Their agenda? When you join forces with another, it's the most important question to ask yourself. If—son of a bitch."

A flash of insight crossed her face. Ignoring Grollner's puzzled look, Lyssa turned toward Mason. "Pallas," she said. "He was present at the Council dinner two years ago, when we talked about Kane and Farida's desire to visit the island again. From there, he only needed to know where to put spies and listeners, and be patient enough to wait for the opportunity."

At Mason's look, she lifted a shoulder. "It's been bothering me," she told him. "I've been working on the question. It just came to me. I thought now might be the optimal time to share.

"He and Belizar drank together, spoke of Russia. Pallas spent time there, centuries ago, before the Industrial Revolution. They spoke of the things they wished were still the same. Innocuous conversation, but Belizar told me at one point Pallas said, 'If you could go back to those times, when vampires and Fae did not mix, and there was no confusion about who is servant and who is Master, it would be better, simpler times, would it not?'"

She turned back to Grollner. "It's one of the dangers of mingling with other races. We recognize our commonalities, but we also forget our differences. Like how good the Fae are at trickery and deception. Pallas is connected to a group of High Fae who resent Tabor's tolerance, and challenge it routinely in his advisory meetings. They were unsettled when Queen Rhoswen and my family alliance turned in a similar direction. They'd felt like they could always count on her animosity toward the vampire world."

She gave Grollner a derisive look. "It pays to do your research before getting into bed with a venomous foe."

Her voice raised. "So we know it's you, Pallas. Do you care to show yourself, or would you prefer to keep skulking in the woods like a coward who won't face his enemies?"

As she spoke, she turned in a broad circle, except for a brief pause when she met Merc's gaze. With purpose. Then she'd completed the circle, and things changed.

The cloaking dropped, and energy flooded the clearing. Overpowering, High Fae energy.

Everyone had to brace against it, foe and ally alike. Kane and Farida's captors hadn't expected it, and Farida's captor was wiping her spit off his face. He stumbled back against the lever. Already at the halfway mark, and well-oiled, the pressure finished the job. The frame dropped.

"No."

With a howl of rage, Mason bowled through the crossbow holders before they expected him. They were knocked aside, even Mason's murderous intentions set aside as he tried to get to his daughter in time.

He was too late. The frame slammed down on the stakes.

Only Farida wasn't there. The restraint was empty. And not just hers. The only thing proving Kane's had held an occupant were four dangling and torn cuffs.

The two vampires who'd been guarding them were on the ground. Dead. Stakes had been ripped from the beds and used to dispatch them.

The startled archers regained their feet and tried to reform ranks. Their weapons' aim was pointed in two directions, one set toward Mason, the second toward Lyssa and the others. Their wild eyes said they'd been well and truly spooked. Only Grollner's roar, reminding them of the presence of their formidable allies, helped steady them.

Lyssa raised a hand, telling Daegan, Gideon and Maddock to hold. To wait. Mason had turned toward her, but even his feral fury banked at her look, his own flickering with calculation. Though it took effort to restrain themselves, not to take advantage of the moment, they obeyed the queen.

"Why do you take my prizes from me?" Grollner snarled at that formless Fae energy.

As the power increased in response, he braced his feet and slashed his hand through the air. "She's right. Don't play these games. She knows it's you. It's too late. You must come forth and help us finish it now."

Slowly the energy gathered into one spot, the northern side of the clearing, behind the guillotine and empty frames. As the power morphed into shapes, it brought Pallas into view of all the assembled.

Pallas, and the army of Fae backing him up.

~

Twelve High Fae. Fucking hell.

Jacob was sure his brother was having the same thought. They were outgunned.

Do not be so sure of that, Jacob.

His lady had dismissed Grollner and was focused on the Fae male a step in front of the others. He had gold hair and silver eyes, and wore the garb of a water Fae. Blue with silver trimmings, a sword and dagger on his belt. She inclined her head. "Pallas."

"Lady Lyssa." The Fae cast an indifferent glance at Grollner. "We took nothing from you, vampire. Pay better attention. The incubus is gone."

As Grollner spun to confirm it, Mason's attention went to the vampire who had a crossbow aimed at this chest. Mason's lips curled back from his fangs. "Without the element of surprise, you can't fire that fast enough to hit me. Take a few lessons from human hunters." His gaze flicked to Gideon.

"A compliment." Gideon raised a brow. "I may faint."

"An indirect one. And faint later," Mason said shortly.

Maddock seemed unnaturally still, his grip firm on his staff. When he met Jacob's gaze, he offered a slight nod, and Jacob felt a tiny fizz of energy. Since the vampires were scanning the area, nostrils flared, all senses on alert, he suspected the sorcerer was projecting a scrambled net of energy that could cloak the children and Merc, wherever they were.

Jacob hadn't seen Merc release them and kill their jailers. Neither had his lady. She wasn't even sure Pallas and his followers had. However, the important thing was Kane and Farida were out of target range, at least for now. His lady's rage was no less than Mason's or his own, though they all maintained their positions. Waiting for the cue to turn this into the bloodbath it was going to have to be.

He didn't know how they'd win against twelve High Fae. But where there was a will, there was a way. Gideon would call that fluffy bunny optimism. Jacob's brother had his own version of a pre-fight pep talk.

Kill all the fuckers before they can kill you.

Jacob, Gideon and Daegan had shifted to a wider formation as the crossbolt holders did the same. From their visibly nervous expressions, the vampires might bolt and leave it to the Fae. They had no chance against Daegan, Lyssa and Mason. Grollner's annoyed expression said he knew it, too. But he knew how much Pallas wanted from this scenario, too, as Pallas confirmed.

"If you are removed, there's no longer a bridge to the vampire world, a family connection to the Unseelie Queen," Pallas told Lyssa. "While we do not share much in common with this primitive creature," he nodded toward Grollner, "we desire to restore our respective worlds to what they were, before your influence changed it in unacceptable ways."

Lyssa sighed. "The key change, the paradigm shift, has already happened. You believe eliminating me will put it back in the box? Our connection is no longer the only one between the Fae and vampire worlds. Or the Fae and human worlds."

"The Queen's backing will ensure we succeed."

"You will not have it if she knows of this."

"You assume she does not?" He gestured at his belt, his garb. "I am of the water Fae. She and I share a similar lineage. Use your eyes, half-breed."

Jacob stepped forward. Lyssa put a hand on his forearm and cocked her head at Pallas. "Name calling. You aren't as sure of yourself as you seem. And you didn't say she does know of it. You sidestepped. Even if I fall here, you will lose. She will take your heads herself."

His lips tightened. "Not if you die here. She will be told the Trads succeeded in murdering you and your children."

"Trads who conveniently no longer exist for questioning." Lyssa sent a significant look toward Grollner, who paled. "Are you honorable enough to allow me to deal with him and his men first, Pallas? You won't have to get your hands dirty with their blood. Then the fight will be between you and us. Agreed?"

A sneer crossed Grollner's face. "You have no power to negotiate anything, Lady Lyssa. You will—"

Pallas inclined his head. "Agreed."

Mason erupted into motion. He came straight at them, taking an arrow in the shoulder as he landed on the one who'd fired it.

"Thank you for the weapon," he said, pulling it out and shoving it into the vampire's chest. He added a vicious twist to the blow to ensure maximum damage to the organ.

In the time it took Mason to put his opponent down, Daegan's katana had whispered free of its sheath and removed two heads. As the Council's enforcer spun, Gideon slid under Daegan's arm and used his wrist crossbolt to kill the one aiming for his Master's back.

Daegan completed the circle, his free hand landing on Gideon's shoulder, twisting him to the right. The next vampire closing in on them had his eyes on Daegan and his lethal blade. Gideon surged up from the crouch Daegan had guided him into and shoved the stake under their enemy's ribs, using the vampire's momentum to rupture the vulnerable organ.

Maddock had conjured a fireball, tossing it up like a baseball player waiting for his turn at bat. It came quickly, two vampires closing in on his position. He deflected their arrows, a thrown knife, plus several bullets from a fired gun. When he launched the sphere of flame, it separated and reformed, two serpents that wrapped around their necks. The elemental garrote severed their heads, the skulls rolling away, engulfed in fire.

Jacob would have given them hell for not letting anyone reach him so he could take his own pound of flesh, but he and his lady had one target on their radar.

Grollner.

The Trad charged to meet her, but she was far swifter. He'd only gone two strides before she was on him. He grappled with her, likely hoping luck would provide him an advantage that simply wasn't there. She was far older, stronger and faster. He'd merely acted on fatalistic courage fueled by the knowledge his cause was lost.

Sliding away like an eel, she slammed him face down on the ground. Jacob closed in, and severed Grollner's cervical vertebra with his knife.

To incapacitate, not kill. His lady had things to say, but they wouldn't take long. Grollner wouldn't have time to heal.

When she was in the mood to embrace the form her Fae blood had given her, it was a winged gargoyle. The echo of it was unmistakable now in the way she perched on Grollner's back, her arms crossed over her knees. When she leaned down, she looked like she was bending down to feed on her prey's juicy eye meat.

Jacob backed off, watching for flank attacks, but each time he thought one of Grollner's vampires would make it to him, one of the other four men intercepted. The few left chose the smart decision. They bolted, but they didn't get far. Several of Pallas's entourage incinerated them with light they could have channeled directly from the sun, no matter that it was currently on the other side of the planet. Poof. That easy.

Yeah, when the fight was engaged with them, it was going to be bad.

An uneasy quiet settled on the clearing. Lyssa's deceptively calm voice penetrated it. "For decades, Trads and the Council have maintained an uneasy truce. One strained by those of your kind who target our female vampires. But you are not a unified people. If a rabid dog strikes at my child, I kill that unfortunate creature and end his suffering. I don't kill all of his brethren. There is no concerted effort among dogs to do harm to human children."

When she was truly angry, all emotion would drop from her voice. And that wasn't the only evidence of it. A polar wind built in the clearing, vortexes that sent shivers up spines, sank into bones. Even Pallas's followers didn't seem immune to it, their gazes shifting around them as if the effect was unexpected, though Pallas remained poker-faced.

Jacob remained silent, standing at his lady's back. The other four drew near to form a circle around them, a protective front. Mason stood near Grollner's head. He wanted to take it, Jacob could tell. But his lady wouldn't allow it.

This one was hers.

"My patience is at an end. You took my son, and my goddaughter. You hurt them." That wind frosted the pine boughs closest to the campground with ice. "You orchestrated the murder of a vampire and his servant, people I considered dear friends. They sacrificed their lives to try and protect our offspring."

The hand she'd clamped over Grollner's shoulder started to morph. That sleek and deadly gargoyle showed itself as it became a powerful claw, with talons that seemed twice as long as her fingers. She stroked the corner of Grollner's widened eye with one, leaving a trail of blood. When he strained to see her face, he saw the shadow of

445

the one her half-Fae blood gave her. Tighter, more feral, a hint of the gray beast.

"You want me to act like a 'Traditional' vampire, savage, acting only on my desires and needs? I will grant your wish, Grollner. You will not live to see it, but I will dedicate myself to annihilating every Trad that exists in our world. Every. Single. Fucking. One."

She tilted her head toward Daegan, who stood, expressionless, watching the exchange. "It will become his number one priority, sanctioned by Council."

"What will that accomplish?" Grollner rasped it, blood bubbling at his lips. Jacob noted his foot twitch, knew his spine was starting to repair. He sent her the message, and received a brief acknowledgement.

Let him think he has a chance, Jacob. It will make crushing his soul even more satisfying.

His lady wasn't feeling merciful. Jacob was fine with that.

"It will send a message that will take decades to forget," she said. "It is far better to be my friend than my enemy. Go to hell, Grollner, and rot there."

She twisted his head and wrenched it from his body, tossing it away and nimbly leaping back as the blood spurted.

In the same movement, her hand returned to its graceful manicured form. She didn't watch the life die out of Grollner's eyes, the body stop twitching. Instead, her gaze met Mason's, to confirm they were both satisfied. Though his gaze was still lit with amber fire, his tone was one of acceptance and respect. "My lady," he said formally.

She glanced at Maddock, Gideon and Daegan. "You have done well. Now comes the real fight."

The one we will likely lose, Jacob.

Not if Kane and Farida are okay.

He wondered if that was how Mal had felt, relieved his children hadn't been on the island. His heart tightened with grief he couldn't yet afford to feel, for the male vampire he'd respected and liked, tremendously, and for Elisa, who had been impossible not to love. If they'd been there, Jacob had no doubt Ruth and Adan would have fought just as fiercely, refusing to back down even in the face of a sure death.

Vampires of "no consequence." For those who sacrificed for and with others, there was no such thing.

We aren't going to lose, my lady, he decided. *Don't be so negative.*

Lyssa shot him a glance, then proceeded back across the clearing, two males in lockstep on either side of her. When she was a few paces from Pallas and the others, she stopped. "Thank you," she said, with courtesy. "There was a great deal of satisfaction in that."

Pallas's gaze flickered toward the trees. "I didn't know incubi had teleporting abilities. Lower magical creatures can surprise us."

"There's a bucket of things you don't know. Otherwise you wouldn't have done something this idiotic."

Gideon of course, standing at Daegan's side. Pallas ignored him, responding as if Lyssa had spoken.

"The Trad, and human sorcerers of unknown identity, will be blamed," he reminded her. "No one will assume the High Fae would be involved in something as crude as this. You will die here, and be unable to tell Rhoswen, Tabor or your Council anything. We will hunt down your young and dispatch them. With the incubus."

Lyssa bared her fangs. "Let's see who's right and who's not."

A few hundred yards from the clearing, concealed by Maddock's anchored cloaking spell, Merc perched in the thick boughs of a pine. Farida was inside the circle of his arm and wing on one side, Kane on the other. Neither teenager had looked away as the queen ripped off Grollner's head. They'd quivered with the desire to be at her side while she did it. Vampires didn't shy from bloodshed.

"We need to join them," Kane said for the twentieth time. Merc had had to restrain him forcibly during the fight with Grollner's forces. "They need help standing against the Fae."

Yeah, they did. But he knew what his charge was.

On their trek through the forest, Lyssa had asked it of him. "Ruth has spoken of your speed. Is it...greater than a vampire's? One of my age, or Mason's?"

"Yes. Exponentially."

Lyssa nodded. "If you see an opportunity to free our children, take it. Get them out of harm's way. You do not leave them until we have prevailed, or until you can deliver them to Council."

She'd paused, her mouth tightening. "I apologize. I know Ruth has given you her marks, but you aren't a servant. You aren't a vampire. I can't command you. I can only ask. I know you're an accomplished fighter. But it is your speed and your ability to fly that I need."

"I will do as you ask." He met her gaze. "I am here to be on your side. Because that is Ruth's side."

Lyssa had moved to face Pallas and his High Fae. Even if the males with her had the same magical power—and only Maddock came close, maybe—they were a fleet of sailboats facing down fighter jets.

Kane sucked in a breath. Waves of power were gathering, pulling oxygen from the air. Winds began to lash the trees and make the trunks sway.

"We are going to help them," the young vampire ordered. He sounded exactly like his mother. Except he wasn't.

He gave the boy cruel honesty. "You're not strong enough, and you will get them killed by dividing their attention between the fight and protecting you."

Anger flashed through Kane's eyes, but so did pain. "They had me out in the yard by the time it happened, but I saw how valiantly they fought. I heard...I heard her cry out when he died. I want their deaths."

"Elisa taught me how to sew a skirt hem," Farida said softly. "I was working on the stitches, right before they attacked."

Merc thought of how Elisa had put him to work in the kitchen. Curving her flour-dusted hand over his to show him how to pinch a pastry crust.

The tree shuddered and Merc increased his grip on them both. The battle had engaged. The clearing lit up like the Circus at the end of a performance, bolts of power, sparks, flashes of light. As he suspected, Maddock and Lady Lyssa held their own on the first barrage, but it wouldn't last. Pallas and his supporters knew what their advantages were, and they weren't in the mood to draw it out. They were employing their Fae magic liberally, making it difficult for the others to get into the action enough to make a difference.

Daegan was the exception. Whomever he fought had to engage

with him directly, countering his swordplay with their own weaponry, as if he was immune to most of their magic.

Merc thought of what he'd heard about Daegan, whispers around the Circus. *Some say he is Lucifer's son. A fallen angel.*

No, not a fallen angel. But if he possessed an angel's blood...

He'd promised Lyssa to protect the children, but to his way of thinking, Kane and Farida would be far better off in the world if their parents were, too.

Ruth would concur.

"If you swear not to leave this tree, I will lend my aid," he told Kane. "You must stay here and protect Farida."

She was strong and tough, but she was also a young female vampire, very much at risk in this environment. This wasn't the only Trad enclave in the area.

"I don't need anyone's protection," Farida said, but when she clasped her hands together, they were visibly shaking.

Merc and Kane exchanged a look, and when Merc rose, pushing out of the tree to hover before them, Kane drew her to his side, the two of them settling in the crook of the branch. "It's all right. I'm not going to let anything happen," he told her.

Farida put her arms around him, her face against his neck. As Kane held her more tightly, her lids lifted to Merc, showing him her somber gaze.

She knew how to keep Kane out of the fight.

"Go," Kane ordered. "Please."

Merc shot away from them. He swooped into the clearing as Pallas was driving Lyssa back, trying to skewer her with showers of ice crystals. She was shielding, blocking, sending back spellwork to pull the ground from beneath his feet, calling rocks and branches to strike him, tangle him up. It would not be enough. He was pure High Fae, and her magic use, though a lot of raw power, didn't have his centuries of honing and skill.

But certain kinds of raw power could prevail against centuries of polish. Which appealed to Merc, because he could imagine how irritating the Fae would find that.

There were reasons he and Ruth got along.

Maddock was trying to hold back five, and Mason was backing him up, doing what he could. He knew some basic protection spellwork, and his strength and speed were formidable. Six were currently engaging Daegan and his blade, Gideon also doing what little he could to assist, just as Jacob was with Lyssa.

Merc went for the head of the snake, barreling toward Pallas. His theory about why Daegan seemed unaffected by certain Fae magic was about to be tested. At this speed, the protection shield Pallas was using to block Lyssa might hit Merc like a brick wall. Or...

Merc went through the shielding like a bullet through smoke. He drove the Fae off his booted feet. Before Pallas stopped rolling, Merc was on top of him, wings beating like a hawk's when landing on prey. It confused the Fae, kept him disoriented as Merc gripped his arms, pulled them back and out of their sockets, his feet snapping Pallas's spine like a twig. He yanked the Fae up, a broken doll.

He would likely heal, but Merc had immobilized him for now. He dropped him, spun and went for the group harassing Maddock, knocking them over like bowling pins. He moved so fast in their ranks, none could see him as he broke more limbs, spines and necks. The echoes of their howls followed him, but Maddock could now handle them, pressing the advantage Merc had offered him.

While the Fae magic was less effective on Daegan, it was preventing him from delivering a killing blow. So he'd adapted, choosing the tactics Merc had. When he had the opportunity, he'd cut off hands, or a leg below the knee, severing bone. The Fae were adapting too, however. Three of them combined forces, and the ground beneath Daegan's feet exploded.

The detonation catapulted him through the air, but he landed on his feet and closed back in like a freight train, with a bloody-fanged snarl.

While he didn't want to disrespect the perseverance, Merc took two of them before Daegan reached them. More cracking, breaking, dropping of bodies. One, taking advantage of his distraction with other opponents, got in a lucky fire spell, burning one wing all the way to the connecting muscle in his back, a searing pain. It hurt like hell but more importantly, it grounded him, a tactical disadvantage.

Then Gideon shocked the Fae—Merc was impressed himself—by coming out of nowhere to jump on his back and plunge his knife into his side like his arm was driven by a jackhammer. As they tumbled to the ground, the Fae twisted, wrapping a barbed wire of flame around the closest thing he could reach, Gideon's chest and right leg. In less than a blink, the human would be in pieces.

Merc yanked the Fae away from Gideon. Though only one wing was functional, the force of his pull took them a few feet in the air and then Merc fell to his back, the Fae writhing upon him. He cracked his neck when the Fae had wrapped that barbed wire around him. Though the flames fizzled out, the burn felt as deep in his flesh as Gideon's knife blade in the Fae's.

It didn't matter. The Fae was disabled.

Merc rose, ignoring the pain, the odd flap of his burned wing. Pallas's supporters littered the clearing. Some draped over Grollner's vampires in those weirdly intimate poses that Merc supposed always happened on battlefields.

Daegan knelt next to Gideon, a hand behind his head, his wrist to his mouth, giving him blood to counter the effect of the Fae's fire. Daegan probably needed some blood himself. They'd all taken hits. Lady Lyssa and Jacob would tend to one another the same way, and Jacob or Gideon would donate to Mason if needed, though the male vampire stood next to Lyssa on his own two feet.

Maddock had collapsed on a stump, his hand over an injury in his side that soaked his fingers with blood, but he was already doing an incantation to stem the blood flow and seal the wound. He would hold until they could deal with things here. Merc would get him back to Charlie for the healing he needed.

Then Merc noticed all of them were staring at him. He hadn't let on how much stronger he would be in a fight with the Fae. Or that their magic couldn't pin him down, block or hold him, even if it could burn or cause injury. But in fairness, he hadn't known that himself, until he tested it. Or the upper limits of his speed, which had made even the Fae unable to see his actions to remove Kane and Farida from their bonds.

He guessed he'd finally have to acknowledge he really was more angel than anything else. *Fuck.* While advantageous for this fight, he wasn't looking forward to admitting Marcellus was right.

However, it might give the senior angel a small smile, and he needed that, with his heart sick over his fortune teller's plight. Because of that, Merc supposed he would suffer the blow to his pride.

A thought struck him then, and he turned, trying to see, an absurd reaction, because even an angel couldn't twist his head around like an owl. He reached behind him, under the wing.

"It's still there," Lyssa said. His gaze snapped to her. "The burn has seared the design, but your flesh will heal and restore what's there. Nothing can remove a binding symbol on a servant's flesh except a removal of the three marks."

"Sometimes it doesn't even disappear if you become a vampire yourself," Jacob added. He met Lyssa's gaze and brushed a lock of hair from her bloodstained cheek.

A groan distracted them, a helpless flailing from one flaccid limb. Merc stalked over and picked up Pallas by the throat. The male was bloody, sweating, putrid. Merc had broken his body badly, but the bitch of immortality was he'd heal despite it. Pallas's eyes burned with hate.

"You are no incubus," he rasped.

"Yes, I am. But I'm something else, too." Merc's grip tightened. "You harmed my female. You took her parents from her."

What he felt wasn't just on Ruth's behalf. Elisa had given him a hug. His first platonic, affectionate, just-because hug. She'd whispered in his ear, "Take care of our girl." Like she believed he could. And would.

Pallas had no idea who he was talking about, but it didn't matter. Merc wasn't saying it for him. "I expect killing him and his supporters would cause problems with King Tabor?"

That question was directed to Lyssa, who'd come with Mason and Jacob to stand beside Merc. Daegan assisted Gideon to his feet, so they, too, could join them. "Are you getting tired of holding him up like that?" Maddock asked from the nearby stump.

"Not particularly." Merc shook the Fae like a baby rattle, and Pallas choked, blood and something more unsightly coming out of his mouth. "He's light. See?"

Lyssa looked not at all displeased with Pallas's discomfort, and her gaze had a reddish tint. The tip of a sharp fang was lengthening again.

"My lady?" Jacob spoke. "I believe Merc needs to know what you want done with him and his companions. The ones that are still alive."

She blinked, and her gaze returned to jade green. "It would go smoother if we had a sanction from King Tabor for it. Perhaps we turn them over to him and let him and Queen Rhoswen handle it."

"But this one is the leader. The one directly responsible for what happened on the island."

Merc glanced at Lyssa. She met his gaze, nodded. "Yes."

Merc returned his attention to Pallas. "It would be wise if you all stepped back," he said.

As Marcellus had taught him about being an angel, it had crossed Merc's mind, wondering if he could weave the incubus power into the angel's, in such a way that the balance the angel side protected was unaffected. A bringing together of darkness and light. Not in conflict with one another, but just the opposite.

He was happy to find out, on an entirely unwilling subject.

The two power sources met within him and circled, like snakes considering a mating dance. After a pause, they drew closer. Then closer. As they began to twine around one another, and determine how they fit, Merc laid his mental hands on them and helped. Then he took the merged power where he desired.

He moved it outside of him, up, twisting it around his arm like Medusa's serpents. Pallas felt it coming, saw it, his eyes widening. When it plunged into him, he cried out, a strangled, horrible noise. Merc didn't look away, watching with satisfaction and critical disinterest. The Fae's cheeks became sunken, his eyes more so, his lips thin and prominent.

What life energy he'd pulled forth held no appeal for him. Merc let it drift away on the wind, inert and useless. When he at last released Pallas and stepped back, the High Fae's limbs were no longer broken. He stood on his own two feet, swaying like a sapling. Upright, but subject to the whims of the breeze. His expression was vacant, his eyes empty.

"You healed his limbs," Lyssa murmured.

"I believe his own healing ability did that. It is exceptionally strong. His mind wasn't. It's gone and will not return. An example to the others while the Queen decides their fate."

He hoped Ruth approved of the compromise. "I'll help you transport them to the Fae world," he told Maddock, who seemed in a rare state of speechlessness. "And then I'm taking you to see Charlie. Or the inside of a hospital."

When Maddock pulled his gaze away from Pallas to answer, the words died on his lips. The others followed the direction of his gaze and similar expressions of astonishment or speculation gripped them.

"What is it?" Merc asked.

"I expect none of you is carrying a mirror," Maddock said dryly. He removed a compact from a pocket of his long coat, and winced as the movement pulled against his injured side. "Not for powdering my nose," he said at Gideon's smirk. "Useful for certain spell work."

He extended it to Merc, the mirror open so Merc could gaze down into it.

His eyes had changed. They were black, with a glimmering hint of silver. There were no whites left.

Like a full angel.

CHAPTER TWENTY-SEVEN

*R*uth stood, helpless and shaking, as Kaela and Garron were escorted out. When the Council followed, she moved to intercept Helga, but the Councilwoman held up a hand. "I know what you are going to say, Lady Ruth. It is regrettable, but until the law changes, it is what it is. Stay here. There's no reason for you to witness this after everything else."

"Why can't they be separated?" Ruth demanded. "Lord Brian can do that, separate a vampire and a servant. He can wipe Garron's mind, send him back to the human world."

Not that either would want that, but compared to the alternative...

"They have likely been together too long for that to be effective, Lady Ruth. But it's also not a matter of incompatibility between Mistress and servant. This is a message, and a punishment. It supports our laws. No matter how much I wish it didn't."

As Helga departed, Ruth spun toward Jessica and Anwyn. The made vampire and Mason's servant were in agreement with Ruth, their expressions torn between horror, anger and denial. For Anwyn, as owner of a BDSM club, it had an additional significance. She knew Dominant and submissive characteristics had no rules other than love itself.

Something Ruth had realized herself, when she saw her parents lying together in their kitchen.

"We have to stop this," she said. "Try to get to Lyssa through your vampires or Gideon. I'll keep doing the same with Merc."

The women nodded. But Anwyn looked between both women, the sable-haired Mistress's expression tense. "We have to go out there. We won't be able to stop them in time if we wait here for a response."

None of them wanted to be present if Ruth's plan failed, but the logic was sound. They hurried after the Council. Ruth's mind was screaming, reaching out, but Merc wasn't answering. Which meant they were in the middle of something as terrible. She'd keep trying. Hoping. Praying.

They came to a halt at the entrance to the courtyard.

Lord Belizar stood formally in the center of the watching Council members. Carola and Helga's faces held regret, but different types. Helga, that it couldn't be stopped, Carola that it had been made necessary, in her opinion, by Kaela's actions. Lords Welles, Walton and Stewart had mixed reactions. Lord Walton seemed to share some of Helga's feelings on it, though less strongly. Welles and Stewart just looked impatient to have it done so they could get back to other Council business.

Belizar's age and experience made it impossible to read his thoughts if he did not care to share them, and since Ruth could tell nothing of what he was thinking, beyond a certain tension in his shoulders, this was one of those times.

Several marked servants stood along the outdoor walkways, their expressions strained. Word had spread. Perhaps Belizar had required a handful to be present. Witnesses to the lesson.

The Council servants were here. With his rugged warrior's appearance, large size, blond hair and blue eyes, Torrence was nicknamed the Viking. Ruth knew he'd been with Helga a long time. Right now, a corpse would have had more expression than he had. Was the compulsion to appear neutral, a proper Council servant, eating him alive inside?

Glancing upward, she saw Debra, Lord Brian's servant, on one of the balconies overlooking the courtyard. Her eyes were filled with emotion, her mouth tight, hands gripping the railing. Lord Brian stood beside her. His expression was grave, and he put a hand on her shoulder.

Even if he felt as Helga did, he would not stop the execution of a sentence in accordance with Council laws.

After all, at the end of the day, it was just a human, right?

Elisa flashed through her mind. Jacob, Gideon, Jessica...all of them. Oh, fucking hell, how could she have ever thought this was okay? Fucking "acceptable."

Her shift of opinion could be a temporary state, having to do with the raw emotions of the last few hours. But she knew that was wrong. Yes, she'd been torn open to the soul, but that had finally balanced her thinking, let her see this from a perspective that had been waiting all this time. Waiting for her to open her fucking eyes.

Lord Belizar spoke to Kaela, his baritone echoing through the courtyard. "A steel stake will be placed in your hands. You will drive it into your servant's chest, ending his life. If you refuse, the honor guard will force you to do it. It will be messy and painful for him. You have brought him to this end. Make it merciful. The Council has no opinion on the quality of his demise, only that it happen now."

"No. *No*." Ruth surged forward, but Lady Helga, giving Lord Belizar an *I have this* look, swiftly covered the ground between her and Ruth and drew her back to the wall of the house. It put them under the balcony where Debra and Brian stood. Anwyn and Jessica held onto Ruth too, the sorrow in their faces showing a heartsick helplessness.

Kaela gazed in the distance over Belizar's shoulder. When he was done speaking, her lips pressed together and she gave a little nod, as if saying something to herself. She turned toward Garron.

They'd shoved him onto his knees. Two holding his shoulders, two ready to hold her. While a wooden stake took the life of a vampire, a metal one was the surest way to end a fully marked human servant. Other than killing their vampire master or mistress.

Mum...Etsi...

When Borgas offered the stake to Kaela, she stared at it. After receiving a short nod from Belizar, Borgas grasped her wrist, lifted her hand and folded her fingers around it. His companion gripped her elbow on the other side, and they moved her toward Garron.

Kaela was rigid dead weight, until the point was at Garron's chest. Then, whatever she'd come to terms with inside her head broke. She began to fight.

Silently, furiously, tears running down her face, fangs bared. She was proving just how hard to beat she could be, a twisting, kicking human mace, delivering blows with arms, legs, elbows and fists. Helga's arms remained tight around Ruth. Lord Brian had come down and was helping her, bidding Jessica to step back as the vampires tried to contain one of their own, same as they were doing in the middle of the courtyard. Debra stood with Jessica, her countenance pale.

"Let me go." She would get free of them, go help Kaela fight. Borgas and his companion grimly tried to quell the overlord's struggles as the other two continued to hold Garron. He was fighting them for a different reason, as best as he could with a broken arm and hand.

"Let her go. *Get your fucking hands off of her.*"

"This is wrong," Kaela shrieked. "He's done nothing to deserve this."

"You're not helping your case, Kaela," Lord Stewart's voice was insanely mild. No more Lady Kaela. She'd been stripped of the overlordship.

With despair, Ruth saw why he seemed unaffected by the battle. Kaela wasn't gaining the upper hand, and she was running out of strength to fight. The blood loss and psychological impact of the firing squad wall she'd been flung against were taking their toll.

Garron's gaze was on her, his expression anguished. Whatever thoughts he was hurling at her, to try to calm her, to stop making it worse on herself, she was having none of it. But then he stopped threatening the guards and went a different way.

"Stop, my lady. *Stop.*"

The command reverberated through the courtyard, as authoritative as Belizar could have done himself. Lady Carola even flinched at the bald evidence of what it said about the human male.

Kaela subsided in Borgas's hold, panting, half sobbing. Not because she agreed with the command, but because Ruth thought whatever else Garron was communicating to her in his mind, reflected in the strong emotions in his expression, made her want to hear his words.

His last words.

He looked toward the Council. "Let me go, and I will help her do it. I swear it."

Belizar met his gaze, and Ruth thought even he couldn't deny what he recognized there. A male, wanting to protect the woman he loved. With his life, if that was the price.

"Lord Belizar," Stewart began, but Belizar lifted a hand.

"Whatever will get it done."

Stewart subsided. When the two guards warily released him and stepped back, Garron's attention went to Borgas.

"Let her go," he said.

Borgas looked toward Belizar. At his slight nod, the guard's face flashed with anger, but he stepped back, letting her go with a scornful expression. "Crawl to your Master," he muttered. "You're an embarrassment."

"Borgas," Carola said sharply.

Kaela didn't seem to hear any of it, and Garron didn't acknowledge the male's insult, either. He simply extended his uninjured hand. "Come to me, my lady."

Kaela came to him, one trembling step at a time. She was still clutching the metal stake, having used it as a weapon. Borgas and the other male were bleeding from several stab wounds.

When Garron clasped Kaela's empty hand, an ease came to her features at the contact. Their fingers laced together.

"I am your Master, always," Garron said quietly. "As well as the man who loves you with a strength no one can put asunder. Ever."

"I will not live without you."

Kaela turned to the Council, her hand still in Garron's. Her shoulders swept back, her chin coming up. "You can't make me submit to the farce of reconditioning if I choose death. Garron's life is the only leverage you have over me, and you are taking that. Bring me a wooden stake. I will end my life, which will end his as well. We die together."

"No," Stewart insisted. "She might change her mind when the sentence is done. If she does not, his wait for her will not be long."

"She has stated her preference," Helga said sharply. "We should respect it."

"The Council has voted, Lady Helga," Walton said, though the tightness of his voice suggested his vote might be wavering. "Let the sentence be carried out as imposed."

"Don't do this to them."

Ruth couldn't bear to see this happen, not today of all days. Not ever. The hoarse plea in her voice didn't win more than a flicker of the other Council's attention, except for Lord Welles's order that she be removed from the courtyard.

But as they began to drag Ruth away, Kaela looked toward her, and offered a nod.

She'd run out of road, her and Garron. The sudden, agonizing peace Ruth saw told her that Stewart was right only about the last part. She was being denied the right to die with Garron, but he would not wait long for her.

Borgas took control of Kaela's grip on the stake again. He'd likely hold her fingers in a bone crushing grip, and make her shove the metal into Garron with violent enthusiasm.

But she was beyond them. Her eyes were upon Garron, and his upon hers. Ruth hoped their last exchanged thoughts shut out all of this.

Belizar was still expressionless. Like a judge awaiting the carrying out of sentence, not taking any joy in it, but not shirking his duty either. Because the rules in the vampire world protected them all. They had to be upheld.

It horrified Ruth, knowing only a few weeks ago she might have felt the same. There was a roaring in her ears as Torrence and Brian pushed her into the library. Helga blocked her escape route, but Ruth grabbed the doorframe and started screaming protests again. They would have to knock her senseless to make her stop.

Merc, please...

Belizar's lips parted. He was going to tell the guards to carry out the sentence. Garron was going to be killed, at Kaela's hands.

No, no, no...

Then the agony in Ruth's mind was invaded, the will of a vampire queen overrunning it like a stampede of kelpies.

"Hold," Ruth shrieked. "Lady Lyssa commands it."

Everything stopped, but only as a teetering-on-the-edge-of-disaster pause. They didn't believe her at first. Until Ruth repeated what Lyssa relayed through Merc's mind link.

"'You hesitated, old friend. I've not seen that happen since the battle in Paris, when you were distracted from the fight by pastry samples and French wine.'"

Belizar's eyes narrowed and he turned to face Ruth. "Tell the queen if she is going to insult me, she should do it in person. And when I have vodka in hand to cushion the blow. Where are they? Are they all right?"

Jessica's soft cry of joy gave them their answer, as Mason obviously spoke in her head. Anwyn gripped her in a tight hug while Ruth drew in a shaky breath. "They've retrieved the children successfully," Anwyn said. "They're on the way here. Everyone's all right. Minor injuries."

It was dizzying, the abrupt change in mood and direction. Lord Brian and Helga held Ruth up as exclamations and cheers passed through the courtyard, embraces exchanged.

That celebration didn't extend to Kaela and Garron. Borgas, his face suffused with frustration, had stepped back at Belizar's gesture, but the honor guard still flanked the vampire and her servant. Kaela swayed forward, Garron's one hand clasping her hip as she dipped her head over his, her hand resting on his shoulder.

It was a pause in the execution. Not a pardon.

Lady Carola confirmed it. Once things settled down, the Council-woman spoke, her gaze flicking to Ruth. "Lady Lyssa, the law is clear. If we address this now, when you return we can handle the far more important issues related to your son's kidnapping. Why command a delay?"

Another pause, as Ruth listened, digested, so she could continue the three-way relay accurately. Now that the immediate danger was past, it took effort not to get distracted by the sensual brush of Merc's voice inside her head, or lose herself to its steadying influence, the strength it provided. For the past few hours, she'd been teetering on the edge of an emotional abyss and having to hold the rope all by herself. Her hands were cramping.

"Lord Mason and I have further insights. For a matter as serious as the execution of an overlord, they should be heard. Lady Kaela, if I may have your word of honor that you will await our arrival and respect our final ruling, then you and your servant will be placed in a guestroom, together, to refresh yourselves."

Kaela straightened and turned. For a moment, she was holding Ruth's gaze, then her expression changed, reflecting the formality of addressing the queen, even if she was not physically present. Her hand remained on Garron's uninjured arm, though. They touched one another without shame, drawing strength from the contact.

Surrounded by enemies, they chose not to pretend otherwise, but her response was filled with respect. "I am ever at my lady's service. Thank you."

Ruth's attention moved to Borgas. It took effort, not to instill a *fuck-you*, middle-finger satisfaction into the next words Lyssa had her convey. Fortunately, Kaela's contemptuous gaze toward the male provided it.

"Borgas, you are dismissed. Confine yourself to your quarters until the Council can address why you dishonored your role as captain of the honor guard. Lionel, take interim command. Get Lady Kaela and Garron fresh clothing. If they are not in far better condition when next this Council sees them, you'll answer to me personally."

Borgas's eyes flashed again, but he remained silent as Lionel executed a short bow to Ruth, as Lyssa's spokesperson. "Yes, my lady."

As they were escorted out, Brian eased Ruth onto a bench in the courtyard. Helga gave her a *behave* look before she rejoined the Council, though it was accompanied by a light shoulder squeeze. Debra brought Ruth a glass of blood. "Brian says you need this," she said.

She did. But with Merc's voice in her head, she knew whose she wanted. And he agreed. Emphatically. "Thank you, but no. I'll be getting some. Soon."

Council adjourned during the wait, but reassembled in the driveway at the front of the estate when the rescue team's arrival was imminent. Jessica stood next to Anwyn, their hands clasped as the two SUVs dispatched to the portal location pulled up with their occupants.

Farida had fallen asleep in her father's arms after he'd given her blood, but as the car came to a stop, she woke. In an instant, she was in her mother's embrace. Lord Mason stepped out and straightened to his formidable height. Though his features were still tight and amber eyes glittering with the fallout from the recent threat, he acknowledged the Council's greeting before he joined his family. Jessica touched the evidence of healed injuries on him, but he spoke assur-ances and kissed her hand before holding his females close.

Anwyn came to the second vehicle, her face suffused with concern as Gideon was helped out by Daegan. "It's Fae magic inflicted. It will heal, but it'll take some time. He's not as indestructible as he thinks he is, but he's impossible to keep out of a fight."

Gideon flicked a burn on Daegan's shirt. "Wonder who else has that problem?"

Anwyn shook her head, but when she wrapped an arm around both of their necks to pull them to her, they answered in kind. Their arms overlapped one another.

Lyssa was speaking to Belizar, but she and Jacob had Kane in between them. Everyone looked as if they'd had a hellish day, but it had ended the right way.

For them, at least.

Ruth pushed aside the selfish thought, noticing Kane was hollow-eyed and quiet. His gaze strayed to Farida frequently, as if he needed to keep confirming she was all right. Farida had her father's amber eyes, but Jessica's curly, thick brown hair and slim build. Her facial features were a mix of both parents.

Ruth expected Kane would do his best to be as strong in the after-math of this as he'd want his parents to believe he was. And he *was* that strong. The details Merc had relayed to her had confirmed it. Even so, Ruth would ask Adan to visit the young vampire at the earliest opportunity. His experience with being kidnapped by the Fae, even though it had happened when he was much younger, might be useful.

God, she wished Adan was here. But she really, really, needed Merc. He'd told her he would be out of range again for a short period as he and Maddock took the Fae to Tabor's court. *After that, I need to get Maddock to Charlie.*

She wanted to act like a child, scream at him to forget all that. Which was embarrassing and pathetic, so she gave him a prompt, if strained response. *Of course. Do what's needed. I'm all right. I...if you get delayed, I'll be back at the island. Come when you can. I'm okay.*

I will be to you soon, Ruth. I will not let you face any of it alone. Even if you insist, I will ignore your wishes.

She'd sought the solitude of Lyssa's rose garden during the

adjournment. At his words, all the feeling in them—caress, reproof...a Master's care, no way she could not sense it, not with him in her soul —she wrapped her arms around herself and pressed her chin to her chest.

Okay. You're not using contractions, by the way.

A sense of laughter was followed by a stirring mental caress. One so intimate it left her wondering just how much range his incubus abilities had, let alone his mind link.

Ruth watched Belizar ruffle Kane's hair. When whatever the male vampire said coaxed a weak but genuine smile from Kane, it surprised Ruth. Jacob had excused himself to come to Ruth's side, probably to make sure she knew why Merc wasn't here. He noted her reaction.

"Belizar's just as scary as he seems," Jacob said. "But he's always had a soft spot for Kane."

"How long do you think it will be...before Merc comes?" Ruth was having trouble keeping her voice steady.

"Right about...now." Jacob gestured upward, and she spun around to see her male. Merc had changed into the black and silver battle skirt. With a spike of alarm, she noted there were practical reasons, other than the meet with the High Fae King. His landing was less graceful than normal, because one of his wings was badly scorched, clumps of feathers missing. He didn't seem bothered about it, though, which should have been reassuring, but it wasn't. The tender healing flesh on other parts of him emphasized how severe the burns had been.

Yet as soon as his feet were on the earth, his hand was out to her. She expected her vampire speed closed that distance, but she didn't remember that. Her urgency to be in his embrace simply transported her where she had to be.

I'm so afraid I'm going to fall apart, Merc. I can't fall apart. Not yet.

All right, you won't. I won't let you.

At what point had she begun to realize she could count on him? Lean on him. Trust him. It didn't matter. It only mattered that it was true. She lifted her head and met his eyes. Her brows rose. "That's new."

"Do you like it, or is it...creepy, as Clara might say?"

"She said she *expected* it to be creepy, the first time she met Marcellus. But it wasn't, and she says his eyes are as expressive as anyone

else's. A person just has to learn to read them, like a new language."
Ruth touched his cheekbone. "Something happened. You feel...
different."

"I'm the same. I've just reallocated what's there in more proper
proportions. You need blood."

"I waited for you, as you told me to do. But I shouldn't have. You
were injured."

"You should always do what I tell you to do," he said.

He'd coaxed a wan smile from her. "In your wildest dreams, that
would be true."

"Lately, some of my most unlikely ones have been within my
grasp." *And I would trade all of them to give you back what you have lost. I
know what it is taking you to stand on your own right now. You will let me
give you blood.*

She pressed her face against his chest again, and he folded both
wings over her. *Hold, my vampire. You have the strength to get through this.
Your queen needs you.*

The meaningful nudge surprised her enough to suck it all back in,
straighten and turn toward Lyssa. Sure enough, the Council head was
looking in their direction, an unspoken bidding that had Ruth
squaring her shoulders and heading that way. Merc followed close
behind.

Lyssa had her arm around Kane. Jacob had returned to them, and
his hand was steady on his son's shoulder. Belizar was speaking to the
vampire queen.

"In all fairness, I told you I was a hammer."

"Yes, you did. But I'm glad you checked its fall when I reached out
to you through Ruth and Merc's link."

"I honor my queen," the Russian said. "But you delay the
inevitable. The law is clear on this."

"Our current laws. Yes." She gave him an enigmatic look. "We
won't delay further. Have them brought back to chambers."

"My lady, you can take your ease first. Rest, have a chance to clean
up, and spend time with your son."

"This comes first. It offers an opportunity to handle another
matter, one that has waited far long enough."

As she turned Kane to face her, Ruth saw Lord Brian and Debra
approaching. "You did well," Lyssa said, her jade gaze resting on

Kane's tired face. Still so young, but the man was there, close beneath the skin. A mix of his father and mother both.

Just as she was. Kohana's words echoed in her mind.

Wherever life takes you, you'll be your father's offspring. And your mother's. You'll learn that's not just a good thing; it's the best thing you've got going for you.

"Lord Brian and Debra will take you and Farida to your quarters and examine you, determine what you need," Lyssa said. "They'll stay until our business is concluded."

"I can..."

"Yes, I know you can be by yourself. But after something like this, shadows lie in wait. Farida will do well in your company until Lord Mason and Jessica can be with her. The Council business we have to address requires the presence of the Council's servants."

Brian gave Kane a slight bow. While Ruth suspected their relationship was usually more informal, Lord Brian was reinforcing the respect that Lyssa's words had telegraphed. Kane was not being treated as a child.

Lord Mason and Jessica brought Farida into the circle, and when Kane reached out a hand to her and Farida took it, their fingers interlocked the way their gazes did.

"John will be sorry he missed all the excitement," Kane told her.

"Our majordomo's son," Jacob murmured to Ruth and Merc. "He's a few years older, but he grew up with Kane. He's at college."

"It's the only reason I'm glad they had a spell to block our minds." Farida squelched the faint tremor in her voice, squaring her shoulders and tossing back her hair. It was as if she was defying anyone, even herself, to treat her like a victim. "John would have lost his mind, knowing we were in trouble, and he wasn't close enough to help."

"He'll make up for it on the back end. Telling us all the smart things we should have done." But then Kane's gaze moved from her to Ruth and stilled. He had peculiar eyes, one green, one blue, the colors shifting with the light. Maybe the two teens had a blood link, because half a heartbeat later, Farida turned toward her as well.

"Your father and mother..." Kane stopped. She saw then he'd thought he'd had the strength to do this, but the words tore something loose inside of him. Suddenly he was swaying on his feet, anguish overwhelming him.

She knew how he felt. She wanted to reach out, to help, but she felt frozen. However, Farida moved under Kane's arm, her hand on his chest, as Jacob steadied the other side.

"It's all right, son," he said quietly. "Maybe later."

When Kane's agonized look met hers, Ruth nodded. "Later's... better. It's okay."

It's not okay, her heart screamed. Merc's grip around her tightened.

Mason shifted into Kane's view, his fingers brushing his daughter's neck. "It will be addressed, Kane. I promise. Trust me."

When Mason looked Ruth's way, the sharpness in his eyes, charged with a grim intent, made Ruth suddenly need Merc's steadying hands on her all the more.

Either from the magic reaching its expiration point, or the breaking of their enemies, Mason had recalled all he'd seen at the sanctuary.

~

As the teenagers were shepherded away by Brian and Debra, the concerned parents watched them go. Jessica stood between Mason and Jacob now, and Jacob touched Jessica's shoulder as Mason held her waist. She gripped both of their hands, but when her gaze met Jacob's, Ruth saw an expression she knew well. The two of them were ready to serve their Master and Mistress, whatever was required.

Whatever reason Lyssa had for doing this now was apparently pretty damn important.

"Good timing," Jacob murmured, drawing Ruth's attention to another SUV pulling up the drive. When it parked, the one absent member of Council emerged.

Lady Danny.

The female vampire was teased by her peers about looking like a 1950s Disney princess, with her blue eyes, blond hair and slim bearing, but those who assumed she'd won a Council position from her friendship with Lady Lyssa didn't pay attention to her history. Like Kaela, she'd fought her way to a Region Master position in Australia, capably managing a diverse and volatile vampire population in her territory until her promotion to Council.

Dev, her servant, was a World War II veteran and had been an itinerant bushman before he'd found his home with her. Like Jacob and most servants who served higher ranking vampires, he was no one to underestimate, either in wits or fighting skills. He shook Jacob's hand as he emerged from the car and held the door for his lady.

Lady Danny offered Lyssa and the other Council members a respectful nod, but the person she went to was Ruth. She took in Ruth's state at a glance. "Your mother told me she thought you had found a worthy male," she said unexpectedly, a tight smile crossing her lips as she glanced at Merc. "Though her father was less willing to admit it, you made a good impression."

Merc's dark gaze flickered. "I'm honored to hear it."

Ruth swallowed. "When did she..."

"She always called me when anything important happened with you or Adan. So a few hours...before."

When Elisa had come to the island in the 1950s, bringing six forcibly turned vampire children to Mal for help, she'd been Danny's second mark on her sheep station in Australia. Which meant Danny might have felt her death as soon as the Fae's magical field was lifted, even before she learned the details from whoever called to give them to her.

Danny put her arms around Ruth and spoke against her ear. "None of us can break right now, and I'm risking it by saying this, but Mal will never let her be anywhere he's not. They're together, Ruth. Always."

"I want Adan here." Ruth spoke against Danny's curtain of blond hair. Dev's strong hand was rubbing her back, offering the same comfort his Mistress was. "But I also don't want him to know yet. I don't ever want him to know, so he doesn't have to hurt like this."

"I know. We'll get through it."

The Council had moved away, heading toward chambers. While it gave them privacy, it was more than that. Business was waiting. Kaela and Garron's fate hung in the balance. Ruth drew back. "I know you have to go. Dev, too. Lyssa wants Council servants there."

"She let me know." Whatever was afoot, there was knowledge of it in Danny's gaze, and in the tense look she and Dev exchanged. The outcome of whatever was planned wasn't certain. Or maybe it was.

Belizar had said as much. The law was the law. The only latitude Ruth could see the Council head having was to put the force of her will behind Kaela's right to take her life with dignity, and leave this life with her servant.

"Ruth?"

Lyssa had paused at the door.

"Yes, my lady?"

"Follow us to chambers. You and Merc."

Her heart quaked at the prospect of seeing the nightmare with Kaela and Garron start all over again. But if Ruth had another chance to speak on Kaela and Garron's behalf, to contribute to them having that one choice, to die together, she wouldn't shirk from it. Even as everything within her wanted to be elsewhere.

I can't watch them die. I can't.

As Danny and Dev headed toward the door, Merc turned Ruth toward him. *I'll spirit them away before they carry out the sentence. They'll never find them.*

The resoluteness in his harsh features told her he would do it. It gave her a whole new flood of feelings to manage, far more welcome. *I thought angels weren't supposed to interfere.*

Still not a hundred percent angel, he told her firmly. *Plus, I already interfered today. I believe in setting new trends.*

She closed her eyes, shook her head. *I know there's a lot of emotional shit happening today.* Her heart and knees trembled with that surfeit, but she used the words and her hold on him, and his on her, to send him the next thought. *But I'm pretty sure I'm in love with you.*

Good. If you weren't, I would be very annoyed with you.

～

"Though Council has voted, the matter of Lady Kaela and her servant Garron is being called back for discussion. Please have them brought before Council."

Lyssa stood at the center chair. The Council members filled the seats on either side of her at the crescent-shaped table, their servants along the wall across from them. Ruth sat in the same chair she'd occupied before, only now Merc stood behind her, his knuckles against the back of her shoulder where his hand gripped the top of the chair.

They weren't the only non-Council members here. Daegan, Anwyn and Gideon were present, as were Lord Brian and Debra, standing a few paces away from her and Merc. Lord Brian gave Ruth a kind but assessing look, making sure she was all right. A reminder that he was a doctor as well as a scientist.

Kaela and Garron were escorted back in. Escorted, not dragged. Though Garron still favored his damaged arm and hand, the breaks were healing, and his wounds were gone, thanks to the nourishment his Mistress had given him. He'd also fed her, because Kaela was no longer pale and she decidedly did not look weak.

The overlord wore ivory-colored slacks and a blue silk blouse, her red hair in an artful twist on her head, business attire for a business meeting. She was composed, though her dignified carriage and expressionless face likely held a wealth of emotions. Garron was in a white dress shirt and black jeans, his face warrior hard, equally impossible to read. Except to his Mistress.

The next person to speak surprised everyone. It drew all eyes toward Ruth.

Because it was Merc.

"I would say something, if it is allowed."

"After what I observed in the Trad compound, I fail to see how I could stop you if it wasn't," Lyssa said dryly. "But since a great debt is owed to you, my lord, the least we can do is allow you to address our Council."

Ruth felt the hitch in Merc's mind at the 'my lord,' from the Council queen. He hadn't expected that. But he let it stand and pressed forward. "When I joined you to retrieve your offspring, I said it was not my angel blood that mattered today. It was what Ruth needed."

His gaze moved briefly to the servants, coming back to Ruth. "From this point forward, it will always be what Ruth needs. I'm her marked servant. I'm also her Master, her protector, the male bound to her in every way. That is what she desires."

He wouldn't state it more blatantly, not without her being on board with it, but she was okay with the closer step to the truth. Hell, with the way she was feeling today, she was ready to wear it on a T-shirt.

I'm a submissive female vampire. If you have a problem with that, go fuck yourself. I'll live or die as who I am.

Merc stroked the sensitive pocket of her collar bone, helping Ruth to settle as he continued. "All the strengths and abilities I have will go toward that. What I have left over can serve angel kind, if that is acceptable to them. If it is not..." his gaze sharpened, "then they will have to deal with it. Thank you. That is all."

Lady Carola pursed her lips. "However we might feel about this pairing, or the reasons behind it, he is more powerful than her. And not of our race. This..."

She looked toward Kaela and Garron with obvious displeasure. "He is human. Weaker. If she subjects herself to his rule on vampire matters..."

"Has there been verifiable evidence presented on that?" Lady Lyssa interjected. "An overlord's actions speak for themselves. When the excesses and failures become too obvious, it is hard to disguise, as her predecessor proved. Most of you felt the disgruntled vampire in her territory had no real proof, and that Lady Kaela has been an exceptional overlord. Correct?"

"It doesn't change the possibility of influence," Carola said. "There is no precedent for this kind of...relationship, and there is a very good reason for that."

"My lords and ladies, may I speak?" Lady Kaela asked.

At Lyssa's questioning brow, Carola shrugged and sat back. "I am done. For the moment."

Lyssa nodded. "You have the floor, Lady Kaela."

"With respect, she's no longer an overlord," Lord Stewart said. "The title was stripped with the ruling.

Lyssa sent Stewart a flat look. "Lady Kaela earned the title. It is my personal decision to continue to respect it."

Lord Stewart's face tightened, but he inclined his head, ceding the point.

"Garron is requesting permission to address you," Kaela said. "I would ask your forbearance in allowing it."

"The question is why would *you* allow it," Carola said sharply. "This is a prime example..."

"A condemned prisoner of the worst sort is allowed last words on the gallows," Lord Walton said unexpectedly. "It is almost inevitable that this day will end with the man's death. I have dealt with Garron many times, and he has always acted appropriately and with courtesy. Give him his two minutes."

Ruth noted various levels of agreement or annoyance on the Council. Belizar's bushy eyebrows drew down when he gave Garron a black stare, but unexpectedly, he nodded. "I do not disagree."

"As head of Council, it's entirely up to me whether or not to allow him to speak, but the input is appreciated." Lyssa arched a brow at Belizar and Walton, but the expression held no rancor. Just the reminder, which they acknowledged, Belizar with a wry twist of his lips.

Lyssa's gaze returned to Kaela and Garron. "You may speak, Garron. Do not abuse the privilege."

"No, my lady." Garron moved to Lady Kaela's side, giving her a look before he bowed to the Council, then straightened.

"From the time Lady Kaela and I met, I sensed two things about her. First, that she was strong and passionate about protecting those in her territory, ruling them fairly with an understanding of what vampires are and are not. And that she was lonely and unhappy, because she craved a certain type of submission. When we met, it was becoming unsustainable to her."

Several Council members shifted uncomfortably at the blatant declaration, but Kaela's face revealed nothing. "She found someone who could serve her the way I do, in both roles, Master and servant," Garron continued. "I'm using the word *serve* deliberately and truthfully."

He looked at Lyssa. "My lady, you know the difference in your own servant, and many vampires choose sexual Dominants for that role, but such servants are never submissive. They serve, because a Dominant *can* serve. Because being the right kind of Dominant is about protecting and caring for his submissive, giving her whatever she needs to be who she is, who she's meant to be."

He looked toward Merc, an acknowledgement of the angel incubus's similar declaration, before returning his attention to Council. "She's a better overlord for finding this sense of completion, this sense that she's not alone in the world. At first, it was difficult. Because of her nature, she felt she was asking me for something she shouldn't. We got past that hurdle, because at a certain point she trusted me enough to believe me.

"She understood that my definition of being a Master was much wider and deeper than she'd realized it could be. It's limited by nothing but the two of us, what we each want and need, and how those wants and needs mesh."

Ruth lifted her hand to cover Merc's. His fingers overlapped hers, tightened.

Garron bowed to Council, then met Kaela's gaze and dropped to one knee before her. He kissed her hand, curled at her side. When her fingers grazed his shaved scalp, he rose and stepped back, into his original position behind her left shoulder.

Guarding her heart, Ruth thought.

"I understand this Council has to weigh what will adversely impact our small population," Kaela said. "And you believe the type of relationship I have with Garron is one of those. You've confirmed your regard for my leadership, and that acknowledgment is appreciated. Please let me finish that service effectively. Give me two weeks to bring my replacement up to speed on matters in my territory, for a seamless transition."

Her attention moved to Daegan. He stood against the wall, just to the right of and behind Lyssa. Gideon and Anwyn were on the opposite wall, aligned with the other servants. Though Kaela's voice faltered at first, she steadied it as she spoke. "Once that's done, send your enforcer. I will not fight or try to evade your sentence. I trust Lord Daegan to handle it efficiently and painlessly. I only ask that it be done with my servant by my side."

Ruth could only imagine what was going on between her and Garron's minds, but unlike before, the calm between them seemed unshakable. In the privacy of that guest room, they'd made their peace with it. Their bond would not be severed by death.

If it could be, love wasn't what Ruth thought it was. Her mind returned to her parents. *I only ask that it be done with my servant by my side.*

Lady Kaela was done. "If we can call the question to a vote..." Lord Stewart started.

Lord Mason rose. "I would like to add some thoughts."

Stewart subsided with a mild look of impatience.

"Proceed, Lord Mason." Lyssa settled back, crossing her legs. She frowned at a blood spot on the cargo pants she was wearing, but then rested her manicured hand on it and gave him her full attention.

Lord Mason turned toward Ruth. "Please pass these words on to your brother when he returns, and must face this terrible loss."

As she understood what was coming, a convulsive jerk went through Ruth's muscles and joints. Merc's unburned wing curved over her shoulder.

"They had immobilized me with their spellwork and already taken Kane, who was out in the yard." Mason held her gaze as he brusquely painted the harsh picture. "Farida was in the lower chambers. The Fae had cloaked their identity, so we could not tell their race."

Mason glanced toward Jessica, whose face was suffused with sadness, reading from his mind what he was saying to the room. She'd adjusted from the wall so she, too, was facing Ruth, as if the two of them together offered the testimonial. And gratitude.

"They told Mal if he would step aside, they would leave him alive. Your father's face had the resoluteness of a hundred armies. Yet there was a calm there, too, as if he drew on the wisdom of creation itself, of the cycles of life and death, and all the paths we walk."

Mason's tiger gaze flashed. "No stronger vampire, no High Fae, could have fought more nobly, more fiercely, to protect my child, than your father did. And your mother was a credit to all servants."

Tears were on Ruth's face, and a tiny noise caught in her throat. She'd risen from her chair and moved forward a pace, feeling as if she needed to be standing. Heedless of their audience, Merc moved with her. He stood behind her, his arms crossed over her chest. The chamber was silent, everyone listening.

"I saw Mal look toward Elisa, before the battle was engaged," Mason continued. "There was a great deal I recognized in that look, as well as things that were treasured feelings, unique to the two of them. They made the decision together. They knew what the cost of the fight would be. The outcome. I saw it."

His gaze moved to the Council and held a beat. "It should have been over in an instant, and yet it wasn't. Though his magical ability was nowhere equal to theirs, never have I seen such an inequal struggle result in such a prolonged fight. His staff fought with him, in the ways that would help the most. Distracting, getting in the way, disrupting. Which meant they knowingly sacrificed themselves."

His face tightened. "Mal used everything he had against the Fae— hand-to-hand combat, magical weaponry and his sharp intelligence— to keep it going as long as he could. Perhaps in the hope that some attempt he'd made to get out a distress call would be answered, though the shielding prevented that."

The active warriors in the room—Daegan, Gideon, Jacob—were tense, as if they could envision the fight, imagine the impossible tactics Mal had used.

"They had wooden stakes, but decapitation ended up being the quickest and safest way...for them. It was an acknowledgement of just how unexpectedly effective his resistance was. Your mother..."

The savage smile on Mason's face made Ruth suck in a startled, pained breath. "She stood in front of the stairs to the rooms below. She watched the fight, her body quivering as if she were feeling each blow. I know she was his sight and ears on every blind front, letting him know what was coming, who was attacking. She was fighting with him, in the best way a servant like her could."

Mason's expression darkened. "When the blade ended him, she grabbed onto the doorway and cried out. She had only moments left, but her gaze speared her enemies. Even though they were cloaked from her view, she showed them the truth of their darkness. Though I didn't know who it was at the time, Pallas ordered another to dispatch her. I think he didn't care to wait for Mal's death to turn that condemning stare away from his soul."

Mason's attention on Ruth was a weighted touch. Though every word was a wound, it was something else, too. "The Fae who approached her saw a human woman who barely reached his chin, one dying before his eyes. He should have known better. She had Mal's knife, that long one he was so fond of. It was hidden in her skirts."

Ruth's hands closed into fists. Her gentle mother who called her *a chuisle mo chroí,* when Ruth needed to hear it most. Heart's beloved, or literally, pulse of my heart. Her gentle, passionate mother.

"She gutted him, twisting the blade and shoving it upward, into his chest." Mason's gaze flashed. "She held onto his shoulder, practically climbing him as she did it."

"Hellfire," someone murmured. Ruth thought it was Gideon.

Mason shook his head. "She knew, as Mal did, that they couldn't keep them from my daughter. But they would not allow it to happen while they had life to stop it."

Ruth saw tears on Danny's face. "She was one of the most remarkable females I've ever met," the blonde said. "In the most unlikely of packages."

"Yes," Mason said. "Another Fae plucked her off the wounded one and tossed her away from him. She landed near the kitchen. I expect that was how she was able to reach Mal before the ending of his life took hers. I did not see that part. They took me away then."

The chamber was silent. Then a chair whispered across the carpeted floor. Belizar rose. Then Walton. And Helga. One by one, they each rose and faced Ruth, Lyssa joining them. They bowed in her direction. So did their servants. Gideon's resolute expression was as clear as spoken words.

That's your inheritance. Nothing will ever break you.

When Lady Kaela and Garron bowed to her, too, a sob escaped Ruth's raw throat.

"Your father and mother have our thanks and eternal regard." Lady Lyssa's voice was thick with emotion. "Their island and their children will be protected and given all the consideration that a fallen hero... and heroine's...should."

Ruth blinked back tears. "Thank you, my lady."

It was all she could manage, but it was all that was needed.

When they took their seats, Merc drawing Ruth back to her own, Mason remained standing. "I expect Lady Carola is wondering how my words connect to Lady Kaela and Garron, but her respect for the moment is keeping her from pointing it out."

Carola's lips twitched, and she made a dismissive gesture, but she wasn't disagreeing. Lord Mason nodded.

"Mal was not our strongest. With his cat sanctuary, he forged a different path than most vampires. Yet can anyone here say he didn't honor the best parts of our race?"

His attention locked on Carola, Stewart and Belizar. "What preserves us as a race? What works against that? What traditions should we allow to die, which should we uphold? Which do we modify to allow more room for growth? Will that turn on us and achieve the opposite? These are difficult questions."

He paused. "Even Lady Kaela submits to your judgment, your

wisdom, understanding the preservation of the race rests in your hands, and she must trust that your wisdom could be greater than her own, because its scope has to be wider than one person's view."

His gaze touched on the California overlord, and Kaela gave him a stiff nod, acknowledging it. "Any governing body given that kind of faith should do their damnedest to honor it," Mason said. "They should question every choice they make, and be sure they have invited in dissenting viewpoints to challenge it."

Carola's lips tightened, but she said nothing, allowing Mason to continue. "I am no different," he said. "Because of today's events, what sticks with me is Mal and Elisa. Who they are, what they sacrificed. Who they chose to be. Mal protected predators who needed help, rather than letting nature take its course on the strong who can no longer defend themselves. He helped them become self-sufficient again where possible, but provided them sanctuary so they could live the best lives available to them when they could not.

"He let his judgment, his practicality, his human *and* vampire sides, help him with those decisions. But in the end, I think he did what all enlightened beings do—he let his soul be his guide. And his heart. Elisa was his heart."

His expression didn't soften. "I have no doubt how much he loved Elisa. She was his servant. He held full command over her, and she was an obedient, loving and submissive soul. She was his soulmate, but he was that to her, too. As I very much believe the optimal vampire and servant relationship should be.

"All these things, accepting more intimate vampire-servant relationships, bonds with other races, it may weaken our species. Or it may strengthen them, after we get through the growing pains. Approved made vampires have to learn to control bloodlust. No one says they should not have been made, at least not during that difficult and dangerous time. The wrong kind of change can destroy a race, the wrong kind of adapting."

His gaze moved around the room, touching on vampires, servants and all. "But the ability to love freely, as oneself? Denying that ability will kill a soul, and if you kill enough souls, you kill the race."

His attention returned to Jessica, held, then came back to Council. "In that last moment, Mal and Elisa decided, as equals, to give their lives to protect a child. To protect the future of our race. So for today, in this moment, I take it as a sign. Let us allow Lady Kaela and Garron to be an opportunity for growth in our race, and see where it leads. Reverse this sentence, which I believe is reactive rather than weighing all the relevant variables."

He paused. "Let us take three moments of silence, not just to honor Mal and his servant, but to contemplate this matter."

There was a shifting throughout the chamber, but the Council members nodded. Some of those in the chamber bowed their heads. Others closed their eyes or gazed meditatively in space. Ruth logged every reaction, holding onto them. She would tell and show all of it to Adan.

As the three minutes were drawing to an end, tapping feet approached the door. At Lyssa's nod, Lionel opened it, and a male Inherited Servant entered. He had sleek dark hair, queued back, a hooked nose, sensual lips and brown eyes. His features were almost obscured by the scrolls he carried, tied with ribbons. He also had a quill and inkwell.

Did we just go back in time? Merc asked.

Ruth shook her head, just as baffled.

"Take a seat behind me, Emrey." Lyssa motioned to the InhServ, then directed her words to the curious Council. "It has been correctly stated that, according to our law, a vampire cannot be submissive to a human servant. But we have a set of directives pending that could change that."

"Lady Lyssa, this was not on the agenda," Lord Stewart said. Lady Carola nodded emphatically, her mouth tight. Lord Belizar's expression had moved to disapproval.

"I'm within my rights to add it. Can anyone claim it hasn't had sufficient time for discussion and revision?"

Some more shifts, a little grumbling, but shrugs showed reluctant agreement with her point.

Emrey unrolled one of the scrolls. Apparently, despite the technological age, the Council still put down new laws, or pending ones, in the same manner as they were done hundreds of years ago. Ruth couldn't deny the sight of the parchment, the careful calligraphy on it, made the proceeding seem more formal. And momentous.

"For years," Lyssa said, "this document has been revised, added to, subtracted from. We've received input from overlords and

Region Masters. In more enlightened moments—like when Lords Belizar, Stewart and Lady Carola have been in more benevolent moods—we've gathered feedback from our more highly placed servants."

Her gaze glinted with some humor. Not much, but what could be managed under the circumstances. "I move that it be read aloud, and the vote called. It is time."

"Yes," Carola said. "I second. It *is* well past time."

Her tone said her vote would not agree with Lyssa's, but the queen didn't show annoyance at the reaction. She merely nodded at Emrey to proceed. The scribe moved in front of the table. Since Kaela and Garron's matter was still pending, they were not invited to move from their position, so he adjusted himself a step to the right, the most direct line of sight available to the Council head.

Kaela had fixed her gaze on Emrey. It was an intense look, one that made him shift a little uneasily. However, he cleared his throat and began, with a strong tenor appropriate to his role. As he read the words, they filled all corners of the chamber, echoing in the rafters above. The gurgling fountain didn't distract from it.

"Servants will have an elected body of seven to represent their interests to the Council...

"Servants desiring separation from their vampire will have the right to petition this committee for that act.

If a vampire desires separation, the servant will not be terminated, unless Council approves it as necessary to protect the race..."

Ruth wondered if Carola, Stewart and Belizar, as well as the other Council members not fully on board with the document, were noting what she did.

Jacob's gaze was locked upon his lady. Lyssa's attention toward him gave that connection enough weight to make it vibrate in the air between them. Jessica's eyes were likewise on her vampire master, her expression reminding Ruth of her history, the horror of her beginnings in the vampire world. How Mason had brought her to love and trust in a Master again.

Even the servants with more traditional connections to their Masters and Mistresses seemed affected. An energy was filling the room. Wonder, uncertainty, hushed anticipation. To many of the vampire and servant relationships here, as well as the servants individually, the words had unique meanings, related to experiences, challenges, intense pain or intimate triumphs,

Aided by the momentous events of these past few hours, the vampires present were stepping into the tide of change. Maybe Lyssa was right, that the timing was right to see who was willing to accept its flow, open themselves to its wisdom in ways they never had been before. Great loss, near loss, it could have that effect. She stood as witness, not just for herself, but for her mother, and her father.

A vampire of any rank has the right to choose whether or not their servant participates in the demands of a social gathering...

She thought of her father's tension about such events, her mother's quiet acceptance. Yes, Elisa had learned she could make it work, find pleasure in serving her Master in such ways, do whatever was required of her. But she and Adan had also recognized, even if they never spoke of it, that Mal worked to keep Elisa's mind on him and his desires, so they could both stand away from the truth.

Many vampires and servants might enjoy it, but Mal had fucking hated those events, even before he had Elisa. And after...sharing her with others was something he never would have voluntarily chosen to do.

The shape of the relationship between vampire and servant is private and not subject to Council rule, as long as there is no proven conflict with his or her loyalty to the preservation of the race, as defined by Council...

The quiver that went through Kaela was strong enough she swayed. Garron didn't move, but when the shudder left her, her body was pressed back against the strength of his, his mouth near the strands of her hair at her temple.

A born vampire's human parent will not be separated from the child unless extraordinary circumstances proving the need are presented to Council. This request can only be submitted by the vampire parent. It cannot be imposed by Council mandate...

A human parent will be honored as such, not merely as the servant of the vampire parent...

Ruth thought of when she and Adan had been told not to call Elisa *Etsi* or *Mum* in front of vampire visitors, because they were supposed to be "old enough" to view her as Mal's servant, not their mother.

All those years Mal and Elisa had to pretend not to be what they were to each other and to their children, in the presence of other vampires, or at those gatherings.

Would the rules radically change things? She heard in the language nuances that might keep many things the same. Enforcement retained plenty of discretion.

Ruth also recalled Elisa's response, that it made no difference. She would be what Mal needed, because she was in his heart and soul. He was her Master, and she loved him. But he loved her, too.

The rules weren't for the Mals and Elisas. They were for those who didn't find their way to that deep bond. They were to protect them from mistakes, from cruelty. The document's most important purpose was acknowledging the servant's right to *have* that protection.

It would also give those like Kaela and Garron, Ruth and Merc, Adan and Catriona, and all vampires and servants, the room to explore what their relationship could be, how it could serve the vampire world as much as themselves, rather than assuming it couldn't.

Making room for change and growth, as Lady Lyssa said. Setting that path down into law was a vital beginning.

The absurdity isn't acknowledging the love between vampire and third marked servant. The absurdity is denying it's always been there, for many of us who have been fortunate enough to discover just how deep and strong that bond can become. I would argue that in most cases, such a bond strengthens the vampire in ways that help protect our race, not weaken it.

Lady Danny had said that, during a late evening fireside chat with her father. Elisa had been brushing Danny's hair, Dev sitting on the hearth, watching firelight glint off his lady's blond locks. The look they shared...there'd been no disagreement in the room that night. Only relief to be among those who understood it.

Ruth had been in her early teens, half asleep with her head on her father's thigh, his hand resting on her hip. She looked toward Danny now. When the female vampire's gaze shifted to Ruth, they were both remembering Elisa. Thinking about how she would have felt about this.

Emrey was done. He rolled up the scroll and stood at attention, waiting for the Council's next direction. Lyssa glanced left and right. "Any final changes? It's been through...how many revisions?"

She glanced at Emrey.

"Two hundred and three, my lady."

"Two hundred and three," she repeated. "For the love of God and Goddess, let's stop flogging this and make a decision. A two thirds majority to pass, as agreed for a change in our laws."

"Agreed," Lord Walton said, and the others nodded.

"If passed," Mason noted, "the language should apply to the matter of Lady Kaela and Garron. To do otherwise would seem more like a vendetta than sound wisdom."

"Alternatively, it is not law until it is passed. So flouting our law is behavior that shouldn't be encouraged. Even if the law is later changed."

"I don't disagree with that," Lord Walton said. "But in light of recent events..." He looked toward Ruth, then Lyssa and Mason. "We have had terrible loss and hard-won victories today, Carola. And nothing about Lady Kaela's behavior suggests she is flouting anything. She kept this matter behind closed doors, between her and her servant, until a member of her own territory saw an opportunity to betray her."

"It is a moot point." Lord Stewart shook his head. "I do not believe it will pass."

"Not to fly in the face of Lord Stewart's conviction, but I vote to approve. Each member indicate yea or nay when called upon." Lyssa glanced to her left. "I will start with you, Lord Belizar."

Belizar drummed thick fingers on the table. His brows were drawn down again, his expression even more forbidding than Ruth suspected was the norm. With his words, however, she realized it was an expression of deep thought, not aggression.

"As everyone knows, I have opposed this document since its inception. Change in our world must be undertaken with great caution. My relationships with my servants do not go outside of traditional boundaries, as I feel is appropriate. My servant is content with that, and I treat him well. With the respect his service deserves."

Vincent, the servant in question, bowed his head in respect to his Master. He was a thin male with steady, sharp gray eyes. Ruth didn't sense disagreement from him about Belizar's assessment.

"Exactly," Lady Carola said. "Wilhelm serves his Mistress as tradition demands, and it is an honor to him."

She received a similar acknowledgement from the handsome blond male standing next to Belizar's servant, but Ruth thought she detected a trace of yearning in his gaze. As if he wished Carola was willing to be more to him. But then it was gone.

"However," Belizar noted, "We have seen matters over these past couple decades that suggest that is not the case for all."

His gaze moved to Jessica, startling Lord Mason's servant, but she straightened under his regard. Lord Mason's attention sharpened on Belizar.

"When I first learned of your treatment under your first master, I was indifferent to it," Belizar said to her. "Until I learned more details. I have seen how you support Lord Mason, with a devotion and intelligence that is a credit to any servant. Your choice was taken from you, but when it was given back, you became everything we desire in a servant. You would have been a good InhServ, Jessica."

"Thank you, my lord. I'm glad to belong to my lord Mason."

"Yes." Belizar glanced at the male in question, noting Mason's narrowed eyes. "Stand down, Lord Mason. I'm paying her a compliment. And you," he acknowledged. His attention returned to Lyssa. "I do not know if I support this document, but I have taken a lot on faith under your leadership, my lady. I have not yet been unacceptably disappointed."

Lyssa's lips twitched. "I will strive to keep meeting those high expectations."

"I suppose you will." Belizar turned to the others. "Walton and Welles, while you are still on the fence, I believe your thinking on it has been altering along the lines of mine. Helga, I know where your mind and vote rests. You made it amply clear earlier."

His gaze shifted from the blond vampire to the tight-lipped Carola and hard-faced Stewart. "You will vote your preference, but we have aligned on many things in the past, and you know my head on these things. I suggest we give it a chance. This Council is an intelligent body, and it feels like time to trust this direction. I vote Yea."

For a full second, not just the Council members, but their servants, were gripped in an obvious shock. Ruth caught a look between Gideon and Jacob that was the equivalent of *holy fuck*. Followed by a mental fist pump.

Garron's hand was on Kaela's shoulder, and her hand flew up to it, their fingers lacing together.

The servant policy passed, 7-2.

CHAPTER TWENTY-EIGHT

*M*erc watched Adan crest the hill. He'd come through the mountain preserve portal a few moments before. An hour ago, he'd spoken in Ruth's head, letting her know he was back from wherever he and Derek had been. Catriona had told him what had happened. His voice had been rough, as he told his sister he was on his way.

I'll walk from the portal. I'll meet you at the house.

Ruth had respected and understood, though as she stood next to Merc on the porch, emotions battered her like an ocean against a lighthouse. These past several days, she'd proven her resilience, again and again. She'd set the house to rights with the staff, ordered replacement glass, even flown her plane for a supply run to the mainland and met with William and Matthew, giving her oath formally to Lord Marshall. As an adult vampire, she'd given it to him some time ago, but due to the circumstances, she'd wanted to reinforce it.

Lord Marshall had told her whatever she needed, she need only ask. William and Matthew had offered to come help with the house and sanctuary. So had Nerida and Miah, whom she'd spoken to on the phone. For now, Ruth had said she and the staff had it covered, but she'd keep them informed about the memorial service that would happen, once Adan returned.

The chores associated with loss were never ending. There were loose ends to tie up, things that had to keep being done. Arrangements for whatever death rituals would be observed. Merc knew it helped Ruth keep the worst of the feelings at bay. If she was moving, staying just ahead of them, she felt she could let them inside her in manageable portions. She'd grabbed that to-do list with both hands. She alternated between stoic numbness and manic activity.

He'd let her follow that strategy, watchful for the moments when it escaped her grasp.

As they crested the hill, Catriona was at Adan's side. Adan stopped, giving his Fae a brief but intense embrace, and left the road to detour toward the field of purple wildflowers. After looking after him for a long moment, Catriona continued toward the house.

Ruth's waves of emotion tripled. Merc had his hand on her shoulder. The staff were drawing comfort from one another, but his vampire had learned to handle so many emotions without sharing them, that wasn't comfortable for her. So those few times she'd lost her hold, she'd gone off on her own to deal with them.

He'd told her he wouldn't respect her wishes on that, and he stuck to that promise. He'd follow, and hold her as she wept and shook in his arms, so hard he was afraid her bones would shatter inside her frame, her muscles tear. It made him wonder how Marcellus had been able to bear it, when those seizures had gripped Clara. It was the worst thing Merc had ever experienced, even worse than his childhood.

He did what he knew Ruth needed. He wrapped her up in arms and wings, his support and yes...love, which he was learning was a painful, wrenching and wondrous thing, but the pain of it didn't matter. What mattered was her. He kept her together as she absorbed the shocking loss in the increments she could manage.

Adan's expression was a wall. The siblings weren't that different. He was doing what Ruth had done, when they'd dealt with the kidnapping and then the Council meeting. He'd contain it until there was no one else that needed his care. He'd contain it until he was sure Ruth was okay.

Ruth left the porch and headed for the field.

Catriona had flown toward the house, her brown, green and golden wings catching the illumination from the pole lights around the outside of the house. Her wings weren't designed for altitude as much as to speed her way, so her toes just cleared the road. As she passed Ruth, she circled her, touched her hair and shoulder. Not impeding her forward progress, but offering the brief comfort before she continued. She landed on the steps, the butterfly-like texture of her wings brushing against Merc's arm. He tightened his wings behind him to give her room to stand at his side.

They said nothing as they watched, but Merc felt Catriona's love and pain for her Master. When Ruth reached the field and they were fifty feet apart, Adan's stride faltered, and he stumbled.

The dam had broken.

In a flash, Ruth had closed the distance and had her arms around him, the two of them kneeling in the field together. As Adan buried terrible moans of grief against her breast, she held him with arms so much stronger than they looked.

"He could not bear Derek or anyone to speak of it." Catriona's voice trembled. "He could not bear a comforting touch."

"He had to come here first. To be with his twin. To accept it is real."

They would help each other, and that too, would help them withstand the onslaught of heartache.

"Yes." Catriona laid a hand on Merc's arm. Simple solidarity. Merc looked down into her gray-green eyes. "We will be everything they need us to be," she said.

A comfort, reassurance and mandate, for them both. He saw the steel in her, this seemingly delicate Fae with her pointed ears and a willow leaf tattoo inked along her temples. He thought of Mason's description of Elisa, and his knowledge of Ruth herself. Warrior-like, even when the body was far more fragile than the will.

During the battle with the Trad and Fae, Merc would not forget how savagely the combatants on their side had fought, not just for vampires...but for family.

Pallas's followers were answering to Rhoswen and Tabor for their presumption. But those were matters for others. Ruth was his priority.

Merc put his hand over Catriona's and saw her surprise at the strength and reassurance he put in the gesture, dialing back the disturbing incubus energy so it couldn't interfere with his message. "Yes. We will."

As Ruth held Adan, he held her, too. Her brother, comforting her as she comforted him. They rocked together on the ground, the purple flowers nodding around them in the quiet wind, the night full of stars. There was a crescent moon. When he wound down, he didn't act embarrassed as he might have in front of someone else. They were twins. They were inside one another. He did sit up, and they kept holding one another, her head on his shoulder, his against her temple.

"We had to go ahead and bury them," she said. "But we're planning a service at the grave."

Kohana and Chumani were in the small family and staff graveyard, formed on the east side of the giant tree whose canopy shaded the picnic tables. It was the gathering spot the staff had always enjoyed, on fair weather days and nights. Kohana and Chumani had spent many good hours there, and the staff still liked including them in their conversations. Mal had said Kohana would want to be where he could keep an eye on things, and Chumani would want to be where she could keep an eye on her beloved giant Sioux.

However, for Mal and Elisa, there had been only one place that fit. The overlook, where Mal could see all the fault lines, and how the cats were doing. See his staff and Ruth move about their tasks, caring for the island he'd loved. Elisa's only desire would be to be close to him.

As Ruth showed that to Adan in his mind, she wiped another river of tears from his cheek. "Did you know this field is where *Etsi* told Da she was carrying us? That she was pregnant?"

"I didn't. She never told me that."

"Women tell one another such things." She paused as a puzzling mix of emotions, shock and uncertainty, flashed over his face. "What? Why is that so startling?"

"It's not...it's just..." Adan released her and drew up his knees so he could prop his elbows on them and scrub his face with his hands. "I'm going to lose it again, Ruth. I'm not sure if I can get this out and hold it together."

She put her arm over his back, her other hand curled around his biceps. Instantly, she shoved her own pain aside as she prepared to fight for her brother, in whatever direction the threat would come. "You don't have to. What is it? Tell me."

"Oh. Hell, no it's nothing bad. Sorry. Just the opposite." He pressed his lips to her hair, cupping her head before he drew back and met her gaze. "Catriona is expecting." His face crumpled. "I was going to tell them...when I got back. She told me just before I left."

"Adan. Oh, Adan." Another flood of tears for them both. She was beginning to think they would never end, that the pain would never ease.

"If I'd come before, I might have been here... They would have had a Light Guardian to defend them..."

"Don't do that to yourself. You can *what if* yourself all day long. Da and Mum wouldn't want you to do that. Oh, Adan. They would have been so happy with your news."

Her attention went to the house. Catriona stood on the rail, gazing up at the night, her wings fluttering like shimmers of golden and green mist. Merc braced his hands on the rail next to her, listening to whatever she was telling him with courteous attention, even though he was fully present in Ruth's mind.

Adan must have let Catriona hear that he'd shared their news with his sister, because Catriona looked in their direction and raised her hand, a tender acknowledgement.

Ruth touched Adan's face again. "He's right here. She's right here. They haven't left us. They'll never leave us." She told herself that every day. A bittersweet comfort that fell far short of what she wanted, but would help, over time. She had to believe that. "They know, Adan. I know they're celebrating for you, overjoyed."

"I can't let go of the selfish bastard, little kid desire to have seen their reaction when we brought them the news. *Etsi* would have danced a jig. Made cookies the size of dinner plates. Da would have insisted that Catriona stay here on the island whenever I was traveling, so they could watch over her. No matter how safe she'd be with Keldwyn in the Fae world, you know he never trusted it much."

"No." They laid back among the flowers and stared up at the sky, their hands clasped. "I don't want to go inside," he said at last, in an aching voice.

"I know. It's truly terrible, the first time."

She didn't mean while it was wrecked and bloodstained, which had been a separate kind of horror, one that would take her years to pack into a closet in her mind and throw away the key.

No. She meant when it was normal, restored, mostly back to the way it was supposed to look, yet it didn't look right at all. "And the second, and third. It's too quiet. But it will be better, with you and Catriona here. How long you can stay?"

Adan turned his head to look at her. "Derek said unless he gets desperate enough to need my pitiful efforts, I can take whatever time I need."

"He's a very encouraging boss."

"Yeah. Being too full of myself is never a problem with him. Like Da..." He swallowed. "I can't say 'was.' I don't want to."

"Then don't. I won't either. As I said, they're still here. I may be too full of pain and anger to really feel it yet, but I have no doubt of it."

Their hands constricted, a flesh and bone knot, reflecting the desire not to let go of the line that connected them to the thought.

"'Even if our decisions bring us to the end of one life, it's only the beginning of another. And those lives are circles that will link, giving your soul everything it needs. When you most doubt it, it will remind you. Because while a lot of things are hard and cruel, that truth never is.'"

His voice got thick again as he spoke the words. He turned his head to meet her eyes. "*Etsi* said that to me, that first time Derek and Ruby brought Jem to the island. You remember that day?"

"I do." They looked back up at the stars for a while longer. Then Adan sat up and gazed down at her with their mother's eyes. Ruth laced her hands over her stomach, knowing he was seeing Mal's gazing back at him from her own face. More reminders. The right kind.

"So Merc is here," he said at last.

"Yes."

"You third marked him."

"Yes." Ruth blew out a breath. "I'm going to run the sanctuary, Adan. He'll do things with Marcellus, for the angels, so he'll come and go for that, but when those things aren't needed, he'll be here. He likes it here."

"Really?"

"Yeah. He's never really had a home. The Circus came closest, but even there they weren't all that sure of him. He tended to be on the outside. I think that's changing, but...he sees me as his home."

"That's the way it's supposed to be, isn't it?" He looked up at the stars.

"Yeah. Mum said that about Da. That he was her home."

"I get it. I wouldn't have, before Catriona. But I do now." He glanced at her. "You and Merc?"

"We're a lot newer than you two. Still...yes, I think so. When I third marked him, it was like my soul recognized his. An, 'oh, there you are,' moment. Does that sound stupid and romantic?"

"Yeah. Doesn't make it less true."

She nudged him, then half-smiled. "He likes helping with the sanctuary chores. He has to cloak his wings so the infirmary cats don't see them; otherwise they try to pull out his feathers while he's feeding or holding them."

Adan managed an answering smile. Their eyes were raw and red, but the smile worked with that. Pain came with the promise of life going on.

No matter how hard that seemed right now.

Adan stayed for two weeks. Then Ruth gently encouraged him and Catriona to return to his Light Guardian duties. They'd set the date for the memorial service, and he'd come back for it, but beyond that, she knew he'd return as often as he could. Grief would be a long roller coaster for both of them, but continuing on with their lives as they were mapped before them, the directions they desired to go and had willingly chosen, would help. It was time for that journey to continue.

Mal and Elisa would want it that way.

Adan's news, that Ruth would soon be an aunt, lifted everyone's spirits. Catriona would be having the first vampire-Fae child since Lyssa, as far as anyone knew. Miracles abounded. Maybe not the one Ruth most wanted, but a reminder that the world kept spinning.

She'd stepped into her father's shoes, taking over management of the sanctuary, helped by Hanska and the staff members who'd loved Mal and Elisa so deeply. For the most part, she handled the jarring daily reminders that they weren't there, but some part of her kept reaching...

She believed what she'd told Adan, that they were still here, a strong echo that connected to whatever afterlife or path they were on now, like a vampire mind link. Elsewhere, but still in touch.

Yet she hadn't felt it the way she wanted to do so. For so many years, they'd been in her head. Within a moment's reach, physically, emotionally. She wanted a reassurance that they had moved beyond those terrible last moments that came to her in too-frequent nightmares.

Sometimes, waiting for that sign, dealing with it all, turned her into a raving lunatic.

~

On good days, Merc could leave Ruth on the island with no concerns. She wouldn't let sadness take her over.

So today here he was, in Shamain, in a meeting with Marcellus's Legion battalion. In his own mind, he'd started out by "sitting in" on the strategy sessions and briefings, at Marcellus's urging. However, before long, Merc had started behaving as if he were a new but vetted member of their ranks. And they were acting the same toward him.

Unsettling as fuck, but that didn't make it less true.

Though Ruth's more limited range meant she couldn't hear or feel him in her mind at a certain distance, he'd learned how to drop into her mind from almost anywhere. So when he was sitting on the Citadel wall, listening to Jonah, the Prime Legion Commander, discuss a problem about another part of the universe, he turned part of his mind toward his vampire.

The sanctuary's business was done for the day, and it was two and a half hours before dawn. She was in her father's office, leaning against the doorway, her forehead against those knife marks Mal had created. As she traced them with her fingers, her nostrils flared and she tilted her head toward the living area.

The blood is still here. Abruptly she pushed off from the wall and headed up the corridor.

Though uneasy with her mood, Merc sensed she was in no danger, and had to tune back into his present surroundings as the battalion took flight.

Nearly two hours later, the matter was done, but what he saw when he checked back into Ruth's head had Merc winging toward the island at near top speed. They were going to fix this mind link thing so it was two-way, regardless of range, so she could hear him when he asked her what the hell was going on, and did she know how close it was to dawn?

He landed in the yard, just as she emerged with bloody hands and another pile of wood, puzzle pieces for jagged holes in the kitchen and living room floor.　　　　.

It was so close to sunrise, she was stumbling.

Her parents' room had become theirs, because the giant bed held the sanctuary's nexus, the canopy crisscrossed with strands of gems, the mattress covered with poached furs of spirits that lent their energy to Mal's protection of the sanctuary cats. Ruth now wore the cat pendant that connected and recharged with those energies while she moved through the sanctuary each night or slept in the bed during the day.

She wanted to feel her father's presence through that carved stone. Through that nexus. She didn't. Sleeping in that bed, she'd been sure they would visit her in her dreams. But all she dreamed about was the blood, and the picture Mason had painted of their last few moments.

She couldn't bear to wait for that contact another moment. And she couldn't take that fucking floor another second.

"I can still smell it in there, sense it," she told him as she flung down the wood. "It has to go, Merc. It's driving me mad...I shouldn't rip up the floors. Mal and Kohana put them down together, but if I don't get rid of those boards...it's in the wood, I can't stand it..."

Merc scooped her up, and when she fought him, snarling and hissing, he dealt with it with a sharp, one-word command. "Stop."

She obeyed, but reluctantly. She vibrated with the desire to resist. He took her back into the house, skirting the impressively large holes she'd created, and moved down the stairs to the vampire living quarters. He didn't go into her parents' room, but to her childhood one, deeper in the earth. She was angry, but while just being cradled in his arms, her eyelids were already drooping, the sun doing its best to claim her consciousness.

"I can't..."

"It will be dealt with," he told her. "You're dealing with everything you should. I will deal with this."

"But—"

"The discussion is over," he told her curtly. "If you make a face, I will spank you."

The startling comment jerked her out of her head, her eyes widening. "You would?"

"I would. You know I would enjoy it."

The tired hopelessness returned, but he took heart from the flash of sexual intrigue, albeit brief, and faint amusement that said she would pull it together after she had some rest. Him being here helped, but she hated that she was dependent on him like that.

Her parents had been murdered only a few weeks ago, changing her whole life. He thought she was doing remarkably well. He'd make that point with her, forcibly, later.

"Can angels visit the dead?"

The question burst from her as he laid her down. He knew it had been hovering in her mind for a while, elusive, kept behind a door, her refusing to ask it. Probably because she already suspected the answer, and couldn't handle another disappointment. He hated to meet those expectations.

"Not Legion angels...or one like me. The wall between the living and the dead is there for important reasons. Reasons even I couldn't argue with. Angels have no access to it. The hope for the day we reunite with loved ones, without the concrete assurance of it...even angels are not exempt from that."

She closed her eyes and turned away, curling into a ball. *I'm sorry, Merc. I knew that. Charlie even told me...with Clara. I'm better than this. Just not today. That goddamn smell...*

He curled his arm around her waist, pulled her closer and lay with her until she fell into the unrelenting arms of daylight sleep. When she was under, he cleaned her hands, checking that they were healing properly. Then he did something he'd never done. He reached out and asked for a favor from Maddock.

Though his communication with Ruth had much deeper levels, Merc had learned an angel had the ability, with practice, to reach out and speak in anyone's mind. It was proving to be a useful tool. And amusing, when Maddock, just rising in his part of the world, started at the unexpected intrusion, sloshing his coffee on his hand. *Goddamn it, Merc...*

The sorcerer nevertheless came through the portal less than an hour later, with Charlie. Charlie went to check on Ruth in her somno-lent state, and Merc and Maddock dealt with the floor.

"It needs to contain the scents she expects. Not a new smell. Not something that stands out as having been replaced for the reasons it's being replaced. No blood or violence from her parents' deaths. Can it be done?"

After a moment of contemplation, Maddock nodded, his expres-sion serious. "I can do it. Mind helping me with the grunt work part?"

"Just tell me what you need."

Maddock might have doubted his sincerity, but an hour later, he no longer did. Merc followed the sorcerer's instruction, starting with bringing the wood back into the living area. It had the scent of her blood on it, too, from where she'd ripped the boards heedlessly off the floor. He laid them back in place, holding them as directed as the sorcerer reversed the damage her strength of purpose had inflicted.

After that, Maddock cast the cleansing smell, lifting out what needed to disappear and restoring to the planks the same scent as what was on the other, unaffected boards. He did the casting throughout the main room and kitchen, everywhere the violence had occurred. When Maddock finished, he had a slight smile on his face.

"Many good memories have been made here. It wasn't difficult to draw on that energy and use it. I'm barely even winded."

Charlie returned. Seeing her sober face, Merc closed in on her. When Maddock shifted between them, Merc brought himself up short and stepped back. "I would never cause her harm," he said.

In the past, he wouldn't have bothered to offer the assurance. He'd wanted to maintain that reserve and distance a dangerous reputation gave him. Connection was more important to him now. Especially if it helped Ruth.

Maddock looked surprised at the obvious sincerity in the admis-sion. He gave Merc a cordial nod, offered in the same tone. "My apologies. You looked a little intense. I'm used to...how you used to be."

Fair enough. Merc looked at Charlie. "How is she?"

"She's emotionally exhausted, stressed and overwhelmed. But only what I would expect for an intense grieving process." Charlie touched Merc's hand.

"You can give her some good news when she wakes. Ruth told

VAMPIRE'S CHOICE

Clara that maybe the physical cost of her visions was the Powers-That-Be's way of telling her she'd done enough. After the vampires retrieved Kane and Farida, she let Maddock embed the blocking spell. She's gained ten pounds and looks happier than I've seen her in a long while. When she comes for the memorial, Ruth will see for herself."

Merc had noted Marcellus looked easier, the past couple times they'd been together. Now he knew why. The senior angel hadn't shared the news, perhaps because he thought celebrating Clara's good fortune wasn't appropriate in the face of Ruth's grief. He'd have to let the angel know that wasn't the case. "Good. I'm glad to hear it."

Charlie's expression told him she could see the toll on Merc as well, because of his feelings for Ruth. That awareness and compassion were unexpected, and caused a heaviness in his chest. The last time those two emotions had been directed his way, they'd come from Elisa.

"You're caring for her properly, Merc," Charlie said soberly. "It will be hard for a while. That's all. She's very strong."

"I know. I just wish I could spare her the pain."

"Stand by her through it. That's more important. Pain shapes us and helps us grow stronger, especially when we have someone with us to get through it."

CHAPTER TWENTY-NINE

*J*acob strode down the island beach. His lady was walking barefoot in the sand, her shoes clasped in her grip as she gazed out at the waves. The memorial for Mal and Elisa had been attended by every Council member, as well as countless others. Knowing what a pain in the ass his stubbornness often caused, Mal would have been amused by the honor. And annoyed, at having so many here to interfere with the sanctuary's daily operations.

Ruth and Adan had stood together before the sculpture of his parents they'd placed a few feet from their grave markers. Evan, the vampire Lord Uthe had sired and who'd become an accomplished artist, had done it. He'd liked coming here to create. Many had found peace and inspiration in the sanctuary Mal had created.

Evan's preferred medium was canvas, but the sculpture proved he was as accomplished with clay. He'd reflected the proud sternness of Mal's features and the strength of character in Elisa's. A mountain lion rested at their feet, Elisa leaning against Mal's side, his head bent toward hers.

One of the Circus members had sung a hymn Elisa favored, and the Native American staff members had followed it up with chants and drumming.

There'd been no speeches. Just the music and unveiling of the statue. Everyone had left something at the base, something that could be blown away in the wind or feed the wildlife without harm. Mal would have been pleased.

At the end, Lyssa had stepped up to the statue. She'd laid a hand on Mal's arm, and Elisa's. She'd bowed her head, and then she'd done something she rarely did, unleashing her Fae magic before an audience.

As the assembled murmured in quiet amazement, flowers grew around the base, curling vines populated with large white moon-flowers.

Then the group dispersed. Some of those new to the sanctuary would visit the cats with the staff, because Ruth had made sure they could see what was done here. Like her father, she stayed cognizant of the funding sources that kept the island thriving.

She would be all right.

His lady on the other hand...

Jacob always paid closer attention to her after losses. Though the likelihood of her succumbing to Ennui was slim at this point, especially with him and Kane in her life, there was such a thing as a natural death, when a soul had simply had enough of loss and change, the wear and tear from a world that made the same mistakes, over and over again, never seeming to learn.

The vigilance to protect one's loved ones from that idiocy could take its toll.

Kane had stood between them during the memorial, his eyes alive with pain. Jacob had kept his hand on his son, a reassurance and reminder. There was nothing he could have done. He was off walking with Adan now, something Ruth had suggested.

As Jacob approached Lyssa on the beach, she spoke. Apparently she wasn't in a mood to be coddled. She preferred to threaten him. "So, this servants' council. You're one of the names they're considering to lead it. Parity, you know, with me as Council head."

"I think it should be Jessica." Jacob gave her an amused look. "Lord Mason proposed the document, after all. His servant would be trusted as its leader, and Jess can handle it. Dev can be a member. He straddles the line well between traditional and less traditional vampire-servant relationships. He understands what vampires can reasonably be asked to do or not do. It should also contain a couple servants not bound to Council members."

Lyssa's lips curved. "I notice you didn't propose your brother."

"With his gift for tact, and his controversial history as a vampire hunter, I don't think he makes the cut. Though I was briefly tempted to throw it out there, just to see his horror at the idea of having to attend regular meetings for...anything."

Jacob looked down the beach, where his brother was body surfing and trying to coax Daegan to come in. Like all vampires with their lack of buoyancy, Daegan was offering a less than enthusiastic response. Anwyn sat in the surf, though, enjoying the rush of it over her excellent legs.

You need to develop some near-sightedness if you want to stay out of trouble.

"You have the most beautiful legs in the universe, my lady. Hers are just...longer."

He laughed as Lyssa kicked water at him, but then he came close enough to stand at her side, nuzzling her hair. "My Mistress can always put out my eyes if that's her choice," he said, half-serious. "We old guard servants aren't likely to cede what we've already given to our vampires, no matter what the new 'Hippiestock' committee proposes."

She touched his throat. As always, his pulse increased, making her even more aware of his blood. And his willingness to give it to her.

"Hippiestock? Did that come from Gideon?"

"Belizar. He surprised me. I figured his knowledge of history stopped at the Bolshevik revolution. He also surprised me when he backed you on the servant proposal."

"He's not immune to change. He just dislikes it intensely." She smiled. "But he's come to see what problems excessive certainty can cause. Stagnation, suppression of ideas that help us grow, adapt. Survive."

Her expression darkened. "I think he realized I wasn't proposing we become softer and gentler with this new law. Just the opposite. We protect our people, what the God and Goddess made us. Kaela has been loyal to me and our kind, and has fought for our people. I was prepared to defend her and Garron with far harsher means, if they'd pushed me to it. Belizar knows I would do the same for him, and for most of the Council members, when it is warranted."

"On that note..." Jacob dipped his head toward Gideon and

Daegan again. "Daegan wants confirmation that you meant it. Exterminating the Trads. Gideon said it would overload his to-do list. He might need to hire additional ninjas."

Lyssa sighed. "I can say I'm still undecided, but that's because I couldn't kill Grollner more than once. You already know the answer, as does Daegan. I would not condemn an entire people to death for the acts of a group." She flashed fangs at her servant. "But I had no problem letting Grollner die with that certainty in his heart."

"There's the female I know and love."

He kissed her hand, and she curved her sharp nails against his cheek, a biting caress. They leaned together, looking at the surf together in silence.

"Love is the only rule between us. Isn't that from a song, or a book. Or both?"

"Thomas told me once that the messages that surface time and again in books, music, all sorts of creative expression, came from the universe first. They can't be stamped out. And when we hear those truths, understand and act upon them, I think the universe smiles. It likely needs those smiles as much as we do."

"Yeah. Maybe more." His blue eyes darkened. "We know loss. But this one has hit particularly fucking hard."

"Yes." Lyssa's expression became that of a concerned mother. One hurting for her child. "Kane thinks him being here, being a target as our son, resulted in this."

"Adan will help him." Jacob held her closer, brushing his lips against her dark hair. "He'll tell him what his father would have said. That Mal wouldn't have changed a thing. Evil doesn't need an excuse, and you can't stop living because it might use an opportunity."

"Yes." They walked together along the beach, and he held her hand. Here, where they'd often been able to be informal, she didn't mind that. He was glad. Jacob watched her bare feet move through the water, and nudged her a little to the left so she didn't step on a jagged-edged shell.

Lyssa looked up at him. Her jade eyes had gone just as sharp and painful. "It hurts me deeply, to know they are not here, Jacob."

"I know." She didn't let her pain show to many, the cost of it to her soul. He closed his arms around her again, held her. Let their hearts beat together. "Ruth will help us mend the tear. She doesn't openly acknowledge it, because she's doing her own grieving, but it's already there. She's her father's daughter. That whole tour thing, after the service."

A smile touched his voice. "Hanska says she's already secured commitments that will increase her quarterly donation projections by nine percent."

"She's her mother's daughter as well." Lyssa drew back. She was composed again, but he was still in her head, staying close. She embraced that intimacy, leaning against him as they walked onward. "I'm glad she has Merc now."

"Yeah. Didn't see that one coming."

The angel incubus had stood behind Ruth during the service. Catriona had stood by Adan's side. A united force that said as well as words the siblings would have formidable support going forward.

"We rarely do." Lyssa took both of his hands, the straps of her shoes over their fingers. She pedaled backwards, giving him a mischievous look that was almost girlish. And beautiful to him. "I was thinking about how Fates bring us together. About our first night together, when I met you at the Eldar. Your presumption that you would be my new servant. Your blue eyes and handsome body. Your earnestness."

As they circled one another, an informal dance in the current, she drew close enough to run her hands down his back, caressing his hips and buttocks. The girl disappeared, replaced by the siren. His temptress. Jacob cinched an arm around her waist.

"I was pretty sure you were going to kill me. Or at least maim me."

"It crossed my mind. But then... Something in you spoke to me, like the truth in those stories and songs. I felt it, knew something meant for us to walk forward together, at least for a little while. And then a little while became much longer."

"Forever, my lady. All eternity." He took down her hair, letting it tumble into his hands. "That's what I promised you. You promised me the same."

Her lips curved. "I did no such thing. Only for as long as you remain tolerable."

"I will always endeavor to please my lady."

She lifted onto her toes to bring her mouth to his. His arms were already tightening to help, the kiss taking them out over the waves, into the sky, and letting them feel the heat of a sun she might never see, but could feel within him.

Perhaps in the end, Lyssa thought, that was what the right servant was. The light and the heat that replaced the sun for a vampire, nourished and helped them see what darkness might keep from them.

She decided to hold that thought to herself. It was always best for a vampire to keep a servant humble, after all. Especially one she knew was the center of her universe.

He'd first crossed her path as her childhood bodyguard in Japan. Then as a knight during the Crusade. Finally, he'd been reborn in this form, forever bound to her soul. If she did share her thought with him, she knew from her head to her tingling toes, what his response would be. No hesitation.

Same goes, my lady. Always and forever.

Three weeks later, Ruth stood on a cliff overlooking the water. The vast, rolling ocean. She'd thought she knew every place on the island, but over the past few weeks she'd endeavored to explore every inch of the terrain, and discovered this new remote viewing perch. From here, she could see the rock formation where she'd waited for Merc's return and found Lord Mason.

The cat pendant at her throat vibrated with the energy that told her everything was tranquil today. As tranquil as an island inhabited by large predators could be. Including herself.

The night sky was full of stars. A smile crossed her face as a section of them blackened into a winged male shape. He was home. Merc landed next to her, his hands already on her waist and the side of her neck to claim the kiss he wanted. She pressed herself against him, opening up to him.

"You're home early."

"I'm able to help these other angels do things more quickly. Efficiently. No wasted time on diplomacy."

She chuckled. "So they're giving you the jobs that require simple speed and violence."

"It seems to be my preferred milieu. But some things I prefer to take my time for..."

His arms slid around her. She saw the silver glimmer of writing and symbols ripple across his forearm, then melt back into the skin. Praises to the Goddess, and protection and guidance for Her warriors. When he wished, they could remain visible. Marcellus had been the angel who awarded them to him, after Merc's first battle in the ranks of the Legion.

Her angel incubus. Who served the Goddess, but also served and cared for Ruth. She remembered the night she'd risen to find he'd taken care of things with the floor, just as he said he would. There was no evidence of violence in her family home. Only the energy vibrations of life itself, and lives well lived.

Tonight, after working at her father's desk on the paperwork that needed managing, she'd decided to leave all that and come here. As she passed through the door, she'd stopped, touching those knife marks Mal had created in his idle pastime of target practice. She'd returned to the desk and picked up Kohana's knife. There was energy there. Strength. She gripped the hilt where her father had gripped it so often, and felt as if she was holding his hand.

Give it time, Charlie had told her. *When you first experience a terrible loss, that's where your mind lights. But over time, it moves to how they lived their lives, what they meant to you. Not how they died. And then...you start to feel other things.*

All these weeks, she'd waited and hoped. Then let it go, knowing it would come in time. And it had.

She'd stood stock still, her heart beating in her ears.

She'd felt them.

The brush of a strong hand, the sense of a smile. The heart-crushing scent of her mother, the strength of her father surrounding her. His hand on her shoulder as he stood just behind her. As they both stood with her.

Tears had squeezed out of her eyes as she wrapped her arms around herself, her hands folding over her collarbone, as if she could overlap their fingers. She held the feeling to her. *I love you both, so much. I love you.*

She let herself think of the one memory worth holding onto from that terrible day. Her father had two tattoos he'd maintained throughout the years, using his blood to anchor the ink, as vampires had to do so it wasn't "healed" or reabsorbed. One was the lioness and feathers art around his biceps. The other was on his side, under his left arm, alongside his heart. The small flower had the same blue color as Elisa's eyes, and the bloom was bordered by two words. *Adan. Ruth.*

Elisa's fingertips had rested on that tattoo. Ruth had zero doubt her mother had intentionally reached for it in her last moment to leave a message for them.

We love you.

It was as she'd told Adan, hoping, wanting to believe, but now she was sure. Everything she did to protect this place, to keep it fulfilling the mission her father had created it for, would weave itself into that echo, making it ever stronger. They would always be here. Willingly. Just like herself.

Adan and her father's worry, about having someone to protect her, to help her, it would extend to the sanctuary's wellbeing too, because Merc loved the island as much as she did.

She'd put the beaded scabbard and that long knife on her belt, to wear it along her thigh. It made her feel balanced.

When it had happened, she knew Merc had seen all of that in her head. He let the beaded strands slide through his knuckles now as she removed the scabbard. At the look of kindled heat in his gaze, she removed her shirt. Then her jeans and the rest of her clothes, leaving them in a neat bundle. Putting her hands behind her back, she dipped her head down. Lowered her eyes.

I love you, Master.

His hands cradled her face, bringing it back up as he lowered his mouth to hers. She leaned against him. He'd taken to wearing his version of Legion wear a lot more often, the black battle skirt, plus an upper body harness loaded with his preferred dagger and a short sword. It was a good look for him. She slid her hands to his taut backside, digging her fingernails into it, her body tightening in anticipation.

"I didn't give you permission to touch me."

He spoke against her ear. Though she'd offered herself to him, and he gave them both pleasure, it was only in the past few days he'd let the Master in him aggressively respond to her again. The only times before then it had shown itself was when he wouldn't allow her to work or push herself too hard.

Maybe he'd known she wasn't ready for the vulnerability that came with bringing it into the intense sexual encounters they shared. But the other night, she'd proven she was more than ready.

During a spirited chase and sparring match, she'd called him some creative names. He'd decided to take offense, holding her over his lap while she struggled and snarled. She'd nearly climaxed from the stinging blows on her ass.

Ruth lifted her hands from him and stepped back. "Did you tell me that I could put my hands on myself?" She slid them along her throat, down to cup her breasts. Even lower, while he dropped to his heels, wings half spread as he watched her with heavy-lidded, heated eyes. "Because I do that quite often, thinking of your hands there instead. Wanting them there. You're away too much."

Which she didn't begrudge him, at all. They both had things they had to do. But she had no trouble using it to tease him like this.

"Perhaps I'll punish you by telling you that every time I take your body for the next few days, the only contact you'll have is my cock driving into your cunt. I will not touch you otherwise. Will not kiss you. I will tell you to touch yourself, command it. Teach you that you can have your hands or mine. You cannot have both."

Her hands stilled, and slowly she removed them, held them out to either side of herself. "I need your touch," she said, her voice throaty. "More than I need pleasure itself."

Merc rose and came to her, sliding his hands to her hips, her backside, lifting her up as she wrapped her legs around him. When she grimaced at the bruising grip of his fingers on her buttocks, he bared his fangs at her. "There are advantages to having a vampire who doesn't heal as fast. You remember your lessons far better."

She would have stuck her tongue out at him now, defying him to do it again, but he captured her mouth, played his tongue around her own, creating more pleasure. She gripped his shoulders, the firm flesh, the heat of him. She needed more of him than she thought anyone could give.

I will prove you wrong, Ruth. As many times as needed for you to learn that lesson, too. Even if we have to fight about it.

Feeling that wicked smile inside him, she responded in kind.

Or want to do so.

WANT MORE? If you haven't read all of the Vampire Queen series stories, you can read Book 1, Lyssa and Jacob's story, for FREE. Or how about another paranormal series? My Arcane Shot trilogy kicks off with a gun-toting witch and a sorcerer in cowboy hat and dragon-skin boots. The first book of the trilogy is also FREE. Check these out below.

CLICK HERE TO READ
VAMPIRE QUEEN'S SERVANT
Or use this BookFunnel link:
https://dl.bookfunnel.com/qnv6rl2rce

CLICK HERE TO READ
ARCANE SHOT
Or use this BookFunnel link:
https://dl.bookfunnel.com/tqo4gmm857

(Note: books are not free at Nook – use the BookFunnel link instead)

Reading this in print format? Use the BookFunnel link or look for the ebooks at your favorite vendor!

Quite a few characters from my series populated this book. Because of that, when you go to the "Also by Joey W. Hill" section, I've added the names of the couples (or trios) attached to each Vampire Queen series title, to help you locate more information about them. For those who belong to other series (like Derek), I've noted their stories as well.

However, before you go on to that, if you're doing a **WTF?!** about the unexpected tragedy in this book, scroll onward to the **Author's Note** that I wrote for all of you. And maybe for me, too.

AUTHOR'S NOTE

When I start to write a story, it's pretty much outlined. It always expands beyond that, but rarely does it go in a direction I didn't see coming.

As you now know, this book had such a turn, and it was a *really* tough one.

I talk about "the muse," and how she and my characters decide where we're going, if I get out of their way. I didn't want to get out of their way for this. I spent several days thinking hard about why the story took this direction, and seeking other possibilities. Even through the editing process, I continued to question it.

Being true to the story you're writing is sometimes a little too much like life outside of a book. When we get hit by loss, we don't know why it has to happen that way, but we have to believe there are reasons for it that will make sense as time goes on—or when we are reunited with that loved one again.

For instance, because of this unexpected turn, the book had several important and positive resolutions for the vampire-servant relationship, which gave that loss meaning.

So in the end, I trusted the muse, that gut creative process that has always guided me. However, because it still hurt like hell to write the scene in question, and I know many fans of the series will feel the same about reading it, I wanted to give you insight into why it unfolded as it did. I hope you'll understand and still love Ruth and Merc's story, because in all other respects I loved their book.

But just so you know, when you reached that spot...I grieved with you.

ABOUT THE AUTHOR

Having penned over fifty acclaimed BDSM contemporary and paranormal titles, which includes six award-winning series, *Joey W. Hill* has been awarded the RT Book Reviews Career Achievement Award for Erotic Romance. A submissive herself, Hill brings authenticity to her intensely emotional love stories.

She is grateful for the support of a wonderful and enthusiastic readership, which allows her to live on her beloved Carolina coast with her even more beloved husband and menagerie of animals.

- On the Web: https://storywitch.com
- Twitter: https://twitter.com/JoeyWHill
- Facebook: https://facebook.com/JoeyWHillAuthor
- Facebook Fan Forum: https://facebook.com/groups/JWHMembersOnly
- MeWe: https://mewe.com/i/joeywhill
- GoodReads: https://www.goodreads.com/author/show/103359.Joey_W_Hill
- BookBub: https://bookbub.com/authors/joey-w-hill
- Amazon: https://amazon.com/Joey-W-Hill/e/B001JSCIW0

ALSO BY JOEY W. HILL

Arcane Shot Series

Arcane Shot (Derek and Ruby)

Arcane Madame (Mikhael and Raina)

Arcane Chaos

Arcane Knight

Daughters of Arianne Series

A Mermaid's Kiss (Jonah and Anna)

A Witch's Beauty (Mina and David)

A Mermaid's Ransom (Dante and Alexis)

Knights of the Board Room Series

Board Resolution

Controlled Response

Honor Bound

Afterlife

Hostile Takeover

Willing Sacrifice

Soul Rest

Knight Nostalgia *(Anthology)*

Mistresses of the Board Room Series

At Her Command

At Her Service

At Her Call

At Her Pleasure

Nature of Desire Series

Holding the Cards

Natural Law

Ice Queen

Mirror of My Soul

Mistress of Redemption

Rough Canvas

Branded Sanctuary

Divine Solace

Worth The Wait

Truly Helpless

In His Arms

Ignition Sequence

Naughty Bits Series

Naughty Bits

Naughty Wishes

Vampire Queen Series

Vampire Queen's Servant (Lady Lyssa and Jacob)

Mark of the Vampire Queen (Lady Lyssa and Jacob, Part 2)

Vampire's Claim (Lady Danny and Dev)

Beloved Vampire (Lord Mason and Jessica)

Vampire Mistress (Daegan, Anwyn and Gideon)

Vampire Trinity (Daegan, Anwyn and Gideon, Part 2)

Vampire Instinct (Mal and Elisa)

Bound by the Vampire Queen (Lady Lyssa and Jacob)

Taken by a Vampire (Evan, Niall and Alanna)

The Scientific Method (Lord Brian and Debra)

Nightfall (Selene and Quinn)

Elusive Hero (Lady Kaela and Garron)

Night's Templar (Fae Lord Keldwyn and Lord Uthe)

Vampire's Soul (Cai and Rand)

Vampire's Embrace (Lord Alistair and Nina)

Vampire Master (Wolf and Ella)

Vampire Guardian (Adan and Catriona)

Vampire's Choice (Merc and Ruth)